MANHATTAN MYSTERIES

ABOUT THE EDITORS

BILL PRONZINI is one of America's finest mystery/suspense writers, as well as one of its leading critics. He has edited or coedited more than 40 anthologies and, with Martin H. Greenberg, has coedited *101 Mystery Stories, Baker's Dozen: 13 Short Mystery Novels,* and others. A longtime resident of San Francisco, he possesses one of the larger collections of pulp magazines in the world.

CAROL-LYNN RÖSSEL WAUGH has coedited a half-dozen mystery anthologies with Martin H. Greenberg. She is also a doll designer and an authority on teddy bears, as well as an artist in other media. Ms. Waugh lives in Winthrop, Maine.

MARTIN H. GREENBERG has justly earned the title "king of the anthologists," with more than 150 to his credit. He is the editor of *On the Diamond: A Treasury of Baseball Stories* and coeditor of *Detectives A to Z, A Treasury of American Horror Stories,* and many others. He is professor of regional analysis and political science at the University of Wisconsin–Green Bay, where he also teaches a course on the history of science fiction.

MANHATTAN MYSTERIES

Edited by Bill Pronzini, Carol-Lynn Rössel Waugh, and Martin H. Greenberg

Avenel Books
New York

Published in 1987 by Avenel Books, distributed by Crown Publishers, Inc.,
225 Park Avenue South, New York, New York 10003

Printed and Bound in the United States of America

Library of Congress Cataloging-in-Publication Data
Manhattan mysteries.
1. Detective and mystery stories, American. 2. New
York (N.Y.)—Fiction. I. Pronzini, Bill. II. Waugh,
Carol-Lynn Rössel. III. Greenberg, Martin Harry.
PS648.D4M36   1987   813'.0872'08327471   86-28720

ISBN 0-517-63179-2
h g f e d c b a

CONTENTS

Introduction:

MYSTERIOUS ISLAND

New York is a city of eight million stories, at least one for every New Yorker. New York is a city noted for its detectives; probably more literary sleuths have been created to walk the streets of Manhattan than any other real estate — and this is without counting shamuses from the other four boroughs. So why aren't the streets safer? I don't know. Nevertheless, New York is my city and I love it.

I'm a native and grew up in the house my great-grandfather built over a century ago on Staten Island. Though a borough of New York City, Staten Island is bucolic in comparison to Manhattan. When I was little, people spoke of "The City" with awe, respect, and fear. It was dangerous, they said, to brave the ferry ride across the bay. You might not survive to make the return trip.

Far from unnerving, these tales fascinated a youngster who mainlined Carolyn Keene and G. K. Chesterton. As soon as I was old enough I began slipping across the bay. It's always been a round trip.

New York has innumerable lures: the buildings, the museums, the shops. But perhaps its biggest lure is the people. In every café, a dozen real-life dramas unfold every hour. Over a cup of coffee, tales of joy and tragedy are spun, threads from which stories are woven. Full of intrigue, free of charge, plots appear. No wonder Manhattan is full of writers. Where else can such a concentration of raw literary material be found?

It is also true that New York has more than its share of crime, adding to its share of story fodder. But no other city in the world has the special mixture that makes for as many varied opportunities for mysterious happenings. No other city has the mesmeric charm to attract so many writers to seek out or invent mystery tales about its citizens. No other city intrigues readers worldwide to vicariously enjoy its thrills and dangers the way New York does.

In this book, my coeditors and I present the finest New York mysteries we have found. They take place yesterday, today, and tomorrow — in almost every neighborhood — and involve people of every class and economic level.

Many of the cases are solved by New York's resident sleuths. Indeed, what other city can boast of such crime fighters as Hildegarde Withers, Jericho, Merlini, "Mom," The Black Widowers, and Ellery Queen, to name just a few. What other city can boast of such crime writers as Isaac Asimov, John Dickson Carr, O. Henry, Ed Hoch, Cornell Woolrich, Stanley Ellin, and "Ellery Queen" to record the sleuths' adventures?

You don't have to be a native to love the mysteries of New York. You don't have to have walked the streets of Manhattan to be enraptured by its promise of adventure, by the possibility that anything could happen. You can visit the city by reading this collection.

If you someday do make the pilgrimage to Manhattan, you will be richly rewarded. Take this book with you and use it as a guide (literary, if not literal) and as a hefty mugger-deterrent.

Perhaps the city will not be exactly as depicted here. Perhaps you will not be able to locate the mysterious landmarks mentioned in these pages, but in searching for them you will probably locate several fine mystery bookstores, filled with more murder and mayhem than is available anywhere else on Earth.

And, if you sit quietly in the right café, you may overhear a one-of-a-kind, custom-made, real-life mystery of your own.

May 1987   Carol-Lynn Rössel Waugh

MANHATTAN MYSTERIES

THE GOOD SAMARITAN

Isaac Asimov

THE BLACK WIDOWERS had learned by hard experience that when Mario Gonzalo took his turn as host of the monthly banquet, they had to expect the unusual. They had reached the point where they steeled themselves, quite automatically, for disaster. When his guest arrived there was a lightening of spirit if it turned out he had the usual quota of heads and could speak at least broken English.

When the last of the Black Widowers arrived, therefore, and when Henry's efficient setting of the table was nearly complete, Geoffrey Avalon, standing, as always, straight and tall, sounded almost lighthearted as he said, "I see that your guest has not arrived yet, Mario."

Gonzalo, whose crimson velvet jacket and lightly striped blue pants reduced everything else in the room to monochrome said, "Well—"

Avalon said, "What's more, a quick count of the settings placed at the table by our inestimable Henry shows that six people and no more are to be seated. And since all six of us are here, I can only conclude that you have not brought a guest."

"Thank Anacreon," said Emmanuel Rubin, raising his drink, "or whatever spirit it is that presides over convivial banquets of kindred souls."

Thomas Trumbull scowled and brushed back his crisply waved white hair with one hand. "What are you doing, Mario? Saving money?"

"Well—" said Gonzalo again, staring at his own drink with a totally spurious concentration.

Roger Halsted said, "I don't know that this is so good. I like the grilling sessions."

"It won't hurt us," said Avalon, in his deepest voice, "to have a quiet conversation once in a while. If we can't amuse each other without a guest, then the Black Widowers are not what once they were and we should prepare, sorrowing, for oblivion. Shall we offer Mario a vote of thanks for his unwonted discretion?"

"Well—" said Gonzalo a third time.

James Drake interposed, stubbing out a cigarette and clearing his throat. "It seems to me, gentlemen, that Mario is trying to say something and is amazingly bashful about it. If he has something he hesitates to say, I fear we are not going to like it. May I suggest we all keep quiet and let him talk."

"Well—" said Gonzalo, and stopped. This time, though, there was a prolonged silence.

"Well—" said Gonzalo again, "I *do* have a guest," and once more he stopped.

Rubin said, "Then where the hell is he?"

"Downstairs in the main dining room—ordering dinner—at my expense, of course."

Gonzalo received five blank stares. Then Trumbull said, "May I ask what dunderheaded reason you can possibly advance for that?"

"Aside," said Rubin, "from being a congenital dunderhead?"

Gonzalo put his drink down, took a deep breath, and said firmly, "Because I thought she would be more comfortable down there."

Rubin managed to get out an "And why—" before the significance of the pronoun became plain. He seized the lapels of Gonzalo's jacket, "Did you say 'she'?"

Gonzalo caught at the other's wrists, "Hands off, Manny. If you want to talk, use your lips, not your hands. Yes, I said 'she'."

Henry, his sixtyish, unlined face showing a little concern, raised his voice a diplomatic notch and said, "Gentlemen! Dinner is served!"

Rubin, having released Gonzalo, waved imperiously at Henry and said, "Sorry, Henry, there may be no banquet. Mario, you damned jackass, *no woman can attend these meetings.*"

There was, in fact, a general uproar. While no one quite achieved the anger and decibels of Rubin, Gonzalo found himself at bay with the five others around him in a semicircle. Their individual comments were lost in the general explosion of anger.

Gonzalo, waving his arms madly, leaped onto a chair and shouted, "Let me speak!" over and over until out of exhaustion, it seemed, the opposition died off into a low growl.

Gonzalo said, "She is not our guest at the banquet. She's just a woman with a problem, an old woman, and it won't do us any harm if we see her *after* dinner."

There was no immediate response and Gonzalo said, "She needn't sit at the table. She can sit in the doorway."

Rubin said, "Mario, if she comes in here, I go, and if I go, damn it, I may not ever come back."

Gonzalo said, "Are you saying you'll break up the Black Widowers rather than listen to an old woman in trouble?"

Rubin said, "I'm saying rules are *rules*!"

Halsted, looking deeply troubled, said, "Manny, maybe we ought to do this. The rules weren't delivered to us from Mount Sinai."

"You, too?" said Rubin savagely. "Look, it doesn't matter what any of you say. In a matter as fundamental as this, one blackball is enough, and I cast it. Either she goes or I go and, by God, you'll never see me again. In view of that, is there anyone who wants to waste his breath?"

Henry, who still stood at the head of the table, waiting with markedly less than his usual imperturbability for the company to be seated, said, "May I have a word, Mr. Rubin?"

Rubin said, "Sorry, Henry, no one sits down till this is settled."

Gonzalo said, "Stay out, Henry. I'll fight my own battles."

It was at this point that Henry departed from his role as the epitome of all Olympian waiters and advanced on the group. His voice was firm as he said, "Mr. Rubin, I wish to take responsibility for this. Several days ago Mr. Gonzalo phoned me to ask if I would be so kind as to listen to a woman he knew who had the kind of problem he thought I might be helpful with. I asked him if it were something close to his heart. He said that the woman was a relative of someone who was very likely to give him a commission for an important piece of work—"

"Money!" sneered Rubin.

"Professional opportunity," snapped Gonzalo. "If you can understand that. And sympathy for a fellow human being, if you can understand *that*."

Henry held up his hand.

"*Please,* gentlemen! I told Mr. Gonzalo I could not help him but urged him, if he had not already arranged a guest, to bring the woman. I suggested that there might be no objection if she did not actually attend the banquet itself."

Rubin said, "And why couldn't you help her otherwise?"

Henry said, "Gentlemen, I lay no claims to superior insight. I do not compare myself, as Mr. Gonzalo occasionally does on my behalf, to Sherlock Holmes. It is only after you gentlemen have discussed a problem and eliminated what is extraneous that I seem to see what remains. Therefore—"

Drake said, "Well, look, Manny, I'm the oldest member here, and the original reason for the prohibition. We might partially waive it just this once."

"No," said Rubin flatly.

Henry said, "Mr. Rubin, it is often stated at these banquets that I am a member of the Black Widowers. If so, I wish to take the responsibility. I urged Mr. Gonzalo to do this and I spoke to the woman concerned and assured her that she would be welcomed to our deliberations after dinner. It was an impulsive act based on my estimate of the characters of the gentlemen of the club.

"If the woman is now sent away, Mr. Rubin, you understand that my position here will be an impossible one and I will be forced to resign as waiter at these banquets. I would have no choice."

Almost imperceptibly the atmosphere had changed while Henry spoke and now it was Rubin who was standing at bay. He stared at the semicircle that now surrounded him and said, rather gratingly, "I appreciate your services to the club, Henry, and I do not wish to place you in a dishonorable position. Therefore, on the stipulation that this is not to set a precedent and reminding you that you must not do this again, I will withdraw my blackball."

The banquet was the least comfortable in the history of the Black Widowers. Conversation was desultory and dull and Rubin maintained a stony silence throughout.

There was no need to clatter the water glass during the serving of the coffee, since there was no babble of conversation to override. Gonzalo simply said, "I'll go down and see if she's ready. Her name, by the way, is Mrs. Barbara Lindemann."

Rubin looked up and said, "Make sure she's had her coffee, or tea, or whatever, downstairs. She can't have anything up here."

Avalon looked disapproving, "The dictates of courtesy, my dear Manny—"

"She'll have all she wants downstairs at Mario's expense. Up here we'll listen to her. What more can she want?"

Gonzalo brought her up and led her to an armchair that Henry had obtained from the restaurant office and that he had placed well away from the table.

She was a rather thin woman, with blunt good-natured features, well dressed and with her white hair carefully set. She carried a black purse that looked new and she clutched it tightly. She glanced timidly at the faces of the Black Widowers and said, "Good evening."

There was a low chorused rumble in return and she said, "I apologize for coming here with my ridiculous story. Mr. Gonzalo explained that my appearance here is out of the ordinary and I have thought, over my dinner, that I should not disturb you. I will go if you like, and thank you for the dinner and for letting me come up here."

She made as though to rise and Avalon, looking remarkably shamefaced, said, "Madame, you are entirely welcome here and we would like very much to hear what you have to say. We cannot promise that we will be able to help you, but we can try. I'm sure that we all feel the same way about this. Don't you agree, Manny?"

Rubin shot a dark look at Avalon through his thick-lensed glasses. His sparse beard bristled and his chin lifted but he said in a remarkably mild tone, "Entirely, ma'am."

There was a short pause, and then Gonzalo said, "It's our custom, Mrs. Lindemann, to question our guests and under the circumstances, I wonder if you would mind having Henry handle that. He is our waiter, but he is a member of our group."

Henry stood motionless for a moment, then said, "I fear, Mr. Gonzalo, that—"

Gonzalo said, "You have yourself claimed the privilege of membership earlier this evening, Henry. Privilege carries with it responsibility. Put down the brandy bottle, Henry, and sit down. Anyone who wants brandy can take his own. Here, Henry, take my seat." Gonzalo rose resolutely and walked to the sideboard.

Henry sat down and said mildly to Mrs. Lindemann, "Madame, would you be willing to pretend you are on the witness stand?"

The woman looked about and her look of uneasiness dissolved into a little laugh. "I never have been and I'm not sure I know how to behave on one. I hope you won't mind if I'm nervous."

"We won't, but you needn't be. This will be very informal and we are anxious only to help you. The members of the club have a tendency to speak loudly and excitably at times, but if they do, that is merely their way and means nothing. —First, please tell us your name."

She said, with an anxious formality, "My name is Barbara Lindemann. Mrs. Barbara Lindemann."

"And do you have any particular line of work?"

"No, sir, I am retired. I am sixty-seven years old as you can probably tell by looking at me—and a widow. I was once a schoolteacher at a junior high school."

Halsted stirred and said, "That's my profession, Mrs. Lindemann. What subject did you teach?"

"Mostly I taught American history."

Henry said, "Now from what Mr. Gonzalo has told me you suffered an unpleasant experience here in New York and—"

"No, pardon me," interposed Mrs. Lindemann, "it was, on the whole, a very pleasant experience. If that weren't so, I would be only too glad to forget all about it."

"Yes, of course," said Henry, "but I am under the impression that you *have* forgotten some key points and would like to remember them."

"Yes," she said earnestly. "I am so ashamed at not remembering. It must make me appear senile, but it was a very *unusual* and *frightening* thing in a way—at least parts of it were—and I suppose that's my excuse."

Henry said, "I think it would be best, then, if you tell us what happened to you in as much detail as you can, and if it will not bother you, some of us may ask questions as you go along."

"It won't bother me, I assure you," said Mrs. Lindemann. "I'll welcome it as a sign of interest. I arrived in New York City nine days ago—from the west coast. I was going to visit my niece, among other things, but I didn't want to stay with her. That would have been uncomfortable for her and confining for me, so I took a hotel room.

"I got to the hotel at about six P.M. on Wednesday and after a small dinner, which was very pleasant, although the prices were simply awful, I phoned my niece and arranged to see her the next day when her husband would be at work and the children at school. That would give us some time to ourselves and then in the evening we could have a family outing.

"Of course, I didn't intend to hang about their necks the entire two weeks I was to be in New York. I fully intended to do things on my own. In fact, that first evening after dinner, I had nothing particular to do and I certainly didn't want to sit in my room and watch television. So I thought—well, all Manhattan is just outside, Barbara, and you've read about it all your life and seen it in the movies and now's your chance to see it in real life.

"I thought I'd just step out and wander about on my own and look at the elaborate buildings and the bright lights and the people hurrying past. I just wanted to get a *feel* of the city, before I started taking organized tours. I've done that in other cities in these recent years when I've been traveling and I've always so enjoyed it."

Trumbull said, "You weren't afraid of getting lost, I suppose."

"Oh, *no*," said Mrs. Lindemann. "I have an excellent sense of direction and even if I were caught up in my sightseeing and didn't notice where I had gone, I had a map of Manhattan and the streets are all in a rectangular grid and numbered—not like Boston, London, or Paris, and I was never lost in those cities. Besides, I could always get in a taxi and give the driver the name of my hotel. Besides, I was sure anyone would give me directions if I asked."

Rubin emerged from his trough of despond to deliver himself of a ringing, "In Manhattan? Hah!"

"Why, certainly," said Mrs. Lindemann, with mild reproof. "I've always heard that Manhattanites are unfriendly, but I have not found it so. I have been the recipient of many kindnesses—not the least of which is the manner in which you gentlemen have welcomed me even though I am quite a stranger to you."

Rubin found it necessary to stare intently at his fingernails.

Mrs. Lindemann said, "In any case, I did go off on my little excursion and stayed out much longer than I had planned. Everything was so colorful and busy and the weather was so mild and pleasant. Eventually, I realized I was terribly tired and I had reached a rather quiet street and was ready to go back. I looked in one of the outer pockets of my purse for my map—"

Halsted interrupted. "I take it, Mrs. Lindemann, you were alone on this excursion."

"Oh, yes," said Mrs. Lindemann. "I always travel alone since my husband died. To have a companion means a perpetual state of compromise as to when to arise, what to eat, where to go. No, no, I want to be my own woman."

"I didn't mean quite that, Mrs. Lindemann," said Halsted. "I mean to ask whether you were alone on this particular outing in a strange city—at night—with a purse."

"Yes, sir. I'm afraid so."

Halsted said, "Had no one told you that the streets of New York aren't always safe at night—particularly, excuse me, for older women with purses who look, as you do, gentle and harmless?"

"Oh, dear, of *course* I've been told that. I've been told that of every city I've visited. My own town has districts that aren't safe. I've always felt, though, that all life is a gamble, that a no-risk situation is an impossible dream, and I wasn't going to deprive myself of pleasant experiences because of fear. And I've gone about in all sorts of places without harm."

Trumbull said, "Until that first evening in Manhattan, I take it."

Mrs. Lindemann's lips tightened and she said, "Until then. It was an experience I remember only in flashes, so to speak. I suppose that because I was so tired, and then so frightened, and the surroundings were so new to me, that much of what happened somehow didn't register properly. Little things seem to have vanished forever. That's the problem." She bit her lips and looked as though she were battling to hold back the tears.

Henry said softly, "Could you tell us what you remember?"

"Well," she said, clearing her throat and clutching at her purse, "as I said, the street was a quiet one. There were cars moving past, but no pedestrians, and I wasn't sure where I was. I was reaching for the map and looking about for a street sign when a young man seemed to appear from nowhere and said, 'Got a dollar, lady?' He couldn't have been more than fifteen years old—just a boy.

"Well, I would have been perfectly willing to let him have a dollar if I thought he needed it, but really, he seemed perfectly fit and reasonably prosperous and I didn't think it would be advisable to display my wallet, so I said, 'I'm afraid I don't, young man.'

"Of course, he didn't believe me. He came closer and said, 'Sure you do, lady. Here, let me help you look,' and he reached for my purse. Well, I wasn't going to let him have it, of course—"

Trumbull said firmly, "No 'of course' about it, Mrs. Lindemann. If it ever happens again, you surrender your purse at once. You can't save it in any case. Hoodlums think nothing of using force and there's nothing in a purse that can be worth your life."

Mrs. Lindemann sighed. "I suppose you're right, but at the time I just wasn't thinking clearly. I held on to my purse as a reflex action, I suppose, and that's when I start failing to remember. I recall engaging in a tug of war and I seem to recall other young men approaching. I don't know how many but I seemed surrounded.

"Then I heard a shout and some very bad language and the loud noise of feet. There was nothing more for a while except that my purse was gone. Then there was an anxious voice, low and polite, saying, 'Are you hurt, madam?'

"I said, 'I don't think so, but my purse is gone.' I looked about vaguely. I think I was under the impression it had fallen in the street.

"There was an older young man holding my elbow respectfully. He might have been twenty-five. He said, 'They got that, ma'am. I'd better get you out of here before they come back for some more fun. They'll probably have knives and I don't.'

"He was hurrying me away. I didn't see him clearly in the dark but he was tall and he wore a sweater. He said, 'I live close by, ma'am. It's either go to my place or we'll have a battle.' I *think* I was aware of other young men in the distance, but that may have been a delusion.

"I went with the new young man quite docilely. He seemed earnest and polite and I've gotten too old to feel that I am in danger of—uh—*personal* harm. Besides, I was so confused and lightheaded that I lacked any will to resist.

"The next thing I remember is being at his apartment door. I remember that it was apartment 4-F. I suppose that remains in my mind because it was such a familiar combination during World War II. Then I was inside his apartment and sitting in an upholstered armchair. It was a rather rundown apartment, I noticed, but I don't remember getting to it at all.

"The man who had rescued me had put a glass into my hand and I sipped from it. It was some kind of wine, I think. I did not particularly like the taste, but it warmed me and it seemed to make me less dizzy—rather than more dizzy, as one would suppose.

"The man appeared to be anxious about my possibly being hurt, but I reassured him. I said if he would just help me get a taxi I would get to my hotel.

"He said I had better rest a while. He offered to call the police to report the incident, but I was adamant against that. That's one of the things I remember *very* clearly. I knew the police were not likely to recover my purse and I did *not* want to become a newspaper item.

"I think I must have explained that I was from out of town because he lectured me, quite gently, on the dangers of walking in the streets of Manhattan. —I've heard so much on the subject in the last week. You should hear my niece go on and on about it.

"I remember other bits of the conversation. He wanted to know whether I'd lost much cash and I said, well, about thirty or forty dollars, but that I had traveler's checks which could, of course, be replaced. I think I had to spend some time reassuring him that I knew how to do that, and that I knew how to report my missing credit card. I had only had one in my purse.

"Finally I asked him his name so that I could speak to him properly and he laughed and said, 'Oh, first names will do for that.' He told me his and I told him mine. And I said, 'Isn't it astonishing how it all fits together, your name, and your address, and what you said back there.' I explained and he laughed and said he would never have thought of that. —So you see I knew his address.

"Then we went downstairs and it was quite late by then, at least by the clock, though, of course, it wasn't really very late by my insides. He made sure the streets were clear, then made me wait in the vestibule while he went out to hail the cab. He told me he had paid the driver to take me wherever I wanted to go and then before I could stop him he put a twenty-dollar bill in my hand because he said I mustn't be left with no money at all.

"I tried to object, but he said he loved New York, and since I had been so mistreated on my first evening there by New Yorkers, it had to be made up for by New Yorkers. So I accepted it—because I knew I would pay it back.

"The driver took me back to the hotel and he didn't try to collect any money. He even tried to give me change because he said the young man had given him a five-dollar bill, but I was pleased with his honesty and I wouldn't take the change.

"So you see although the incident began very painfully, there was the extreme kindness of the Good Samaritan young man and of the taxi driver. It was as though an act of unkindness was introduced into my life in order that I might experience other acts of kindness that would more than redress the balance. And I *still* experience them—yours, I mean.

"Of course, it was quite obvious that the young man was not well off and I strongly suspected that the twenty-five dollars he had expended on me was far more than he could afford to throw away. Nor did he ask my last name or the name of my hotel. It was as though he knew I would pay it back without having to be reminded. Naturally, I would.

"You see, I'm quite well-to-do really, and it's not just a matter of paying it back. The Bible says that if you cast your bread upon the waters it will be returned tenfold, so I think it's only fair that if he spent twenty-five dollars, he ought to get two hundred and fifty back, and I can afford it.

"I returned to my room and slept so soundly after all that; it was quite refreshing. The next morning, I arranged my affairs with respect to the credit card and the traveler's checks and then I called my niece and spent the day with her.

"I told her what had happened but just the bare essentials. After all, I had to explain why I had no bag and why I was temporarily short of cash. She went on and *on* about it. I bought a new purse—this one—and it wasn't till the end of the day when I was in bed again that I realized that I had not made it my business to repay the young man *first thing*. Being with family had just preoccupied me. And then the real tragedy struck me."

Mrs. Lindemann stopped and tried to keep her face from crumpling, but she failed. She began to weep quietly and to reach desperately into her bag for a handkerchief.

Henry said softly, "Would you care to rest, Mrs. Lindemann?"

Rubin said, just as softly, "Would you like a cup of tea, Mrs. Lindemann, or some brandy?" Then he glared about as though daring anyone to say a word.

Mrs. Lindemann said, "No, I'm all right. I apologize for behaving so, but I found I had forgotten. I don't remember the young man's address, *not at all*, though I must have known it that night because I talked about it. I don't remember his first name! I stayed awake all night trying to remember, and that just made it worse. I went out the next day to try to retrace my steps, but everything looked so different by day—and by night, I was afraid to try.

"What must the young man think of me? He's never heard from me. I took his money and just vanished with it. I am worse than those terrible young hoodlums who snatched my purse. I had never been kind to *them*. They owed *me* no gratitude."

Gonzalo said, "It's not your fault that you can't remember. You had a rough time."

"Yes, but *he* doesn't know I can't remember. He thinks I'm an ungrateful thief. Finally I told my nephew about my trouble and he was just thinking of employing Mr. Gonzalo for something and he felt that Mr. Gonzalo might have the kind of worldly wisdom that might help. Mr. Gonzalo said he would try, and in the end—well, here I am.

"But now that I've heard myself tell the story I realize how hopeless it all sounds."

Trumbull sighed.

"Mrs. Lindemann, please don't be offended at what I am about to ask, but we must eliminate some factors. Are you sure it all really happened?"

Mrs. Lindemann looked surprised. "Well, of *course* it really happened. My purse was *gone!*"

"No," said Henry, "what Mr. Trumbull means, I think, is that after the mugging you somehow got back to the hotel and then had a sleep that may have been filled with nightmares so that what you remember now is partly fact and partly dream—which would account for the imperfect memory."

"No," said Mrs. Lindemann firmly, "I remember what I do remember perfectly. It was not a dream."

"In that case," said Trumbull, shrugging, "we have very little to go on."

Rubin said, "Never mind, Tom. We're not giving up. If we choose the right name for your rescuer, Mrs. Lindemann, would you recognize it, even though you can't remember it now?"

"I hope so," said Mrs. Lindemann, "but I don't know. I've tried looking in a phone directory to see different first names, but none seemed familiar. I don't think it could have been a very common name."

Rubin said, "Then it couldn't have been Sam?"

"Oh, I'm certain that's not it."

"Why Sam, Manny?" asked Gonzalo.

"Well, the fellow was a Good Samaritan. Mrs. Lindemann called him that herself. Sam for Samaritan. His number and street may have represented the chapter and verse in the Bible where the tale of the Good Samaritan begins. You said his name and address fitted each other and that's the only clue we have."

"Wait," put in Avalon eagerly, "the first name might have been the much less common one of Luke. That's the gospel in which the parable is to be found."

"I'm afraid," said Mrs. Lindemann, "that doesn't sound right, either. Besides, I'm not *that* well acquainted with the Bible. I couldn't identify the chapter and verse of the parable."

Halsted said, "Let's not get off on impossible tangents. Mrs. Lindemann taught American history in school, so it's very likely that what struck her concerned American history. For instance, suppose the address were 1812 Madison Avenue and the young man's name was James. —James Madison was President during the War of 1812."

"Or 1492 Columbus Avenue," said Gonzalo, "and the young man was named Christopher."

"Or 1775 Lexington Avenue and the name Paul for Paul Revere," said Trumbull.

"Or 1623 Amsterdam Avenue and the name Peter," said Avalon, "for Peter Minuit, or 1609 Hudson Street and the name Henry. In fact, there are many such named streets in lower Manhattan. We can never pick an appropriate one unless Mrs. Lindemann remembers."

Mrs. Lindemann clasped her hands tightly together. "Oh, dear, oh, *dear,* nothing sounds familiar."

Rubin said, "Of course not, if we're going to guess at random. Mrs. Lindemann, I assume you are at a midtown hotel."

"I'm at the New York Hilton. Is that midtown?"

"Yes. Sixth Avenue and 53rd Street. The chances are you could not have walked more than a mile, probably less, before you grew tired. Therefore, let's stick to midtown. Hudson Street is much too far south and places like 1492 Columbus or 1812 Madison are much too far north. It would have to be midtown, probably west side—and I can't think of anything."

Drake said, through a haze of cigarette smoke, "You're forgetting one item. Mrs. Lindemann said it wasn't just the name and address that fit but what the young man said back there—that is, at the site of the rescue. What did he say back there?"

"It's all so hazy," said Mrs. Lindemann.

"You said he called out roughly at the muggers. Can you repeat what he said?"

Mrs. Lindemann colored. "I could repeat *some* of what he said, but I don't think I want to. The young man apologized for it afterward. He said that unless he used bad language the hoodlums would not have been impressed and would not have scattered. Besides, I know I couldn't have referred to *that* at all."

Drake said thoughtfully, "That bites the dust then. Have you thought of advertising? You know, 'Will the young man who aided a woman in distress—' and so on."

"I've thought of it," said Mrs. Lindemann, "but that would be *so* dreadful. He might not see it and so many impostors might try to make a claim. —Really, this is so dreadful."

Avalon, looking distressed, turned to Henry and said, "Well, Henry, does anything occur to you?"

Henry said, "I'm not certain. —Mrs. Lindemann, you said that by the time you took the taxi it was late by the clock but not by your insides. Does that mean you arrived from the west coast by plane so that your perception of time was three hours earlier?"

"Yes, I did," said Mrs. Lindemann.

"Perhaps from Portland, or not too far from there?" asked Henry.

"Why, yes, from just outside Portland. Had I mentioned that?"

"No, you hadn't," interposed Trumbull. "How did you know, Henry?"

"Because it occurred to me, sir," said Henry, "that the young man's name was Eugene, which is the name of a town only about a hundred miles south of Portland."

Mrs. Lindemann rose, eyes staring. "My goodness! The name *was* Eugene! But that's marvelous. How could you possibly tell?"

Henry said, "Mr. Rubin pointed out the address had to be in midtown Manhattan on the west side. Dr. Drake pointed out your reference to what the young man had said at the scene of the rescue, and I recalled that one thing you reported him to have said was that you had better go to his place or there'd be a battle.

"Mr. Halsted pointed out that the address ought to have some significance in American history and so I thought it might be 54 West 40th Street, since there is the well-known election slogan of '54-40 or fight,' the election of 1844, I believe. It would be particularly meaningful to Mrs. Lindemann if she were from the northwest since it pertained to our dispute with Great Britain over the Oregon Territory. When she said she was indeed from near Portland, Oregon, I guessed that the rescuer's name might be Eugene."

Mrs. Lindemann sat down, "To my dying day I will never forget this. That *is* the address. How could I have forgotten it when you worked it out so neatly from what little I did remember."

And then she grew excited. She said, "But it's not too late. I must go there *at once*. I must pay him or shove an envelope under his door or something."

Rubin said, "Will you recognize the house if you see it?"

"Oh, yes," said Mrs. Lindemann. "I'm sure of that. And it's apartment 4-F. I remembered that. If I knew his last name I would call but, no, I want to *see* him and explain."

Rubin said mildly, "You certainly can't go yourself, Mrs. Lindemann. Not into that neighborhood at this time of night after what you've been through. Some of us will have to go with you. At the very least, I will."

Mrs. Lindemann said, "I very much dislike inconveniencing you, Mr. Rubin."

"Under the circumstances, Mrs. Lindemann," said Rubin, "I consider it my duty."

Henry said, "If I know the Black Widowers, I believe we will all accompany you, Mrs. Lindemann."

MOM SINGS AN ARIA

James Yaffe

IT WAS ONE of the greatest disappointments of my mother's life that I never turned out to be a musical genius. For a couple of years, when I was a kid, Mom made me take violin lessons. At the end of the first year I played a piece called "Rustling Leaves." At the end of the second year I was still playing "Rustling Leaves." Poor Mom had to admit I wasn't another Jascha Heifetz, and that was the end of my musical career.

Mom has always been crazy about music herself. She did a little singing when she was a girl, and might have done something with her voice — instead she got married, moved up to the Bronx, and devoted herself to raising a future Lieutenant in the New York City Homicide Squad. But she still listens regularly to the Saturday afternoon broadcasts of the Metropolitan Opera, and she can still hum along with all the familiar arias. That was why — when my wife Shirley and I went up to the Bronx the other night for our regular Friday dinner — I knew Mom would be interested in my latest case.

"You're a music lover, Mom," I said. "Maybe you can understand how a man could love music so much that he'd commit murder for it."

"This is hard to understand?" Mom said, looking up from her roast chicken. "Why else did I stop your violin lessons? Once, while you were playing one of your pieces, I happened to take a look at your teacher, Mrs. Steinberg — and on her face was murder if I ever saw it!"

"You don't mean that literally, do you, Mother?" Shirley said. "A woman wouldn't *really* feel like murdering a little boy because he played the violin badly."

15

"People can have plenty feelings that were never in your psychology books at college," Mom said. "Believe me, in my own family—my Aunt Goldie who thought the pigeon outside her window was actually her late husband Jake—"

Mom went into detail, and her story was fascinating. Then she passed the chicken a second time, and I was able to get back to my murder.

"Have you ever seen the standing-room line at the Metropolitan Opera House?" I said. "Half an hour before every performance the box office sells standing-room tickets at two-fifty each, on a first-come first-served basis. The opera lovers start lining up outside the house hours ahead of time. They stand on their feet for three hours *during* the opera! Talk about crazy human motives!"

"People with no ears in their heads," Mom said, "shouldn't be so quick to call other people crazy." And she gave me one of those glares which has been making me feel like a naughty little five-year-old ever since I *was* a naughty little five-year-old.

I turned my eyes away and pushed on. "Well, there are certain people who show up on the opera standing-room line night after night, for practically every performance throughout the season. These 'regulars' are almost always at the head of the line—they come earlier than anyone else, wait longer, and take the best center places once they get inside the house. And since most of them have been doing this for years, they know each other by name, and they pass the time gossiping about the opera singers and discussing the performances. You could almost say they've got an exclusive little social club all their own—only their meeting place isn't a clubhouse, it's the sidewalk in front of the Met. Anyway, you couldn't imagine a more harmless collection of old fogeys—the last group on earth where you'd expect to find a murderer!"

"Even an opera lover has to have a private life," Mom said. "He enjoys himself with the beautiful music—but he's still got business troubles or love troubles or family troubles waiting for him at home."

"That's just it, Mom. If one of these standing-room regulars had gone home and killed his wife or his mother-in-law or his business partner, this would just be another routine case. But what happened was, he killed one of the other people in the standing-room line."

Mom was looking at me with her eyes narrowed—a sure sign that I had interested her. "The two oldest regulars in the standing-room line," I said, "the charter members of the club, are Sam Cohen and Giuseppe D'Angelo. Cohen used to be a pharmacist, with his own drug store on the West Eighty-third Street. He retired fifteen years ago, after his wife died, and turned the management of the store over to his nephew, though he went on living in the apartment above it. As soon as he retired, he started going to the opera almost every night of the season.

"D'Angelo was in the exterminating business out in Queens— insects, rodents, and so on—but *he* retired fifteen years ago too. His wife is alive, but she doesn't care for music, so he's been in the habit of going to the opera by himself—almost every night of the season, just like Cohen.

"The two old men met on the standing-room line fifteen years ago, and have seen each other three or four nights a week ever since—but only at the opera, never anywhere else. As far as we know, they've never met for a drink or a lunch, they've never been to each other's homes, and they've never seen each other at all in the summer, when the opera is closed.

"Opera is the biggest thing in both their lives. Cohen's mother was a vocal coach back in Germany, and he cut his teeth on operatic arias— D'Angelo was born and brought up in the city of Parma, which they tell me is the most operatic city in Italy—"

"I've read about Parma," Mom said. "If a tenor hits a bad note there, they run him out of town."

"How horrible!" Shirley said. "It's positively, uncivilized!"

Mom shrugged. "A little less civilization here in New York, and maybe we wouldn't hear so many bad notes."

I could see the cloud of indignation forming on Shirley's face—she never *has* caught on to Mom's peculiar sense of humor. I hurried on, "Well, the two old men both loved opera, but their opinions about it have always been diametrically opposed. So for fifteen years they've been carrying on a running argument. If Cohen likes a certain soprano, D'Angelo can't stand her. If D'Angelo mentions having heard Caruso sing *Aida* in 1920, Cohen says that Caruso never sang *Aida* after 1917.

"And the old men haven't conducted these arguments in nice soft gentlemanly voices either. They yell at each other, wave their arms, call each other all sorts of names. 'Liar' and 'moron' are about the tamest I can think of. In spite of their bitterness, of course, these fights have never lasted long—before the night is over, or at least by the time of the next performance, the old men always make it up between them—"

"Until now?" Mom said.

"I'll get to that in a minute, Mom. Just a little more background first. According to the other regulars on the standing-room line, the fights between Cohen and D'Angelo have become even more bitter than usual in recent years. They've been aggravated by a controversy which has been raging among opera lovers all over the world. Who's the greatest soprano alive today—Maria Callas or Renata Tebaldi?"

Mom dropped her fork and clasped her hands to her chest, and on her face came that ecstatic almost girlish look which she reserves exclusively for musical matters. "Callas! Tebaldi! Voices like angels, both of them! That Callas—such fire, such passion! That Tebaldi—such beauty, such sadness! To choose which one is the greatest—it's as foolish as trying to choose between noodle soup and borscht!"

"Cohen and D'Angelo made their choices, though," I said. "D'Angelo announced one day that Tebaldi was glorious and Callas had a voice like a rooster—so right away Cohen told him that Callas was divine and Tebaldi sang like a cracked phonograph record. And the argument has been getting more and more furious through the years.

"A week ago a climax was reached. Callas was singing *Traviata,* and the standing-room line started to form even earlier than usual. Cohen and D'Angelo, of course, were right there among the first. Cohen had a bad cold—he was sneezing all the time he stood in line—but he said he wouldn't miss Callas' *Traviata* if he was down with double pneumonia. And D'Angelo said that personally he could live happily for the rest of his life without hearing Callas butcher *Traviata*—he was here tonight, he said, only because of the tenor, Richard Tucker."

"That Richard Tucker!" Mom gave her biggest, most motherly smile. "Such a wonderful boy—just as much at home in the *schul* as he is in the opera. What a proud mother he must have!" And Mom gave me a look which made it clear that she still hadn't quite forgiven me for "Rustling Leaves."

"With such a long wait on the standing-room line," I said, "Cohen and D'Angelo had time to whip up a first-class battle. According to Frau Hochschwender—she's a German lady who used to be a concert pianist and now gives piano lessons, and she's also one of the standing-room regulars—Cohen and D'Angelo had never insulted each other so violently in all the years she'd known them. If the box office had opened an hour later, she says they would have come to blows.

"As it turned out, the performance itself didn't even put an end to their fight. Ordinarily, once the opera began, both men became too wrapped up in the music to remember they were mad at each other—but this time, when the first act ended, Cohen grabbed D'Angelo by the arm and accused him of deliberately groaning after Callas' big aria. 'You did it to ruin the evening for me!' Cohen said. He wouldn't pay attention to D'Angelo's denials. 'I'll get even with you,' he said. 'Wait till the next time Tebaldi is singing!' "

"And the next time Tebaldi was singing," Mom said, "was the night of the murder?"

"Exactly. Three nights ago Tebaldi sang *Tosca*—"

"*Tosca!*" Mom's face lighted up. "Such a beautiful opera! Such a sad story! She's in love with this handsome young artist, and this villain makes advances and tries to force her to give in to him, so she stabs him with a knife. Come to think of it, the villain in that opera is a police officer."

I looked hard, but I couldn't see any trace of sarcasm on Mom's face.

"Those opera plots are really ridiculous, aren't they?" Shirley said. "So exaggerated and unrealistic."

"Unrealistic!" Mom turned to her sharply. "You should know some of the things that go on—right here in this building. Didn't Polichek the janitor have his eye on his wife's baby sitter?"

Another fascinating story came out of Mom, and then I went on. "Anyway, for the whole week-end before *Tosca,* D'Angelo worried that Cohen would do something to spoil the performance for him. He worried so much that the night before, he called Cohen up and pleaded with him not to make trouble."

"And Cohen answered?"

"His nephew was in the room with him when the call came. He was going over some account books and didn't really pay attention to what his uncle was saying—at one point he heard Cohen raise his voice angrily and shout out, 'You can't talk me out of it! When Tebaldi hits her high C in the big aria, I'm going to start booing!"

Mom shook her head. "Terrible—a terrible threat for a civilized man to make! So does D'Angelo admit that Cohen made it?"

"Well, yes and no. In the early part of the phone conversation, D'Angelo says he and Cohen were yelling at each other so angrily that neither of them listened to what the other one was saying. But later on in the conversation—or so D'Angelo claims—Cohen calmed down and promised to let Tebaldi sing her aria in peace."

"Cohen's nephew says he didn't?"

"Not exactly. He left the room while Cohen was still on the phone—he had to check some receipts in the cash register—so he never heard the end of the conversation. For all he knows Cohen *might* have calmed down and made that promise."

"And what about D'Angelo's end of the phone conversation? Was anybody in the room with him?"

"His wife was. And she swears that he *did* get such a promise out of Cohen. But of course she's his wife, so she's anxious to protect him. And besides she's very deaf, and she won't wear a hearing aid—she's kind of a vain old lady. So what it boils down to, we've got nobody's word except D'Angelo's that Cohen didn't intend to carry out his threat."

"Which brings us," Mom said, "to the night Tebaldi sang *Tosca?*"

"Cohen and D'Angelo both showed up early on the standing-room line that night. Frau Hochschwender says they greeted each other politely, but all the time they were waiting they hardly exchanged a word. No arguments, no differences of opinion—nothing. And her testimony is confirmed by another one of the regulars who was there—Miss Phoebe Van Voorhees. She's an old lady in her seventies, always dresses in black.

"Miss Van Voorhees came from a wealthy New York family, and when she was a young woman she used to have a regular box at the opera—but the money ran out ten or twelve years ago, and now she lives alone in a cheap hotel in the East Twenties. and she waits on the standing-room line two nights a week. She's so frail-looking you wouldn't think she could stay on her feet for five minutes, much less five hours—but she loves opera, so she does it."

"For love," Mom said, "people can perform miracles."

"Well, Miss Van Voorhees and Frau Hochschwender both say that Cohen and D'Angelo were unusually restrained with each other. Which seems to prove that they were still mad at each other and hadn't made up the quarrel over the phone, as D'Angelo claims—"

"Or maybe it proves the opposite," Mom said. "They *did* make up the quarrel, and they were so scared of starting another quarrel that they shut up and wouldn't express any opinions."

"Whatever it proves, Mom, here's what happened. On cold nights it's the custom among the standing-room regulars for one of them to go to the cafeteria a block away and get hot coffee for the others—meanwhile they hold his place in the line. The night of Tebaldi's *Tosca* was very cold, and it was D'Angelo's turn to bring the coffee.

"He went for it about forty-five minutes before the box office opened, and got back with it in fifteen or twenty minutes. He was carrying four cardboard containers. Three of them contained coffee with cream and sugar—for Frau Hochschwender, Miss Van Voorhees, and D'Angelo himself. In the fourth container was black coffee without sugar—the way Cohen always took it.

"Well, they all gulped down their coffee, shielding it from the wind with their bodies—and about half an hour later the doors opened. They bought their tickets, went into the opera house, and stood together in their usual place in the back, at the center.

"At eight sharp the opera began. Tebaldi was in great voice, and the audience was enthusiastic. At the end of the first act all of the standing-room regulars praised her—except Cohen. He just grunted and said nothing. Frau Hochschwender and Miss Van Voorhees both say that he looked pale and a little ill.

" 'Wait till she sings her big aria in the second act,' D'Angelo said. 'I hope she sings it good,' Cohen said—and Frau Hochschwender says there was a definite threat in his voice. Miss Van Voorhees says she didn't notice anything significant in his voice—to her it just sounded like an offhand remark. Then the second act began, and it was almost time for Tebaldi's big aria—"

"Such a beautiful aria!" Mom said. *"Vissy darty.* It's Italian. She's telling that police officer villain that all her life she's cared only for love and for art, and she never wanted to hurt a soul. She tells him this, and a little later she stabs him." And in a low voice, a little quavery but really kind of pretty, Mom began to half sing and half hum— *"Vissy darty, vissy damory—"* Then she broke off, and did something I had seldom seen her do. She blushed.

There was a moment of silence, while Shirley and I carefully refrained from looking at each other. Then I said, "So a few minutes before Tebaldi's big aria, Cohen suddenly gave a groan, then he grabbed hold of Frau Hochschwender's arm and said, 'I'm sick—' And then he started making strangling noises, and dropped like a lead weight to the floor.

"Somebody went for a doctor, and D'Angelo got down on his knees by Cohen and said, 'Cohen, Cohen, what's the matter?' And Cohen, with his eyes straight on D'Angelo's face, said, 'You no-good! You deserve to die for what you did!' Those were his exact words, Mom—half a dozen people heard them.

"Then a doctor came, with a couple of ushers, and they took Cohen out to the lobby—and D'Angelo, Frau Hochschwender, and Miss Van Voorhees followed. A little later an ambulance came, but Cohen was dead before he got to the hospital.

"At first the doctors thought it was a heart attack, but they did a routine autopsy—and found enough poison in his stomach to kill a man half his age and twice his strength. The dose he swallowed must've taken two to three hours to produce a reaction—which means he swallowed it while he was on the standing-room line. Well, nobody saw him swallow *anything* on the standing-room line except that container of hot black coffee."

"And when the doctors looked at the contents of his stomach?"

"They found the traces of his lunch, which *couldn't* have contained the poison or he would've died long before he got to the opera house—and they found that coffee—and that was all they found. So the coffee had to be what killed him."

"And since that old man D'Angelo is the one who gave him the coffee, you naturally think he's the murderer."

"What else can we think, Mom? For five minutes or so—from the time
he picked up the coffee at the cafeteria to the time he gave it to Cohen
at the opera house—D'Angelo was alone with it. Nobody was watching
him—he could easily have slipped something into it. And nobody *else*
had such an opportunity. Cohen took the coffee from D'Angelo, turned
away to shield the container from the cold wind, and drank it all down
then and there. Only D'Angelo *could* have put the poison into it."

"What about the man at the cafeteria who made the coffee?"

"That doesn't make sense, Mom. The man at the cafeteria would have
no way of knowing who the coffee was meant for. He'd have to be a
complete psycho who didn't care *who* he poisoned. Just the same, though,
we checked him out. He poured the coffee into the container directly
from a big urn—twenty other people had been drinking coffee from the
same urn. Then in front of a dozen witnesses he handed the container to
D'Angelo without putting a thing in it—not even sugar, because Cohen
never took his coffee with sugar. So we're right back to D'Angelo—he
has to be the murderer."

"And where did he get it, this deadly poison? Correct me if I'm wrong,
but such an item isn't something you can pick up at your local supermarket."

"Sure, it's against the law to sell poison to the general public. But
you'd be surprised how easy it is to get hold of the stuff anyway. The
kind that killed Cohen is a common commercial compound—it's used to
mix paints, for metallurgy, in certain medicines, in insecticides. Ordinary
little pellets of rat poison are made of it sometimes, and you can buy
them at your local hardware store—a couple of dozen kids swallow them
by accident in this city every year. And don't forget, D'Angelo used to
be in the exterminating business—he knows all the sources, it would be
easier for him to get his hands on poison than for most people."

"So you've arrested him for the murder?" Mom said.

I gave a sigh. "No, we haven't."

"How come? What's holding you up?"

"It's the motive, Mom. D'Angelo and Cohen had absolutely no connection with each other outside of the standing-room line. Cohen didn't leave
D'Angelo any money, he wasn't having an affair with D'Angelo's wife,
he didn't know a deep dark secret out of D'Angelo's past. There's only
one reason why D'Angelo could have killed him—to stop him from booing
at the end of Renata Tebaldi's big aria. That's why he committed the
murder. I'm morally certain of it, and so is everyone else in the Department. And so is the D.A.'s office—but they won't let us make the arrest."

"And why not?"

"Because nobody believes for one moment that we can get a jury to believe such a motive. Juries are made up of ordinary everyday people. They don't go to the opera. They think it's all a lot of nonsense—fat women screaming at fat men, in a foreign language. I can sympathize with them—I think so myself. Can you imagine the D.A. standing up in front of a jury and saying, 'The defendant was so crazy about an opera singer's voice that he killed a man for disagreeing with him!' The jury would laugh in the D.A.'s face."

I sighed harder than before. "We've got an airtight case. The perfect opportunity. No other possible suspects. The dying man's accusation— 'You no-good! You deserve to die for what you did!' But we don't dare bring the killer to trial."

Mom didn't say anything for a few seconds. Her eyes were almost shut, the corners of her mouth were turned down. I know this expression well—her "thinking" expression. Something always comes out of it.

Finally she looked up and gave a nod. "Thank God for juries!"

"What do you mean, Mom?"

"I mean, if it wasn't for ordinary everyday people with common sense, God knows *who* you experts would be sending to jail!"

"Mom, are you saying that D'Angelo *didn't*—"

"I'm saying nothing. Not yet. First I'm asking. Four questions."

No doubt about it, whenever Mom starts asking her questions, that means she's on the scent, she's getting ready to hand me a solution to another one of my cases.

My feelings, as always, were mixed. On the one hand, nobody admires Mom more than I do—her deep knowledge of human nature acquired among her friends and neighbors in the Bronx; her uncanny sharpness in applying that knowledge to the crimes I tell her about from time to time.

On the other hand—well, how ecstatic is a man supposed to get at the idea that his mother can do his own job better than *he* can? That's why I've never been able to talk about Mom's talent to anybody else in the Department—except, of course, to Inspector Milner, my immediate superior, and only because he's a widower, and Shirley and I are trying to get something going between Mom and him.

So I guess my voice wasn't as enthusiastic as it should have been, when I said to Mom, "Okay, what are your four questions?"

"First I bring in the peach pie," Mom said.

We waited while the dishes were cleared, and new dishes were brought. Then the heavenly aroma of Mom's peach pie filled the room. One taste of it, and my enthusiasm began to revive. "What *are* your questions, Mom?"

She lifted her finger. "Number One: you mentioned that Cohen had a cold a week ago, the night Maria Callas was singing *Traviata*. Did he still have the same cold three nights ago, when Tebaldi was singing *Tosca?*"

By this time I ought to be used to Mom's questions. I ought to take it on faith that they're probably not as irrelevant as they sound. But I still can't quite keep the bewilderment out of my voice.

"As a matter of fact," I said, "Cohen *did* have a cold the night of the murder. Frau Hochschwender and Miss Van Voorhees both mentioned it—he was sneezing while he waited in line, and even a few times during the performance, though he tried hard to control himself."

Mom's face gave no indication whether this was or wasn't what she wanted to hear. She lifted another finger. "Number Two: after the opera every night, was it the custom for those standing-room regulars to separate right away—or did they maybe stay together for a little while before they finally said good night?"

"They usually went to the cafeteria a block away—the same place where D'Angelo bought the coffee that Cohen drank—and sat at a table for an hour or so and discussed the performance they'd just heard. Over coffee and doughnuts—or Danish pastry."

Mom gave a nod, and lifted another finger. "Number Three: at the hospital you naturally examined what was in Cohen's pockets. Did you find something like an envelope—a small envelope with absolutely nothing in it?"

This question really made me jump. "We did find an envelope, Mom. Ordinary stationery size—it was unsealed, and there was no address or stamp on it. But how in the world did you—"

Mom's fourth finger was in the air. "Number Four: how many times this season is Renata Tebaldi supposed to sing *Tosca?*"

"It was Tebaldi's first, last, and only performance of *Tosca* this season," I said. "The posters in front of the opera house said so. But I don't see what that has to do with—"

"You don't see," Mom said. "Naturally. You're like all the younger generation these days. So scientific. Facts you see. D'Angelo was the only one who was ever alone with Cohen's coffee—so D'Angelo must have put the poison in. A fact, so you see it. But what about the *people* already? Who is D'Angelo—who was Cohen—what type human beings? This you wouldn't ask yourself. Probably you wouldn't even understand about my Uncle Julius and the World Series."

"I'm sorry, Mom. I never knew you *had* an Uncle Julius—"

"I don't have him no more. That's the point of the story. All his life he was a fan from the New York Yankees. He rooted for them, he bet money on them, and when they played the World Series he was always there to watch them. Until a couple of years ago when he had his heart attack, and he was in the hospital at World Series time.

" 'I'll watch the New York Yankees on television,' he said. 'The excitement is too much for you,' the doctor said. 'It'll kill you.' But Uncle Julius had his way, and he watched the World Series. Every day he watched, and every night the doctor said, 'You'll be dead before morning.' And Uncle Julius said, 'I wouldn't die till I know how the World Series comes out!' So finally the New York Yankees won the World Series—and an hour later Uncle Julius went to sleep and died."

Mom stopped talking, and looked around at Shirley and me. Then she shook her head and said, "You don't follow yet? A man with a love for something that's outside himself, that isn't even his family—with a love for the New York Yankees or for Renata Tebaldi—in such a man this feeling is stronger than his personal worries or his personal ambitions. He wouldn't let anything interrupt his World Series in the middle, not even dying. He wouldn't let anything interrupt his opera in the middle—not even murdering."

I began to see a glimmer of Mom's meaning. "You're talking about D'Angelo, Mom?"

"Who else? Renata Tebaldi was singing her one and only *Tosca* for the year, and for D'Angelo, Renata Tebaldi is the greatest singer alive. Never— in a million years, never—would he do anything to spoil this performance for himself, to make him walk out of it before the end. Let's say he *did* want to murder Cohen. The last time in the world he'd pick for this murder would be in the middle of Tebaldi's *Tosca*—her one and only *Tosca!* Especially since he could wait just as easy till after the opera, when the standing-room regulars would be having cake and coffee at the cafeteria— he could just as easy poison Cohen *then*."

"But Mom, isn't that kind of far-fetched, psychologically? If the average man was worked up enough to commit a murder, he wouldn't care about hearing the end of an opera first!"

"Excuse me, Davie—the average man's psychology we're not talking about. The opera lover's psychology we are talking about. This is why you and the Homicide Squad and the District Attorney couldn't make heads and tails from this case. Because you don't understand from opera lovers. In this world they don't live—they've got a world of their own. Inside their heads things are going on which other people's heads never even dreamed about. To solve this case you have to think like an opera lover."

"To solve this case, Mom, you have to answer the basic question: if

D'Angelo didn't poison that coffee who *could* have?"

"Who says the coffee was poisoned?"

"But I told you about the autopsy. The poison took two to three hours to work, and the contents of Cohen's stomach—"

"The contents of his stomach! You should show a little more interest in the contents of Cohen's pockets!"

"There was nothing unusual in his pockets—"

"Why should a man carry in his pocket an empty unsealed envelope, without any writing on it, without even a stamp on it? Only because it wasn't empty when he put it there. Something was in it—something which he expected to need later on in the evening—something which he finally took out of the envelope—"

"What are you talking about, Mom?"

"I'm talking about Cohen's cold. An ordinary man, he don't think twice about going to the opera with a cold. What's the difference if he sneezes a little? It's only music. But to an opera lover, sneezing during a performance, disturbing people, competing with the singers—this is worse than a major crime. A real opera lover like Cohen, he'd do everything he could to keep his cold under control.

"Which explains what he put in that envelope before he left his home to go to the opera house. A pill, what else? One of these new prescription cold pills that dries up your nose and keeps you from sneezing for five-six hours. And why was the envelope empty when you found it in his pocket? Because half an hour before the box office opened, he slipped out his pill and swallowed it down with his hot black coffee."

"Nobody *saw* him taking that pill, Mom."

"Why should anybody see him? Like you explained yourself, to drink his coffee he had to turn his body away and shield the container from the wind."

I was beginning to be shaken, no doubt about it. But Shirley spoke up now, in her sweet voice, the voice she always uses when she thinks she's one up on Mom. "The facts don't seem to bear you out, Mother. All the witnesses say that Mr. Cohen went on sneezing *after* the opera had begun. Well, if he really did take a cold pill, as you believe, why didn't it have any effect on his symptoms?"

A gleam came to Mom's eyes and I could see she was about to pounce. The fact is that Shirley never learns.

So to spare my wife's feelings I broke in quickly, before Mom could open her mouth. "I'm afraid that confirms Mom's theory, honey. The reason why the cold pill didn't work was that it wasn't a cold pill. It looked like one on the outside maybe, but it actually contained poison."

"I always knew I didn't produce a dope!" Mom said, with a big satisfied smile. "So now the answer is simple, no? If Cohen was carrying around a poison pill in his pocket, where did he get it? Who gave it to him? Why should he think it was a cold pill? Because somebody told him it was. Somebody he thought he could trust—not only personally but professionally. 'Give me some of that new stuff, that new wonder drug, that'll keep me from sneezing during the opera—' "

"His nephew!" I interrupted. "My God, Mom, I think you're right. Cohen's nephew *is* a pharmacist—he manages the drug store that Cohen owned. He has access to all kinds of poison and he could make up a pill that would look like a real cold pill. And what's more, he's the only relative Cohen has in the world. He inherits Cohen's store and Cohen's savings."

Mom spread her hands. "So there you are. You couldn't ask for a more ordinary, old-fashioned motive for murder. Any jury will be able to understand it. It isn't one bit operatic."

"But Mom, you must've suspected Cohen's nephew from the start. Otherwise you wouldn't have asked your question about the empty envelope."

"Naturally I suspected him. It was the lie he told."

"What lie?"

"The night before the opera D'Angelo called up Cohen and tried to make up their quarrel. Now, according to the nephew, Cohen made a threat to D'Angelo over the phone. 'When Tebaldi hits her high C in the big aria, I'm going to start booing!' A terrible threat—but Cohen never could have made it."

"I don't see why not—"

"Because Cohen was an opera lover, that's why. A high C—in the *Vissy darty* from *Tosca* there isn't any such note. A high B flat is what the soprano is supposed to sing at the end of this aria. If Tebaldi ever made such a mistake—which in a million years she couldn't do—the conductor would have a conniption fit and Cohen would hide his head in shame. People who are ignoramuses about opera—people like Cohen's nephew—they never *heard* of anything except the high C. But an opera lover like Cohen—he positively couldn't get so mixed up. Now excuse me, I'll bring in the coffee."

Mom got to her feet, and then Shirley called out, "Wait a second, Mother. If his nephew committed the murder, why did Cohen accuse D'Angelo of doing it?"

"When did Cohen accuse D'Angelo?"

"His dying words. He looked into D'Angelo's face and said, 'You no-good! You deserve to die for what you did!'"

"He looked into D'Angelo's face—but how do you know it was D'Angelo he was seeing? He was in delirium from the weakness and the pain, and before his eyes he wasn't seeing any D'Angelo, he wasn't seeing this world that the rest of us are living in. He was seeing the world he was looking at before he got sick, the world that meant the most to him—he was seeing the world of the opera, what else? And what was happening up there on the stage just before the poison hit him? The no-good villain was making advances to the beautiful heroine, and she was struggling to defend herself, and pretty soon she was going to kill him—and Cohen, seeing that villain in front of his eyes, shouted at him, 'You no-good! You deserve to die for what you did!' "

Mom was silent for a moment, and then went on in a lower voice, "An opera lover will go on being an opera lover—right up to the end."

She went out to the kitchen for the coffee, and I went to the phone in the hall to call the Homicide Squad.

When I got back to the table, Mom was seated and the coffee was served. She took a few sips, and then gave a little sigh. "Poor old Cohen—such a terrible way to go!"

"Death by poisoning *is* pretty painful," I said.

"Poisoning?" Mom blinked up at me. "Yes, this is terrible too. But the worst part of all—the poor man died fifteen minutes too soon. He never heard Tebaldi sing the *Vissy darty.*"

And Mom began to hum softly.

THE WOMAN I ENVIED
George Baxt

I'D HAVE LEFT my husband except I loved our apartment. I suppose that sounds like a facetious statement, but it happens to be quite honest. We married almost forty years ago when falling in love and marrying was less expensive. Abner was considered a genius and I was looked upon as an oddity. I had read Marx and Engels when others were reading Tiffany Thayer and Edna Ferber. We were both twenty years of age and we married in haste because there was a war hanging over our heads like the sword of Damocles. My best friend offered us her studio for a honeymoon, then Abner went off to war—the European theater (theater, what a tame appelation for that bloody arena!)—leaving behind a pregnant bride. Rebecca Berger, aged twenty. Another kind friend gave me a job as a clerk in his bookstore on the Upper West Side of my beloved New York City. I had no idea at the time, and this is the truth, that it was a Communist front. I just thought it was intellectually advanced and I met a lot of interesting people, some of whom went on to literary and theatrical fame, some to notoriety, and most to oblivion. I wish I had joined the oblivions but it's too late now.

My baby was born on Christmas Eve and that made me feel biblical, so I called him Aaron Moses. I went back to work almost immediately, except this time as the editor at a small publishing house that specialized in what would some years in the future be referred to as inflammatory and anti-American. Actually, some of what we published was quite good and about a dozen of the books are today represented on the back lists of other houses. Of course they're no longer radical. They're minor classics.

When the war was over and Abner came home to our vast barn of an apartment on Riverside Drive where the rent was delightfully modest, we were, like too many other wartime couples, strangers. He took pride in our son, who was now three years old and resented this peculiar older man's intrusion, but he didn't quite relish living off his wife, who was now earning a heathy salary. There was also a live-in housekeeper, Natasha Brown, a lovely black lady whose mother had named her after Rudolph Valentino's second wife, Natasha Rambova. I thought that was rather cute. Adner said it was degrading and once he said it I knew we were going to be in trouble.

My name was becoming an important one in literary circles. Rebecca Walsh Berger. I had found, nursed, and published an impressive list of young writers. No need to inscribe them here. You can buy my autobiography when it comes off the presses next autumn. Anyway, my life, my triumphs and my tragedies, are not what this story is all about. What I'm doing now is laying the groundwork so you'll understand the horror I shall eventually unveil.

In time, because I worked very hard at it, Abner and I grew comfortable together. It wasn't the youthful passion of our courting days, but what there was was serviceable. I introduced Abner to a film producer who was negotiating the rights to one of my writer's novels—Jack Dresden's remarkable *Bloody Castanets*, about Franco and the Spanish Civil War, which of course was never filmed because the Franco government protested vehemently—and they took to each other immediately. Norman Lubin, the producer, took Abner to Hollywood, where they traded their lofty beliefs and ideals for a series of innocent, inane comedies that made Mr. Lubin a millionaire and provided Abner with a steady income. He wasn't a good enough business man to demand a percentage, but then not being good enough was always Abner's shortcoming. Still, he began to earn the respect of the film industry, which was not yet reeling from the shattering competition the television industry would soon offer.

And since he was spending most of his time on the West Coast and I spent most of my time on the East Coast, we both took lovers.

But by the time our son Aaron went off to private school, Natasha had left me and I was alone. No son, no housekeeper, no husband, no lover. There was plenty to occupy my mind, however. There was something called the House Unamerican Activities Committee, for instance. The witch hunt found Abner and me among the victims. Abner's innocuous films were somehow branded Communistic. (Watching them occasionally on late-night television I'm still astonished at how lamebrained those scripts were.) And while loathsome gossip columnists were pilorying

Abner on the West Coast, I was being assailed in the East as the Red Queen. My company bravely stood by me and ignored the hundreds of anonymous phone calls and hate letters directed at me. But when poor Abner was sent to jail for refusing to name names, the jig, as they sometimes say, was up. Actually, I would have dug in my heels and continued resisting, but then Aaron was brutally beaten by some of his classmates because his mother and father were "dirty Commy reds."

I removed him from school. I visited Abner in jail. I couldn't kiss him goodbye because there was a glass barrier between us, but then there had always been barriers between us. I sublet our gorgeous apartment to a dimwitted young woman who was earning a fortune writing books about her funny funny life as a school teacher. (You might remember Rachel Goddard. She was stabbed to death by one of her students after he learned how to read.) I took Aaron to England, and after a few months of hardship I set up a television producing company. In five years I was a millionaire. Aaron was my associate producer, the youngest in the business. (After serving a year and a day in jail, poor Abner got a job managing a luncheonette in Queens. He couldn't get a passport to join us in London.)

I held onto the Riverside Drive apartment and when the building went cooperative I bought it for what would be considered a steal today. In a letter from my then tenant Miss Goddard I learned that the apartment next door had been bought by a psychiatrist, Daniel Ostrer. Well, it was certainly big enough to be divided into offices and residence. But why did I feel uneasy as I read and reread Rachel Goddard's letter about Doctor Ostrer? I didn't know the man, let alone what he looked like. I did know from Rachel that he was in his early forties, that his wife was a quiet woman named Ethel, and that they had a teenaged daughter named Rosalie who was very polite when encountered in the hallway or the elevator. Rachel also let me know that a laundry room had been installed in the basement.

Abner now had his passport but no inclination to join me in London. Instead he went to Hollywood again. At about the same time, Aaron decided it was time to fly the nest and he too took wing for Hollywood, where you all know he became a multimillionaire television producer (due in part to his lack of any taste). In London, my world slowly disintegrated. My lawyers robbed me of almost all my millions (without even knowing the numbers of the Swiss accounts) and the type of television I was producing fell out of favor. It was time to go home. All the witch hunters were dead. And so was my tenant, Miss Goddard.

When I returned to New York, I wasn't exactly poverty-stricken. I still owned residual interests in my television series and there were the dozens

of paintings I had bought in Europe in addition to my strongbox filled
with jewelry. And in no time Dame Fortune once again favored me through
a new East Coast film company, the owner of which, Dominic D'amigo,
persuaded me to join as a full partner once we began our affair. It didn't
bother me that I then became known as "The Queen of Pornography."

But then, right after I redid the apartment from top to bottom, Dominic
was found at the wheel of his car in a parking lot in Canarsie with four
bullets in his head. And right after I took possession of the film company,
Abner came home from Hollywood to die.

"It's terminal," he told me, "and I'm frightened."

I put my arms around him and kissed him on the lips. Oh, his hair
was white and there was a pink tonsure that was a bit shiny when the sun
hit it and his face was wrinkled and his skin was the color of a baked
potato and his hands trembled and he hadn't done anything of note professionally in years, but I knew I'd take care of him. I didn't realize he might
go into years of remission, which he did, and become such a painful
thorn in my side.

And I was tired. Very tired.

One day as I left the apartment, locked the door behind me, and crossed
to the elevator, the door to the adjoining apartment opened and out stepped
a very pretty woman with two children, a boy and a girl. I guessed the
woman to be in her early thirties and the boy and the girl about six or
seven years old, possibly twins. The elevator came and I held the door
open while the woman attended to the four locks on her door. I only had
one lock because I'd long ago assumed a devil-may-care attitude toward
the percentages in being robbed or mugged on the street.

"Oh, thank you so much," she said in a velvet voice as she herded
the youngsters into the elevator. The children smiled politely, but there
was something weird about them. They were too perfectly behaved. They
didn't chatter or misbehave the way most kids that age do. He was a
perfect little gentleman and she was a perfect little lady—and the mother,
now that I got a closer look at her, was perfection. Not a hair out of
place, just a trace of make up on her face because with that glorious skin
who needed artificial embellishments? Her suit was exquisite and magnificently tailored. It had cost plenty. I introduced myself.

She smiled and said almost shyly, "I'm Rosalie Appleby. This is my
son Nicholas and this is my daughter Evangeline." Nicholas smiled and
Evangeline hung her head. With a name like that, I didn't blame her.
"You've been back from England quite a while now, haven't you?"

I told her yes and asked if she knew what had become of the doctor
who had had her apartment.

"That was my father. Doctor Ostrer. He was a psychoanalyst. He and mother went to live in Florida after his breakdown, so my husband, the children, and I moved in. Daddy gave the place to us." I felt there was something she wanted to ask me, but we had arrived at the lobby. She let me precede her family out of the elevator. The doorman, who was an Iranian student, held the door open for us and we walked out into a blaze of sunshine.

"Going shopping?" I asked her.

"Just to the supermarket," she said. Dressed to the nines just to go to the supermarket? "Are you going to your office?"

"Yes I am."

"I wish I was going to an office." Had her voice trembled then? I'm not sure. It was so many months ago. I only remember being preoccupied with why the doorman had suddenly held the door open for us when usually I had to struggle with it on my own while he concentrated on his comic book. Then I remembered. It was only seven weeks until Christmas.

"I've never had a job," Rosalie Appleby said wistfully.

"You *have* a job," I told her, "you're a mother. You're raising two perfectly lovely children." I tried not to sound like Betty Furness giving a consumer report, but I wasn't succeeding. What I was saying I was saying halfheartedly. She obviously felt trapped. *Felt* trapped, hell, she *was* trapped. Of all the strange times and places for me to have a sudden and much-needed flash of self-awareness—at that moment I realized what a lucky woman I had been. Despite the trials, the tribulations, the vicissitudes, and mental tortures I had endured, I understood now that I had lived one hell of an exciting life. And that I would like nothing better than to change places with her!

I said it out loud. "I wish I was going to the supermarket with my children. I wish I was a young married woman with a loving husband. Oh, dear Mrs. Appleby, count your blessings."

"You're so sweet," she said. "I hope we get to know each other better." Then she took the children each by a hand and they went marching off to the supermarket while I flagged a cab and directed him to my world of carnal sin.

That night when I got home Abner told me Rosalie Appleby had invited us over for a drink. He was stretched out on the couch in the living room, reading a murder mystery and looking very healthy. It was a bit after seven. "Too late now, isn't it?" I asked.

"No," said Abner. "She said she puts the kids to bed at seven."

"Seven! Surely not in this day and age. Only pioneer families put their children to bed at seven."

"Please, Rebecca." His voice was suddenly weak and belonged to a martyr. "She said seven. It's after that now. If you're interested in a drink with the Applebys, go ring their bell and join them."

"What about you?"

"I'm not up to it."

"Aren't you feeling well?"

"How do you think a dying man feels?"

"I don't know. I've never been a dying man." I went to the bedroom and changed into a superb new pants suit. When I returned to the living room, Abner was sitting up watching a game show on television. "Change your mind and come with me," I said. "I'd like your opinion of Rosalie Appleby and her children." I told him about my morning encounter.

"No, thanks," he said. "I'd rather watch TV. Are we eating in or out?"

"I'll let you know when I get back."

Rosalie Appleby greeted me like a long lost friend. Victor Appleby was a knockout. He was easily ten or fifteen years older than his wife. Had she married a father figure? He was a stockbroker who jogged five miles every morning before going to work. His hair was chestnut brown and fell in seductive waves around his ears like Prince Valiant. His eyes—magnificent eyes—were Paul Newman-blue and sparkling. His trim mustache married his goatee and he looked as distinguished as a presidential candidate. He was well over six feet, and I could see through his smoking jacket and body-hugging trousers that here was a physical specimen to set any maiden's heart aflutter. Or the heart of a next-door neighbor pushing sixty, albeit reluctantly.

And *she* envied *me?*

I forget what we talked about. All I know is that when I finally got back to my own apartment Abner was on the verge of succumbing to starvation. I threw together a meal of hamburger and salad but had little appetite for it. I had fed my full on Victor Appleby.

I saw a lot of the Applebys. Rosalie and I did our laundry together in the basement room most Saturdays. The children remained proper and boring. I had a feeling that they were perplexed not only by adults but by childhood. They never played games. All they did was read books—but I mean very impressive books for their age: Freud and Jung and Norman Mailer. When I asked Rosalie about it, she explained, "They've been precocious since birth." Some explanation.

I often had them in for dinner or brunch or drinks and Victor was most sympathetic to Abner's condition. His father and a younger brother had both succumbed to terminal illnesses. Once, when we were alone in the kitchen, he kissed me lightly on the cheek. I said something stupid like "Thank you, kind sir," but he wasn't blind. He could see my face ablaze with not-too-restrained passion.

Then one day he invited me to lunch. We met at a quiet Italian restaurant in the East Thirties, chosen by him, I'm sure, because it was discreet and we weren't likely to run into mutual acquaintances such as my husband (who wouldn't have given a damn) or his wife (who would have). After out first martini, he got down to cases. Living with Rosalie, it seems, was like living with a time bomb. She was suicidal and had repressed their children. (I wasn't blind.) I was saving Rosalie's life, Victor said.

"Me? What have I done?"

"You told her you envy her. Rosalie has never been envied. She's like her mother, who always thought every other woman in the world had a better life than she did. She would have traded places with most of her husband's woman patients. Rosalie's the same. Envy, envy, envy! If I hear that word again—"

I reached across the table and took his hand. He reacted warmly. His skin was pure velvet and my mouth went dry. "I'm glad I've helped Rosalie," I managed to say.

Very softly, he said, "Rebecca." For the first time I liked the sound of my name. Then he mentioned a hotel on East Fortieth Street that rented rooms by the hour, no questions asked. Lunch was cancelled. We found a more fulfilling sustenance elsewhere.

That afternoon with Victor changed everything. Though I continued to act my role of envying Rosalie, I secretly despised her. Victor and I were stealing hours together wherever and whenever possible. He rented a car and kept it in a garage near our apartment building and we soon knew dozens of motels outside of the city—across the George Washington Bridge in New Jersey, over the Henry Hudson Bridge in Connecticut. If Abner suspected anything, he couldn't care less. If Rosalie suspected anything, she had missed her vocation as an actress.

One Saturday morning, wheeling my soiled laundry from the apartment into the hall, I was astonished to see Rosalie waiting for the elevator, dressed as though she'd been invited to a coronation.

"Hi," I said. "No laundry this morning?"

"No," she answered. "I have an appointment in New Jersey. I've rented a car." That sent a prickle of guilt and apprehension up my spine. "Victor's in Chicago," she added. "The children are with my in-laws."

I almost blurted, "I know Victor's in Chicago—he begged me to meet him there." The elevator arrived and the descent seemed forever.

"You certainly look terrific," I told her. "Where in New Jersey are you heading?"

"Hackensack."

Hackensack! "Why Hackensack?" I said.

"I want to purchase something there."

"Something they only sell in Hackensack?" I wasn't trying to be funny. There was something too weird and other-worldly about our conversation. She didn't reply to my question. We had arrived at the lobby and she was hurrying out. I continued down to the basement.

That night Abner looked all too healthy and I told him so. "I'm getting this new treatment," he explained.

"What new treatment?"

"It was discovered in the mountains of Peru by a missionary for the Seventh Day Adventists. In those parts they live to be over a hundred." I winced and hoped he didn't notice. "It's a culture from goat cheese and llama blood."

"Illegal, I'm sure."

"Well, don't I look better?"

"Yes," I agreed glumly.

Then we heard the shot. It could have been automobile backfire. But there was no use kidding ourselves—it had come from the next apartment, Rosalie and Victor's apartment. I shouted, "That was gunfire!" We ran into the hall, where we were joined by other neighbors. A man was pounding on the door to the Appleby apartment, shouting something inane like "Open up in there!" The building superintendant, Mr. Janowski, arrived and used his passkey. We followed him into the apartment.

Rosalie was in the den. There was a bullet wound in her head. She was seated at the desk, and except for the blood, she was impeccably attired. On the floor at her feet lay a small handgun—the object, no doubt, that she had gone to Hackensack to purchase.

Abner phoned for the police. Other neighbors came in. A few shrieked with horror, others sobbed. We located Victor in Chicago.

And so that was the end of the woman I envied.

It was in all the newspapers. Victor was shattered by the tragedy. I made the funeral arrangements, though there were relatives and other friends who might have been accommodating.

At the funeral, Victor spoke a lovely eulogy I had ghosted for him. Rosalie's parents, who had flown up from Florida, stood at the graveside, he frail and somewhat tottering, she tall as a flagpole and just as imposing. Contrary to Victor's description, her face reflected strength and positive thinking. It was easier to figure out Rosalie now. After the services, we returned to Victor's apartment, where caterers I had hired served a tasteful lunch complimented by several excellent wines. Over the next few days I supervised the removal of Rosalie's belongings, choosing several worthy charities for the donations.

Abner's new treatment wasn't doing him that much good. It gave him better color, but he was losing weight and energy rapidly. Victor and I no longer had to resort to grubby little motels. We could have our clandestine meetings in his own apartment right next door.

But I found my thoughts dwelling on Rosalie. "Victor," I said one evening. "About Rosalie."

"What about her?"

"Her suicide. Was it anything I said?"

"No, cutie," answered Victor, snuggling me in his arms, "it's what you didn't say."

"What do you mean?"

"From the day we started our affair, you stopped telling her how much you envied her. The day before I went to Chicago, she said to me, 'Rebecca has changed. Have you noticed?' I asked her in what way she thought you had changed. She said, 'She's looking younger and younger every day. Her voice has new color in it and her skin seems to have taken on a fresh life. It's as though she and I have changed places. I don't think she envies me any longer. I think she's got what she's wanted.' "

"What did you say to that?"

"I didn't say anything. I went to Chicago."

Well, Abner did die. Although it was expected, it was unexpected. He was found dead sitting on a bench along Riverside Drive where he sometimes sat and fed the pigeons. Victor and I were married and for auld lang syne we spent our wedding night in one of the motels we used to frequent. I sold my business to a syndicate of lascivious Arabs. Now Victor goes to his office and I stay home writing and trying to look after his children. I've sold several short stories, there's my autobiography due next autumn, and at present I'm plotting a very overheated novel.

At first we talked of joining our two apartments into one huge apartment, but Victor decided his held too many memories of Rosalie, so we rented it to a very attractive writer named Miranda Braggiotti. I believe she's famous for several books on the occult and Victor thinks she dabbles in witchcraft.

It's too amusing what happened when I met her at the elevator this morning with Nicholas and Evangeline morosely in tow. She gave us a strange, mysterious look and said to me, "You know something, Mrs. Appleby?" I can hear her voice now—soft, insinuating, somewhat menacing. "I envy you very much."

NEW YORK BLUES

Cornell Woolrich

IT'S SIX O'CLOCK; my drink is at the three-quarter mark—three-quarters down not three-quarters up—and the night begins.

Across the way from me sits a little transistor radio, up on end, simmering away like a teakettle on a stove. It's been going steadily ever since I first came in here, two days, three night ago; it chisels away the stony silence, takes the edge off the being-alone. It came with the room, not with me.

Now there's a punctuation of three lush chords, and it goes into a traffic report. "Good evening. The New York Municipal Communications Service presents the 6:00 P.M. Traffic Advisory. Traffic through the Holland and Lincoln Tunnels and over the George Washington Bridge, heavy westbound, light eastbound. Traffic on the crosscut between the George Washington and Queens-Whitestone Bridges, heavy in both directions. Traffic through the Battery Tunnel, heavy outbound, very light inbound. Traffic on the West Side Highway, bumper to bumper all the way. Radar units in operation there. Traffic over the Long Island Expressway is beginning to build, due to tonight's game at Shea Stadium. West 70th Street between Amsterdam and West End Avenues is closed due to a water-main break. A power failure on the East Side I.R.T. line between Grand Central and 125th Street is causing delays of up to forty-five minutes. Otherwise all subways and buses, the Staten Island Ferry, the Jersey Central, the Delaware and Lackawanna, and the Pennsylvania Railroads, and all other commuter services, are operating normally. At the three airports, planes are arriving and departing on time. The next regularly scheduled traffic

39

advisory will be given one-half hour from now—"

The big week-end rush is on. The big city emptying itself out at once. Just a skeleton crew left to keep it going until Monday morning. Everybody getting out—everybody but me, everybody but those who are coming here for me tonight. We're going to have the whole damned town to ourselves.

I go over to the window and open up a crevice between two of the tightly flattened slats in one of the blinds, and a little parallelogram of a New York street scene, Murray Hill section, six o'clock-evening hour, springs into view. Up in the sky the upper-echelon light tiers of the Pan Am Building are undulating and rippling in the humidity and carbon monoxide ("Air pollution index: normal, twelve percent; emergency level, fifty percent").

Down below, on the sidewalk, the glowing green blob of a street light, swollen to pumpkin size by foreshortened perspective, thrusts upward toward my window. And along the little slot that the parted slats make, lights keep passing along, like strung-up, shining, red and white beads. All going just one way, right to left, because 37th Street is westbound, and all going by twos, always by twos, headlights and tails, heads and tails, in a welter of slowed-down traffic and a paroxysm of vituperative horns. And directly under me I hear a taxi driver and would-be fares having an argument, the voices clearly audible, the participants unseen.

"But it's only to Fifty-ninth Street—"

"I don't *ca-a-are,* lady. Look, I already tolje. I'm not goin' up that way. Can'tje get it into your head?"

"Don't let's argue with him. Get inside. He can't put you out."

"No, but I can refuse to move. Lady, if your husband gets in here he's gonna sit still in one place, 'cause I ain't budgin'."

New York. The world's most dramatic city. Like a permanent short circuit, sputtering and sparking up into the night sky all night long. No place like it for living. And probably no place like it for dying.

I take away the little tire jack my fingers have made and the slats snap together again.

The first sign that the meal I phoned down for is approaching is the minor-key creak from a sharply swerved castor as the room-service waiter rounds a turn outside my door. I'm posted behind a high-backed wing chair, with my wrists crossed over the top of it and my hands dangling like loose claws, staring a little tensely at the door. Then there's the waiter's characteristically deferential knock. But I say, "Who is it?" anyway, before I go over to open it.

He's an elderly man. He's been up here twice before and by now I know the way he sounds.

"Room service," comes through in that high-pitched voice his old age has given him.

I release the double lock, then I turn the knob and open the door.

He wheels the little white-clothed dinner cart forward into the room, and as the hall perspective clears behind him I get a blurred glimpse of a figure in motion, just passing from view, then gone, too quickly to be brought into focus.

I stand there a moment, holding the door to a narrow slit, watching the hall. But it's empty now.

There's an innocuous explanation for everything. Everything is a coin that has two sides to it, and one side is innocuous but the other can be ominous. The hall makes a right-angle turn opposite my door, and to get to the elevators, those whose rooms are back of this turn have to pass the little setback that leads to my door.

On the other hand, if someone wanted to pinpont me, to verify which room I was in, by sighting my face as I opened the door for the waiter, he would do just that: stand there an instant, then quickly step aside out of my line of vision. The optical snapshot I'd had was not of a figure in continuous motion going past my point of view, but of a figure that had first been static and then had flitted from sight.

And if it's that, now they know which room I'm in. Which room on which floor in which hotel.

"Did you notice anyone out there in the hall just now when you came along?" I ask. I try to sound casual, which only makes me not sound casual.

He answers with a question of his own. "*Was* there somebody out in the hall, sir?"

"That's what I asked you, did you see anyone?"

He explains that years of experience in trundling these food-laden carts across the halls have taught him never to look up, never to take his eyes off them, because an unexpected bump on the floor under the carpet might splash ice water out of the glass and wet the tablecloth or spill consommé into its saucer.

It sounds plausible enough. And whether it is or not I know it's all I'm going to get.

I sign the check for the meal, add the tip, and tell him to put it on the bill. Then just as he turns to leave I remember something I want to do.

"Just a second; that reminds me." I shoot one of my cuffs forward and twist something out of it. Then the other one. And I hold out my hand to him with the two star-sapphire cuff links he admired so much last night. (Innocently, I'm sure, with no venal intent.)

He says I'm not serious, I must be joking. He says he can't take anything like that. He says all the things he's expected to say, and I override them. Then when he can't come up with anything else, he comes up with, half hopefully (hopeful for a yes answer): "You tired of them?"

"No," I say quite simply, "no—they're tired of me."

He thanks me over and thanks me under and thanks me over again, and then he's gone, and I'm glad he's gone.

Poor old man, wasting his life bringing people their meals up to their rooms for thirty-five, forty-odd years. He'll die in peace, though. Not in terror and in throes of resistance. I almost envy him.

I turn my head a little. The radio's caroling *Tonight,* velvety smooth and young and filled with plaintive desire. Maria's song from "West Side Story." I remember one beautiful night long ago at the Winter Garden, with a beautiful someone beside me. I tilt my nose and breathe in, and I can still smell her perfume, the ghost of her perfume from long ago. But where is she now, where did she go, what did I *do* with her?

Our paths ran along so close together they were almost like one, the one they were eventually going to be. Then fear came along, fear entered into it somehow, and split them wide apart.

Fear bred anxiety to justify. Anxiety to justify bred anger. The phone calls that wouldn't be answered, the door rings that wouldn't be opened. Anger bred sudden calamity.

Now there aren't two paths anymore; there's only one, only mine. Running downhill into the ground, running downhill into its doom.

*Tonight, tonight—there will be no morning star—*Right, kid, there won't. Not for me anyway.

There's a tap at the door, made with the tip of a key, not the tip of a finger. The voice doesn't wait, but comes right through before the signal has a chance to freeze me stiff. A woman's voice, soft-spoken, reassuring. "Night maid."

I wait a second to let a little of the white drain from my face before she sees me, and then I go over and let her in.

Her name is Ginny. She told me last night. I asked her, that's why she told me. I wanted to hear the sound of somebody's name, that's why I asked her. I was frightened and lonely, that's why I wanted to hear the sound of somebody's name.

On her face the beauty of two races blends, each contributing its individual hallmark. The golden-warm skin, the deep glowing eyes, the narrow-tipped nose, the economical underlip.

While she's turning back the bedcovers in a neat triangle over one corner I remark, "I notice you go around the outside of the room to get to the bed, instead of cutting across the middle, which would be much shorter. Why do you?"

She answers plausibly, "People are often watching their television sets at this time, when I come in, and I don't want to block them off."

I point out, "But mine isn't on, Ginny."

I see how the pupils of her eyes try to flee, to get as far away from looking at me as possible, all the way over into their outside corners. And that gives it away. She's afraid of me. The rumors have already reached her. A hotel is like a beehive when it comes to gossip. *He never leaves his room, has all his meals sent up to him, and keeps his door locked all the time.*

"I want to give you something," I say to her. "For that little girl of yours you were telling me about."

I take a hundred-dollar bill out of the wallet on my hip. I fold the bill a few times so that the corner numerals disappear, then thrust it between two of her fingers.

She sees the "1" first as the bill slowly uncoils. Her face is politely appreciative.

She sees the first zero next—that makes it a ten. Her face is delighted, more than grateful.

She sees the last zero. Suddenly her face is fearful, stunned into stone; in her eyes I can see steel filings of mistrust glittering. Her wrist flexes to shove the bill back to me, but I ward it off with my hand up-ended.

I catch the swift side glance she darts at the fifth of rye on the side table.

"No, it didn't come out of that. It's just an impulse—came out of my heart, I suppose you could say. Either take it or don't take it, but don't spoil it."

"But why? What for?"

"Does there have to be a reason for everything? Sometimes there isn't."

"I'll buy her a new coat," she says huskily. "A new pink coat like little girls all seem to want. With a little baby muff of lamb's wool to go with it. And I'll say a prayer for you when I take her to church with me next Sunday."

It won't work, but—"Make it a good one."

The last part is all she hears.

Something occurs to me. "You won't have to do any explaining to her father, will you?"

"She has no father," she says quite simply. "She's never had one. There's only me and her, sir."

Somehow I can tell by the quick chip-chop run of her feet away from my door that it's not lost time she's trying to make up; it's the tears starting in her eyes that she wants to hide.

I slosh a little rye into a glass—a fresh glass, not the one before; they get rancid from your downbreaths that cling like a stale mist around the inner rim. But it's no help; I know that by now, and I've been dousing myself in it for three days. It just doesn't take hold. I think fear neutralizes alcohol, weakens its anesthetic power. It's good for small fears; your boss, your wife, your bills, your dentist; all right then to take a drink. But for big ones it doesn't do any good. Like water on blazing gasoline, it will only quicken and compound it. It takes sand, in the literal and the slang sense, to smother the bonfire that is fear. And if you're out of sand, then you must burn up.

I have it out now, paying it off between my fingers like a rosary of murder. Those same fingers that did it to her. For three days now I've taken it out at intervals, looked at it, then hidden it away again. Each time wondering if it really happened, hoping that it didn't, dreading that it did.

It's a woman's scarf; that much I know about it. And that's about all. But whose? Hers? And how did I come by it? How did it get into the side pocket of my jacket, dangling on the outside, when I came in here early Wednesday morning in some sort of traumatic daze, looking for room walls to hide inside of as if they were a folding screen. (I didn't even know I had it there; the bellboy who was checking me in spotted it on the way up in the elevator, grinned, and said something about a "heavy date.")

It's flimsy stuff, but it has great tensile strength when pulled against its grain. The strength of the garotte. It's tinted in pastel colors that blend, graduate, into one another, all except one. It goes from a flamingo pink to a peach tone and then to a still paler flesh tint—and then suddenly an angry, jagged splash of blood color comes in, not even like the others. Not smooth, not artificed by some loom or by some dye vat. Like a star, like the scattered petals of a flower. Speaking of—I don't know how to say it—speaking of violence, of struggle, of life spilled out.

The blood isn't red any more. It's rusty brown now. But it's still blood all the same. Ten years from now, twenty, it'll still be blood; faded out, vanished, the pollen of, the dust of, blood. What was once warm and moving. And made blushes and rushed with anger and paled with fear. Like that night—

I can still see her eyes. They still come before me, wide and white and glistening with fright, out of the amnesiac darkness of our sudden, unpremeditated meeting.

They were like two pools of fear. She saw something that I couldn't see. And fear kindled in them. I feared and I mistrusted, but I couldn't bear to see my fear reflected in her eyes. From her I wanted reassurance, consolation; only wanted to draw her close to me and hold her to me, to lean my head against her and rest and draw new belief in myself. Instead she met my fear with her fear. Eyes that should have been tender were glowing with unscreaming fear.

It wasn't an attack. We'd been together too many times before, made love together too many times before, for it to be that. It was just that fear had suddenly entered, and made us dangerous strangers.

She turned and tried to run. I caught the scarf from behind. Only in supplication, in pleading; trying to hold on to the only one who could save me. And the closer I tried to draw her to me, the less she was alive. Until finally I got her all the way back to me, where I wanted her to be, and she was dead.

I hadn't wanted that. It was only love, turned inside out. It was only loneliness, outgoing.

And now I'm alone, without any love.

And the radio, almost as if it were taking my pulse count, electro-graphing my heartbeats, echoes them back to me: *For, like caressing an empty glove, Is night without some love, The night was made for—*

The hotel room ashtrays are thick glass cubes, built to withstand cracking under heat of almost any degree. I touch my lighter to it, to the scarf compressed inside the cube. The flame points upward like a sawtoothed orange knife. There goes love. After a while it stops burning. It looks like a black cabbage, each leaf tipped by thin red lines that waver and creep back and forth like tiny red worms. Then one by one they go out.

I dump it into the bathroom bowl and flip the lever down. What a hell of a place for your love to wind up. Like something disemboweled.

I go back and pour out a little more. It's the seatbelt against the imminent smash-up, the antidote for terror, the prescription against panic. Only it doesn't work. I sit there dejectedly, wrists looping down between my legs. I'm confused; I can't think it out. Something inside my mind keeps fogging over, like mist on a windshield. I use the back of my hand for a windshield wiper and draw it slowly across my forehead a couple times, and it clears up again for a little while.

"Remember," the little radio prattles. "Simple headache, take aspirin. Nervous tension, take—"

All I can say to myself is: there *is* no fix for the fix you're in now.

Suddenly the phone peals, sharp and shattering as the smashing of glass sealing up a vacuum. I never knew a sound could be so frightening, never knew a sound could be so dire. It's like a short circuit in my nervous system. Like springing a cork in my heart with a lopsided opener. Like a shot of sodium pentathol up my arm knocking out my will power.

All I keep thinking is: this is it. Here it is. It's not a hotel-service call, it can't be, not at this hour any more. The waiter's been and gone, the night maid's been and gone. It can't be an outside call, because nobody on the outside knows I'm here in the hotel. Not even where I work, where I used to work, they don't know. This is it; it's got to be.

How will they put it? A polite summons. "Would you mind coming down for a minute, sir?" And then if I do, a sudden preventive twisting of my arm behind my back as I step out of the elevator, an unnoticeable flurry tactfully covered up behind the backs of the bellboys—then quickly out and away.

Why don't they come right up here to my door and get me? Is it because this is a high-class hotel on a high-class street? Maybe they don't want any commotion in the hall, for the sake of the other guests. Maybe this is the way they always do it.

Meanwhile it keeps ringing and ringing and ringing.

The damp zigzag path my spilled drink made, from where I was to where I am now, is slowly soaking into the carpet and darkening it. The empty glass, dropped on the carpet, has finished rocking on its side by now and lies still. And I've fallen motionless into the grotesque posture of a badly frightened kid. Almost prone along the floor, legs sprawled out in back of me in scissors formation, just the backs of my two hands grasping the edge of the low stand the phone sits on, and the rim of it cutting across the bridge of my nose so that just two big staring straining eyes show up over the top.

And it rings on and on and on.

Then all at once an alternative occurs to me. Maybe it's a wrong-number call, meant for somebody else. Somebody in another room, or somebody in this room who was in it before I came. Hotel switchboards are overworked places; slip-ups like that can happen now and then.

I bet I haven't said a prayer since I finished my grammar school final-exam paper in trigonometry (and flunked it; maybe that's why I haven't said a prayer since), and that was more a crossed-fingers thing held behind my back than a genuine prayer. I say one now. What a funny thing to pray for. I bet nobody ever prayed for a wrong number before, not since telephones first began. Or since prayers first began either.

Please, make it a mistake and not for me. Make it a mistake.

Suddenly there's open space between the cradle and the receiver, and I've done it. I've picked it up. It's just as easy as pulling out one of your own teeth by the roots.

The prayer gets scratched. The call is for me, it's not a wrong number. For me all right, every inch of the way. I can tell from the opening words. Only—it's not the one I feared; it's friendly, a friendly call no different from what other people get.

A voice from another world, almost. Yet I know it so well. Always like this, never a cloud on it; always jovial, always noisy. When a thing should be said softly, it says it loudly; when a thing should be said loudly, it says it louder still. He never identifies himself, never has to. Once you've heard his voice, you'll always know him.

That's Johnny for you—the pal of a hundred parties. The bar-kick of scores of binges. The captain of the second-string team in how many foursome one-night stands? Every man has had a Johnny in his life sometime or other.

He say's he's been calling my apartment since Wednesday and no answer; what happened to me?

I play it by ear. "Water started to pour down through the ceiling, so I had to clear out till they get it repaired . . . No, I'm not on a tear . . . No, there's nobody with me, I'm by myself . . . Do I? Sound sort of peculiar? No, I'm all right, there's nothing the matter, not a thing."

I pass my free hand across the moist glisten on my forehead. It's tough enough to be in a jam, but it's tougher still to be in one and not be able to say you are.

"How did you know I was here? How did you track me to this place? . . . You went down the yellow pages, hotel by hotel, alphabetically. Since three o'clock yesterday afternoon? . . . Something to tell me?"

His new job had come through. He starts in Monday. With a direct line, and two, count 'em, two secretaries, not just one. And the old bunch is giving him a farewell party. A farewell party to end all farewell parties. Sardi's, on 44th. Then they'll move on later to some other place. But they'll wait here at Sardi's for me to catch up. Barb keeps asking, Why isn't your best-man-to-be here with us?

The noise of the party filters through into my ear. Ice clicking like dice in a fast-rolling game. Mixing sticks sounding like tiny tin flutes as they beat against glass. The laughter of girls, the laughter of men. Life is for the living, not the already dead.

"Sure, I'll be there. Sure."

If I say I won't be—and I won't because I can't—he'll never quit pestering and calling me the rest of the night. So I say that I will, to get off the hook. But how can I go there, drag my trouble before his party, before his friends, before his girl? And if I go it'll just happen there instead of here. Who wants a grandstand for his downfall? Who wants bleachers for his disgrace?

Johnny's gone now, and the night goes on.

Now the evening's at its noon, its meridian. The outgoing tide has simmered down, and there's a lull—like the calm in the eye of a hurricane—before the reverse tide starts to set in.

The last acts of the three-act plays are now on, and the after-theater eating places are beginning to fill up with early comers; Danny's and Lindy's—yes, and Horn & Hardart too. Everybody has got where they wanted to go—and that was out somewhere. Now everybody will want to get back where they came from—and that's home somewhere. Or as the coffee-grinder radio, always on the beam, puts it at about this point: *New York, New York, it's a helluva town, The Bronx is up, the Battery's down, And the people ride around in a hole in the ground—*

Now the incoming tide rolls in; the hours abruptly switch back to single digits again, and it's a little like the time you put your watch back on entering a different time zone. Now the buses knock off and the subway expresses turn into locals and the locals space themselves far apart; and as Johnny Carson's face hits millions of screens all at one and the same time, the incoming tide reaches its crest and pounds against the shore. There's a sudden splurge, a slew of taxis arriving at the hotel entrance one by one as regularly as though they were on a conveyor belt, emptying out and then going away again.

Then this too dies down, and a deep still sets in. It's an around-the-clock town, but this is the stretch; from now until the garbage-grinding trucks come along and tear the dawn to shreds, it gets as quiet as it's ever going to get.

This is the deep of the night, the dregs, the sediment at the bottom of the coffee cup. The blue hours; when guys' nerves get tauter and women's fears get greater. Now guys and girls make love, or kill each other, or sometimes both. And as the windows on the "Late Show" title silhouette light up one by one, the real ones all around go dark. And from now on the silence is broken only by the occasional forlorn hoot of a bogged-down drunk or the gutted-cat squeal of a too sharply swerved axle coming around a turn. Or as Billy Daniels sang it in "Golden Boy": *While the city sleeps, And the streets are clear, There's a life that's happening here—*

In the pin-drop silence a taxi comes up with an unaccompanied girl in it. I can tell it's a taxi, I can tell it's a girl, and I can tell she's unaccompanied; I can tell all three just by her introductory remark.

"Benny," she says. "Will you come over and pay this for me?"

Benny is the hotel night-service man. I know his name; he brought drinks up to the room last night.

As the taxi drives away paid, Benny reminds her with aloof dignity, "You didn't give me my cut last week." Nothing personal, strictly business, you understand.

"I had a virus week before last," she explains. "And it took me all last week to pay off on my doctor bills. I'll square it with you tonight." Then she adds apprehensively, "I'm afraid he'll hurt me." Not her doctor, obviously.

"Na, he won't hurt you," Benny reassures.

"How would you know?" she asks not unreasonably.

Benny culls from his store of call-girl sponsorship experience. "These big guys never hurt you. They're meek as mice. It's the little shrimps got the sting."

She goes ahead in. A chore is a chore, she figures.

This of course is what is known in hotel-operational jargon as a "personal call." In the earthier slang of the night bellmen and deskmen it is simply a "fix" or a "fix-up." The taxi fare of course will go down on the guest's bill, as "Misc." or "Sundries." Which actually is what it is. From my second-floor window I can figure it all out almost without any sound track to go with it.

So much for the recreational side of night life in the upper-bracket-income hotels of Manhattan. And in its root-origins the very word itself is implicit with implication: recreate. Analyze it and you'll see it also means to reproduce. But clever, ingenious Man has managed to sidetrack it into making life more livable.

The wafer of ice riding the surface of my drink has melted freakishly in its middle and not around its edges and now looks like an onion ring. Off in the distance an ambulance starts bansheeing with that new broken-blast siren they use, scalp-crimping as the cries of pain of a partly dismembered hog. Somebody dead in the night? Somebody sick and going to be dead soon? Or maybe somebody going to be alive soon—did she wait too long to start for the hospital?

All of a sudden, with the last sound there's been all night, I can tell they're here. Don't ask me how, I only know they're here. It's beginning at last. No way out, no way aside and no way back.

Being silent is their business, and they know their business well. They make less sound than the dinner cart cruching along the carpeted hall, than Ginny's stifled sob when I gave her that hundred-dollar bill, than the contestants bickering over the taxi. Or that girl who was down there just a little while ago on her errand of fighting loneliness for a fee.

How can I tell that they're here? By the absence of sound more than by its presence. Or I should say, by the absence of a complementary sound—the sound that belongs with another sound and yet fails to accompany it.

Like:

There's no sound of arrival, but suddenly two cars are in place down there along the hotel front. They must have come up on the glide, as noiselessly as a sailboat skimming over still water. No sound of tires, no sound of brakes. But there's one sound they couldn't quite obliterate—the cushioned thump of two doors closing after them in quick succession, staccato succession, as they spilled out and siphoned into the building. You can always tell a car door, no other door sounds quite like it.

There's only one other sound, a lesser one, a sort of follow-up: the scratch of a single sole against the abrasive sidewalk as they go hustling in. He either put it down off-balance or swiveled it too acutely in treading at the heels of those in front of him. Which is a good average, just one to sound off, considering that six or eight pairs of them must have been all going in at the same time and moving fast.

I've sprung to my feet from the very first, and I'm standing there now like an upright slab of ice carved in the outline of a man—burning-cold and slippery-wet and glassy with congealment. I've put out all the lights— they all work on one switch over by the door as you come in. They've probably already seen the lights though if they've marked the window from outside, and anyway what difference does it make? Lighted up or dark, I'm still here inside the room. It's just some instinct as old as fear: you seek the dark when you hide, you seek the light when the need to hide is gone. All the animals have it too.

Now they're in, and it will take just a few minutes more while they make their arrangements. That's all I have left, a few minutes more. Out of a time allotment that once stretched so far and limitlessly ahead of me. Who short-changed me, I feel like crying out in protest, but I know that nobody did; I short-changed myself.

"It," the heartless little radio jeers, "takes the worry out of being close."

Why is it taking them such a long time? What do they have to do, improvise as they go along? What for? They already knew what they had to do when they set out to come here.

I'm sitting down again now, momentarily; knees too rocky for standing long. Those are the only two positions I have left; no more walking, no more running, no more anything else now. Only stand up and wait or sit down and wait. I need a cigarette terribly bad. It may be a funny time to need one, but I do. I dip my head down between my outspread legs and bring the lighter up from below, so its shine won't glow through the blind-crevices. As I said, it doesn't make sense, because they know I'm here. But I don't want to do anything to quicken them. Even two minutes of grace is better than one. Even one minute is better than none.

Then suddenly my head comes up again, alerted. I drop the cigarette, still unlit. First I think the little radio has suddenly jumped in tone, started to come on louder and more resonant, as if it were spooked. Until it almost sounds like a car radio out in the open. Then I turn my head toward the window. It is a car radio. It's coming from outside into the room.

And even before I get up and go over to take a look I think: there's something familiar about it, I've heard it before, just like this, just the way it is now. This sounding-board effect, this walloping of the night like a drum, this ricochet of blast and din from side to side of the street, bouncing off the house fronts like a musical handball game.

Then it cuts off short, the after-silence swells up like a balloon ready to pop, and as I squint out it's standing still down there, the little white car, and Johnny is already out of it and standing alongside.

He's come to take me to the party.

He's parked on the opposite side. He starts to cross over to the hotel. Someone posted in some doorway whistles to attract his attention. I hear it up at the window. Johnny stops, turns to look around, doesn't see anyone.

He's frozen in the position in which the whistle caught him. Head and shoulders turned inquiringly half around, hips and legs still pointed forward. Then a man, some anonymous man, glides up beside him from the street.

I told you he talks loud; on the phone, in a bar, on a street late at night. Every word he says I hear; not a word the other man says.

First, "Who is? What kind of trouble?"

Then, "You must mean somebody else."

Next, "Room 207. Yeah, that's right, 207."

That's my room number.

"How'd you know I was coming here?"

Finally, "You bugged the call I made to him before!"

Then the anonymous man goes back into the shadows, leaving Johnny in mid-street, taking it for granted he'll follow him as he was briefed to do, commanded to do.

But Johnny stands out there, alone and undecided, feet still one way, head and shoulders still the other. And I watch him from the window crevice. And the stakeout watches him from his invisible doorway.

Not a crisis arises. Not in my life, because that's nearly over; but in my illusions.

Will he go to his friend and try to stand by him, or will he let his friend go by?

He can't make it, sure I know that, he can never get in here past them; but he *can* make the try, there's just enough slack for him to do that. There's still half the width of the street ahead of him clear and untrammeled, for him to try to bolt across, before they spring after him and rough him up and fling him back. It's the token of the thing that would count, not the completion.

But it doesn't happen that way, I keep telling myself knowingly and sadly. Only in our fraternity pledges and masonic inductions, our cowboy movies and magazine stories, not in our real-life lives. For, the Seventeenth Century humanist to the contrary, each man *is* an island complete unto himself, and as he sinks, the moving feet go on around him, from nowhere to nowhere and with no time to lose. The world is long past the Boy Scout stage of its development; now each man dies as he was meant to die, and as he was born and as he lived: alone, all alone. Without any God, without any hope, without any record to show for his life.

My throat feels stiff, and I want to swallow but I can't. Watching and waiting to see what my friend will do.

He doesn't move, doesn't make up his mind, for half a minute, and that half a minute seems like an hour. He's doped by what he's been told, I guess. And I keep asking myself while the seconds are ticking off: What would *I* do? If there were me down there, and he were up here: What would *I* do? And I keep trying not to look the answer in the face, though it's staring at me the whole time.

You haven't any right to expect your friends to be larger than yourself, larger than life. Just take them as they are, cut down to average size, and be glad you have them. To drink with, laugh with, borrow money from, lend money to, stay away from their special girls as you want them to stay away from yours, and above all, never break your word to once it's been given.

And that is all you have the obligation to have, all you have the right to expect.

The half minute is up, and Johnny turns, slowly and reluctantly, but he turns, and he goes back to the opposite side of the street. The side opposite to me.

And I knew all along that's what he would do, because I knew all along that's what I would have done too.

I think I hear a voice say slurredly somewhere in the shadows, "That's the smart thing to do," but I'm not sure. Maybe I don't, maybe it's me I hear.

He gets back in the car, shoulders sagging, and keys it on. And as he glides from sight the music seems to start up almost by itself; it's such second nature for him to have it on by now. It fades around the corner building, and then a wisp of it comes back just once more, carried by some cross-current of the wind: *Fools rush in, Where wise men never dare to go*—and then it dies away for good.

I bang my crushed-up fist against the center of my forehead, bring it away, then bang it again. Slow but hard. It hurts to lose a long-term friend, almost like losing an arm. But I never lost an arm, so I really wouldn't know.

Now I can swallow, but it doesn't feel good any more.

I hear a marginal noise outside in the hall, and I swing around in instant alert. It's easy enough to decipher it. A woman is being taken from her room nearby—in case the going gets too rough around here in my immediate vicinity, I suppose.

I hear them tap, and then she comes out and accompanies them to safety. I hear the slap-slap of her bedroom slippers, like the soft little hands of children applauding in a kindergarten, as she goes hurrying by with someone. Several someones. You can't hear them, or her, but I know they're with her. I even hear the soft *sch sch* of her silk wrapper or kimono as it rustles past. A noticeable whiff of sachet drifts in through the door seam. She must have taken a bath and powdered herself liberally just moments ago.

Probably a nice sort of woman, unused to violence or emergencies of this sort, unsure of what to bring along or how to comport herself.

"I left my handbag in there," I hear her remark plaintively as she goes by. "Do you think it'll be all right to leave it there?"

Somebody's wife, come to meet him in the city and waiting for him to join her. Long ago I used to like that kind of woman. Objectively, of course, not close-up.

After she's gone, another brief lull sets in. This one is probably the last. But what good is a lull? It's only a breathing spell in which to get more frightened. Because anticipatory fear is always twice as strong as present fear. Anticipatory fear has both fears in it at once—the anticipatory one and the one that comes simultaneously with the dread happening itself. Present fear only has the one, because by that time anticipation is over.

I switch on the light for a moment, to see my way to a drink. The one I had is gone—just what used to be ice is sloshing colorlessly in the bottom of the glass. Then when I put the recharged glass down again, empty, it seems to pull me after it, as if it weighed so much I couldn't let go of it from an upright position. Don't ask me why this is, I don't know. Probably simple loss of equilibrium for a second, due to the massive infusion of alcohol.

Then with no more warning, with no more waiting, with no more of anything, it begins. It gets under way at last.

There is a mild-mannered knuckle rapping at the door. They use my name. A voice, mild-mannered also, says in a conciliatory way, "Come out please. We want to talk to you." Punctilious, I guess, would be a better word for it. The etiquette of the forcible entry, of the break-in. They're so considerate, so deferential, so attentive to all the niceties. Hold your head steady, please, we don't want to nick your chin while we're cutting your throat.

I don't answer.

I don't think they expected me to. If I had answered, it would have astonished them, thrown them off their timing for a moment.

The mild-voiced man leaves the door and somebody else takes his place. I can sense the shifting over more by intuition than by actual hearing.

A wooden toolbox or carryall of some sort settles down noisily on the floor outside the door. I can tell it's wooden, not by its floor impact but by the "settling" sound that accompanies it, as if a considerable number of loose and rolling objects in it are chinking against its insides. Nails and bolts and awls and screwdrivers and the like. That tells me that it's a kit commonly used by carpenters and locksmiths and their kind.

They're going to take the lock off bodily from the outside.

A cold surge goes through me that I can't describe. It isn't blood. It's too numbing and heavy and cold for that. And it breaks through the skin surface, which blood doesn't ordinarily do without a wound, and emerges into innumerable stinging pin pricks all over me. An ice-sweat.

I can see him (not literally, but just as surely as if I could), down on one knee, and scared, probably as scared as I am myself, pressing as far back to the side out of the direct line from the door as he can, while the others, bunched together farther back, stand ready to cover him, to pile on me and bring me down if I should suddenly break out and rush him.

And the radio tells me sarcastically to "Light up, you've got a good thing going."

I start backing away, with a sleepwalker's fixity, staring at the door as I retreat, or staring at where I last saw it, for I can't see it in the dark. What good would it do to stay close to it, for I can't hold it back, I can't stop it from opening. And as I go back step after step, my tongue keeps tracking the outside outline of my lips, as if I wondered what they were and what they were there for.

A very small sound begins. I don't know how to put it. Like someone twisting a small metal cap to open a small medicine bottle, but continuously, without ever getting it off. He's started already. He's started coming in.

It's terrible to hear that little thing move. As if it were animate, had a life of its own. Terrible to hear it move and to know that a hostile agency, a hostile presence, just a few feet away from me, is what is making it move. Such a little thing, there is almost nothing smaller, only the size of a pinhead perhaps, and yet to create such terror and to be capable of bringing about such a shattering end-result: entry, capture, final loss of reason, and the darkness that is worse than death. All from a little thing like that, turning slowly, secretively, but avidly, in the lockplate on the door, on the door into my room.

I have to get out of here. Out. I have to push these walls apart, these foursquare tightly seamed walls, and make space wide enough to run in, and keep running through it, running and running through it, and never stopping. Until I drop. And then still running on and on, inside my head. Like a watch with its case smashed open and lying on the ground, but with the works still going inside it. Or like a cockroach when you knock it over on its back so that it can't ambulate any more, but its legs still go spiraling around in the air.

The window. They're at the door, but the window—that way out is still open. I remember when I checked in here the small hours of Wednesday, I didn't ask to be given a room on the second floor, they just happened to give me one. Then when I saw it later that day in the light, I realized the drop to the ground from one of the little semicircular stone ledges outside the windows wouldn't be dangerous, especially if you held a pillow in front of you, and remembered to keep your chin tilted upward as you went over. Just a sprawling shake-up fall maybe, that's all.

I pull at the blind cords with both hands, and it spasms upward with a sound like a lot of little twigs being stepped on and broken. I push up the window sash and assume a sitting position on the sill, then swing my legs across and I'm out in the clear, out in the open night.

The little stone apron has this spiked iron rail guard around it, with no space left on the outer side of it to plant your feet before you go over. You have to straddle it, which makes for tricky going. Still, necessity can make you dexterous, terror can make you agile. I won't go back inside for the pillow, there isn't time. I'll take the leap neat.

The two cars that brought them here are below, and for a moment, only for a moment, they look empty, dark and still and empty, standing bumper to bumper against the curb. Someone gives a warning whistle—a lip whistle I mean, not a metal one. I don't know who, I don't know where, somewhere around. Then an angry, ugly, smoldering, carbound orange moon starts up, lightens to yellow, then brightens to the dazzling white of a laundry detergent commercial. The operator guiding it slants it too high at first, and it lands above my head. Like a halo. *Some* halo and *some time* for a halo.Then he brings it down and it hits me as if someone had belted me full across the face with a talcum powder puff. You can't see through it, you can't see around it.

Shoe leather comes padding from around the corner—maybe the guy that warded off Johnny—and stops directly under me. I sense somehow he's afraid just as I am. That won't keep him from doing what he has to do, because he's got the backing on his side. But he doesn't like this. I shield my eyes from the light on one side, and I can see his anxious face peering up at me. All guys are scared of each other, didn't you know that? I'm not the only one. We're all born afraid.

I can't shake the light off. It's like ghostly flypaper. It's like slapstick-thrown yoghurt. It clings to me whichever way I turn.

I hear his voice talking to me from below. Very near and clear. As if we were off together by ourselves somewhere, just chatting, the two of us.

"Go back into your room. We don't want you to get hurt." And then a second time: "Go back in. You'll only get hurt if you stand out here like this."

I'm thinking, detached as in a dream: I didn't know they were this considerate. Are they always this considerate? When I was a kid back in the Forties, I used to go to those tough-guy movies a lot. Humphrey Bogart, Jimmy Cagney. And when they had a guy penned in, they used to be tough about it, snarling: "Come on out of there, yuh rat, we've got yuh covered!" I wonder what has changed them? Maybe it's just that time has moved on. This is the Sixties now.

What's the good of jumping now? Where is there to run to now? And the light teases my eyes. I see all sorts of interlocked and colored soap bubbles that aren't there.

It's more awkward getting back inside than it was getting out. And with the light on me and them watching me there's a self-consciousness that was missing in my uninhibited outward surge. I have to straighten out one leg first and dip it into the room toes forward, the way you test the water in a pool before you jump in. Then the other leg, and then I'm in. The roundness of the light beam is broken into long thin tatters as the blind rolls down over it, but it still stays on out there.

There are only two points of light in the whole room—I mean in addition to the indirect reflection through the blind, which gives off a sort of phosphorescent haziness—two points so small that if you didn't know they were there and looked for them, you wouldn't see them. And small as both are, one is even smaller than the other. One is the tiny light in the radio which, because the lens shielding the dial is convex, glows like a miniature orange scimitar. I go over to it to turn it off. It can't keep the darkness away any more; the darkness is here.

"Here's to the losers," the radio is saying. "Here's to them all—"

The other point of light is over by the door. It's in the door itself. I go over there close to it, peering with my head bowed, as if I were mourning inconsolably. And I am. One of the four tiny screwheads set into the corners of the oblong plate that holds the lock is gone, is out now, and if you squint at an acute angle you can see a speck of orange light shining through it from the hall. Then while I'm standing there, something falls soundlessly, glances off the top of my shoe with no more weight than a grain of gravel, and there's a second speck of orange light at the opposite upper corner of the plate. Two more to go now. Two and a half minutes of deft work left, maybe not even that much.

What careful planning, what painstaking attention to detail, goes into extinguishing a man's life! Far more than the hit-or-miss, haphazard circumstances of igniting it.

I can't get out the window, I can't go out the door. But there *is* a way out, a third way. I can escape inward. If I can't get away from them on the outside, I can get away from them on the inside.

You're not supposed to have those things. But when you have money you can get anything, in New York. They were on a prescription, but that was where the money came in—getting the prescription. I remember now. Some doctor gave it to me—sold it to me—long ago. I don't remember why or when. Maybe when fear first came between the two of us and I couldn't reach her any more.

I came across it in my wallet on Wednesday, after I first came in here, and I sent it out to have it filled, knowing that this night would come. I remember the bellboy bringing it to the door afterward in a small bright-green paper wrapping that some pharmacists use. But where is it now?

I start a treasure hunt of terror, around the inside of the room in the dark. First into the clothes closet, wheeling and twirling among the couple of things I have hanging in there like a hopped-up discotheque dancer, dipping in and out of pockets, patting some of them between my hands to see if they're flat or hold a bulk. As if I were calling a little pet dog to me by clapping my hands to it. A little dog who is hiding away from me in there, a little dog called death.

Not in there. Then the drawers of the dresser, spading them in and out, fast as a card shuffle. A telephone directory, a complimentary shaving kit (if you're a man), a complimentary manicure kit (if you're a girl).

They must be down to the last screwhead by now.

Then around and into the bathroom, while the remorseless dismantling at the door keeps on. It's all white in there, white as my face must be. It's dark, but you can still see that it's white against the dark. Twilight-colored tiles. I don't put on the light to help me find them, because there isn't enough time left; the lights in here are fluorescent and take a few moments to come on, and by that time they'll be in here.

There's a catch phrase that you all must have heard at one time or another. You walk into a room or go over toward a group. Someone turns and says with huge emphasis: "*There* he is." As though you were the most important one of all. (And you're not.) As though you were the one they were just talking about. (And they weren't.) As though you were the only one that mattered. (And you're not.) It's a nice little tribute, and it don't cost anyone a cent.

And so I say this to them now, as I find them on the top glass slab of the shallow medicine cabinet: *There* you are. Glad to see you—you're important in my scheme of things.

As I bend for some running water, the shower curtain twines around me in descending spiral folds—don't ask me how, it must have been ballooning out. I sidestep like a drunken Roman staggering around his toga, pulling half the curtain down behind me, while the pins holding it to the rod above tinkle like little finger cymbals, dragging part of it with me over one shoulder, while I bend over the basin to drink.

No time to rummage for a tumbler. It's not there anyway—I'd been using it for the rye. So I use the hollow of one hand for a scoop, pumping it up and down to my open mouth and alternating with one of the nuggets from the little plastic container I'm holding uncapped in my other hand. I've been called a fast drinker at times. Johnny used to say—never mind that now.

I only miss one—that falls down in the gap between me and the basin to the floor. That's a damned good average. There were twelve of them in there, and I remember the label read: *Not more than three to be taken during any twenty-four-hour period.* In other words, I've just killed myself three times, with a down payment on a fourth time for good measure.

I grab the sides of the basin suddenly and bend over it, on the point of getting them all out of me again in rebellious upheaval. *I* don't want to but they do. I fold both arms around my middle, hugging myself, squeezing myself, to hold them down. They stay put. They've caught on, taken hold. Only a pump can get them out now. And after a certain point of no return (I don't know how long that is), once they start being assimi-lated into the bloodstream, not even a pump can get them out.

Only a little brine taste shows up in my mouth and gagging a little, still holding my middle, I go back into the other room. Then I sit down to wait. To see which of them gets to me first.

It goes fast now, like a drumbeat quickening to a climax. An upended foot kicks at the door, and it suddenly spanks inward with a firecracker sound. The light comes fizzing through the empty oblong like gushing carbonation, too sudden against the dark to ray clearly at first.

They rush in like the splash of a wave that suddenly has splattered itself all around the room. Then the lights are on, and they're on all four sides of me, and they're holding me hard and fast, quicker than one eyelid can touch the other in a blink.

My arms go behind me into the cuffless convolutions of a strait jacket. Then as though unconvinced that this is enough precaution, someone standing back there has looped the curve of his arm around my throat and the back of the chair, and holds it there in tight restraint. Not choking-tight as in a mugging, but ready to pin me back if I should try to heave out of the chair.

Although the room is blazing-bright, several of them are holding flashlights, all lit and centered inward on my face from the perimeter around me, like the spokes of a blinding wheel. Probably to disable me still further by their dazzle. One beam, more skeptical than the others, travels slowly up and down my length, seeking out any bulges that might possibly spell a concealed offensive weapon. My only weapon is already used, and it was a defensive one.

I roll my eyes toward the ceiling to try and get away from the lights, and one by one they blink and go out.

There they stand. The assignment is over, completed. To me it's my life, to them just another incident. I don't know how many there are. The man in the coffin doesn't count the number who have come to the funeral. But as I look at them, as my eyes go from face to face, on each one I read the key to what the man is thinking.

One face, soft with compunction: Poor guy, I might have been him, he might have been me.

One, hard with contempt: Just another of those creeps something went wrong with along the way.

Another, flexing with hate: I wish he'd show some fight; I'd like an excuse to—

Still another, rueful with impatience: I'd like to get this over so I could call her unexpectedly and catch her in a lie; I bet she never stayed home tonight like she told me she would.

And yet another, blank with indifference, its thoughts a thousand miles away: And what's a guy like Yastrzemski got plenty of other guys haven't got too? It's just the breaks that's all—

And I say to my own thoughts, dejectedly: Why weren't you that clear, that all-seeing, the other night, that terrible other night? It might have done you more good then.

There they stand. And there I am, seemingly in their hands but slowly slipping away from them.

They don't say anything. I'm not aware of any of them saying anything. They're waiting for someone to give them further orders. Or maybe waiting for something to come and take me away.

One of them hasn't got a uniform on or plainclothes either like the rest. He has on the white coat that is my nightmare and my horror. And in the crotch of one arm he is up-ending two long poles intertwined with canvas.

The long-drawn-out death within life. The burial-alive of the mind, covering it over with fresh graveyard earth each time it tries to struggle through to the light. In this kind of death you never finish dying.

In back of them, over by the door, I see the top of someone's head appear, then come forward, slowly, fearfully forward. Different from their short-clipped, starkly outlined heads, soft and rippling in contour and gentle. And as she comes forward into full-face view, I see who she is.

She comes up close to me, stops, and looks at me.

"Then it wasn't—you?" I whisper.

She shakes her head slightly with a mournful trace of smile. "It wasn't me," she whispers back, without taking them into it, just between the two of us, as in the days before. "I didn't go there to meet you. I didn't like the way you sounded."

But someone was there. I came across someone there. Someone whose face became hers in my waking dream. The scarf, the blood on the scarf. It's not my blood, it's not my scarf. It must belong to someone else. Someone they haven't even found yet, don't know even about yet.

The preventive has come too late.

She moves a step closer and bends toward me.

"Careful—watch it," a voice warns her.

"He won't hurt me," she answers understandingly without taking her eyes from mine. "We used to be in love."

Used to? Then that's why I'm dying. Because I still am. And you aren't any more.

She bends and kisses me, on the forehead, between the eyes. Like a sort of last rite.

And in that last moment, as I'm straining upward to find her lips, as the light is leaving my eyes, the whole night passes before my mind, the way they say your past life does when you're drowning: the waiter, the night maid, the taxi argument, the call girl, Johnny—it all meshes into start-to-finish continuity. Just like in a story. An organized, step-by-step, timetabled story.

This story.

SMALL HOMICIDE

Ed McBain

HER FACE WAS small and chubby, the eyes blue and innocently rounded, but seeing nothing. Her body rested on the seat of the wooden bench, one arm twisted awkwardly beneath her.

The candles near the altar flickered and cast their dancing shadows on her face. There was a faded, pink blanket wrapped around her, and against the whiteness of her throat were the purple bruises that told us she'd been strangled.

Her mouth was open, exposing two small teeth and the beginnings of a third.

She was no more than eight months old.

The church was quiet and immense, with early-morning sunlight lighting the stained-glass windows. Dust motes filtered down the long, slanting columns of sunlight, and Father Barron stood tall and darkly somber at the end of the pew, the sun touching his hair like an angel's kiss.

"This is the way you found her, Father?" I asked.

"Yes. Just that way." The priest's eyes were a deep brown against the chalky whiteness of his face. "I didn't touch her."

Pat Travers scratched his jaw and stood up, reaching for the pad in his back pocket. His mouth was set in a tight, angry line. Pat had three children of his own. "What time was this, Father?"

"At about five-thirty. We have a six o'clock mass, and I came out to see that the altar was prepared. Our altar boys go to school, you understand, and they usually arrive at the last moment. I generally attend to the altar myself."

"No sexton?" Pat asked.

"Yes, we have a sexton, but he doesn't arrive until about eight every morning. He comes earlier on Sundays."

I nodded while Pat jotted the information in his pad. "How did you happen to see her, Father?"

"I was walking to the back of the church to open the doors. I saw something in the pew, and I . . . well, at first I thought it was just a package someone had forgotten. When I came closer, I saw it was . . . was a baby." He sighed deeply and shook his head.

"The doors were locked, Father?"

"No. No, they're never locked. This is God's house, you know. They were simply closed. I was walking back to open them. I usually open them before the first mass in the morning."

"They were unlocked all night?"

"Yes, of course."

"I see." I looked down at the baby again. "You . . . you wouldn't know who she is, would you, Father?"

Father Barron shook his head again. "I'm afraid not. She may have been baptized here, but infants all look alike, you know. It would be different if I saw her every Sunday. But . . ." He spread his hands wide in a helpless gesture.

Pat nodded, and kept looking at the dead child. "We'll have to send some of the boys to take pictures and prints, Father. I hope you don't mind. And we'll have to chalk up the pew. It shouldn't take too long, and we'll have the body out as soon as possible."

Father Barron looked down at the dead baby. He crossed himself then and said, "God have mercy on her soul."

I was sipping my hot coffee when the buzzer on my desk sounded. I pushed down the toggle and said, "Levine here."

"Dave, want to come into my office a minute? This is the lieutenant."

"Sure thing," I told him. I put down the cup and said, "Be right back," to Pat, and headed for the Skipper's office.

He was sitting behind his desk with our report in his hands. He glanced up when I came in and said, "Sit down, Dave. Hell of a thing, isn't it?"

"Yes," I said.

"I'm holding it back from the papers, Dave. If this breaks, we'll have every mother in the city telephoning us. You know what that means?"

"You want it fast."

"I want it damned fast. I'm pulling six men from other jobs to help you and Pat. I don't want to go to another precinct for help because the bigger this gets, the better its chances of breaking print are. I want it quiet and small, and I want it fast." He stopped and shook his head, and then muttered, "Goddamn thing."

"We're waiting for the autopsy report now," I said. "As soon as we get it, we may be able to—"

"What did it look like to you?"

"Strangulation. It's there in our report."

The lieutenant glanced at the typewritten sheet in his hands, mumbled, "Uhm," and then said, "While you're waiting, you'd better start checking the Missing Persons calls."

"Pat's doing that now, sir."

"Good, good. You know what to do, Dave. Just get me an answer to it fast."

"We'll do our best, sir."

He leaned back in his leather chair, "A little girl, huh?" He shook his head. "Damn shame. Damn shame." He kept shaking his head and looking at the report, and then he dropped the report on his desk and said, "Here're the boys you've got to work with." He handed me a typewritten list of names. "All good, Dave. Get me results."

"I'll try, sir."

Pat had a list of calls on his desk when I went outside again. I picked it up and glanced through it rapidly. A few older kids were lost, and there had been the usual frantic pleas from frantic mothers who should have watched their kids more carefully in the first place.

"What's this?" I asked. I put my forefinger alongside a call clocked in at eight-fifteen. A Mrs. Wilkes had phoned to say she'd left her baby outside in the carriage, and the carriage was gone.

"They found the kid," Pat said. "Her older daughter had simply taken the kid for a walk. There's nothing there, Dave."

"The Skipper wants action, Pat. The photos come in yet?"

"Over there." He indicated a pile of glossy photographs on his desk. I picked up the stack and thumbed through it. They'd shot the baby from every conceivable angle, and there were two good close-ups of her face. I fanned the pictures out on my desk top and phoned the lab. I recognized Caputo's voice at once.

"Any luck, Cappy?"

"That you, Dave?"

"Yep."

"You mean on the baby?"

"Yeah."

"The boys brought in a whole slew of stuff. A pew collects a lot of prints, Dave."

"Anything we can use?"

"I'm running them through now. If we get anything, I'll let you know."

"Fine. I want the baby's footprints taken and a stat sent to every hospital in the state."

"Okay. It's going to be tough if the baby was born outside, though."

"Maybe we'll be lucky. Put the stat on the machine, will you? And tell them we want immediate replies."

"I'll have it taken care of, Dave."

"Good. Cappy, we're going to need all the help we can get on this one. So . . ."

"I'll do all I can."

"Thanks. Let me know if you get anything."

"I will. So long, Dave. I've got work."

He clicked off, and I leaned back and lighted a cigarette. Pat picked up one of the baby's photos and glumly studied it.

"When they get him, they should cut off his . . ."

"He'll get the chair," I said. "That's for sure."

"I'll pull the switch. Personally. Just ask me. Just ask me and I'll do it."

The baby was stretched out on the long white table when I went down to see Doc Edwards. A sheet covered the corpse, and Doc was busy typing up a report. I looked over his shoulder:

The McBain Brief

POLICE DEPARTMENT

City of New York

Date: June 12, 1953

From: Commanding Officer, Charles R. Brandon, 77th Pct.

To: Chief Medical Examiner

SUBJECT: DEATH OF Baby girl (unidentified)

Please furnish information on items checked below in connection

with the death of the above named. Body was found on June 12,

1953   at Church of the Holy Mother,

1220 Benson Avenue, Bronx, New York
_____

Autopsy performed or examination made? _____Yes_____

By Dr. ____James L. Edwards, Fordham Hospital Mortuary_____

_____

Date: _____June 12, 1953_____ Where? ___Bronx County_____

Cause of death: _____Broken neck_____

Doc Edwards looked up from the typewriter.

"Not nice, Dave."

"No, not nice at all." I saw that he was ready to type in the *Result of chemical analysis* space. "Anything else on her?"

"Not much. Dried tears on her face. Urine on her abdomen, buttocks, and genitals. Traces of Desitin and petroleum jelly there, too. That's about it."

"Time of death?"

"I'd put it at about three A.M. last night."

"Uh-huh."

"You want a guess?"

"Sure."

"Somebody doesn't like his sleep to be disturbed by a crying kid. That's my guess."

"Nobody likes his sleep disturbed," I said. "What's the Desitin and petroleum jelly for? That normal?"

"Yeah, sure. Lots of mothers use it. Mostly for minor irritations. Urine burn, diaper rash, that sort of thing."

"I see."

"This shouldn't be too tough, Dave. You know who the kid is yet?"

"We're working on that now."

"Well, good luck."

"Thanks."

I turned to go, and Doc Edwards began pecking at the typewriter again, completing the autopsy report on a dead girl.

There was good news waiting for me back at the office. Pat rushed over with a smile on his face and a thick sheet of paper in his hands.

"Here's the ticket," he said.

I took the paper and looked at it. It was the photostat of a birth certificate.

U.S. NAVAL HOSPITAL   St. Albans, N.Y.   Birth Certificate

This certifies that _____Louise Ann Dreiser_____was born to

_____Alice Dreiser_____ in this hospital at _____4:15 P.M._____ on

the _____tenth_____ day of_____November, 1952_____

Weight _____7_____ lbs. _____6_____ozs.

In witness whereof, the said hospital has caused this certificate to be issued, properly

signed and the seal of the hospital hereunto affixed.

Gregory Freeman, Lt(jg) MC USN
Gregory Freeman, LTJG MC USN
_____
Attending Physician

Frederick L. Mann
Frederick L. Mann, CAPTAIN MC
_____
Commanding Officer USN

"Here's how they got it," Pat said, handing me another stat. I looked at it quickly. It was obviously the reverse side of the birth certificate.

The McBain Brief

Baby's Footprint   (Permanent Evidence of Identity)

Left foot   Right foot

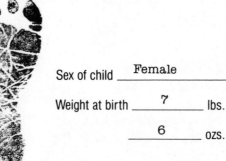

Sex of child _____Female_____

Weight at birth _____7_____ lbs.

_____6_____ ozs.

Certificate of birth should be carefully preserved as record of value for future use:

1. To identify relationship

2. To establish age to enter school

There were several more good reasons why a birth certificate should be kept in the sugar bowl, and then below that:

Official registration at _____ 148-15 Archer Avenue,

Jamaica, L.I., N.Y.

Mother's left thumb   Mother's right thumb

"Alice Dreiser," I said.

"That's the mother. Prints and all. I've already sent a copy down to Cappy to check against the ones they lifted from the pew."

"Fine. Pick one of the boys from the list the Skipper gave us, Pat. Tell him to get whatever he can on Alice Dreiser and her husband. They have to be sailors or relations to get admitted to a naval hospital, don't they?"

"Yeah. You've got to prove dependency."

"Fine. Get the guy's last address, and we'll try to run down the woman, or him, or both. Get whoever you pick to call right away, will you?"

"Right. Why pick anyone? I'll make the call myself."

"No, I want you to check the phone book for any Alice Dreisers. In the meantime, I'll be looking over the baby's garments."

"You'll be down at the lab?"

"Yeah. Phone me, Pat."

"Right."

Caputo had the garments separated and tagged when I got there.

"You're not going to get much out of these," he told me.

"No luck, huh?"

He held out the pink blanket. "Black River Mills. A big trade name. You can probably buy it in any retail shop in the city." He picked up the small pink sweater with the pearl buttons. "Toddlers, Inc., ditto. The socks have no markings at all. The undershirt came from Gilman's here in the city. It's the largest department store in the world, so you can imagine how many of these they sell every day. The cotton pajamas were bought there, too."

"No shoes?"

"No shoes."

"What about the diaper?"

"What about it? It's a plain diaper. No label. You got any kids, Dave?"

"One."

"You ever see a diaper with a label?"

"I don't recall."

"If you did, it wasn't in it long. Diapers take a hell of a beating."

"Maybe this one came from a diaper service."

"Maybe. You can check that."

"Safety pins?"

"Two. No identifying marks. Look like five-and-dime stuff."

"Any prints?"

"Yeah. There are smudged prints on the pins, but there's a good partial thumbprint on one of the pajama snaps."

"Whose?"

"It matches the right thumbprint on the stat you sent down. Mrs. Dreiser's."

"Uh-huh. Did you check her prints against the ones from the pew?"

"Nothing, Dave. None of her, anyway."

"Okay, Cappy. Thanks a lot."

Cappy shrugged. "I get paid," he said. He grinned and waved as I walked out and headed upstairs again. I met Pat in the hallway, coming down to the lab after me.

"What's up?" I asked.

"I called the Naval Hospital. They gave me the last address they had for the guy. His name is Carl Dreiser, lived at 831 East 217th Street, Bronx, when the baby was born."

"How come?"

"He was a yeoman, working downtown on Church Street. Lived with his wife uptown, got an allotment. You know the story."

"Yeah. So?"

"I sent Artie to check at that address. He should be calling in soon now."

"What about the sailor?"

"I called the Church Street office, spoke to the commanding officer, Captain"—he consulted a slip of paper—"Captain Thibot. This Dreiser was working there back in November. He got orders in January, reported aboard the U.S.S. Hanfield, DD 981, at the Brooklyn Navy Yard on January fifth of this year."

"Where is he now?"

"That's the problem, Dave."

"What kind of problem?"

"The Hanfield was sunk off Pyongyang in March."

"Oh."

"Dreiser is listed as missing in action."

I didn't say anything. I nodded, and waited.

"A telegram was sent to Mrs. Dreiser at the Bronx address. The Navy says the telegram was delivered and signed for by Alice Dreiser."

"Let's wait for Artie to call in," I said.

We ordered more coffee and waited. Pat had checked the phone book, and there'd been no listing for either Carl or Alice Dreiser. He'd had a list typed of every Dreiser in the city, and it ran longer than my arm.

"Why didn't you ask the Navy what his parents' names are?" I said.

"I did. Both parents are dead."

"Who does he list as next of kin?"

"His wife. Alice Dreiser."

"Great."

In a half hour, Artie called in. There was no Alice Dreiser living at the Bronx address. The landlady said she'd lived there until April and had left without giving a forwarding address. Yes, she'd had a baby daughter. I told Artie to keep the place staked out, and then buzzed George Tabin and told him to check the Post Office Department for any forwarding address.

When he buzzed back in twenty minutes, he said, "Nothing, Dave. Nothing at all."

We split the available force of men, and I managed to wangle four more men from the lieutenant. Half of us began checking on the Dreisers listed in the phone directory, and the rest of us began checking the diaper services.

The first diaper place I called on had a manager who needed only a beard to look like Santa Claus. He greeted me affably and offered all his assistance. Unfortunately, they'd never had a customer named Alice Dreiser.

At my fourth stop, I got what looked like a lead.

I spoke directly to the vice-president, and he listened intently.

"Perhaps," he said, "perhaps." He was a big man, with a wide waist, a gold watch chain straddling it. He leaned over and pushed down on his intercom buzzer.

"Yes, sir?"

"Bring in a list of our customers. Starting with November of 1952."

"Sir?"

"Starting with November of 1952."

"Yes, sir."

We chatted about the diaper business in general until the list came, and then he handed it to me and I began checking off the names. There were a hell of a lot of names on it. For the month of December, I found a listing for Alice Dreiser. The address given was the one we'd checked in the Bronx.

"Here she is," I said. "Can you get her records?"

The vice-president looked at the name. "Certainly, just a moment." He buzzed his secretary again, told her what he wanted, and she brought the yellow file cards in a few minutes later. The cards told me that Alice Dreiser had continued the diaper service through February. She'd been late on her February payment, and had cancelled service in March. She'd had the diapers delivered for the first week in March but had not paid for them. She did not notify the company that she was moving. She had not returned the diapers they'd sent her that first week in March. The company did not know where she was.

"If you find her," the vice-president told me, "I'd like to know. She owes us money."

"I'll keep that in mind," I said.

The reports on the Dreisers were waiting for me back at the precinct. George had found a couple who claimed to be Carl's aunt and uncle. They knew he was married. They gave Alice's maiden name as Grant. They said she lived somewhere on Walton Avenue in the Bronx, or at least *had* lived there when Carl first met her, they hadn't seen either her or Carl for months. Yes, they knew the Dreisers had had a daughter. They'd received an announcement card. They had never seen the baby.

Pat and I looked up the Grants on Walton Avenue, found a listing for Peter Grant, and went there together.

A bald man in his undershirt, his suspenders hanging over his trousers, opened the door.

"What is it?" he asked.

"Police officers," I said. "We'd like to ask a few questions."

"What about? Let me see your badges."

Pat and I flashed our buzzers and the bald man studied them.

"What kind of questions do you want to ask?"

"Are you Peter Grant?"

"Yeah, that's right. What's this all about?"

"May we come in?"

"Sure, come on in." We followed him into the apartment, and he motioned us to chairs in the small living room. "Now, what is it?" he asked.

"Your daughter is Alice Dreiser?"

"Yes," he said.

"Do you know where she lives?"

"No."

"Come on, mister," Pat said. "You know where your daughter lives."

"I don't," Grant snapped, "and I don't give a damn, either."

"Why? What's wrong, mister?"

"Nothing. Nothing's wrong. It's none of your business, anyway."

"Her daughter had her neck broken," I said. "It is our business."

"I don't give a . . ." he started to say. He stopped then and looked straight ahead of him, his brows pulled together into a tight frown. "I'm sorry. I still don't know where she lives."

"Did you know she was married?"

"To that sailor. Yes, I knew."

"And you knew she had a daughter?"

"Don't make me laugh," Grant said.

"What's funny, mister?" Pat said.

"Did I know she had a daughter? Why the hell do you think she married the sailor? Don't make me laugh!"

"When was your daughter married, Mr. Grant?"

"Last September." He saw the look on my face, and added, "Go ahead, you count it. The kid was born in November."

"Have you seen her since the marriage?"

"No."

"Have you ever seen the baby?"

"No."

"Do you have a picture of your daughter?"

"I think so. Is she in trouble? Do you think she did it?"

"We don't know who did it yet."

"Maybe she did," Grant said softly. "She just maybe did. I'll get you the picture."

He came back in a few minutes with a picture of a plain girl wearing a cap and gown. She had light eyes and straight hair, and her face was intently serious.

"She favors her mother," Grant said, "God rest her soul."

"Your wife is dead?"

"Yes. That picture was taken when Alice graduated high school. She graduated in June and married the sailor in September. She's . . . she's only just nineteen now, you know."

"May we have this?" He hesitated and said, "It's the only one I've got. She . . . she didn't take many pictures. She wasn't a very . . . pretty kid."

"We'll return it."

"All right," he said. His eyes began to blink. "She . . . If she's in trouble, you'll . . . you'll let me know, won't you?"

"We'll let you know."

"Kids . . . kids make mistakes sometimes." He stood up abruptly. "Let me know."

We had copies of the photo made, and then we staked out every church in the neighborhood in which the baby was found. Pat and I covered the Church of the Holy Mother, because we figured the suspect was most likely to come back there.

We didn't talk much. There is something about a church of any denomination that makes a man think rather than talk. Pat and I knocked off at about seven every night, and the night boys took over then. We were back on the job at seven in the morning, every morning.

It was a week before she came in.

She was a thin girl, with the body of a child and a pinched, tired face. She stopped at the font in the rear of the church, dipped her hand in the holy water, and crossed herself. Then she walked to the altar, stopped before an idol of the Virgin Mary, lighted a candle, and knelt before it.

"That's her," I said.

"Let's go," Pat answered.

"Not here. Outside."

Pat's eyes locked with mine for an instant. "Sure," he said.

She knelt before the idol for a long time, and then got to her feet slowly, drying her eyes. She walked up the aisle, stopped at the font, crossed herself, and then walked outside.

We followed her out, catching up with her at the corner. I pulled up on one side of her and Pat on the other.

"Mrs. Dreiser?" I asked.

She stopped walking. "Yes?"

I showed my buzzer. "Police officers," I said. "We'd like to ask some questions."

She stared at my face for a long time. She drew a trembling breath then, and said, "I killed her. I . . . Carl was dead, you see. I . . . I guess that was it. It wasn't right—his getting killed, I mean. And she was crying." She nodded blankly. "Yes, that was it. She just cried all the time, not knowing that I was crying inside. You don't know how I cried inside. Carl . . . he was all I had. I . . . I couldn't stand it anymore. I told her to shut up and when she didn't I . . . I . . . ."

"Come on now, ma'm," I said.

"I brought her to the church." She nodded, remembering it all now. "She was innocent, you know. So I brought her to the church. Did you find her there?"

"Yes, ma'm," I said. "That's where we found her."

She seemed pleased. A small smile covered her mouth and she said, "I'm glad you found her."

She told the story again to the lieutenant. Pat and I checked out and on the way to the subway, I asked him, "Do you still want to pull the switch, Pat?"

He didn't answer.

THE GENTLEMAN FROM PARIS

John Dickson Carr

Carlton House Hotel
Broadway, New-York
14th April, 1849

MY DEAR BROTHER:

Were my hand more steady, Maurice, or my soul less agitated, I should have written to you before this. *All is safe:* so much I tell you at once. For the rest, I seek sleep in vain; and this is not merely because I find myself a stranger and a foreigner in New-York. Listen and judge.

We discussed, I think, the humiliation that a Frenchman must go to England ere he could take passage in a reliable ship for America. The *Britannia* steam-packet departed from Liverpool on the second of the month, and arrived here on the seventeenth. Do not smile, I implore you, when I tell you that my first visit on American soil was to Platt's Saloon, under Wallack's Theatre.

Great God, that voyage!

On my stomach I could hold not even champagne. For one of my height and breadth I was as weak as a child.

"Be good enough," I said to a fur-capped coachman, when I had struggled through the horde of Irish immigrants, "to drive me to some fashionable place of refreshment."

The coachman had no difficulty in understanding my English, which pleased me. And how extraordinary are these "saloons"!

The saloon of M. Platt was loud with the thump of hammers cracking ice, which is delivered in large blocks. Though the hand-coloured gas-

globes, and the rose-paintings on the front of the bar-counter, were as
fine as we could see at the Three Provincial Brothers in Paris, yet I confess
that the place did not smell so agreeably. A number of gentlemen, wearing
hats perhaps a trifle taller than is fashionable at home, lounged at the
bar-counter and shouted. I attracted no attention until I called for a sherry
cobbler.

One of the "bartenders," as they are called in New-York, gave me a
sharp glance as he prepared the glass.

"Just arrived from the Old Country, I bet?" said he in no unfriendly tone.

Though it seemed strange to hear France mentioned in this way, I smiled
and bowed assent.

"Italian, maybe?" said he.

This bartender, of course, could not know how deadly was the insult.

"Sir," I replied, "I am a Frenchman."

And now in truth he was pleased! His fat face opened and smiled like
a distorted, gold-toothed flower.

"Is that so, now!" he exclaimed. "And what might your name be?
Unless"—and here his face darkened with that sudden defensiveness and
suspicion which for no reason I can discern, will often strike into American
hearts—"unless," said he, "you don't want to give it?"

"Not at all," I assured him earnestly. "I am Armand de Lafayette, at
your service."

My dear brother, what an extraordinary effect!

It was silence. All sounds, even the faint whistling of the gas-jets,
seemed to die away in that stone-flagged room. Every man along the line
of the bar was looking at me. I was conscious only of faces, mostly with
whiskers under the chin instead of down the cheek-bones, turned on me
in basilisk stare.

"Well, well, well!" almost sneered the bartender. "You wouldn't be no
relation of the *Marquis* de Lafayette, would you?"

It was my turn to be astonished. Though our father has always forbidden
us to mention the name of our late uncle, due to his republican sympathies,
yet I knew he occupied small place in the history of France and it puzzled
me to comprehend how these people had heard of him.

"The late Marquis de Lafayette," I was obliged to admit, "was my
uncle."

"You better be careful, young feller," suddenly yelled a grimy little
man with a pistol buckled under his long coat. "We don't like being
diddled, we don't."

"Sir," I replied, taking my bundle of papers from my pocket and
whacking them down on the bar-counter, "have the goodness to examine

my credentials. Should you still doubt my identity, we can then debate the matter in any way which pleases you."

"This is furrin writing," shouted the bartender. "*I* can't read it!" And then—how sweet was the musical sound on my ear!—I heard a voice addressing me in my own language.

"Perhaps, sir," said the voice, in excellent French and with great stateliness, "I may be able to render you some small service."

The newcomer, a slight man of dark complexion, drawn up under an old shabby cloak of military cut, stood a little way behind me. If I had met him on the boulevards, I might not have found him very prepossessing. He had a wild and wandering eye, with an even wilder shimmer of brandy. He was not very steady on his feet. And yet, Maurice, his manner! It was such that I instinctively raised my hat, and the stranger very gravely did the same.

"And to whom," said I, "have I the honour . . . ?"

"I am Thaddeus Perley, sir, at your service."

"Another furriner!" said the grimy little man, in disgust.

"I am indeed a foreigner," said Perley in English, with an accent like a knife. "A foreigner to this dram-shop. A foreigner to this neighbourhood. A foreigner to—" Here he paused, and his eyes acquired an almost frightening blaze of loathing. "Yet I never heard that the reading of French was so *very* singular an accomplishment."

Imperiously—and yet, it seemed to me, with a certain shrinking nervousness—M. Perley came closer and lifted the bundle of papers.

"Doubtless," he said loftily, "I should not be credited were I to translate these. But here," and he scanned several of the papers, "is a letter of introduction in English. It is addressed to President Zachary Taylor from the American minister at Paris."

Again, my brother, what an enormous silence. It was interrupted by a cry from the bartender, who had snatched the documents from M. Perley.

"Boys, this is no diddle," said he. "This gent is the real thing!"

"He ain't!" thundered the little grimy man, with incredulity.

"He is!" said the bartender. "I'll be a son of a roe (*i.e., biche*), if he ain't!"

Well, Maurice, you and I have seen how Paris mobs can change. Americans are even more emotional. In the wink of an eye hostility became frantic affection. My back was slapped, my hand rung, my person jammed against the bar by a crowd fighting to order me more refreshment.

The name of Lafayette, again and again, rose like a holy diapason. In vain I asked why this should be so. They appeared to think I was joking, and roared with laughter. I thought of M. Thaddeus Perley, as one who could supply an explanation.

But in the first rush towards me M. Perley had been flung backwards. He fell sprawling in some wet stains of tobacco juice on the floor, and now I could not see him at all. For myself, I was weak from lack of food. A full beaker of whisky, which I was obliged to drink because all eyes were on me, made my head reel. Yet I felt compelled to raise my voice above the clamour.

"Gentlemen," I implored them, "will you hear me?"

"Silence for Lafayette!" said a big but very old man, with faded red whiskers. He had tears in his eyes, and he had been humming a catch called "Yankee Doodle." "Silence for Lafayette!"

"Believe me," said I, "I am full of gratitude for your hospitality. But I have business in New-York, business of immediate and desperate urgency. If you will allow me to pay my reckoning . . ."

"Your money's no good here, monseer," said the bartender. "You're going to get liquored-up good and proper."

"But I have no wish, believe me, to become liquored-up! It might well endanger my mission! In effect, I wish to go!"

"Wait a minute," said the little grimy man, with a cunning look. "What *is* this here business?"

You, Maurice, have called me quixotic. I deny this. You have also called me imprudent. Perhaps you are right; but what choice was left to me?

"Has any gentleman here," I asked, "heard of Madame Thevenet? Madame Thevenet, who lives at number 23 Thomas Street, near Hudson Street?"

I had not, of course, expected an affirmative reply. Yet, in addition to one or two snickers at mention of the street, several nodded their heads.

"Old miser woman?" asked a sportif character, who wore chequered trousers.

"I regret, sir, that you correctly describe her. Madame Thevenet is very rich. And I have come here," cried I, "to put right a damnable injustice!"

Struggle as I might, I could not free myself.

"How's that?" asked half a dozen.

"Madame Thevenet's daughter, Mademoiselle Claudine, lives in the worst of poverty at Paris. Madame herself has been brought here, under some spell, by a devil of a woman calling herself . . . Gentlemen, I implore you!"

"And I bet you," cried the little grimy man with the pistol, "you're sweet on this daughter what's her name?" He seemed delighted. "Ain't you, now?"

How, I ask of all Providence, could these people have surprised my secret? Yet I felt obliged to tell the truth.

"I will not conceal from you," I said, "that I have in truth a high regard for Mlle. Claudine. But this lady, believe me, is engaged to a friend of mine, an officer of artillery."

"Then what do you *get* out of it? Eh?" asked the grimy little man, with another cunning look.

The question puzzled me. I could not reply. But the bartender with the gold teeth leaned over.

"If you want to see the old Frenchie alive, monseer," said he, "you'd better git." (*Sic*, Maurice). "I hearn tell she had a stroke this morning."

But a dozen voices clamoured to keep me there, though this last intelligence sent me into despair. Then up rose the big and very old man with the faded whiskers: indeed, I had never realised how old, because he seemed so hale.

"Which of you was with Washington?" said he, suddenly taking hold of the fierce little man's neckcloth, and speaking with contempt. "Make way for the nephew of Lafayette!"

They cheered me then, Maurice. They hurried me to the door, they begged me to return, they promised they would await me. One glance I sought—nor can I say why—for M. Thaddeus Perley. He was sitting at a table by a pillar, under an open gas-jet; his face whiter than ever, still wiping stains of tobacco-juice from his cloak.

Never have I seen a more mournful prospect than Thomas Street, when my cab set me down there. Perhaps it was my state of mind; for if Mme. Thevenet had died without a sou left to her daughter: you conceive it?

The houses of Thomas Street were faced with dingy yellow brick, and a muddy sky hung over the chimney-pots. It had been warm all day, yet I found my spirit intolerably oppressed. Though heaven knows our Parisian streets are dirty enough, we do not allow pigs in them. Except for these, nothing moved in the forsaken street save a blind street-musician, with his dog and an instrument called a banjo; but even he was silent too.

For some minutes, it seemed to me, I plied the knocker at number 23, with hideous noise. Nothing stirred. Finally, one part of the door swung open a little, as for an eye. Whereupon I heard the shifting of a floor-bolt, and both doors were swung open.

Need I say that facing me stood the woman whom we have agreed to call Mademoiselle Jezebel?

She said to me: "And then, M. Armand?"

"Madam Thevenet!" cried I. "She is still alive?"

"She is alive," replied my companion, looking up at me from under the lids of her greenish eyes. "But she is completely paralysed."

I have never denied, Maurice, that Mlle. Jezebel has a certain attractiveness. She is not old or even middle-aged. Were it not that her complexion is as muddy as was the sky above us then, she would have been pretty.

"And as for Claudine," I said to her, "the daughter of madame—"

"You have come too late, M. Armand."

And well I remember that at this moment there rose up, in the mournful street outside, the tinkle of the banjo played by the street-musician. It moved closer, playing a popular catch whose words run something thus:

> *Oh, I come from Alabama*
> *With my banjo on my knee;*
> *I depart for Louisiana*
> *My Susannah for to see.*

Across the lips of mademoiselle flashed a smile of peculiar quality, like a razor-cut before the blood comes.

"Gold," she whispered. "Ninety thousand persons, one hears, have gone to seek it. Go to California, M. Armand. It is the only place you will find gold."

This tune, they say, is a merry tune. It did not seem so, as the dreary twanging faded away. Mlle. Jezebel, with her muddy blond hair parted in the middle and drawn over her ears after the best fashion, faced me implacably. Her greenish eyes were wide open. Her old brown taffeta dress, full at the bust, narrow at the waist, rustled its wide skirts as she glided a step forward.

"Have the kindness," I said, "to stand aside. I wish to enter."

Hitherto in my life I had seen her docile and meek.

"You are no relative," she said. "I will not allow you to enter."

"In that case, I regret, I must."

"If you had ever spoken one kind word to *me*," whispered mademoiselle, looking up from under her eyelids, and with her breast heaving, "one gesture of love—that is to say, of affection—you might have shared five million francs."

"Stand aside, I say!"

"As it is, you prefer a doll-faced consumptive at Paris. So be it!"

I was raging, Maurice; I confess; yet I drew myself up with coldness.

"You refer, perhaps, to Claudine Thevenet?"

"And to whom else?"

"I might remind you, mademoiselle, that the lady is pledged to my good friend Lieutenant Delage. I have forgotten her."

"Have you?" asked our Jezebel, with her eyes on my face and a strange hungry look in them. Mlle. Jezebel added, with more pleasure:

"Well, she will die. Unless you can solve a mystery."

"A mystery?"

"I should not have said mystery, M. Armand. Because it is impossible of a solution. It is an Act of God!"

Up to this time the glass-fronted doors of the vestibule had stood open behind her, against a darkness of closed shutters in the house. There breathed out of it an odour of unswept carpets, a sourness of stale living. Someone was approaching, carrying a lighted candle.

"Who speaks," called a man's voice; shaky, but as French as Mlle. Jezebel's. "Who speaks concerning an Act of God?"

I stepped across the threshold. Mademoiselle, who never left my side, immediately closed and locked the front doors. As the candle-glimmer moved still closer in gloom, I could have shouted for joy to see the man whom (as I correctly guessed) I had come to meet.

"You are M. Duroc, the lawyer!" I said. "You are my brother's friend!"

M. Duroc held the candle higher, to inspect me.

He was a big, heavy man who seemed to sag in all his flesh. In compensation for his bald head, the greyish-brown moustache flowed down and parted into two hairy fans of beard on either side of his chin. He looked at me through oval gold-rimmed spectacles; in a friendly way, but yet frightened. His voice was deep and gruff, clipping the syllables, despite his fright.

"And you—," *clip-clip;* the candle-holder trembled—"you are Armand de Lafayette. I had expected you by the steam-packet today. Well! You are here. On a fool's errand, I regret."

"But why?" (And I shouted it at him, Maurice.)

I looked at mademoiselle, who was faintly smiling.

"M. Duroc!" I protested. "You wrote to my brother. You said you had persuaded madame to repent of her harshness towards her daughter!"

"Was that your duty?" asked the Jezebel, looking full at M. Duroc with her greenish eyes. "Was that your right?"

"I am a man of law," said M. Duroc. The deep monosyllables rapped, in ghostly bursts, through his parted beard. He was perspiring. "I am correct. Very correct! And yet—"

"Who nursed her?" asked the Jezebel. "Who soothed her, fed her, wore her filthy clothes, calmed her tempers, endured her interminable abuse? *I* did!"

And yet, all the time she was speaking, this woman kept sidling and sliding against me, brushing my side, as though she would make sure of my presence there.

"Well!" said the lawyer, "It matters little now! This mystery . . ."

You may well believe that all these cryptic remarks, as well as reference to a mystery or an Act of God, had driven me almost frantic. I demanded to know what he meant.

"Last night," said M. Duroc, "a certain article disappeared."

"Well, well?"

"It disappeared," said M. Duroc, drawn up like a grenadier. "But it could not conceivably have disappeared. I myself swear this! Our only suggestions as to how it might have disappeared are a toy rabbit and a barometer."

"Sir," I said, "I do not wish to be discourteous. But—"

"Am I mad, you ask?"

I bowed. If any man can manage at once to look sagging and uncertain, yet stately and dignified, M. Duroc managed it then. And dignity won, I think.

"Sir," he replied, gesturing with the candle towards the rear of the house, "Madame Thevenet lies there in her bed. She is paralysed. She can move only her eyes or partially the lips, without speech. Do you wish to see her?"

"If I am permitted."

"Yes. That would be correct. Accompany me."

And I saw the poor old woman, Maurice. Call her harridan if you like.

It was a square room of good size, whose shutters had remained closed and locked for years. Can one smell rust? In that room, with faded green wall-paper, I felt I could.

One solitary candle did little more than dispel shadow. It burned atop the mantelpiece well opposite the foot of the bed; and a shaggy man, whom I afterwards learned to be a police-officer, sat in a green-upholstered arm-chair by an unlighted coal fire in the fireplace grate, picking his teeth with a knife.

"If you please, Dr. Harding!" M. Duroc called softly in English.

The long and lean American doctor, who had been bending over the bed so as to conceal from our sight the head and shoulders of Madame Thevenet, turned round. But his cadaverous body—in such fashion were madame's head and shoulders propped up against pillows—his cadaverous body, I say, still concealed her face.

"Has there been any change?" persisted M. Duroc in English.

"There has been no change," replied the dark-complexioned Dr. Harding, "except for the worse."

"Do you want her to be moved?"

"There has never been any necessity," said the physician, picking up his beaver hat from the bed. He spoke dryly. "However, if you want to learn anything more about the toy rabbit or the barometer, I should hurry. The lady will die in a matter of hours, probably less."

And he stood to one side.

It was a heavy bed with four posts and a canopy. The bedcurtains, of some dullish-green material, were closely drawn on every side except the long side by which we saw Madame Thevenet in profile. Lean as a post, rigid, the strings of her cotton nightcap tightly tied under her chin, Madame Thevenet lay propped up there. But one eye rolled towards us, and it rolled horribly.

Up to this time the woman we call the Jezebel had said little. She chose the moment again to come brushing against my side. Her greenish eyes, lids half-closed, shone in the light of M. Duroc's candle. What she whispered was: "You don't really hate me, do you?"

Maurice, I make a pause here.

Since I wrote the sentence, I put down my pen, and pressed my hands over my eyes, and once more I thought. But let me try again.

I spent just two hours in the bedroom of Madame Thevenet. At the end of the time—oh, you shall hear why!—I rushed out of that bedroom, and out of number 23 Thomas Street, like the maniac I was.

The streets were full of people, of carriages, of omnibuses, at early evening. Knowing no place of refuge save the saloon from which I had come, I gave its address to a cab-driver. Since still I had swallowed no food, I may have been light-headed. Yet I wished to pour out my heart to the friends who had bidden me return there. And where were they now?

A new group, all new, lounged against the bar-counter under brighter gaslight and brighter paint. Of all those who smote me on the back and cheered, none remained save the ancient giant who had implied friendship with General Washington. *He*, alas, lay helplessly drunk with his head near a sawdust spitting-box. Nevertheless I was so moved that I took the liberty of thrusting a handful of bank-notes into his pocket. He alone remained.

Wait, there was another!

I do not believe he had remained there because of me. Yet M. Thaddeus Perley, still sitting alone at the little table by the pillar, with the open gas-jet above, stared vacantly at the empty glass in his hand.

He had named himself a foreigner; he was probably French. That was as well. For, as I lurched against the table, I was befuddled and all English had fled my wits.

"Sir," said I, "will you permit a madman to share your table?"

M. Perley gave a great start, as though roused out of thought. He was now sober: this I saw. Indeed, his shiver and haggard face were due to lack of stimulant rather than too much of it.

"Sir," he stammered, getting to his feet, "I shall be—I shall be honored by your company." Automatically he opened his mouth to call for a waiter; his hand went to his pocket; he stopped.

"No, no, no!" said I. "If you insist, M. Perley, you may pay for the second bottle. The first is mine. I am sick at heart, and I would speak with a gentleman."

At these last words M. Perley's whole expression changed. He sat down, and gave me a courtly nod. His eyes, which were his most expressive feature, studied my face and my disarray.

"You are ill, M. de Lafayette," he said. "Have you so soon come to grief in this—this *civilized* country?"

"I have come to grief, yes. But not through civilization or the lack of it." And I banged my fist on the table. "I have come to grief, M. Perley, through miracles or magic. I have come to grief with a problem which no man's ingenuity can solve!"

M. Perley looked at me in a strange way. But someone had brought a bottle of brandy, with its accessories. M. Perley's trembling hand slopped a generous allowance into my glass, and an even more generous one into his own.

"That is very curious," he remarked, eyeing the glass. "A murder, was it?"

"No. But a valuable document has disappeared. The most thorough search by the police cannot find it."

Touch him anywhere, and he flinched. M. Perley, for some extraordinary reason, appeared to think I was mocking him.

"A document, you say?" His laugh was a trifle unearthly. "Come, now. Was it by any chance—a letter?"

"No, no! It was a will. Three large sheets of parchment, of the size you call foolscap. Listen!"

And as M. Perley added water to his brandy and gulped down about a third of it, I leaned across the table.

"Madame Thevenet, of whom you may have heard me speak in this café, was an invalid. But (until the early hours of this morning) she was not bedridden. She could move, and walk about her room, and so on. She had been lured away from Paris and her family by a green-eyed woman named the Jezebel.

"But a kindly lawyer of this city, M. Duroc, believed that madame suffered and had a bad conscience about her own daughter. Last night, despite the Jezebel, he persuaded madame at last to sign a will leaving all her money to this daughter.

"And the daughter, Claudine, is in mortal need of it! From my brother and myself, who have more than enough, she will not accept a sou. Her affianced, Lieutenant Delage, is as poor as she. But, unless she leaves France for Switzerland, she will die. I will not conceal from you that Claudine suffers from that dread disease we politely call consumption."

M. Perley stopped with his glass again half-way to his mouth.

He believed me now; I sensed it. Yet under the dark hair, tumbled on his forehead, his face had gone as white as his neat, mended shirt-frill.

"So very little a thing is money!" he whispered. "So very little a thing!"

And he lifted the glass and drained it.

"You do not think I am mocking you, sir?"

"No, no!" says M. Perley, shading his eyes with one hand. "I knew myself of one such case. She is dead. Pray continue."

"Last night, I repeat, Madame Thevenet changed her mind. When M. Duroc paid his weekly evening visit with the news that I should arrive today, madame fairly chattered with eagerness and a kind of terror. Death was approaching, she said; she had a presentiment."

As I spoke, Maurice, there returned to me the image of that shadowy, arsenic-green bedroom in the shuttered house; and what M. Duroc had told me.

"Madame," I continued, "cried out to M. Duroc that he must bolt the bedroom door. She feared the Jezebel, who lurked but said nothing. M. Duroc drew up to her bedside a portable writing-desk, with two good candles. For a long time madame spoke, pouring out contrition, self-abasement, the story of an unhappy marriage, all of which M. Duroc (sweating with embarrassment) was obliged to write down until it covered three large parchment sheets.

"But it was done, M. Perley!

"The will, in effect, left everything to her daughter, Claudine. It revoked a previous will by which all had been left (and this can be done in French law, as we both know) to Jezebel of the muddy complexion and the muddy yellow hair.

"Well, then! . . .

"M. Duroc sallies out into the street, where he finds two sober fellows who come in. Madame signs the will, M. Duroc sands it, and the two men from the street affix their signatures as witnesses. Then *they* are gone. M. Duroc folds the will lengthways, and prepares to put it into his carpet-bag. Now, M. Perley, mark what follows!

" 'No, no, no!' cries madame, with the shadow of her peaked nightcap wagging on the locked shutters beyond. 'I wish to keep it—for this one night!'

" 'For this one night, madame?' asks M. Duroc.

" 'I wish to press it against my heart,' says Madame Thevenet. 'I wish to read it once, twice, a thousand times! M. Duroc, what time is it?'

"Whereupon he takes out his gold repeater, and opens it. To his astonishment it is one o'clock in the morning. Yet he touches the spring of the repeater, and its pulse-beat rings one.

" 'M. Duroc,' pleads Madame Thevenet, 'remain here with me for the rest of the night!'

" 'Madame!' cries M. Duroc, shocked to the very fans of his beard. 'That would not be correct.'

" 'Yes, you are right,' says madame. And never, swears the lawyer, has he seen her less bleary of eye, more alive with wit and cunning, more the great lady of ruin, than there in that green and shadowy and foul-smelling room.

"Yet this very fact puts her in more and more terror of the Jezebel, who is never seen. She points to M. Duroc's carpet-bag.

" 'I think you have much work to do, dear sir?'

"M. Duroc groaned. 'The Good Lord knows that I have!'

" 'Outside the only door of this room,' says madame, 'there is a small dressing-room. Set up your writing-desk beside the door there, so that no one may enter without your knowledge. Do your work there; you shall have a lamp or many candles. Do it,' shrieks madame, 'for the sake of Claudine and for the sake of an old friendship!'

"Very naturally, M. Duroc hesitated.

" '*She* will be hovering,' pleads Madame Thevenet, pressing the will against her breast. '*This* I shall read and read and read, and sanctify with my tears. If I find I am falling asleep,' and here the old lady looked cunning, 'I shall hide it. But no matter! Even *she* cannot penetrate through locked shutters and a guarded door.'

"Well, in fine, the lawyer at length yielded.

"He set up his writing-desk against the very doorpost outside that door. When he last saw madame, before closing the door, he saw her in profile with the green bed-curtains drawn except on that side, propped up with a tall candle burning on a table at her right hand.

"Ah, that night! I think I see M. Duroc at his writing-desk, as he has told me, in an airless dressing-room where no clock ticked. I see him, at times, removing his oval spectacles to press his smarting eyes. I see him returning to his legal papers, while his pen scratched through the wicked hours of the night.

"He heard nothing, or virtually nothing, until five o'clock in the morning. Then, which turned him cold and flabby, he heard a cry which he describes as being like that of a deaf-mute.

"The communicating door had not been bolted on Madame Thevenet's side, in case she needed help. M. Duroc rushed into the other room.

"On the table, at madame's right hand, the tall candle had burnt down to a flattish mass of wax over which still hovered a faint bluish flame. Madame herself lay rigid in her peaked nightcap. That revival of spirit last night, or remorse in her bitter heart, had brought on the last paralysis. Though M. Duroc tried to question her, she could move only her eyes.

"Then M. Duroc noticed that the will, which she had clutched as a doomed religious might clutch a crucifix, was not in her hand or on the bed.

" 'Where is the will?' he shouted at her, as though she were deaf too. 'Where is the will?'

"Madame Thevenet's eyes fixed on him. Then they moved down, and looked steadily at a trumpery toy—a rabbit, perhaps four inches high, made of pink velours or the like—which lay on the bed. Again she looked at M. Duroc, as though to emphasize this. Then her eyes rolled, this time with dreadful effort, towards a large barometer, shaped like a warming-pan, which hung on the wall beside the door. Three times she did this before the bluish candle-flame flickered and went out."

And I, Armand de Lafayette, paused here in my recital to M. Perley.

Again I became aware that I was seated in a garish saloon, swilling brandy, amid loud talk that beat the air. There was a thumping noise from the theatre above our heads, and faint strains of music.

"The will," I said, "was not stolen. Not even the Jezebel could have melted through locked shutters or a guarded door. The will was not hidden, because no inch of the room remains unsearched. *Yet the will is gone!*"

I threw a glance across the table at M. Perley.

To me, I am sure, the brandy had given strength and steadied my nerves. With M. Perley I was not so sure. He was a little flushed. That slightly wild look, which I had observed before, had crept up especially into one eye, giving his whole face a somewhat lopsided appearance. Yet all his self-confidence had returned. He gave me a little crooked smile.

I struck the table.

"Do you honour me with your attention, M. Perley?"

"What song the Sirens sang," he said to me, "or what names Achilles assumed when he hid himself among women, although puzzling questions, are not beyond *all* conjecture."

"They are beyond *my* conjecture!" I cried. "And so is this!"

M. Perley extended his hand, spread the fingers, and examined them as one who owns the universe.

"It is some little time," he remarked, "since I have concerned myself with these trifles." His eyes retreated into a dream. "Yet I have given some trifling aid, in the past, to the Prefect of the Parisian police."

"You are a Frenchman! I knew it! And the police?" Seeing his lofty look, I added: "As an amateur, understood?"

"Understood!" Then his delicate hand—it would be unjust to call it claw-like—shot across the table and fastened on my arm. The strange eyes burned towards my face. "A little more detail!" he pleaded humbly. "A little more, I beg of you! This woman, for instance, you call the Jezebel?"

"It was she who met me at the house."

"And then?"

I described for him my meeting with the Jezebel, with M. Duroc, and our entrance to the sick-room, where the shaggy police-officer sat in the arm-chair and the saturnine doctor faced us from beside the bed.

"This woman," I exclaimed, with the room vividly before my eyes as I described it, "seems to have conceived me (forgive me) a kind of passion. No doubt it was due to some idle compliments I once paid her at Paris.

"As I have explained, the Jezebel is *not* unattractive, even if she would only (again forgive me) wash her hair. Nevertheless, when once more she brushed my side and whispered, 'You don't really hate me, do you?' I felt little less than horror. It seemed to me that in some fashion I was responsible for the whole tragedy.

"While we stood beside the bed, M. Duroc the lawyer poured out the story I have recounted. There lay the poor paralytic, and confirmed it with her eyes. The toy rabbit, a detestable pink colour, lay in its same position on the bed. Behind me, hung against the wall by the door, was the large barometer.

"Apparently for my benefit, Madame Thevenet again went through her dumb-show with imploring eyes. She would look at the rabbit; next (as M. Duroc had not mentioned), she would roll her eyes all around her, for some desperate yet impenetrable reason, before fixing her gaze on the barometer.

"It meant . . . what?

"The lawyer spoke then. 'More light!' gulped out M. Duroc. 'If you must have closed shutters and windows, then let us at least have more light!'

"The Jezebel glided out to fetch candles. During M. Duroc's explanation he had several times mentioned my name. At first mention of it the shaggy police-officer jumped and put away his clasp-knife. He beckoned to the physician, Dr. Harding, who went over for a whispered conference.

"Whereupon the police-officer sprang up.

" 'Mr. Lafayette!' And he swung my hand pompously. 'If I'd known it was you, Mr. Lafayette, I wouldn't 'a' sat there like a bump on a log.'

" 'You are an officer of police, sir,' said I. 'Can *you* think of no explanation?'

"He shook his head.

" 'These people are Frenchies, Mr. Lafayette, and you're an American,' he said, with somewhat conspicuous lack of logic. '*If* they're telling the truth—'

" 'Let us assume that!'

" 'I can't tell you where the old lady's will is, he stated positively. 'But I can tell you where it ain't. It ain't hidden in this room!'

" 'But surely . . . !' I began in despair.

"At this moment the Jezebel, her brown-taffeta dress rustling, glided back into the room with a handful of candles and a tin box of the new-style Lucifer matches. She lighted several candles, sticking them on any surface in their own grease.

"There were one or two fine pieces of furniture; but the mottled-marble tops were chipped and stained, the gilt sides cracked. There were a few mirrors, creating mimic spectral life. I saw a little more clearly the faded green paper of the walls, and what I perceived to be the partly open door of a cupboard. The floor was of bare boards.

"All this while I was conscious of two pairs of eyes: the imploring gaze of Madame Thevenet, and the amorous gaze of the Jezebel. One or the other I could have endured, but both together seemed to suffocate me.

" 'Mr. Duroc here,' said the shaggy police-officer, clapping the distressed advocate on the shoulder, 'sent a messenger in a cab at half-past five this morning. And what time did we get here? I ask you and I tell you! Six o'clock!'

"Then he shook his finger at me, in a kind of pride and fury of efficiency.

" 'Why, Mr. Lafayette, there's been fourteen men at this room from six this morning until just before you got here!'

" 'To search for Madame Thevenet's will, you mean?'

"The shaggy man nodded portentously, and folded his arms.

" 'Floor's solid.' He stamped on the bare boards. 'Walls and ceiling? Nary a inch missed. We reckon we're remarkable smart; and we are.'

" 'But Madame Thevenet,' I persisted, 'was not a complete invalid until this morning. She could move about. If she became afraid of' "—the name of the Jezebel choked me—" 'if she became afraid, and *did* hide the will . . .'

" 'Where'd she hide it? Tell me!'

" 'In the furniture, then?'

" 'Cabinet-makers in, Mr. Lafayette. No secret compartments.'

" 'In one of the mirrors?'

" 'Took the backs of 'em off. No will hid there.'

" 'Up the chimney!' I cried.

" 'Sent a chimney-sweep up there,' replied my companion in a ruminating way. Each time I guessed, he would leer at me in a friendly and complacent challenge. 'Ye-es, I reckon we're pretty smart. But we didn't find no will.'

"The pink rabbit also seemed to leer from the bed. I saw madame's eyes. Once again, as a desperate mind will fasten on trifles, I observed the strings of the nightcap beneath her scrawny chin. But I looked again at the toy rabbit.

" 'Has it occurred to you,' I said triumphantly, 'to examine the bed and bedstead of Madame Thevenet herself?'

"My shaggy friend went to her bedside.

" 'Poor old woman,' he said. He spoke as though she were already a corpse. Then he turned round. 'We lifted her out, just as gentle as a newborn babe (didn't we, ma'am?). No hollow bedposts! Nothing in the canopy! Nothing in the frame or the feather-beds or the curtains or the bedclothes!'

"Suddenly the shaggy police-officer became angry, as though he wished to be rid of the whole matter.

" 'And it ain't in the toy rabbit,' he said, 'because you can see we slit it up, if you look close. And it ain't in that barometer there. It just—ain't here.'

"There was a silence as heavy as the dusty, hot air of this room.

" 'It is here,' murmured M. Duroc in his gruff voice. 'It must be here!'

"The Jezebel stood there meekly, with downcast eyes.

"And I, in my turn, confess that *I* lost my head. I stalked over to the barometer, and tapped it. Its needle, which already indicated, 'Rain; cold,' moved still further towards that point.

"I was not insane enough to hit it with my fist. But I crawled on the floor, in search of a secret hiding-place. I felt along the wall. The police-officer—who kept repeating that nobody must touch anything and he would take no responsibility until he went off duty at something o'clock—the police-officer I ignored.

"What at length gave me pause was the cupboard, already thoroughly searched. In the cupboard hung a few withered dresses and gowns, as though they had shrivelled with Madame Thevenet's body. But on the shelf of the cupboard . . .

"On the shelf stood a great number of perfume-bottles: even today, I fear, many of our countrymen think perfume a substitute for water and soap; and the state of madame's hands would have confirmed this. *But*, on the shelf were a few dusty novels. There was a crumpled and begrimed copy of yesterday's New-York *Sun*. This newspaper did not contain a will, but it did contain a black beetle, which ran out across my hand.

"In a disgust past describing, I flung down the beetle, and stamped on it. I closed the cupboard door, acknowledging defeat. Madame Thevenet's will was gone. And at the same second, in that dim green room—still badly lighted, with only a few more candles—two voices cried out.

"One was my own voice:

" '*In God's name, where is it?*'

"That other was the deep voice of M. Duroc:

" '*Look at that woman! She knows!*'

"And he meant the Jezebel.

M. Duroc, with his beard-fans a-tremble, was pointing to a mirror; a little blurred, as these mirrors were. Our Jezebel had been looking into the mirror, her back turned to us. Now she dodged, as at a stone thrown.

"With good poise our Jezebel writhed this movement into a curtsy, turning to face us. But not before I also had seen that smile—like a razor-cut before the blood comes—as well as full knowledge, mocking knowledge, shining out of wide-open eyes in the mirror.

" 'You spoke to me, M. Duroc?' She murmured the reply, also in French.

" 'Listen to me!' the lawyer said formally. 'This will is *not* missing. It is in this room. You were not here last night. Something has made you guess. You know where it is.'

" 'Are you unable to find it?' asked the Jezebel in surprise.

" 'Stand back, young man!' M. Duroc said to me. 'I ask you something, mademoiselle, in the name of justice.'

" 'Ask!' said the Jezebel.

" 'If Claudine Thevenet inherits the money to which she is entitled, you will be well paid; yes, overpaid! You know Claudine. You know that!'

" 'I know it.'

" 'But if the new will be *not* found,' said M. Duroc, again, waving me back, 'then you inherit everything. And Claudine will die. For it will be assumed—'

" 'Yes!' said the Jezebel, with one hand pressed against her breast. 'You yourself, M. Duroc, testify that all night a candle was burning at madame's bedside. Well! The poor woman, whom *I* loved and cherished, repented of her ingratitude towards me. She burnt this new will at the candle-flame; she crushed its ashes to powder and blew them away!'

" 'Is that true?' cried M. Duroc.

" 'They will assume it,' smiled the Jezebel, 'as you say.' She looked at me. 'And for you, M. Armand!'

"She glided closer. I can only say that I saw her eyes uncovered; or, if you wish to put it so, her soul and flesh together.

" 'I would give you everything on earth,' she said. 'I will not give you the doll-face in Paris.'

" 'Listen to me!' I said to her, so agitated that I seized her shoulders. 'You are out of your senses! You cannot give Claudine to me! She will marry another man!'

" 'And do you think that matters to me,' asked the Jezebel, with her green eyes full on mine, 'as long as you still love her?'

"There was a small crash as someone dropped a knife on the floor.

"We three, I think, had completely forgotten that we were not alone. There were two spectators, although they did not comprehend our speech.

"The saturnine Dr. Harding now occupied the green arm-chair. His long thin legs, in tight black trousers with strap under the boot-instep, were crossed and looked spidery; his high beaver hat glimmered on his head. The police-officer, who was picking his teeth with a knife when I first saw him, had now dropped the knife when he tried to trim his nails.

"But both men sensed the atmosphere. Both were alert, feeling out with the tentacles of their nerves. The police-officer shouted at me.

" 'What's this gabble?' he said. 'What's a-gitting into your head?'

"Grotesquely, it was that word 'head' which gave me my inspiration.

" 'The nightcap!' I exclaimed in English.

" 'What nightcap?'

"For the nightcap of Madame Thevenet had a peak; it was large; it was tightly tied under the chin; it might well conceal a flat-pressed document which—but you understand. The police-officer, dull-witted as he appeared, grasped the meaning in a flash. And how I wished I had never spoken! For the fellow meant well, but he was not gentle.

"As I raced round the curtained side of the bed, the police-officer was holding a candle in one hand and tearing off madame's nightcap with the other. He found no will there, no document at all; only straggly wisps of hair on a skull grown old before its time.

"Madame Thevenet had been a great lady, once. It must have been the last humiliation. Two tears overflowed her eyes and ran down her cheeks. She lay propped up there in a nearly sitting position; but something seemed to wrench inside her.

"And she closed her eyes forever. And the Jezebel laughed.

"That is the end of my story. That is why I rushed out of the house like a madman. The will has vanished as though by magic; or is it still there by magic? In any case, you find me at this table: grubby and dishevelled and much ashamed."

For a little time after I had finished my narrative to M. Perley in the saloon, it seemed to me that the bar-counter was a trifle quieter. But a faint stamping continued from the theatre above our heads. Then all was hushed, until a chorus rose to a tinkle of many banjos.

> *Oh, I come from Alabama*
> *With my banjo on my knee;*
> *I depart for Louisiana . . .*

Enough! The song soon died away, and M. Thaddeus Perley did not even hear it.

M. Perley sat looking downwards into an empty glass, so that I could not see his face.

"Sir," he remarked almost bitterly, "you are a man of good heart. I am glad to be of service in a problem so trifling as this."

"*Trifling!*"

His voice was a little husky, but not slurred. His hand slowly turned the glass round and round.

"Will you permit two questions?" asked M. Perley.

"Two questions? Ten thousand!"

"More than two will be unnecessary." Still M. Perley did not look up. "This toy rabbit, of which so much was made: I would know its exact position on the bed?"

"It was almost at the foot of the bed, and about the middle in a crossways direction."

"Ah, so I had imagined. Were the three sheets of parchment, forming the will, written upon two sides or upon only one?"

"I had not told you, M. Perley. But M. Duroc said: upon one side only."

M. Perley raised his head.

His face was now flushed and distorted with drink, his eyes grown wild. In his cups he was as proud as Satan, and as disdainful of others' intelligence; yet he spoke with dignity, and with careful clearness.

"It is ironic, M. de Lafayette, that I should tell you how to lay your hand on the missing will and the elusive money; since, upon my word, I have never been able to perform a like service for myself." And he smiled, as at some secret joke. "Perhaps," he added, "it is the very simplicity of the thing which puts you at fault."

I could only look at him in bewilderment.

"Perhaps the mystery is a little *too* plain! A little *too* self-evident!"

"You mock me, sir! I will not . . ."

"Take me as I am," said M. Perley, whacking the foot of the glass on the table, "or leave me. Besides—" here his wandering eye encountered a list of steam-sailings pasted against the wall—"I—I leave tomorrow by the *Parnassus* for England, and then for France."

"I meant no offence, M. Perley! If you have knowledge, speak!"

"Madame Thevenet," he said, carefully pouring himself more brandy, "hid the will in the middle of the night. Does it puzzle you that she took such precautions to hide the will? But the element of the *outré* must always betray itself. The Jezebel *must not* find that will! Yet Madame Thevenet trusted nobody—not even the worthy physician who attended her. If Madame were to die of a stroke, the police would be there and must soon, she was sure, discover her simple device. Even if she were paralysed, it would ensure the presence of other persons in the room to act as unwitting guards.

"Your cardinal error," M. Perley continued dispassionately, "was one of ratiocination. You tell me that Madame Thevenet, to give you a hint, looked fixedly at some point near the foot of the bed. Why do you assume that she was looking at the toy rabbit?"

"Because," I replied hotly, "the toy rabbit was the only object she could have looked at!"

"Pardon me; but it was *not*. You several times informed me that the bed-curtains were closely drawn together on three sides. They were drawn on all but the 'long' side towards the door. Therefore the ideal reasoner, without having seen the room, may safely say that the curtains were drawn together at the foot of the bed?"

"Yes, true!"

"After looking fixedly at this point represented by the toy, Madame Thevenet then 'rolls her eyes all round her'—in your phrase. May we assume that she wishes the curtains to be drawn back, so that she may see something *beyond* the bed?"

"It is—possible, yes!"

"It is more than possible, as I shall demonstrate. Let us direct our attention, briefly, to the incongruous phenomenon of the barometer on another wall. The barometer indicates, 'Rain; cold.' "

Here M. Perley's thin shoulders drew together under the old military cloak.

"Well," he said, "the cold is on its way. Yet this day, for April, has been warm outside and indoors, oppressively hot?"

"Yes! Of course!"

"You yourself," continued M. Perley, inspecting his finger-nails, "told me what was directly opposite the foot of the bed. Let us suppose that the bed-curtains are drawn open. Madame Thevenet, in her nearly seated position, is looking *downwards*. What would she have seen?"

"The fireplace!" I cried. "The grate of the fireplace!"

"Already we have a link with the weather. And what, as you have specifically informed me, was in the grate of the fireplace?"

"An unlighted coal fire!"

"Exactly. And what is essential for the composition of such a fire? We need coal; we need wood; but primarily and above all, we need . . ."

"Paper!" I cried.

"In the cupboard of that room," said M. Perley, with his disdainful little smile, "was a very crumpled and begrimed (mark that; not dusty) copy of *yesterday's* New-York *Sun*. To light fires is the most common, and indeed the best, use for our daily press. That copy had been used to build yesterday's fire. But something else, during the night, was substituted for it. You yourself remarked the extraordinarily dirty state of Madame Thevenet's hands."

M. Perley swallowed the brandy, and his flush deepened.

"Sir," he said loudly, "you will find the will crumpled up, with ends most obviously protruding up, under the coal and wood in the fireplace grate. Even had anyone taken the fire to pieces, he would have found only what appeared to be dirty blank paper, written side undermost, which could never be a valuable will. It was too self-evident to be seen— Now go!"

"Go?" I echoed stupidly.

M. Perley rose from his chair.

"Go, I say!" he shouted, with an even wilder eye. "The Jezebel could not light that fire. It was too warm, for one thing; and all day there were police-officers with instructions that an outsider must touch nothing. But now? *Madame Thevenet kept warning you that the fire must not be lighted, or the will would be destroyed!"*

"Will you await me here?" I called over my shoulder.

"Yes, yes! And perhaps there will be peace for the wretched girl with— with the lung-trouble."

Even as I ran out of the door I saw him, grotesque and pitiful, slump across the table. Hope, rising and surging, seemed to sweep me along like the crack of the cabman's whip. But when I reached my destination, hope receded.

The shaggy police-officer was just descending the front steps.

"None of us coming back here, Mr. Lafayette!" he called cheerily. "Old Mrs. What's-her-name went and burnt that will at a candle last night—Here, what's o'clock?"

The front door was unlocked. I raced through that dark house, and burst into the rear bedroom.

The corpse still lay in the big, gloomy bed. Every candle had flickered almost down to its socket. The police-officer's clasp-knife, forgotten since he had dropped it, still lay on bare boards. But the Jezebel was there.

She knelt on the hearth, with the tin box of Lucifer matches she had brought there earlier. The match spurted, a bluish fire; I saw her eagerness; she held the match to the grate.

"A Lucifer," I said, "in the hand of a Jezebel!"

And I struck her away from the grate, so that she reeled against a chair and fell. Large coals, small coals rattled down in puffs of dust as I plunged my hands into the unlighted fire. Little sticks, sawed sticks; and I found it there: crumpled parchment-sheets, but incontestably madame's will.

"M. Duroc!" I called. "M. Duroc!"

You and I, my brother Maurice, have fought the Citizen-King with bayonets as we now fight the upstart Bonapartist; we need not be ashamed of tears. I confess, then, that the tears overran my eyes and blinded me. I scarcely saw M. Duroc as he hurried into the room.

Certainly I did not see the Jezebel stealthily pick up the police-officer's knife. I noticed nothing at all until she flew at me and stabbed me in the back.

Peace, my brother: I have assured you all is well. At that time, faith, I was not much conscious of any hurt. I bade M. Duroc, who was trembling, to wrench out the knife; I borrowed his roomy greatcoat to hide the blood; I must hurry, hurry, hurry back to that little table under the gas-jet.

I planned it all on my way back. M. Perley, apparently a stranger in this country, disliked it and was evidently very poor even in France. But *we* are not precisely paupers. Even with his intense pride, he could not refuse (for such a service) a sum which would comfort him for the rest of his life.

Back I plunged into the saloon, and hurried down it. Then I stopped. The little round table by the pillar, under the flaring gas-jet, was empty.

How long I stood there I cannot tell. The back of my shirt, which at first had seemed full of blood, now stuck to the borrowed greatcoat. All of a sudden I caught sight of the fat-faced bartender with the gold teeth, who had been on service that afternoon and had returned now. As a mark of respect, he came out from behind the bar-counter to greet me.

"Where is the gentleman who was sitting at that table?"

I pointed to it. My voice, in truth, must have sounded so hoarse and strange that he mistook it for anger.

"Don't you worry about that, monseer!" said he reassuringly. "*That's* been tended to! We threw the drunken tramp out of here!"

"You threw . . ."

"Right bang in the gutter. Had to crawl along in it before he could stand up." My bartender's face was pleased and vicious. "Ordered a bottle of best brandy, and couldn't pay for it." The face changed again. "Goddel-mighty, monseer, what's wrong?"

"*I* ordered that brandy."

"*He* didn't say so, when the waiter brought me over. Just looked me up and down, crazy-like, and said a gentleman would give his I.O.U. Gentleman!"

"M. Perley," I said, restraining an impulse to kill that bartender, "is a friend of mine. He departs for France early tomorrow morning. Where is his hotel? Where can I find him?"

"Perley!" sneered my companion. "That ain't even his real name, I hearn tell. Gits high-and mighty ideas from upper Broadway. But his real name's on the I.O.U."

A surge of hope, once more, almost blinded me. "Did you keep that I.O.U?"

"Yes, I kepp it," growled the bartender, fishing in his pocket. "God knows why, but I kepp it."

And at last, Maurice, I triumphed!

True, I collapsed from my wound; and the fever would not let me remember that I must be at the dock when the *Parnassus* steampacket departed from New-York next morning. I must remain here, shut up in a hotel-room and unable to sleep at night, until I can take ship for home. But where I failed, you can succeed. He was to leave on the morrow by the *Parnassus* for England, and then for France—so he told me. You can find him—in six months at the most. In six months, I give you my word, he will be out of misery forever!

"*I.O.U.*" reads the little slip, "*for one bottle of your best brandy, forty-five cents. Signed Edgar A. Poe.*"

I remain, Maurice,
Your affectionate brother,
Armand

THE LORD OF CENTRAL PARK

Avram Davidson

THIS ALL TOOK place a while back . . .

It was a crisp evening in middle April.

Cornelius Goodeycoonce, the river pirate, headed his plunder-laden boat straight at an apparently solid wall of pilings, steering with the calm of a ferryboat captain nearing a slip, and cut his motor.

Up in Central Park, where he was kipped out in a secluded cave, Arthur Marmaduke Roderick Lodowicke William Rufus de Powisse-Plunkert, 11th Marquess of Grue and Groole in the Peerage of England, 22nd Baron Bogle in the Peerage of Scotland, 6th Earl of Ballypatcoogen in the Peerage of Ireland, Viscount Penhokey in the Peerage of the United Kingdom, Laird of Muckle Greet, Master of Snee, and Hereditary Lord High Keeper of the Queen's Bears, heard a familiar beat of wings in the night and held out a slice of bread just in time to catch a medium-rare charcoal-broiled steak.

Not a mile away the Grand Master of the Mafia, Don Alexander Borjia, admired for the ten-thousandth time the eternally enigmatic smile on the lips of the *original* Mona Lisa, which hung, as it had for 50 years, on the wall of the Chamber of the order's Grand Council. A certain foreign visitor, who called himself Tosci, came down the gangway ladder on the side of the yacht which in daylight flew the flag of the landlocked nation whose citizenship he claimed, and got gingerly into the launch which was to bear him to shore.

Daisy Smith, in her trim and tiny bachelor-girl apartment, prepared herself a tunafish sandwich without enthusiasm, and reflected how much more—how very much more—she would rather be preparing, say, roast beef and potatoes for a young man, if only she knew a young man she considered worth preparing roast beef and potatoes for.

And across the North River, on the Jersey shore, a thin line of green still hugged the outline of the cliffs; and over that, a thin line of blue. And then the night rolled all the way down, and the lines of light were lost . . .

The momentum of Cornelius's boat carried it swiftly toward the bulkhead. A crash seemed inevitable. Then Cornelius picked up an oar and prodded one certain timber well below the waterline. Instantly a section of the pilings swung open, just wide enough and just high enough for the boat to pass through; then it swung shut once more.

The boat proceeded onward in gathering darkness as the light from the river dimmed behind it. Gauging the precise instant when the momentum would cease to propel his boat against the mild current of Coenties Kill—walled in and walled over these 150 years—the man lowered his oar and began to pole. The eyes of an alligator flashed briefly, then submerged.

Presently a light showed itself some distance off, then vanished, reappeared, vanished once more in the windings of the sluggish creek, and finally revealed itself, hissing whitely, as a Coleman lamp. It sat on a stone lip of what had been a fairly well frequented landing in the days when De Witt Clinton was Mayor and Jacob Hays was High Constable of the City of New York. Cheap as labor had been in those days—and fill even cheaper—it had been less expensive to vault up rather than bury the Kill when the needs of the growing metropolis demanded the space. Experience had proved that to be the case when other Manhattan "kills" or streams, refusing meekly to submit to burial, had flooded cellars and streets.

The Goodeycoonce-the-river-pirate of that time had noted, marked, mapped, and made the private excavations. They were an old, old family, loath to change what was even then an old family trade.

"Well, now, let's see—" said the present-day Cornelius. He tied up. He unloaded his cargo onto a pushcart, placed the lamp in a bracket, and slowly trundled the cart over the stone paving of the narrow street, which had echoed to no other traffic since it lost the light of the sun so long ago.

At the head of the incline the path passed under an archway of later construction. The Goodeycoonce-of-that-time, trusting no alien hand, had learned the mason's trade himself, breaking in onto a lovely, dry, smooth tunnel made and abandoned forever by others—the first, last, and short-lived horse-car subway. The wheels of the pushcart fitted perfectly into the tracks, and the grade was level.

Granny Goodeycoonce was reading her old Dutch family Bible in the snug apartment behind her second-hand store. That is, not exactly *reading* it; it had been generations since any member of the family could actually read Dutch; she was looking at the pictures. Her attention was diverted from a copperplate engraving of the she-bear devouring the striplings who had so uncouthly mocked the Prophet Elisha with the words, *Go up baldhead* ("Served them right!" she declared. "Bunch of juvenile delinquents!"), by a thumping from below.

She closed the Book and descended to the cellar, where her only grandchild was hauling his plunder up through the trap door.

"Put out that *lamp*, Neely!" she said sharply. "Gasoline costs *money!*"

"Yes, Granny," the river pirate said obediently.

Denny the Dip stared in stupefaction at the sudden appearance of a steak sandwich's most important ingredient. Then he stared at the winged visitor which had appeared a second after the steak. The winged visitor stared back—or, perhaps "glared" would be the *mot juste*—out of burning yellow eyes. "Cheest!" said Denny the Dip.

There had been a time when, so skillful was The Dip, that he had picked the pocket of a Police Commissioner while the latter was in the very act of greeting a Queen. (He had returned the wallet later, of course, via the mails, out of courtesy, and, of course, minus the money.) But Time with her winged Flight, and all that—age and its concomitant infirmities, much aggravated by a devotion to whatever Celtic demigod presides over the demijohn—had long rendered The Dip unfit for such professional gestures.

For some years now he had been the bane of the Mendicant Squad. His method was to approach lone ladies with the pitch that he was a leper, that they were not to come any nearer, but were to drop some money on the sidewalk for him. This, with squeaks of dismay, they usually did. But on one particular evening—this one, in fact—the lone lady he had approached turned out to be a retired medical missionary; she delivered a lecture on the relative merits of chaulmoogra oil and the sulfonamides in the treatment of Hansen's Disease ("—not contagious in New York, and never was—"), expressed her doubts that The Dip suffered from anything worse than, say, ichthyosis; and the paper she gave him was neither Silver Certificate nor Federal Reserve Note, but the address of a dermatologist.

Her speech had lasted a good quarter of an hour, and was followed by some remarks on Justification Through Faith, the whole experience leaving Denny weak and shaken. He had just managed to totter to one of those benches which a benevolent municipality disposes at intervals along Central Park West, and sink down, when he was espied by the 22nd Baron and 11th Marquess aforesaid, Arthur Marmaduke et cetera, who was walking his dog, Guido.

The dog gave Denny a perfunctory sniff, and growled condescendingly. Denny, semisubliminally, identified it as a whippet, reidentified it as an Italian greyhound, looked up suddenly and whimpered, "Lord Grey and Gore?"

"Grue and Groole," the dog's master corrected him. "Who the juice are you?" The dog was small and whipcord-thin and marked with many scars. So was his master. The latter was wearing a threadbare but neat bush jacket, jodhpurs, veldt-schoen, a monocle, and a quasi-caracul cap of the sort which are sold three-for-two-rupees in the Thieves' Bazaar at Peshawar. He scowled, peered through his monocled eye, which was keen and narrow, the other being wide and glassy.

"Cor flog the flaming crows!" he exclaimed. "Dennis! Haven't seen you since I fingered that fat fool for you aboard the *Leviathan* in '26. Or was it '27? Demned parvenu must have had at least a thousand quid in his wallet, which you were supposed to divide with me fifty-fifty, but didn't; eh?"

"Sixty-forty in my favor was the agreement," Denny said feebly. "Have you got the price of a meal or a drink on yez, perchance?"

"Never spend money on food or drink," said the Marquess primly. "Against my principles. Come along, come along," he said, prodding The Dip with his swagger stick, "and I'll supply you with scoff and wallop, you miserable swine."

The Dip, noting the direction they were taking, expressed his doubt that he could make it through the Park.

"I don't live *through* the Park, I live *in* the Park, mind your fat head, you bloody fool!" They had left the path and were proceeding—master and hound as smoothly as snakes, Denny rather less so—behind trees, up rocks, between bushes, under low-hanging boughs. And so came at last to the cave. "Liberty Hall!" said the Marquess. "After you, you miserable bog-oaf."

A charcoal fire glowed in a tiny stove made from stones, mud, and three automobile license plates. A kettle hummed on it, a teapot sat beside it, in one corner was a bed of evergreen sprigs covered with a rather good Tientsin rug woven in the archaic two blues and a buff, and a Tibetan butter-lamp burned on a ledge. There was something else in the cave, something which lunged at Denny and made fierce noises.

"Cheest!" he cried. "A baby eagle!" And fell back.

"Don't be a damned fool," his host exclaimed pettishly. "It's a fully grown falcon, by name Sauncepeur . . . There, my precious, there, my lovely. A comfit for you." And he drew from one of his pockets what was either a large mouse or a small rat and offered it to the falcon. Sauncepeur swallowed it whole. "Just enough to whet your appetite, not enough to spoil the hunt. Come, my dearie. Come up, sweetheart, come up."

The Marquess had donned a leather gauntlet and unleashed the bird from the perch. Sauncepeur mounted his wrist. Together they withdrew from the cave; the man muttered, the bird muttered back, a wrist was thrown up and out, there was a beating of wings, and the falconer returned alone, stripping off his gauntlet.

"Now for some whiskey . . . Hot water? Cold? Pity I've no melted yak butter to go with—one grew rather used to it after a bit in Tibet; cow butter is no good—got no body. What, straight? As you please."

Over the drink the 11th Marquess of Grue and Groole filled in his visitor on his career since '25—or was it '26? "Poached rhino in Kenya, but that's all over now, y'know. What with the Blacks, the Arabs, and the East Injians, white man hasn't got a prayer in that show—poaching, I mean. Ran the biggest fantan game in Macao for a while, but with the price opium's got to, hardly worthwhile.

"Signed a contract to go find the Abominable Snowman, demned Sherpas deserted only thirty days out, said the air was too thin for their lungs that high up, if you please, la-de-da—left me short on supplies, so that when I finally found the blasted *yeti*, I had to eat it. No good without curry, you know, no good at all.

"Lost m'right eye about that time, or shortly after. Altercation with a Sikh in Amritsar. Got a glass one. Lid won't close, muscle wonky, y'know. Natives in Portuguese East used to call me Bwan-a-Who-Sleeps-With-One-Eye-Waking; wouldn't come within a hundred yards after I'd kipped down for the night."

He paused to thrust a Sobranie black-and-gold into a malachite cigarette holder and lit it at the fire. With the dull red glow reflected in his monocle and glass eye, smoke suddenly jutting forth from both nostrils, and the (presumably) monkey skull he held in one hand for an ashtray as he sat cross-legged in the cave, the wicked Marquess looked very devilish indeed to the poor Dip, who shivered a bit, and surreptitiously took another peg of whiskey from the flask.

"No, no," the Marquess went on, "to anyone used to concealing himself in Mau Mau, Pathan, and EOKA country, avoiding the attention of the police in Central Park is child's play. Pity about the poor old Fakir of Ipi, but then, his heart always was a bit dicky. Still, they've let Jomo out of jail. As for Colonel Dighenes—"

And it was brought to the attention of the bewildered Dip that the Marquess had fought *for*, and not against, the Mau Maus, Pathans, EOKAs, et cetera. The nearest he came to explaining this was, "Always admired your Simon Girty chap, y'know. Pity people don't scalp any more—here, give over that flask, you pig, before you drink it all. It's a point of honor with me never to steal more than one day's rations at a time.

"Travel light, live off the country. I was one of only two white men in my graduating class at Ah Chu's College of Thieves in Canton. Took my graduate work at Kaffir Ali's, Cairo. I suppose you little reck, miserable fellow that you are, that *I was the last man to be tried by a jury of his peers before the House of Lords!* True, I did take the Dowager's Daimler, and, true, I sold it—lost the money at baccarat—never trust an Azerbaijanian at cards, but—"

He stopped, harkened to some sound in the outer darkness. "I fancy I hear my saucy Sauncepeur returning. 'What gat ye for supper, Lord Randall, my son?'—eh? Chops, steak, Cornish rock hen, what? Curious custom you Americans have—charcoal grills on your balconies. Though, mind, I'm not complaining. Bread ready? *Ahhh*, my pretty!"

The steak was just fine, as far as Denny the Dip was concerned, though Lord Grue and Groole complained there was a shade too much garlic. "Mustn't grumble, however—the taste of the Middle Classes is constantly improving."

The man who called himself Tosci rose to his feet.

"Don Alexander Borgia, I presume?" he inquired.

"No, no, excuse me—Borjia—with a 'j'," the Grand Master corrected him. The Grand Master was a tall, dark, handsome man, with a head of silvery gray hair. "The Grand Council is waiting," he said, "to hear your proposition. This way."

"I had no idea," Tosci murmured, impressed, "that the headquarters of the Mafia were quite so—quite so—" He waved his hand, indicating an inability to find the *mot juste* to fit the high-toned luxury and exquisite good taste of the surroundings.

"This is merely the Chamber of the Grand Council," said Don Alexander. "The actual headquarters, which we are required by our charter to maintain, is in back of a candy store on Mulberry Street. The dead weight of tradition, huh? Well, pretty soon that time will come of which the political philosophers have predicted, when the State shall wither away. 'No more Tradition's chains will bind us,' yeah? After you." Don Alexander took his seat at the head of the table and gestured the visitor to begin.

The latter gazed at the assembled Masters of the Mafia, who gazed back, unwinking, unblinking, but not—he was quite sure—unthinking.

After a moment he began, "*Signori*—" and paused; "then, *Fratelli*—" —and was interrupted by Grand Master Borjia.

"Excuse me, Hare Tosci, or Monsoon Tosci, or however you may in your country, but evidently you have fallen victim to the false delusion that the Mafia is a strictly Eyetalian organization, which I have no hesitation in saying it is an erroneous concept and a misinformation disseminated by the misinformed press, see? I would like it clearly understood that you should get it through your head we of the sorely misconstrued and much maligned Mafia do not discriminate in any way, shape, or form, against race, creed, color, national origin, or, uh, what the hell is the other thing which we don't discriminate against in any way, shape, or form, somebody?"

"Previous kahn-dition of soivitood," said a stocky Grand Councilor, wearing a Brooks Brothers suit, two cauliflower ears, and an eyepatch.

"Yeah. Thanks very much, Don Lefty McGonigle."

"Nat a-tall," said Don Lefty, with a slight blush, as he bent his slightly broken nose toward the orchid in his buttonhole—one of three flown up for him daily from Bahia. " ' Rank is but d'guinea stamp, an' a man's a man for all dat,' " he added. "A quotation from d' poet Boyns; no offensive ettnic connotations intended."

"Exactly," said the Grand Master, a slight scowl vanishing from his distinguished features. "Our Grand Council is a veritable microcosm of American opportunity, as witness, besides myself, Don Lefty McGonigle, Don Shazzam X—formerly Rastus Washington—Don Gesú-María Gomez, Don Leverret Lowell Cabot, Don Swede Swanson, Don Tex Thompson, Don Morris Caplan, and Don Wong Hua-Fu, which he's the Temporary Member of the Permanent Representation of the Honorable Ten Tongs—in a word, a confraternity of American business and professional men devoted to the study of the Confucian classics, the Buddhist Scriptures, and the art of horticulture as it might be exemplified by the peaceful cultivation of the *ah-peen* poppy."

He paused and drew breath. "The Mafia," he continued, "despite the innumerous slanders and aspersions cast upon it by scoffers, cynics, and the ever-present envious, is no more than a group of humble citizens of the world, determined to provide, besides certain commercial services, a forum wherein or whereby to arbitrate those differences which the lack of communication—alas, all too prevalent in our society—might otherwise terminate untowardly; as to its supposed origins in romantic Sicily, who, indeed, can say? What's on your mind, Tosci?" he concluded abruptly.

Mr. (or Herr, or Monsieur, or whatever way they say in his country) Tosci blinked. Then he smiled a small noncommittal smile, appropriate to the citizen of a neutral nation.

"As you are aware, my country is landlocked," he began. "Despite, or perhaps because of this situation, the question of providing a merchant marine of our own arises from time to time. It has arisen lately. My company, the *Societé Anonyme de la Banque de la Commerce et de l'Industrie et pour les Droites des Oeuvriers et des Paysans*, known popularly and for convenience as *Paybanque*, is currently interested in the possibilities of such a project.

"It is those 'certain commercial services' of the Mafia, of which you spoke, that we propose to engage. Our merchant marine headquarters in the New World would naturally be located in the New York City port area. Although at the present time the North River, or such New Jersey areas as Hoboken or Bayonne are most heavily favored by shipping, it was not always so. It is our opinion that excellent possibilities exist along the East River side of Manhattan, particularly the lower East River.

"It is our desire therefore that you provide us with a land, sea, and air survey, largely but not exclusively photographic in nature, engaging for the duration of the survey more or less centrally located quarters on the waterfront area in this locale. Something in the neighborhood of the Williamsburg Bridge would be ideal. Our representatives would participate with you, though the home office, so to speak, would remain aboard my yacht.

"This portfolio," he went on, placing it on the table and opening it, "contains a more detailed description of our proposal, as well as the eleven million dollars in United States Treasury Notes which your Northern European contact informed us would be your fee for considering the proposal. If you are agreeable to undertake the work, we can discuss further terms."

He ceased to speak. After a moment the Grand Master said, "Okay. We will leave you now." After Tosci had departed, Don Alexander asked, "Well, what do you think?"

"An Albanian Trotskyite posing as a Swiss Stalinist. If you ask me, I think he wants to blow up the Brooklyn Navy Yard," Don Morris Caplan said.

"Of course he wants to blow up the Brooklyn Navy Yard," Borjia snapped. "That was obvious right from the beginning—I can spot them Albanian deviationists a mile away. Now the point is: Do we *want* the Brooklyn Navy Yard blown up? It is to this question, my esteemed fellow colleagues, which we must now divert our attention."

*   *   *   *

Events went their traditional way in the Goodeycoonce household. Granny had dressed herself up as though for a masquerade, the principal articles of costume consisting of a tasseled cap, a linen blouse with wide sleeves, a pair of even wider breeches, and wooden shoes; all these articles were very, very old. She next picked up a pipe of equally antique design, with a long cherrywood stem and a hand-painted porcelain bowl, and this she proceeded to charge with genuine Indian Leaf tobacco which she had shredded herself in her chopping bowl. The tobacco was purchased at regular intervals from the last of the Manahatta Indians—that is, he was one-eighth Last-of-the-Manahatta-Indians, on his mother's side—who operated the New Orleans Candle and Incense Shop on Lexington Avenue. ("*I* don't know what them crazy White folks want with that stuff," he often said; "they could buy *grass* for the same price.") Granny struck a kitchen match, held it flat across the top of the pipe bowl, and began to puff.

Neely seated himself and took up a spiral notebook and a ballpoint pen. A scowl, or rather a pout, settled on his usually good-natured countenance.

First Granny coughed. Then she gagged. Then she inhaled with a harsh, gasping breath. Then she turned white, then green, then a bright red which might have startled and even alarmed Neely, had he not seen it all happen so often before. Presently she removed the pipe. Her face had taken on an almost masculine appearance. She rolled up one hand into a somewhat loose fist, then the other, then she placed one in alignment with the other and lifted them to her eyes and peered through her simulated telescope.

Neely, in a tone of voice obviously intended as mockery, or at least mimicry, said, " 'To arms, to arms! Blow der drums and beat der trumpet! De dumdam Engels ships ben gesailing up de River!' "

The eye which was not looking through the "telescope" now looked at him, and there was something cold and cruel in it. Neely's own eyes fell. After a moment he mumbled, "Sorry, Oude Piet. I mean Oom Piet. I mean, *darn it*, Heer—um—Governor—ah—Your Highness."

The eye glared at him, then the "telescope" shifted. After a while a heavily accented and guttural voice, quite unlike his grandmother's usual tones, came from her throat and announced, in a businesslike drone, "Shloop by der vharf in Communipaw. Beaver pelts—"

Neely clicked his tongue in annoyance. "You're in the wrong century, darn it, now!" he cried. Again, the cold old eye glared at him. But he stood his ground. "Come on, now," he said. "A promise is a promise. What would the *Com*pany say?"

The "telescope" shifted again. The drone recommenced. "Pier Dvendy-

Zeven—Durkish Zigarettes—Zipahi brand—watchman gedding dronk—"
Neely's ballpoint scribbled rapidly. *"That's* the ticket!" he declared.

Daisy Smith finished the tunafish sandwich (no mayonnaise—a girl
has to watch those calories every single *minute*) and washed the dish.
For dessert she had half a pear. Then the question could no longer be
postponed—what was she going to do that evening. It had all seemed so
simple, back in Piney Woods, New Jersey: she would take her own savings,
all $80 plus the $500 or so, most of it in old-fashioned long bills, but
including the $100 Liberty Bond, which had been found in the much-
mended worsted stocking under Uncle Dynus' mattress after his funeral
(the note found with it—thise is four *Dasi*—seemed to make traffic with
the Surrogate's Court unnecessary), and come to New York. There she
would find, in the order named, an apartment, a job, and Someone-To-Go-
Out-With.

She had found the first two without much trouble, but the third, which
she had thought would proceed from the second, did not materialize. Her
employer, Mr. Katachatourian, was the nicest old man in the world, but,
though a widower, he was *old*; somehow the importing of St. John's
bread—his business—didn't seem to attract *young* men. And if, from time
to time, with trepidation, he took a flyer on a consignment of sesame
seeds, or pistachio nuts, it helped Daisy's prospects not at all. The jobbing
of sesame seeds, or pistachio nuts, attracted exactly the same sort of
gentlemen as did the jobbing of St. John's bread—either middle-aged and
married, or elderly.

Once, to be sure, and once only, Daisy had made a social contact from
her job. Mr. Imamoglu, one of the largest exporters of St. John's bread
on the eastern Aegean littoral, had come to New York on business, had
dropped in to see his good customer, The Katachatourian Trading Company,
and had immediately fallen in love with Daisy. With true Oriental opulence
he took her out every night for a week. He took her to the opera, to the
St. Regis, to the Horse Show at Madison Square Garden, to Jack
Dempsey's restaurant, to a Near Eastern night club on Ninth Avenue, to
Hamburger Heaven, to a performance of *Phèdre* in the original French,
to the Bowery Follies, and to a triple-feature movie house on 42nd Street
which specialized in technicolor Westerns, of which Mr. Imamoglu was
inordinately fond.

Then he proposed marriage.

Well, the prospect of living in a strawberry-ice-cream-pink villa in the
fashionable suburb of Karsiyaka across the picturesque Bay from the
romantic port of Izmir, where she would be waited on, hand and foot,

by multitudes of servants, *did* appeal to Daisy. But although Mr. Imamoglu assured her that both polygamy and the harem were things of the past in Turkey, that, in fact, neither veil nor *yashmak* could be procured for love or money in all his country, still, you know, *after all*. And furthermore, Mr. Imamoglu was somewhat on in years; he must have been in his thirties.

And besides, she didn't love him.

So Daisy said No.

The departure of the semidisconsolate exporter left Daisy's evenings emptier than before. Go to church? Why, bless you, of course she went to church, every single Sunday, sometimes twice, and met a number of young men who played the organ or were in the choir or conducted a Sunday-school class. Most of them lived in the YMCA and were careful to explain to Daisy that it would be many, many years before they could even begin to *think* of marriage; and their ideas of a social evening were quite different from Mr. Imamoglu's; they would arrange to meet her somewhere after supper and then go to a free illustrated lecture on the Greenland missions; followed by a cup of coffee or a coke, followed by a chaste farewell at the subway kiosk.

Sometimes a girl thought she might just as well be back in Piney Woods, New Jersey.

What, then, to do tonight? Wash her hair? Watch TV? Catch up on her letters? Mending? Solo visit to a movie? She decided to take a walk.

A few blocks from her apartment she saw a familiar trio leaning in familiar stances against a wall. They nudged one another as they saw Daisy coming, as they had the first time and as they did every time. By now she knew there would be no wolf whistles, no rude proposals.

"Good evening, miss."

"G' evening, miss."

"Evening, miss."

"Good evening," Daisy said, pausing. "Oh, look at your new hats!" she exclaimed. "White fedoras. My goodness. Aren't they nice."

The three men beamed and smirked, and readjusted their brims. "All the big fellows wear white fedoras," said the leader of the trio, whose name was Forrance.

"The big fellows?"

"Sure. Like on that, now, TV show, *The Unthinkables*. Al—Lucky—Baby Face—*you* know."

As Forrance mentioned these people his two associates pursed lips and nodded soberly. One was quite small and suffered from nosebleeds. ("Must be a low pressure area comin' down from Canada," he would mumble; "I c'n alwees tell, Omma reggella human brommeter.") He was known, quite simply, as Blood.

His companion, as if in compensation, was obese in the extreme. ("A glanjalla condition," was his explanation; he indignantly denied gluttony. Taxed with overeating, he pleaded a tapeworm. "It's not f' me," was his indignant cry, over a third helping of breaded pork chops and French fries; "it's f' the woim!") Not unexpectedly he was called Guts. Now and then he pretended that it was an acknowledgement of personal courage.

"Al?" Daisy repeated. "Lucky? Baby Face? White fedoras? *The Unthinkables?* But *you're* not *gangsters?*" she burst out. "*Are you?*" For, as often as she had seen them, she had never thought to ask their trade.

Forrance drew himself up. Blood slouched. Guts loomed. A look of pleased importance underlay the grim look they assumed at the question. "Listen," Forrance began, out of the side of his mouth, an effect instantly spoiled by his adding, "miss."

"Listen, miss, you ever hear of—" he paused, glanced around, drew nearer—"the Nafia?" He thrust his right hand into his coat pocket. So did his two lieutenants. Daisy said, No, she never did; and at once the three were cast down. Was it, she asked helpfully, anything like the Mafia? Forrance brightened, Blood brightened, Guts brightened.

"*Sump*thing like the Mafia," said Forrance. "Om really very surprised you never—but you're from outatown, aintcha?"

"But what do you *do?*" Daisy demanded, mildly thrilled, but somehow not in the least frightened.

"We control," said Forrance impressively, "*all the gumball and Indian nut machines south of Vesey Street!*"

"My goodness," said Daisy. "Uh—are there many?"

"We are now awaiting delivery of the first of our new fleet of trucks," said Forrance formally.

"*Well,*" said Daisy, "Lots of luck. I've got to go now. Good night."

"Good night, miss."

"G' night, miss."

"Night, miss."

The crisp air was so stimulating that Daisy walked a considerable distance past her usual turning-around point, and then decided to come home by a different route, window shopping on the way. And in one window she noted many good buys in linoleum and tarpaulins, ships' chandlery, bar-and-grill supplies, and various other commodities; but somehow nothing she really *needed* just at the moment.

Then the flowered organdy caught her eye, but the bolt of blue rayon next to it was just as adorable. She looked up at the sign. THE ALMOST ANYTHING SECOND-HAND GOODS AND OUTLET STORE, it said. Wondering slightly, Daisy opened the door and went in. A bell tinkled. After a moment another door opened and a tall vigorous-looking woman, whose brown hair was turning gray, came in from the back. She smiled politely on seeing Daisy.

"I thought I might get some of that organdy in the window, the one with the flowers, enough for a dress."

"Yes, isn't it lovely? I'll get it for you right away. Was there anything else in the window you liked, while I'm there? Leather goods, outboard motors, canned crabmeat?"

"No, just—"

"Seasoned mahogany, yerba maté, manila hemp? Turkish cigarettes— Sipahi brand?"

"No, just the organdy, and, oh, maybe that blue rayon?"

"That's lovely, too. You have very good taste."

While the lady was reaching into the window, the door at the back opened again and a voice said, "Granny," and then stopped. Daisy turned around. She saw a well-made young man with a healthy open countenance and light brown hair which needed combing. He wore a peacoat, corduroy trousers, and a woolen cap. He stared at Daisy. Then he smiled. Then he blushed. Then he took off his cap.

Daisy instantly decided to buy, not just enough material for a dress, but both entire bolts, plus so large an amount of leather goods, outboard motors, canned crabmeat, seasoned Honduras mahogany, yerba maté manila hemp, and Turkish Sipahi cigarettes as would leave the proprietor no choice but to say, "Well, you can never carry all that by yourself; my grandson will help you take it home,"—or words to that effect.

What actually happened was quite different. The lady emerged from the window with the bolts of cloth and said, "I really don't know which is the lovelier," then noticed the young man and said, "Yes, Neely?"

"I finished the, uh, you-know," said the young man. He continued smiling at Daisy, who was now smiling back.

"Then start stacking the Polish hams," his grandmother directed crisply. "Smash up all those old crates, pile the raw rubber up against the north wall, but not too near the Turkish cigarettes because of the smell. Go on, now."

"Uh—" said Neely, still looking at the new young customer.

"And when you're finished with that," his grandmother said, "I want all the cork fenders cleaned, and the copper cable unwound from the big reel onto the little ones."

"Uh—"

"Now, never mind. Uh—you go and do as I say, or we'll be up all night . . . Neely!"

For a moment the young man hesitated. Then his eyes left Daisy and caught his grandmother's glance. He looked down, swallowed, scraped his boots. "Well?" Neely threw Daisy a single quick glance of helplessness, wistfulness, and embarrassment. He said, "Yes, Granny," turned and went out the door.

Daisy, her purchase under her arm, walked home full of indignation. "There are no young men any more!" she told herself vexedly. "If they're *men*, they're not young, and if they're *young*, they're just not *men*. 'Yes, Granny!' How do you like *that*? Oh, I'd 'Yes, Granny' him!" she declared. "I'd show *him* who was boss!" she thought, somewhat inconsistently.

"Milksop!" she concluded. She was surprised to realize that, in her annoyance, she had bought only the flowered organdy. There was really no help for it; much as she despised the grandmother and grandson, if she wanted that blue rayon she would have to revisit THE ALMOST ANYTHING SECOND-HAND GOODS AND OUTLET STORE a second time. Too bad, but it wasn't really *her* fault, was it?

The man called Tosci stepped from the yacht's launch onto the gangway ladder and was steadied by a stubble-faced man in dungarees. "Thank you, boatswain," he said.

"Did you enjoy your visit ashore, M. Tosci?" the bosun asked.

"Ah, New York is such a stimulating city," said Tosci, going up the ladder. "One simply cannot absorb it on a single visit."

He handed his hat to the man, who followed him to his cabin, where he tossed the hat aside, and turned on a device which not only blanked out the sound of their actual conversation against any electronic eavesdropping, but supplied a taped innocuous conversation to be picked up by such devices instead.

"Well?" the "boatswain" demanded.

Tosci shrugged. "Well, Comrade Project Supervisor," he said, "they took the Treasury Notes and said they would let us know. One really could not expect more at the moment."

"I suppose not," the Project Supervisor said gloomily. "Do you think they will '*take the contract*,' as I believe the phrase goes?"

"Why should they not, Comrade Project Supervisor? How could they resist the temptation? We are, after all, prepared to go as high as a *hundred* and eleven million dollars. It would take them a long time to collect a hundred and eleven million dollars from their, how do they call it, 'numbers racket'."

"About a week and a half; not more. Well, well, we shall see. Meanwhile, I am hungry. You took your time coming back."

"I am sorry, Comrade Project Supervisor, but—"

"No excuses. Bring me my supper now. And see that the cabbage in the borscht is not soggy as it was last night, and that there are no flies in the yogurt. Do you hear?"

"Yes, Comrade Project Supervisor," said Tosci.

Don Sylvester Fitzpatrick, Second Vice-President of the Mafia (Lower Manhattan Branch) and son-in-law of Don Lefty McGonigle, sat brooding in his tiny office in the wholesale foodstuffs district. Despite his title he was a mere petty don in the hierarchy; well did he know that it was rumored he owed even this to nepotism, and these circumstances rankled (as he put it) in his bosom. "A man of my attainments, which they should put him in the front ranks of enterprise," he muttered, "and what am I doing? I'm in charge of the artichoke rake-off at the Washington Market!" Don Sylvester laughed bitterly; Don Sylvester sulked.

Meanwhile, in the Grand Chamber Council, discussion among the senior dons went on apace.

"Blowing up the Brooklyn Navy Yard," said Don Tex Thompson reflectively, "might be just the thing the national economy is in need of. Unemployment among skilled laborers went up seven-point-oh-nine percent in the last fortnightly period, and among unskilled laborers the figure scores an even higher percentile. The Mafia," he said, "cannot remain indifferent to the plight of the workingman."

"Not if it is to retain that position of esteem and preeminence to which it is rightly entitled," said Don Morris Caplan.

"To say nothing of the excellent effect upon our National Defenses of clearing out all that obsolete equipment and replacing it with the newest devices obtainable through modern science," Don Shazzam X (formerly Rastus Washington) declared. "The Congress could scarcely refuse appropriations in such circumstances."

Don Wong Hua-Fu pursed his thin lips and put the tips of his six-inch fingernails together in church-steeple fashion. "The Honorable Ten Tongs do include sound common stocks in the various heavy-metals industries in their portfolio. Still," he said, "we must consider the great burdens already borne by the widows and orphans who constitute the majority of American taxpayers."

And Don Leverret Lowell Cabot pointed out another possible objection. "We cannot neglect our own heavy commitments in the Brooklyn Navy Yard area," he said. "As part of our responsibility to the men who man our country's ships we have, need I remind the Grand Council, leading interests in the bars, restaurants, night clubs, strip-joints, clip-joints, and gambling hells of the area—to say nothing of the hotels used for both permanent and temporary residence by the many charming ladies who lighten the burdens of the sea-weary sailors."

"It's a problem, believe *me*," sighed Don Gesú-María Gomez. "Little does the public know of our problems."

"Decisions, decisions, decisions!" Don Swede Swanson echoed the sigh.

"Gen-tle-men, gen-tle-men," said Don Lefty McGonigle, a note of mild protest in his hoarse voice. "Aren't we being a lit-tul pre-ma-chua? *We* are not being asked to blow up duh Brooklyn Navy Yahd dis minute. *We* are not even being asked to *decide* if it should be blown up dis minute. All we are being asked to do, gen-tle-men, is to decide if we are going to make a soyvey of de Iowa East Trivva estuary from d' point of view of its amen-i-ties as a pos-si-ble headquarters faw moychant marine offices. I yap-peal to you, Grand Master, am I creckt?"

Don Alexander Borjia tore his eyes away from the Mona Lisa on the wall. The lineaments of La Gioconda never ceased to entrance him, and there was the added fillip to his pleasure that the rest of the world naively thought the original still hung in the Louvre, little realizing that this last was a mere copy, painted, true, by Leonardo, but by Leonardo in his ancient age. The switcheroo had been arranged by Don Alexander's father, the late Grand Master Don Cesár Borjia, before the First World War. Copies of masterworks of art, stolen at various times from museums and private collectors around the world, adorned the other walls. But Don Alexander Borjia's favorite remained the Mona Lisa.

"Don Lefty McGonigle is correct," he said. "Take the contract for the survey, charge them eighty-seven million dollars for it, and when it comes time for a decision on the *big* question, so we'll leave them know further. All in favor say *Aye*. Opposed, *Nay*. The Ayes got it."

There was a silence.

"A foyda question," said Don Lefty finally. He fingered the cabochon emerald which nestled in his watered-silk four-in-hand, and fiddled with his eyepatch.

"Speak."

"Whom is to be ap-poin-ted to take over d' soyvey?"

"Whom did you have in mind?"

"A young man which he oughta be given more responsibility than he's being given, to wit, my son-in-law, the Second Vice-President of the Mafia, Lower Manhattan Branch. Woddaya say, gen-tle-men?"

The pause which followed this suggestion seemed faintly embarrassed. Then Don Swede Swanson was heard to express the opinion that Don

Sylvester FitzPatrick couldn't find the seat of his pants in the dark with both hands.

Don Lefty turned to him and pressed both his hands to his chest. "You wound me!" he exclaimed, his voice deep with suppressed emotion. "Night afta night I come home an' my liddle Philomena is eating huh haht out. 'Daddy, Daddy, Daddy,' she asks, weeping, 'what has everybody got against poor Sylvester? Din't he soyve his apprenticeship the same as everybody else? Isint he loyal? Trustwoythy? Coyteous? Kind? So why, afta twelve years, is he still only in chahge of ahtichokes at Wahshington Mahket?'

"An' ya know what? I don't know what to say ta huh! *If* fit was a matta of money, so I'd buy him a sand-and-gravel company, or a broory. But it's a matta of tra-*di*-tion, gen-tle-men! All of youse got sons. I ain't got no son! All I got is my liddle Philomena. A bee-uty in thuh Hollywood sense a thuh woid she may not be, but she yiz the yimage of huh sainted mother, rest her soul, an' huh husband is like a son ta me, so when ya spit on *him*, gen-tle-men, it's like ya spitting on *me!*"

Throats were cleared, eyes wiped, noses blown. Don Alexander essayed to speak, but was prevented by emotion. At last the silence was broken by Don Swede Swanson. "So let it be Sylvester," he said huskily. There was a chorus of nods.

"Of course, there is one hazard of the chase involved in my sweet Sauncepeur's snaffling hot broils off these outdoor grills," Lord Grue and Groole observed. "It—shall I sweeten the air in here a bit? I've a packet of frankincense that my friend, Osman Ali the Somali, sent me not long ago; I wouldn't *buy* incense, of course," he said, sprinkling the pale yellow grains on the glowing embers. A pungent odor filled the cave.

Denny the Dip coughed. The Marquess donned his gauntlet and examined the falcon's talons, particularly about the pads. "It makes the poor creature's petti-toes sore. I've experimented with various nostra and it's my considered opinion that Pinaud's Moustache Wax is above all things the best. Is there anything more left in the flask? Shall we kill it, as you say over here? Ah, good show."

With a gesture he motioned to Denny to take the bed; he himself reclined on a tiger skin which was stored during the day in a dry niche. Thus settled, he grew expansive. "Ah, it's not what I've been accustomed to, me that used to have my own shooting lodge in the grouse season, waited on, hand and foot, by a dozen Baloochi servants; well, and now here I am, like a bloody eremite, living on me wits and the $5.60 I get from home each week."

Denny lifted his head. "You're a remittance man?" he inquired.

"Sort of remittance man, you might say, yes. Me nevew, Piers Plunkert, pays me two quid a week, not so much to stay away as to stay alive. 'Avoid alcohol, Uncle,' he writes, 'and mind you wear your wooly muffler when the north wind blows.' It's not filial piety, mind, or avuncular piety, or anything like it. You see, if I pop off, *he* becomes the twelfth Marquess of Grue and Groole, and all the rest of that clobber—the mere thought of it makes his blood run cold. No, he's not a Labour M.P.; his fix is worse than that. He's one of the *Angry Young Men!*

"Struth! Lives in a filthy little room in South Stepeny, aild composes very bad, very blank verse damning The Establishment, under the pseudonym of 'Alf Huggins.' Well, now, I ask you—would *you* pay any attention to an Angry Young Man named Lord Grue and Groole? No, of course you wouldn't. And neither would anyone else.

"Once a year I threaten suicide. 'It doesn't matter about me, my boy,' I write. '*You* will carry on the name and title.' My word, what a flap that puts him in! *Always* good for ten quid pronto via cablegram."

A sound, so dim and distant that it failed to reach the ear of Denny the Dip, caused the peerless peer to break off discourse and raise his head. "Bogey," he announced. "Policeman, to you. Weighs about a hundred and sixty and has trouble with his left arch. Neglects his tum, too—hear it rumble!"

Denny strained, could hear nothing but the traffic passing through the park, its sound rising and falling with the wind, like surf. He murmured, "What a talent you got, Grooley! What a team we'd make!"

"A team we certainly will *not* make!" the peer snorted. "But, as to your playing squire to my knight, hmm, well, we'll consider it. I plan to take a brisk walk in the morning, down to the Battery and vicinage. We'll see if you can stand the pace—no sinecure being gunbearer, as it were, to the man who outwalked The Man-Eater of Mysore. And another thing—" He thwacked The Dip across the feet with his swagger stick. "No more of this 'Grooley!' Call me Sahib, Bwana, Kyrios, or M'lord."

"Hmm," murmured Lord Grue and Groole, pausing and looking in the shop window. "I find that curious. Don't *you* find that curious, Denny?"

Denny, panting and aching from the long trek down from Central Park, was finding nothing curious but his inability to break away and sink to rest. "Wuzzat, Gr—I mean Bwana?" he moaned. He was bearing, in lieu of gun, the Marquess' swagger stick.

"Use your *eyes*, man! There, in the window. What do you see?"

The Dip wiped the sweat out of his eyes. "Leather goods?" he inquired.

"Outboard motors? Canned crabmeat?" The Marquess clicked his tongue, and swore rapidly in Swahili (Up-Country dialect). "Seasoned Honduras mahogany?" The Dip continued hastily. "Flowered organdy? Blue rayon? Manila hemp?"

"*Ahah!* Just so, a great lovely coil of Manila hempen rope. Notice anything odd about it? *No?* You were pulling the wrong mendicant dodge, you should've used a tin cup. You really don't see that scarlet thread running through it, so cleverly and closely intertwined that it cannot be picked out without spoiling the rope? You *do* see it; good. No use to ask if you know what it means; you don't, so I'll tell you. It means that rope was made by and for the Royal Navy. It is *never* sold, so it must have been stolen. No one would dare fence it in Blighty, so they've shipped it over here. Clever, I call that. Must look into this."

He entered the shop, followed by Denny, who sank at once into a chair. The dog Guido, looking as cool and fresh as his master, stood motionless. Mrs. Goodeycoonce emerged from the back.

"Afternoon, ma'am," said Lord Grue and Groole, touching the brim of his quasi-caracul cap, and giving her no chance to speak. "My name is Arthur Powisse, of the Powisse Exterminating Company. Allow me to offer you my card—dear me, I seem to have given the last one away; ah, well, it doesn't signify. This is my chief assistant, Mr. Dennis, and the animal is one of our pack of trained Tyrolean Rat Hounds. We have just finished a rush job at one of the neighborhood warehouses, and, happening to pass by and being entranced by your very attractive window display, thought we would drop in and offer you an estimate on deratting your premises."

Mrs. Goodeycoonce opened her mouth, but the Marquess swept on. "I anticipate your next comment, ma'am. You are about to say, 'But I keep a clean house'—and so you do, so you obviously do. But do your *neighbors?* Aye, there's the rub; they don't, alas. Around the corner is an establishment of the type known as, if you will pardon the expression, a common flophouse—the sort of place where they throw fishbones in the corner and never sweep up. Three doors down is the manufactory of Gorman's Glossy Glue Cakes, a purely animal product, on which *ratus ratus* thrives, ma'am, simply *thrives!*"

Something flickered in Granny Goodeycoonce's eyes which seemed to indicate she had long been aware of the proximity of Gorman's Glossy Glue Cakes, particularly on very warm days, and found in it no refreshment of soul whatsoever.

"How often at night," Lord Grue and Groole waxed almost lyrical, "when all should be quiet, must you not have heard Noises, eh?—and attributed them to the settling of the timbers, the expansion and contraction of the joists and beams. Not a bit of it! *Rats!*" His voice sank to a whisper. "Oh, the horror of it! First one gray shadow, then another—"

He took a step forward, she took one backward, he advanced, she retreated. "Then great grisly waves of them, first in the foundations, then in the cellar, then—does this door lead to the cellar? I had better examine it."

Later that evening found the Marquess and his bearer deep in the shadowy doorway of an empty warehouse. "It was the advent of that offensively wholesome-looking young chap, her grandson, that broke the spell," the Marquess mused. "Said she'd consider it. No matter. I saw the cellar. Those crates and crates of Polish hams! Those bales of raw rubber! Turkish Sipahi Cigarettes! That infinite variety of portable, sea-borne merchandise!

"It can only mean one thing: the people are pukka river pirates. I know the signs—seen them on the Thames, the Nile, Hoogli, Brahmapootra, Whampoa, Pei-Ho—*eheu fugaces*. Nice setup she's got there—snug shop, tidy house, fine figger, and a widow woman, I'm sure—no sign of a husband and anyone can see she's not the divorcing type. Hmm, well Question is: How does the lad get the stuff there? How do river pirates *usually* get the stuff there? Just so."

And they had walked along the waterfront, the Marquess examining the water as intently as one of the inhabitants of the Sundra Straits peering for *bêche-de-mer*, The Dip plodding along to the rear of Guido, as sunken beneath the weight of the swagger stick as if it had been an elephant gun. He reflected on the day he might have spent, conning old ladies out of coins, and on a certain bat-cave he knew of, where an ounce and a quarter of Old Cordwainer retailed for the ridiculous sum of 21 cents. But there was that about the Marquess which said *Hither to me, caitiff, and therein fail not, at your peril*; therefore Denny plodded meekly.

"Ho," said His Lordship, stopping, and pointing at the filthy waters of the East River, which, in a happier time, lined with forests and grassy meads, were thick with salmon, shad, cod, ale-wives, herring, sturgeon, and all fruits of the sea; now the waters were merely thick. "Observe," said His Lordship. "You see how—there—the oil slick, orange peel, bad bananas, and other rubbish floats down with the tide. Whereas the flotsam rides more or less straight out from under us and joins the current at a right angle. The *main* current, that is. Let's have a dekko," he declared, and shinnied down the side of the wharf timbers almost to the water's edge.

His enthusiasm, as he clambered up, almost communicated itself to

The Dip. "Whuddaya see, Sahib?" he asked, craning.

"Enough. Tonight, when the eyes of the Blessed Houris in Paradise, yclept 'stars' in our rude Saxon Tongue, shine as clearly as this filthy air will allow them to, we shall follow young Mr. Goodeycoonce. Here are rupees, or whatever the juice they call them—'quarters'? Just so. Go thou and eat, and return within the hour. As for me, a strip of biltong will do, and fortunately I took care to refill the flask. They make good whiskey in Belfast, I must say, cursed Orangemen though they be." He raised his drink and waved it across a trickle in the gutter. "To the King over the water"—and drank. His glass eye glittered defiance to all the House of Hanover.

All was quiet in the kitchen behind THE ALMOST ANYTHING SECOND-HAND GOODS AND OUTLET STORE. Granny Goodeycoonce was pasting in her scrapbook the latest letter she had received in reply to a message of congratulations sent on the birthday of one of the Princesses of the Netherlands. It read, as did all the others in the scrapbook: *The Queen has read your letter with interest and directs me to thank you for your good wishes.* And it was signed, as nearly as could be made out, Squiggle Van Squiggle, Secretary.

"Gee," said Neely, looking up from a trade journal he was reading, "here's a bait business for sale on Long Island, on the North Shore." There was no answer. He tried again. "And a boat basin in Connecticut. 'Must be sold at once,' the ad says, 'to settle estate.' Gee."

His grandmother capped the tube of library paste. "I suppose Princess Beatrix will be getting engaged pretty soon," she observed. "I wonder who to. How old is the Crown Prince of Greece? No, that wouldn't do, I suppose; he'll be *King* of Greece some day, and she'll be Queen of Holland. Hmm." She knit her brows, deep in the problems of dynasty.

"They could be combined," Neely suggested.

Granny Goodeycoonce looked up, amazed. "What, Greece and *Holland?*"

"No, I mean a bait business and a boatyard. People," he explained enthusiastically, "would buy *bait to* fish with from their *boats.* And—"

She clicked her tongue. "The idea! A Goodeycoonce becoming a fishmonger!"

"Better than being a river pirate," he mumbled.

"Never let me hear you use that word again!" she snapped. "The very idea! Have you *no* respect for the traditions of the family? Why, it makes my blood boil! And don't you forget for one minute, young man, that I am a Goodeycoonce by descent as well as by marriage; don't you forget *that!*"

"Fat chance," Neely muttered.

His grandmother opened her mouth to release a thunderbolt, but at that moment there came a thud from the cellar, followed by a clatter.

"Oh, my land," Granny whispered, a hand at her throat. "Rats! I should've listened to that Limey. Is the door to the cellar locked?"

Answer was superfluous, for at that moment the door swung open and in stepped the Limey himself, more properly described as Arthur Marmaduke Roderick Lodowicke William Rufus de Powisse-Plunkert, Baron Bogle, Earl of Ballypatcoogen, Viscount Penhokey, Laird of Muckle Greet, Master of Snee, 11th Marquess of Grue and Groole in the Peerage of England, and Hereditary Lord High Keeper of the Queen's Bears. "Good evening, all," he said.

Neely went pale. "I knew it!" he cried, "I knew we couldn't go on getting away with it forever, not after almost three hundred years! That exterminator story was just a dodge—he must be from the Harbor Patrol, or the Coast Guard!"

The Marquess took his swagger stick from the quivering Denny (who had made the underground voyage with his head under his coat, for fear of bats), and smacked it gently into the palm of his hand. "You know, I resent that very much," he said, a touch of petulance in his voice. "I will have you know that I am no copper's nark, common informer, or fink. I—"

"You get out of my house," said Granny Goodeycoonce, "or I'll—"

"Call the police? Oh, I doubt that, my good woman; I doubt that entirely. How would you explain all those cork fenders in the cellar? The copper cable, raw rubber, Turkish Sipahi cigarettes, Polish hams? To say nothing of enough sailcloth to supply a regatta, a ton of tinned caviar, five hundred *oka* of Syrian arrack, twenty canisters of ambergris, several score pods of prime Nepauli musk, and, oh, simply ever so many more goodies—all of which, I have no hesitation in declaring, are the fruits of, I say not theft, but of, shall I say, impermissive acquisition. Eh?"

Granny Goodeycoonce, during the partial inventory, had recovered her aplomb. "Well, you simply couldn't be more wrong," she said, a smile of haughty amusement on her lips. " 'Impermissive'? Poo. We have the best permission anyone could ever want. Neely, show this foreign person our permission."

Still pale, and muttering phrases like *I'll be an old man when I get out*, Neely unlocked an antique cabinet in one corner of the room and removed a flat steel case, which he handed to his grandmother. She opened it with a key of her own, and reverently extracted a parchment document festooned with seals, which she displayed to the Marquess with the words: "Look, but don't touch."

He fixed his monocle firmly in his good eye and bent over. After a while he straightened up. "Mph. Well, I must confess that my knowledge of Seventeenth Century Dutch orthography is rather limited. But I *can* make out the name of Van Goedikoentse, as well as that of Petrus Stuyvesant. Perhaps you would be good enough to explain?"

Nothing could have pleased Granny more. "*This*," she said in tones both hushed and haughty, "is a Patent from the Dutch West India Company, granting to my great-great-great-great-great-great-great-grandfather, Nicolaes Jacobus Van Goedikoentse, *and* 'to his heirs forever,' the right of collecting customs in the harbor port of Nieuw Amsterdam. It was granted in return for Myn Heer Van Goedikoentse's valiant help in resisting the insolent British demand for surrender in 1662. Governor Stuyvesant promised he would never forget."

For a moment no word broke the reverent silence. Then, slowly, Lord Grue and Groole removed his cap. "And naturally," he said, "your family has never recognized that surrender. Madam, as an unreconstructed Jacobite, I honor them for it, in your person." He gravely bowed. Equally gravely, Mrs. Goodeycoonce made a slight curtsy. "Under no circumstances," he went on, "would I dream of betraying your confidence. As a small effort to amend for the sins of my country's past I offer you my collaboration—my very, very *experienced* collaboration, if I do say so."

Three hundred years (almost) of going it alone struggled in Mrs. Goodeycoonce's bosom to say No. At the same time she was plainly impressed with Lord Grue and Groole's offer—to say nothing of his manner. It took her a while to reply. "Well," she said finally, "we'll see."

Don Sylvester FitzPatrick, Second Vice-President of the Mafia (Lower Manhattan Branch), was nervous. The survey was almost finished, and the Grand Council still hadn't made up its mind about blowing up the Brooklyn Navy Yard. In fact, it was even now debating the project in their Chamber, at the window of the anteroom to which Don Sylvester now sat. Elation at being at long last removed from the artichoke detail had gradually given way to uneasiness. Suppose they *did* decide to blow it up? Would the United States Government take the same broad view of this as the Dons did? Visions of being hanged from the yardarm of, say, the USS *Missouri*, danced like sugar plums in Sylvester's head.

A flutter from the crates at his foot distracted his attention. In one was a black pigeon, in one was a white. Very soon the mysterious Mr. Tosci would appear with $87,000,000 in plain, sealed wrappers, and be told the Grand Council's decision. Even now the Mafiosi bomb squads were standing by at the ready in Brooklyn. Informed only that morning that police had put the traditional, semiannual wire tap on the Mafiosi phones, the Mafiosi had brought out the traditional, semiannual pigeon post.

"Now, remember," Don Lefty McGonigle had instructed his son-in-law, "d' black boid has d' message *Bombs Away* awready in d' cap-sool fastened to its foot. And d' white boid's got d' message *Everyt'ing Off* inscribed on d' paper in d' cap-sool on *its* foot. Ya got dat?"   •

"Yeah, Papa," said Don Sylvester, wiping his face.

"So when ya get d' woid, *Yes*, ya leddout d' *black* pigeon. But if ya get d'woid, *No*, den ya leddout d' *white* pigeon. An' nats all dere's to it. Okay?"

"Okay, Papa."

"Om depending on you. Philomena is depending on you. So don't chew be noivous."

"No, Papa," said Don Sylvester.

When Forrance told Daisy that the "Nafia" was awaiting delivery of the first of its new fleet of trucks he was speaking optimistically. The new truck was "new" only in the sense that it was newer than the one it replaced, a 1924 Star, which had to be thawed out with boiling water in cold weather and cranked by hand before it would start, in all weather. The Nafia treasury had suffered a terrible blow when the Cherry Street Mob, in the mid-fifties, took over the distribution of birch beer south of Vesey Street—during the course of which epic struggle Guts had his ears boxed and Blood suffered a sympathetic nasal hemorrhage; as a result, the treasury could only afford to have the single word NAFIA painted on the side panels. Still it was *some*thing.

"Rides like a dream, don't it," Forrance said, as they headed along South Street one bright afternoon.

"No, it don't," said Blood. "It liss."

"Whaddaya mean, 'it liss'?"

"I mean, like it liss ta one side. Look—"

Guts said, "He's right, boss. It *does* liss. Them new gumball machines ain't equally distribitted. They all slide to one side."

Forrance halted the truck with a grinding of gears. "All right," he said resignedly; "then let's take'm all out and put'm back in again, but *evenly* this time."

So the smallest criminal organization in New York got out of its fleet of trucks to unload and reload its gumball machines.

*   *   *   *

Tosci paused on the deck of the yacht to receive his superior's final instructions. "I have counted the money," he said. "Eighty-six million in negotiable bearer bonds, and one million in cash."

"Very well. Perhaps they will have time to spend it all before we Take Over; perhaps not. I have instructed the Chief Engineer to test the engines in order that we can leave as soon as the decision is made. They *say* the bombs are set for four hours, but who knows if we can believe them?"

As if to confirm his fears, the Chief Engineer at this moment rushed on deck, grease and dismay, in equal parts, showing on his face.

"The engines won't start!" he cried.

"They *must* start!" snapped the Project Supervisor. "Go below and see to it!" The Chief, with a shrug, obeyed. The Project Supervisor scowled. "An odd coincidence—if it is a coincidence," he said. "Personally, I have never trusted sailors since the Kronstadt Mutiny." To conceal his nervousness he lifted his binoculars to his eyes, ordering Tosci not to leave the ship for the time being. Scarcely had he looked through the glasses when an exclamation broke through his clenched lips.

"There is a truck on the waterfront," he cried, "with the Mafia's name on it! And three men are lifting something from it. Here—" he thrust the glasses at Tosci—"see what you can make of it."

Tosci gazed in bewilderment. "Those machines," he said. "I've never seen anything like them. I don't understand—why should the Mafia be unloading such strange devices so near our ship?"

Suspicion, never far below the surface of the Project Supervisor's mind, and usually right on top of it, burst into flames. "They must be electronic devices to keep our engines from functioning!" he cried. "They think to leave us stuck here in the direct path of the explosions, thus destroying alien witnesses! Clever, even admirable—but we cannot allow it. Come—" he seized Tosci by the arm holding the portfolio in which the bonds and money were—"to the launch! We must see about this!" Together they rushed down the gangway ladder into the boat.

"White pigeon if it's No," Don Sylvester mumbled. "Black pigeon if it's Yes. White, No. Black, Yes. I got it." But he was still nervous. Suppose he fumbled his responsibilities at the crucial moment—*suppose he bungled the job?* For the hundredth time his fingers examined the catches on the cage, lifted one up a fraction of an inch, closed it, then lifted the other—and there was a sudden sound from the cage.

Don Sylvester's startled fingers flew to his mouth. The catch snapped up. The black pigeon hopped out, fluttered to the window sill, cooed again, and—as Sylvester made a frantic lunge for it—spread its wings and flew out. It soared up, up, up, circled once, circled twice, then flew off toward Brooklyn.

Sylvester stared at the air in wordless horror. Then he stared at the door of the Grand Council Chamber. Any moment now, it might open. He tiptoed over and listened.

"I say *no!*" a voice declared.

"And I say *yes!*" declared a second voice.

Helplessly, his eyes roamed the anteroom, fell at length on the telephone. Regardless of possible wiretaps, he quickly and fearfully dialed a number. "Hello?" he whispered hoarsely. "Hello, Philomena? Listen, Philomena—"

The black pigeon flapped its way toward Brooklyn with leisurely strokes, thinking deep pigeonic thoughts. Now and then it caught an updraft and coasted effortlessly. It was in no hurry. But, of course, it really was not very far to Brooklyn, as a pigeon flies . . .

"Easy does it—watch my toes, ya dope—down, down."

"Good afternoon, boys," said Daisy. "I just came out to mail a letter to Turkey. Did you know that airmail is ten cents cheaper to the west bank of the Hellespont, because it's in Europe? Oooh—gumballs! Let me see if I have a penny—"

"No, let me see if I got one, Miss—no, lem*me* see, Forry—aa, *c'mon, I* gotta have one—"

While the three Nafiosi were plunging in their pockets, the yacht's launch drew up to the pier. Out of it came Tosci, the Project Supervisor, and three crewmen. "What are you up to?" Tosci shouted.

"What's it to you?" Forrance countered.

"I order you to remove those machines from this area at once!"

Instantly truculent, Forrance thrust out his jaw. "Nobody orders the Nafia what to do with its machines," he said. "Anyways, not south of Vesey Street," he amended.

"Put them on the truck and see that they are driven away," Tosci instructed a crewman, who began to obey, but was prevented by Blood. The crewman swung, Blood's nose, ever sensitive, began, and Daisy, aroused, cried, "You let him alone!" and wielded her pocketbook with a will. The crewman staggered. Guts, gauging his distance to a nicety, swung his ponderous belly around and knocked them down.

"Take the girl," shouted the Project Supervisor, in his own language. "She is undoubtedly their moll. We will keep her aboard as a hostage."

And while he, Tosci, and one of their men engaged the tiny syndicate in combat, the other two sailors hustled Daisy into the launch, muffling her cries for help.

Mrs. Goodeycoonce, Neely, Denny, Guido, and Lord Grue and Groole were out for a walk. No decision had yet been made on the noble lord's proposal, but nevertheless everyone seemed to be growing somewhat closer. The Marquess was telling about the time that he rescued the Dowager Begum of Oont from the horrid captivity in which she had been placed by her dissolute nephew, the Oonti Ghook. All listened in fascination, except the dog Guido, who had heard the story before.

So taken up in his account was the Marquess that he absent-mindedly abstracted from his pocket a particularly foul pipe (which respect for the lady had normally prevented his smoking in her presence), and proceeded to charge it with the notoriously rank tobacco swept up for sale to the inhabitants of the lower-income quarters of Quetta; and struck a match to it. At the first unconsidered whiff Mrs. Goodeycoonce coughed. Then she gagged, then she inhaled with a harsh, gasping breath. And next she turned white, green, and bright red.

Neely was the first to notice. "Granny!" he said. "Granny?" Then, "It must be your pipe—"

The Marquess was overcome with confusion and remorse. "Terribly sorry," he declared. "I'd knock the dottle out, except that's all it *is*, you know—dottle, I mean. I say, Mrs. Goodeycoonce—oh, I *say*."

But Mrs. Goodeycoonce's face had taken on an almost masculine appearance. She rolled up first one fist, loosely, and then the other, placed them in alignment, lifted them to her eyes, and peered out upon the River. And in a gutturally accented and heavy voice quite unlike her usual tones she declared, "Zound der alarm! Beat to qvarters! *Zo, zo, wat den duyvel!*"

The Marquess' eagle-keen eyes followed her glance and immediately observed something very much amiss upon the waters.

"Stap my vitals, if I don't believe a gel is being forced aboard that vessel over there," he said. "Bad show, that. What?"

Instantly the possessing spirit of Peter Stuyvesant vanished and was replaced by that of Mrs. Goodeycoonce. She uttered a cry. "White slavery, that's what it must be! And in broad daylight, too. Oh, the brazen things! What should we do?"

Neely hauled an old-fashioned but quite authentic and brass-bound telescope from his pocket and swung it around. As he focused in and recognized Daisy, struggling desperately while being taken up the gangway, he uttered a hoarse shout of rage.

" 'Do'?" he yelled. "We've got to save her! Come on! My boat! Let's go!"

The black pigeon passed over City Hall, dallied for a few moments in the currents around the Woolworth Building, and then pressed on in the general direction of Sand Street . . .

As Neely's boat zoomed under the bow of the yacht, the Marquess kicked off his shoes, seized the anchor chain, and swarmed up like a monkey. Neely and Denny were met at the foot of the gangway ladder by two crewmen, who shouted, gesticulated, and menaced them with boathooks. But in a moment the boatmen's attention was diverted by a tumult from above. Part of this was caused by Lord Grue and Groole who, darting from one place of concealment to another, called out (in different voices) battle cries in Pathan, Kikuyu, and Demotic Greek; and part of it was caused by the alarm of the crew at being boarded—so they thought—by a host of foes.

While their opponents' attention was thus distracted, Denny and Neely gained the deck where Neely at once knocked down the first sailor he saw. Denny's contribution was more circumspect. Noting an oily rag in a corner he took out a match. In a moment clouds of black smoke arose.

"Fire!" cried the Dip. "Fire! *Fire!*"

Part of the crew promptly swarmed down the ladder into Neely's boat and cast off. The rest jumped over the side and commenced swimming briskly toward the nearer shore.

"Hello!" Neely shouted, stumbling along the passageways, opening doors. "Hello, hello! Where are you?"

A muffled voice called, he burst in, and there was Daisy, gagged and bound, struggling in a chair. Neely cut her loose, removed the gag, and—after only a very slight hesitation, perhaps natural in a shy young man of good family—kissed her repeatedly.

"*Well*," said Daisy tremulously, as he paused for breath, and then to herself, "I guess he's not such a milksop after all."

On deck Denny the Dip and the Marquess stomped out the smoldering rag, though not, however, in time to avoid having attracted two police boats, a Coast Guard cutter, the Governor's Island ferry, a Hudson River Dayliner, and the New York City Fireboat, *Zophar Mills*, all of which converged on the yacht.

"Thank you, thank you," called out the Marquess, between cupped hands. "We don't require any assistance, the fire is out. You will observe, however, that officers and crew have abandoned the ship, which means that she is now, under maritime law, by right of salvage, the property of myself and my associates, both *in personam* and *in rem*."

The failure of the engines to start, it was ascertained after a careful scrutiny, was owing to the intrusion of a large waterbug into one of the oil lines; this was soon set right. An attempt of a floating delegate of the Masters, Mates, and Pilots Union to question the Marquess' right to take the helm of the salvaged vessel was quickly terminated by the revelation that he possessed a first-class navigation certificate in the Siamese Merchant Marine. The delegate addressed him henceforth as "Captain," and on departing, offered him the use of all the amenities of the Union Hall.

It was while seeing this personage off that Lord Grue and Groole observed a familiar shadow on the deck of the yacht, and, taking off his quasi-caracul and waving it, lured Sauncepeur down from what the poet Pope once so prettily described as "the azure realms of Air."

"She has clutched a quarry," he observed. "Well-footed, my pretty, well-trussed. Let me have pelt, dearie—nay, don't mantle it—there. Good. You shall have new bewits, with bells, and silver varvels to your jesses, with my crest upon them. Hel-lo, *hel*-lo, what have you *done*, you demned vulture? You've taken a carrier pigeon!" He opened the message capsule. "*Bombs Away*," he read. "Rum, very rum. Doubtless the name of a horse, and some poor booby of a bookmaker has taken this means of evading the puritanical Yankee laws dealing with the dissemination of racing intelligence. Hmm, well, not my pidjin. Haw, haw!" he chuckled at the pun. "Denny!" he called.

"Yes, M'Lord?"

The Marquess tossed him the bird. "A pigeon for the pot. See that Sauncepeur gets the head and the humbles; afterwards she's to have a nice little piece of beefsteak, and a bone to break."

That, in a way, concludes the story. The epilogue is brief. Don Lefty McGonigle, though heartbroken at the abrupt and (to him mysterious) disappearance of his son-in-law and daughter, takes some comfort in the frequent picture postcards that Philomena sends him from such places as Tahiti, Puntas Arenas, Bulawayo, and other locales where the Mafia's writ (fearsomely hard on deserts) runneth not. The Nafia (originally organized in 1880 under the full name of the National Federal of Independent Artisans, or "Wide Awake" or Chowder and Marching Society as part of the presidential campaign of General Winfield Scott Hancock, whose famous declaration that "the tariff is a local issue" insured his defeat by General J. Abram Garfield)—the Nafia still controls all the gumball and Indian nut machines south of Vesey Street, and revels in the publicity resultant from its members' brief incarceration, along with

Tosci, the Project Supervisor, and the three crewmen. The Cherry Street Mob would not *dream* of muscling in on a syndicate whose pictures were in all the papers in connection with a portfolio containing $87,000,000; it is the Mob's belief that the fight was caused by the Nafia's attempting to hijack this sum.

Cornelius ("Neely") and Daisy Goodeycoonce have purchased, out of their share of the salvage money, one of the most up-and-coming bait-and-boatyard businesses on Long Island Sound. Granny Goodeycoonce at first was reluctant, but on learning that Daisy's mother was a Van Dyne, of the (originally) Bergen-o-Zoom, Holland, Van Dynes, she extended her blessings. It remains her view, however, that the family profession of nocturnal customs collecting is merely in abeyance, and will be kept in trust, as it were, for the children.

Granny is, in fact, for the first time in her life, no longer a Goodeycoonce, but Mistress of Snee, Lady of Muckle Greet, Baroness Bogle, Countess Ballypatcoogen, Viscountess Penhokey, Marchioness of Grue and Groole—and, presumably, Lord High Keeperess of the Queen's Bears—although on this last point Debrett's is inclined to be dubious. The fact that the older couple has chosen to go on a prolonged honeymoon with their yacht to the general vicinage of the Sulu Sea where, those in the know report, the opportunities for untaxed commerce (coarsely called "smuggling" by some) between the Philippines, Indonesia, and British North Borneo are simply splendid, is doubtless purely coincidental.

One thread (or at most two) in the gorgeous tapestry we have woven for the instruction of our readers remains yet untied. This is the question of what happened to Tosci and his Project Supervisor after the release from brief confinement on unpressed charges of assault.

It is unquestionably true that their pictures were in all the papers. It is equally true, and equally unquestionable, that the Mafia frowns on publicity for those connected with its far-flung operations. Rumors that the two men were fitted for concrete spaceshoes and subsequently invited to participate in skindiving operations south of Ambrose Light, no matter how persistent, cannot be confirmed.

Mr. Alexander Borjia, businessman and art connoisseur, questioned by a Congressional investigating committee, said (or at any rate, read from a prepared statement): "My only information about the so-called Mafia comes from having heard that it is sometimes mentioned in the Sunday supplements of sensation-seeking newspapers. I do not read these myself, being unable to approve of the desecration of the Lord's Day which their publication and distribution necessarily involve. Nor can I subscribe to the emphasis such journals place upon crime and similar sordid subjects, which cannot but have an unfortunate effect upon our basically clean-living American youth."

It was at or about this point that Senator S. Robert E. Lee ("Sourbelly Sam") Sorby (D., Old Catawba), chose to light up his famous double-bowl corncob pipe, of which it has been said that the voters of his native state sent him to Washington because they could not stand the smell of it at home. Mr. Borjia (evidently as unimpressed as the Old Catawba voters by Senator Sorby's statement that the mixture was made according to a formula invented by the Indians after whom the State was named)—Mr. Borjia coughed, gagged, gasped, turned white, green, red; and after leveling an imaginary telescope consisting of his own loosely rolled fists, proceeded (in a strange, guttural, and heavily accented voice quite unlike his own) to describe what was even then going on in the secret chambers of the Mafia in such wealth of detail as to make it abundantly clear to the Executive, the Judicial, and the Legislative branches of the Government (as well as to himself, when with bulging eyes he subsequently read the transcripts of his own "confession") that he must never be allowed outside any of the Federal caravanserais in which he has subsequently and successively been entertained.

And there let us leave him.

A CRAVING FOR ORIGINALITY
Bill Pronzini

CHARLIE HACKMAN WAS a professional writer. He wrote popular fiction, any kind from sexless Westerns to sexy Gothics to oversexed historical romances, whatever the current trends happened to be. He could be counted on to deliver an acceptable manuscript to order in two weeks. He had published 9,000,000 words in a fifteen-year career, under a variety of different names (Allison St. Cyr being the most prominent), and he couldn't tell you the plot of any book he'd written more than six months ago. He was what is euphemistically known in the trade as "a dependable wordsmith," or "a versatile pro," or "a steady producer of commercial commodities."

In other words, he was well-named: Hackman was a hack.

The reason he was a hack was not because he was fast and prolific, or because he contrived popular fiction on demand, or because he wrote for money. It was because he was and did all these things with no ambition and no sense of commitment. It was because he wrote without originality of any kind.

Of course, Hackman had not started out to be a hack; no writer does. But he had discovered early on, after his first two novels were rejected with printed slips by thirty-seven publishers each, that (a) he was not very good, and (b) what talent he did possess was in the form of imitations. When he tried to do imaginative, ironic, meaningful work of his own he failed miserably; but when he imitated the ideas and visions of others, the blurred carbon copies he produced were just literate enough to be publishable.

Truth to tell, this didn't bother him very much. The one thing he had always wanted to be was a professional writer; he had dreamed of nothing else since his discovery of the Hardy Boys and Tarzan books in his pre-teens. So from the time of his first sale he accepted what he was, shrugged, and told himself not to worry about it. What was wrong with being a hack, anyway? The writing business was full of them—and hacks, no less than nonhacks, offered a desirable form of escapist entertainment to the masses; the only difference was, his readership had nondiscriminating tastes. Was his product, after all, any less honorable than what television offered? Was he hurting anybody, corrupting anybody? No. Absolutely not. So what was wrong with being a hack?

For one and a half decades, operating under this cheerful set of rationalizations, Hackman was a complacent man. He wrote from ten to fifteen novels per year, all for minor and exploitative paperback houses, and earned an average annual sum of $25,000. He married an ungraceful woman named Grace and moved into a suburban house on Long Island. He went bowling once a week, played poker once a week, argued conjugal matters with his wife once a week, and took the train into Manhattan to see his agent and editors once a week. Every June he and Grace spent fourteen pleasant days at Lake George in the Adirondacks. Every Christmas Grace's mother came from Pennsylvania and spent fourteen miserable days with them.

He drank a little too much sometimes and worried about lung cancer because he smoked three packs of cigarettes a day. He cheated moderately on his income tax. He coveted one of his neighbors' wives. He read all the current paperback bestsellers, dissected them in his mind, and then reassembled them into similar plots for his own novels. When new acquaintances asked him what he did for a living he said, "I'm a writer," and seldom failed to feel a small glow of pride.

This was the way it was for fifteen years—right up until the morning of his fortieth birthday.

Hackman woke up on that morning, looked at Grace lying beside him, and realized she had put on at least forty pounds since their marriage. He listened to himself wheeze as he lighted his first cigarette of the day. He got dressed and walked downstairs to his office, where he read the half page of manuscript still in his typewriter (an occult pirate novel, the latest craze). He went outside and stood on the lawn and looked at his house. Then he sat down on the porch steps and looked at himself.

I'm not just a writer of hack stories, he thought sadly, I'm a liver of a hack life.

Fifteen years of cohabiting with trite fictional characters in hackneyed fictional situations. Fifteen years of cohabiting with an unimaginative wife in a trite suburb in a hackneyed lifestyle in a conventional world. Hackman the hack, doing the same things over and over again; Hackman the hack, grinding out books and days one by one. No uniqueness in any of it, from the typewriter to the bedroom to the Adirondacks.

No originality.

He sat there for a long while, thinking about this. No originality. Funny. It was like waking up to the fact that, after forty years, you've never tasted pineapple, that pineapple was missing from your life. All of a sudden you craved pineapple; you wanted it more than you'd ever wanted anything before. Pineapple or originality—it was the same principle.

Grace came out eventually and asked him what he was doing. "Thinking that I crave originality," he said, and she said, "Will you settle for eggs and bacon?" Trite dialogue, Hackman thought. Hackneyed humor. He told her he didn't want any breakfast and went into his office.

Originality. Well, even a hack ought to be able to create something fresh and imaginative if he applied himself; even a hack learned a few tricks in fifteen years. How about a short story? Good. He had never written a short story; he would be working in new territory already. Now how about a plot?

He sat at his typewriter. He paced the office. He lay down on the couch. He sat at the typewriter again. Finally the germ of an idea came to him and he nurtured it until it began to develop. Then he began to type.

It took him all day to write the story, which was about five thousand words long. That was his average wordage per day on a novel, but on a novel he never revised so much as a comma. After supper he went back into the office and made pen-and-ink corrections until eleven o'clock. Then he went to bed, declined Grace's reluctant offer of "a birthday present," and dreamed about the story until 6:00 A.M. At which time he got up, retyped the pages, made some more revisions in ink, and retyped the story a third time before he was satisfied. He mailed it that night to his agent.

Three days later the agent called about a new book contract. Hackman asked him, "Did you have a chance to read the short story I sent you?"

"I read it, all right. And sent it straight back to you."

"Sent it back? What's wrong with it?"

"It's old hat," the agent said. "The idea's been done to death."

Hackman went out into the back yard and lay down in the hammock. All right, so maybe he was doomed to hackdom as a writer; maybe he just wasn't capable of *writing* anything original. But that didn't mean he couldn't *do* something original, did it? He had a quick mind, a good grasp of what was going on in the world. He ought to be able to come up with at least one original idea, maybe even an idea that would not only satisfy his craving for originality but change his life, get him out of the stale rut he was in.

He closed his eyes.

He concentrated.

He thought about jogging backward from Long Island to Miami Beach and then applying for an entry in the Guinness Book of World Records.

Imitative.

He thought about marching naked through Times Square at high noon, waving a standard paperback contract and using a bullhorn to protect man's literary inhumanity to man.

Trite.

He thought about adopting a red-white-and-blue disguise and robbing a bank in each one of the original thirteen states.

Derivative.

He thought about changing his name to Holmes, finding a partner named Watson, and opening a private inquiry agency that specialized in solving the unsolved and insoluble.

Parrotry.

He thought about doing other things legal and illegal, clever and foolish, dangerous and harmless.

Unoriginal. Unoriginal. Unoriginal.

That day passed and several more just like it. Hackman became obsessed with originality—so much so that he found himself unable to write, the first serious block he had had as a professional. It was maddening, but every time he thought of a sentence and started to type it out, something would click in his mind and make him analyze it as original or banal. The verdict was always banal.

He thought about buying a small printing press, manufacturing bogus German Deutsche marks in his basement, and then flying to Munich and passing them at the Oktoberfest.

Counterfeit.

Hackman took to drinking a good deal more than his usual allotment of alcohol in the evenings. His consumption of cigarettes rose to four packs a day and climbing. His originality quotient remained at zero.

He thought about having a treasure map tattooed on his chest, claiming to be the sole survivor of a gang of armored car thieves, and conning all sorts of greedy people out of their life savings.

Trite.

The passing days turned into passing weeks. Hackman still wasn't able to write; he wasn't able to do much of anything except vainly overwork his brain cells. He knew he couldn't function again as a writer or a human being until he did something, *anything* original.

He thought about building a distillery in his garage and becoming Long Island's largest manufacturer and distributor of bootleg whiskey.

Hackneyed.

Grace had begun a daily and voluble series of complaints. Why was he moping around, drinking and smoking so much? Why didn't he go into his office and write his latest piece of trash? What were they going to do for money if he didn't fulfill his contracts? How would they pay the mortgage and the rest of their bills? What was the *matter* with him, anyway? Was he going through some kind of midlife crisis or what?

Hackman thought about strangling her, burying her body under their acacia tree in the back yard—committing the perfect crime.

Stale. Bewhiskered.

Another week disappeared. Hackman was six weeks overdue now on an occult pirate novel and two weeks overdue on a male-action novel; his publishers were upset, his agent was upset; where the hell were the manuscripts? Hackman said he was just polishing up the first one. "Sure you are," the agent said over the phone. "Well, you'd better have it with you when you come in on Friday. I mean that, Charlie. You'd better deliver."

Hackman thought about kidnapping the star of Broadway's top musical extravaganza and holding her for a ransom of $1,000,000 plus a role in her next production.

Old stuff.

He decided that things couldn't go on this way. Unless he came up with an original idea pretty soon, he might just as well shuffle off this mortal coil.

He thought about buying some rat poison and mixing himself an arsenic cocktail.

More old stuff.

Or climbing a utility pole and grabbing hold of a high-tension wire.

Prosaic. Corny.

Or hiring a private plane to fly him over the New Jersey swamps and then jumping out at two thousand feet.

Ho-hum.

Damn! He couldn't seem to go on, he couldn't seem not to go on. So what was he going to do?

He thought about driving over to Pennsylvania, planting certain carefully faked documents inside Grace's mother's house, and turning the old bat in to the F.B.I. as a foreign spy.

Commonplace.

On Friday morning he took his cigarettes (the second of the five packs a day he was now consuming) and his latest hangover down to the train station. There he boarded the express for Manhattan and took a seat in the club car.

He thought about hijacking the train and extorting $20,000,000 from the state of New York.

Imitative.

When the train arrived in Manhattan he trudged the six blocks to his agent's office. In the elevator on the way up an attractive young blonde gave him a friendly smile and said it was a nice day, wasn't it?

Hackman thought about making her his mistress, having a torrid affair, and then running off to Acapulco with her and living in sin in a villa high above the harbor and weaving Mexican *serapes* by day and drinking tequila by night.

Hackneyed.

The first thing his agent said to him was, "Where's the manuscript, Charlie?" Hackman said it wasn't ready yet, he was having a few personal problems. The agent said, "You think you got problems? What about my problems? You think I can afford to have hack writers missing deadlines and making editors unhappy? That kind of stuff reflects back on me, ruins my reputation. I'm not in this business for my health, so maybe you'd better just find yourself another agent."

Hackman thought about bashing him over the head with a paperweight, disposing of the body, and assuming his identity after first gaining sixty pounds and going through extensive plastic surgery.

Moth-eaten. Threadbare.

Out on the street again, he decided he needed a drink and turned into the first bar he came to. He ordered a triple vodka and sat brooding over it. I've come to the end of my rope, he thought. If there's one original idea in this world, I can't even imagine what it is. For that matter, I can't even imagine a partly original idea, which I'd settle for right now because maybe there isn't anything completely original any more.

"What am I going to do?" he asked the bartender.

"Who cares?" the bartender said. "Stay, go, drink, don't drink—it's all the same to me."

Hackman sighed and got off his stool and swayed out onto East 52nd Street. He turned west and began to walk back toward Grand Central, jostling his way through the mid-afternoon crowds. Overhead, the sun glared down at him between the buildings like a malevolent eye.

He was nearing Madison Avenue, muttering clichés to himself, when the idea struck him.

It came out of nowhere, full-born in an instant, the way most great ideas (or so he had heard) always do. He came to an abrupt standstill. Then he began to smile. Then he began to laugh. Passersby gave him odd looks and detoured around him, but Hackman didn't care. The idea was all that mattered.

It was inspired.

It was imaginative.

It was meaningful.

It was original.

Oh, not one-hundred-percent original—but that was all right. He had already decided that finding total originality was an impossible goal. This idea was close, though. It was close and it was wonderful and he was going to do it. Of course he was going to do it; after all these weeks of search and frustration, how could he *not* do it?

Hackman set out walking again. His stride was almost jaunty and he was whistling to himself. Two blocks south he entered a sporting goods store and found what he wanted. The salesman who waited on him asked if he was going camping. "Nope," Hackman said, and winked. "Something *much* more original than that."

He left the store and hurried down to Madison to a bookshop that specialized in mass-market paperbacks. Inside were several long rows of shelving, each shelf containing different categories of fiction and nonfiction, alphabetically arranged. Hackman stepped into the fiction section, stopped in front of the shelf marked "Historical Romances," and squinted at the titles until he located one of his own pseudonymous works. Then he unwrapped his parcel.

And took out the woodsman's hatchet.

And got a comfortable grip on its handle.

And raised it high over his head.

And—

Whack! Eleven copies of *Love's Tender Fury* by Allison St. Cyr were drawn and quartered.

A male customer yelped; a female customer shrieked. Hackman took no notice. He moved on to the shelf marked "Occult Pirate Adventure," raised the hatchet again, and—

Whack! Nine copies of *The Devil Daughter of Jean Lafitte* by Adam Caine were exorcised and scuttled.

On to "Adult Westerns." And—

Whack! Four copies of *Lust Rides the Outlaw Trail* by Galen McGee bit the dust.

Behind the front counter a chubby little man was jumping up and down, waving his arms. "What are you doing?" he kept shouting at Hackman. "What are you doing?"

"Hackwork!" Hackman shouted back. "I'm a hack writer doing hackwork!"

He stepped smartly to "Gothic Suspense." And—

Whack! Five copies of *Mansion of Dread* by Melissa Ann Farnsworth were reduced to rubble.

On to "Male Action Series," and—

Whack! Ten copies of Max Ruffe's *The Grenade Launcher/23: Blowup at City Hall* exploded into fragments.

Hackman paused to survey the carnage. Then he nodded in satisfaction and turned toward the front door. The bookshop was empty now, but the chubby little man was visible on the sidewalk outside, jumping up and down and semaphoring his arms amid a gathering crowd. Hackman crossed to the door in purposeful strides and threw it open.

People scattered every which way when they saw him come out with the hatchet aloft. But they needn't have feared; he had no interest in people, except as bit players in this little drama. After all, what hack worth the name ever cared a hoot about his audience?

He began to run up 48th Street toward Fifth Avenue, brandishing the hatchet. Nobody tried to stop him, not even when he lopped off the umbrella shading a frankfurter vendor's cart.

"I'm a hack!" he shouted.

And shattered the display window of an exclusive boutique.

"I'm Hackman the hack!" he yelled.

And halved the product and profits of a pretzel vendor.

"I'm Hackman the hack and I'm hacking my way to glory!" he bellowed.

And sliced the antenna off an illegally parked Cadillac limousine.

He was almost to Fifth Avenue by this time. Ahead of him he could see a red signal light holding up crosstown traffic; this block of 48th Street was momentarily empty. Behind him he could hear angry shouts and what sounded like a police whistle. He looked back over his shoulder. Several people were giving pursuit, including the chubby little man from the bookshop; the leader of the pack, a blue uniform with a red face atop it, was less than fifty yards distant.

But the game was not up yet, Hackman thought. There were more bookstores along Fifth; with any luck he could hack his way through two or three before they got him. He decided south was the direction he wanted to go, pulled his head around, and started to sprint across the empty expanse of 48th.

Only the street wasn't empty any longer; the signal on Fifth had changed to green for the eastbound traffic.

He ran right out in front of an oncoming car.

He saw it too late to jump clear, and the driver saw him too late to brake or swerve. But before he and the machine joined forces, Hackman had just enough time to realize the full scope of what was happening—and to feel a sudden elation. In fact, he wished with his last wish that he'd thought of this himself. It was the crowning touch, the final fillip, the *coup de grâce;* it lent the death of Hackman, unlike the life of Hackman, a genuine originality.

Because the car that did him in was not just a car; it was a New York City taxi cab.

Otherwise known as a hack.

THE DAY OF THE BULLET

Stanley Ellin

I BELIEVE THAT in each lifetime there is one day of destiny. It may be a day chosen by the Fates who sit clucking and crooning over a spinning wheel, or, perhaps, by the gods whose mill grinds slow, but grinds exceedingly fine. It may be a day of sunshine or rain, of heat or cold. It is probably a day which none of us is aware of at the time, or can even recall through hindsight.

But for every one of us there is that day. And when it leads to a bad end it's better not to look back and search it out. What you discover may hurt, and it's a futile hurt because nothing can be done about it any longer. Nothing at all.

I realize that there is certain illogic in believing this, something almost mystical. Certainly it would win the ready disfavor of those modern exorcists and dabblers with crystal balls, those psychologists and sociologists and case workers who—using their own peculiar language to express it—believe that there may be a way of controlling the fantastic conjunction of time, place, and event that we must all meet at some invisible crossroads on the Day. But they are wrong. Like the rest of us they can only be wise after the event.

In this case—and the word "case" is particularly fitting here—the event was the murder of a man I had not seen for thirty-five years. Not since a summer day in 1923, or, to be even more exact, the evening of a summer day in 1923 when as boys we faced each other on a street in Brooklyn, and then went our ways, never to meet again.

We were only twelve years old then, he and I, but I remember the date because the next day my family moved to Manhattan, an earthshaking event in itself. And with dreadful clarity I remember the scene when we parted, and the last thing said there. I understand it now, and know it was that boy's Day. The Day of the Bullet it might be called—although the bullet itself was not to be fired until 35 years later.

I learned about the murder from the front page of the newspaper my wife was reading at the breakfast table. She held the paper upright and partly folded, but the fold could not conceal from me the unappetizing picture on the front pace, the photograph of a man slumped behind the wheel of his car, head clotted with blood, eyes staring and mouth gaping in the throes of violent and horrifying death.

The picture meant nothing to me, any more than did its shouting head-line—RACKETS BOSS SHOT TO DEATH. All I thought, in fact, was that there were pleasanter objects to stare at over one's coffee and toast.

Then my eye fell on the caption below the picture, and I almost dropped my cup of coffee. *The body of Ignace Kovac,* said the caption, *Brooklyn rackets boss who last night—*

I took the paper from my wife's hand while she looked at me in astonishment, and studied the picture closely. There was no question about it. I had not seen Ignace Kovac since we were kids together, but I could not mistake him, even in the guise of this dead and bloody hulk. And the most terrible part of it, perhaps, was that next to him, resting against the seat of the car, was a bag of golf clubs. Those golf clubs were all my memory needed to work on.

I was called back to the present by my wife's voice. "Well," she said with good-natured annoyance, "considering that I'm right in the middle of Walter Winchell—"

I returned the paper to her. "I'm sorry. I got a jolt when I saw that picture. I used to know him."

Her eyes lit up with the interest of one who—even at secondhand—finds herself in the presence of the notorious. "You did? When?"

"Oh, when the folks still lived in Brooklyn. We were kids together. He was my best friend."

My wife was an inveterate tease. "Isn't that something? I never knew you hung around with juvenile delinquents when you were a kid."

"He wasn't a juvenile delinquent. Matter of fact—"

"If you aren't the serious one." She smiled at me in kindly dismissal and went back to Winchell who clearly offered fresher and more exciting tidings than mine. "Anyhow," she said, "I wouldn't let it bother me too much, dear. That was a long time ago."

It was a long time ago. You could play ball in the middle of the street then; few automobiles were to be seen in the far reaches of Brooklyn in 1923. And Bath Beach, where I lived, was one of the farthest reaches. It fronted on Gravesend Bay with Coney Island to the east a few minutes away by trolley car, and Dyker Heights and its golf course to the west a few minutes away by foot. Each was an entity separated from Bath Beach by a wasteland of weed-grown lots which building contractors had not yet discovered.

So, as I said, you could play ball in the streets without fear of traffic. Or you could watch the gas-lighter turning up the street lamps at dusk. Or you could wait around the firehouse on Eighteenth Avenue until, if you were lucky enough, an alarm would send the three big horses there slewing the pump-engine out into the street in a spray of sparks from iron-shod wheels. Or, miracle of miracles, you could stand gaping up at the sky to follow the flight of a biplane proudly racketing along overhead.

Those were the things I did that summer, along with Iggy Kovac who was my best friend, and who lived in the house next door. It was a two-story frame house painted in some sedate color, just as mine was. Most of the houses in Bath Beach were like that, each with a small garden in front and yard in back. The only example of ostentatious architecture on our block was the house on the corner owned by Mr. Rose, a newcomer to the neighborhood. It was huge and stuccoed, almost a mansion, surrounded by an enormous lawn, and with a stuccoed two-car garage at the end of its driveway.

That driveway held a fascination for Iggy and me. On it, now and then, would be parked Mr. Rose's automobile, a gray Packard, and it was the car that drew us like a magnet. It was not only beautiful to look at from the distance, but close up it loomed over us like a locomotive, giving off an aura of thunderous power even as it stood there quietly. And it had *two* running-boards, one mounted over the other to make the climb into the tonneau easier. No one else around had anything like that on his car. In fact, no one we knew had a car anywhere near as wonderful as that Packard.

So we would sneak down the driveway when it was parked there, hoping for a chance to mount those running-boards without being caught. We never managed to do it. It seemed that an endless vigil was being kept over that car, either by Mr. Rose himself or by someone who lived in the rooms over the garage. As soon as we were no more than a few yards down the driveway a window would open in the house or the garage, and a hoarse voice would bellow threats at us. Then we would turn tail and race down the driveway and out of sight.

We had not always done that. The first time we had seen the car we had sauntered up to it quite casually, all in the spirit of good neighbors, and had not even understood the nature of the threats. We only stood there and looked up in astonishment at Mr. Rose, until he suddenly left the window and reappeared before us to grab Iggy's arm.

Iggy tried to pull away and couldn't. "Leggo of me!" he said in a high-pitched, frightened voice. "We weren't doing anything to your ole car! Leggo of me, or I'll tell my father on you. Then you'll see what'll happen!"

This did not seem to impress Mr. Rose. He shook Iggy back and forth—not hard to do because Iggy was small and skinny even for his age—while I stood there, rooted to the spot in horror.

There were some cranky people in the neighborhood who would chase us away when we made any noise in front of their houses, but nobody had ever handled either of us or spoken to us the way Mr. Rose was doing. I remember having some vague idea that it was because he was new around here, he didn't know yet how people around here were supposed to act, and when I look back now I think I may have been surprisingly close to the truth. But whatever the exact reasons for the storm he raised, it was enough of a storm to have Iggy blubbering out loud, and to make us approach the Packard warily after that. It was too much of a magnet to resist, but once we were on Mr. Rose's territory we were like a pair of rabbits crossing open ground during the hunting season. And with just about as much luck.

I don't want to give the impression by all this that we were bad kids. For myself, I was acutely aware of the letter of the law, and had early discovered that the best course for anyone who was good-natured, pacific, and slow afoot—all of which I was in extra measure—was to try and stay within bounds. And Iggy's vices were plain high spirits and recklessness. He was like quicksilver and was always on the go and full of mischief.

And smart. Those were the days when at the end of each school week your marks were appraised and you would be reseated according to your class standing—best students in the first row, next best in the second row, and so on. And I think the thing that best explains Iggy was the way his position in class would fluctuate between the first and sixth rows. Most of us never moved more than one row either way at the end of the week; Iggy would suddenly be shoved from the first row to the ignominy of the sixth, and then the Friday after would just as suddenly ascend the heights back to the first row. That was the sure sign that Mr. Kovac had got wind of the bad tidings and had taken measures.

Not physical measures, either. I once asked Iggy about that, and he said, "Nah, he don't wallop me, but he kind of says don't be so dumb, and, well—you know—"

I did know, because I suspect that I shared a good deal of Iggy's feeling for Mr. Kovac, a fervent hero worship. For one thing, most of the fathers in the neighborhood "worked in the city"—to use the Bath Beach phrase—meaning that six days a week they ascended the Eighteenth Avenue station of the B.-M.T. and were borne off to desks in Manhattan. Mr. Kovac, on the other hand, was a conductor on the Bath Avenue trolley-car line, a powerful and imposing figure in his official cap and blue uniform with the brass buttons on it. The cars on the Bath Avenue line were without side walls, closely lined with benches from front to back, and were manned by conductors who had to swing along narrow platforms on the outside to collect fares. It was something to see Mr. Kovac in action. The only thing comparable was the man who swung himself around a Coney Island merry-go-round to take your tickets.

And for another thing, most of the fathers—at least when they had reached the age mine had—were not much on athletics, while Mr. Kovac was a terrific baseball player. Every fair Sunday afternoon down at the little park by the bay there was a pick-up ball game where the young fellows of the neighborhood played a regulation nine innings on a marked-off diamond, and Mr. Kovac was always the star. As far as Iggy and I were concerned, he could pitch like Vance and hit like Zack Wheat, and no more than that could be desired. It was something to watch Iggy when his father was at bat. He'd sit chewing his nails right through every windup of the pitcher, and if Mr. Kovac came through with a hit, Iggy would be up and screaming so loud you'd think your head was coming off.

Then after the game was over we'd hustle a case of pop over to the team, and they would sit around on the park benches and talk things over. Iggy was his father's shadow then; he'd be hanging around that close to him, taking it all in and eating it up. I wasn't so very far away myself, but since I couldn't claim possession as Iggy could, I amiably kept at a proper distance. And when I went home those afternoons it seemed to me that my father looked terribly stodgy, sitting there on the porch the way he did, with loose pages of the Sunday paper around him.

When I first learned that I was going to have to leave all this, that my family was going to move from Brooklyn to Manhattan, I was completely dazed. Manhattan was a place where on occasional Saturday afternoons you went, all dressed up in your best suit, to shop with your mother at Wanamaker's or Macy's, or, with luck, went to the Hippodrome with your father, or maybe to the Museum of Natural History. It had never struck me as a place where people *lived*.

But as the days went by my feelings changed, became a sort of apprehensive excitement. After all, I was doing something pretty heroic, pushing off into the Unknown this way, and the glamor of it was brought home to me by the way the kids on the block talked to me about it.

However, none of that meant anything the day before we moved. The house looked strange with everything in it packed and crated and bundled together; my mother and father were in a harried state of mind; and the knowledge of impending change—it was the first time in my life I had ever moved from one house to another—now had me scared stiff.

That was the mood I was in when after an early supper I pushed through the opening in the hedge between our back yard and the Kovacs', and sat down on the steps before their kitchen door. Iggy came out and sat down beside me. He could see how I felt, and it must have made him uncomfortable.

"Jeez, don't be such a baby," he said. "It'll be great, living in the city. Look at all the things you'll have to see there."

I told him I didn't want to see anything there.

"All right, then don't," he said. "You want to read something good? I got a new Tarzan, and I got *The Boy Allies in England.* You can have your pick, and I'll take the other one."

This was a more than generous offer, but I said I didn't feel like reading, either.

"Well, we can't just sit here being mopey," Iggy said reasonably. "Let's do something. What do you want to do?"

This was the opening of the ritual where by rejecting various possibilities—it was too late to go swimming, too hot to play ball, too early to go into the house—we would arrive at a choice. We dutifully went through this process of elimination, and it was Iggy as usual who came up with the choice.

"I know," he said. "Let's go over to Dyker Heights and fish for golf balls. It's pretty near the best time, anyhow."

He was right about that, because the best time to fish for balls that had been driven into the lone water hazard of the course and never recovered by their owners was at sunset when, chances were, the place would be deserted but there would still be enough light to see by. The way we did this kind of fishing was to pull off our sneakers and stockings, buckle our knickerbockers over our knees, then slowly and speculatively wade through the ooze of the pond, trying to feel out sunken golf balls with our bare feet. It was pleasant work, and occasionally profitable, because the next day any ball you found could be sold to a passing golfer for five cents. I don't remember how we came to fix on the price of five cents as a fair one, but there it was. The golfers seemed to be satisfied with it, and we certainly were.

In all our fishing that summer I don't believe we found more than a total of half a dozen balls, but thirty cents was largesse in those days. My share went fast enough for anything that struck my fancy: Iggy, however, had a great dream. What he wanted more than anything else in the world was a golf club, and every cent he could scrape together was deposited in a tin can with a hole punched in its top and its seam bound with bicycle tape.

He would never open the can, but would shake it now and then to estimate its contents. It was his theory that when the can was full to the top it would hold just about enough to pay for the putter he had picked out in the window of Leo's Sporting Goods Store on 86th Street. Two or three times a week he would have me walk with him down to Leo's, so that we could see the putter, and in between he would talk about it at length, and demonstrate the proper grip for holding it, and the way you have to line up a long putt on a rolling green. Iggy Kovac was the first person I knew—I have known many since—who was really golf crazy. But I think that his case was the most unique, considering that at the time he had never in his life even had his hands on a real club.

So that evening, knowing how he felt about it, I said all right, if he wanted to go fish for golf balls I would go with him. It wasn't much of a walk down Bath Avenue; the only hard part was when we entered the course at its far side where we had to climb over mountains of what was politely called "fill." It made hot and smoky going, then there was a swampy patch, and finally the course itself and the water hazard.

I've never been back there since that day, but not long ago I happened to read an article about the Dyker Heights golf course in some magazine or other. According to the article, it was now the busiest public golf course in the world. Its eighteen well-kept greens were packed with players from dawn to dusk, and on weekends you had to get in line at the clubhouse at three or four o'clock in the morning if you wanted a chance to play a round.

Well, each to his own taste, but it wasn't like that when Iggy and I used to fish for golf balls there. For one thing, I don't think it had eighteen holes; I seem to remember it as a nine-hole layout. For another thing, it was usually pretty empty, either because not many people in Brooklyn played golf in those days, or because it was not a very enticing spot at best.

The fact is, it smelled bad. They were reclaiming the swampy land all around it by filling it with refuse, and the smoldering fires in the refuse laid a black pall over the place. No matter when you went there, there was that dirty haze in the air around you, and in a few minutes you'd find your eyes smarting and your nose full of a curious acrid smell.

Not that we minded it, Iggy and I. We accepted it casually as part of the scenery, as much a part as the occasional Mack truck loaded with trash that would rumble along the dirt road to the swamp, its chain-drive chattering and whining as it went. The only thing we did mind sometimes was the heat of the refuse underfoot when we climbed over it. We never dared enter the course from the clubhouse side; the attendant there had once caught us fishing in the pond trying to plunder his preserve, and we knew he had us marked. The back entrance may have been hotter, but it was the more practical way in.

When we reached the pond there was no one else in sight. It was a hot, still evening with a flaming-red sun now dipping toward the horizon, and once we had our sneakers and stockings off—long, black cotton stockings they were—we wasted no time wading into the water. It felt good, too, as did the slick texture of the mud oozing up between my toes when I pressed down. I suspect that I had the spirit of the true fisherman in me then. The pleasure lay in the activity, not in the catch.

Still, the catch made a worthy objective, and the idea was to walk along with slow, probing steps, and to stop whenever you felt anything small and solid underfoot. I had just stopped short with the excited feeling that I had pinned down a golf ball in the muck when I heard the sound of a motor moving along the dirt track nearby. My first thought was that it was one of the dump trucks carrying another load to add to the mountain of fill, but then I knew that it didn't sound like a Mack truck.

I looked around to see what kind of car it was, still keeping my foot planted on my prize, but the row of bunkers between the pond and the road blocked my view. Then the sound of the motor suddenly stopped, and that was all I needed to send me splashing out of the water in a panic. All Iggy needed, too, for that matter. In one second we had grabbed up our shoes and stockings and headed around the corner of the nearest bunker where we would be out of sight. In about five more seconds we had our stockings and shoes on without even bothering to dry our legs, ready to take flight if anyone approached.

The reason we moved so fast was simply that we weren't too clear about our legal right to fish for golf balls. Iggy and I had talked it over a couple of times, and while he vehemently maintained that we had every right to—there were the balls, with nobody but the dopey caretaker doing anything about it—he admitted that the smart thing was not to put the theory to the test, but to work at our trade unobserved. And I am sure that when the car stopped nearby he had the same idea I did: somebody had reported us, and now the long hand of authority was reaching out for us.

So we waited, crouching in breathless silence against the grassy wall of the bunker, until Iggy could not contain himself any longer. He crawled on hands and knees to the corner of the bunker and peered around it toward the road. "Holy smoke, look at that!" he whispered in an awed voice, and waggled his hand at me to come over.

I looked over his shoulder, and with shocked disbelief I saw a gray Packard, a car with double running-boards, one mounted over the other, the only car of its kind I had ever seen. There was no mistaking it, and there was no mistaking Mr. Rose who stood with two men near it, talking to the smaller one of them, and making angry chopping motions of his hand as he talked.

Looking back now, I think that what made the scene such a strange one was its setting. Here was the deserted golf course all around us, and the piles of smoldering fill in the distance, everything seeming so raw and uncitylike and made crimson by the setting sun; and there in the middle of it was this sleek car and the three men with straw hats and jackets and neckties, all looking completely out of place.

Even more fascinating was the smell of danger around them, because while I couldn't hear what was being said I could see that Mr. Rose was in the same mood he had been in when he caught Iggy and me in his driveway. The big man next to him said almost nothing, but the little man Mr. Rose was talking to shook his head, tried to answer, and kept backing away slowly, so that Mr. Rose had to follow him. Then suddenly the little man wheeled around and ran right toward the bunker where Iggy and I were hidden.

We ducked back, but he ran past the far side of it, and he was almost past the pond when the big man caught up with him and grabbed him, Mr. Rose running up after them with his hat in his hand. That is when we could have got away without being seen, but we didn't. We crouched there spellbound, watching something we would never have dreamed of seeing—grownups having it out right in front of us the way it happens in the movies.

I was, as I have said, twelve years old that summer. I can now mark it as the time I learned that there was a difference between seeing things in the movies and seeing them in real life. Because never in watching the most bruising movie, with Tom Mix or Hoot Gibson or any of my heroes, did I feel what I felt there watching what happened to that little man. And I think that Iggy must have felt it even more acutely than I did, because he was so small and skinny himself, and while he was tough in a fight, he was always being outweighed and overpowered. He must have felt that he was right there inside that little man, his arms pinned tight behind his back by the bully who had grabbed him, while Mr. Rose hit him back and forth with an open hand across the face, snarling at him all the while.

"You dirty dog," Mr. Rose said. "Do you know who I am? Do you think I'm one of those lousy small-time bootleggers you double-cross for the fun of it? *This* is who I am!" And with the little man screaming and kicking out at him he started punching away as hard as he could at the belly and face until the screaming and kicking suddenly stopped. Then he jerked his head toward the pond, and his pal heaved the little man right into it headfirst, the straw hat flying off and bobbing up and down in the water a few feet away.

They stood watching until the man in the water managed to get on his hands and knees, blowing out dirty water, shaking his head in a daze, and then without another word they walked off toward the car. I heard its doors slam, and the roar of the motor as it moved off, and then the sound faded away.

All I wanted to do then was get away from there. What I had just seen was too much to comprehend or even believe in; it was like waking up from a nightmare to find it real. Home was where I wanted to be.

I stood up cautiously, but before I could scramble off to home and safety, Iggy clutched the back of my shirt so hard that he almost pulled me down on top of him.

"What're you doing?" he whispered hotly. "Where do you think you're going?"

I pulled myself free. "Are you crazy?" I whispered back. "You expect to hang around here all night? I'm going home, that's where I'm going."

Iggy's face was ashy white, his nostrils flaring. "But that guy's hurt. You just gonna let him stay there?"

"Sure I'm gonna let him stay there. What's it my business?"

"You saw what happened. You think it's right to beat up a guy like that?"

What he said and the way he said it in a tight, choked voice made me wonder if he really had gone crazy just then. I said weakly, "It's none of my business, that's all. Anyhow, I have to go home. My folks'll be sore if I don't get home on time."

Iggy pointed an accusing finger at me. "All right, if that's the way you feel!" he said, and then before I could stop him he turned and dashed out of concealment toward the pond. Whether it was the sense of being left alone in a hostile world, or whether it was some wild streak of loyalty that acted on me, I don't know. But I hesitated only an instant and then ran after him.

He stood at the edge of the pond looking at the man in it who was still on his hands and knees and shaking his head vaguely from side to side. "Hey, mister," Iggy said, and there was none of the assurance in his voice that there had been before, "are you hurt?"

The man looked slowly around at us, and his face was fearful to behold. It was bruised and swollen and glassy-eyed, and his dripping hair hung in long strings down his forehead. It was enough to make Iggy and me back up a step, the way he looked.

With a great effort he pushed himself to his feet and stood there swaying. Then he lurched forward, staring at us blindly, and we hastily backed up a few more steps. He stopped short and suddenly reached down and scooped up a handful of mud from under the water.

"Get out of here!" he cried out like a woman screaming. "Get out of here, you little sneaks!"—and without warning flung the mud at us.

It didn't hit me, but it didn't have to. I let out one yell of panic and ran wildly, my heart thudding, my legs pumping as fast as they could. Iggy was almost at my shoulder—I could hear him gasping as we climbed the smoldering hill of refuse that barred the way to the avenue, slid down the other side in a cloud of dirt and ashes, and raced toward the avenue without looking back. It was only when we reached the first street-light that we stopped and stood there trembling, our mouths wide open, trying to suck in air, our clothes fouled from top to bottom.

But the shock I had undergone was nothing compared to what I felt when Iggy finally got his wind back enough to speak up.

"Did you see that guy?" he said, still struggling for breath. "Did you see what they did to him? Come on, I'm gonna tell the cops."

I couldn't believe my ears. "The cops? What do you want to get mixed up with the cops for? What do you care what they did to him, for Pete's sake?"

"Because they beat him up, didn't they? And the cops can stick them in jail for fifty years if somebody tells them, and I'm a witness. I saw what happened and so did you. So you're a witness too."

I didn't like it. I certainly had no sympathy for the evil-looking apparition from which I had just fled, and, more than that, I balked at the idea of having anything to do with the police. Not that I had ever had any trouble with them. It was just that, like most other kids I knew, I was nervous in the presence of a police uniform. It left me even more mystified by Iggy than ever. The idea of any kid voluntarily walking up to report something to a policeman was beyond comprehension.

I said bitterly, "All right, so I'm a witness. But why can't the guy that got beat up go and tell the cops about it? Why do we have to go and do it?"

"Because he wouldn't tell anybody about it. Didn't you see the way he was scared of Mr. Rose? You think it's all right for Mr. Rose to go around like that, beating up anybody he wants to, and nobody does anything about it?"

Then I understood. Beneath all this weird talk, this sudden access of nobility, was solid logic, something I could get hold of. It was not the man in the water Iggy was concerned with, it was himself. Mr. Rose had pushed *him* around, and now he had a perfect way of getting even.

I didn't reveal this thought to Iggy, though, because when your best friend has been shoved around and humiliated in front of you, you don't want to remind him of it. But at least it put everything into proper perspective. Somebody hurts you, so you hurt him back, and that's all there is to it.

It also made it much easier to go along with Iggy in his plan. I wasn't really being called on to ally myself with some stupid grownup who had got into trouble with Mr. Rose; I was being a good pal to Iggy.

All of a sudden, the prospect of walking into the police station and telling my story to somebody seemed highly intriguing. And, the reassuring thought went, far in back of my head, none of this could mean trouble for me later on, because tomorrow I was moving to Manhattan anyhow, wasn't I?

So I was right there, a step behind Iggy, when we walked up between the two green globes which still seemed vaguely menacing to me, and into the police station. There was a tall desk there, like a judge's bench, at which a gray-haired man sat writing, and at its foot was another desk at which sat a very fat uniformed policeman reading a magazine. He put the magazine down when we approached and looked at us with raised eyebrows.

"Yeah?" he said. "What's the trouble?"

I had been mentally rehearsing a description of what I had seen back there on the golf course, but I never had a chance to speak my piece. Iggy started off with a rush, and there was no way of getting a word in. The fat man listened with a puzzled expression, every now and then pinching his lower lip between his thumb and forefinger. Then he looked up at the one behind the tall desk and said, "Hey, sergeant, here's a couple of kids say they saw an assault over at Dyker Heights. You want to listen to this?"

The sergeant didn't even look at us, but kept on writing. "Why?" he said. "What's wrong with your ears?"

The fat policeman leaned back in his chair and smiled. "I don't know," he said, "only it seems to me some guy named Rose is mixed up in this."

The sergeant suddenly stopped writing. "What's that?" he said.

"Some guy named Rose," the fat policeman said, and he appeared to be enjoying himself a good deal. "You know anybody with that name who drives a big gray Packard?"

The sergeant motioned with his head for us to come right up to the platform his desk was on. "All right, kid," he said to Iggy, "what's bothering you?"

So Iggy went through it again, and when he was finished the sergeant just sat there looking at him, tapping his pen on the desk. He looked at him so long and kept tapping that pen so steadily—tap, tap, tap—that my skin started to crawl. It didn't surprise me when he finally said to Iggy in a hard voice, "You're a pretty wise kid."

"What do you mean?" Iggy said. "I saw it!" He pointed at me. "He saw it, too. He'll tell you!"

I braced myself for the worst and then noted with relief that the sergeant was paying no attention to me. He shook his head at Iggy and said, "I do the telling around here, kid. And I'm telling you you've got an awful big mouth for someone your size. Don't you have more sense than to go around trying to get people into trouble?"

This, I thought, was the time to get away from there, because if I ever needed proof that you don't mix into grownup business I had it now. But Iggy didn't budge. He was always pretty good at arguing himself out of spots where he was wrong; now that he knew he was right he was getting hot with outraged virtue.

"Don't you believe me?" he demanded. "For Pete's sake, I was right there when it happened! I was this close!"

The sergeant looked like a thundercloud. "All right, you were that close," he said. "Now beat it, kid, and keep that big mouth shut. I got no time to fool around any more. Go on, get out of here."

Iggy was so enraged that not even the big gold badge a foot from his nose could intimidate him now. "I don't care if you don't believe me!" he said. "There's plenty other people'll believe me. Wait'll I tell my father. You'll see!"

I could hear my ears ringing in the silence that followed. The sergeant sat staring at Iggy, and Iggy, a little scared by his own outburst, stared back. He must have had the same idea I did then. Yelling at a cop was probably as bad as hitting one, and we'd both end up in jail for the rest of our lives. Not for a second did I feel any of the righteous indignation Iggy did. As far as I was concerned, he had led me into this trap, and I was going to pay for his lunacy. I guess I hated him then even more than the sergeant did.

It didn't help any when the sergeant finally turned to the fat policeman with the air of a man who had made up his mind.

"Take the car and drive over to Rose's place," he said. "You can explain all this to him, and ask him to come along back with you. Oh yes, and get this kid's name and address, and bring his father along, too. Then we'll see."

So I had my first and only experience of sitting on a bench in a police station watching the pendulum of the big clock on the wall swinging back and forth, and recounting all my past sins to myself. It couldn't have been more than a half hour before the fat policeman walked in with Mr. Rose and Iggy's father, but it seemed like a year. And a long, miserable year at that.

The surprising thing was the way Mr. Rose looked. I had half expected them to bring him in fighting and struggling, because while the sergeant may not have believed Iggy's story Mr. Rose would know it was so.

But far from struggling, Mr. Rose looked as if he had dropped in for a friendly visit. He was dressed in a fine summer suit and sporty-looking black and white shoes and he was smoking a cigar. He was perfectly calm and pleasant, and, in some strange way, he almost gave the impression that he was in charge there.

It was different with Iggy's father. Mr. Kovac must have been reading the paper out on the porch in his undershirt, because his regular shirt had been stuffed into his pants carelessly and part of it hung out. And from his manner you'd think that he was the one who had done something wrong. He kept swallowing hard, and twisting his neck in his collar, and now and then glancing nervously at Mr. Rose. He didn't look at all impressive as he did at other times.

The sergeant pointed at Iggy. "All right, kid," he said, "now tell everybody here what you told me. Stand up so we can all hear it."

Since Iggy had already told it twice he really had it down pat now, and he told it without a break from start to finish, no one interrupting him. And all the while Mr. Rose stood there listening politely, and Mr. Kovac kept twisting his neck in his collar.

When Iggy was finished the sergeant said, "I'll put it to you straight out, Mr. Rose. Were you near that golf course today?"

Mr. Rose smiled. "I was not," he said.

"Of course not," said the sergeant. "But you can see what we're up against here."

"Sure I can," said Mr. Rose. He went over to Iggy and put a hand on his shoulder. "And you know what?" he said. "I don't even blame the kid for trying this trick. He and I had a little trouble some time back about the way he was always climbing over my car, and I guess he's just trying to get square with me. I'd say he's got a lot of spirit in him. Don't you, sonny?" he asked, squeezing Iggy's shoulder in a friendly way.

I was stunned by the accuracy of this shot, but Iggy reacted like a firecracker going off. He pulled away from Mr. Rose's hand and ran over to his father. "I'm *not* lying!" he said desperately and grabbed Mr. Kovac's shirt, tugging at it. "Honest to God, Pop, we both saw it. Honest to God, Pop!"

Mr. Kovac looked down at him and then looked around at all of us. When his eyes were on Mr. Rose it seemed as if his collar was tighter than ever. Meanwhile, Iggy was pulling at his shirt, yelling that we saw it, we saw it, and he wasn't lying, until Mr. Kovac shook him once, very hard, and that shut him up.

"Iggy," said Mr. Kovac, "I don't want you to go around telling stories about people. Do you hear me?"

Iggy heard him, all right. He stepped back as if he had been walloped across the face, and then stood there looking at Mr. Kovac in a funny way. He didn't say anything, didn't even move when Mr. Rose came up and put a hand on his shoulder again.

"You heard your father, didn't you, kid?" Mr. Rose said.

Iggy still didn't say anything.

"Sure you did," Mr. Rose said. "And you and I understand each other a lot better now, kiddo, so there's no hard feelings. Matter of fact, any time you want to come over to the house you come on over, and I'll bet there's plenty of odd jobs you can do there. I pay good, too, so don't you worry about that." He reached into his pocket and took out a bill. "Here," he said, stuffing it into Iggy's hand, "this'll give you an idea. Now go on out and have yourself some fun."

Iggy looked at the money like a sleepwalker. I was baffled by that. As far as I could see, this was the business, and here was Iggy in a daze, instead of openly rejoicing. It was only when the sergeant spoke to us that he seemed to wake up.

"All right, you kids," the sergeant said, "beat it home now. The rest of us got some things to talk over."

I didn't need a second invitation. I got out of there in a hurry and went down the street fast, with Iggy tagging along behind me not saying a word. It was three blocks down and one block over, and I didn't slow down until I was in front of my house again. I had never appreciated those familiar outlines and the lights in the windows any more than I did at that moment. But I didn't go right in. It suddenly struck me that this was the last time I'd be seeing Iggy, so I waited there awkwardly. I was never very good at saying goodbyes.

"That was all right," I said finally. "I mean Mr. Rose giving you that dollar. That's as good as twenty golf balls."

"Yeah?" said Iggy, and he was looking at me in the same funny way he had looked at his father. "I'll bet it's as good as a whole new golf club. Come on down to Leo's with me, and I'll show you."

I wanted to, but I wanted to get inside the house even more. "Ahh, my folks'll be sore if I stay out too late tonight," I said. "Anyhow, you can't buy a club for a dollar. You'll need way more than that."

"You think so?" Iggy said, and then held out his hand and slowly opened it so that I could see what he was holding. It was not a one dollar bill. It was, to my awe, a five dollar bill.

That, as my wife said, was a long time ago. Thirty-five years before a photograph was taken of little Ignace Kovac, a man wise in the way of the rackets, slumped in a death agony over the wheel of his big car, a bullet hole in the middle of his forehead, a bag of golf clubs leaning against the seat next to him. Thirty-five years before I understood the meaning of the last things said and done when we faced each other on a street in Brooklyn, and then went off, each in his own direction.

I gaped at the money in Iggy's hand. It was the hoard of Croesus, and its very magnitude alarmed me.

"Hey," I said. "That's five bucks. That's a lot of money! You better give it to your old man, or he'll really jump on you."

Then I saw to my surprise that the hand holding the money was shaking. Iggy was suddenly shuddering all over as if he had just plunged into icy water.

"My old man?" he yelled wildly at me, and his lips drew back showing his teeth clenched together hard, as if that could stop the shuddering. "You know what I'll do if my old man tries anything? I'll tell Mr. Rose on him, that's what! Then you'll see!"

And wheeled and ran blindly away from me down the street to his destiny.

THE CRIME OF THE CENTURY

R. L. Stevens

RAGGER WAS SEATED on a wood piling, staring out through the evening mist at the calm beauty of New York harbor, when he heard someone approaching. It could only have been Edith, but he felt his muscles tense nevertheless. He let one hand slide along his waist to the sandbag he carried on his belt, ready to spring to the attack if it should be a policeman or Pinkerton guard assigned to the pier area.

But it was Edith.

"This is a dangerous place at night," she cautioned. "Someone could rob you and toss your body into the water."

"I can take care of myself. I came down here for the view."

"What can you see in all this mist?"

"My girl, I can see a half million dollars."

"A half—"

"I am going to commit the crime of the century—a crime that will put my name in the history books alongside that of John Wilkes Booth."

"You mean you're going to shoot President Cleveland!"

Ragger chuckled at the idea. Cleveland had only been in office three months, since his inauguration on March 4, 1885. "He ain't even had time to make enemies yet, girl!"

"But you won't get into the history books unless you're caught."

"I'll write 'em from South America after it's all over and tell them who I am."

"South America? Can I go with you, Ragger?"

159

"'Course you can go with me! What do you think I'm telling you about it for?"

"When's all this going to happen?"

"In about ten days, give or take a day. I'm meeting tomorrow with some boys that are goin' to help me. There's lots of plannin' to be done."

"The crime of the century . . . What is it, Ragger?"

"You'll find out soon enough, my girl."

The following evening Ragger and Edith crossed the new bridge to the city of Brooklyn and met four men in a waterfront tavern, gathering in a private upstairs room where they wouldn't be disturbed. One of them, Andy Crews, had been a friend of Ragger's since their Navy days together. The other three were tough-looking seamen anxious to make a crooked dollar. Andy had had little trouble recruiting them for the job.

Ragger looked them over and asked, "What're your names?"

"Haskel," a rough-looking bald man answered.

"Peters." A young one, but already carrying the scars of battle on his face.

"Fernandez." This last from a dark-skinned Spaniard.

"Good. I'm Ragger and this is Edith, my woman. That's all you need to know about us. If the job is successful you'll be paid twenty-five thousand dollars each." He could see their faces light up at the sum. It was as much as they'd normally make in many years.

"Who do we have to kill?" Haskel asked with a grin.

"With luck, nobody. We're going to be pirates. We're going to intercept a ship as she approaches the shore, board her, and remove her cargo."

"What is it—gold bullion?" the young one, Peters, asked.

"Something better than bullion. You'll know when the time comes and not before." He turned to Andy Crews. "What luck have you had with a boat?"

Andy shook his head. "Not good, Ragger. I've got one that can be handled by this small a crew, and it has a good strong winch on board. But have you figured out the timing on this operation?"

Andy Crews was an educated man who worried about things like timing. Ragger often scoffed but usually followed his advice. "What about the timing?" he asked with a frown.

"There are two hundred and twenty large crates to be removed from the ship—correct?"

"That's right. That's the word I got from my man who'll be on board."

"Well, the boat I have for us could barely hold one hundred crates on its deck without capsizing. It would have to make two or more likely three trips to the ship—all while we held the crew captive. The thing would take days—just the unloading would take days! And while we went back and forth to shore you'd be virtually alone on the *Isère* with your prisoners."

It was the first time the name of the French ship had been mentioned. Ragger glanced at the three men but he saw at once that the name meant nothing to them. "All right," he said finally. "Any better suggestion?"

"Yes," Crews said. "Instead of my coming with you as originally planned, I could remain on shore. You'd have these three plus your man on board the *Isère* to seize the ship, while Edith held our little cutter alongside. You know my fondness for pigeons. When the ship is secure you could release a pigeon which would fly back to me here at the tavern as a signal."

"Are they trained for that?"

Andy Crews nodded. "I have some trained ones as good as any used during the war. When I receive the signal, I would then announce that the ship's cargo was being held for $500,000 ransom. If the money was not paid at once, we would threaten to scuttle or blow up the *Isère*."

Ragger admitted it made sense. The transfer of the cargo had always bothered him, and this way it could be avoided. "All right," he decided. "It's agreed. But we'll be depending on you. How will you notify us that the ransom has been paid?"

"Your man on the *Isère* is to fire a rocket when the ship is in sight of Sandy Hook. I will do the same. When the money is paid, I will fire a rocket from Sandy Hook—and you can leave the ship."

"With the Revenue Cutter Service in pursuit!" Edith predicted.

"No, I'll take care of that," Andy Crews promised. "I'll say we've left one man on board the ship, to scuttle her if you're pursued. By the time they get out there and find it's not true, we'll all be far away."

The plan sounded good to Ragger. "We'll go look at your boat tomorrow."

"When's this supposed to happen?" Fernandez wanted to know.

"Sometime around a week from Wednesday, June seventeenth. The ship is due about then. We'll have to be out there every day next week watching for her, watching for the rocket signal from my man on board."

Later, after more talk, Ragger ordered drinks for everyone. The scheme that would make him famous was under way, and he had a feeling nothing could stop it.

When the three hired men had gone, Ragger asked Andy Crews, "Are you sure you can trust them?"

"I'm sure. For that much money they'd kill their own mothers."

Ragger downed the rest of his rum. "How about guns?"

"Model 1873 carbines for you and the three of them. Winchesters—the best made. Plus standard-issue U.S. Cavalry model revolvers, caliber 44/40, to carry in a belt holster."

"That's Indian-fighting gear!"

"You'll be thankful for it. Those French seamen just might decide to put up a fight. I got you some smoke bombs too, to confuse things when you come alongside."

Ragger chuckled. "Andy, my boy, I'm glad to see you've kept up your contacts with the military."

Some hours later, back at Ragger's dingy two-room apartment on Delancey Street, Edith asked him, "What is it, Ragger? I want to know what it is we're stealing."

"First of all, we're not stealing it—only holding it for ransom. And second, it's best you don't know quite yet."

"Andy knows, doesn't he?"

"Sure. Andy has to know. But nobody else right now."

"How do you know they'll pay a half million for it? I can't think of anything but gold that'd be worth near that much!"

"The contents of those crates are actually valued at $450,000, but I'm sure they'll pay a half million to have it safe and sound."

"How're you splitting the money?"

"Twenty-five thousand to each of those three, like you heard, plus the same to a French seaman named Vascal who's on the ship. Andy's getting one hundred thousand because he's my key man. And that leaves three hundred thousand for you and me and South America."

"That must be more money than there is in the world!"

"Oh, there's lots of money in the world for them that can get it. Them with the brains."

The next day they went down to the Brooklyn docks and looked over the boat Andy had selected. It was a cutter like the ones the government used for its coastal patrol, single-masted like a sloop but having the mast farther astern. "A good fast ship," Andy said. "You could probably outrun them with this even if they did decide to chase you."

"Yes," Ragger agreed. "I like it. But I doubt if even a hundred crates would have fit on this deck space. You must have known I'd go along with the change of plan when you picked it out."

"It's the only way that makes sense, Ragger. But the boat's only rented for next week, so there wasn't that much to lose if you overruled me."

"What'd you tell the owner?"

"That we were going deep-sea fishing. Of course he didn't believe me, but he didn't care. Probably figures we're running in illegal aliens or something."

In the wheelhouse Ragger turned to Edith. "Do you think you could handle it while we're on board the *Isère?* Just hold steady alongside in case we have to make a quick exit?"

She tried the wheel. "I think so. Give me some practice while we're out sailing around."

"It might be several hours or even a day," Andy Crews cautioned her. "But once the French crew is subdued and locked up Ragger could relieve you."

For the next few nights they went over the plans again and again, figuring every angle, trying to anticipate every response the police could make. "After I deliver my ransom demand we enter the crucial phase," Andy said. "If they decide to ignore me and order the Revenue Cutters or the Navy after you, we're all in big trouble."

"They won't chance it," Ragger said with assurance. "I'd scuttle the ship and they know it. And that's one thing I'm sure they won't risk. I know how politicians react."

Andy snickered. "You've been reading books."

"And newspapers. I may not be as smart as you, Andy, but I'm no dope an' don't you forget that! This whole scheme was my idea. It's *me* that's goin' down in the history books."

"Along with John Wilkes Booth," Edith remarked.

"Now what in hell is gettin' at *you?*"

"Nothing, Ragger, nothing. It's just that you keep harping so much on wanting to commit the crime of the century. Sometimes I think those history books are more important to you than the money!"

"Come on," Andy said. "It won't do us any good to fight among ourselves."

Ragger calmed down. They were both right, of course. He hadn't come all this way with his planning to let it fly out the window. "All right," he said. "We take her out next Monday, armed and ready to go."

Cutting through the early morning mists off Sandy Hook, the boat made better headway than Ragger had expected. "When we get back I'll have to compliment Andy," he told Edith. "It's got speed and it handles well. Want to try the wheel for a bit?"

They traded places and he watched her steering. "I can manage it," she decided.

"Good! You'll do fine."

They cruised back and forth the entire day without catching sight of the ship they awaited. Finally, heading in to the dock in Brooklyn, Edith asked, "You're sure it's due now?"

"Around Wednesday. I just wanted to make sure it didn't arrive ahead of schedule. Vascal has no way to communicate their progress to me."

On Tuesday morning they went out again.

The three in the crew were more at ease this time, and they joked among themselves as the cutter headed east toward the Atlantic shipping lanes. Ragger had a feeling in his bones that this would be the day. He kept his carbine ready while he used a spyglass to scan the horizon for ships.

"I told Andy we might stay out all night and sleep on the boat," he said to Edith. "I can't take a chance on missing the *Isère*."

Edith gave the wheel to Peters and came over to where Ragger stood. "This thing means a great deal to you, doesn't it?"

"Of course! It means we'll be rich."

"We'll be rich if you can trust Andy Crews."

He looked hard at her, seeking some meaning in her spray-swept face. "I'd trust Andy with my life."

"That's just what you're doing, Ragger."

He put down the spyglass. "What are you trying to tell me?"

"He's planning to collect the half million and take off for South America with all of it."

"That's crazy, I don't believe it!"

She took a deep breath. "He asked me to go with him, Ragger. He wants me to leave you aboard the *Isère* and sail the cutter to Sandy Hook to meet him."

"I don't believe it," Ragger said again.

But somehow he did.

It would be Andy Crews then who had committed the crime of the century, Andy Crews whose name went down in the history books.

"Ragger?"

"We're heading home," he decided suddenly, barking orders at young Peters. "I'll deal with Andy."

It was near evening when the cutter docked, and Ragger headed for the Brooklyn tavern where they had held the first full meeting. He knew Andy Crews would be waiting there for the carrier pigeon that would tell him they had seized the *Isère*.

Andy was in the upstairs room alone. He turned toward the door as Ragger entered, a look of surprise on his face. "What's wrong? What are you doing back here?"

"You know what's wrong, Andy."

Crews saw the carbine in Ragger's hands, and he went for his own gun, screaming in the same instant, "For God's sake, don't shoot! I don't know what you're—"

Ragger fired once, and the bullet toppled Andy Crews backward. Then, suddenly, there was the sound of police whistles. Ragger turned, tried to run, but already the room was filling with men.

The Commissioner of Police looked up from his desk as Edith Murphy entered. He smiled and extended his hand. "That was a fine job you did, Miss Murphy. You forestalled a very serious crime."

She smiled slightly. "The crime of the century, Ragger called it."

"I suppose it might well have been, if they'd gotten away with it. When I assigned you to him six months ago, I never dreamed he was into anything more than some waterfront crime."

"Oh, Ragger had big ideas—there's no doubt of that. But I never thought it would end in murder. I had to get the cutter back to port before the French ship appeared, and that lie about Andy Crews was the only way I could think of."

"Crews was a bad one—he won't be missed. Maybe your lie even had a bit of truth to it. We discovered he had booked a passage to South America. Anyway, the whole thing's much simpler this way. We've charged Ragger with second-degree murder and we're sure of a quick conviction. The business about the *Isère* and its cargo need never come out."

She walked to the window, thinking still of her days with Ragger. "So he'll go to prison for killing a man in a barroom brawl, and his name will be forgotten after all. Not exactly the crime of the century that he planned on."

"No," the Commissioner agreed. "But you'll get a promotion for this, even so. A fine bit of work."

She was staring out toward New York harbor, though she couldn't see it from the window. She was staring as Ragger had stared on that misty night just ten days ago.

The *Isère* had reached Sandy Hook on June 17, and soon an army of workmen would begin assembling the contents of those 220 large crates.

And one day next year, on an island in the harbor, the Statue of Liberty would be dedicated.

THE BACK STAIRWAY
Hal Ellson

HIS LAST FIFTEEN cents. Gordon looked at the coins on his palm, went to the stand, and bought a frankfurter. He ate it quickly and walked on. A few minutes later he found himself in Times Square.

A moving ribbon of lights flashed the news high up on the Times Building. A gaping crowd stood in the street.

MARTIAL LAW PROCLAIMED IN CONGO.

So what? thought Gordon, and noticed a man in the crowd watching him. He was struck by his face, by the look in his eyes. Finally he turned and looked directly at him.

The man walked away. Five minutes later he returned. Gordon was still there. The man asked him for a cigarette.

"Haven't got any," Gordon answered. "In fact, I'm broke."

"No job?"

"No job."

"Then how about a cup of coffee?"

Gordon hesitated, then nodded his head. They went to the Automat, had coffee, and came out.

The man glanced at the crowd on the sidewalk. "Plenty of people."

"Yes."

"My name's Tony."

"Mine's Gordon."

"Doing anything special?"

"No."

"Care to take a ride uptown a way? I've got to pick up something at my room."

"All right."

They boarded a bus and rode uptown.

"What business are you in?" Tony asked.

"None. I'm on the loose," Gordon answered, and produced a big switch-blade he was carrying.

"What's that for?"

"I always carry it, and I know how to use it."

Tony nodded. Gordon casually put the knife back in his pocket. He wasn't afraid, but he wanted to make sure Tony knew he had it.

They left the bus and went to a cheap rooming house in the Fifties, between Eighth and Ninth Avenues. Tony went up and came down and they returned to Times Square. They had another coffee and some pie in a restaurant and walked around, talking of fighters.

At eleven they knew as much of each other as they cared to tell, and they were back at the rooming house.

"Where're you sleeping tonight?" Tony asked.

"I don't know."

"Want to come up to my place?"

Gordon hesitated, but he didn't know where else he could go and nodded his head.

Tony took the elevator. Gordon walked up the back stairs—four flights.

Tony was waiting at the door to his room. He laughed when he saw Gordon panting.

"Another flight and I wouldn't have made it," Gordon said.

"Well, it's done. Come on in."

They entered the room and Gordon looked around. It was a real dive, with a single bed, faded yellow walls, and no pictures.

Tony was watching him. Their eyes finally met.

"Not so nice, but it could be worse," Tony remarked and sat down on the bed.

Gordon took a chair. They talked some more. Finally Tony said, "I guess you're wondering what I do for a living."

"That's none of my business."

"Well, I'm a crap-game hustler."

"You make a living at it?"

"I manage to get by."

Gordon nodded. His face showed doubt.

"You don't believe I hustle, do you?" Tony said. "Well, I don't blame you. I guess both of us have doubts about each other."

"You were wondering about me?"

"About the knife."

"What about it?"

Tony grinned. "I had an idea you were a character. Some kind of clip artist."

"No, the knife is just for protection."

Tony nodded and yawned. "Getting late," he said. "I'm going to turn in. What about you?"

"I could use some sleep."

"Good."

Tony stood up. Gordon did too, and they both prepared for bed. Tony hid his wallet in the bottom drawer of the bureau.

Gordon noticed and thought, That's how much he trusts me, but I can't blame him—he's probably thinking about the knife.

They slept in the same bed that night.

Gordon awoke the next afternoon. Tony was gone. He didn't return until evening.

It went like that: Tony hustled for money while Gordon remained in the room most of the time, waiting for evening. No demands were made on him. He could leave when he wished, or stay. It was up to him.

"When you find a job, we'll split the expenses." That was all Tony had said.

He's a nice guy, Gordon thought, but he still had doubts about him. Besides, this was too good to last. As for finding a job, daily he promised himself he'd look for one, but he never did. All day he stayed in the room, sleeping and reading. At night, when he went out to eat with Tony, he always used the back stairway so the rooming house proprietor wouldn't see him.

Two weeks passed, then he and Tony had a minor argument. Tony left in a huff. Gordon heard his steps fade away on the stairs.

The quiet of the house came back, a deep silence. Suddenly the room seemed too small.

He finished his cigarette, undressed, and doused the light. Darkness filled the room. Immediately those four dingy walls, already so close, seemed to be moving in on him.

Quietly he went to the window and lifted the shade. The window was closed. Tony's work. He flung it open and felt the night air moving into the room.

There was nothing to see outside but a single, tiny bathroom light that was no more than a slit in a blank wall. The sky was dark and aloof.

He went back to bed, but he couldn't sleep. Woven into the cool air drifting through the window were fragmented sounds and the soft, sonorous purring of the city—a nocturnal eddying that seemed like the very life-breath of the vast network of life outside. It was a quiet yet morbid sound.

He closed his eyes. Quick and soft, then, footsteps echoed in the hall, passed, and someone whispered, "Hurry!" The whisper was so close he sat bolt-upright.

A door closed down the hall. Then there was nothing but silence.

The footsteps didn't bother him. He was used to them. People came and went anonymously here. He expected them, as he used to expect the attendants in the institution which he'd left—men making the rounds at night, a flashlight spraying the dormitory walls, footsteps all through the night. Voices.

But the whispered "Hurry!" that had been so close to him moments ago turned his body cold. Now he felt the speaker was in the room and standing beside him. It was someone he knew, and his flesh turned into ice.

But no one was there.

His heart slowed its beat again. He waited, then looked about the room.

A nebulous whiteness swirled like smoke in the dark. It's the mirror, he told himself. But he was still frightened and half expected someone to appear before him.

No one did. He waited for the footsteps to pass through the hall once more. They didn't and the door which had closed didn't open.

This wasn't an unreasonable sequence. Doors opened, closed, or were left ajar here. Footsteps came and went, fragments of conversation threaded the narrow corridor, and no one in all the world could decipher the comings and goings, or guess what was happening within this rat nest.

The thought was heartening, but it didn't help for long. He couldn't shake off the fear. Once more his heart began to pound.

The walls of the room were closing in again. He couldn't breathe, couldn't do anything but wait to be crushed. His nails sank into the flesh of his palms.

Suddenly he remembered the Blue Room—so called for the single bulb that lit its bleak interior. The patients in the hospital never said much about it, and none wanted to be sent there. Gordon had told himself he'd never be.

He went there for fighting with another patient. Vividly now he remembered the two attendants who met him—the one who spoke, and the one with the glove.

He saw the glove too late. It exploded in his face and he fell to the floor.

A week later he returned to his regular ward, tame as a fly, remembering nothing but the feeling of walls that threatened to crush him.

Now he understood why this room bothered him, why all the rooms he'd stayed in did. This knowledge released him from the fear he'd hidden from himself and he was able to lie back on the cot again.

But immediately his thoughts returned to the Blue Room. He saw the blue light, the gloved hand; he saw himself sprawled on the floor and the attendant standing over him.

Suddenly he began to shiver. With immense effort he brought himself under control.

That's the past. They'll never get me back there. But why am I afraid? he asked himself; and he had his answer in the question—fear of being brought back to the hospital.

I'm not insane, he told himself; but who believes it of himself if he is?

It was better not to think like this and he rolled over. Oddly, he heard no footsteps, but the door of the room opened and closed so quietly that he thought he was dreaming. A chill set him trembling. Someone was in the room.

If it were Tony, he thought, he'd have switched on the light.

The light didn't go on. He held his breath and waited. The one who'd entered moved across the room. He wanted to scream.

"Tony?"

"You awake?"

"Yes."

The switch clicked on the wall, the light blazed. Gordon looked up, blinking his eyes.

"What's wrong with you?" Tony said.

"Nothing. Why didn't you put the light on before?"

"I thought you were sleeping."

"Couldn't," Gordon answered. He sat up and looked at the brown paper bag Tony was holding.

"Coffee? I brought back two containers."

Gordon nodded. "You came back early."

"I had to make it fast tonight."

He took the containers from the bag, then met Gordon's eyes. There was an expression in them that Gordon had never seen before. He looked away. Tony handed him a container.

It was bitter coffee. He drank it anyhow. That way he didn't have to speak. The two of them sat like strangers till they emptied the containers.

Then Tony stretched out on the bed. Gordon knew he was watching him.

Waiting for me to speak, he thought. It's my move.

"You hustled up a game?" he said.

Tony nodded, a faint smile on his face.

"That was real fast."

"Real fast, but too close for comfort."

"What's that mean?"

Tony smiled unpleasantly. A long scar on the side of his face seemed unnaturally white.

"Too close for comfort," he said again.

"What was?"

"Getting the money."

He couldn't have got it running a floating dice game tonight. He'd been gone too short a while.

"What happened?" Gordon asked.

"I rolled a guy."

"You're kidding."

"Not at all. It looked easy. The guy was drunk. I followed and got him in a side-street next to a theater alley," Tony went on. "A real tough baby. I belted him and he wouldn't go down. I almost busted my hand on him."

He lifted his right hand. It was swollen. "So I had to get tough," he said calmly as he examined his hand.

"How tough?"

"I mugged him." Tony raised his eyes. "It was him or me. I had to do it."

Gordon was stunned, but his face showed nothing. A moment later the real shock came.

"I think I killed the guy."

"You're joking."

"No. The guy finally went down in a lump, but he started to yell. I had to give him an extra squeeze. Something cracked. It felt like his windpipe."

The coffee came burning up in Gordon's throat. He didn't want to believe this.

"How could you be sure?" he asked.

"Because I happen to know. I killed a man like that in the war," Tony said almost casually, as if the experience hadn't touched him at all.

Perhaps it hadn't. Gordon wasn't sure. Oddly now, he no longer felt shocked and couldn't explain this to himself.

At any rate, nothing had changed. Tony was still the same person. He didn't look like a murderer. Gordon thought of several attendants he'd known at the hospital. Their faces were inhuman. Tony's was only hard and knowing.

"Anyway," he said at last, "I've got the money for the room, so we don't have to sleep in the gutter."

This, too, was put casually, and its full meaning didn't hit Gordon for several moments. Then he felt sick. For he realized he was at least partly responsible for what had happened.

He looked at Tony and saw no sign that he felt anything. It had been merely an accident. Anyway, he'd killed before, in the war. Tonight it had probably been much simpler.

Tony was undressing now. Gordon kept watching him, and he didn't seem worried. At last he lay down on the bed. He glanced at the light, then at Gordon.

"Going to sit up all night?" he asked.

"No."

"What's the trouble?"

"Suppose the cops find out what happened?"

"Don't worry about it. They won't. Nobody saw me, and I didn't leave anything behind."

"They still might find out."

"How?"

"I don't know. Sometimes they do."

"What's the matter? Scared?"

"No."

"You don't have to be. It's my concern."

"Maybe we ought to blow out of here."

Tony smiled. "You are scared. Want to leave?"

Gordon didn't answer; but he wasn't afraid—at least, not for himself.

"We're good for another week in this dump," Tony went on. "And I'm starting to like the place. Not that it's anything like home."

The last words stung Gordon. Home? He'd never had one, never would now. It would go on like this forever—a succession of cheap rooming houses and hotels.

Oh, God, he thought, and stood up. Tony was still smoking. That kept him from switching off the light. But Tony understood why he was waiting.

"Put it out," he said.

The light went off. The eye of the cigarette glowed in the dark.

"Pretty cool after the rain," Tony said.

"Is that why you closed the window?"

Tony laughed. A moment later the glowing end of the cigarette made an arc and vanished, snuffed out in a tray. The springs of the bed complained. Silence followed. Within a minute Tony was fast asleep.

He always went off like that, and Gordon envied him. Apparently the mugging meant nothing at all to him.

It couldn't have, thought Gordon, remembering the coffee. After killing a man, he'd picked up the containers on his way back to the room.

The silence was deadly now. Gordon waited, hoping to hear a sound outside, or in the hall. Nothing broke the quiet. The whole city had gone down in a cloud of dust.

For Gordon the city returned sometime beyond noon and in the same cell-like room. Tony had left. The house leaked sounds. The city's daytime clamor rose drowsily toward the pale summer sky.

Another day of heat and emptiness. It was better to sleep . . .

It was always gray in the room. When he opened his eyes again, the gray was deeper. A wavering figure stood in it and finally came into focus.

A policeman. Another stepped through the door. Then the man who owned the rooming house. His thick-lensed glasses gleamed dully.

"What's wrong?" Gordon asked, jumping out of bed.

The first policeman said, "Get your clothes on. You'll find out soon enough."

The second policeman went to the bureau, picked up a wallet, and examined it.

"This is it," he said, and pulled open the top drawer of the bureau. His hand went in. He lifted a big switch-blade knife and held it up.

"And this clinches it," he said.

Gordon's heart dropped. "Wait," he said. "There's been a mistake."

"And you made it," said the first policeman. "Get dressed."

"But the knife . . ."

"It's not yours?"

"It is, but . . ."

"It killed a man. That's his wallet."

Gordon was stunned, but he understood now—the argument last night with Tony.

Tony had used his knife on the man he'd killed and left the wallet behind to put the guilt on him. It was all clear now.

"Tony," he shouted. "He did it."

"Who's Tony?"

"We roomed together here. He's the one. Last night . . ."

The policeman turned to the old man who owned the rooming house.

"Know anybody named Tony?" he asked.

The old man stared through his thick-lensed glasses, shook his head slowly, and pointed at Gordon. "I only rent one to a room, and that's the fellow," he said.

"No, that's not true," Gordon cried out. "You've never seen me before. You couldn't have."

"Couldn't have? You think I'm blind because of these glasses?"

"It's not your eyes. But you never saw me because I always used the back stairway."

The old man's jaw fell slack. "The back stairway?"

Gordon nodded and smiled. "So you wouldn't know there were two of us in the same room," he said, and turned to the policeman.

The policeman cleared his throat and frowned at the old man whose mouth was agape again. "What about that?" the policeman asked him.

The old man hesitated, as if uncertain of himself; then he raised his voice. "I live here twenty years. I should know," he said, and paused.

"Know what?" said the policeman.

"There is no back stairway in this house."

THE HAWK AND THE DOME OF HELL

S. S. Rafferty

As THE LIVING-ROOM clock ting-tanged four A.M. throughout the humid second-floor flat, Tess Fenley lay alone in the back bedroom counting cricket chirps. She ticked off the obligatory fifteen seconds on her fingertips while counting the insects' rhythmic clicking in the yard below. Having counted forty-five chirps, she then added the magic number thirty-seven and arrived at the temperature in New York City.

Eighty-two degrees! The penny press was calling it the worst heat wave in late June since 1868. The memory of that terrible summer thirteen years ago when sunstroke had carried off her Aunt Nellie and hundreds of others convinced Tess that she shouldn't wear a corset today.

Her momentary mental diversion into temperature and weather was actually a ruse to keep her mind from the horrible thoughts that had kept her awake since her husband had left the house an hour before. A policeman's wife learned early on to expect midnight calls to duty, but this one was dreadfully different. Captain John Fenley wasn't fighting mere criminals this time; he was fighting the Devil himself. Tess's recall of the newspaper weather reports brought with it other headlines of the past few days, headlines that underscored her feeling of dread.

THIRD TUNNEL WORKER
DIES MYSTERIOUSLY
Police Baffled

SUBWAY DIGGING UNLEASHES
PRETERNATURAL FORCES
SAYS OCCULTIST

"SEAL WALL ST. TUNNEL"
*Clergy Fear Dome of
Hell Cracked*

CLARION CABLES
JULES VERNE
FOR ADVICE

ROGAN REFUSES TO HALT
TUNNEL WORK
Charges "El" Owners' Plot

FENLEY NABS
EMBEZZLER IN CHICAGO
Returns to City Today

As she lay in the heat, Tess knew that today's headlines would say the best detective on the Metropolitan Bureau (and hero of Bull Run) had been assigned to the case. In all probability, she thought, he hadn't gone directly to Wall and Broadway, but had made a detour to Copley Mews on Thirteenth Street to pick up Dr. Amos Phipps, the police department consultant. Today's headlines wouldn't call the doctor by name, however, since they delighted in calling him The Hawk, a title Phipps abhorred.

The crude elevator plummeted down the dark shaft with deadfall speed, causing Fenley to question the judgment of the winchman far above on Broadway. Then suddenly, with a stomach-wrenching jolt, the carriage stopped dead in the gloom of a dimly lit tunnel.

"Orpheus descending," Phipps mused as Fenley raised the safety bar and stepped out onto the rock-dusted tramway.

"Huh?" he grunted.

"Stygian darkness, Captain—then the underworld. We go forward to our metamorphoses."

"If you please, Doctor," Fenley snapped testily, "I've had three hours' sleep in the last thirty-six. I'm in no mood for—"

"Captain Fenley!" a voice called from somewhere up the tracks.

"That you, Binabee?" Fenley's voice cannonaded off the vaulting.

"Yes, sir." The voice drew nearer. As their eyes grew accustomed to the half light and shadows from the flambeaux along the bulkhead, the figure of a man coming down the tramway took shape. He was tall and trim and wore the traditional detective's billycock hat with its iron lining. As he drew nearer, he gave a rather halfhearted salute. "Sergeant Binabee, sir, of the Broadway Squad."

"Yes, I remember you," Fenley said. "You've been on this from the start."

"Aye, Captain, and I'm sure glad to see you and the doctor on the case. It's a gold-plated baffler."

Suddenly a clamor of voices could be heard far up the tunnel. As the noise came closer, the words became clearer.

"Flanagan—" it was an angry growl "—if you mention that hissing sound to me once more, I'll fire you on the spot."

"On my mother's grave, Mr. Rogan," an Irish brogue pleaded, "I swear I heard a hissin' sound when I came down here on my inspection tour. 'Twas louder than a snake."

"It's either blarney or booze," a third voice said. "Either way, it only confuses the issue, Flanagan."

"That's Mr. Rogan, the owner, the tunnel boss, and the Irishman who found the body," said Binabee. "I've got my eye on him."

The three men now stood before them. Each wore a miner's cap with headlamp affixed. The shortest of the trio, a very corpulent man, wore a fine linen cloth duster which covered him like a tent from neck to boot-spats. By contrast, the other two wore scuffed leather trousers and exposed powerful biceps and forearms under rolled-up shirtsleeves.

"This is terrible, Fenley," the man in the duster said with exasperated grimness. "I told the Commissioner this afternoon that you personally should have taken up the case immediately."

"Mr. Rogan," Fenley replied, trying to hide his anger with a level tone of voice. "As he must have told you, I had just come off a difficult case in Chicago and I needed sleep."

"We understand there's been another murder." Phipps attempted to head off a squabble with the interruption. As a doctor he could tell Fenley was still close to exhaustion, and as an alienist, he knew how that could alter a normally calm demeanor.

The taller of the men in work clothes, sensing the tension between the detective and the financier, said, "There has, sir. Excuse me, Major Fenley, we've met before. I'm George Lockwood. I was with you at Petersburg."

The man's friendly tone had a soothing effect on the situation. Fenley almost smiled. "Lockwood? Oh yes, Lieutenant Lockwood, Forty- eighth

Pennsylvania, wasn't it? Colonel Pleasant's sappers. It's nice to see you again, Lockwood. I'm afraid I'm only a captain now."

"Yes, Captain. I'm tunnel boss on this project. Flanagan—" he turned to the other workman "—why don't you take Mr. Rogan topside for a cup of tea?" Then, to the financier, "You're going to take a chill down here, sir. I can handle things."

"I suppose you're right, George," Rogan grumped and stepped into the lift. "But make damn sure that cowboy of a winchman goes slow, you hear?"

Before the car ascended, Fenley motioned Binabee to join the two men in the carriage. The person who finds the body bears watching. When they were behind the bar, Flanagan tugged the signal rope and they were gone.

"You'll have to forgive the old man, gentlemen," Lockwood said. "He's at his wits' end. It's understandable, of course. He's got his last cent invested in this idea. I thought it best to get him off the premises and out of your hair."

"It appears you were also anxious to get the Flanagan fellow out of the picture," Phipps said.

Lockwood gave him a quizzical look.

"Oh, forgive me." Fenley turned to his companion. "This is Dr. Phipps, our police consultant."

"Yes, I've heard of The Hawk," Lockwood said, proffering a hand.

"It's a soubriquet I disdain," Phipps said mechanically.

"Maybe so, Doctor, but it fits. You've got a quick eye. Yes, I wanted to get Flanagan out of here. Mr. Rogan was capable of ascending alone."

"Do you suspect Flanagan?"

"Not necessarily, Doctor. I just didn't want him spouting off and accusing the Welshman again. From the confused expressions on your faces, I suspect you're not yet aware of the facts in the case."

"I've been out of the city for a week," Fenley explained, "and Dr. Phipps doesn't read the newspapers."

"And precious little information he'd get from them, although they did report that you tracked that embezzler to Chicago and were bringing him back."

"Suppose you fill in the empty spaces for us, Lockwood. What's this about a Welshman? And where's the new corpse?"

"Some four hundred yards up the Broadway cut, sir. I'll explain as we go along."

As they started down one leg of the tunnel and turned north (or so Lockwood said—Fenley and Phipps had lost all sense of direction)

Lockwood explained. "As you probably know, we've been at this project for over a year and were making damn little progress, mostly because the local help is inexperienced at underground work."

He stopped and picked up a flat piece of shale-like rock. "This is schist. New York is sitting on miles of it. It makes for good building foundations, but it's hell to tunnel through because it splits easily along certain planes. Four months ago Mr. Rogan sent me out to Pennsylvania to recruit coal miners, but I could only get about forty men to come to New York. They're worth their weight in gold, these Irishmen—tough, know the ins and outs of shoring up and blasting. If you overlook their drinking and pugnaciousness, of course. But forty men weren't enough, so Mr. Rogan sent me off to Wales and I signed up twenty-four men from the collieries over there.

"That's when the trouble started. The two groups just didn't get along and it didn't take long for bad blood to build up. Finally, I decided to split up the crews—the Welsh working nights and the Irish days, on alternating weekly shifts.

"The new system was about to start when we found the body of one of the Welshmen, Chaley Morgan, in one of the Broadway-side cut tunnels. Your people, Captain Fenley, saw it as the result of some squabble with one of the Irishmen. A day later we found Lemus Dunn's body in the Wall Street let. A revenge murder, your Sergeant Binabee figured, and I agreed with him."

"And the third death?"

"Well, Doctor, that's where it started to get muddled. Yesterday afternoon we found the body of young Carl Dietter, my assistant engineer who was neither Irish not Welsh and was universally liked by all the men.

"To be on the safe side, I've given the crews two days off till we get to the bottom of it. Mr. Rogan raised hell about my stopping the work, but under the circumstances I did it anyway. It's damn strange though. This latest death certainly makes a hash of the revenge motive."

"How so?"

"Didn't they tell you?" Lockwood asked, stopping and looking at both men with amazement. "This one's a woman."

"A woman!" Fenley said with a start.

"Egad," Phipps muttered to himself, "Orpheus finds his Eurydice."

"What was a woman doing down here?" Fenley demanded.

"I haven't the slightest idea, Captain. But she's down here, sure enough."

The coroner's man was known to Fenley. Dr. Brinze was a no-nonsense forensicist, completely devoid of humor or guile—which made his preliminary cause-of-death so surprising to the Captain.

"I tell you, Fenley," Brinze said, "the woman died of acute fright. There isn't a mark on her."

"Well," Fenley said, "she could have had a bad heart."

"I see what you mean, Dr. Brinze." Phipps observed. "The eyes are popped open, the jaw locked in a death scream. May I suggest, however, that minute care be taken during the autopsy to detect any snake bites on the body."

"You believe there are snakes down here?" Brinze asked in disbelief.

"It's unlikely, but the person who found the body said he heard a hissing noise."

"Ach, that Irisher." Brinze shook his head. "But, to satisfy you, we'll look." He paused. "We *always* take minute care at Bellevue, Doctor," he admonished.

"Of course. What was the cause of death in the other cases, Dr. Brinze?"

"Well, the *cause* was getting their throats torn open. It's what caused the *wounds* that has us stymied—and, I might add, what feeds this hysteria the newspapers have been churning up."

"Torn open, Doctor?"

"It's unscientific, but it's the only way to describe it. In each case, the larynx was ripped out with great force."

"An animal of some kind?"

"I will not speculate, Captain. The Coroner's Department has taken the position that the determination of the agency of death is a police matter."

"Thank you, Doctor. I'll need photographs of the woman's face for identification. Could you do the autopsy immediately—say by noon?"

"We will proceed with care, not haste, Captain," Brinze said icily. "May we move the body?"

As Brinze and the morgue wagoners disappeared down the tunnel with the stretcher Fenley turned to Phipps. "Bit of a stick, isn't he?"

"With good reason. He's a matter-of-fact scientist who has bumped into an inexplicable situation. It's frustrating for him."

"Well, you're a scientist too. Are you frustrated?"

"Not yet, Captain. But I'm sure we're in for a bit of confusion before we're through."

Within half an hour, in spite of his fatigue, or possibly because the excitement dissipated it, Captain Fenley had marshalled his forces and his wits. Twenty uniformed men of the crack Broadway Squad, split into two groups each headed by a sergeant, stood in casual ranks listening to his orders. Several of the younger men could be observed casting suspicious eyes at the tunnel's overhead as if expecting it to crash down at any moment. Fenley was saying:

"Now, each sergeant has a map. We're standing under the corner of Wall Street and Broadway. One party will proceed north on Broadway until you reach the curve at Canal Street and then follow it east to the Bowery. The other party will go east across Wall to Pearl Street and then north. The completed tunnel will be like a big circle, only the section above Pearl isn't connected yet, so you won't meet."

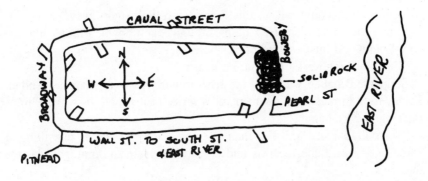

"Keep your eyes skinned and listen to your sergeants. I want every inch of it covered, including the side tunnels you'll find along the way. That's where the entrances up to the street will eventually go. Carry on."

As the two groups took their assigned routes, Phipps came down the tunnel from his reexamination of the side cut in which the woman's body had been found. "Are you looking for anything special, Captain?" he asked.

"Anything I can get. I'd like to prove this woman was a jade working her trade down here."

"A prostitute in the tunnel?"

"Doctor, one of the main things I learned in the army was that the only two things that can't be kept out of an encampment are prostitution and dysentery. These miners are hard-working men with lusty appetites. At least it gives us a reason for her being down here."

Phipps was shaking his head in disbelief. "You *do* need sleep, my friend. The dead woman's clothes were of good quality—her hands were well cared for and meticulously manicured."

"A gentlewoman?"

"No, a working girl. In fact, a telegrapher." He observed Fenley wryly. "I can see I've jarred you a bit. Her hands, Captain, were so well taken care of that my attention was drawn to them. But despite all the cosmetic care, she couldn't hide the callusing of her right index finger. I suspect she might have suffered from what is known as Morse Finger, a spasmodic contraction of the digit that works the telegraph key."

"Well, I'll be damned," Fenley groaned. Then: "You'd think Brinze would have caught on to that."

"He undoubtedly will. However, you now have a line of inquiry as far as occupation goes."

"And we can start right here in the financial district, where hundreds of telegraphers are employed." The police officer rubbed his hands with satisfaction. It was a factual crumb in a case that appeared to be thoroughly devoid of solid evidence.

"I think we should talk to this Flanagan fellow right away."

"I had the same idea. He's being brought back down. I didn't like the way Lockwood hustled him out of here."

"I'm more interested in what he heard."

Sergeant Binabee was with the Irish miner when the shaft descended. Fenley took him aside and whispered a series of instructions while Phipps interrogated Flanagan.

"*Sean* Flanagan, sir," the man answered Phipp's initial question. "I came over as a babe in arms and consider myself an American despite the brogue."

"As well you are. I understand, Sean, that you heard something when you found the woman. Tell me about it."

"Well, sir, I pulled the night-watch trick since the two-day layoff started. I was to tour the tunnel every morning checkin' for water seepage, cracks, things like that. Well, I started up the Broadway leg checkin' the bulkheads when I found her. It was then I heard it."

"Hissing?"

"Yes, but not exactly. It was a deeper sound, more like steam escapin' in spurts."

"Could you determine where the sound came from, Sean?"

"Sound is as tricky a thing in a tunnel as it is in a mine, sir. It echoes off the bulkheads—it's hard to tell exactly where it's comin' from."

"We were thinking along the lines of a snake?"

The idea provoked laughter from the miner. "If it was a snake, sir, it had to be the biggest reptile on all the face of the earth."

"Who found the other bodies, Sean?"

"Chaley Morgan was found by a couple of fellas. Lemus Dunn was found by his brother, Danny. And the boss found the Dietter kid."

"Mr. Rogan?"

"No, Lockwood. He's the real boss of this job. Knows his business too."

While Flanagan talked, Fenley, having dispatched Binabee, joined them.

"How did you get along with the Welshmen, Sean?" Phipps asked.

"Me personal? I can take some and leave others."

"How did Lemus Dunn feel about them?"

"Well, he was a greenhorn and a bit thick. In general, most of the lads from the old country didn't get along with the Taffies, but both sides was greenhorns to fellas like myself—Americans, that is. Dr. Phipps, I have a hunch these questions are leading to this talk of hatred and revenge killings between the men. It's pure slag. If a miner—any miner, Taffy or Mick—has a beef, settles it with this." He held up a hamlike fist. "Not by sneakin' up on a man and mauling him like an animal."

"Thanks for your insights, Sean," Phipps said. He paused. "I'd like you to do me a favor."

"To be sure, sir."

"I'd like you to visit Mr. Barnum's menagerie—"

The miner looked shocked at the suggestion. "That's mighty tony society for the likes of me, Doctor."

"The Captain's men will make sure you're given every consideration. What I would like you to do is walk through the menagerie with your eyes closed. Take your time and listen to the sounds of the various beasts. If you hear any sound resembling the hissing you heard when you found the woman, tell the detective accompanying you. But don't open your eyes. Understand?"

"Yes, sir."

"Then Captain Fenley will arrange it. Right, Captain?"

Fenley replied affirmatively and detailed another plainclothesman to accompany Flanagan in the Barnum experiment. Phipps heaved a sigh. "What's your next move, Captain?"

"Well, I think we should get a few solid facts under our belts. Let's get Rogan's thoughts while Binabee's boys are covering the woman's identification. Hey, there, Lockwood," he said to the tunnel boss, who had been leaning casually on an empty tram cart, "where would Mr. Rogan be at this time of day?"

"Going on ten— Only one place. The Stock Exchange."

"Give my sergeant the addresses of the miners. We'll have to talk to them all."

"Sure thing. But most of them will be using the days off to make extra money on other construction jobs."

"Tunnels?"

"No, Captain—" the ex-sapper smiled "—we're the only tunnel in town. But there are lots of job sites looking for experienced men who speak English and understand rigging. There are several new buildings going up right here on Wall Street."

"By the way, Lockwood, don't you have a guard or watchman at the pithead?"

"In a manner of speaking, but they're usually either asleep or sneaking off to some gin mill. If you're asking if it's difficult to sneak down here, it isn't."

Five minutes later Fenley and Phipps emerged at the pithead into the bright hot sunshine of Wall and Broadway. Fenley started off toward the East River and had gone a few yards before he realized he was alone. Turning, he found his companion standing precariously on one leg, shaking pebbles from his shoe.

"Serves you right, wearing those fancy European slippers in a tunnel, Doctor."

"Pumps," Phipps corrected him as he put the shoe back on his foot and walked on. "And much more comfortable than those heavy boots of yours."

Fenley shrugged, but in his soul he knew the shoes were a sort of symbol of their divergent approaches to crime—he relying on dogged legwork, Phipps leaning toward tailored intellectualism. He enjoyed Phipps's company, of course. And the man was a damned good cook, although Fenley would never tell his wife about their bachelor braiser dinners. He had a fine mind too, but at times he went too far. This Orpheus stuff, for instance, and all this la-di-da about metamorphoses and Eurydice. Phipps always played it too fancy—his shoes, his food, his methods of detection.

As they walked along the north side of Wall Street, Fenley noticed excavation work ahead where the new Sub-Treasury Building would rise next to the U.S. Assay Office. "We'd better cross to the south side, Doctor. I see more pebbles in your future. The way they're building up the area down here, I can see where Rogan's subway *could* make a fortune."

Behind them, at the Broadway foot of this canyon of commerce, the bell tower of Trinity Church began to toll ten o'clock. Each stroke seemed to accentuate the mounting human energy all across the eight-block strip to the swift East River. Here were the great life insurance companies, the U.S. Customs House, the Cotton Exchange, the Assay Office, Wells and Standard Oil, the Petroleum Exchange, all housed in magnificently solid buildings, each new one outmatching its neighbors in one superlative or other—largest, tallest, widest, most opulent. Architectural records fell with each new ground-breaking.

Between New and Broad Streets, at 13 Wall, a high block-long marble building, an elderly concierge opened its brassbound oak doors and waited patiently, his pocket watch in one hand and a clapper bell in the other. As the tower sent out the tenth toll over its sleepy graveyard, the concierge violently clanged his handbell. "The market is open!" he shouted to the milling crowd much as a railway conductor would hail "All aboard!"

The New York Stock Exchange, the drive piston of the country's—the world's—commerce, now chugged into action that would see thirty million dollars change hands before 3:00 P.M. Within its great hall, 1,200 silkhatted men would shout bids above the tumult and make lightning-fast mental calculations toward their next moves in the wild game that had a language all its own.

As Fenley and Phipps turned into the building and headed across the marble hall toward the door to the trading floor, they found their way blocked by the concierge. "Have to use the visitors' gallery, gents," he said, pointing to a stairway. When Fenley showed his shield and stated his business, the small man said with a triumphant smile, "Still don't cut no ice, but I can tell Mr. Rogan you're here, Captain."

Moments later, Rogan came hurrying off the trading floor. In broad daylight and dressed in striped trousers and morning coat, he cut a more imposing figure than he had in the tunnel. His irritability hadn't changed, however; it had, in fact, increased.

"Twenty points," he muttered. "The market opened only minutes ago, and I'm down twenty points already. I lost twelve yesterday and never bounced back."

When Fenley asked who his business enemies might be, a sardonic smile crossed Rogan's pudgy face. "Any one of 1,199 men," he said in a low tone. "Any seat holder on this Exchange. Don't be fooled by these tailored clothes and clean fingernails, fellows. I've done my time with a pick and shovel. You see, it's called the Exchange, but it's really an exclusive gentlemen's club, and they don't see me as a gentleman. And maybe I'm not. Hell, I never claimed to be. I've dug mines, peddled coal oil, run carnies and cooch shows, and never saw the inside of a schoolroom, never mind a college. They all got their noses out of joint when I finally wangled a seat. Cost me forty thousand dollars, but I got it and I aim to keep it. I got the jump on 'em too, with this underground scheme. *That* burned 'em good and proper."

"Could you narrow it down a bit, Mr. Rogan—1,199 suspects is a big chunk."

"You can start and stop with Gervase Brumm of Elevated Transit, for my money. My underground system will put the kibosh on his noisy, stinking cattlecars, so he has plenty to lose. If he had his way the sun would never shine again on New York streets, with all these ugly girders and tracks overhead.

"And don't think those fine gentlemen are above murder. You don't know what goes on behind Wall Street doors, my lads. Don't forget the Gould and Fisk shenanigans back in Sixty-nine. Brumm is no better. And he hates me. He even blackballed me at the Yacht Club for spite. *Me,* turned down by a bunch of Sunday sailors! *Me,* who's been a ship's master in my time! Hell, I own a seagoing schooner, not a toy boat like the rest of them."

"He's a bit of buccaneer, isn't he?" Phipps observed when they were back on the street.

"Tough-minded, certainly. You have to admire a fellow who pulls himself up by his bootstraps. You know, these murders may stop work on the tunnel, but somehow I don't think anything will stop Rogan. He's liable to dig the damn thing himself just to prove his point.

"Well, I don't relish bothering Gervase Brumm—he's a high muckety-muck around town and will resent an interview—but we have to look at all sides and the business-revenge idea can't be ignored."

They started eastward again toward the elevated Transit Line offices at the East River foot of Wall Street. As they strolled along, an occasional and welcome breeze came up from the water. Fenley reviewed the case aloud. "We've more angles than a miter box in this thing," he said. "Let's say the first two deaths were tradeoffs between the Irish and Welsh miners and somehow the well-liked assistant engineer took sides and was killed. That would neaten it up if it weren't for the lady telegrapher. She's the fly in the ointment."

"She might well be the answer to the whole matter," Phipps muttered.

"Yes. Once we get Brumm out of the way we can concentrate on her. I sure wish my prostitute theory held up though."

"There's another aspect to this that bears investigation."

"Which is?"

"The Molly Maguires."

"The Pennsylvania miners' secret society?" Fenley asked.

"More a clan of killers who terrorized mine owners a few years back."

"But neither Rogan not Lockwood mentioned any labor problems. The Welsh and the Irish hate each other, not the company."

"I was thinking that a few Maguires salted among the crew by an outside party would be insurance that the subway would fail."

"Which brings us back to Gervase Brumm—at whose door we've just arrived," Fenley announced.

*   *   *   *

"Rogan sounds a mite like 'rogue' to me, gentlemen," Gervase Brumm said from behind a desk that seemed to take up half his large office. He was bald and sported old-fashioned muttonchop whiskers. "And rogue he is. Of course, I understand, Captain Fenley, that you have to follow up on all sorts of information, even if it is lies. So let me tell you about Rogue Rogan. Along with being a bit of a pirate—and I mean real South Sea piracy—he's also the biggest damn fool this side of the equator.

"Take this subway scheme, for example. When my syndicate decided to develop a transit system, we considered tunneling, but the engineers turned it down as impractical. If you were going to go underground, the best method would be to dig open trenches, lay the trackage, roof over the cut, and backfill. But even that's impractical, so we went with the elevated concept. Mark my words, men, Rogan is out to swindle—and swindle he will, unless you can catch onto him."

"We understand, sir," Fenley said, "that if the project fails, he will lose everything. So why would he cut his own throat by failing deliberately?"

"That I can't say. But if he does fail, I hope his scurvy boat goes up for sale. I'll buy it and sink it." He got to his feet and pointed out the window to the river twelve stories below. Fenley and Phipps raised themselves out of their chairs to follow his finger's path. "See that God-awful scow?" Brumm pointed to a dilapidated schooner docked at the foot of Wall Street. "He berths her there just to annoy me. I even tried to buy the dock, and found he owns it."

"Mr. Brumm, I noticed on the lobby directory that Elevated Transit Lines is just one of your holdings," Phipps said.

"Oh, my syndicate is quite diversified, Doctor."

"Yes, and it's quite impressive. Rails, coal, commodities—is that coal mining or coal shipping?"

"Both," Brumm said with a gusty laugh. "No use owning a railroad unless you own a few coal mines, you know. Well, gentlemen, I hope I've allayed any fears that I am the author of Rogan's difficulties." He laughed again. "Elephants don't strike at gnats."

As they rose to go Fenley said, "I know you're a churchgoing man, Mr. Brumm. What do you think of this Dome of Hell idea?"

"Well, sir, I can't say yes and I can't say no, but if there's a God in heaven there's got to be a Devil, and why not in a rogue's tunnel?"

They were headed back to Broadway when Phipps said, "Sergeant Binabee has a list of the tunnel workers by now. I suggest you look it over and wire the Altoona police. I noticed on the directory as we left that Brumm's coal mines are based there. You'll want to know if any of the tunnel workers ever worked for Brumm. And that includes Lockwood, the tunnel boss."

"Well, now, I *know* Lockwood. He's a fine officer."

"Spare me, Captain. Battlefield acquaintances give a one-sided perspective. I'm really most interested in why the one expert engineer was sent away from the job to recruit workers when anyone could have done it."

"That's not necessarily true. It's dangerous work down there, and he'd want a hand-picked crew. I would. But I'll check it anyway. And when we get the lady telegrapher's picture, we'll make the Brumm offices our first stop. But you know, Doctor, old Brumm really hasn't any money motive. He's got more than a body could count."

"I often think that one of the inherent dangers of having great wealth is that it allows time for the full development of our baser instincts—in this case, jealousy or hate. Poor people are so involved in their own survival that— Fenley, isn't that one of the Broadway Squad hurtling toward us?"

A young uniformed officer was running so fast he almost streaked by them. Fenley's large hands halted him. "If you're going to run, young fellow, get out in the street with the horses," he said.

"Oh Captain Fenley, I was on my way to the Elevated Transit offices for you! Sergeant Binabee tracked you down through Mr. Rogan. You'd better come back to the tunnel right away, sir."

"What's the problem, lad?"

"They found the footprints of a monster down there, sir!"

STRANGE PAW PRINT FOUND
IN TUNNEL ROCK DUST
BY BROADWAY SQUAD

PREHISTORIC ANIMAL, SAY
UNIVERSITY EXPERTS
OF FRESH PRINT

ANCIENT BEASTS ROAM
CENTER OF EARTH
Come Up Through Tunnel

MAYOR ORDERS TUNNEL
CLOSED IN MOVE TO
QUIET PUBLIC HYSTERIA
Seeks Federal Troops to
Patrol City Streets

NOT FLESH EATERS,
SAYS PROF
But Tunnel Deaths
Belie His Theory

"The madness and delusion of the crowd," Phipps said, shaking his head at the latest fiction from the presses along Park Row. He and Fenley had established temporary headquarters at Precinct One, a short walk from Wall Street. He placed the latest headline on Fenley's desk.

FENLEY THEORY THAT
PRINT IS A FAKE
CALLED PREPOSTEROUS
Experts Sneer
Tunnel Searched in Vain

Fenley scowled and tossed the paper aside with disgust. "Damned experts," he muttered. "I'll show 'em yet. We've drawn some good leads in your absence, Doctor. What have you been up to?"

"Nothing much. I was over at the Met. I had lunch with Max Alvary."

Fenley looked blank.

"Alvary, the opera star. He opened in *Siegfried* in the Fall. They've been losing money on Italian operas, so they're mounting a German season. Do you like Wagner, Captain?"

Fenley spluttered and said the only Wagner he knew was serving thirty years for bank robbery.

"You said some leads have developed?" Phipps asked.

Fenley nodded. "It seems Lockwood once worked for Brumm's company in the Altoona area, but the Irish miners worked in other mines. But here's an interesting angle. Sean Flanagan was long suspected of Molly Maquire activity, but the Altoona force and the mine-company police could never prove anything against him."

"Excellent," Phipps said without excitement. "Anything else?"

"Yes, as a matter of fact—"

He was interrupted by a knock on the door. "She's here," Binabee said, poking his head in.

"Let's have her," Fenley ordered.

The young woman was obviously nervous as she was ushered into the room and offered a chair.

"We appreciate your cooperation, Miss—"

"Cooper, sir. Mary Cooper. I doubt I can really be of much help, beyond telling you that the girl in the picture this gentleman showed me is Carla Tuttle. We lived in the same boarding house and were telegraphers at Western Union's Pine Street office. And that's about all I can tell you, gentlemen."

"Up until now, young lady," Fenley said sternly, "you haven't told us a blessed thing. The information you've just confirmed was given us by the manager of your Pine Street branch. Why didn't you come forward when the girl failed to come home two nights ago?"

Mary Cooper's mouth quivered slightly and she shifted her gaze to Phipps in a silent appeal for help.

"I think, Captain, we can assume that Miss Cooper seriously believed Miss Tuttle had been called out of town. Or—" Phipps addressed the young woman "—was there another good reason for her absence?"

"There was," she said excitedly. "There most certainly was!" She turned her attention back to Fenley with reassurance. "I thought she had moved up her elopement by a week."

"I see," Fenley said, supressing a grin at Phipps. They often played friend-and-foe with people under investigation. And Fenley always ended up being the bad hat. "Go on, Miss Cooper—who was she eloping with?"

"I don't know." Anticipating renewed antagonism from Fenley, she hastened to be emphatically sincere. "I swear I don't know her gentleman's name, sir. She was very secretive about it, so I didn't pry. All I know is that she was to elope with a professional man over the Fourth of July weekend. The Fourth falls on Monday, so they would have had the long weekend."

"Professional man?" Fenley's eyebrows rose in surprise. "Did she mention what profession, Miss Cooper?"

"No, she never did."

"*Never?* Come, Miss Cooper, you were roommates—friends. It's hard to believe you two didn't share intimacies."

"We weren't really friends, sir. Miss Brooke, the landlady, just put her in with me in a take-it-or-leave-it fashion. Clara was a closemouthed type, except for the one evening she told me about her elopement. I thought she was just trying to get a rise out of me at first, but then I saw she was serious. She said that after July third she'd never have to touch a telegraph key again because she was marrying a professional man who worked on Wall Street. She asked me not to say anything when she didn't show up for work after the holiday."

"My, my, that *is* secretive. Didn't she realize inquiries would eventually be made as to her whereabouts?"

"You're echoing my very words to her, sir. She said they'd need only seventy-two hours and then the world could know, for all she cared. I assumed his family was well off and would have opposed the match. She was an orphan, she said."

The rest of the interrogation, despite Phipps's kid-glove questioning, produced no further information and Mary Cooper was released. While she had been at the Old Slip precinct house Binabee's men had thoroughly searched the room she had shared with Clara Tuttle and questioned all the other roomers. There wasn't a trace of evidence to link the dead woman with any man, professional or otherwise.

Both men spent the remainder of the afternoon reviewing the case, trying to fit Clara Tuttle into the jumble of characters involved.

"Damned if I can make any sense of it," Fenley said. "Maybe she has no connection with the tunnel. Could be some Johnny who didn't want to get married took advantage of the mysterious doings down there to get rid of her and cover his motive."

"So he took her down there and scared her to death, saying 'Boo' in the dark?" Phipps chided. "I'm afraid not, my friend. She is definitely a part of the whole Dome mystery, and I still think she's the most valuable piece on the board. Is the tunnel sealed off as yet?"

"No, but if the Mayor has his way that shaft will soon be filled with twenty tons of cement."

"Rogan fights to the end, eh? Well, good for him. Once it's sealed, the case becomes unsolvable."

"It's not Rogan who's doing the fighting. In fact, he's about done in financially. The main pressure is coming from old P. T. Barnum. He wants to trap one of the monsters for his circus. It's just another of his publicity stunts, of course, but he has the governor's ear. Eventually we'll have every crackpot in creation showing up with one scheme or other. Just before you came back from your operatic luncheon, there was a fellow in here from out west named Cody who wanted a permit to hunt down there. He calls himself Buffalo Bill, no less."

He sighed. "Well, I'm for having all the miners in for requestioning. Maybe we can shake something loose. It looks like another all night to-do, Doctor."

"I wish you good fortune, Captain."

"Oh, you're not going to be here *again?* Another opera?"

"No, I'm going to a lecture at Columbia and then have a large supper with friends from Holland. By the way, would anyone require a permit to hunt down there?"

"I'd sure hate to be the fool who signed one."

"You may well be yet, Captain. By the bye, when you're questioning the workers, would you kindly ask them if they are ever troubled by foot blisters?"

"Sure, Doctor," was the wary reply. "Right foot or left?"
"Either," Phipps said seriously, and departed.

The next afternoon the headlines reflected the final defeat of Charles
Rogan, financier.

ROGAN TO SEAL TUNNEL HIMSELF
Apologizes to Public
for Panicking City
Action Lauded by Mayor
Cement Pours Tomorrow

The group of men who crowded into the Mayor's office shortly after
the headlines appeared was led by Dr. Amos Phipps.
"Well, I won't sign it," the Mayor insisted. "It's damned dangerous."
Motley was an apt description of the group—they were as diverse in
background as they were in appearance. There was the corpulent and
ebullient Phineas T. Barnum, wearing a well tailored suit and vest. A tall
man in his early thirties—William Cody—wore the broad-brimmed slouch
hat of the plainsman. Phipps and Fenley, of course, displayed their usual
distinctive tastes in haberdashery, one European cut, the other off-the-rack
rumpled. Possibly the most discordant note in the group was Sean Flanagan, still in leather pants, flannel shirt, and boots.
Phipps pressed the issue with the Mayor. "It's more dangerous if you
don't sign it, Your Honor. If there are risks these men are willing to take
them."
It was Barnum's threat to bring in the Governor—and the President, if
necessary—that finally got the permit signed.

Later that evening the five men approached the tunnel pithead, showed
the permit to the Federal officer, and entered the elevator car.
"I think, Mr. Barnum," Phipps said, "it would be better if you remained
on top. I don't know what we're going to bump into down there." The
offer was made in deference to Barnum's age, which was close on seventy.
"That's why we have these repeater rifles, isn't it, young fellow?"
Barnum asked with bravado. "I wouldn't miss it for the world—not that
I have the slightest idea of what we're doing, or why."
"That make four of us," Fenley groused. "Only Dr. Phipps seems to
know."
When they reached the bottom, they found that many of the torches
along the tunnel wall had gone out through neglect. The few that remained

lit here and there created a confusion of flicker and shadow—an eerie chiaroscuro.

"I can go back up and get some kerosene for the torches," Flanagan offered.

"No we have enough light for our purpose," Phipps murmured.

"What next?" Fenley asked. "The squad has been over these tunnels with a fine-toothed comb. Shall we split up—half of us take the Broadway leg and the other half the Wall Street leg?"

"No, Captain, we're interested only in the Wall Street end. Try to move quietly now."

They started off, Phipps and Cody leading, and were a few yards under Wall Street when they heard it.

"Jay-sus," Flanagan whispered, "the hissing again!"

Down the tunnel there was indeed a hissing sound—not unlike a steam engine, but somehow less rhythmic, less mechanical. It had the naturalness of breathing. Suddenely Cody was at the alert, his rifle at the ready. Phipps had seen it too, as the thing—a tail possibly—slithered into a side cut.

"What in tarnation—" Cody started to say. A head darted out for only a split second, but long enough to burn it into a man's memory for a lifetime. It was the head of a gargoylelike creature covered with brown scales. When it opened its bright red mouth it showed vicious sawlike teeth.

Each man was riveted in his place by a curious force that blended stark terror and awed disbelief into one moment of inaction.

"Watch it!" Fenley shouted as the head now grew a body at least ten feet long from its ugly head to its slithery tail. It looked to weigh as much as three hundred pounds yet it moved with lightning speed.

Cody started the fusillade of fire that tore into the breast flesh, sending spurts of blood onto the shale-dust floor. Each man had emptied his rifle in seconds, and the thing now lay dead just six feet from them.

"Reload, men!" Fenley gave the command in his old military style. "There may be more of them."

"God help us," Flanagan said, making the sign of the cross.

"I think not, Captain," Phipps assured him.

Barnum had taken a torch from its fixture and was examining the beast. "It's a shame it had to be killed," he lamented. "Gentlemen, this would have been the attraction to end all attractions. Bigger than the Wild Man of Borneo and the Siamese twins rolled into one. But what in blue blazes is it? It looks like a lizard."

"Precisely, Mr. Barnum," Phipps explained. "A giant lizard called the monitor, or Komodo dragon. If you had an *authentic* Wild Man of

Borneo he'd know of it, since this beast is found on the nearby island of Java."

"Well, I'll be dundered. I've got to get me one. Are they man eaters?"

"According to the Dutch zoologist I dined with last night, they have been known to eat a wild pig or a small deer at times. I felt it best to take no chances on when this beast had last eaten."

"So *this* is what frightened Clara Tuttle to death," Fenley observed. "But how about the dead men?"

"Ah, that's a different kind of monster," Phipps said. "Let's get to work, Flanagan."

Skirting the beast's body, they followed Phipps further up the Wall Street tunnel until they came to a large gatelike structure that blocked their way. Closer examination showed it was made of wood and it was easily unhinged from the bulkhead. While Flanagan and Cody took it down, Phipps explained that the temporary gate was to keep the lizard in the far end of the tunnel. Once the gate was removed, Phipps was on his way again, and for the first time Fenley noticed that he was pacing off the distance. Then suddenly he stopped, turned to the north wall, and said to Flanagan, "It's here someplace, Sean. Let your seasoned eye do its work."

The Irishman held a torch close to the wall and examined it with infinite care. Then he stopped, ran his fingers over something, turned, and smiled. "This must be it. The seaming ain't natural," he said. He tugged at a piece of sharp shale and a door suddenly swung open, revealing another tunnel. This led back to a small crude lift, big enough to hold two men. Far above there was a clanking sound.

Fenley started to speak, but was shushed by Phipps, who beckoned them back to the main tunnel.

"Close it up, Flanagan. We'll wait for him here."

"May I ask who we're waiting for?"

"Why, Captain, I thought you knew, since you supplied the vital insight into the case." Phipps didn't finish for just then the tunnel wall reopened and an amazed Charles Rogan, dressed in miner's gear, walked into The Hawk's trap.

"Good evening, Mr. Rogan," Phipps said gaily. "Putting the finishing touches on the shaft yourself, I see. Too bad we had to interrupt before the Fourth of July. Now shall we walk down the rest of the tunnel to where you secretly ascend to your dock on the East River?"

"You've got nothing on me, Phipps," Rogan glowered. "I've done nothing illegal."

"Triple murder? Attempted robbery? Come, man, you're through, and you know it."

"Robbery? What robbery, Doctor?" Fenley asked.

"The robbery that was the purpose of this elaborate subway system. You see, gentlemen, we are standing under thirty million dollars in gold."

"There's no gold to be mined in New York," Barnum interjected.

"Oh, yes there is, sir," Phipps corrected. "Directly above us is the U.S. Assay Office, into which Mr. Rogan here had a shaft dug by Chaley Morgan and Lemus Dunn under the direction of Carl Dietter, the assistant engineer. Clever of you to use an Irish and a Welsh miner, supposed enemies, for the heavy work, Mr. Rogan. When they outlived their usefulness they were killed as part of the plot to get the tunnel shut down. Tearing their throats out was crude but effective."

"You can't prove a thing, Phipps," Rogan said confidently. "As far as I'm concerned there *was* a plot to rob the Assay. I uncovered this secret shaft tonight."

"And the Komodo dragon? Did it come up from the bowels of hell? How did you get past it? Come, Rogan, you're caught red-handed. The beast is yours, trapped by your schooner crew on Java and kept aboard the ship until it was needed in the final days of the plot. After you had used the tunneling skills of Morgan, Dunn, and Dietter, you killed them and put the finishing touches on the secret shaft yourself, using the dragon to scare off anyone who might venture down here while you worked and leading it back to the ship when the night's work was over.

"Now you would be correct in saying that all I've said is universally applicable and circumstantial, except for your one crucial mistake. You forgot that people fall in love and confide in each other. Carl Dietter was affianced to Clara Tuttle, the foolish girl who ventured down here seeking an answer to her lover's death and met deadly terror instead. You were as amazed as anyone else when her body was found, although you must have suspected she had seen the dragon. But it offered no problem, you thought, because it further compounded the mystery. That, Rogan, was your downfall. Dietter had told his future wife all about your plans for the Fourth of July, and she in turn told a friend, a Miss Mary Cooper.

"There were, of course, other clues that pointed to you. When Lockwood pushed for a night shift, you had to act because you needed an empty tunnel to complete the Assay Office shaft. Thus Morgan was killed ahead of schedule, probably with the help of Dunn and Dietter. Then, you were always sending Lockwood away on recruitment."

Phipps stopped. The smirk on Rogan's face had turned to a dark scowl so fierce it distracted everyone's attention long enough to give Rogan time to produce a derringer from inside his shirt—but not quickly enough to stop Cody's reaction shot that sent Rogan's body into a heap in the rock dust.

After the Broadway Squad had rounded up the five-man crew of Rogan's schooner and Flanagan had found the secret East River shaft, Barnum insisted on buying dinner at Rector's, where the group looked more motley than ever among the society diners.

"So you were working when I thought you were playing," Fenley said to Phipps, who was forking an oyster.

"Even when I went to the Met," he replied. "You see, in the second act of *Siegfried* the hero slays Fafner, the dragon. It's quite a dramatic moment. It's possible that's where Rogan got the idea in the first place. Anyway, through Alvary, the star of the opera, I talked with the creators of the stage dragon. In their opinon, the print wasn't man-made. Well, if it wasn't faked, and it couldn't possibly be a prehistoric beast, then it had to be something alive.

"Zoology provided the answer through the Dutch scientist who had worked on Java. The South Seas aspect put Rogan into focus. The question was why he would wreck his own subway plan. Brumm told us about engineering difficulties in deep tunneling, so I conjectured that the project was meant to fail from the beginning. But what would he want with an abandoned tunnel under Wall Street? Then I remembered my foot blisters, and it became clear."

"You did ask me to find out if the miners ever got blisters," Fenley said, "but I thought you were pulling my leg."

"Not at all. I said you gave me the vital insight, and you did. You recall I got some pebbles in my shoe while in the tunnel? Then, when we were passing the Sub-Treasury Building construction site you cautioned me to avoid picking up any more of them. That started a sequence of inquiry. Geologists at the Columbia School of Mines agreed that the pebbles found in the shale tunnel actually came from sub-surface soil—about twenty feet down—in the Wall Street area. They could have gotten there only if someone was digging a shaft to the surface. Deserted tunnel, the Assay Office loaded with gold, a three-day national holiday, a convenient schooner at tide's turning. It was simple once the plot was 'unearthed.' "

Pebbles, Fenley thought as he toyed with his food. Blisters. Phipps had been dangling the clue so his associate could share in the solution. And he would have, if Phipps weren't so damn fancy.

THE BEATINGS

Evan Hunter

AUGUST WAS A shimmering canopy of heat, August was the open mouth of a blast furnace, August was a hot cliché, all the hot clichés, and the city wore August like a soiled flannel shirt.

And in August, the bars were serving tall Tom Collinses or gin and tonics to polite society who drank to chase the heat. No one on the Bowery drank to chase the heat. Winter and Summer were twin seasons on the Bowery, merged together in a heavy fog of persistent memories. You drank to squash the memories, but the drink only strengthened them.

And in the brotherhood of wine, you somehow began to feel a sense of real brotherhood. Everything else was gone then. Your Trina was gone, and your agency was gone, and your life was gone, all poured down the sink like a bottle of sour wine. The others had nothing, too. The others were only faces at first, but the faces began to take on a meaning after a while, the members of your exclusive fraternity, the cast of the living dead. These were your brothers. Louse-infected, bearded, rumpled, sweating, empty hulks of men, they were nonetheless your brothers. The world above 14th Street was a fantasy. The Bowery was your life, and its inhabitants were your friends and neighbors.

If your name is Matt Cordell, there's something inside you that makes you a part of your friends and neighbors.

My name is Matt Cordell.

* * * *

My friend and neighbor owned a very bloody face. My friend and neighbor was called Angelo, and he tried to talk but his lips were puffed and bleeding, and the teeth in the front of his mouth had been knocked out. He had never looked pretty, Angelo, but his face was almost unrecognizable now, and the words that trailed from his ruptured mouth were indistinct and blurred.

"Who did it?" I asked. I was only another face in the ring of faces surrounding Angelo. The faces were immersed in an alcoholic haze, but the sight of Angelo was evaporating the stupor. We crowded around him like bettors in a floating crap game. He shook his head and drops of blood splashed to the sidewalk.

"Don't know," he mumbled. "Didn't see. Couldn't . . ."

"What do you mean, you don't know?" Danny asked. Danny was tall and thin, a wino who'd been on the Bowery for as long as I could remember. The rumble had it that Danny used to be a professor of history in a swank upstate girl's college until he'd got into some kind of trouble. Danny did not like violence. His dislike showed in the sharp angle of his shaggy brows, the tight line of his mouth.

"Didn't see who," Angelo mumbled. He shook his head. "Just like that. Fast."

"Were you carrying money?" I asked.

Angelo tried to smile, but his broken mouth wouldn't let him. "Money? Me? No, Matt. No money."

"A jug, then? Did you have a jug on you?"

"No."

"Then why would anyone . . ." Danny started.

"I don't know," Angelo said, puzzled. "I got hit on the back of the head, and then I was down . . ."

"Like what happened to Fritzie," Farvo said. Farvo was a fat man who blinked a lot. He blinked because he was trying to shut out the sight of a wife who'd shot herself in the head while he watched. We all knew why he blinked and so we never mentioned it. Men can become good neighbors when their common mortar is despair.

"And Diego got it like that too," Marty said. "Just like that, with nobody around. It's crazy, that's all."

"Do you think the cops, maybe?" Danny asked.

"No," I said.

"Why not?"

"Why should it be the cops? They've got no reason for wholesale beatings. This is about the sixth guy in two weeks."

"The cops are good at this kind of thing," Farvo said, blinking.

"Only when they've got a reason."

"Cops don't need no reason," Marty said.

No one answered him. We got Angelo to his feet, and we took him to the Professor. The Professor had once been a chemist, until he began sampling the drugs he'd handled. He still knew how to dress a cut. He'd helped me once, and he helped Angelo now, and when he was through with his bandages, he asked, "What are we going to do, Matt?"

"I don't know," I said.

"This is a community, you know," he said. "It may be the world's worst community, and maybe its citizens are all pigs, but that's no reason to turn it into a slaughterhouse."

"No," I said.

"You ever run into anything like this before? You used to run a detective agency. Did you ever . . ."

"No, nothing exactly like it," I said.

"So what are we going to do?"

"Keep our eyes open," I said. "We'll find whoever's responsible."

"You think he'd leave us alone," the Professor said sadly. "You'd think we got enough troubles."

"Yeah," I said.

Our troubles got bigger. Farvo turned up the next night. Farvo wasn't blinking, and he'd never blink again. Farvo had been beaten to death.

There had been a beating a long, long time ago. A private detective named Matt Cordell had found his wife in the arms of one of his operatives, a man named Garth. He had used the butt end of a .45 on him. The police hadn't liked the idea. The police had lifted Cordell's license, and Garth had taken Cordell's wife, Trina. He'd been left with nothing, nothing at all. Nothing but the bottle.

I started the way I had to start, in the streets. I kept my eyes open and my ears open, and the August sun didn't help my job because the August sun was very hot. When a shirt is dirty it sticks like glue. When your soles are thin, the pavement scorches up through them. When you need a haircut, your hair mats to your forehead, clinging and damp. I took to the streets, and I thought of gin and tonics and fancy restaurant-bars. I talked to Fritzie first.

Fritzie's arm was still in a cast. Fritzie's face had not been hurt too badly, except for the bridge of his nose, which was still swollen. The back of his head carried a large patch, and you could see the bald spot surrounding it, where the doctors had shaved his hair to get at the cut.

"Farvo's dead," I told him. "Did you know that?"

"Yeah," Fritzie said. "I heard."

"We figure the same guy who's been doing the rest. You think so?"

"It could be," Fritzie said.

"Did you get a look at the guy?"

"No," Fritzie said.

"Where'd it happen."

"On Houston. I'd made a big kill, Matt. Six bits from some society guy and his broad. You shoulda seen this broad, Matt, diamond clips in her hair, and her bubs all spilling out the front of her dress. It was her got him to give me the six bits."

"Go ahead, Fritzie."

"I got a jug, you know? Some cheap stuff, but what the hell, all wine tastes the same."

"So?"

"So I killed the jug, and I was walking down Houston, and that's when the El fell down."

"Did you see who hit you?"

"I told you. No. I got hit on the back of the head." Fritzie's hand went up to the patch, his fingers touching it gingerly.

"What happened then?"

"I fell down, and the son of a bitch kicked me in the face. That's how I got this nose. It's a wonder it didn't come out the hole in the back of my head." Fritzie shook his head forlornly.

"Then what?"

"Then nothing, as far as I'm concerned. That was all she wrote, Matt. I blacked out. When I come to, I see my arm there next to my side, but it's pointing up in the wrong direction, as if it was glued on wrong at the elbow. Matt, it hurt like a bastard."

"What'd you do?"

"I went to the clinic. They said I had a compound fracture. They set it for me. It was no picnic, man."

"You have any money on you?"

"Hell, no," Fritzie said. He paused and touched his patch again. "What do you think, Matt?"

"Jesus," I said, "I don't know."

Detective-Sergeant Thomas Randazzo was a good-looking man in a brown tweed suit. The uniformed cop led me into his office, and Randazzo rose, smiled, and offered me his hand, which I took.

"Cordell, huh?" he said.

"Yes," I told him.

"What's on your mind, Cordell?"

"A man named Gino Farvo was beaten to death a few nights ago," I said. "I was wondering . . ."

"We're working on it now," Randazzo said, still smiling pleasantly.

"Have you got anything yet?"

"Why?" he said.

"I'm working on it, too."

"You?" Randazzo's eyebrows quirked in smiling curiosity.

"Yes," I said. "Me."

"I thought your license had been yanked."

"I'm working on it as a private citizen."

"Maybe you'd better leave it to us," Randazzo said politely.

"I'm interested in it," I said. "These men are my friends. These men . . ."

"What do you mean, these men?"

"Farvo isn't the first," I said. "He just happens to be the most."

"Oh, I see." Randazzo paused. "So naturally, you're interested."

"Yes," I said.

Randazzo smiled. "Forget it, Cordell. We'll take care of it."

"I'd rather . . ."

"Cordell, you've had enough headaches with the police department. No look, seriously, I'm not trying to be a smart guy. I know all about that time with your license, and I know all about your wife this last time."

"What's that got to do with it?"

"Nothing. She wants to kill . . . what was his name? . . . Garth, yes, that's okay with me. But I know what it must have done to you, and . . ."

"That's all water under the bridge," I said. I didn't tell Randazzo that Trina had tried to set me up as a patsy in the Garth kill. I didn't tell him that she'd worn out her second husband, pumped him full of bullets in the bathtub, and then tried to hang the frame on me. Randazzo didn't have to know about that. And he didn't have to know how I'd felt about it, how it seemed like the end of the world, worse than the first time, much worse. Or how I'd come out of it with the feeling that nothing further could happen to me. Garth was dead now, and Trina was set for the chair, and that was it, all the memories washed away, except they could never be washed away. The motive gone, but the results remaining by force of habit. I didn't tell Randazzo all that.

"Water under the bridge," he said. "Fine and good, Cordell. Don't mess in this, please. I appreciate your offer of help, no, honestly, I really do. But you've had enough to do with cops. You've had enough to last you a lifetime." He paused. "Why don't you get out of the Bowery, Cordell?"

"I like the Bowery," I said.

"Have you ever tried to get your license back?"

"No."

"Why not?"

"That's my business. Randazzo, have you got any leads on this Farvo thing? Anything at all? Anything I can . . ."

Randazzo shook his head. "I'm sorry, Cordell. I don't want you in this."

"Okay," I said.

"You understand? It's for your own good."

"Sure."

"Don't be sore at me. I'm just . . ."

"I'm not sore at you."

"No?"

"No. I'm sore at whoever killed Farvo."

I talked to Diego, who had been beaten very badly a few weeks back. Diego had been the first, and we hadn't thought too much about it at the time, until the beatings took on the look of an epidemic. Diego was from Puerto Rico, and he didn't talk English too well. The scars on his face had healed by this time, but whoever had beaten him had left scars deep in his eyes that time would never remove.

"Why you bother me, Matt?" he asked. "I know nothing. I swear."

"Farvo was killed," I said.

"So? Me, I am not killed. Matt, I do not want another beating. Leave me out, Matt."

"Diego," I said, "I'm trying to piece together . . ."

"I don't care what you try to do. I don't want more trouble, Matt."

"Look, you stupid bastard, what makes you think this is the end?"

"Huh?" Diego asked.

"You going to stay inside all day and all night? You never going to come up for air? What makes you think you won't get another beating some night when you're lushed up and roaming the streets? You *might* be Farvo, next time."

"No," Diego said, shaking his head. "Matt, I don't know nothing anyway. Even I want to help you, I can't."

"You didn't see who hit you?"

"No."

"Tell me what happened."

"I don't remember."

"Diego, if you know something, you'd better tell me. You'd damn well better tell me, or you'll get another beating, right this minute, and this time you won't be so lucky."

Diego tried to smile. "Oh, come on, Matt. Don't talk like that, man."

"What do you say, Diego?"

He must have seen something in my eyes. He looked at me quickly, and then ducked his head.

"I dinn see nobody, Matt," he said.

"Were you struck from behind?"

"Yes."

"With what?"

"Something hard. I don't know what. Hard like a rock."

"A gun?"

"I don't know."

"What happened then?"

"I fell down."

"Unconscious?"

"No."

"What happened?"

"He grab me under the arms and pull me off the sidewalk. Then he kick me."

"He put you down and kicked you?"

"I don't know. It's hard to remember, Matt. He drag me, an' then I get a kick. An' then I get another kick. An' then he starts hitting me on the face, an' kicking me all the time."

"He kept kicking you and hitting you?"

"Like he have ten arms an' legs, Matt. All over me. Hard." Diego shook his head, remembering.

"Did he say anything to you?"

"No. Yes, wait a minute. Yes, he say something."

"What did he say?"

"He say, 'Come on, bum' and then he laugh."

"What did his voice sound like?"

"Well, it was high first, an' then it get low later."

"He spoke twice?" I asked.

"Yes. Yes, I think so. Twice, or maybe more. It's hard to remember. He was hit me all this time."

"What did he say the second time."

"He say 'I got him'."

"And his voice was lower you say?"

"Yes, lower. Lower than the first time."

" 'I got him.' Is that what he said? When was this?"

"When he start hitting me in the face."

"Did he steal anything from you—"

"I got nothing to steal, Matt," Diego said.

"I figured," I said. "Were you lushed when he got you?"

Diego smiled. "Sure," he said.

There were no further beatings for three weeks. This wasn't hard to work out. Whoever had killed Farvo apparently realized the heat was on. In three weeks, the cops would have lost their interest. In three weeks, Farvo would be just another grave with wilted flowers, Farvo would be just another name in the Open File. So for three weeks, the community that was the Bowery lived its normal life. For three weeks, my friends and neighbors went unmolested. But we waited, because we knew the beater would strike again, as soon as things cooled down. Once a pattern is established, it's difficult to break.

I waited along with the rest, but I waited harder. I waited by walking the streets at night. I walked down all the dark streets, staying away from the brightly-lighted areas. I walked with a simulated roll in my step. Sometimes I sang loudly, the way a drunk will sing when he's on a happy toot. I lurched along crazily, and I grabbed at brick walls for support, and I hoped someone would hit me on the back of the head, but no one did. It's not fun being bait. It's not fun when you know a fractured skull can be in the cards. And suspecting what I now suspected, it was even less fun. But I set myself up as a target, and I did my heavy drinking during the day so that I could be cold sober while play-acting the drunk at night.

For three weeks, nothing happened.

The hottest day of the year came at the tail end of August, as if Summer were making a last bid for recognition before Autumn piled in. It was a bitch of a day, and even liquor couldn't kill the pain of the heat. The night wasn't any better. The night closed in like a damp blanket, smothering the city with darkness. There wasn't a breeze blowing. The heat lay on the rooftops, baked in the bricks, shimmered on the asphalt. The heat was a plague that hovered over the city, a life-choking thing that stuck in the nostrils and suffocated the throat.

I started at ten.

I put on my drunken walk, and I staggered up the streets, stopping to panhandle every now and then, making it look legit in case I was being tailed. I didn't think whoever'd killed Farvo was the tailing kind of killer, but I played it safe anyway. The heat made me want to scream. It crawled up my back and under my armpits and into my crotch. It left me dry and tired, and it made me wish I was really drunk instead of just playing at it.

I didn't hit pay dirt until twelve-thirty.

The street was very dark. It lay like a black nightstick between the buildings, dark and straight and silent. There was no one on the street. I looked down it, and then I huddled against the wall for a second, like a drunk trying to clear his head, and then I started down it, walking crazily, stumbling once or twice. I passed an alleyway between the buildings, and I stopped against the wall just past the alleyway, hoping to draw something out of the black opening. I drew nothing.

I started walking again, and I stumbled again, and then I got to my feet and burped and I said "Son 'fa bitch" like a drunk cursing at the world in general. I didn't have to act very hard.

I passed a second alleyway, and I saw the shadow snake out over the brick wall an instant before the pipe hit the back of my head. I'd been waiting for the blow for three weeks, and I rolled with it now, my thick matted hair cushioning the strike a little, the roll taking away some of the power behind it, but not all of it, the pain still rocking my head and erupting in a sort of yellow flash. But the pain passed before I dropped to the sidewalk, and my head was clear because Farvo's killer was about to try the act again, the act that was always good for an encore.

I lay there like a dead man, and then there were footsteps coming from the alleyway, and I felt hands under my armpits, and then a high voice said, "Come on, bum," and the voice trailed away into a delighted kind of laughter, an almost hysterically ecstatic laughter.

My heels dragged along the sidewalk, and I tensed myself, waiting for what was coming, ready for it. The hands under my armpits released their grip, and my back hit the concrete, and then a shoe lashed out, catching me on the shoulder, hurting me, but I didn't make my play, not even then. Another kick came, and I tried to roll with it, waiting, listening in the darkness.

"I got him," the voice said, and it was a lower voice, just the way Diego had said, but it sure as hell wasn't the same voice that had spoken first. And then, out of the darkness, a third voice said, "Come on, come on," and I figured the full cast was there then, so I went into action.

The "I got him" voice was starting to straddle me, ready to use the fists he'd used on Diego and Farvo and all the other boys. I didn't wait for him to finish his straddle, and I didn't waste a lot of time with him. I jack-knifed my leg, and then I shot out with my foot, and I felt the sole of my shoe collide with his crotch, and I was sure I'd squashed his scrotum flat. He let out a surprised yell, and the yell trailed away into a moan of anguish. He dropped to the pavement, clutching at his pain, and I got to my feet and said, "Hello, boys."

I'd underestimated their numbers. There were four of them, I saw, and four was a little more than I'd bargained for. I-Got-Him was rolling on the ground, unable to move, but the other three with him were very much able to move, and two of them were blocking the mouth of the alleyway now. The third was a big hulking guy who stood across from me on the opposite wall.

"Having a little sport, boys?" I said.

They couldn't have been more than eighteen or nineteen years old. They were big boys, and the summer heat had put a high sheen of sweat on the young muscles that showed where their tee shirts ended.

"He ain't drunk," one of the boys in the alley mouth said.

"Not drunk at all," I told him. "Does that spoil the kicks?"

"Let's get out of here, Mike," the other boy blocking the alley mouth said.

The boy opposite me kept looking at me. "Shut up," he said to the boys. "What's your game, mister?"

"What's yours, sonny?"

"I'm asking the questions."

"And I've got the answers, sonny. All of them. I figured you for just one crazy bastard at first. One crazy bastard with strong fists and feet. But then things began getting a little clearer, and I began to figure you for more than one crazy bastard. I asked myself *why?* Why beat up bums, guys with no money? Sure, roll an uptown lush, but why a Bowery bum? It figured for nothing but kicks then, kicks from a deadly dull summer. And then I asked myself, who's got time on their hands in the summer?" I paused. "What high school do you go to, sonny?"

"Take him," Mike said, and the two boys rushed in from the alley mouth, ready to take me.

The boys were amateurs. The boys had got their training in street fights or school fights, but they were strictly amateurs. It was almost pitiful to play with them, but I remembered what they'd done to Farvo, just for kicks, just for the laughs, just for the sport of beating the hell out of a drunken bum, and then I didn't care what I did to them.

I gave the first boy something called a Far-Eastern Capsize. As he rushed me, I dropped to one knee and butted him in the stomach with my head. I swung my arms around at the same time, grabbing him behind both knees, and then raising myself from one knee and snapping him back to the pavement. He screamed when he tried to break his fall with his hands, spraining them, and then his head hit the concrete, and he wasn't doing any more screaming. I pulled myself upright just as his pal threw himself onto my back, and I didn't waste any time with him, either. I went into a Back Wheel, dropping again to my knees, surprising the hell out of him. Before he got over his surprise, I had the little finger of his left hand between my own hands, and I shoved it back as far as it would go, and then some. He was too occupied with the pain in his hand to realize that I was tugging on it, or that his body was beginning to lean over my head. I snapped to my feet again, and he went down butt over teacups, and then I reached down for him and drove my fist into his face with all my might.

Mike was huddled against the wall. Mike was the leader of these pleasure-seekers, and I saved the best for Mike. I closed in on him slowly, and he didn't at all like the turn of events, he didn't at all like being on the other end of the stick for a change, even though he carried a lead pipe.

"Listen," he said. "Listen, can't we . . ."

"Come on, bum," I said, and then I really closed in.

Detective Sergeant Randazzo was very happy to close the case. He was so happy that he asked me afterwards if I wouldn't like him to buy me a drink. I said no thanks, and then I went home to the Bowery, and that night we all sat around and passed a wine jug, me and Danny and Angelo and Diego and the Professor and Marty and oh, a lot of guys.

My friends and neighbors.

A PLACE OF HER OWN

Joyce Harrington

IF YOU ASKED me when she first showed up on the corner, I couldn't tell you. One day she just started being a regular part of the scenery, like Carvel's and Waldbaum's, and then she was always there. Summer and winter, rain or shine, she was there sitting on the sidewalk like patience on a monument. In the good weather she'd sometimes go across the street to the opposite corner where there was a tree and a mailbox and sit between them. But most of the time she would be scrunched down in a little covered-over space, like a shallow cave, right between Carvel's and the bank. That was her place.

I was surprised that the bank let her stay there where everybody going in or coming out could see her. Not good for business, if you know what I mean. I thought about saying something to the manager, but it wasn't my bank.

Once in a while she'd be gone. The first time I went by and she wasn't there I said to myself, "Oh boy! A good thing. Somebody picked her up. The police or the loony squad. Either way, a good thing. She's not making a disgrace of the neighborhood."

But the next day she was back, crouching in her cave, drinking coffee from a paper container and staring around with her crazy eyes. I can tell you, it gave me a shock to have those eyes staring at me when I wasn't expecting it, but I just walked on as if nothing had happened. I never missed a day of work in my life, and the only times I was ever late was when the subway got itself messed up. By the time I got to the station my heart had stopped pounding and all I could think about was squeezing onto the train.

After that I was always ready for her. I could see from a block away if she was there, and I could walk fast and keep my eyes looking the other way. Or I could walk on the other side of the street. But ready or not, something always made me look at her. Not right in the face, but at some part of her clothes or her feet or the top of her head. I couldn't go by without one quick look.

She always wore a coat, summer and winter. Sometimes she had it all buttoned up, other times slung over her shoulders like a model in a magazine. Underneath the coat she wore sweaters. Even on summer days when the temperature got in the nineties and everybody else was dying from the heat, sweaters. And baggy dirty slacks. I got the impression she wore a couple pairs of slacks at once. She looked like a great big bundle of old clothes. If you didn't look at her face, you could just walk by like she was some pile of garbage waiting to be picked up.

I took my vacation in August and went to Ohio to visit my married daughter, Ellen. I have to go to her. She won't come to visit me. When she got married, she said to me, "Momma, I hope you won't be hurt, but I'm getting out of this crummy town and I'm never coming back."

Well, I'm not hurt. Why should I be? It's pretty where she lives. Grass and trees around the house. Everything clean. She has a nice new car to drive around in. The kids, God bless them, almost grown up and never sick a day in their lives. Only they hardly remember me from one visit to the next. Their other grandmother lives nearby. She's a nice lady, I guess. The kids show me all the presents she gives them—ten-speed bicycles, a record player for Kathy, Timmy's racing-car setup in the basement. Those are nice things to give your grandchildren. I brought them presents, too—small things I could carry on the plane. Nothing special.

This time Ellen said to me, "Momma, you've been working over thirty years in that store. You could retire anytime you want. Wouldn't you like to stop working and come and live with us?"

She doesn't understand. It's not just a store. After her father died, rest his soul, I was lucky to get a job there. Ellen was only five years old. What does she remember about that time? But I remember how frightened I was the day I walked into the Personnel Office. Artie was a good man, but he didn't leave any insurance or anything else. He never expected to be taken off so young. So I had to get a job, quick, and I'd never worked a day in my life.

I was so nervous that day when they showed me how to work the cash register. Artie used to give me just enough money to buy food with and everything else he took care of himself. So it scared me to have all that money that wasn't mine passing through my hands every day. But I got used to it after a while, and I got used to having money of my own, too. So much for the rent, so much to live on, so much to save. And it's a good thing I saved because when Ellen got grown up, she wanted to go to college and that's where she met her husband. So it all worked out. If it wasn't for the store, Ellen wouldn't be living in her pretty house, with a dentist for a husband and two fine kids, and she ought to understand that.

Sometimes I think she's a little ashamed of me. Once, when I was there visiting, she had some of her neighbors over for coffee in the afternoon, and when she introduced me, she said, "This is my mother. She's a buyer for a big New York department store." Well, it was only a little lie, but I felt my face getting red. I couldn't correct her. That would only have made things worse. So I just smiled and hoped nobody would be interested enough to ask me any questions about my job. They weren't. Fact of the matter is, I am a saleswoman in the Ladies Foundations Department and that's where I've been for over 30 years. I'm not ashamed of it even if Ellen is.

When my vacation was over and she was driving me to the airport, she brought it up again. "You're too old to keep on working, Momma," she said. "Peter and I talked it over and we'd be happy to give you a home with us. I worry about you all alone in that awful little apartment. There's so much violence these days. You'd be safe out here with us."

Well, I had to bite my tongue to keep from saying what I wanted to say. The "awful little apartment" had been my home for more years than I had worked in Ladies Foundations. It was the home that Artie and I made together when we were young and I wasn't about to leave it now that I'm old. It had been Ellen's home, too, although she didn't seem to want to remember that she'd had some happy times there and there was always good nourishing food on the table.

What I said was, "I still have your bedroom suite. Good as new. Maybe Kathy would like to have it for her room. I could ship it out."

She laughed. "My God, Momma! Get rid of it. Give it to the Salvation Army. All pink ruffles and flounces, wasn't it? I can't believe I used to pretend I was some kind of movie star in that room. No, thanks. But whenever you're ready, you just get rid of all that junky old furniture and we'll set you up with a room of your own, a television, everything you need. Peter says we might be able to put in a swimming pool next year."

I thought about those things on the plane, and I thought about what I would really want to do with myself when the time came that I wouldn't be getting on the subway every morning and going to the store. It wasn't yet, but it would be soon. Three more years? It would be nice being right there to watch Kathy and Timmy grow up and get married. But the fact of the matter is that outside of Ellen herself, I've never been around teen-aged kids very much. They seem kind of large and noisy. And I have a television.

Small, but perfectly good. I got it on sale at the store, which, with my discount, made it a very good buy. And what would an old lady like me want with a swimming pool? I haven't been in swimming since Ellen was 15 and we went for a week to the Jersey shore, and even then I only got my feet wet up to my knees.

I took a cab from the airport. Expensive, but I was tired and the next day was already Monday and the end of my vacation. I'd have to go back to work. It was a heavy evening, humid and overcast, and the whole world was a dirty gray color. By the time we got off the expressway, it had begun to rain and the cab driver, like everyone else trying to squeeze through the weekend traffic, was scowling and muttering curses. For a moment I thought maybe Ellen was right and I ought to pack up and leave all this behind.

But then we swung onto a familiar street and home was only a few blocks away. I leaned forward to give the driver directions and through the rain-streaked windshield I saw her. She was crouched down in that little sheltered corner by the bank, a sheet of plastic tucked in around her knees. All around her she had boxes and shopping bags tied with string, and parked at one side she had a Waldbaum's shopping cart piled high with God knows what kind of rubbish. And right in the middle of all this she squatted, staring out into the rain. She stared right into the cab as we drove by and I felt sure she recognized me. It seemed as if she shouted something, but I couldn't hear her.

The driver said, "Which way, lady?"

So I told him where to turn, and in less than a minute I was paying him off with a good tip because he helped me carry my luggage up to the door. Before he left, he said, "How do I get out of this crummy neighborhood?" So I told him that and then I dragged my luggage indoors.

Home. I looked around the lobby and it was just the same as it always was. But for some reason I began to remember that years ago there used to be a red-leather settee and a couple of armchairs over against the wall. There was nothing there now. I couldn't remember when they'd been taken away. Then I remembered that on the wall, over the settee, there used to be a picture. Horses, I think. Or sailboats. Something outdoorsy. Now, if you looked very closely you could just about make out where it had hung, but the wall was so dirty everything had blended into the same shade of grimy green. The floor was dirty, too, and not just because it was raining and people had been tracking it up with wet feet. Whatever happened to the rubbber mat the super used to put down when it rained? I guess a lot of things had changed over the years, and I'd never noticed.

I pushed the button for the elevator, and while I was waiting I glanced over at the mailboxes. My neighbor across the hall, Mrs. Finney, had been picking up my mail while I was away, so there was no reason for me to check my mailbox. Still, I noticed that some of the little metal doors were bent and hanging loose. Not mine, but some of the others. How long had they been like that? And why didn't the super get them fixed?

Next to the mailboxes a sign had been taped to the wall. From where I stood I could read the big print at the top. It said: ATTENTION ALL TENANTS, and there was a lot of small print underneath. I was about to go and look at it, but the elevator door opened, so I dragged my luggage on and pushed the button for the sixth floor.

I don't know if it was because I was so tired, or because of the change coming from Ellen's pretty house with the trees and grass around it, or because I was finally seeing things the way they really were, but when I got inside my apartment and turned on the lights I could have cried. Nothing had changed in my apartment. Everything was just as I had left it. It wasn't even dusty or bad-smelling because Mrs. Finney, when she brought in the mail, would always open the windows and give the place a quick once-over, which I would do the same for her when she was away. No, it was something else, something inside me that turned on like a searchlight and made everything look shabby and old. Worn out. Like Ellen said, junk.

The living-room suite, that Artie and I bought with the money his folks gave us for a wedding present, was covered with summer slipcovers just like every summer. The slipcovers weren't as old as the furniture. I got new ones every few years or so from the store. How long ago did I get these? Whatever, there were holes in them and the brown plush underneath was showing through. That made me think of the places on the couch cushions and the arms where the brown plush was worn down to the shiny material. Old, right? Junk.

Same thing with the rug, the coffee table, the bookcase with Ellen's old books in it, even the draperies at the windows. Everything was old, shabby, faded, chipped, ready for the junk collector. Even the television was an old black-and-white set that I'd bought back in the days of Uncle Miltie and Howdy Doody. For Ellen.

I went into Ellen's room. I don't know what made me keep her room just the way she'd left it. Maybe I always thought she'd come back for a visit, in spite of what she said. The bedroom suite was a present I got for her when she started high school, so she'd feel like a young lady, no longer a baby, and have girl friends over to visit. I remember how proud she had been of her room.

This time I didn't turn on the overhead light. Maybe that's what made the living room look so awful. I walked into the room to where there were two little pink-shaded lamps sitting on the vanity table. I turned on one of those instead. The room was small, I have to admit that—smaller than the room I'd stayed in at Ellen's house. And most of it was taken up with the bed. I'll never forget the look on her face the day the delivery truck from the store came and the men carried that furniture upstairs and even helped put the bed together. When she saw them put the canopy on top, I thought she would never stop smiling and dancing around and squealing. "Oh, Momma! It's beautiful! I love it!" Those were her exact words. I guess people change.

Now, in the rosy glow from the vanity lamp, I could see that the canopy was sagging and the pink quilted bedspread and dust ruffle had turned the color of old underwear. The pink net skirt on the vanity table, which I'd made myself, was droopy and frayed at the bottom, and the white paint on the bedposts and on the chifforobe was dingy and gray. Maybe if I scrubbed it down . . .

The door buzzer sounded. I got my face ready with a smile because right now it would be very good to have some company and forget all this gloom that was making me feel like a worn-out piece of junk myself. But before I got to the door I took the smile away just in case it was some creep going through the building looking for old ladies to molest. Don't laugh. It happened in the next block. Thank God the landlord put peepholes in all our doors. I looked through and it was Mrs. Finney from across the hall.

Right away when she came in she said, "Did you eat yet, Lillian? I brought some Danish."

That's Grace Finney. Always worrying about whether people got enough to eat. A good person.

"I ate on the plane, but I could have some Danish. Why don't I make some coffee?"

She followed me into the kitchen, and again I noticed things, like the worn spot on the linoleum in front of the sink and the scars on the table that made it look like it had been through the wars. But I put it all out of my mind so I could tell Grace about Ellen and her family and how well they were doing. She put the Danish down on the table while I filled the kettle and got out the instant coffee.

"Did you read your mail yet?" she asked. "No. I can see you didn't. Wait a minute."

And she raced out to the living room where the mail was stacked on the coffee table and came back waving an envelope.

"Wait'll you see this," she said. "And there's nothing we can do about it. Not a damn thing."

It was unusual for Grace Finney to swear. She prided herself on being a lady and got her hair done every Saturday morning at Gwen's around the corner. So it must be something really bad.

I looked at the envelope.

"Open it. Open it," she said.

It hadn't come through the mail. There was no stamp on it and no address. Only my name, Mrs. Lillian Curry, written out in big black letters.

"We all got one," she said. "It came right after you left. It's a shame. A crying shame. Read it."

I opened the envelope. Inside was a single sheet of paper. I pulled it out and right away across the top I saw: ATTENTION ALL TENANTS.

"What is this?" I said. "I saw it downstairs but I didn't stop to read it."

"Read," she commanded. "You'll cry. If I tell you, I'll get so mad I don't know what I'll do. Old Mr. Zukowski in 2D, when he read it, he had a heart attack and he's still in the hospital. Nobody knows if he'll ever get out alive."

So I read. And then I turned the kettle off. And then I sat down on a kitchen chair, the one that wobbled a little. Coming on top of the way I was feeling, I didn't know whether to laugh or cry over what the piece of paper said. I guess it's safe to say I was stunned, because I just sat there with my head going around and the words on the paper getting all blurry when I tried to read it again to make sure it was really true.

What it boiled down to was this. The building had been sold and the new owner was going to tear it down. All the other apartment buildings on the block, too. In place of a lot of rundown little buildings he was going to put up a brand-new giant building with lots more apartments. We all had to get out within two months, because after that all the services would be shut off. We could all come back if we wanted to and get apartments in the new building. At the end they tried to take the curse off it by saying what a great thing it was for the neighborhood and how projects like this would help put an end to urban decay.

Urban decay. Junk. Everything was turning into junk. They wanted to turn us all over to the junk collectors. Buildings, bedroom suites, people, even an old dog wouldn't be safe. Could they give me a new body, a new life to live in the new building? I could feel words choking in my throat, and I must have made some kind of noise, because Grace was shaking me and bending over to stare in my face.

"Are you all right?" she demanded. "Don't you go having a heart attack on me. Here, I'll make the coffee."

She rattled around and pretty soon a cup of black coffee was on the table beside the Danish.

"Eat," she said. "It's from Dubin's."

So I ate a bite of Danish and I sipped some coffee. And I have to admit I felt better, but still not clear in my head.

"I'm leaving," said Grace. "I'm not waiting around while this place turns into a ghost building and the scavengers start breaking the windows and stealing the pipes off the walls. The moving truck is coming in the morning. I found a place out in Queens. The rent is more, but at least it's clean and they won't be tearing it down around my ears. You ought to leave, too."

"But I just got back."

"Yeah, I know. It's a shock. You need a little time to get used to the idea. But don't wait too long. You know what happens to empty buildings. It's not safe."

"Where is safe? Ellen wants me to go out and live with them. She says it's safe."

"She's a good daughter, Ellen. You ought to go. I wish I had a daughter like that. All I have is that bum, my son, who can't even hold a job. Forty years old and still trying to figure out what to do with his life. Well, I have to go. I still have a lot of packing to do. I just didn't want you to be alone when you got the news. You'll be all right now? Have the rest of the Danish for breakfast."

I sat there at the table for a while. The coffee got cold and a roach got brave and ran across the drainboard. I didn't even get up to chase him. I always keep my kitchen spotless, no food lying around, so the roaches won't come. But they come anyway. You can't get away from them in these old buildings. Maybe the new building wouldn't have any roaches. Maybe I could find a place to stay in the neighborhood, a room somewhere nearby, and move into the new building when it gets finished.

That's what the piece of paper said, that we could all move back in and have nice new apartments. But what about the rent? New apartments don't come cheap. And what would I do with my furniture in the meantime? How long does it take to build a giant apartment house? A year, two years? Come to think of it, how would my junky old furniture look in a brand-new apartment? Come to think of it, would I live that long?

I shivered. It wasn't cold, only like the old saying goes, somebody was walking on my grave. Wherever that would be. I'd never thought about that before, but now it came through like a *Daily News* headline. A place to die. I wouldn't be looking for a place to live. I'd be looking for a place to die.

It was crazy, but the thought made me feel better. I wrapped the Danish up in plastic and put it in the breadbox. And then I went to polish my shoes. Tomorrow was Monday, and I never went to work on Monday without polishing my shoes.

In the morning I put on a black dress. I know things are different now, but back when I started working in the store we all had to wear black dresses and I never got out of the habit. Sometimes I'll wear brown or navy blue, but that's as far as I go. Not like some of the other girls who wear pantsuits in turquoise or lavender. It wouldn't be right.

I ate the rest of the Danish I had started and had a cup of coffee. There wasn't much else to eat, and I would have to stop at Waldbaum's on my way home. There was one Danish left over, so I put it in a bag to take with me for my coffee break. When I left the building, the moving truck was already in front and Grace Finney's upright piano was standing on the sidewalk. She could only play *Chopsticks,* but she'd bought it years ago when her boy said he wanted to study music. He'd never even learned *Chopsticks,* but Grace hung on to the piano and used to let Ellen play whenever she wanted to. I walked away fast. I didn't want to be late for work on my first morning back from vacation.

The subway station was three blocks away, and as soon as I turned the corner I saw her. I didn't see her exactly, but I saw her shopping cart parked in its usual place outside the bank, so I knew she was there. I kept on walking fast, and I kept watching the toes of my shiny black shoes going one, two, one, two in front of me. I didn't look up when I passed her, and I don't know what made me do it, but I put the bag with the Danish in it on top of the mound of old junk in her shopping cart. I was trembling so bad when I got to the change booth, I could hardly pick up my tokens.

Th. only thing different about the store when I got there was that they had the new fall merchandise on display. When I had left, they were getting rid of the last of the summer stuff. But Ladies Foundations doesn't change much from season to season. A girdle is a girdle, even though they keep coming out with new kinds of fabrics and new styles. It felt good to be back, and right away before the opening bell rang I started checking over the shelves and drawers so I'd know if we were running low on any sizes.

Miss Kramer, the floor manager, came by before I'd gotten very far, and she said: "Good morning, Lillian. Welcome back. Did you have a good vacation? I'd like to see you in my office if you have a few minutes."

So I said, "Good morning. Thanks. Yes. I'll come right now."

I followed her across the floor and into the corridor behind the fitting rooms where her office was, all the way wondering what she wanted to talk to me about. It had been over a year since my last raise, so maybe that was it. I could sure use a raise if I was going to have to find a new apartment. I had a little money saved up, but the way prices were going higher all the time, it was getting harder and harder to save anything.

"Sit down, Lillian," she said.

So I sat down in the little straight chair in front of her desk and she sat down in the swivel chair behind her desk. She looked at me for a second and then she started flipping through some cards in a metal box. She pulled one out.

"Lillian," she said, "you've been with us for over thirty years."

"Yes," I said, feeling proud and smiling a little. It was sure to be a raise. It always started like that; how long you've been there and what a good employee you were and how you've earned a little extra in your paycheck.

"And you've been in Ladies Foundations all that time," she went on. "You've received five letters of commendation from the President, your attendance record is perfect, and your sales record is steady."

I just nodded and held my breath. I couldn't say a word. It was coming now. I just wondered how much it would be. My hands were getting clammy and I wished I had brought a handkerchief.

Miss Kramer took a deep breath, bulging out her chest, and looked at the wall behind my head. "Lillian," she said, "you're sixty-two years old. Have you thought about how you will spend your retirement years?"

"What!" I said. "No! There's plenty of time for that."

"Well, that's just the point," she said. "There isn't plenty of time. We're cutting back on staff, and we'd like you to take early retirement."

It was like a knife cutting into my heart, cutting off the blood, cutting off the air to my lungs. I couldn't breathe. I got cold all over. There was a pain somewhere inside that wouldn't stay still and wouldn't let go.

I must have scared Miss Kramer. She must have thought I was going to faint or have a stroke or something. She got up out of her chair and ran around her desk and held me by the shoulders.

"Lillian," she whispered, "are you all right? Do you want to lie down?"

"No," I said. And I shook myself a little, so she would let go. I couldn't let her see that I was weak enough to fall off the chair, so I held on to the seat with both hands.

She backed off a little but kept her eyes glued to my face. "Do you understand, Lillian?" she said. "You've worked a long time and you've been a good employee, but now it's time for you to take it easy. You'll get your pension and you'll always have your discount. And we'll keep up your medical insurance. We're not going to throw you out and forget about you. You'll always be a member of the family."

"No," I said. "I won't go. You can't make me. What about my regulars? They always ask for me."

"Lillian, nothing lasts forever. If I were you, I'd be glad to have a chance to rest and do what I want to do. Don't you have a daughter and grandchildren somewhere out west? Think how glad they would be if you could spend more time with them."

"No. I don't want to go out there and be an old lady stuck in a room with nothing to do. I've always worked. I'm a good worker. You said so yourself. These young kids, what do they know? Here one day and gone the next. Not me. I'm not going. You can't make me go. I'll talk to the President. He knows you can't run that department without me."

She sighed and sat back down in her chair. "Lillian," she said, "don't make it hard for yourself." She picked up a sheaf of papers and handed it to me. "Here's your retirement computation all made out and signed by the President. He'd like to wish you well himself, but he's out of town this week. Now if you'll just hand in your identification card, I'll give you your final paycheck and you'll be free to pursue a life of leisure."

"Just like that? Out?" I couldn't believe it. "You don't even want me to work today? Out on the street? No place to go? Nothing to do? After I polished my shoes?"

"There'll be a Christmas party for retirees. You'll get an invitation. Now if you'll excuse me, we're getting ready for Labor Day and you know what that means."

"You couldn't let me stay and help out?"

She didn't answer. Now I really wished I had brought a handkerchief. But I held back the tears and we walked back to my counter. I got out my pocketbook, handed her my I.D. card, and she gave me the check and that was that.

I stood there behind the counter for a minute, but then I started feeling funny, like I didn't belong which, of course, I didn't any more. I walked around to the other side of the counter, trying to feel like a customer, but that didn't feel right either. I wanted to say goodbye to the other girls in the department, but I was afraid that if I did I'd really start crying and that wouldn't do any good. So I just drifted away across the floor as if I was only going to the ladies room or the cafeteria for a cup of coffee.

That was the way to do it—a little bit at a time. I walked around the floor, through Sleepwear and Daywear and Robes, and I saw a lot of familiar faces behind the counters getting ready for business. But I might have been invisible for all the notice they took of me. I guess the word had got around.

By the time I got to the escalators, customers were beginning to spread through the store, so I just went along following this group or that group. All morning I wandered through the store, up and down the escalators, visiting all my favorite departments. But I didn't buy anything and I didn't speak to a soul. At lunchtime I ran out to the bank and cashed my check. I couldn't eat in the employees' cafeteria any more, but I did the next best thing. I ate in the restaurant on the fifth floor.

In the afternoon I spent a lot of time looking at things that Kathy and Timmy would like. And then I went to Home Furnishings and thought about how I would like my new apartment to look. I stayed there until quitting time.

After I got off the subway, I stopped at Waldbaum's. I bought a barbecued chicken, some cottage cheese, a head of lettuce, and two tomatoes. The street was full of people going in and out of shops and hurrying home from work. I was hurrying home from work, too, but not so fast that I didn't notice her. She was in her usual corner by the bank, staring and smirking at the people going by. I stopped, and for the first time I looked right at her. She didn't like that. She shook her fist at me and growled some words I couldn't understand.

I said, "Do you want something to eat?"

I didn't wait for her to answer. I think she was as surprised as I was that I had spoken to her. I pulled the barbecued chicken out of the bag and stooped to lay it in her lap. Getting that close to her was a revelation. She smelled. Well, of course, she did, poor thing. There aren't any bathtubs on street corners. Then I went home.

The moving truck was gone, and that meant Grace was gone. There really wasn't anyone else in the building I was on friendly terms with. No mail in the mailbox. Who was there to write to me except once in a while Ellen and once a month Con Edison? The building already seemed deserted. My footsteps made a hollow sound in the lobby and the elevator groaned like it had rheumatism. I wondered how many besides Grace had already moved out. Maybe I was the only one left.

I made a little cottage-cheese salad for my supper and went to bed as soon as I had washed my plate and one fork. Ellen was right about one thing, I wasn't getting any younger. My black shoes were good and strong and had low heels, but even so, my feet hurt and my legs ached clear up to my knees from standing up and walking around all day. I fell asleep thinking about the Labor Day sales and how busy we would be at the store.

In the morning I got up and took a shower just like always, put on my black dress and my black shoes that still had a good shine to them, and got ready to go to the store. I always put on a little makeup, not a lot because an old lady with a face full of makeup looks like death warmed over, but just enough to show I cared about my appearance. This morning I took a good hard look at myself. I had gray hair, and so did she. Blue eyes, both of us. My skin, wrinkles and all, was pale and soft with only a few age spots, while hers was coarse and red. Otherwise, we might have been sisters. I wondered if she'd eaten the chicken.

When I left the building, a man was hauling in the garbage cans. He wasn't the regular super, but I stopped to talk to him anyway.

"Where's Victor? Is he sick?"

"Who?"

"Victor. The super."

"Gone. All the supers gone. The whole block. They fired all the supers. Me, I just come around and do the garbage cans. But not for long. Another week or two, then no more. You got garbage, you gotta get rid of it yourself. Better you should get out, lady. You got a place to go, go. It ain't safe around here no more. Last night they broke in next door and cleaned out the empty apartments. Light fixtures, toilets, it's a wonder they don't take the wallpaper off the walls. Damn ripoff artists!"

He sent the garbage cans crashing down into the areaway as if they were the thieves in question. I walked away toward the subway. I certainly didn't want to be late today, not with Labor Day coming up next weekend. A place to go. I always had a place to go. The store was my place. I would always be safe there.

When I got to the corner by the bank, she was standing up. I think she was waiting for me. I had never seen her on her feet before, and I was surprised to see how tall she was. Somehow I'd always thought of her as bent and stunted, a dwarf, but she was at least as tall as I am, maybe an inch or two taller.

"Wait," she croaked. She rummaged in her shopping cart and came up with a bright yellow bundle. "Take it."

"No," I said. Even though it was a summer morning and already hot and sticky, I felt a chill.

"Take it," she growled, and shoved it into my hands.

I shook it out. It was one of her sweaters, a yellow orlon cardigan, wrinkled and raveling, with buttons missing.

"Put it on."

She looked so fierce that I didn't want to risk making her angry with me. I put it on. The surprising thing was that my flesh didn't crawl from contact with the filthy thing. Instead, I felt a kind of warmth spreading all through my shaking body.

"Nice," she said. "You keep it."

I said, "Thank you. I have to go now." And I went on to the subway.

The guard wouldn't let me go in the employees' entrance. I had to go around to the front and wait for the store to open. That was the first thing. The second thing was that after I'd been in the store for about an hour I noticed one of the store detectives following me. I knew her, a nice girl who'd helped me out several times when ladies would try to put on two or three girdles and walk out.

I stopped and said, "Why are you following me?"

"I'm not following you," she said.

"Yes, you are. Do you think I'm going to steal something?"

"No," she said. "Look, Mrs. Curry, why don't you go home. They're afraid you might do something crazy. They saw you walking around yesterday and we all have orders to watch out for you."

"Do I look crazy?" I asked her.

"No," she said, but her voice wavered and I could see her taking in the yellow sweater. Then I realized that I'd forgotten to put on any makeup that morning and maybe I hadn't even combed my hair.

"Okay," I said. I wasn't going to wait around for a third thing to happen, and I could see Miss Kramer sailing across the floor with a hard look on her face. I got on the down escalator.

It was strange getting on the subway in the middle of the day. No crowds, I even got a seat. I noticed that people avoided sitting next to me. The yellow sweater was like some kind of magical cloak that made a little wall of privacy between me and everyone else. I thought that over all the way home, that and the fact that the store really wasn't my place any more and I would have to find some place that was mine.

When I got to the corner near the bank there she was. Some kids were teasing her, bouncing a ball off the wall and making it go as close to her as they could without actually hitting her. She crouched in her corner with her eyes closed, trying to ignore them, but her lips were moving a mile a minute and she sure wasn't saying her prayers. I felt sorry for her and at the same time glad, because for some reason when I stopped at Waldbaum's I had picked up double what I needed for my dinner. Two little steaks instead of one, not sirloin or anything like that. Just minute steaks, but they taste okay if you put some steak sauce on them. Two nice potatoes to bake in the oven and some frozen peas. I guess I was thinking that I could eat one steak today and one tomorrow, but now I thought, "Why not have some company? Mrs. Finney is gone and there's nobody to talk to, and maybe this one could do with a decent meal. It would be my good deed for the day."

I shooed the kids away. They went, but not before they called me some names I'd never heard before and I thought I had heard everything. When

I turned back to look at her, she was looking at me. And smiling. At least, I think it was a smile, but it was hard to tell because one side of her mouth went up and the other side went down and there were a couple of teeth missing in the middle. But she seemed friendly enough.

I said, "Hi. Was the chicken okay?"

She growled something and started rummaging in one of her boxes. What she pulled out was a plastic bag, the kind that hot-dog buns come in, and she handed it to me still growling and smiling and getting very excited. I looked in the plastic bag. It was full of chicken bones, big ones and little ones, all the meat chewed off clean as a whistle. I guess she was saying thank you and wanted me to know that she had really polished off that chicken.

"Well," I said, "that's nice."

I didn't know what to do with the chicken bones. I didn't want to put them in the trash barrel on the corner right in front of her eyes, just in case she meant them as a present for me and I would hurt her feelings. So I put them in my Waldbaum's shopping bag. Her smile got even bigger, and she started nodding and making gobbling noises and pointing at my shopping bag. I got the idea.

"You want something else to eat?"

Oh, boy! Talk about hitting the jackpot! Her eyes got bright and nearly bugged out of her head, and spit started drooling down the corners of her mouth.

"Well, okay," I said, "but you'll have to come home with me so I can cook it."

That stopped her. She closed her eyes, sank back into her corner, and pulled her coat collar up around her ears.

"Suit yourself," I said. She was acting like a little kid, so I'd just have to treat her like one. "Come or don't come. It's up to you. I'm going now."

I crossed the street, but I hadn't got more than half a block away before I heard the shopping cart rattling and bumping along behind me. And that's the way we went home, me walking along in front pretending I didn't know she was following, and her pushing her shopping cart loaded up with everything she owned, which was junk.

When we got inside the lobby of my building, I kept on pretending she wasn't there, and when the elevator came I got on it and so did she without saying a word. But when we finally got inside my apartment I couldn't keep it up any more.

"Well, here we are," I said.

She didn't say anything, but she started looking around and picking things up and putting them down. I didn't mind because it was all going to have to go anyway, and if she broke something what did it matter because it was all just as much junk as what she had in her shopping cart. Which was parked just inside the door.

"I'm going to cook now," I said. "The bathroom's over there if you want to wash up."

So I went in the kitchen and did what I had to do. Potatoes in the oven, set the table, get out the frying pan. I had some sherry left over from Christmas. I'm not much of a drinking person, but every once in a while I liked to have a glass or two with Mrs. Finney. Might as well get rid of it, I thought. So I went into the living room to ask if she'd like some. She wasn't there. I thought maybe she got nervous and left. Nothing to be nervous about. But then I saw the shopping cart still there, and not only that, but she had put my pair of china robins that I'd won at the bingo at church years ago right on top of the heap of stuff in the cart.

"Well, that's okay," I said to myself, "if it makes her happy. It all has to go and it might as well go that way."

She came out of the bathroom and her face was about ten degrees cleaner, although the rest of her still didn't smell too good.

"Want some sherry?" I asked her.

She smiled that crazy crooked smile and croaked out a word that sounded like "Yes."

So back in the kitchen I went and got out some glasses and the bottle, and while I was doing that I got so angry because a couple of roaches crawled out of the breadbox.

"Dammit!" I said, although I hardly ever swear, and I quick got the roach powder out from under the sink. Boy, did I let them have it! I buried them in it. And I watched them curl up and tip over on their backs with their legs waving in the air. And then I poured the sherry. I had to stir hers around a lot because the way it is with oil and vinegar, it's the same with sherry and roach powder.

It wasn't that I thought she was a roach or something horrible. She was really kind of nice to have around. She didn't talk too much, and she had a sense of obligation which she showed by giving me her yellow sweater. The only thing was, there wouldn't be room for the two of us in the corner by the bank, and I didn't want to leave the old neighborhood, not even to go to Queens where Grace Finney was.

Well, she drank her sherry up right away, in one gulp, and held out her glass for more. So I went back in the kitchen to get her some more. And then some more. Pretty soon the bottle was empty. So was the roach-powder box.

I threw them both in the garbage and checked on the potatoes baking in the oven. They weren't done yet. I went back in the living room and she was sort of toppled over on the couch kind of snoring and blowing bubbles out of the side of her mouth.

I said, "If you're tired, why don't you come and lie down?"

I pulled her up and made her get off the couch. It wasn't easy, what with her being almost a dead weight and the smell and all. But I took her in my bedroom and let her flop down on my bed. She looked at me once, and I think she looked kind of happy. She gave a little growl and closed her eyes and that was that.

The potatoes still weren't done, so I decided the least I could do was make her look halfway decent. I took her shoes off. She was wearing an old pair of sneakers with holes at the toes, tied with string. No socks. Her ankles were crusty with dirt. I got a basin of hot water and soap and towels and a scrub brush. It was hard work, getting all those clothes off her and cleaning her up. And it was sad how thin she was underneath everything. I washed her like a baby and when I got finished she was as clean and fresh as a baby. I even washed her hair. And then I dressed her in one of my own flannel nightgowns and straightened her out on the bed and covered her up. She looked like she was sleeping, so I tiptoed out of the room.

Boy, was I hungry! By then the potatoes were done, so I put both steaks in the frying pan and boiled up the water for the peas. And believe it or not I ate everything. Every bite. Then I cleaned up the kitchen, because you never can tell. I wouldn't want to go off and leave a mess behind for someone else to see. I'd been thinking about it all, you see, and what I thought was this. She had a place in the world and now she didn't need it any more. I had no place in the world and I needed one. Now I would take her place, and she could have my old place, which was no place.

And what would happen when they find her? Who can tell the difference between one old lady and another? Who cares? They'll write to Ellen and tell her, "We found your mother." Maybe she'd come, maybe she wouldn't. Maybe she'd cry a little, and have the body shipped out there to be buried. I don't want to be buried out there, dead or alive. If she comes here and says, "That's not my mother," they'll say, "Then who is she? We found her in your mother's apartment." But she won't come. Anyway, maybe they'll never find her. If I know them, they'll just tear the building down and cart the rubble off to New Jersey, her included.

And all the time I'll be laughing. I'll be there in my corner. She'll be there. We'll be there. I never knew her name. That's all right, though.

We'll have a new name. Or no name. Who needs a name? I have this nice shopping cart and a place to go to.

She's always there, crouching down in the little covered-over space next to the bank on the corner. Rain or shine, winter or summer, she's there watching the people go by. It's not a bad life, and you learn a lot about human nature. It's amazing, the good stuff that people throw away. If it gets cold, there are places to go to keep warm, but after a while you get so you don't feel the cold. One thing, though. I always keep my shoes polished.

THE MEDICAL FINGER

Ellery Queen

IN WATCHING OVER the special interests of women since early Roman times, the queen of heaven has had more names, shapes, and identities than the notorious Sophie Lang. As Caprotina, Juno was worshiped by female slaves; as Sospita, the savior, she was invoked by women in their perils; under titles like Cinxia, Unxia, and Pronuba, she played the leading role in the ritual of marriage; as Iuno Lucina, her protection was implored by occupants of the labor stools; and on the Matronalia, the married ladies with their maiden daughters met at her temple in a grove on the Esquiline and made offerings. Also, not to be sentimental about it, Juno is found represented as a war goddess—a fine recognition by the ancients that, where the fairer sex is concerned, all is not moonlight and roses. The animals sacred to her were the goose, which is silly; the peacock, which is beautiful; the cuckoo, which has a monotonous voice and lays its eggs in other birds' nests; and the serpent, whose nature is too well-known for indictment. She is the goddess of advice and of money—of all things peculiarly interesting to women; and, of course, ever since the hapless judgment of Paris, when—as Hera—Juno was outbribed by Aphrodite, she has been the most jealous and unforgiving of the deities.

In short, Juno is all things to all women, and that is why the poet Ovid has Juno say that the month of June was named in her honor—June being the season of the year most favorable to marriages. "Prosperity to the man and happiness to the maid when married in June" was a proverb in ancient Rome. Multimillions of the sisterhood have put their maiden faith in it ever since, and the elder daughter of Richard K. Troy of Sutton Place and Palm Beach was no exception. She had always wanted a June wedding, and she got one—not quite, perhaps, as she had dreamed. But the calendar was right, she was dressed as a bride, and there was a ring—so the old saying came true, if only for a very short time.

Her father had named her Helen, for Richard K. Troy was that most dangerous of people, a practising sentimentalist. To Mr. Troy, in the beginning was the word; and since he had an easy vocabulary and a cliché for everything, he had made his fortune in the greeting-card business. His first child's name was a sentimental inspiration of his youth, and when Helen Troy grew to be a marvelously beautiful young woman, her father was not surprised; it was simply another proof, in the whole argument of his life, of the word made flesh.

He always regretted that he had not had the foresight to perform a similar service for his younger daughter Effie, the selection of whose name he had imprudently left to his wife. Mrs. Troy had leaned heavily toward propriety; and Euphemia, the dictionary told her, signified "of good report." Effie indeed grew up to be well spoken of, but the trouble was she entered conversations very seldom, being plain and always looking as if she were about to get down on all fours. Effie was Mr. Troy's cross.

But Helen was the apple of his eye—"the golden apple," he liked to say whimsically. "You'll remember that was the real reason the Trojan War was fought, haha!" Peaceable as he was, Mr. Troy said it not without a glow; an army of young men had fought over Helen from the time she was beginning to bud above the waist, and she arrived at Junoesque maturity by stepping lightly over a battlefield littered with bloodied noses and broken hearts. Mr. Troy had a moment of uneasiness after Mrs. Troy died when Helen, the vigilant mothereye finally lidded over, promptly trifled with the wrong kind of man. But Helen laughed and assured her father that she could handle the fellow, and Mr. Troy was fatuous enough to let the moment pass.

That was a mistake.

Victor Luz was a chunky young European with sprouting black eyebrows and really formidable hands. They were the hands of a peasant and he was ashamed of them, because his father—who was attached to one of the United Nations delegations—came from a Louvre of aristocrats and had long slim golden fingers like women's cigarette holders. Victor had come to the United States as a college student. At Princeton he had been persuaded to put his hands to use, and as he was agile and athletic, with a naturally lethal left hook, he had no difficulty making the boxing team. But intercollegiate competition brought out the depressing fact that when he was hurt, Luz forgot the rules and became a killing animal, gouging and punching wildly low and all but using his powerful teeth. In one bout he rolled to the mat with his opponent, a bewildered junior from Rutgers, and he was disqualified and dropped from the team. But he was charming and handsome, with continental manners and a great deal of money, and he was a social success from the moment he sublet a bachelor apartment · on Park Avenue after his graduation. He made rare appearances at Lake Success, where he was known vaguely to have some connection with his country's delegation. But he was seen regularly at horse shows and hunt clubs and he was a favorite of café society—even being interviewed under his full name, which included a titular prefix, by Sherman Billingsley himself on the Stork Club television program.

Luz was introduced to the Troys by Henry Middleton Yates, who had known him at Princeton and now sold bonds for a Wall Street house. Yates had been in love with Helen Troy since his first crew-cut. He was one of the warriors whose nose had been bloodied, but his heart remained intact; being a born bond salesman, Henry was undiscourageable. Long after most of his rivals had consoled themselves with lesser prizes, he was still in dogged pursuit of the Troy beauty. Helen was fond of him; he was good-natured, good-looking, comfortably manageable, and he had just the right promise of static electricity; she might, in fact, have married him long before if the battle had still not warmed her blood a little and . . . of course . . . her mother had approved, which she had not. Henry was aware of the two impediments to his happiness, but he was patient; he knew time would remove both of them. When Mrs. Troy died, Henry was ready. He threw Victor Luz at Helen.

Henry was a planner, and his plan depended on his knowledge of Helen and his shrewd appraisal of her state of mind. Adoration at arm's length would not satisfy her forever, and there were signs that the Trojan wars were palling. What she needed, he reasoned, was a final passage of arms, in which her appetite for conquest would be glutted. Victor Luz, thought Henry, was just the man for the job. Luz could hardly fail to be smitten, and Helen would lead him on automatically. There was no danger that she would fall in love with him or that his name would tempt her to do something silly: Luz was too foreign for Helen's emotional tastes and she was too sensible to sell her freedom for a title. He would amuse her for a while; then she would drop him, expecting him to accept his dismissal, as the others had done, with a broken heart but a sporting smile. What she would not know until it was too late was that Luz, when balked, forgot the rules. So he would be a bad loser, and the whole episode would end disagreeably. Henry was sure such an experience at this period in

Helen's life would drop her, finally and gratefully, into his lap.

And that was a mistake also, even though it all came to pass exactly as Henry hoped.

He brought Victor Luz to the Troy house, Luz was enchanted, Helen was interested, they began to see a great deal of each other, Luz pressed an ardent courtship, Helen played with him until her interest dribbled away, she broke it off—and Luz hung on. Helen looked at him then really for the first time. There was something alarming in the quality of his persistence, the quivering intensity of a sealed tank building up a pressure. He did not hang on like a gentleman, unobtrusively. He took to following her, threatening her escorts with violence, sending her wild notes, hounding her on the telephone, proposing suicide pacts, weeping on the garden wall outside her bedroom window, jumping out at her from doorways in broad daylight and falling at her feet. The climax came one night at El Morocco, when Luz made a scene so outrageous and humiliating that Helen fled in tears—into Henry's arms.

As far as Henry Middleton Yates was concerned, that was the end of the play. Unfortunately, Victor Luz was following a script of his own.

The morning after the scandalous scene in the night club, Richard K. Troy was peacefully finishing his decaffeinized coffee when his younger daughter Euphemia came in and said with unfamiliar vivacity, "Victor Luz is in the library asking for you."

"That fellow?" said Mr. Troy, frowning. "What's he want?"

"I don't know, Daddy," said Effie. "But he looks awfully stiff and correct. Maybe he wants to apologize for last night."

"I suppose I ought to punch him in the nose," said her father helplessly. "Where's Helen?"

"She won't see him. Anyway, she's in the garden with Henry Yates. I'll bet Henry would punch him in the nose!"

"I'm entirely capable of handling my children's affairs," said Mr. Troy, sounding the reverse; and he went to the library unhappily.

Victor Luz was seated on the edge of a chair, knees spread slightly, big hands grasping suède gloves and a Homburg over the head of a furled umbrella. His dark skin was quite yellow. He rose immediately.

"See here, Luz–" began Mr. Troy with a scowl.

"Mr. Troy," said Luz, "I call this morning for two purposes. I wished to abase myself before your daughter for having been so gauche as to make a public scene last night. But she will not see me. Therefore, sir, I address my apologies to you."

"Well, ah, yes. Yes, I see," said Mr. Troy.

"The second purpose of my visit is to seek your permission to ask your daughter's hand in marriage," said Victor Luz. "I am madly in love with Helen, Mr. Troy. I cannot—"

"—live without her. Yes, yes," sighed Mr. Troy. "It's surprising, though, how many of you fellows manage to survive. Mr. Luz, my only mission in life is to see my daughters happy. If Helen thinks you'd do it, it doesn't matter what I think. Go ahead and ask her."

"Ah, you are a great man!" cried Luz joyfully.

"Not at all," said Mr. Troy with a grin. "I'm just passing the buck to more capable hands."

But Luz was rapidly soliloquizing, "I have spoken to her of my love, of her beauty, and so on, but the word marriage . . . How could she have failed to misunderstand? I'll ask her now!"

At this moment the library door opened and the fair Helen appeared, followed by Henry Middleton Yates. Behind Henry hovered Effie, trembling.

Luz blinked as if at an unbearable radiance. He went to her swiftly, engulfing her hand. "Helen, I must speak to you!"

Helen laughed, withdrawing her hand and wiping it carefully with her handkerchief. Then she went up to her father and she said, "Dad, Henry has something to say to you."

"Henry," said Mr. Troy. "Oh! Oh, yes, yes."

"I've asked Helen to marry me, Mr. Troy," said Henry Middleton Yates, "and she's said yes. Is it kappazootic with you?"

Mr. Troy looked bewildered. For a cry came from an unexpected quarter, the throat of his daughter Effie. After that single noise, Effie became silent and mousier than ever; then she scurried down the hall as if cats were after her. Helen looked thoughtful and Henry Yates blank.

It was all too much for Mr. Troy, especially since in the very next instant Henry Yates was on his back on the library floor, giving a credible imitation of a man fighting for his life. He had been bowled over by the ninepin head of Victor Luz, and Luz now had his great hands about Henry's throat and was banging Henry's head against the floor. Mr. Troy was conscious of his daughter Helen making some unpleasantly shrill sounds.

"Descendant of body lice!" shouted Luz, his dark skin now magenta. "You will never have her! I will kill her first!"

Henry gurgled something indignant, and Helen whacked Luz's head with the handle of his umbrella. Mr. Troy found himself growing strong with anger, and then he found himself throttling Victor Luz so vigorously that, between the grip on his throat and the blows on his head, Luz released his hold on poor Henry Yates and fell back blanched and impotent.

Helen was on her knees beside her gasping cavalier, crooning solace. Luz got to his feet, fumbling for his umbrella. He did not look at either of them.

"I said I would kill her," he said in a bubbly voice to no one in particular, "and if she marries Yates I will."

"But that isn't all of it, Mr. Queen," Mr. Troy said a month later. "When my prospective son-in-law got to his feet, he knocked the fellow kicking, and you'd have thought that would be the end of it. But it was only the beginning."

"More threats?" said Ellery. "Or actual attempts on your daughter's life?"

"No, no, it was the beginning of an entirely new relationship. I don't pretend to understand young people nowadays," said Mr. Troy, using his handkerchief. "In my day he'd have been horsewhipped or put in jail, and no amount of crawling on his—I beg your pardon, Miss Porter, is it?—but this has really got me down."

"I don't think we follow, Mr. Troy," said Nikki.

"Why, he no sooner recovered from Henry's knockout than Luz was a changed man. Butter wouldn't melt in his mouth. Sucking dove—ate humble pie as if he enjoyed it. Apologized practically on his knees. Positively embarrassed me. The next day he sent Helen a bushel of orchids with the inscription, *With Best Wishes for the Coming Event, Your friend, Victor Luz*—he wouldn't go very far in the greeting-card business, I'm afraid, haha!—and he sent Henry Yates a case of sixty-five-year-old cognac; and the result of all this was that within a week Helen had forgiven him and Henry was saying he wasn't such a bad fellow after all."

"And within two weeks?" asked Ellery. "Because it's evident it didn't stop there."

"You're darned right it didn't," said Mr. Troy indignantly. "Within two weeks Helen had invited him to the wedding, because Luz gave a big party at the Versailles at which Helen and Henry were guests of honor and, as I understand it, spent most of the evening proposing champagne toasts to their happiness."

"How very sweet," exclaimed Nikki.

"Mr. Troy, I think, Nikki," said Ellery, "detects a sour note."

"Mr. Queen, I yield to no man in loving-kindness," said Mr. Troy earnestly, "but I tell you this man isn't to be trusted. I consider myself a judge of character, and I saw his face when he heard that Helen was going to marry Henry Yates. There was murder there, and not good clean murder, either, Mr. Queen."

"—and he's going to be at your daughter's wedding"—murmured Ellery.

"He's not only going to be at it," said Mr. Troy, waving, "he's to be best man!"

There was a silence.

"Oh, dear," said Nikki, "How did he get to be that?"

"He's stuck close to Henry ever since the fight in my library," said Mr. Troy wildly, "and apparently he's made Henry feel that the only way Henry can show there are no hard feelings is to let him be best man at the wedding. I've appealed to Helen, but she's walking on clouds these days and she thinks it's simply too romantic! I tell you, it's enough to—"

"When and where is the wedding, Mr. Troy?" asked Ellery thoughtfully. "And what kind of wedding will it be?"

"Quiet, Mr. Queen, very quiet. My wife died recently and of course a big church wedding is out of the question. I wanted Helen to wait a few months, but June starts on Friday, and she insists on a June wedding— June weddings *are* lucky, of course—and she won't wait another year till next June. So it's to be at home, with a very small and select guest list—immediate family and a few friends—this coming Saturday. . . . I'd have gone to the police, Mr. Queen," said Mr. Troy glumly, "except that . . . Would you consider coming to the wedding to sort of keep an eye on things?"

"I really don't think you have much to worry about, Mr. Troy," said Ellery with a smile, "but if it will ease your mind—all right."

"Thank you!"

"But wouldn't this man Luz," asked Nikki, "be suspicious of the presence of a complete stranger?"

"Let him!" said Mr. Troy violently.

"Mr. Troy's right, Nikki. If Luz knows he's being watched, he's much less likely to try anything. If, of course," added Ellery indulgently, "he has any such intention."

Indulgent or not, Ellergy did not wait for Saturday to make the acquaintance of Victor Luz. He set about getting to know him immediately, by remote control. In addition, Ellery confided in Inspector Queen, and the Inspector assigned Sergeant Thomas Velie of his staff to special duty, which consisted in following Mr. Luz conspicuously wherever he went. The Sergeant executed his assignment as ordered, grumbling at the affront to his professional pride. As a result, by the day of the Troy-Yates nuptials, Ellery had an approximate knowledge of Mr. Luz's life and habits, and

Mr. Luz had the certain knowledge that he was being shadowed. As for the dossier on Luz, Ellery found nothing in it of interest beyond repeated evidences that Luz had a beastly temper and went berserk occasionally, and that he came from a long line of European noblemen with a history of elegant sadism and, in the older days, refined savagery toward peasants, *pour le sport*. For the rest, Luz lived well and honorably on his father's money, and his personal life was neither more nor less questionable than that of any other young Park Avenue bachelor.

Nevertheless, because he was thorough, Ellery arranged for Sergeant Velie to attend the wedding, too.

"Acting the part of a detective," Ellery explained.

"What d'ye mean, acting?" growled the Sergeant.

"Private detective, Sergeant, ostensibly watching the wedding presents."

"Oh," said Sergeant Velie; but he went to the wedding glowering.

The June day was as rare as any bride could have yearned for. It was a garden wedding, with the high Troy walls invisible under thousands of roses and the river invisible beyond the walls. The bride's gown was by Mainbocher, the floral decorations and bouquets were by Max Schling, the catering was by the Ritz, the presiding clergyman was a bishop, and there were no more than three dozen wedding guests. And Juno Regina smiled down from the battlements of heaven.

As far as Ellery could see, he was merely wasting an afternoon healthily. He and Velie, in striped trousers, had arrived early and they had elaborately searched the house and grounds, making sure that Mr. Luz saw them at their labors. Mr. Luz had paled slightly on seeing the heroic figure of Sergeant Velie, and he had made some remark to the bride's father.

"Oh, detectives," said Mr. Troy, trying to sound careless; but he turned away nervously.

Luz had bitten his lip and then, impeccable in his cutaway, he had gone upstairs to the rooms set aside for the groom. When he found Ellery at his heels, he ground his teeth. Ellery waited patiently outside the door. When Luz, after a long time, emerged with Henry Yates, Ellery followed them downstairs.

"Who the devil is that?" he heard Yates ask Luz.

"A detective, Mr. Troy said."

"What on earth for?"

In the crowded room downstairs Ellery nodded to Sergeant Velie, and Sergeant Velie collided with Luz.

"Here, fellow! What are you doing?" cried Luz angrily.

"Pardon," said the Sergeant; and he reported to Ellery that their man was not heeled.

Neither man took his eyes off Luz for an instant.

When the ceremony began, Ellery was in the front row of chairs, directly behind Luz. Sergeant Velie was in the doorway of the reception room off the terrace, one hand tucked under his coat in Napoleon's classic pose.

Ellery concentrated on the best man, letting the bishop's murmur trickle over him. It had all long since begun to seem unreal and silly. Luz stood a little behind and to the side of the groom, looking properly solemn, and quite conscious of the watchful stranger behind him. Yates's big body was between him and Helen Troy; he could not possibly have reached her without interception. And the bride was too beautiful in her wedding gown to give credence to thoughts of death—far more beautiful than any woman there, in particular her maid of honor, who was her sister Euphemia and seemed precariously on the verge of tears. And Mr. Troy, to the side of the bride, kept his beetled glance directly on the best man, as if challenging him to violate the loveliness of the moment by so much as a thought.

Too silly for words . . .

"And now the ring, if you please," the bishop was saying.

The groom turned to the best man, and the best man's fingers automatically went to the left-hand lower pocket of his vest. They probed. They probed more. They stopped probing, petrified. A horrified titter ran through the garden. Victor Luz began to search frantically through all his pockets. The bishop glanced heavenward.

"For—for God's sake, Victor," whispered Henry Yates. "This is no time for a gag!"

"Gag!" choked Luz. "I assure you . . . I could have sworn . . ."

"Maybe you left it in your topcoat!"

"Yes. Yes! But where . . . ?"

Effie Troy stretched her skinny neck their way and whispered, "Your topcoat's in the clothes closet in the upstairs hall, Victor. I put it there myself when you got here."

"Hurry up," groaned the groom. "Of all the idiot . . . Darling, I'm so sorry . . . Bishop, please forgive . . ."

"It's quite all right, young man," sighed the bishop.

"Won't be a minute," stammered Luz. "So terribly sorry . . ."

Ellery pinched his nose, so when Victor Luz disappeared in the reception room Sergeant Velie clumped after him.

When Luz emerged from the house Ellery quietly rose and made his way to the terrace, where the Sergeant stood waiting. Luz was advancing across the lawn holding a ring aloft shamefacedly, and everyone was smiling. He handed it to Henry Yates with careful ceremony, looking relieved. The bishop, looking martyred, resumed.

"Now if you will repeat after me . . ."

"What did Luz do, Sergeant?" asked Ellery.

"Went upstairs to a hall closet, fished around in a man's topcoat, came up with the ring—"

"That's all he did?"

"That's all. Just beat it back downstairs with it."

They watched.

"It's all over!"

"And I had to miss my Turkish bath for this." Sergeant Velie sounded disgusted.

Ellery hurried out onto the lawn. The bride and groom were surrounded by laughing people, kissing and being kissed, shaking hands, everyone talking at once. The newly minted Mrs. Henry Middleton Yates had never looked more mythically happy, her sister Effie more realistically plain, the groom more dazedly successful, the bride's father more puzzled and relieved. As for Luz, he had quietly congratulated the bride and groom and he was now on the edge of the crowd, smiling and saying something to the white-cheeked Effie, whose eyes were tragically on her sister's husband. Mr. Troy was conversing animatedly with the bishop. Waiters were beginning to wheel out veritable floats of tables, and others were beginning to circulate with portable bars. Two photographers were busily setting up. The sun was mild and the flowers sugared the air. A barge beyond the river wall hooted its good wishes.

Ellery shrugged. Now that Helen Troy was safely Mrs. Yates, the gyrations of the past two hours seemed infantile. He would have to see Mr. Troy . . .

"Darling! What's the matter?"

The voice was the groom's. Ellery craned. The mob around the couple had stopped milling with a curious suddenness. Mr. Troy and the bishop had turned inquiringly.

With violence, Ellery shoved through the crowd.

"Henry . . ." The bride was leaning against her husband. Her cheeks were chalky under the make-up. She had a hand to her eyes.

"What is it, dearest? . . . *Helen!*"

"Catch her!" Ellery shouted.

But the bride was already on the grass in a broken white pile, staring into the sun.

Inspector Queen was definitely a menace that day. He had an unusually bitter altercation with Dr. Prouty of the medical examiner's office, a few searing words for the bewildered Sergeant Velie, and deathly subtemperatures for his son. Having already been exposed to absolute zero in the person of Richard K. Troy before the poor man was put to bed by his physician, Ellery was thorougly refrigerated. He hung about the proceedings like a fugitive drip of stalactite, ignored. Effie Troy was in her room in hysterics, in care of a nurse; Henry Yates sat on a chair in the reception room vacantly, drinking brandy by the water glass and not even looking up when addressed; Victor Luz was in Troy's library chainsmoking under the murderous eye of Sergeant Velie; there was no one to talk to, no one at all. Ellery wandered miserably about, yearning for Nikki Porter.

About the only thing everyone agreed on without argument was that it had been the quickest June marriage in society history.

Finally, after a century, the Inspector beckoned.

"Yes, Dad!" Ellery was at his father's side like an arrow. "Why the freeze-out?"

Inspector Queen looked positively hostile.

"I still don't know how it happened." Ellery sounded dazed. "She just dropped, Dad. She was dead in a few minutes."

"Seven minutes from the time the poison was administered," the Inspector said frigidly.

"How? She hadn't had time to eat or drink anything!"

"Directly into the bloodstream. With this." And the Inspector opened his fist. "And you let him!"

"Her wedding ring?"

The ring gleamed on his father's palm. It was a plain, very broad, and massive gold band.

"You can handle it. The sting's removed."

Ellery shook his head, then he seized the ring and scrutinized it fiercely. He looked up, incredulous.

"That's right," nodded the Inspector. "A poison ring. Hidden automatic spring on the inner surface of the band that ejects a hollow needle point under pressure. Like the fang of a snake. And this was loaded, brother. Right after the ceremony everybody was congratulating her, kissing her, shaking her hand. . . . Quite a gimmick. The handshaker exerts just the right amount of pressure on the hand wearing the ring, and wham—a dead bride in seven minutes. If she felt the sting, she was too excited to call attention to it. I've heard of the kiss of death, but the handshake of death—that's a new one!"

"Not so new," muttered Ellery. "Poison rings go back at least to the time of Demosthenes. And Hannibal, who killed himself with one. But those weren't like this. This is the *anello della morte* with reverse Venetian. In the medieval model the hollow point was in the bezel and scratched the person with whom the wearer of the ring was shaking hands. This one pricks the wearer."

"Medieval. Europe." The Inspector sounded very grim; he was an incurable softie, and the sight of the beautiful young corpse in her wedding gown under the June sun had infuriated him. "It's an antique; I've had it expertized. This is the kind of cute gadget a European blueblood like Luz might have had in his family locker for centuries."

"It's also the kind of thing you might pick up in a Third Avenue pawnshop," said Ellery. "Is it an exact duplicate—except for the mechanism—of the ring Yates had bought?"

"I haven't been able to get much out of Yates, but I gather it's not quite the same. It wouldn't be. Yate's ring, of course, is gone. The killer counted on the excitement and tension of the ceremony preventing Yates from noticing that the poison ring was a bit different when Luz handed it to him. Yates bought his ring two weeks ago and showed it to all of them except Helen, so the killer had plenty of time to dig up a poison ring resembling it . . . if he didn't have one handy all the time."

"When did Yates turn the regular ring over to Luz?"

"Last night. Luz claims, of course, that he knows nothing about this poison ring. He says—he *says*—when he went upstairs to the hall closet during the ceremony and fished around in his topcoat and felt the ring, he just took it out and hurried downstairs with it without taking a good look at it, and Velie confirms that."

"And then he handed it to Yates, who may have palmed it," said Ellery.

"Yates? The *groom*? Palmed it? I don't—"

"Suppose Henry Yates had the poison ring concealed in his hand. Luz hands him the innocent ring; Yates palms it and puts the poison ring on Helen's finger."

The Inspector seemed to pop from all directions. "Are you out of your mind? That boy want to kill the girl he was marrying? And what a girl! And in such a way!"

"I don't say he did, but you'll find," said Ellery, "that Helen Troy came into a wad of money, the instant she got married, by the will of her mother, who had an independent fortune. And Henry Yates is, after all, merely a bond salesman—a very smart bond salesman, incidentally, or he'd never have snagged the Troy girl. And you can't ignore the corollary fact that such a time and method of murdering his bride would give Yates the perfect fall guy . . . the man who handed him the ring, the man who had been rejected by the bride, the man who had actually threatened to kill her if she married Yates. Not to mention the psychological advantages to Yates in picking such a time for his crime—"

Inspector Queen said through his dentures: "You know what your trouble is, son? A degenerate imagination."

"It's not imagination at all. It's logic."

"It's rot!"

"And then there's Effie Troy," Ellery continued absently. "Effie is hopelessly in love with Yates—a strabismic jackass could see that. And it was Effie, by her own admission, who hung Luz's topcoat in the upper hall closet. Velie says none of the wedding guests or hired help had access to that closet, Dad. He had the staircase in view the whole time and he says only Luz and the immediate family used those stairs from the time Luz arrived at the house."

The Inspector fixed his son with a stern and glittering eye. "Then you don't believe Luz did this?"

"I don't see anything that pins it on him. There are at least two other possible theories, either of which makes as much sense."

"To you on cloud eighty-eight," rasped his father. "To my simple brain it's simple. Luz threatened to kill Helen Troy if she married Yates. That's motive—"

"One motive," said Ellery patiently. "There are at least two others."

"As best man Luz had charge of the wedding ring and had the best chance to substitute the poison ring for the real one. That's opportunity."

"One opportunity, and only equally as good as Effie Troy's and Henry Yates's," mumbled Ellery.

"Luz shook hands with the bride right after the ceremony—"

"So did a dozen or more other people."

The Inspector glared, turning an eggplant color. "If no evidence to the contrary turns up in the next twenty-four hours," he snarled, "father of a genius or no father of a genius, I'm arresting Luz for the murder of that girl!"

It must be faced: Ellery did not shine in the Troy-Yates-Luz case. In a lesser way, that June wedding was as unlucky for him as for the bride. Not only had he failed to prevent the tragedy he had been commissioned to guard against, not only was he an honorless prophet in his own house, but he found that he had suddenly lost caste in the eyes of his secretary. Nikki was Juno's messenger to her mortal sex; licit love and blessed betrothal had no more fanatical advocate on earth. The murder of a beautiful bride on her wedding day—more, with the first holy kiss of her husband still warm on her lips—struck Miss Porter as a more inhuman crime than the drawing and quartering of newborn babes. She was all for applying vigilante law to the monster Luz—she was positive he was a monster—and after reading the details in the Sunday paper she came to the Queen apartment, notwithstanding it was her day off, expressly to whip Mr. Queen into the proper bloodthirsty frame of mind . . . after telling him, of course, what she thought of his bungling.

"How could you have let it happen, Ellery?" cried Miss Porter scathingly. "Under your celebrated nose! When you were supposed to be *watching.*"

"Surely," said Mr. Queen wearily, "I can be forgiven for not anticipating that somebody was going to bump her off with a wedding ring? Even geniuses—to quote a certain relative of mine—can't be expected to think of wedding rings as dangerous weapons. We're not living in the days of the Borgias, Nikki." Ellery jumped up and began to walk about violently. "It was diabolical. The whole body of myth and folk belief that surrounds the institution of marriage got in the way. Did you ever hear of the medical finger?"

"What an odd way to change the subject," said Miss Porter coldly.

"It is the subject. The medical finger was what centuries ago the English called the third finger—not counting the thumb; their leeches used that finger in stirring drugs and potions—"

"Educational," began Nikki.

"—and it was believed that that finger was connected directly with the heart by a special nerve and that poisonous substance could come in contact with it without giving a warning. And that's the finger, Nikki, wedding rings are worn on."

"And poetic," finished Nikki, "but, considering what happened, a lot of malarkey, don't you agree? And it hardly puts Victor Luz where he belongs, does it? Why isn't he in the clink? Why did the Inspector grill poor Effie Troy and that poor, poor Henry Yates last night till all hours? What is everybody waiting for?—What's the matter?"

For Ellery had stopped in the middle of the room, stealthy-still and staring as if he were peering into the fourth dimension and being revolted by what he saw there.

"Ellery, what's wrong?"

Ellery came back to the solar system with an unmistakable shudder. "Wrong?" he said feebly. "Did I say anything is wrong?"

"No, but you looked—"

"Electrified, Nikki. I'm always electrified by my own stupidity. Get Dad on the phone," he muttered. "Try headquarters. I've got to talk to him . . . God help me."

"He's tied up," Nikki said when she had put the phone down. "He'll call you back."

Ellery backed into a chair and fumbled unseeingly for his cigarettes. "Nikki, a premise of this case has been that the pressure of a handshake, exerted a certain way, was required to release the spring in the poison ring. When you shake hands with somebody, which hand do you offer?"

"Which hand do I offer?" said Nikki. "My right, of course."

"And which hand does the other person offer?"

"His right. He has to."

"But on which hand does a woman wear her wedding ring?"

"Her . . . left."

"Merest detail, you see. Trivial. The only thing is, it solves the case and, of course, I forgot it until just now." From his tone, Nikki expected him to produce scorpions and irontipped whips. "How could a normal right-handed handshake have released that poisoned needle, when the ring was on Helen's left hand?"

"Impossible," said Nikki excitedly. "So it wasn't done by a handshake at all!"

"That's not the alternative, Nikki—it had to be done by a handshake. The alternative is that, since the poisoned ring was on Helen's left hand, *it was her left hand which was shaken.*"

Nikki looked blank.

"Don't you see? In the press of people around her just after the ceremony, the murderer came up and extended his left hand, forcing Helen to extend hers."

"So what?"

"So the murderer was left-handed."

Miss Porter considered this. "Come, come," she said at last, with no respect at all. "Being a wedding ring, it *had* to be on her left hand, therefore the killer *had* to give her a left-handed handshake, therefore he isn't necessarily left-handed at all."

The master, sorely tried as he was, managed a smile. "His crime, Nikki, necessitated a left-handed handshake. The brain is modified and restrained by the nature of the machine it runs. If a right-handed man were planning a crime that depended on the use of a hand, he'd instinctively plan a crime that depended on the use of his right hand. The very conception of a left-handed crime indicates a left-handed criminal." Ellery shrugged. "When the bishop asked for the ring during the ceremony and the groom turned to his best man, *his best man's hand automatically went to the lower left-hand pocket of his vest.* Had he been right-handed, he would have searched, or pretended to search, his right-hand pocket, because a right-handed man—when he has a free choice of sides and there are no conditioning factors present—will automatically reach for a right-side pocket. Victor Luz automatically reached for a left-side pocket, so he's left-handed.

"So for once," Ellery sighed, "logic comes to the support of a circumstantial case. Luz meant his threat, and left the ring in his topcoat deliberately to make it look later as if someone else could have switched rings, not merely himself. Dad was ri—"

The telephone rang.

"Ellery?" It was Inspector Queen's sharp voice.

"Dad—" began Ellery, inhaling manfully.

But the Inspector said, "I told you Luz was our man. Dumb as hell, besides. We traced that poison ring to an antique shop on Madison Avenue, and when Luz was faced with the evidence he broke. I've just got through blotting the ink on his signed confession. All that fancy big-brain stuff about Henry Yates and Effie Troy! What did you want, Ellery?"

Ellery swallowed. Then he said, "Nothing, Dad," humbly and hung up.

THE CORPSE IN THE STATUE OF LIBERTY

William Irish

SHE WAVED A dishmop at me. Not threateningly but to point up her argument. "And that's why you're no further than you are," she went on. "Ten years from now you'll still be a second-grader, picking up loiterers, pinching pickpockets."

"What should I do?" I said chaffingly. "Let them go?" I tweaked the dial and the pale-blue light flickered off the screen, left it looking like blank white paper. "Just because you don't like ball games."

"In your line, it's not what you do with your working-time that counts, it's what you do with your off-time. Tee-vee and beer, beer and tee-vee, that's all you ever think of whenever you have any time to yourself."

"Is that bad?" I wondered academically.

"Why don't you improve your mind? Why don't you read a book?"

"And wind up being one of these guys that needs glasses? In my job I've got to keep my eyesight unimpaired."

"Why don't you go to a museum once in a while? The city's full of museums. Look at the art works and statues."

I grinned. "That's dirty," I said firmly. "I did that once when I was twelve. I'm a grown man now."

"You're not a bit funny," she said. She took the dishmop back into the two-by-four closet—excuse me, kitchen—with her. She was hurt. A special kind of emotion, meaning I was the one who felt guilty. It never failed to transfer itself that way.

I went in there after her. Not in, just outside; it couldn't hold two at once. "Are you serious?"

"You know I am. I don't mind doing dishes, but I want to do them with elbow room and where there's a view."

"And looking at statues'll bring that?" I was willing but bewildered. I seemed to have her there for a minute. "It's just a step," she tried to explain. "A step in the right direction. It doesn't have to be statues. It could be anything. It's not the *thing*, it's what it does for you."

I was still bound to be funny. "You said statues, and it's going to be statues." I reached for my hat and showed it to her in my hand. "Look. I've got my hat."

"You'll probably get as far as Donovan's on the corner," she said skeptically.

I put down fifty cents next to her on the edge of the drainboard. "Cover that?"

"I don't have fifty cents," she said primly. "And I don't like betting anyway." But she was trying to keep the corners of her mouth turned down, and not completely managing.

I put down another fifty cents. "There's yours." I dipped my mouth to the back of her bent neck. "I'll tell you all about it when I come back. I may never do it again all the rest of my life, but right now, just this once, just this one time, I'm going out of here and I'm going to look at statues. Look at statues for all I'm worth."

She was trying not to but I could hear her laughing before I closed the door.

We were only seven months married, that was why.

Standing in the subway car riding downtown, my strap-dangling hips doing a lazy rumba-grind, forward and back, forward and back, to the jiggling of the train floor, I was hit by a sudden bright idea. Instead of getting a piecemeal education, a little at a time, looking at a lot of small-sized statues, why not look at just one large statue, the bigger the better, get my education in one big solid chunk, and get it over with then and there? Look at the time and energy I'd save. Then I could always say to her, scornfully complacent, "Why, sure I've looked at a statue. I've looked at it from every angle. No one in this whole city has ever looked harder at such-and-such a statue than I have. You have an educated husband, young lady. You don't appreciate him."

I started to make up a mental list, while the local stations went by like tracer bullets in the dark outside the car windows. I didn't know much about the large public statues of New York. In fact, this was the absolute first time they had ever crossed my mind, much less lingered within it, in twenty-eight years of incessant, nonstop thinking. I had a hard time getting any for my list. All of them had some drawback.

General Sherman's statue, in the plaza opposite the park entrance at Fifth and Fifty-ninth. *N-naa*. Not enough to it. Just a man on horseback. What could that do for you?

The statue of Columbus, in the middle of Columbus Circle. *N-n-nope*. Traffic conditions made it too hazardous to stand still and concentrate. Also, it was too high up to be easily studied; perched on the top of a long skinny column. I'd get knocked over or I'd get a stiff neck.

The Soldiers' and Sailors' Monument on Riverside Drive. Ineligible; it was a monument, not a statue. Had to be a single statue, not a plural one.

What else? There must be more, in a city this size. Wasn't there one down at the foot of Fifth Av—? No, that was an arch. Disqualified. There was one in the park, honoring some watchmaker, Bulova or Boliva, but I wasn't sure just where, and the park was too big to go around in looking for it.

And then it hit me. Or rather I should say, it soaked through. It had been there in front of my face the whole time, right on this grubby subway car with me, but my inner thoughts had kept my eyes dialed off channel, I guess, like sometimes happened on the screen at home. I hadn't been getting a clear picture.

The car placard neatly slotted into place above the window right before me said *GIVE!* in big letters, and then some small print about what they wanted the money for, and over at the side the figure of a draped woman, in blue, holding aloft a torch, with red rays streaking out all around it.

The Statue of Liberty, of course. What bigger? What better? A whole college course, in one huge lump! I'd come back from this one about like with a Ph.D. Man, I'd be *ed*ucated!

I stayed on to the end of the line, the Battery station at the island's tip, chased upstairs, crossed over to the ferry house, and put down the money for one round-trip ticket down to Bedloe's Island and back. It wasn't very expensive, either; one of the few things in town that must have stayed down at where it was before the war. When I compared it to a haircut, or a string of beers at Donovan's, I said to myself wonderingly: "Gee, education is cheap! That is, if you know how to go about getting it."

The little ferry that takes you down the bay to the Statue berthed, and everyone got aboard. There were roughly about ten others making the excursion with me. I didn't bother counting heads, but that was the impression I got with my inattentive mind's eye: just a shade under a dozen. After a brief wait for possible latecomers—of whom there were none—the ferry whistle gave a fragile bleat, and we were under way.

I'd never even seen the bay before, or if I had, I hadn't looked at it good. The waters made little scallops all around, as far as the eye could reach, as if a hundred thousand silver fish were poking their fins above the surface and then dipping them down again. Behind me, the skyscrapers were all bunched together on the very outermost tip of the island, like a collection of lonely totem poles huddling together to keep one another company. New York. I wonder what it's like *not* to come from New York, and see it from the bay like that; if it's like that when you *do* come from there, and see it like that.

The Statue came gliding over the water, getting slowly bigger all the time. First it was about the size of your thumb, and it kept going up and up and up into the harbor sky, until it was as tall as an office building. It was pea green, just like it is on the postcards that strangers send home from New York (never New Yorkers).

I know it did something to me, all right, just to look at it. It made me think about things I hadn't thought about in years; about being an American, and how glad I was I was. It made me feel in a way that I hadn't felt since I was a kid, almost. I don't know how to put it; sort of patriotic, and sort of romantic, and sort of daydreamy, making me want to do something that was of more service to my country than what I was doing. I mean, like being a jet pilot, or at least an FBI agent, instead of just a humdrum, everyday city detective.

But then on second thought, I cancelled that last wish out, because I remembered an FBI agent that I *had* known, sort of casually, a couple of years back. He'd spent six months, he told me, working on a hair, a single hair. Matching it up against other hairs. I remember I was standing chatting with him on the street one day when a woman in a pony-tail hairdo, wearing a scraggly fur coat, and leading a big fuzzy dog, happened to go by. His eyes sort of crossed, and his knees buckled, and I caught him just before he went down. I managed to get him into a taxi and turned him in at a hospital. He was all right again pretty soon, because the doctor who treated him was bald-headed and the nurses all wore their caps well down below their ears whenever they came into his room. They fed him lots of eggs and grapefruit and other smooth-surfaced things like that, and they let him play all the billiards he wanted.

The ferry nosed Liberty Island finally, and tied up at a long pier built on piles, that thrust out into the water. Our group got off, and made way for another small crowd waiting there to get on and go back up the bay to the city. The round trip, it seems, is only made once every hour.

The statue was even more towering than it had seemed, once you got up close under it. The stone base alone was six-stories high, and after that there was nothing but statue all the rest of the way up, until your eye got tired of following it. There was just room enough left over on the foreground of the island for a little green lawn with cannon balls for markers, a couple of cement paths and some benches. But on the other side, away from the city, there were a group of two-story brick houses, lived in by the maintenance staff, I suppose. Or perhaps the quarters of the commanding brass, this being an Army preserve.

Anyway, we went into the statue's interior through a thick, brutal-looking sheet-metal door painted black, and down a long electrically lighted stone corridor, and after a couple of turns came to an elevator. A spick-and-span one, too, that looked as if it had just been installed. This only went up as far as the top of the pedestal, and after that you had to walk the other seventeen stories. If you did, you were now inside the statue itself. Those curving thicknesses around you were the reverse side of the goddess' draperies. They do these things well in France, I must admit. The staircase was a spiral one only wide enough to let one person through at a time, and toiling up it was hard work, even for me with my trimmed-down weight and springy leg muscles. But several times on the way up a little platform would open out suddenly before you, with an ordinary park bench placed there to rest on.

Each time I got to one of these stopping places, there was always the same fat man sitting there heaving on the bench, with not much room left over for anybody else. When I say fat, I mean anywhere from two hundred and fifty pounds up. Probably more up than otherwise. My first impulse was to laugh; they always strike you as funny, I don't know why. But this was no laughing matter; I had sense enough to realize that right away. He had no business being in such a place and trying such a thing.

The second time I squeezed in next to him on the bench, he turned and looked at me dolorously for a long time, while he fanned himself, hat in hand. Finally, when he'd gotten over wheezing sufficiently to be able to articulate, he said, simply but poignantly, "This is murder."

Funny, you can hear that expression a hundred times a day, and it never means a thing. Then again, you can hear it just once, and it comes back to you later, and you remember you heard it. This was that once, the hundred-and-first time.

I said, not unnaturally, "Then why do you do it?"

"I wanted to show her I could," was all he answered.

His wife, I supposed, but I didn't ask him.

He heaved a jellylike sigh and looked down at himself. Not down, out and around. "When you're fat," he said—and there in capsule-form, I suppose, was the whole tragedy of his life—"when you're fat, you're always the one sitting at the table when they dance, you're always the one left behind when they climb."

What could I say to that? I'm not fat.

"Will she believe you, when you tell her you made it?" I brow-lifted at him.

"She's right along with me, to make sure I don't cheat." His answer surprised me; I hadn't noticed him with anyone. But for that matter, how could I say that? I hadn't noticed him even by himself.

"She go up ahead?" I asked unnecessarily. She wasn't here, so she must have.

"She's waiting for me up there now. Got tired poking along, I guess. To her it's no problem. She floats like a feather when she walks."

That gave me a picture of her, to some extent. Not that I wanted one, but it did.

I only asked him one more question, idly. Or is it ever idly that you ask? "Whose idea was it, yours or hers?"

"Mine," he said first. Then he said second, "Well, I don't know; you know how those things come up." Then, third, he said, "Mine, it was."

Hers, I said to myself, only he doesn't know it.

I was rested long before he was, so I got up and left him with a consoling, "Well, it'll be easier coming down," and went on up.

At the very top you had to push through a little turnstile, and then you were finally up in the head of the statue. The crown or tiara she wears, with those big spikes sticking out, has windows running from side to side in a half-circle. I picked the nearest one and stuck my head out through it. You could see for miles. All New York was like some little toy game that children were playing at. The skyscrapers were mostly stubby now, like worn-down sticks of white and gray and tan chalk. The boats in the harbor were the size of matchboxes. When I craned my neck and looked straight down, the cannon balls on the lawn below looked like raisins in a pudding.

I stayed there awhile like that, dreaming the dreams you do in such a place. In the beginning there were people at nearly all the other windows, but one by one they drifted down again, until there was no one left any more but the woman standing alone at the next window over from mine. I noticed her as I turned away to go down myself. Amusing herself by inscribing her initials on the thick stone facing of the window embrasure, which was about a foot deep and wider at the outside than at the inside, the tiara being a semicircle as I've said. That was nothing; they all do that, whenever they visit any monument or point of interest like this. The window facings were all loaded with names, initials, dates, addresses; crawling with them, every square inch. They looked like bugs, going at all different angles, that have all stopped moving for a second as your eye falls on them. She was using an eyebrow pencil to do hers. I could see the little gold cylinder in her hand.

By that time we were the last two up there. By that token, I figured her to be the wife of the poor fat fellow who was suffering so down below there. She was the only one still up here, so she must be waiting for him to finally make the top and join her. Privately, I had my doubts that he ever would make it, but it was none of my business either way. The ferry was on its way back from the Battery to pick us up by this time, so I started down myself and left her alone up there behind me. She didn't even turn her head at the clatter my shoes made on the corrugated-iron stair slats. Lost in a world of her own, dreaming her kind of dreams just like I'd dreamed my own kind standing there myself like that. I wondered idly for a moment what her kind were like; that her husband was thin, I suppose, and could lead her a marvelous mambo.

I looked her over from the back, and then my head dipped down out of sight, and she was over. The heels of her stockings were arrows, pointing as if to show which way was up. Her dress was like a glove worn on the body instead of on the hand. Her hair was the color of charcoal, with a little help, I guess. The back of her neck looked like that of a man who needs a haircut. I've heard my wife call this the Italian cut. They stick their heads in front of an electric fan, I guess, and when it gets blown every which way, that's it.

She was some eyeful. I wouldn't have married her on a bet.

You went down by a different staircase than you came up. I mean it was the same spiral structure, but a different branch of it. You were on the outside track this time, and there was no partition between, just a handrail. There were lights all along the stairs at regular intervals, of course. There had to be, or the place would have been pitch-dark. Some were just ordinary house bulbs, others were small searchlights turned outward against the lining of the statue, which was painted silver. In other words, anyone who was going up while you were coming down had to pass you in full view, almost rub elbows with you; there was no other way. And no one did, I was alone on that staircase the whole time. The entire boatload who had come out with me were down below by this time, except for Slenderella, waiting up there all alone for her man.

He'd quit, as I'd expected him to, and gone on down again without trying any more. He wasn't there where I'd left him, when I got down level with the first resting platform. The first on the way down, the last on the way up. Something caught my eye, though, just as I was making the turn that took me below it. I stepped back, and reached under the rail, and pulled out a discarded hat, which had rolled under the bench.

The shadow wouldn't let you see it from above; it was only when your face got down to flooring-level like mine was now that you could make it out.

I looked it over. It was his all right, I'd seen him swinging it in his hand to try to make some air. The sweat band was as soaked as a just-used bathing cap. It was a Knox, and P.C. were the initials.

I thought: "He sure must have been in bad shape, if he even had to leave this behind him, climb down without it. Maybe he had a dizzy spell or something, from overexertion." I took it with me and went on down, to try to locate him and hand it back to him.

When I got to where the elevators started from, and the car had come up for me, I asked the operator: "What happened to that fat fellow, know the one I mean? Anything go wrong with him? I picked up his hat on the stairs just now."

"I haven't seen him," he said. "He must be still up there."

"He isn't, I tell you," I insisted. "I just came down from there myself. You must have taken him down without noticing."

"How can you take him down without noticing?" he protested, not unreasonably.

"Well, how can he still be up there without me noticing?" I argued. "It works both ways."

"Tell you where he might be," he suggested. "Outside there on that parapet that runs all around us, here where we are now. Right out through there, see it? They all go out there for a last look through the telescope before they get back in the car to go down."

"Well, hold your car up here for me a minute until I find out." I went out and made a complete circuit of the place, then doubled back and did it the other way around. It was a sort of terrace that ran around the top of the base, protected by a waist-high stone ledge on all four sides. It was a great deal lower than the head of Miss Liberty, of course, but still quite high. There wasn't a soul on it.

I went back inside. "Nothing doing," I told the operator. "You sure you didn't take him down in your car without knowing it?"

"How you going to do that?" he said. "When he got on the first time he almost flattened me against my own door squeezing by. I woulda felt it just as much the second time. I ain't seen him since."

"Are there any lavatories or rest rooms along those stairs?"

"Naw," he said. "We ain't got any."

"Don't say 'ain't' so much," I corrected him. "This is a cultural monument."

"Why ain't ain't all right?" he wanted to know artlessly.

I squeezed my eyes tight and grimaced painfully. "Now it's coming in twos. Because ain't isn't all right."

"But you just said it y—"

"Because isn't ain't all right," I hurriedly reshuffled it.

"But you keep saying it y—"

"Because isn't isn't all right," I finally straightened it out.

"But you said it was ain't that ain't all right. Now you say it's isn't that ain't all right."

I took one of those deep-down safety-valve sighs. I dropped my voice confidentially, like you do reasoning with a kid brother. I even placed my hand on his shoulder—mostly because I didn't trust it and I wanted it where I could keep my eye on it. "Look," I pleaded with him. "I don't want to hit you. You're younger than I am. You're earning an honest living. You probably have a mother. But you use that word once more!"

He just gulped, and gave me big round goggle-eyes.

I simmered down finally. "How'd we get on this grammar-kick anyway?" I wanted to know testily. "We've got a problem. Or at least I have. Let's get back to it."

"Yes-s, s-sir," he whispered cautiously, as though checking every word before it got out, to make sure a you-know-what hadn't slipped in among them unaware.

"Do you think, maybe," I suggested, "he walked down the rest of the way, from here, without waiting for you?"

"No, sir," he said with conviction. "None of them have ever done that yet, in all the years I've been on this job. That's what the elevator's here for. Even kids have had enough leg-work to wear them out by the time they get back down to this point again."

"It just doesn't add up, that's all," I said dissatisfiedly. "Better take me on down to the bottom, to see if I can find out anything down there."

He started to throw the switch, then held it for a moment. I saw his face light up, as if a very agreeable, one might almost say welcome, thought had just occurred to him. "Sa-ay," he drawled hopefully, "maybe he—You don't suppose he—? Maybe that's why you can't find him!"

I knew what he was driving at. "What're you trying to tell me, he took a jump over for himself?" I said scornfully. "Those observation windows up in the head are only slits; nobody could squirm through them. The stairs are all closed in. That leaves only this terrace outside here, and for him even that would be a physical impossibility. The ledge is too wide even for him to get up on it, much less across and over. If he pushed his middle up against it, his arms would be held too far back to even get a grip on it. And as far as lifting himself. . . ."

His face dropped disappointedly. "They never try anything from here," he complained. "They always pick bridges and stuff like that instead."

"You're a nice cheerful customer," I rebuked him. "I'm going to call you Suicide Johnny. Why you so anxious to—?"

"Aw, you don't know how monotonous it gets," he confided disgruntedly. "All day long all I do is shinny up and down this shaft. They get on, they get off. Then more get on. Then *they* get off. Nothing ever happens here."

"I think you need watching," I told him severely.

I couldn't reform him. "Even when I break for lunch," he rebelled, "what do I get to see? Sea gulls and water. Water and sea gulls. Just once, if something would only happen around here! Just once!"

"Cheer up," I told him disapprovingly. "Unless I find that guy somewhere around down below, it looks like your wish is building itself up to come true, right here, now and today!"

When he let me out at ground-level I made straight for the concession pavilion down near the pier, where most of the ten who had come out with me were hanging around buying postcards and ice-cream cones, waiting for the ferry to pull in. It wasn't more than fifty yards away by this time, coasting in a big half-circle from the right to get into position, with its engine already cut off.

The fat man wasn't in the refreshment house; one look inside from the doorway told me that. I asked one or two of the others if they'd seen him since they'd come out of the statue. Nobody had, although plenty had noticed him inside earlier, toiling up the stairs, just as I had.

"He must be around someplace," one of them reassured me indifferently. "Couldn't very well get off the island until the ferry came back for him."

"No kidding?" I remarked brittlely. "And here I've been thinking the whole time he went up in a puff of smoke, from overheating his bearings too much on those stairs!"

I went around to the other side of the base, along the cement footpaths with the cannon-ball trim. No rotund party in sight. I inquired at the dispensary at the back of the island, and even at one or two of the brick cottages the caretakers lived in, thinking he might have stopped in at either the one or the other, because of illness respectively or out of curiosity. No sign of him anywhere.

I completed my circuit of the terraced lawn that surrounds the statue and returned to the front of it again. It had dawned on me by now that I was going to a whale of a lot of trouble just to return a man's hat to him, but it wasn't the hat, of course. It was his complete disappearance that was an irritant, that kept sparking me on in spite of myself. It was the size of the man that burned me more than anything. I wouldn't have been so annoyed if it had been somebody less—how shall I say?—palpable, but to be as big as all that and then to turn into nothing. I wouldn't buy it.

The ferry was in when I got back and the passengers were straggling up the long, almost horizontal gangplank. It hadn't brought anybody out with it this trip, as the statue was closed to visitors after 4:30 each day and this was its last round trip.

I shoved the hat at one of the soldiers on pier duty as I went by. "Turn this in at the lost-and-found for me, will you? I can't find the owner, and I'm sick of carrying it around with me."

"Hand it in at the other end, at the Battery," he instructed me. "That's where they come and claim things."

So I was still stuck with it. But I was so dead sure of spotting its owner on the ferry, this being its last trip back, that I hung onto it without arguing any further about it. The landing platform was rolled back and we started to nose up the bay.

"He's got to be on here," I insisted to myself. "He's not spending the night back there on the island. And nothing that floats came to take him off between the time we all landed originally and just now, when the ferry called back for us." There could be no argument about that, because the ferry only made its run once every hour, and it was the only one in service.

So I started to hunt for him high and low, all over the wallowing craft. In the "saloon"—or whatever they call the between-decks part of a ferry—a couple of youngsters were sitting one on each side of their father, swinging their legs over the edge of the long bench that ran all around it, the way youngsters love to do. And a man who didn't give a hoot about the skyline outside was reading the sports column in the *Mirror*. (I wondered what he'd made the excursion for in the first place.) Nobody else.

On the port deck, which was getting the better view on this leg of the trip, the other half-dozen were sitting in chairs, just like they would on a transatlantic greyhound, only without rugs and without the stewards with the consommé, trying to kid themselves they were on an ocean trip. He wasn't there, either.

Then when I went around to the starboard deck (only maybe it was the port and the first one was the starboard; don't expect too much from a guy who has never been any farther out to sea than Coney Island all his life), there was the Lollobrigida-type brunette, whom I'd last seen mooning alone up on the observation platform of the statue, sitting all by herself staring broodingly at New Jersey. Not that I blamed her; to have to stare at Jersey is enough to make anyone brood.

She was the only person on that side. Which was maybe why she was on that side, for all I know. I walked slowly past her once and took her in, without turning to stare too much. She took in well. I mean, all of it was nice restful eye-work, every detail. There's a word I have for her. I used to think there wasn't any such word, but now I know there is. I first came across it in a fashion magazine my wife subscribed to. She left it open on the table, and there was a picture of a bikini—not just a bikini, but a bikini with someone in it—and underneath it said *svelt*. Just like that. Naturally, I figured the typesetter was Swedish and he'd printed his stuff with an accent. What he'd wanted to put down was *swell*, and it came out *svelt*. What do you want from a Swede, maybe only in this country six months. But my wife, after first rapping the back of my head with her knuckles, so that my nose mashed against the photograph (I was bending quite close to the bikini), and jerking the magazine away, told me solemnly there was such a word. And not to bother my head with it, because it wasn't going to be of any possible future use to me in my work. She hoped. She canceled her subscription to that particular magazine soon after, incidentally, and just let *The Christian Science Monitor* come into the house from then on.

So this deck-decorator was svelt, that was for her.

Now, I had no absolute proof that she had even made the excursion with him at all. Trying to recall, I wasn't even sure I'd seen her at all near him on the outward trip. She certainly hadn't at any time been right up next to him. True, because of his figure, you couldn't *get* right up next to him, you had to stand out at a certain distance, so that didn't prove anything, one way or another. The only thing I could be positive of was that he *had* had a wife with him, because he'd mentioned it to me on the stairs, so somebody had to be his wife. But which somebody? Everybody else was with somebody else already. Svelt looked like she was elected.

I stopped up at the other end of the narrow little deck and turned and started back toward her. Her eyes wouldn't admit they saw me. When I tried to corner them, they leaned over the other way as far as they could get, where there wasn't any me.

I stopped short right in front of her, tipped my own hat and said: "Pardon me, but I've got your husband's hat here." And held it out toward her.

She looked me up and down, and a lot of little icicles went tinkling along the deck. "That's a very good trick if you have," she said. "Because I haven't any husband—and therefore he hasn't any hat." And she gave me a look with pins and needles in it—all coming my way. "Clear? And I'm not interested in picking one up off a ferryboat in the bay!"

I couldn't help resenting this, particularly since I was looking at it from my own point of view, not hers, and you can't see two points of view at once. "Don't get *me* wrong," I growled. "I am a husband already. Somebody else's."

She hinted at a philosophical shoulder shrug without giving one. "That can't be helped; some women are just more unfortunate than others, that's all," she said with misleading compassion.

It took it awhile to sink in. Like some of those slow-working acids, when a drop gets on you. Then when it did, I didn't do much with it anyway. No man is ever a match for a woman in repartee. They have the claws, we just have the fists. "Oh yeah?" I said like they did in 1925. And "Is zat so?" like they did in 1927. And I finally came up with the 1940 snapper, "Hubba hubba." After that I quit, while I was still behind.

All of this was enough to sour a saint. First there's a fat man and a wife and a hat. (But not all three of them together at the same time.) Then there's no fat man. Next there's no wife, either. And it wouldn't have surprised me, before I was through, to find out there was no hat as well; that I was just holding my thumb pinched against my middle finger.

I unhitched a pencil. "Mind giving me your name?"

"I certainly would," was all she said.

I went through the bit with the badge, corny as it was. "I'm asking you as a detective, not as a would-be admirer."

She mumbled something that sounded like "Detective shmetective."

I'd never had it regarded in exactly that light before. It wasn't good for my ego. But then she wasn't good for my ego from first to last anyway. She had me over some sort of a psychological barrel, I don't know what it was. Maybe that business about being so svelt.

"Now do you mind?"

"Much as ever. But if you must have it, here goes. Just so you'll go 'way and leave me alone." She threw back the lid of her handbag and started fishing around inside, looking for identification I guess. Then she got taken up looking at her own reflection in the mirror and didn't go ahead. "I didn't expect a third degree like this, so I'm not prepared."

"One question isn't a third degree."

"Just having you hang around me is a penal sentence," she said charmingly.

I just waited.

"My name's Colman. Alice Colman. Address, Van Raalte Apartments, Tarrytown. Satisfactory?"

"For now," I said briefly.

"Oh, there's going to be more?"

"Let's hope not."

"You don't mean that," she said angrily. "You do hope there's going to be more. And if you've got any way of working it, you'll see to it that there's more. That's you police fellows, every time. That's how you earn your keep, by going around making something out of it, even when there's nothing to start with."

"We don't get paid for doing piecework," I remonstrated mildly.

She swung her legs around to get up, with a furious little clop of the heels.

"You mean you didn't notice this very hefty man on the way over?"

"How could you miss? He got in the way of the view half the time. But why marry me off to him, and turn me into his hat-check girl in the bargain?"

"Just asking," I said imperturbably.

"Just getting answered," she said heatedly.

And with that, our cordial little interview was over. She whisked herself off down the deck as if she couldn't stand me another minute. I watched her go, but I let her go. What could I hold her on, giving back-talk to an officer? She was svelt to the end. And I mean that just in the way you think you're mistaken in thinking I do.

When the ferry had tied up at the South Ferry landing, I stationed myself at the lower end of the plank ahead of everyone and stopped them one by one as they tried to go past. "Police Department . . . Name, please . . . Address . . . Anything to corroborate it, please?" And I took care of the inevitable "What's wrong, officer? What is it for?" with a reassuring "Just routine." What did they know if it was or wasn't, fortunately.

That way, at least I now had the identities of everyone who had been on the outing—all, of course, but the one identity that had started the whole thing in the first place, by being missing. And he was still missing, very much so. He had definitely not made the trip back on the ferry. And since he definitely *had* made the trip out on it, he had to be back there on the island or in the water around it. It figured. Alive, dead, or in a state between the two.

The last one off was the black-haired vamp, although I shouldn't classify her that way; she noticeably hadn't tried to vamp me. I'll put it this way: the last one off was the black-haired potential vamp.

She stopped. We looked at each other. We didn't like each other.

"You're going to hear about this," she said darkly. "I'm not through."

"You're very lucky," I told her with unruffled dignity (that was what it was meant for; I hope it came out like that), "if you don't hear about it first, even before I do."

"I'm going to call up right now!" she vowed, flouncing determinedly on her way.

"Next of kin of Wagner," I murmured sarcastically.

I pocketed my dossier of identities, went around to the ticket office in the ferry building. It was closed by now, of course, but they were still in there, counting out the day's receipts or something. I pounded on the little side door, and at first they thought it was a holdup, jumped like anything.

"It's all right, Police Headquarters. Let me in a minute."

I recognized the one who had sold me my own ticket, and therefore serviced our entire boatload, and singled him out. "Look, this last trip out, the one that went just now, do you remember selling a ticket to a very fat man? Puffy cheeks like this?" I blew my own up with air. "Blue suit, brown hat?"

No trouble there. "Sure do. I remember calculating the ferry's chances of foundering, with him on it."

"Yeah, but here comes the gimmick. How many did he buy, one or two?"

I had him there. "Wait a minute, now. Give me time, I'll get it. I've been selling them all day long."

"I know you have," I said. "But I want it, so try for it."

"I remember I had an argument about change—" he groped. "But I'm not sure now if it was with him, or somebody else."

"Don't you usually know who it's with, when you have an argument?" I wanted to know with a touch of asperity.

"But when one face follows another, sometimes the argument slips a cog, and lands on the one before, or the one after. That is, later when you try to recollect."

Movable arguments, I thought impatiently. Like on ball bearings.

"I can't make the connection," he said, palming his eyes a minute. "Wait, now. Just wait."

"I am," I said. "That all I've been doing, for the past seven-and-a-half minutes."

"It's coming back to me now," he said. "He gave me a five-dollar bill. . . ."

"The fat man?"

"No, the man I had the argument with. I'm not sure yet if it was the fat man or not. He gave me a five-dollar bill. . . ."

"That's ten he gave you already," I said nastily.

"No, five," he said, startled, and that nearly threw him in itself. He had a sick mind.

"He claimed I was a dollar short on the change I gave him. I said,

'Buddy, when I went to school, two times thirty-five made seventy, and five from seventy. . . .' "

"Never mind the sound track," I pleaded, almost agonized. "He did buy two tickets; you've just told me as much."

"Who?" he said blankly.

"Oh, no!" I groaned, all down inside of me.

Something else had just occurred to him, though. He turned his head away from me sharply. "Hey, Lou! You know what just came to me? I think I underchanged him sixty-five cents! That must be that sixty-five short we came across just now."

I quit. I gave up. I only wanted to die. Or at least, to get out of there alive, and then go off quietly and die someplace else.

"Why don't you try out for Police Training School?" I all but sobbed, as I opened the door and seeped weakly out. "They're awfully short of tackling dummies right now."

He just looked after me, hurt.

I hustled outside to the ferry again. It was still there, but readying to go wherever it is they go when they're laid up for the night. A couple of tattooed arms tried to bar my way up the gangplank. (Even on ferries they go in for tattooing, it seems.)

"Got to see the captain." The badge was getting oxidized from so much exposure to the damp waterfront air.

He came out of the deckhouse just then struggling into a lumberjacket, evidently going ashore to catch up on his suds. He looked sort of beery. But the badge didn't mean a thing to him. He was used to being in authority, even if it was only on a ferry.

"You're out of your head!" he boomed down to me, and it bounced off the buildings at the foot of Bowling Green and seemed to turn the whole harbor into an echo chamber. "This craft's asleep for the night. She's not going anywhere."

At least he didn't say "ain't." I told him about the hefty passenger who had made a one-way trip on a two-way outing.

"Well, then rustle up a police launch. That's what they're for. That stepped-on piece of tin you keep waving doesn't mean a thing. I take my orders from the company." And he executed the most graceful U-turn spit over the rail I had ever seen, a regular salivary horseshoe.

I wasn't sure I pulled enough weight to commandeer a police launch, and (whisper it low) wasn't even quite sure how to go about it; two facts which I preferred to keep to myself, if at all possible.

I went back down again, had it out hot and heavy with one of the agents in the ferry house; had him in turn telephone one of his superiors, get his okay, and then sign an order for me to take back and show the captain.

"Here's your instructions, admiral." He was drooling by this time and looking longingly in the direction of the dives along South Street.

He turned around and hollered an order, and back we plugged.

He wanted to know how long I was going to be, when I loped off again at the other end.

"Your orders were to bring me here and back," I reminded him. "So you just stay put until I show up again."

He sure could swear, in a sort of internal-combustion key; he had it pitched just right, so that you could get the sense of the words but they weren't loud enough to pin him down on it. But you knew you were being sworn at, the way his mouth slowly rotated.

The thick, chilly looking black metal doors that led into the base were already closed tight by this time. I had to get another permit from the commanding officer on the island, and two soldiers were detailed to come with me (I suppose so I wouldn't try to shoplift the statue). Suicide Johnny was routed out to run us up in the elevator. His blotchy face lighted up like a rashy sunrise when he saw me. He knew something bad was up. And boy, he liked something bad something awful.

"Gee!" he said gleefully, throwing the switch in the car. "This is the day I've been waiting for!"

"What do you feed this boy, red meat?" I asked one of the GI's. "We'll go up to the top," I said when we got out of the car. "And work our way down from there. Anyway, I want to take a closer look at some of those initials and names scrawled on the stonework up there."

"Aw, them!" said one of the soldiers contemptuously. "Every rubberneck that ever came out here since the place was built takes a crack at that."

We climbed all that weary way back again and finally stood there, panting like four forges going at once.

I had a close look, first of all, at what my friend—and I use the word loosely—Alice Colman had written, at the window next to the one I'd been standing at myself originally. She'd made it easy for me to pick out her work. Or I suppose she hadn't known there would be any me around to pick out her work. Second supposition: she'd wanted to make it easy for somebody else to pick it out. She'd used an eyebrow pencil and the mark it left was dark and greasy, different from the thin gray lead-pencil marks of the rest of them. It stood out like a freshly inked headline above columns of fine print.

It was an impersonal sort of thing, at first glance. Too impersonal. If it was going to be that impersonal, why do it at all? It didn't say Alice

Colman; it didn't say any name; it didn't say A.C., it didn't say any initial. It didn't even say Alice, and it didn't even say A. It was just eight numbers in a row. Oh yes, and one letter stuck in the middle of them, as if it had got in there by mistake. Like so:

$$424254W51$$

It wasn't a telephone number, because that only has five numbers, and two letters for the exchange, and they come in the beginning and not in the middle. Anyway, she wasn't the promiscuously flirty type. Besides, she wouldn't have had to write her phone number on a wall, even if she were. All she would have had to do was blink once, with one eye at that, and one whole exchange of the telephone company would have promptly broken down from overwork.

I tried decoding them. That's what you do with numbers.

I turned to one of the bored pfc's. "What's today's date?"

"Twenty-third," he said grudgingly. I could tell what he was thinking. Some detective. Doesn't even know the day of the month.

That's what I'd figured it for, too. But she seemed to have gotten her dates mixed. Well, you can't go to jail for that.

Assuming that she'd meant the date (and I had to begin somewhere) that left me with a four and a space after it. This was August, and four stands for April, so it wasn't part of the date, didn't go with it.

"How much more time you going to be?" one of the soldiers chafed.

Then I got it. That gave it to me. It was the hour. Four o'clock. She'd visited this place at four o'clock, and she wanted the world to know about it.

That left—but all I had to do was look at it, and it resolved itself automatically. Three numerals, a letter, and two more. A New York street address, what else? Two-fifty-four West Fifty-first. And not her own, either, which she'd given me as the Van Raalte Apartments, Tarrytown.

A date. I mean the other kind now: an appointment. That must be it. And that straightened out the supposed error in the day of the month. It was for tomorrow, not for today. Now it cleaned itself up like this: four o'clock tomorrow, at Two-fifty-four West, etc.

I thought to myself, you're pretty good. I might as well think it, nobody else was going to. "Let's go down," I told the GI's. "I want a look at that bench he was sitting on the last time." By this time they both hated me heartily from the guts outward, but that's one thing about the Army, they do what they're detailed to do. They turned and led the way.

We never got there, though. About midway between the head and where the bench was—in other words at about where the statue's shoulder came—

there was a slit or crevice in the stair facing, with a chain across it bearing a placard *PUBLIC NOT ADMITTED*. I had of course noticed this twice before: the first time I came up, and then later when I had originally gone back down to look for him. Maybe the chain had thrown me off, the undisturbed chain stretched across it. More likely it was this, though: until you stood directly before it, it looked far slimmer and more inaccessible than it actually was, the way the lights slurred past it and made it seem no more than a tuck on the inside of the lady's gigantic metal draperies. They tricked the eye, the way lights so often do gliding over a curved, a nonflat surface.

I stopped and asked them what it was.

"That used to lead up into the arm and torch formerly, sort of a branch staircase to this main one. The arm started weakening little by little, so they shut the whole thing off while they get ready to repair it. It's boarded up solid just a little ways past the ch— Hey!" he broke off. "Where you going? You can't do that!"

"I'm going just that little ways between the chain and where the boarding is," I told him, spanning the cable with one leg. "If the arm lasted this long, one more person won't hurt it, I don't weigh enough. Throw your lights up after me."

The thing was a spiral, just like the other staircase that led to the head. Or rather, it started out to be, but at the very first half-turn-around it took, the boarding had already shown up, sealing it from top to bottom. That half-turn, however, cut off their lights, which shone in a straight line like any lights would. A pie-slice wedge of blackness was left down in one lower corner which they couldn't eliminate, no matter how they maneuvered the torches.

"Come on a little nearer with those things!" I called impatiently. "Come past the chain!"

They wouldn't budge. "Against orders." That's the Army for you.

I came back down a few steps and grabbed a torch for myself. "Well, if you won't, I will." I jumped on up again and washed out the stubborn black silt clinging to the corner with the thin beam in my hand, as if it were a thin jet of water played from a nozzle.

There he was. Sure was. As the saying goes, big as life. Only it didn't fit this case. Big as death would have been better. And tucked in just as neatly as though the space had been measured off for him ahead of time. In a slumped sitting position on the turn of the steps, back propped against the boarding, legs drawn up under him to help keep him propped. Head over. I touched the side of his neck. He was as cold already as the metal statue that made a tomb for him.

"Got him," I told them laconically.

"What's he doing up there?" one of them wanted to know inanely.

That's always been a hard one to answer. What are they doing, after they've come to a full stop? "Waiting around," I said dryly, "with no place to go any more."

They got it, and they gasped.

I had a call put in for the medical examiner, and then the remaining GI and I waited it out for him to arrive. Which was quite a piece of waiting-out. When he finally got there he had two men from the Morgue with him, with a stretcher. He examined him, okayed it, and they got started with him.

"Multiple fracture, blunt instrument," he said, backing out of their way.

It wasn't easy, even for two of them.

The thing that had done it was lying under him when they got him up off the steps and brought him down—a wicked-looking iron bar wrapped in a stiffened, blood-brown piece of rag. The wound—it was a deadly looking thing—was on the side of the head just over the ear. He hadn't bled much, outside of the first splash on the padded weapon itself. The little there was after that had clung closely to the skin, running down behind the jawbone and into the collar of his shirt, hence nothing on the ground around the bench where the attack had occurred. The only thing I could see around there, when I got down and pored over it, were the two shiny ribbonlike tracks his heels had made as he was dragged backwards into the hiding place. It hadn't been a subtle crime. Just somebody came up the stairs, iron bar already at the ready, swung—and that was it.

The two pallbearers loved the job. They must have lost ten pounds apiece in sweat, getting him down those seventeen stories of narrow, spiral staircase. When they were down at the elevator you could hear their heaving all the way up where I was. When I got down myself, Suicide Johnny, with the body propped in his car and the two stretcher men in a state of collapse alongside of it, was wreathed in smiles. His fondest dream had come true; something had at last happened. "Wow!" he kept saying over and over, "A stiff! Wow! A real live stiff! Right here under my eyes."

"How can a stiff be live?" I snapped at him disapprovingly.

After I'd seen them safely en route with him, I went back inside the statue again alone, for what I hoped was the last time, and decided to make Suicide Johnny useful, since he seemed to be enjoying himself so. "Come on up with me," I said, "you man-eating young cannibal."

He nearly jumped out of his shoes with alacrity. "Wow!" he said starry-eyed. "I'm helping a real detective!"

The fellows on the squad, I thought wryly, sometimes have grave doubts about that. But I didn't disillusion him; life is tough enough on the young.

When we got up to the head I took out my notebook, where I had the ten names I'd collected from the excursionists. "You take a pencil," I told Suicide, "and hold the book. Call out those names you've got there one at a time. Real slow. Each time I find one that matches here around the windows, you cross off the corresponding one there in the book. That's all."

"Why?" he said, fish-mouthed.

"Because there's going to be one too many."

"On the window?"

"No, stupe," I said with real old-fashioned courtesy, "in the book. A guy doesn't commit a murder, and then right after that scratch his initials in the vicinity."

This wasn't paperwork really; you might better call it stone-work. When we got through, we had nine of the ten names. Three of the ten were just initials. Initials were a risk, because they might have been put there previously by others, might have stood for altogether different names than the ones they appeared to match up with in the book. But the breaks were our way: two of them were triple initials, that is the middle initial was given, too; and two of those in the book had given middle initials, too. So where all three clicked, that was enough. The third belonged to a woman evidently of Slavic ancestry, and they were unusual enough in themselves to pass on the strength of that alone. Law of averages, I mean. Nobody else was likely to have them. X-Z. Xenia Zoruboff was the name.

"Now, which one's left over?" I asked Suicide.

He screwed up his face and read off: "Vincent Scanlon, 55 Amboy Street, Brooklyn; real estate."

"On circumstantial alone, that's my guy. Only, his name isn't Scanlon, he doesn't live on Amboy Street, and he's not in real estate."

"Hully mackerel!" cried the enraptured Johnny. "You not only can tell which one the guy *is,* but you can even tell what his name *isn't* and where he *don't* live and what kind of a job he *hasn't* got!"

"Good boy," I murmured inattentively. "Not an ain't in a carload." I took the note book, held it open before me, and did my damnedest to try to visualize whoever it was had given me that name. Wouldn't work, wouldn't come clear. Lost in the shuffle among the nine others.

"Let's go back down," I said wearily. "I didn't get anything out of that. Only what I already knew before I came up: that one of the ten gave me a spiked name."

He was deflated, I could see. I'd disappointed him. I'd struck out, on his score card. He started the car down slowly, with his head hanging to match it. But even that slow motion, snail-like as it was, was disturbing to my faculties (all right, put quotes around the word), which were trying to mesh. I cut my hand at him and said: "Hold the car here a minute, right where it is."

He stopped it, looked at me expectantly awhile, finally asked: "What's here?"

"Nothing," I said. "But I want to think. And it's easier to think when you're standing still."

He didn't think much of thinking, I could tell. Probably because he wasn't too avid a practitioner of it himself. He watched my face carefully for a while, and then, since no neon signs or anything flashed on the outside of it to show thinking was going on, lost interest altogether, took out a furled newspaper he had stashed away behind the control lever, spread it and lost himself behind it.

And then, just like in the story books—". . . *So I started to hunt for him high and low, all over the wallowing ferry. In the saloon a couple of youngsters were sitting one on each side of their father, swinging their legs. And a man who didn't give a hoot about the skyline outside was reading the sports column in the* Mirror. *I wondered what he'd made the excursion in the first place for. . . ."*

That was him right there. The man who didn't give a hoot about the skyline outside—naturally not—and kept the lower half of his face covered up behind a newspaper. And now I knew what he'd made the excursion in the first place for, didn't have to wonder any more. To commit murder, what else?

"Let's go," I said to Johnny. "I've got him now."

"All of him?"

"Lots of him. Got his eyes, got the sort of a wavy line that runs across his forehead, that deepens when he reads. Got the shape of the rims of his ears, got the way his hair looks just over and around them. Got the way his hatbrim slants across the front of his head. What more do I want? Do I have to have his whole face? You have to do a *little* work in this business."

He shook his head. "I could never be a detective," he said forlornly. "I ain't smart enough."

"To be a detective, son," I said, taking leave of him, "you have to be dumb to start off with, not smart. Otherwise you never would try to be a detective in the first place." And I forgave him the final ain't, as a sort of parting present. We were outside the statue by that time, anyway.

I made two phone calls as soon as I got ashore. One to my house and one to a person or persons unidentified at a number unknown. I made the one to my house first, being a coward like most men are where their opposite numbers are concerned.

I was in bad odor. I don't mean literally, but at the other end of the phone.

"I suppose you're sitting up with a sick statue, that's the one this time!"

"No, but—"

"You go out of here at two o'clock in the afternoon and—! Well, *stay* out! You're not coming back here! I'm going to take my embroidery scissors and rip your pillow full of gashes and empty out all the feathers. You can sleep with the old police comissioner for all I c—"

"Oh, he's not that way," I tried to expostulate in all fairness. "Anyway, I never use my own, I always use—"

This was high-octane gasoline on an acetylene torch. "Vulgar thing!" she stormed. "You did so! You did, too! A week ago last—" Then she thought maybe she better unremember.

"You missed me!" I cried joyfully. "And I thought you never noticed."

She hung up in my ear, and nearly took the ear with her.

My second call was to a much calmer lady. "This is police business. Can you give me a listing, an identification, to go with. . . ." And I carefully read out to her Alice Colman's eyebrow-pencil notation, just as I'd transcribed it into my pocket notebook from the statue's window coping: "Two-five-four West Five-one."

"I'm sorry, officer, but it's impossible for us to work that way. We can only get you the number from the name; we can't get you the name from the number. It would take weeks to check through the directories."

I didn't have weeks, so it was up to my own feet to play the part of Information, Dial 411. She gave me my dime back at least, which I thought was rather regular of her.

I did it by taxi. How else, from the tip of the island to the Fifties? It would have been some fare, too, if I'd have been paying for it. He'd brought me up Eighth, and it seemed to lie east of there, so I got off at the corner, Five-one being a westbound street. I took it on my own feet down the opposite, the odd-numbered side.

I needn't have tried to be so cagey. It hit me right smack in the face, bright as a California supermarket on opening night, before I'd even got within three building-lengths of it. *"Capital Bus Terminal,"* it said.

So that was it. They weren't holing up here; they were going to blow out together. They'd carefully stayed away from each other on the ferry, and ditto once they were ashore in Manhattan; now they were teaming up again as per the timetable on the statue. My own private name for this gambit is the rubber-band gimmick. First they stretch wide apart, then they snap back together again. It's old. But so are cops.

I asked the man at the ticket window what he had going out at four.

"Going out where?" he said.

"That's what I'm asking," I said patiently. "Where *to?*"

"Yes, but you've got to tell me where you want to go *to,* first; then I tell you what time it leaves. That's the way we do it."

"I'd like to tell *you* where to go *to,"* I said between slowly grinding teeth. I paid off each word on a fingertip, to make it simpler for him. "Where do the busses that pull out at four head for?"

He was going to make it tough for me to the end. "A.M. or P.M.?" he said doggedly.

The statue hadn't specified. "Make it A.M.," I said. "That's the nearest four coming up from now. Just the big ones," I added.

"Big busses?"

"No, big places."

He told me Boston and Philly.

"Take an aspirin and get some sleep," I told him, turning away. "You'll be all right."

He stood up in his seat and leaned out after me. "No, you take an aspirin!" he squawked. "In fact, an aspirin would have to take something for *you!* You'd give an aspirin a headache!"

I saw him come in at three thirty. Three twenty-five, to be exact. No sign of her yet. I was on the last row of benches, back against the wall, where nobody could sit behind me, everyone had to sit in front. I was asleep. People do that in bus waiting rooms, especially at that hour of the night. Well, let's say my clothes were in sleeping position. My hat brim all the way down, almost into my upended coat collar. Just a slit between, to look out through.

He must have had their tickets already. He took a preliminary seat first, close to the door, so that he could jump up again and beat it outside fast if he needed to. From there he carefully cased the place, around on all sides. He looked at everyone, me included. Me he passed over very briefly, I was just a slumped mass. One man glanced back at him, and that alarmed him for a minute, I could see. At least, it took his attention off me. Then the man's wife came in, carrying a baby in arms, and they started a loud argument together, so that reassured him. He changed seats, went farther to the back, where he'd be less conspicuous. He put the newspaper up in front of him, but it was too late for that to do him any good now. They never know when they're being watched and when they're not, and they always play it wrong.

No her. No she. One of those two has to be right. It got to be twelve-to, and then ten, and then eight. I wasn't enjoying myself at all. One of the toughest things to do is stay in a relaxed, inert position when you're all tense and taut inside. I felt like I needed a piano tuner; every nerve was out of key. But then, he was having it just as bad; it was written all over him. Even the back of his neck was pale. And I could see the newspaper quivering even from where I was sitting.

I could have gone over and picked him up easy as you lift a rabbit by the ears, sure. But I didn't want him alone, didn't dare touch him alone. I wanted to wait until she got there, and where the aitch was she? Six-to, the clock said now—five-to—four. Maybe she'd walked out on him, too, and was going to stand him up. A woman who would arrange to have her husband put out of the way wouldn't think twice about welshing out on her accomplice, if it seemed to better her own chances of getting away.

Departure time was at hand. The sprinkling of late-night travelers stirred, got up from their seats, got their things together, moved outside to the bus platform, fell into two lines, one for each bus, and slowly climbed in, one by one. He was very much in the middle of all of them. But she was nowhere in sight.

I was on my feet, too, now, and strolling out there after him—but very uneasy. I should have had somebody else on this with me. I saw his foot go up to the bottom bus step, and then he poised that way, knee raised, waiting for the person ahead of him to clear the way. It was the Boston one. I got on the end of that line, about four down from him.

He was in now. Through the windshield glass, I saw him go down the aisle and take a seat all the way at the back. I was third from the door now. Then I was second from the door. I had to make up my mind pretty quick what I wanted to do.

I thought the wrong thing. It seemed right, but it wasn't. I thought: maybe she's on the Philly bus, the next one up. Maybe she got on there by mistake, without my seeing her, while I've been watching this one. I quit the boarding line, which now consisted of only one other person beside myself, and went on up the platform and cased the other bus. She wasn't on that one, either. But the mistake was to move so far away from the first one. Two whole bus-lengths, and then an empty gap of about one more bus-length in between. It was too far for me to get back on time and head her off.

The door of the ladies' rest room gave a clap that attracted my attention— but that was only as it slammed back closed, and she was already better than halfway to her mark. She must have been hiding in there for hours, long before he ever showed up. And after all, what safer place? I had I'd say, roughly, better than twice the distance she had to cover to get there even with her, and I couldn't make it, nobody could have.

Did you ever see a woman run? Sure you have, and laughed. So have I, and so have I laughed. The hip swing, the choppy too-short steps. But never for her life, never for her freedom, not like this one did. She came on like a streak. Like an arrow. Like whatever goes fast and true. She knew just where she was going, and she went. And on high heels yet.

Even her timing was split-second perfect. She just skinned through the door after it was already past the halfway-closed mark. Five more pounds on her and she'd have gotten wedged. Ten seconds sooner and I could have made it in after her. She belonged at the Olympic Games, not on a New York City bus platform. I take that back. She belonged in jail.

So there I was, and there was the bus, and there they both were. And in just that order, with the bus very much in between us. I wasted time hammering the door. By that time he'd started rolling and was already easing down the incline toward the street.

He snarled something to me. "I'm on a schedule, and you're out of luck. Take the next one." I suppose it was that anyway; I could only see his jaws meshing through the glass.

The first window on my side was open about eight inches from the bottom for ventilation. The second one was not.

But there was a man behind it, and they'll co-operate more often than a woman will in a roughhouse play like this. I motioned to him and he threw his open about halfway up. I thrust an arm through each opening, twined them around together on the inside, folded my legs up against the side of the bus so my feet wouldn't drag, and just hung on there and let myself be carried along like a barnacle.

The man sitting there reached out, grabbed me by one shoulder, and gave me a hoist. I got my whole head in, and that one shoulder. Then I brought the other one around in after the first one. All that was left outside was my legs now, and they've got to go where the rest of me goes; nothing else they can do.

"Stop the bus," I panted. "This is an arrest."

"I'll stop," the driver agreed, "because I don't want to see you kill yourself. But if this is just a trick to keep from missing the bus, I'll turn you over to the nearest policeman."

"You'll have to turn me over to myself then," I said, going down all over the floor like a lot of loose bricks, "because *I'm* the nearest policeman. And I want to get even nearer."

I tackled him first, naturally. He'd bolted from his seat, and he tried to jump over me—had to—to get to the door. I just grabbed him by one leg as he went over me, and he did a nose dive and stunned himself face down on the bus aisle. So the rest was just attaching the cuff links.

She'd been sitting farther forward, and she *had* got to the door by that time. She was beating at it with her hands.

"Hold that woman!" I yelled to the driver. "She's under arrest too!"

He didn't have to put a hand on her. He just kept from opening the door, and she was held trapped there, like a goldfish in a bowl. I blew a whistle out one of the windows, and finally attracted the attention of a patrolman, and between the two of us we got them both off and started them on their way.

We pushed him around a little when we got him down in the station-house basement, and he broke very easy. Like a balloon if you jab it with a pin. The lights bothered him, and his guilty conscience bothered him, and he was more afraid of getting hurt than he actually was hurt. Just a couple of shoves back and forth did it.

"She set the thing up," he yelped. "I met her in a bar about a year ago, and she slowly built it up to me. We used to meet about once a week or so. And she kept working on me, and working on me."

"And how about you working on her?" somebody said.

He shrugged matter-of-factly. "She's a gal and I'm a guy. What'd you expect us to do with our time, twiddle our thumbs?"

"You twiddled your thumbs, all right. Upside down."

"How'd you come to pick the statue?" I asked him.

"We didn't pick it. It just worked out that way. We'd been all set for weeks before, but we never could get him in the right place at the right time. Then she calls me suddenly yesterday morning and tips me off she's steering him to the Statue of Liberty. 'See what you can do there,' she said. 'It must be gloomy inside, and you ought to be able to work something out. Wait around by the ferry slip, and stick close behind us when you see us show up.'

"So I did. I had brought along a chunk of lead pipe, and I hung back down below until everybody had gone up and the stairs were clear. Then I found him alone on one of the benches, where she'd purposely left him behind, with his tongue practically hanging out. A couple of swings with the pipe, and that was it. Then I rolled him into that little cranny there, so he couldn't be seen when the people came down again."

I let the others put the finishing touches to him, and I went up and started working on her. You don't manhandle women arrestees, of course. That's all you need. Try it and you get them automatically acquitted. But you can "interrogate" them (no, that doesn't mean what you think) and draw your own conclusions.

There was a matron present, as there has to be by law.

"Your partner," I told her, "has spilled the beans."

She was going to be the know-nothing type. "What partner?" she said. "And what beans?"

I offered her a cigarette, and she took it. I waited a couple of minutes. I could see she was tired and letdown after the long-sustained tension.

"All right," I said. "So you won't tell me. Then I'll tell you."

"Will you?" she purred, lazing smoke through her diminutive nostrils and watching it go with her head tilted back. "Go ahead."

"He weighed two-hundred-ninety, three hundred," I said.

"Did he?" she said.

"You got a little tired of packing that much excess husband around."

"Really?" she said.

"He made good money."

"Is that a crime?"

"No, a motive. And he banked it all in your name."

This time she just blinked. She didn't say anything.

She didn't have to.

She threw away her cigarette half finished, as if just then remembering that it had come from a policeman. She brushed off her skirt, as if to imply it had been a very dirty cigarette. "You people haven't got a thing on me."

"We never do at the start," I answered equably. "But put your money on us at the finish."

Someone else took over the questioning, and I went home.

I was in real trouble there.

"I wrapped up a case," I explained, by way of preliminary softening up.

"A case of what—Rheingold?"

Then when it was all over with and explained away, and we were arm in arm and cheek to cheek, I nearly blew the whole thing again.

"Gee, I'd like to go to Egypt," I said wistfully.

"Egypt!" she all but screamed.

"Because if statues are a help to you in your work, think of the promotion I could get down *there*. They've got the Sphinx."

THE COP AND THE ANTHEM

O. Henry

ON HIS BENCH in Madison Square Soapy moved uneasily. When wild geese honk high of nights, and when women without sealskin coats grow kind to their husbands, and when Soapy moves uneasily on his bench in the park, you may know that winter is near at hand.

A dead leaf fell in Soapy's lap. That was Jack Frost's card. Jack is kind to the regular denizens of Madison Square, and gives fair warning of his annual call. At the corners of four streets he hands his pasteboard to the North Wind, footman of the mansion of All Outdoors, so that the inhabitants thereof may make ready.

Soapy's mind became cognisant of the fact that the time had come for him to resolve himself into a singular Committee of Ways and Means to provide against the coming rigour. And therefore he moved uneasily on his bench.

The hibernatorial ambitions of Soapy were not of the highest. In them there were no considerations of Mediterranean cruises, of soporific Southern skies or drifting in the Vesuvian Bay. Three months on the Island was what his soul craved. Three months of assured board and bed and congenial company, safe from Boreas and bluecoats, seemed to Soapy the essence of things desirable.

For years the hospitable Blackwell's had been his winter quarters. Just as his more fortunate fellow New Yorkers had bought their tickets to Palm Beach and the Riviera each winter, so Soapy had made his humble arrangements for his annual hegira to the Island. And now the time was come. On the previous night three Sabbath newspapers, distributed beneath his

coat, about his ankles and over his lap, had failed to repulse the cold as
he slept on his bench near the spurting fountain in the ancient square. So
the Island loomed big and timely in Soapy's mind. He scorned the provi-
sions made in the name of charity for the city's dependents. In Soapy's
opinion the Law was more benign than Philanthropy. There was an endless
round of institutions, municipal and eleemosynary, on which he might
set out and receive lodging and food accordant with the simple life. But
to one of Soapy's proud spirit the gifts of charity are encumbered. If not
in coin you must pay in humiliation of spirit for every benefit received
at the hands of philanthropy. As Caesar had his Brutus, every bed of
charity must have its toll of a bath, every loaf of bread its compensation
of a private and personal inquisition. Wherefore it is better to be a guest
of the law, which though conducted by rules, does not meddle unduly
with a gentleman's private affairs.

Soapy, having decided to go to the Island, at once set about
accomplishing his desire. There were many easy ways of doing this. The
pleasantest was to dine luxuriously at some expensive restaurant; and
then, after declaring insolvency, be handed over quietly and without uproar
to a policeman. An accommodating magistrate would do the rest.

Soapy left his bench and strolled out of the square and across the level
sea of asphalt, where Broadway and Fifth Avenue flow together. Up
Broadway he turned, and halted at a glittering café, where are gathered
together nightly the choicest products of the grape, the silkworm and the
protoplasm.

Soapy had confidence in himself from the lowest button of his vest
upward. He was shaven, and his coat was decent and his neat black,
ready-tied four-in-hand had been presented to him by a lady missionary
on Thanksgiving Day. If he could reach a table in the restaurant unsus-
pected success would be his. The portion of him that would show above
the table would raise no doubt in the waiter's mind. A roasted mallard
duck, thought Soapy, would be about the thing—with a bottle of Chab-
lis, and then Camembert, a demi-tasse and a cigar. One dollar for the
cigar would be enough. The total would not be so high as to call forth
any supreme manifestation of revenge from the café management; and
yet the meat would leave him filled and happy for the journey to his
winter refuge.

But as Soapy set foot inside the restaurant door the head waiter's eye
fell upon his frayed trousers and decadent shoes. Strong and ready hands
turned him about and conveyed him in silence and haste to the sidewalk
and averted the ignoble fate of the menaced mallard.

Soapy turned off Broadway. It seemed that his route to the coveted island was not to be an epicurean one. Some other way of entering limbo must be thought of.

At a corner of Sixth Avenue electric lights and cunningly displayed wares behind plate-glass made a shop window conspicuous. Soapy took a cobblestone and dashed it through the glass. People came running around the corner, a policeman in the lead. Soapy stood still, with his hands in his pockets, and smiled at the sight of brass buttons.

"Where's the man that done that?" inquired the officer excitedly.

"Don't you figure out that I might have had something to do with it?" said Soapy, not without sarcasm, but friendly, as one greets good fortune.

The policeman's mind refused to accept Soapy even as a clue. Men who smash windows do not remain to parley with the law's minions. They take to their heels. The policeman saw a man half way down the block running to catch a car. With drawn club he joined in the pursuit. Soapy, with disgust in his heart, loafed along, twice unsuccessful.

On the opposite side of the street was a restaurant of no great pretensions. It catered to large appetites and modest purses. Its crockery and atmosphere were thick; its soup and napery thin. Into this place Soapy took his accusive shoes and telltale trousers without challenge. At a table he sat and consumed beefsteak, flapjacks, doughnuts and pie. And then to the waiter he betrayed the fact that the minutest coin and himself were strangers.

"Now, get busy and call a cop," said Soapy. "And don't keep a gentleman waiting."

"No cop for youse," said the waiter, with a voice like butter cakes and an eye like the cherry in a Manhattan cocktail. "Hey, Con!"

Neatly upon his left ear on the callous pavement two waiters pitched Soapy. He arose, joint by joint, as a carpenter's rule opens, and beat the dust from his clothes. Arrest seemed but a rosy dream. The Island seemed very far away. A policeman who stood before a drug store two doors away laughed and walked down the street.

Five blocks Soapy travelled before his courage permitted him to woo capture again. This time the opportunity presented what he fatuously termed to himself a "cinch." A young woman of a modest and pleasing guise was standing before a show window gazing with sprightly interest at its display of shaving mugs and inkstands, and two yards from the window a large policeman of severe demeanour leaned against a water plug.

It was Soapy's design to assume the role of the despicable and execrated "masher." The refined and elegant appearance of his victim and the contiguity of the conscientious cop encouraged him to believe that he would soon feel the pleasant official clutch upon his arm that would insure his winter quarters on the right little, tight little isle.

Soapy straightened the lady missionary's ready-made tie, dragged his shrinking cuffs into the open, set his hat at a killing cant and sidled toward the young woman. He made eyes at her, was taken with sudden coughs and "hems," smiled, smirked and went brazenly through the impudent and contemptible litany of the "masher." With half an eye Soapy saw that the policeman was watching him fixedly. The young woman moved away a few steps, and again bestowed her absorbed attention upon the shaving mugs. Soapy followed, boldly stepping to her side, raised his hat and said:

"Ah there, Bedelia! Don't you want to come and play in my yard?"

The policeman was still looking. The persecuted young woman had but to beckon a finger and Soapy would be practically en route for his insular haven. Already he imagined he could feel the cozy warmth of the station-house. The young woman faced him and, stretching out a hand, caught Soapy's coat sleeve.

"Sure, Mike," she said joyfully, "if you'll blow me to a pail of suds. I'd have spoke to you sooner, but the cop was watching."

With the young woman playing the clinging ivy to his oak Soapy walked past the policeman overcome with gloom. He seemed doomed to liberty.

At the next corner he shook off his companion and ran. He halted in the district where by night are found the lightest streets, hearts, vows and librettos. Women in furs and men in greatcoats moved gaily in the wintry air. A sudden fear seized Soapy that some dreadful enchantment had rendered him immune to arrest. The thought brought a little of panic upon it, and when he came upon another policeman lounging grandly in front of a transplendent theatre he caught at the immediate straw of "disorderly conduct."

On the sidewalk Soapy began to yell drunken gibberish at the top of his harsh voice. He danced, howled, raved and otherwise disturbed the welkin.

The policeman twirled his club, turned his back to Soapy and remarked to a citizen.

"'Tis one of them Yale lads celebratin' the goose egg they give to the Hartford College. Noisy; but no harm. We've instructions to lave them be."

Disconsolate, Soapy ceased his unavailing racket. Would never a policeman lay hands on him? In his fancy the Island seemed an unattainable Arcadia. He buttoned his thin coat against the chilling wind.

In a cigar store he saw a well-dressed man lighting a cigar at a swinging light. His silk umbrella he had set by the door on entering. Soapy stepped inside, secured the umbrella and sauntered off with it slowly. The man at the cigar light followed hastily.

"My umbrella," he said, sternly.

"Oh, is it?" sneered Soapy, adding insult to petit larceny. "Well, why don't you call a policeman? I took it. Your umbrella! Why don't you call a cop? There stands one on the corner."

The umbrella owner slowed his steps. Soapy did likewise, with a presentiment that luck would again run against him. The policeman looked at the two curiously.

"Of course," said the umbrella man—"that is—well, you know how these mistakes occur—I—if it's your umbrella I hope you'll excuse me—I picked it up this morning in a restaurant—If you recognise it as yours, why—I hope you'll—"

"Of course it's mine," said Soapy, viciously.

The ex-umbrella man retreated. The policeman hurried to assist a tall blonde in an opera cloak across the street in front of a street car that was approaching two blocks away.

Soapy walked eastward through a street damaged by improvements. He hurled the umbrella wrathfully into an excavation. He muttered against the men who wear helmets and carry clubs. Because he wanted to fall into their clutches, they seemed to regard him as a king who could do no wrong.

At length Soapy reached one of the avenues to the east where the glitter and turmoil was but faint. He set his face down this toward Madison Square, for the homing instinct survives even when the home is a park bench.

But on an unusually quiet corner Soapy came to a standstill. Here was an old church, quaint and rambling and gabled. Through one violet-stained window a soft light glowed, where, no doubt, the organist loitered over the keys, making sure of his mastery of the coming Sabbath anthem. For there drifted out to Soapy's ears sweet music that caught and held him transfixed against the convolutions of the iron fence.

The moon was above, lustrous and serene; vehicles and pedestrians were few; sparrows twittered sleepily in the eaves—for a little while the scene might have been a country churchyard. And the anthem that the organist played cemented Soapy to the iron fence, for he had known it well in the days when his life contained such things as mothers and roses and ambitions and friends and immaculate thoughts and collars.

The conjunction of Soapy's receptive state of mind and the influences about the old church wrought a sudden and wonderful change in his soul. He viewed with swift horror the pit into which he had tumbled, the degraded days, unworthy desires, dead hopes, wrecked faculties and base motives that made up his existence.

And also in a moment his heart responded thrillingly to this novel mood. An instantaneous and strong impulse moved him to battle with his desperate fate. He would pull himself out of the mire; he would make a man of himself again; he would conquer the evil that had taken possession of him. There was time; he was comparatively young yet; he would resurrect his old eager ambitions and pursue them without faltering. Those solemn but sweet organ notes had set up a revolution in him. Tomorrow he would go into the roaring downtown district and find work. A fur importer had once offered him a place as driver. He would find him tomorrow and ask for the position. He would be somebody in the world. He would—

Soapy felt a hand laid on his arm. He looked quickly around into the broad face of a policeman.

"What are you doin' here?" asked the officer.

"Nothin'," said Soapy.

"Then come along," said the policeman.

"Three months on the Island," said the Magistrate in the Police Court the next morning.

JERICHO AND THE CARDBOARD BOX

Hugh Pentecost

IT WAS A Sunday morning when Jericho found the box outside the door of his studio in Jefferson Mews in Greenwich Village. It was an almost square cardboard carton designed to hold twelve quart bottles of whiskey. The name of the distiller was stamped on the side and on the top of the carton. The top was closed and held in place by packaging tape. It rested on top of the Sunday *Times* and the Sunday *News* which Jericho had home-delivered. It appeared to be intended for Jericho though it wasn't addressed to him in any way. He moved it, realizing that it didn't contain its original contents of liquor—it was much too light for that. But if it wasn't meant for him, why else would it be there?

John Jericho is a giant of a man, six feet four inches tall with a body that is 240 pounds of hard, conditioned muscle. His hair, his beard and mustache, are a flaming red, which gives him the look of an ancient Viking warrior. He has been called an "original," and he is—no duplicate, no carbon copy anywhere. He is, by profession, an artist. His paintings, noted for their vivid colors, their enormous vitality that seems to leap at you from the canvas, are to be seen in museums and private collections all over the world.

But Jericho is more than a gifted painter. Some art critics say his works suffer because they always carry a message. The message, in a world of violence and terror, of assassinations and mass murders, is an outcry against man's inhumanity to man. But he is more than just the conveyer of messages. He confronts evil where he can find it and fights it eye to eye, toe to toe. The fact that he is alive and well and living in Greenwich

Village in New York City tells you all you need to know about those confrontations. There are people who love him, and there are people who hate his guts.

A gift from someone he had helped was not unusual. He picked up the newspapers and the cardboard carton and carried them into the studio. He was wearing only a terry-cloth robe over his naked body, fresh from a shower. From the kitchen off his skylighted studio came the pleasant aroma of fresh cooked bacon and coffee.

He picked up a palette knife from the table beside his easel and slit the strips of package tape on the carton. He opened the box. He stepped back, taking a deep breath to fight off a wave of nausea.

"Time to put in your eggs, love?" a pleasant girl's voice called to him from the kitchen.

"Stay out of here, Marla!" Jericho called out, his voice harsh.

He looked into the open carton once more. Leering up at him from a bed of bloodied newspaper was the severed head of an old woman.

Lieutenant Mark Kreevich, Manhattan Homicide, is one of a new breed of cops. He is a man with a law degree. He is a man with sophisticated tastes in the arts; he can talk painting or literature or the theater. He is also a man dedicated to "law and order," but not the cliché kind of law and order paid lip service by politicians. It is his belief that people have a right to live without fear; if possible, crime should be prevented rather than solved after the fact.

It is not illogical that this slim, intense, highly competent crime fighter was the official John Jericho called when he had recovered from the first shock of seeing what was in the cardboard box. Kreevich and Jericho were long-standing friends, dating back to a murder case on which their paths had crossed some years ago.

Kreevich, his face looking, for the moment, as though it was carved out of stone, turned away from the open carton. "You know who she is?" he asked.

"Yes and no," Jericho said.

"Meaning?"

"She's an old bag lady who haunts this part of town," Jericho said. "I don't know her name or anything about her. I've spoken to her on the street."

"About what?"

" 'Good morning,' 'Have a good day.' That sort of thing."

A girl came out of the kitchen. She looked like what she was, a beautiful fashion model. She had long red hair that she wore shoulder-length, an elegant figure, high cheekbones, a wide generous mouth, bright blue eyes. She was carrying two mugs of coffee which she put down on the table next to the carton, keeping her eyes averted.

"What's a bag lady, Johnny?" she asked.

"She's an old crone who lives, God knows where, in the neighborhood—probably in some deserted building or cellar. You see her on the street, always carrying paper bags, sifting through trash and garbage, always searching for something that will contribute to survival. A scavenger." Jericho glanced at Kreevich. "You remember Marla Rivers, Mark."

The detective managed a thin smile. "We all had too many drinks at Connolly's Bar and Grill a few months back," he said.

"You don't like Picasso," Marla said.

"I admire him but I don't want to live with him," Kreevich said.

"Sugar? Cream?" Marla asked him.

"In this kind of situation I take it black," Kreevich said. He took a sip of the hot coffee. "Without the rest of the lady it's impossible to tell what happened to her. Did the beheading kill her or was it done afterward? The thing that interests me, Johnny, is why your doorstep on a summer Sunday morning?"

"It beats me," Jericho said.

The front doorbell buzzer rang.

"That could be Captain Cardwell of the local precinct," Kreevich said. "I asked him to join me here—Department protocol."

Captain Tom Cardwell was a gray-haired man with cold, slate-gray eyes. He looked a little bulky, out of shape, in his police captain's uniform. Jericho knew him. The part of Greenwich Village in which Jefferson Mews is located is somewhat old-fashioned in today's world. It is like a small town, where everyone knows everyone, everyone speaks to everyone, almost everyone knows what everyone else does. Police in this area, unlike most of the city, are still regarded as friends and allies, not the enemy.

Tom Cardwell, near retirement age Jericho guessed, had spent his whole career in this part of town. He was feared by some, liked and respected by many. Under his command, drunks were usually taken home, not thrown into jail; people in trouble often went to him for help. Down-and-outers, an old bag lady like the one whose head was in the box, were not molested so long as they didn't make themselves obnoxious to other residents. Cardwell's precinct was considered to be too gently paternalistic by the higher-ups in the department, but the crime rate was low and he was allowed to run things his own way.

Cardwell acknowledged an introduction to Marla Rivers as though he had never seen her before, though Jericho would have bet he knew that she spent frequent weekends here in this studio. Cardwell knew everything that went on in his own little world.

Kreevich took the Captain over to the carton and opened the lid. Cardwell looked down and they could hear his breath whistle.

"Sarah Watson!" he said.

"You know her?" Kreevich asked.

"Lived down here for years," Cardwell said. "Bag lady. Never did anybody any harm that I know of. What kind of swine would do this?"

"What kind of swine would put it in a box and leave it for me?" Jericho asked.

"You know Sarah?" Cardwell asked.

"The way I know a hundred people in this neighborhood," Jericho said. "I wave, I say hello. Don't know names." He glanced at the carton. "I never heard her name until you just mentioned it."

"Looks so old," Kreevich said.

"In her eighties, I imagine," Cardwell said. "She was already part of the picture in this neighborhood when I was assigned to this precinct thirty-five years ago. Even then she was living out of garbage cans." He shook his head. "Ten days from retirement and this gets dropped in my lap."

"Living out of garbage cans?" Marla sounded shocked. "Aren't there organizations that take care of people like that? The Salvation Army, for instance?"

Cardwell allowed himself a bitter little chuckle. "Tough old bird, Sarah Watson. Wouldn't have her life any other way. Fought off an army of do-gooders in her time. Not starving to death, you understand. Would you believe she was a crazy, wild horse player? Every day of her life, betting on the nags, putting down her two bucks."

"That old woman?" Marla asked.

"Yes, didn't miss a day," Cardwell said. "Before we had Off Track Betting she knew where to find an illegal bookie. I understand she does pretty well—did pretty well. They say she picked winners for dozens of people every day in this area."

"A Damon Runyon character," Kreevich said.

Cardwell squared his shoulders. "Job now is to—to find the rest of her," he said. "I'd like to send a man up here to fingerprint that carton before we move it, Mr. Jericho."

"Sure. Of course I handled it, not dreaming—"

"You won't mind letting my man take your prints so we can separate them from any others that may be on the carton?"

"Of course not."

"Is it okay if I use your telephone?" Cardwell asked. "You'll have to live with—with that—for another half hour."

"Not exactly the kind of Sunday I'd planned," Jericho said to Marla Rivers. They were alone in the studio with the carton. Kreevich had taken off with Captain Cardwell.

"There will be other Sundays, other days, love," Marla said. Her cool fingers touched his bearded cheek. "You don't have any idea why—that—that horror was left for you to find?"

"Two explanations," he said. "First, it wasn't meant for me at all. Just put down at random, somewhere, anywhere. Happened to be outside my door, but not meant for anyone in particular. Someone just getting rid of it."

"You believe that?"

"No," Jericho said, scowling. "Second, it was meant to tell me something, but I can't read the message yet."

"But if you didn't know her, if she wasn't even a casual acquaintance—?"

"Somebody knows something about me," Jericho said.

"What, Johnny?"

"That I never let a violence go unpunished if I can help it."

"Why you? Why not the police?"

"Good question," Jericho said.

Two detectives came from the precinct house with fingerprint equipment. They dusted the carton and took off what they found. Many different prints, they told Jericho. He submitted to having his own prints taken, and the two detectives left, carrying the carton and its grisly contents with them.

"Alone at last!" Marla said, but somehow it wasn't funny.

"Interesting to know when it was left outside my door," Jericho mused.

"It wasn't there when we came in from dinner, which was about ten thirty." Her eyes widened. "It was put there while we were—!"

"Yes, darling," Jericho said. "I've always said that the ultimate siren for the hydrogen bomb could sound while I was with you and I wouldn't hear it."

"Flattery will get you anything," Marla said. "What about the paper boy?"

"What about him?"

"He'd know whether the carton was there when he brought the Sunday papers. Then you'd know something about when it was left."

Jericho bent down and kissed her. "I may have to marry you to make you a permanent partner. See you when I get back!"

* * * *

The word was evidently out in the neighborhood. When Jericho reached the street a dozen people were grouped across the way, obviously interested in Number 16. He was instantly surrounded by people babbling questions. He had no answers, not yet. One thing he learned from his inquisitive neighbors. The story was already being broadcast on the local radio stations. *Bag lady decapitated in Jefferson Mews.*

Jericho walked down the block to Angelo Gambini's newspaper and notion store on the corner. Angelo, a stout, always smiling man, was not himself this morning. He crossed himself when he saw Jericho come in from the street.

"Mr. Jericho! I hear it on the radio. Someone leave you Sarah Watson's head in a box. *Dio mio!*"

"I wanted to talk to your boy, Tony," Jericho said. "I want to ask him if the box was there when he delivered the papers. If the box was brought after he delivered, then it was brought in daylight. If so, the person who delivered it could have been seen."

"Oh, it is there when Tony take you your papers," Angelo said. "When he hear about it on the radio Tony tell me. I send him straight down to report to Captain Cardwell."

"Report what?"

"That the box is there when he come with your papers. He lift it up and put papers under. His fingerprints, they are on the box, so I know he must tell Cardwell before he is suspected of something."

So the carton could have been delivered any time in the night, after ten thirty when Jericho and Marla had come in from dinner. Darkness, in the early hours of the morning, would have reduced any risk that the deliverer had to run.

"Who were Sarah Watson's close friends?" Jericho asked.

Angelo shrugged. "She have many friends," he said. "But close friends? Who knows? She give tips to many people on the horse races. If tips pay off, the people give her ten percent of winnings. You never know from looking at her, walking around in rags and carrying paper bags, that she may be better off than some fine gentlemen we see going to office."

"Carried her money with her?"

Angelo laughed. "She come in to buy something she have to half undress to pay for it. Money inside stockings, inside underclothes. I kid her about being a stripper. 'Nothing much to look at when you're eighty,' she tell me."

"So people knew she carried money. Could be a motive for attacking her, and killing her if she resisted."

Angelo nodded. "You find the body, if there's no money on it you'll know."

"No real close friends?" Jericho persisted.

"There is old Dave Morris," Angelo said. "Old-time Bowery bum. Drink anything that you can light a match to—canned heat, you name it. I suppose he's around sixty, but he look older. Sarah treat him like a kid—like maybe she is his nursemaid. Pull him out of alleys when he is drunk so cops not find him, scrounge food for him, find places where he sleep it off. I say he owes her that he's alive. I suppose you say that's close."

"Where can I find him?" Jericho asked.

"Who knows? No regular place to stay. He may not know what happen. He sure don't have a radio."

At that moment the little radio on the shelf behind Angelo announced local news: "The police have made an arrest in the case of the Greenwich Village bag lady who was found murdered early this morning. David Morris, a down-and-outer, has been charged with the murder and decapitation of Sarah Watson. More details as they develop."

"Well, I guess he know what happen," Angelo said.

Captain Cardwell was in good humor when Jericho walked into his office at the precinct house.

"We got lucky," he said.

"You're certain Morris is guilty?" Jericho asked.

"You won't believe what I've got to tell you," Cardwell said. "Radio did the job for us. Fred Thomas, who is vice-president in charge of the branch of the Waring Trust Company here in the Village, heard the news and called me. Five days ago—last Tuesday—Sarah Watson opened an account at his bank. Would you like to guess how much?"

"A few hundred dollars?"

Cardwell picked up a note from his desk.

"Sixty-one thousand two hundred and forty-two dollars and eighty-nine cents."

"You're kidding!"

"Exactly that amount. Mr. Thomas was just as astounded as you are. In cash, mind you! Old, old lady. He asked her what would become of the money if anything happened to her. Did she have a will? She didn't, but she made out a will right there in his office, instructed by the bank's lawyer, and all duly signed, and she left the whole wad, sixty-odd thousand bucks, to David Morris. You need a better motive for a down-and-out bum?"

"That's all you've got? A motive?"

Cardwell laughed cheerfully. "Just the beginning," he said. "We found Morris, potted to the gills, passed out cold, in the cellar of a deserted house on West 12th Street. Blood all over his clothes. We carted him back here, too drunk to talk. We fingerprinted him. Would you believe his prints are all over that carton that was left outside your front door?"

"Does he admit he left it for me?"

"He doesn't say anything yet that makes any sense. But I don't think we need him to talk. The Medical Examiner is making tests. If the blood on his clothes matches Sarah Watson's, and I'll bet my life it does, it's open and shut."

"Have you found Sarah's body?"

"Still looking. We'll come up with it."

Jericho brought his fist down on Cardwell's desk. "Why would he deliver that head to me? May I talk to him?"

"It won't do any good," Cardwell said. "He makes no sense. But if you can stand the smell—"

The cell was reasonably clean; toilet, basin, a cot on which appeared to be a bundle of old rags. The smell of stale booze was almost overpowering.

"Morris!" Jericho said sharply.

The rags moved. A bleary-eyed, unshaved face turned into view. "Mr. Jericho." It was like the whisper of a prizefighter who has been hit many times on the Adam's apple.

"You sent me a bizarre message," Jericho said.

Dave Morris' rumpled head moved up and down in the affirmative.

"You killed Sarah Watson?"

The head shook in an almost vigorous negative.

"Do you have a lawyer, Morris? Because they've got you nailed to the barn door."

Again the negative head shake. Then: "A lawyer wouldn't be any use."

"Why did you leave that carton outside my studio?"

The rags propped themselves up on an elbow. A bony finger beckoned Jericho close. "Don't you know," Morris whispered, "that this cell is bugged?" The rags sank back on the cot, then turned away.

Back in Cardwell's office the Captain spread his hands in an I-told-you-so gesture. "Has to present a defense whether he wants to or not. The court will appoint someone." He chuckled. "Pretty smart cookie to know we had him wired for sound."

"Smarter than me," Jericho said, irritated that he hadn't been told.

"Played a hunch," Cardwell said. "Thought he might spill something."

Fred Thomas, manager and vice-president of the Village Branch of the Waring Trust Company, was not a stranger to Jericho. The artist kept a checking account at the bank. There had been a time when the Zabriskis, who ran a mom-and-pop fruit-and-vegetable store, had come to Jericho for help. They needed $2000 for repairs to their refrigeration system. Would Jericho go on a note for them at the bank? Jericho would, and went to the bank to talk to Fred Thomas.

"You don't have to go on a note for the Zabriskis," Thomas said. "I know them—they're part of my community. Their credit is good with me. Of course, if they asked for my advice I'd be bound to tell them they're involved in a losing war. The big chain supermarkets are going to roll over them, as certainly as death and taxes. But unless they insist on an opinion I'm not going to hurt their pride. Forty years in that one store—"

Jericho registered Thomas in the back of his mind as a good man. He needed the banker's help now.

Thomas lived in a ground-floor garden apartment on Jane Street. He didn't seem altogether surprised to see Jericho outside his front door.

"I had a feeling you might be wanting to talk to me, Mr. Jericho," he said. "Please come in." He led the way to the garden where the Sunday newspapers were scattered about. He waved Jericho to a high-backed wicker armchair. He was a pleasant-faced, sandy-haired man in his forties. "What a shocking business for you! Old Sarah's head in a cardboard box? But Captain Cardwell informs me they've got their man. I'm having iced coffee. Would you care for some? Or a drink?"

"Iced coffee would be perfect," Jericho said. "Black." He waited for Thomas to come back from the kitchen with a tall cool drink. "You once told me this was 'your community'," he said. "Can you guess why Dave Morris—after he had killed Sarah Watson, if he did—would cut off her head, put it in a box, and carry it to my front door?"

" 'If he did'? Is there any doubt that he did?"

"Morris won't talk to me in his jail cell. He's afraid the place is bugged. And it is. Which means he won't tell me what he knows where the police can overhear him."

"But if he didn't kill Sarah, and he knows something—?"

"Tell me about Sarah and her bank account, and her will," Jericho said.

Fred Thomas shook his head, like a man who didn't believe. "Do you realize, Jericho," he asked, "that Sarah Watson has been scrounging the streets and alleys of this part of town since long before either of us was born? I can remember her as a kid. We were all a little scared of her, I suppose because she was 'different'. I thought of her as an old woman when I was five years old. That's too damned many years ago. But she was alive and apparently going strong only yesterday. I said hello to her on the street."

"About her bank account," Jericho said.

"That was last Tuesday," Thomas said. "Would you believe that beyond a good morning here and there I'd never had any conversation with her. Oh, as a kid I used to shout insults at her when I'd see her fumbling around in someone's garbage. That's all. Now she asked to see me. I think my secretary would have turned her away—rags, paper bags, not smelling like a bed of violets. I happened to come out of my office, saw her, and invited her in.

" 'You wanted to see me, Miss Watson,' I said. 'Is it Miss or Mrs.?' 'The way it is today it's Ms.,' she said. 'I want to open an account in your bank, Freddie Thomas, even though you threw a rock at me the other day.'

" 'Forty years ago, Ms. Watson,' I said.

" 'A Watson never forgets,' she said. 'I thought of a savings account.'

" 'No problem,' I said. 'How much do you want to start with, Ms. Watson?'

"So help me, then she began to pull some packages wrapped in brown paper out of her bags. Then she pulled up her skirt and rolled down her stockings. More packages. Then she began unbuttoning her blouse, or shirt waist, or whatever you call it. I wondered if I ought to call for help! More packages. I'd expected a deposit of fifty, maybe a hundred dollars. You know how much it was from Cardwell—over sixty thousand! I suggested that she consider buying some government bonds, renting a safety-deposit box, and keeping the bonds in the bank. So she put ten thousand in a savings account, bought bonds with the balance, and rented a box. She shoved a few hundred dollars—loose change I suppose you'd call it—back in one of her paper bags.

" 'You carry this kind of money around with you in—in those bags?'

" 'Where else?' she said. 'All my life. But recently some creep has been trying to con me out of my money and I decided I better put it somewhere safe.'

" 'Con you? What kind of con?' I asked her.

" 'Fifty Gs would buy me an option on an Atlantic City hotel, which, when it was turned into a gambling casino, would return ten times my investment. I know something about gambling. Been a gambler all my life. But I just don't trust this creep. Never have trusted his kind. I decided if I didn't hand over the money he might try to take it away from me by force. I'm getting a little old to defend myself against a grown man.' That's when the will business came up. With the help of the bank's attorney she made out a will naming this Dave Morris."

"So, obviously, Dave Morris isn't the man who was trying to con her," Jericho said.

"But if she told Morris he was her heir—" Thomas shrugged.

"Nothing else about the con man? What do you suppose she meant by 'his kind'?"

"A con artist—someone trying to sell her the Brooklyn Bridge," Thomas said.

"So she tells Dave Morris, a down-and-out bum, that he's going to inherit over sixty thousand dollars," Jericho said. "In order to get it quick, he kills her. Then he cuts off her head, puts it in a box, carries the box with his fingerprints all over it to my front door. I'm a stranger to him. Why?"

"It's beyond me," Thomas said.

"I'm a stranger, but he knows my reputation," Jericho said. "Suppose Sarah Watson told him about the con man, told Morris who the con man is? He thinks the con man killed her trying to take the money she no longer had on her person. Morris brings me the severed head, hoping I'll dig out the truth."

"A big-time con man," Thomas said. "He knew how much cash she carried around with her. He was after fifty grand, not just the few bucks most people imagined she might have as the proceeds from her two-dollar horse bets."

"And that con man isn't Dave Morris," Jericho said. "She left him her money. Someone who knew her habits, someone who could make a realistic guess about the money she'd gotten her hands on over all the years."

"A confidant?" Thomas suggested.

"Or a spy," Jericho said.

Captain Tom Cardwell didn't seem surprised to see Jericho outside his front door when he opened it.

"They told me at the precinct you'd gone home," Jericho said.

"Sunday's supposed to be my day off," Cardwell said. "With the Watson case wrapped up I came home. Come in."

The living room was a hodge-podge of old but comfortable-looking furniture. Things looked clean but in disorder. Cardwell seemed to read Jericho's thoughts.

"Living without a woman, things pile up," he said. "My wife died seven years ago. We bought this old house back in the days when you could buy property on a policeman's wages. When I retire next month I'm going to convert the three top floors into apartments and rent 'em out. Have to, to keep things going in today's economy." He waved to a chair. "Sit down, Mr. Jericho. Coffee?"

Jericho sat, accepting the offer of coffee. "Any luck finding the body?" he asked.

"Not yet," Cardwell said. "My men have searched every vacant building in the area. I've got the harbor police looking for it in the river. It could have been taken there and dumped." He came back from a sideboard with a mug of coffee he'd poured from an electric percolator. He handed the mug to Jericho.

"It occurred to me there's one place your men might not look," Jericho said, his face suddenly rock-hard.

"Oh? Where?" Cardwell asked.

"Here, in this house," Jericho said.

Cardwell's slate-gray eyes seemed to freeze, the coffee mug raised halfway to his mouth. "What the hell are you talking about?" His voice had a harsh, rasping sound.

"It would never occur to cops to look in the private home of their precinct captain."

"Well, I should hope not," Cardwell said, trying to smile.

"I suggest you were sure they wouldn't," Jericho said.

"I think you must be off your rocker," Cardwell said.

"Dave Morris knew," Jericho said. "How was it? She had an appointment here to close your mythical deal for an Atlantic City hotel. Dave, having been told she'd already put the money in the bank, came with her to make sure all went well when she told you it was no deal. He waited for her outside. She didn't come out. He waited for you to go somewhere and then got into the house. Where? In the basement? He found her, head chopped off."

"That's wild!" Cardwell said.

"To Dave Morris cops are the privileged enemy. He figured if he told the cops he'd found a body in your house they'd cover it up and nail him somehow. That's why he wouldn't talk to me in that bugged cell in the precinct house. He took the head, put it in a box he probably found in your basement. I checked, you buy liquor by the case, Captain. Morris brought the box to me, the only person he could think of who might help him. He didn't dare face me because he thought I might come to you and you'd still have a chance to cover up."

"Why would I do such a thing?" Cardwell asked. He sounded hollow.

"You've worked this precinct your whole career," Jericho said. "You had quite proper reasons for watching the activities of an old bag lady like Sarah Watson. In time you realized that she was really raking in money with her racing bets. You kept it to yourself at first, because once you were a decent, honest man. If anyone knew what she was carrying around she'd be a constant target for muggers. But now, with retirement at hand, with your tastes calling for more money than your pension would supply, you tried a con game on her. Invest in an Atlantic City casino and her money would multiply by ten. She almost bought it, but maybe you were too persuasive, maybe your smile was too sincere. So she put her money in the bank and came to tell you 'no deal.' All your dreams shattered by this crazy old woman. You killed her. God knows why you cut off her head. It must have been quite a shock when you came home after your tour of duty and found her head gone."

"Her blood is all over Morris," Cardwell said.

"Sure it is. He handled the bloody head while drunk, clumsy, scared out of his wits. Shall we go down in the cellar, Captain, and have a look at the body?" Jericho stood up.

"You crazy fool, you're driving me to do this, you know," Cardwell said. There was a police special in his hand, aimed straight at Jericho. "You're right, of course. She burned me up, refusing the deal, calling me names. I put the slug on her. I hit her, knocked her flat. She got up, and from inside her bag she produced a knife. It was a butcher's knife, a foot and a half long, sharp as a razor. She came at me. Eighty years old! She started at me with that knife and I grabbed it away from her. She was on me, clawing at me, and I took a swing at her with the knife." He choked. "It was like cutting a flower off its stem with a sickle."

"So let's go down in the cellar and find what's left of her," Jericho said.

"I'm afraid you're not going anywhere, Mr. Jericho."

The mug of coffee flew straight into Cardwell's face. Then Jericho's smashing blow to Cardwell's jaw sent the policeman down, where he lay twitching like a broken mechanical toy.

Jericho went to the phone and dialed a number. He asked for Lieutenant Kreevich, his friend at Homicide.

"Mark? Jericho here. Look, friend, I've either solved a murder or I'm a candidate for a long stay in one of your better jails." He gave him Cardwell's address. "Bring a shovel, Mark. We may need to do some digging. And issue an order for Dave Morris' release."

"Anything else?" Kreevich asked, in a wry voice.

"Call Marla at my place, if you will, and tell her I'll be along when you're through with me."

He put down the phone. Cardwell made an effort to sit up. Jericho put his foot on the policeman's chest and held him down.

"To quote you, chum," Jericho said. "I'm afraid you're not going anywhere. Not anywhere."

THE MAN WHO CAME BACK
Edward D. Hoch

NEW YORK IS a sweatbox in August, and Paul Conrad often wondered why the city didn't simply shut down for the month as Paris did. This August seemed especially bad, with daily temperatures above ninety, and it was no wonder that he thought often of his sister with her cottage on Fire Island. He thought of her, and then went back to his drawing board to work on the winter ad campaigns.

He'd been working nights all month, if only because the office was air-conditioned. After work there was nothing awaiting him but a hot and lonely bachelor's apartment, with a bar or a movie as the only likely alternatives. He was between girls at the moment, much to his sister's displeasure. She felt that any man of 31 should be bringing up a family. Helen, two years younger and already on her second husband, had three children from her first marriage, with another on the way.

This night, alone in the agency art department, he was hunched over his drawing board when the telephone rang.

"Paul Conrad?"

"Speaking."

"Paul, I took a chance on catching you there, when nobody answered at the apartment."

"Who's this?" The voice was familiar, and yet some barrier of his mind kept him from identifying it.

"Ralph," the voice answered.

Ralph. He sat down hard, clutching the telephone as if it might suddenly fly away. "Ralph Jennings?" he whispered, though now he recognized the voice and knew the impossible was true. "You're *alive!*"

"I have to see you, Paul. Tonight."

"Where are you?"

"The Manhattan Manor Motel. It's over on the west side, near the river."

"I'll find it. Are you using your own name?"

"Sure." He hesitated a moment on the other end of the line and then added, "Paul . . . don't tell Helen. Not yet."

"Don't worry, I won't."

He hung up and sat staring at the phone for several minutes. Ralph Jennings, his sister's first husband, had returned from a watery grave after five years. The only trouble was, Helen now had another husband.

No, he wouldn't tell Helen.

The motel room was neat and modern, an impersonal room, but Paul Conrad barely noticed it as he faced the man he'd never expected to see again.

"What happened?" he asked, though he wanted to ask why. *Why did you disappear, why did you come back now, why did you call me? Why?*

"I fell off the boat, just like the newspapers said, but I didn't drown."

"I can see that," Paul said.

Ralph Jennings smiled. He'd always been quick with a smile, always the charming young man with the bright future. Helen hadn't been able to resist him. "I made it to shore somehow, but I was dazed and didn't remember clearly. It took me a couple of days before I was myself, and by that time Finley had told everybody I'd drowned. I didn't know what to do."

"So you did nothing."

Jennings averted his eyes. "Well, I guess so."

"What have you been doing for five years?"

"Sailing, mostly. I've been working on a cruise ship out of Miami. I always liked the sea, you know. We make several runs each year between the various Caribbean ports, and to Bermuda. I only get to New York in the summer."

He was talking too fast, telling too much, and yet not enough. "What do you want me to do, Ralph? Helen's remarried, you know."

"I know. I saw it in the papers last winter. You probably won't believe this, but every year when I got to New York I'd say to myself maybe this summer I'll call her. This year, with the remarriage and all, I figured I should. But the shock might hit her pretty hard—that's why I called you first."

"Weren't you ever curious about your three children?"

"Sure. Sure I was curious." His eyes were pleading, but somehow to Paul the pleading wasn't quite sincere enough. "You must think I'm some sort of a monster."

"You disappeared and let Helen think you were dead. You left your three children without a father."

Jennings ran a hand through his dark hair. "They had the insurance."

"Which will now have to be paid back."

"I don't know, Paul. I don't know what I was thinking of! So I was wrong! What can I do about it now?"

"Helen's pregnant, you know."

"I didn't know. How could I? Who is this guy, Paul?"

"Jack Winegood. He makes a pretty fair living as news director on one of the smaller New York radio stations. A good enough living so they can afford a cottage on Fire Island."

"Is that where she is now?"

Paul nodded. "Do you really want her to know you're still alive?"

"Of course! We've got to get this thing worked out."

Paul sighed and stood up. "I'll go talk to her, see how she's feeling. The police might take a dim view of your defrauding the insurance company, you know."

"*I* didn't get the money. And she was acting innocently. She didn't know I was alive."

"How long will you be in town?"

"The ship sails the first of next week, but I'll stay longer if necessary."

"It's too late to see her tonight," Paul decided. "I'll take off from work tomorrow and go see her in the morning. Stay close to your phone around noon."

"Right." He held out his hand. "And thanks, Paul."

"Don't thank me. You're in big trouble, as if you didn't know it."

The street was still hot, but he didn't really notice. On the way back to the apartment he stopped for a couple of stiff drinks.

In the morning he drove out to Long Island's south shore and took one of the summer ferries over to Fire Island. The day was clear and a breeze off the ocean was just strong enough to make the heat bearable. He strolled along the boardwalk until he reached his sister's cottage, then went out through the sand to where he saw them at the water's edge. Helen was there with the three children and another woman, enjoying a morning swim in the salty surf.

As he approached, Helen stood up to greet him. "Playing hooky from work? This is only Friday, isn't it?" The white one-piece bathing suit was flat against her stomach, with no sign as yet of her pregnancy. At 29, she still looked like a college girl, and acted like one sometimes, too.

"How are you, Sis? Just thought I'd take a run out to see you."

"Great! Do you remember Sharon O'Connell? She was a bridesmaid at my first wedding."

Yes, he remembered Sharon O'Connell: tall and graceful and eternally sad, a serious girl in a world that needed one. He shook hands with her, noted the absence of a wedding ring on her left hand, and wondered what she'd been doing with herself. "I didn't recognize you at first. How've you been, Sharon?"

"Fine. Just fine, Paul. It's been a long time."

"You working in New York?"

She nodded, studying him through heavy eye makeup that seemed out of place on the morning beach. "I still do a little modeling, though both the years and the pounds are catching up with me. I went to a party here last night and ran into Helen. She invited me to spend the night, since Jack was working."

He turned to his sister. "Jack's in town?"

Helen nodded. "Covering the U.N. thing. He hopes to get out for the weekend."

"I wonder if Sharon would excuse us for a few moments, Helen. There's something I want to talk to you about. A family sort of thing."

Sharon rose to her feet on cue and grabbed the children's grasping hands. "Sure, you two go ahead. I'll take the kids for a run down the beach."

Paul watched her go, the long tanned legs kicking up sand as she ran. He was remembering that she'd once dated Ralph Jennings, a long time ago when they'd all been younger.

"Now, what's all the mystery?" Helen wanted to know.

"I'm afraid I've got a bit of surprising news for you. Last night—" He was interrupted by the ringing of the telephone in the cottage. Helen ran to answer it and he slipped out of his sport jacket, relaxing on the sand. Far off down the beach, Sharon and the children splashed noisily along the surf.

Helen came back after a few moments, her face pale even through the suntan. "That was Jack," she said.

"What's the matter?" His heart pounded with sudden apprehension.

"He said . . . he said Ralph was alive. He said Ralph was alive until this morning, but that somebody had murdered him."

Ralph Jennings had died in the motel room where Paul had met him. He'd been shot in the forehead at close range, with a small-caliber pistol that made little noise. It appeared that he'd just opened the door to admit his murderer when he was shot. Another guest had discovered his body near the half-open door around eight a.m., and Jack Winegood had been covering the story for his station when Ralph's identity was determined.

Paul left Helen at the cottage with Sharon and the children, and caught the next ferry to the mainland. An hour later he was with Jack Winegood in his office.

"How's Helen taking it, Paul?" the big man asked. Jack was not a great deal unlike Ralph Jennings, though he'd always lacked Ralph's twinkle of charm. He was a businessman, and his business was the news.

"She's stunned, of course." Paul told Winegood about Ralph's phone call, and their meeting of the previous night at the motel.

Helen's husband nodded as he listened. "The police will want to talk with you. That may have been the last time he was seen alive."

Paul had already considered the possibility, and he didn't like it. To his knowledge, on the previous evening he was the only one who knew that Ralph Jennings was still alive—and certainly that was one of the prerequisites for the killer: to know Ralph Jennings was alive. "You'd better get out there with Helen," he told Winegood. "I'll see the police."

He didn't, however, go directly to the police. They would only tie him up with hours of questioning or worse. There was somebody he wanted to talk with first.

Oat Finley had been a neighborhood character when Paul and Helen were growing up on the New Jersey coast. He'd come back from the war to open a boat charter service that allowed him plenty of time to sit on the dock and smoke his pipe. There had been those who spoke of an old war injury, of Oat being not quite right, but he'd always been friendly enough to Paul and his sister.

When Helen married Ralph Jennings, a strange sort of friendship had developed between Jennings and Oat. Before long, Jennings had bought a share of the failing charter-boat business, and he spent many nights and weekends on the water with Oat. It had been on one of those trips, five years ago, that he'd fallen overboard in the dark, and Oat Finley had reported him dead.

Paul hadn't seen Oat recently, but he knew where to find the man. The charter-boat service was still in operation, though now it had been moved to Staten Island, where its main customers were weekend fishermen who traveled out into the Atlantic with a collection of exotic lures and a couple of cases of beer.

It was midafternoon when Paul walked down the sagging wooden ramp to the deck of the *Brighter II* and called out to Oat Finley, "How are you, Oat? Remember me?"

Though Oat couldn't have been more than forty, he had a slow way about him that constantly brought forth guesses regarding his age, placing it anywhere over fifty. His hair was already gray, and the weather-beaten lines of his face seemed almost like old leather when he turned to smile at Paul.

"Conrad, aren't you? Helen's brother."

"That's right. Haven't seen you in a number of years now, Oat."

"Been that long?" Oat bit on his pipe. "What can I do for you? Give you a good price if you want to rent the boat."

Paul sat down on a canvas deck chair opposite him. "I came about Ralph Jennings, Oat."

"Ralph Jennings?"

"He's dead."

The wrinkled eyelids closed for a moment, then opened to meet his gaze. gaze.

"Ralph Jennings has been dead for five years," he said finally.

Paul shook his head. "No, Oat. Only for about ten or eleven hours."

The expression of friendly indifference didn't change. "He drowned."

"You thought he drowned, but he swam to shore. He's been alive all these years, working on a cruise ship. Last evening he called me and told me about it. Then sometime during the night he was murdered."

"What do you want from me?"

"I thought Ralph might have phoned you yesterday, too."

"He didn't. To me, he's been dead for five years, ever since that night on the boat. I don't know about anything else."

"Just what happened that night? Where were you bound?"

"I told all that when it happened. One of our boats, the *Brighter* it was, had developed engine trouble. We'd worked on it most of the day and took it out for a run to see if we'd gotten the kinks out. It was still making a funny noise, and Ralph leaned over the engine to try and spot the trouble. Just then we hit a swell and he went over the side. I swung the boat around, but in the darkness I couldn't find him."

"All right," Paul said. "And you haven't heard anything from him since?"

"What would I hear from a dead man?"

It was useless to explain any more. Paul thanked him and climbed back to the dock, feeling the sweat beginning to roll down the small of his back. He had visited Oat Finley and learned nothing at all. Now there was nobody left but the police.

Paul returned to the city and told his story to a calm and well-dressed detective who asked questions in a quiet voice and wrote everything down. They even gave him a cup of coffee, and when he left the station house it was with a relieved feeling that the worst was over.

"Hello, there," a voice spoke from the shadows as he was opening his car door.

"What?" He turned and saw Sharon O'Connell leaning against the car next to his. "Well! This is unexpected."

"I always do the unexpected," she answered with a smile. "I spotted your car and decided to wait."

He wanted to ask how she knew what his car looked like, but instead he said, "Let's get a cup of coffee, then."

"I could use a drink a lot better, if you're buying."

"Sure."

She drove her own car, following him to a nearby bar that was reasonably quiet for a Friday night. Over two tall, frosty glasses he studied her carefully cool image and asked, "All right. You wanted to talk to me. What about?"

"Now that's a romantic opening!"

"My brother-in-law was murdered this morning. I'm not feeling romantic. You shouldn't, either, if memory serves. Didn't you date Ralph at one time?"

"My good man, that was a lifetime ago! He married your sister nearly ten years back. I went with him in college."

"Still—"

"Still, nothing! Besides, I didn't come here to talk about me. It's about your sister."

"Helen? What—?" Suddenly he was afraid of what was coming. He signaled the waiter for two more drinks.

"I told you I spent the night at Fire Island with her, but that's not strictly true. I met her at this party and came back to the cottage with her, but then she asked me to look after the children and she went out again. She was gone for three hours, Paul."

"Did you tell this to the police?"

"Of course not. Do you think . . . Paul, would that have been time enough for her to drive into Manhattan and back?"

He thought about it and nodded. "Just barely. Are you implying that Helen drove into town and killed Ralph Jennings?"

"Of course not! I'm just telling you because that's what the police might think if they get wind of this. Helen is a friend of mine, and I think she needs help. I think you're the only one who can reach her right now."

"What about her husband?"

"Oh, sure! I'm going to go to Jack Winegood and tell him his wife was away from home for three hours in the middle of the night! While he was working! How do you think that would sound?"

"Better than murder, I suppose. You know, another man might be her only alibi if this thing gets out."

"How's it going to get out?"

He played with his glass, forming moist circles on the table. "Things have a way of getting around. If there's another man, he might talk. And if she took the ferry, several people must have seen her."

Sharon leaned back in her chair. "So now you can worry about it, too."

"Did she get a phone call while you were with her last night?"

"No. Not after we got back to the cottage. This all seemed to have been set up before."

He knew he'd have to face Helen with his knowledge. They'd never had secrets from one another, not all through childhood when they confided their innermost thoughts while hanging upside down from the big elm in Grandmother's yard. "All right," he said finally. "Thanks, I think."

"Is there anything I can do to help, Paul?"

"I guess not. Except . . . Well, you knew Ralph pretty well at one time."

"So did you."

"I know, but not the same way. Sometimes I wonder if I really knew him at all." He paused, not knowing how to put it into words. "Sharon, did he ever give you any hint that he might have been involved in something not exactly honest?"

"What do you mean?" Her eyes sharpened with something like apprehension.

"He'd been hiding for five years. Why? Was he hiding from Helen, or something else? If it was from Helen, why would he have come back this summer? Not just because he suddenly heard about her marriage. Examine the thing logically, Sharon. The news of her marriage brought him out into the open, therefore it couldn't have been hatred or dislike of my sister that kept him away."

"Maybe he reappeared just to make more trouble for her."

"Then why did he call me first, to ease the shock? Why didn't he just barge in on her—or better still, call her husband?"

Sharon O'Connell lit a cigarette. "Maybe he did call Jack. He was in town last night, remember. Jack could have killed him."

Paul tried to examine his current brother-in-law objectively. Yes, he could imagine Jack Winegood committing murder; but would he have shot Ralph Jennings, a man he'd never met, as soon as Ralph opened the door of his room? "I doubt it," he told Sharon.

"Then it gets back to Helen, doesn't it? There's no one else he would have called."

"I'll talk to her," Paul said. "Tomorrow."

"I'm driving back to Fire Island tonight, if you want to come along."

"Sure," he decided suddenly. "Helen and Jack have a guest room. I'll stay with them overnight."

The ride out was uneventful, and he began to regret having left his own car in town. Now he'd be stranded out there till Jack drove in sometime the following day, and he didn't know just when that might be.

"Looks like rain," Sharon said on the ferry, glancing up at the stars as they gradually faded from view behind a curtain of clouds.

"Summer storm. In another month we'll be having hurricanes."

"You're a dreamer, Paul. You always were. Only most of your dreams are nightmares." She gazed out at the rippling waters. "Why don't you get married and settle down?"

"Is that a proposal, or are you just filling in for Helen with the kid-sister bit?"

"Neither one. I like you, that's all."

"You liked Ralph, too," he reminded her, awaiting her reaction.

"Sure I did. I liked a lot of guys back in those days."

"What was it about Ralph? Why didn't you two ever hit it off?"

She turned her eyes toward him, just for an instant. "Maybe Helen came along. That's what you wanted me to say, wasn't it?"

"No."

"Maybe I left those kids alone last night, and took the ferry in myself. Maybe I killed him, because he'd come back to Helen again. That's what you're thinking, isn't it?"

"No."

"Damn you, Paul Conrad! You never change, do you?"

"How should I change? Should I go away and disappear for five years, like Ralph did? Should I jump over the side right now?"

They were mostly silent for the rest of the trip across, and Sharon left him before he reached his sister's cottage. It was night on Fire Island, but it was a Friday night, and there were parties in progress in some of the cottages. He found Helen and Jack alone on their porch with tall glasses clinking of ice cubes, and he settled into a chair opposite them.

"Can you put me up for the night?" he asked Helen. "I'll ride in with Jack tomorrow."

"Sure. How'd you get out here?"

"Sharon drove me. I ran into her at the police station."

"Anything new?" Helen asked.

"Jack probably knows as much as I do."

Jack Winegood shifted in his wicker chair. "The police think it might have been a sneak thief who thought the room was empty and panicked when he found Jennings there."

"Sure. Guys come back from the dead every day to get killed by hotel thieves."

Winegood shrugged. "Stranger things 'have happened."

"Jack, get Paul a drink, will you? We've been sitting here talking and he doesn't even have a glass."

Winegood mumbled something and disappeared into the cottage. It was the chance for which Paul had been waiting. He stared into the darkness at the glowing tip of his sister's cigarette. "Sharon says you were away from here last night."

"What? Oh, I guess I went up to the store for something."

"Are you in trouble, Helen?" he asked, wishing he could see her face more clearly.

"Why should I be?"

"You'd have been in trouble if Ralph had lived. You'd have had one husband more than allowed."

"So I'd have hired myself a good lawyer."

"Helen . . . I don't think I ever asked you this before. Did you still love Ralph when he disappeared?"

"He was the father of my children."

"But did you still love him?"

The screen door slammed and Jack Winegood reappeared with Paul's drink. "Hope you felt like gin, boy. The Scotch is all gone."

"Fine." He wondered how much of the conversation Helen's husband had heard, but he didn't particularly care.

"You'd better get some sleep if you're driving in with me tomorrow. I have to be at the station by nine."

"I'll be ready."

He sipped his drink, tasting the burning coolness of the gin going down. When Helen and Jack went in to bed, he decided to stay up a while longer, and strolled down the beach with his glass, feeling the warmth of the sand as it sifted into his shoes. There was a moon now, and the threat of a storm had passed. He remembered Sharon, and headed for the cottage where she was staying, but there was a party going on there. A girl who might have been Sharon was laughingly fighting off a shadowy young man on the front steps.

Paul felt old and tired and went back to his bed.

By noon on Saturday he was back at the police station, seeking out the young detective who'd questioned him. The man's name was Rivers, and he remembered Paul with a casual greeting. He was still well dressed, but this time he didn't offer Paul any coffee.

"You've remembered something else, Mr. Conrad?" he asked pleasantly.

"Not exactly. I just had an idea that might help you."

"Oh? What's that?"

"Well, if Ralph's killer wasn't just a sneak thief—if it was someone who *knew* Ralph was still alive and back in New York—then Ralph must have phoned him as he did me. Hotels and motels keep a record of calls made by guests, don't they?"

The detective smiled slightly. "They usually record the total number of local calls made, and the individual telephone numbers in the case of long-distance calls."

"Then you can check—"

"We have checked, Mr. Conrad."

"Well?"

"Ralph Jennings placed only one call from his room, and that would have been the local call to you. It looks as if you were the only person who knew he was still alive."

After that, Paul had one more angle to try—the nagging suspicion that something other than Helen had kept Ralph in hiding during the past five years. Something else, and that something else just might have been an illicit undertaking of some sort. He'd always been suspicious of the amount of time Jennings spent on the boat with Oat Finley.

He found Jack Winegood at the station, checking the news ticker for the latest out of Washington. "I was wondering if you could help me, Jack. You've got an in with the police."

His brother-in-law blinked and put down the yellow sheets of news bulletins. "What do you want?"

"Can you find out if a man named Oat Finley has a police record? Either here or in New Jersey?"

"Finley? Wasn't he on that boat with Jennings five years ago?"

"That's right. He lives out on Staten Island now."

"You're trying to solve this murder all by yourself, aren't you? Mind telling me why?"

"I'd rather not, Jack."

Winegood studied him a moment longer. "Look, I didn't want to mention it in the car coming in this morning . . . I guess maybe you and I haven't been the closest of friends, but I heard part of your conversation with Helen last night. I know you're doing this for her, and I appreciate it."

"Then you'll check on Oat Finley?"

"Wait in my office. If he has a record in New York City, I can get the information over the telephone. New Jersey will be tougher."

Paul went into the office where he'd met with Winegood just twenty-four hours earlier, when both of them were still shocked by the news of Ralph's reappearance and murder. He dropped into one of the sticky leather armchairs and lit a cigarette, prepared for a lengthy wait while Winegood was busy on the phone. The office was a reflection of the man, drab and ordinary, with occasional flashes of interest in the form of framed and autographed pictures. A former mayor, a current senator—the newsmakers. On his desk was a paperweight in the shape of a microphone.

Winegood returned in ten minutes. "That was a good guess," he said. "Oat Finley's been arrested twice. The first time was eight years ago, on suspicion of running contraband Scotch whisky into the country from a ship ten miles offshore. The charges were finally dismissed because of some problem with the evidence—illegal search and seizure. Two years ago, Federal agents grabbed him on a similar charge—this time selling whisky without a tax stamp on it. He was convicted, but received a suspended sentence for a first offense."

"Interesting."

"Here's something even more interesting. Did you know it was Finley who identified Jennings' body yesterday morning? A card in Jennings' wallet listed him as next of kin."

"I'll be damned!" Paul moved to the edge of the chair, feeling the rush of excitement through his veins. It was a long shot, but it had paid off. "I talked to him yesterday and he never mentioned it. In fact, he pretended to know nothing about Jennings surviving the boat accident."

"He knew, all right."

"I guess he did." Suddenly the pieces were dropping into place for Paul. "When I talked with Ralph, he mentioned that he was dazed after the accident. The water wouldn't have done that, but a hit on the head might have. I think Ralph was in on Oat's smuggling activities. He must have known about them, with all the time he spent on the boat with Oat Finley. Something happened that night five years ago, and Oat tried to kill him. Ralph was scared and decided to play dead, until he heard about Helen's remarriage to you. Then he decided to return and straighten things out—and Oat killed him again."

"Where is this guy?" Winegood asked.

"Staten Island. I'm going out there."

"So am I, Paul."

"I think I can handle him."

Jack Winegood smiled. "I'm still a newsman, and this is the best story I've had all summer. I'm sticking with it."

They left together, and headed through Brooklyn toward the bridge to Staten Island.

Oat Finley's boat was there, bobbing gently against the dock, but he was nowhere in sight. Paul squinted into the sun and finally settled on a bald little man who ran a hot-dog stand at one end of the pier.

"How's the fishing, Pop?"

"Good, I guess. Don't fish much myself."

"We wanted to rent a boat. Oat Finley's boat."

"That one out there, with the big mast. Nice one, but he don't rent it much."

"You seen him around today?"

"Not in the last hour or two."

"Where does he live, when he's not on the boat?"

"Got an apartment with a nephew of his, up on the hill. That red brick building."

"The nephew been around today?"

The bald man shook his head. "He usually works the boat with Oat, but I ain't seen him in a couple of days."

Paul climbed the hill, with Winegood behind, thinking as he always did that Staten Island was a place apart. Even the bridge, stretching across the harbor entrance like some steel umbilical, had fed the island only with greater numbers, but not yet with the peculiar turmoil that was the real New York.

"Wait outside," Paul told Winegood when they reached the apartment building. "He might try to get away."

"All right."

Paul went up the steps carefully, wishing he had some weapon, then remembering that this was Oat Finley—old Oat, the neighborhood character. No one to fear, even if he were a murderer.

"Oat!" He knocked softly on the door, then louder. "Oat!"

The door was unlocked. Oat had never been one for locking doors. He stepped in, ready for anything except what he saw.

Oat Finley was seated in a chair facing the door, staring at him with three eyes. The third eye was a bullet hole, and old Oat wasn't needing any of them to see.

Downstairs, Paul found Jack Winegood still waiting. "He's dead, murdered. Not too long ago."

The blood drained from Winegood's face, and he seemed to sway.

Paul steadied him. "I know how you feel. If Oat Finley was guilty, that meant Helen was innocent. Now we're back where we started, only worse."

"She's my wife, Paul."

"And she's my sister. I think . . . " He was staring back down the hill at the shoreline, watching one of the crafts pull slowly away from the dock. He couldn't be mistaken. It was Oat Finley's *Brighter II*. "Jack! Stay here and call the police!" he shouted, already running down the hill.

"Where are you—?"

Paul couldn't hear any more. He was running with the momentum of a downhill race, his eyes never leaving the sleek white hull as it moved slowly, but with gaining speed, through the choppy waters of the Lower Bay. It might have been heading for Fire Island, or for a thousand other points on the opposite shore.

"Quick!" Panting, gasping for breath. "What's the fastest boat I can rent here?"

"Well, mister, I've got a speedboat over there that's pretty fast."

"Can you catch the *Brighter II*?"

"Oat Finley's barge? Any day in the week!"

"Here's ten bucks if you catch it right now."

"You're on, mister."

The man knew his craft, sent it kicking through the crests as if driven by a fury. Within five minutes they were gaining, closing the gap with the *Brighter II*.

"He thinks it's a race," the man told Paul. "He's speeding up."

"Catch him!"

"I saw it go out, but that's not Oat on board."

"I know," Paul said. He no longer had to ask who it was.

"Clouding up. Looks like a storm to the east."

Spray in his face, salty to his tongue, Paul didn't bother to answer. They were overtaking the *Brighter II* again, and this time they would catch her.

"When you're close enough, I'm going to jump for it," Paul told the man.

"Damn fool stunt! Give me my ten bucks first!"

He handed the man his money, then stood upright, grasping the sticky windshield. "Get a little closer."

"You'll kill yourself, mister."

Paul waited another instant, until he felt he could almost touch the sleek silvery side of the other craft. Then he launched himself into space, clawing for a handhold. One foot hit the water, and he thought he'd be grabbed under, but then he was pulling himself over the railing, rolling into the stern of the craft.

He got shakily to his feet and clawed his way forward to the tiny cabin. He knew there'd be a gun, and when he saw it pointed at him he felt no fear.

"Hello, Ralph," he said above the roar of the engines. "Back from the dead a second time?"

Ralph Jennings didn't lower the gun. He kept his left hand on the wheel, but his eyes and the pistol were both on Paul. "You had to come after me, didn't you?"

"Helen's in trouble, Ralph. They're going to think she did it."

The eyes were hard and cold above the gun. "They'll know soon enough it wasn't me that got killed. I only needed to confuse things until I could get to that rat Finley and catch him off guard."

"I know about all that, Ralph."

"How, Paul? How'd you know?"

"I didn't tumble for a long time, not till just a few minutes ago, in fact, when I saw the way you were handling this boat. But I should have. Of course I didn't see the body, and neither did Helen. Winegood might have seen it while he was reporting the killing, but he'd never met you. And this morning I learned that Oat Finley had identified the body! That really set me to thinking. I'd already figured out how you and Finley were running whisky ashore from ships and selling it tax-free back in the old days. Your story about being dazed after the accident made me think that it wasn't an accident at all, but a case of thieves falling out. Finley tried to kill you, and you decided to go into hiding rather than call the police and get yourself deeper into trouble."

The craft hit a swell, and Ralph had to steady himself. "Keep talking."

"So this summer, finally, you came back. Helen had remarried, and I guess you realized you weren't being fair to her. You phoned me, and then you phoned Oat Finley, because you knew he'd find out you'd returned. You were more clever with those phone calls than you realized. The police check showed you'd only made one local call from your room. This baffled me, till I realized that there wouldn't have been a Staten Island phone book in your room. You could have called Information, but instead I suppose you went down to the lobby, looked up the number, and called Oat from there."

"You're smart, Paul. Wasting your time in the art business."

"Oat Finley knew you were going to have to tell everything about your disappearance, including his attempt to kill you and his illegal smuggling business. He was already on a suspended sentence, and he knew it would mean prison for him. You figured he'd try to kill you again Thursday night, but what you didn't figure was that instead of coming himself he'd send his nephew—who'd taken over as his criminous partner after you disappeared."

"You're guessing now."

"Not at all! You were ready for something, killed the nephew, and switched identification with him, to confuse things till you could kill Finley and be safe from him. But in switching wallets you must have missed a card he carried listing Oat Finley as his next of kin. When I heard that the police called Finley to identify the body, I should have known right away it wasn't you. You wouldn't be listing your would-be murderer as next of kin. Apparently this card didn't have the nephew's own name on it, because the police only needed Finley's word to be convinced the body was yours. Of course, the truth would come out quickly enough if they checked the fingerprints or showed the body to Helen, but you needed only a few hours. Finley gave you more time than you expected, because he saw an advantage to himself in identifying the dead man as you—he could kill you later and throw your body in the ocean, and the police would never untangle the thing. He must have figured his nephew wouldn't be missed. He could always make up a story to cover his absence."

Ralph suddenly swerved the boat, scanning the harbor area with a quick eye. "Talk faster, Paul. I'm getting impatient."

"You got to Finley this morning, before he could find you, and killed him. When I found his body, the pieces began to fit together. The first dead man was a kin of Finley's, and a nephew was missing. If the dead man was the nephew, I figured you'd killed them both—otherwise, why go into hiding again right after reappearing? When I was chasing the boat just now, I could see it was in the hands of someone who knew it. That made it you for sure. Now tell me where you're going."

"Away. Just away."

"You think you can? Even if the police don't go checking fingerprints, some newspaper's bound to print your picture from five years ago. The cops will know quickly enough that it's not your body, that you set up the scene in the motel room to look like you were shot opening the door. They've probably got a pickup out for you already."

"Then Helen won't have to worry." He stared down at the gun in his hand, as if seeing it for the first time. "I thought Oat was just running untaxed whisky, and I helped him with it. Then one night I discovered there was heroin in the cases, too. I wanted out, and that's when he tried to kill me. That's why he sent his nephew to kill me, too. I don't feel guilty about killing either of them."

The craft hit another harbor swell, throwing Ralph off balance. Paul went at him, trying for the gun, but he wasn't fast enough. There was a single shot and Ralph Jennings crumpled into the corner. By the time Paul tore his shirt away, Ralph's blood was on them both. He tried to speak, and then died in Paul's arms as the *Brighter II* cruised unmanned in widening circles.

Paul looked down at his sister, playing in the sand with her youngest child. "Do you want to tell me where you were that night, Helen?" he asked her quietly.

"I've told Jack, and he's the only one who needs to know. It was just a messy little Fire Island affair, and it's over now."

"I'm glad. Jack's a pretty decent guy."

She nodded. "Maybe this summer hasn't been so bad after all."

Paul kicked at the sand with his bare foot. Down the beach he could see Sharon O'Connell walking toward them. "Maybe not," he agreed.

HILDEGARDE WITHERS IS BACK

Stuart Palmer

A MUFFLED DIN sounded in the anteroom, and then the door banged open and an unexpected guest backed her way into the Inspector's office, fending off the uniformed guardian of the gates with handbag and umbrella. "Oscar! *Do* something!" she cried.

"Hildegarde Withers, as I live and breathe!" gasped the grizzled skipper of Homicide, managing to get out of his swivel chair and restore some semblance of order. "Don't mind the sergeant, he's a new man and didn't know you from Adam—I mean, Eve. If you'd let me know you were coming to town I'd have had the welcome mat out. But I thought you were safely retired, and busy with your African daisies out in California."

"African *violets,* Oscar." The schoolteacher was preening her feathers like a ruffled Buff Orpington. "And if you dare to add insult to injury by making one of your characteristic snide remarks about my new hat—"

"That's a *hat?* I thought it was a fallen soufflé!"

"This is hardly the time for persiflage. Not when I've just flown all the way across the country to come to your aid on the Barth case."

"By broomstick? Well, dear lady, we've been getting along pretty well here at Centre Street without any amateur help since you quit being self-appointed gadfly to the Police Department—" Here Inspector Oscar Piper broke into a slow double-take. "The *what* case?"

"Barth, Cecily Barth. You do recall the name?"

"It may ring a bell somewhere, but just now—"

"Oscar, I sometimes think that you are being intentionally dense! Cecily Barth happens to have been one of Hollywood's most famous stars in her

311

day. You yourself must have been just about the right age to have had a schoolboy crush on her, back when she was the Love Goddess of the Silver Screen, unquote."

"I used to be a Tom Mix fan, myself," he said almost apologetically.

"But even you must have seen some of the recent newspaper publicity about how the great independent television producer Mr. Boris Abbas is producing the life story of Cecily Barth as a special on filmed TV, bringing a famous Hollywood writer here to do the script in collaboration with Cecily herself, testing dozens of young sexpot actresses to play the leading role, and so on and so forth."

The Inspector carefully relighted his cigar. "Oh, *that* one! I've got the flimsies here somewhere. Yeah, right here. You call it the Barth case, but it was some scenario writer name of Gary Twill who did the Dutch Act out of his hotel window late yesterday afternoon. According to all reports, it was a simple case of suicide."

"Suicide is never simple! Oscar, most criminologists agree that falls from high windows, like drownings from canoes, are automatically suspect. Perfect murders, perhaps. I am quite aware of the fact that you police don't believe there is any such thing as the perfect murder, but remember, if it were perfect, you wouldn't know of it! And Gary Twill's death was no suicide, I'll wager a pretty penny. I feel it in my bones."

"Of which you have a complete set," Oscar Piper put in unkindly but accurately, softening the wisecrack with a Hibernian-type grin. "Look, Hildegarde old girl, I'm personally delighted to have you back in town and tonight will joyfully buy you a spaghetti dinner at any place you name. I think I know just how bad you're itching to make like the old firehorse at the sound of the siren, but believe me, this case just ain't it!"

"*Isn't* it," she corrected automatically.

"Okay, *isn't.* This Hollywood writer, the guy named Twill, had been out of work a while and he got this plush assignment to come to New York and do a TV script, with free hotel room and everything—and then it all went blooie. He had a thing going with the boss's playgirl-type secretary and he had a contract and he lost them both at the same time, the girl *and* the job. So he did the Dutch Act, like I said. What more do you want, chimes?"

"A suicide note or an eyewitness would help. Oscar, there is more here than meets the eye. I have known some screenwriters in my time—Los Angeles is crawling with them. They don't take their lives when they lose a girl, or a job either; they feel sure that another one, girl or job, will be along in a minute. Meanwhile, like Miniver Cheevy, they keep on drinking."

"Miniver *who?*"

"A character in an almost forgotten poem by an almost forgotten poet named Edwin Arlington Robinson. No matter. I became interested in this case because of a certain letter which was shown to me over a week ago by a neighbor of mine out in Santa Monica, a Mrs. Marcia Connell, whose three children are usually trampling down my flowerbeds. She happens to be the niece and presumably the only blood relation of the once glamorous Cecily Barth.

"I've caught glimpses of the old lady arriving on Christmas and birthdays, in an ancient Cadillac with equally ancient chauffeur, to deliver presents to her grandniece and grandnephews. Lady Bountiful—but she *never* has helped when Marcia needed a new washer and dryer or the children's teeth needed straightening. And I've seen Cecily mentioned in the newspapers; she's a fanatic anti-vivisectionist, makes speeches for the SPCA and Humane Society drives, and once—before arthritis totally crippled her below the belt and confined her to a wheel chair—she even tried to lead a protest march against the Chicago stockyards because of what she considered cruelty in slaughtering methods. Quite a personality, Oscar. Would you care to read the letter she wrote to her niece, a week or more ago?"

"Yes, but not very much," said Oscar Piper. Nevertheless he meekly accepted the note, neatly typed on Hotel Harlow Towers stationery, and read:

Darling,

Rain rain rain here in New York, and I wish I was home in my own house in Coldwater Canyon where I belong. I hope Jack is still working at Douglas and bringing home his paycheck intact. And darling Loramae and Timmy and Ricky! I hope to be back home for Christmas, but if I am still tied up here I have just oodles of goodies I've collected in these wonderful toy stores like Schwarz's, all wrapped and ready.

The script goes well, except that Gary Twill, the writer—who is right handy in the room next to my suite—is sometimes a bit stubborn and wants documentation for things that happened instead of trusting my memory, which as you know is perfect. I usually get my way, however. He does the structure and first draft of the scenes and then we hash them over and finally I type up the finished version and correct the dialogue and so forth. We are now on the final scenes.

I confess I'll be glad when it's over. The weather has been so nasty that I don't have Felicio, the most obliging Puerto Rican bellboy, push my wheel chair out on any more shopping trips. I don't feel so safe in this big town, either. Somebody doesn't want this film released—I've had some threatening phone calls and so has Mr. Abbas and Gary Twill.

And I tell you, dear, I can almost smell Death around this hotel—close to me and coming closer. When I tell my fortune with the cards, I get the Queen of Spades or some other dismal symbol almost every time—and you know what that means!

I rescued a lost forlorn black kitten in an alleyway and sneaked it into the hotel—you know black cats are lucky! I named him Asmodeus, and I intend to bring him back with me and present him to our darlings.

If I ever come back! Marcia, I have a terrible presentiment that Death hovers over this old hotel—I mean it! Just as soon as the TV script is finished and approved by Mr. Abbas—a very strange man but you know producers, almost always the enemies of talent—and as soon as the picture is completely cast and costumes picked, I am getting out of here. Maybe I'll come back when they actually start shooting and maybe I won't. This Lilith Lawrence who is to play me looks the part all right—she is beautiful enough—but she underacts terribly. I hate to say it about anybody but I fear she's a Method actress!

Must close now—room service will be bringing up my dinner and I have to lock Asmodeus in the closet as the little black devil will dash out through any open door and then I have to chase him, in my wheel chair, yet—unless Felicio or Gary Twill is around to help.

Don't worry about what I said—at my age Death is only a heartbeat away anyhow. And I know how to protect myself. I have a very authentic-looking pistol that shoots ammonia, plus some other precautions, like a chain on the door.

Kiss the dear kiddies for me.

> Your affectionate
> Auntie Cecily

The Inspector handed back the letter and shrugged. "Sounds like some kind of a nut," he observed. "And I thought black cats were supposed to be *un*lucky."

"I am not interested in primitive superstitions, Oscar. During the Dark Ages in Europe—and even in England during the witchcraft hunts—hundreds of thousands of cats were tortured and killed because they were thought to be witches' familiars, and rats and mice overran the land. How any cats survived I'll never know, but I prefer dogs myself, particularly big Standard poodles like my dear old Talley, who is languishing in a boarding kennel at the moment."

The Inspector looked at his watch pointedly.

"Very well, Oscar, we'll get down to cases. Perhaps Cecily is a bit of a psychic, or has some ESP precognition power. Coming events do cast their shadows before: Abraham Lincoln foresaw his own death in a dream, and the day before President Kennedy was assassinated a clairvoyant ran all over Washington trying to get to somebody and warn him not to go to Dallas."

"Coincidence," said Oscar Piper.

"Perhaps. But suppose somebody actually *doesn't* want Cecily's life story to come out—somebody who knew her 'way back when and has since, shall we say, reformed and hoped that the wild oats would stay buried?"

"Come off it! The old dame is strictly a has-been! Who cares about scandals that happened more than forty years ago? It's ancient history. And how would knocking off the writer—or Cecily either—prevent Mr. Abbas from making the picture anyway?"

"I don't know—yet! But I have all the newspaper clippings here in my handbag. There is something rotten, and I don't mean in Denmark. I'm not just working on a hunch, or on my so-called feminine intuition either. Oscar, how deeply have you looked into this Gary Twill death?"

"Things have changed in the Police Department, Hildegarde. I'm strictly administrative now, and other men on precinct level do the legwork. I'm supposed to be an Inspector."

"Well, then—*inspect!*"

"Hildy, why are you getting the wind up and making all these waves?"

"I'll tell you exactly why. I only got into town this morning—I tried to phone you from the airport and got a fast brushoff from that uniformed ape in your outer office. He told me you were in conference!" She sniffed. "You were not to be disturbed!"

"That's right, I was down having a look at the morning lineup."

"I got another brushoff at the Hotel Harlow Towers, where Cecily Barth is too tied up to see anybody, and so on. But I had noticed that Gary Twill, the man you say committed suicide, was reported by hotel employees to have gone out on a brief errand shortly before he died. He returned with a paper bag which he took up to his room. Right?"

"According to these reports, right. But it all fits. He thought he needed some Dutch courage—"

"I do wish, Oscar, you would stop insulting the people of Holland. And why should Gary Twill go out in the rain? Why buy liquor himself when he could have called room service and had drinks sent up from the bar and charged to Mr. Abbas? Or at least sent a bellboy out on his errand? It just doesn't fit! So having nothing better to do, I provided myself with a newspaper photograph of Twill—who, I must say, was a distinctive-looking man well over six feet, with prematurely white hair—and I went out cruising the neighborhood shops to see if I could discover the *real* purpose of his last errand." She paused dramatically.

"And so what?"

"So *this!* He not only bought a bottle of champagne at a package store on Sixth Avenue, but he also stopped in at a travel agency on Fifth and purchased a first-class airplane ticket to Los Angeles on the 11:00 P.M. flight! Now, don't tell me that a man who intends to die the hard way would go out and spend almost $200 on a plane ticket that he didn't intend to use!"

The Inspector frowned. "Then something must have happened to push him over the edge—"

"Exactly! Something—or someone."

"I mean, to make him change his mind." But Oscar Piper was not quite as sure as he had been a few moments before.

"These are deep waters, Oscar. And getting deeper. If we could only look back in Time, and see Yesterday . . ."

It was late morning on a rainy Wednesday. Or a rainy morning on a late Wednesday. Gary Twill wasn't quite sure and didn't care which. He opened his bloodshot eyes somewhat gingerly, to survey the ceiling of his hotel room, wishing fervently that he were far, far away from this dingy pad, far from the darling if slightly demented old bat of a Cecily—he sometimes thought of her as "Nightmare Alice"—in the next suite, far from Boris Abbas in his office up in the penthouse furnished in silver and black upholstery, and most particularly far from Janey Roberts, Valkyrie-cum-vixen.

Far from Manhattan. The big city, to a native Californian, always seemed dirty, raw, and cold—when it wasn't dirty, hot, and humid. Twill had worked almost all night on the final sequence of *The Thousand and One Loves of Cecily Barth*—a title he loathed, but maybe he could talk Abbas into changing it later. He had turned the final ten pages over to Cecily for her to read and approve and type up the final version with two carbons; it kept her feeling that she was a part of it all to bang it out on her portable electric typewriter, and she could do nice clean copy. She was to take it up to Abbas, or at least leave it with Janey for the great man to read later. Anyway, the damn thing was done, finis, complete.

What a wild assignment! What a wild collaboration, with this crazy old relic who fancied herself as a writer because she'd taken some correspondence course in screenwriting and had turned out a dozen or so dramas that never even got to first base with movie or TV story editors! But today not even a former Oscar winner could pick and choose his assignments; there was eighty percent unemployment in the Writers Guild West.

The big man sat up in his tangled blankets and sighed, ruffling his almost white but still very curly locks. Then he fumbled for the phone and called down to room service for breakfast—not that his stomach was really awake yet.

After a while the ubiquitous Felicio rolled in a cart bearing a pot of coffee, orange juice, some cold toast and obviously colder eggs. Felicio also wore his hopeful Puerto Rican smile, beneath the nose which had been flattened during some earlier attempts to become the terror of the welterweights—but you had to give the guy credit for trying.

Sometimes he was very trying, like now. For he had another manuscript with him; Twill could see it sticking out of a pocket. The Great American short story again. "Oh God!" moaned the man in the bed. "Not today!"

"But you have feenish the job. You will go back soon to Hollywood. You take my manuscript and show it to Mr. Goldwyn like you promise?"

"Yes, yes. Just leave it on the bureau."

Gary Twill might just as well have said "wastebasket"—and the hypersensitive Felicio sensed it immediately. He withdrew into his Latin sheath, with injured dignity. "I guess it was all just kidding, no?" There was a sentence or two in mumbled Spanish, too fast for Gary Twill to catch— except for one or two words, and those not customarily found in Spanish-English tourist dictionaries. The door closed behind Felicio, and none too gently.

Twill sighed and shrugged. These would-be authors! He really should not have jollied Felicio along—now he'd probably made another enemy in this God-forsaken place. Twill drank the orange juice and a few sips of the cold coffee, then went back to a troubled sleep, from which he was rudely awakened around 2:00 P.M. by the sound of a key in the door and the entrance of a somewhat oversize but very blonde and very curvaceous young woman whose secret Mona Lisa smile boded no particular good.

She had been here many times before, under happier circumstances. It was obvious that at this moment she was not on loving dalliance bent, to put it mildly. "You could have knocked, Janey dear," he said, as he drew a sheet over the bare and exposed portions of his muscular figure.

"I could have knocked with a hammer on your thick skull, buster," said Jane. "With joy and gusto. But as it happens I just dropped by to return your room key, and to be the first to bring you some good news. Good from my point of view at least. Not from yours."

"Don't be unkind when I have a king-size hangover. What happened? Didn't Cecily approve the script! She's already okayed all but the last ten pages."

"Oh, she typed up the last scene real neat, and she said she approved the whole thing. She'd do anything for you, Lover Boy, like most women. But when His Nibs read your hunk of tripe—"

"Rewrite required?" asked Gary Twill, moaning.

"Rewrite my sainted painted toenails! Mr. Abbas read it and then he blew up and he said—and I quote—that it is the most misbegotten, unshootable, useless one hundred and eighty pages of junk that he has ever seen, even in a lifetime involved with writers who can't write, and that it turns out to be sophomoric fantasy instead of the objective semi-documentary biography he hired you to do, and that if he could he'd hold up your check and that he fervently wished someone would restrain him from coming down here and strangling you with his bare hands for wasting over four grand of his hard-earned money and then delivering a package of pure garbage!"

Jane was enjoying this, Gary Twill suddenly discovered. She was trying to get a bit of her own back, as our British cousins say. But he was now fairly wide-awake. "Come now; what was so wrong with the damn script?"

"You ought to know! You fictionized the whole thing!"

"Suddenly I feel confused—I didn't think it was fiction. But dear sweet love, knock it off! So what if Abbas puts another writer on the final, shooting version of the script? Forgive and forget; come back to Hollywood with me and live it up a little! We fit together so good—you make me happy!"

"Slap-happy," said Jane. "Mister Twill, I wouldn't go to Hollywood with you if by any chance I wanted to go to Hollywood and you were the accredited, uniformed driver of a brand-new Greyhound bus! I don't mess around with a guy who's already had three wives!"

"Two, and both legally divorced. I only pay token alimony." He sighed, the handsome if slightly raddled face looking hurt. "You shouldn't insist on taking it so seriously. I should have told you in the beginning, I know. But please, baby—I got a headache. I worked all night. Everybody hates me. Cecily thinks I didn't do her amours full justice, now you say Abbas isn't satisfied with the script, and Felicio hates me because I don't flip over his short stories cribbed from O. Henry—"

"And don't forget Lilith Lawrence, buster!"

"Lilith? Hell, she got the part, didn't she? She's set to play Cecily, thanks to me."

"And you soft-talked her into testing for the role on the Beautyrest, which got her into trouble with her agent who happens also to be her boy friend, a guy even bigger than you are and considerably stronger if not meaner, by the name of Hymie Rose. Keep out of dark alleys, darling, while you're still in Manhattan."

"You *do* give a damn, then, Janey, darling!" Gary Twill said hopefully.

"Not for you, for Hymie. He might just possibly get caught, though it would be justifiable homicide in my book, you—you rat-fink!" Jane went out, slamming the door behind her.

Twill winced and then slid out of bed, stark naked. He paused to take a medicinal gulp from the almost-empty bottle of whiskey on the bureau and then—when the warm glow had hit his insides to a satisfactory degree—set about showering, shaving, and putting on some clothes. He'd phone Abbas pretty soon and find out how much Janey, in her vicious, holier-than-thou mood, had exaggerated the foul-up with the script. Probably she had exaggerated quite a lot, because while it wasn't going to be nominated for an Emmy it was still a damn good piece of work, considering what there had been to work with. Cecily's life story almost outstripped *Fanny Hill* and *Forever Amber* combined.

When Gary Twill was half dressed he stopped short, sniffing. There was a strange smell in the air. It wasn't Janey's too liberal sprinkling of "My Sin," or the breakfast eggs, or Cecily's damn cat that had its litter box in the otherwise unused connecting bathroom; it was something else— something Gary couldn't identify.

"New York just smells, I guess," he said to himself. "Too many people too close together." Being an essentially factual and objective man, he did not once consider the odor to be the smell of death, nor did he—for all his sensitivity—hear the beating of dark, invisible wings overhead.

"Here goes," he said aloud, and finished the bottle. Then he mentally girded his loins, put on his armor, and went down the hall and up the elevator to the penthouse. Abbas had both his offices and his living quarters here, plus a tiny and somewhat bedraggled patio and garden outside, forty stories above the street.

Miss Bixby, the built-in receptionist, was a dour old doll, a sort of birdlike old biddy from whom he had never even been able to win a smile. Not at least until this afternoon, when she told Gary Twill that the great man was much too busy to see him, and that his severance check would be mailed to his agent. Gary Twill ruefully chalked up another sworn enemy, but he headed for the inner door.

It was locked. "He's got Miss Lawrence and her agent in there now," proffered Miss Bixby. "And I don't think waiting around will do you any good, frankly. Jane distinctly said that I was to tell you not to wait."

But Gary Twill waited anyway, reading an old magazine from the coffee table without actually seeing it. After a while the inner door opened and Lilith Lawrence—the spitting image of Cecily Barth at 25, even to the dark sleek hair and the billowy hips—emerged, closely followed by her agent. Hymie was a robust, sharply dressed man with close-shaved but darkish-blue chin and cheeks, who looked straight through Gary Twill and headed for the exit. Lilith Lawrence (born Mae Klotz) hesitated for a moment, giving the writer her sweetest smile.

"So sorry, Gary darling," she trilled. "But .that's the way the ball bounces, isn't it? I only—" Hymie Rose grasped her by the elbow and propelled her hastily out of the place.

"So now can I see Abbas?" Twill demanded of the woman at the desk.

She shrugged and picked up the phone. After a moment she put it down and said, "Mr. Abbas says to tell you that he's very busy and that your room rent is paid up only through today and that if you keep hanging around and bothering him I am to call Mr. Durkin, who as you know is the house detective, and have you forcibly eee-jected!"

"I get the message," said Gary Twill. "Have a good time at the next coven." He departed, with whatever dignity was left to him. Which was not too much.

As he rode down in the elevator he decided to travel westward under the alias of George Spelvin or something; no use letting everybody in the trade who read *Daily Variety* and its "NY to LA and LA to NY" column know that screenwriter Gary Twill had flopped in the big city and was returning ahead of time with his tail between his legs . . .

In Inspector Piper's office Miss Hildegarde Withers was holding forth. "But don't you see, Oscar, this man Twill was out of his element here in New York. He was surrounded by people he didn't understand and who didn't understand him. This independent producer, Mr. Abbas, is reputed throughout show business to be a man of violent temper. According to the newspaper accounts, in his earlier days he was a professional wrestler in Hungary and a protégé of Sandor Szabo, whoever that was—"

"Just one of the greatest mat men in history," said Piper, brightening.

"You see? If he became enraged at his writer—?"

"Hildegarde, you're tilting at windstorms."

"It's *windmills,* if you insist on quoting from books you've never read! Abbas is a possibility, anyway. He had the physical ability to throw anybody through a window or over a parapet. And then there is this Jane Roberts person, the blonde Amazon type. With whom Gary Twill was for a time intimate, to put it politely. A woman scorned, Oscar—you know how dangerous they are."

"Dream on, dream on. In this day and age women don't kill for that, not good-looking ones, anyway."

The spinster schoolteacher was consulting her sheaf of newspaper clippings. "Then what about Lilith Lawrence, the girl chosen to play the part of the young Cecily in the TV film? Here's a nightclub photo of her and Gary Twill, holding hands at someplace called El Morocco and looking very fatuously at one another. A girl as physically equipped as Lilith must have plenty of boy friends, some of whom might have resented a Hollywood writer getting into the act, as the phrase goes. An obvious jealousy motive. And there is also the unpleasant Mr. Durkin, the house detective, who was very nasty to me this morning when I tried to see Cecily. According to the newspaper stories he had had several altercations with Twill over noise and high jinks in the hotel room. He's a suspect to be reckoned with."

"He's also an ex-cop," Piper said. "I remember vaguely that there was some beef connected with his leaving the Force. That I will look into, if you insist. But don't let me stop you—go on with your brain-washing."

"I think you mean brain-storming, but no matter. You're a real Mr. Malaprop, Oscar. There is also this bellboy named Felicio Bonaventura, who keeps cropping up in the affair and who seems to have told each reporter a different story. Anyway, not one of these people has an airtight alibi for the time of the murder—if it was, as I believe, a murder."

"But do they *need* alibis? And while you're making up your list, better put down dear old Cecily Barth, too. I don't see any motive for her—but you never know. And the wheel chair can be only a prop, and she can really walk as good as anybody else—"

"As *well*, Oscar! And I think you have been watching too many old movies on the Late Late Show. Even if it weren't for her crippling arthritis, even if she could get out of the wheel chair and walk, how on earth could she—a frail woman weighing less than a hundred pounds—throw a big man out of a window?"

"It's your frammis," said Oscar Piper. "Personally, I think it was the butler. Only I guess there really isn't any butler in our cast of characters, is there?"

"You're not being very funny. And you haven't explained the bottle of champagne or the airline ticket. I think the ticket alone proves that my worst suspicions are justified."

"Do you ever have any *best* suspicions?" He grinned, and chose a fresh cigar. "Hildegarde, I'm very fond of you, but sometimes you're nuttier than a fruit cake."

"In case you don't know it, there are some new recipes for fruit cake.

Remember, Oscar, that Cecily Barth did step on a lot of toes in her heyday, and no doubt she made a lot of enemies. In her time as a movie queen she was, according to legend, no better than she should be, leading men on and then throwing them aside—"

"Like a worn-out glove?"

"—and wrecking many a marriage and many a career. Her life story, if presented on television, might just possibly ruin certain people who have since grown mature and respectable. Suppose for a moment that she, and not Gary Twill at all, was the intended victim? Remember Cecily's letter to her niece? Suppose Gary Twill had been trying to protect her, and somehow got too close to the truth?"

"My supposer isn't quite that active nowadays, Hildegarde. But let's look at this thing seriously for a moment. It just *has* to be suicide. Twill was a big, powerful, athletic-type man and nobody could have thrown or pushed him out of a hotel window, not without a hell of a lot of commotion anyway."

"Unless he was knocked unconscious first, perhaps?"

"You're *reaching,* Hildegarde. No, I have a hunch he took the easy way out."

"Suicide is 'easy'?" she snapped. "That could only be suggested by someone who has never experienced it. Oh, you know what I mean! And my dear Oscar, time was when if I came into your office with a bee in my bonnet, you'd have come instantly alive, grabbed your hat and a handful of those dreadful stogies, and we'd have taken off on the chase."

"Time *was,*" admitted the Inspector soberly. "I'm strictly desk level now; I don't actually go out on cases and try to do the work of the precinct men. And remember, neither of us is as young as we used to be."

"Speak for yourself, Oscar!" And Miss Withers gathered herself and her belongings together and made an abrupt exit, slamming the door so hard that, out in the anteroom, the sergeant swallowed his gum.

Thirty seconds later the sergeant had another shock, as he saw the skipper erupt from the inner office, hat and topcoat and cigars in hand. "Closed for the day," Inspector Oscar Piper barked in passing. "Hold the fort. I got to take off and try to keep my best friend from becoming her own worst enemy." He hurried out into the main hallway—where he found Miss Hildegarde Withers leaning against the bulletin board with a patient yet cryptic smile on her somewhat equine visage.

"So here we go again," she said. "Better late than never."

A little later the two oddly assorted sleuths climbed out of a taxi at the Hotel Harlow Towers, that once plush and now slightly run-down hostelry on Central Park South. They stood on the sidewalk, a chill autumnal wind whipping about their ankles, at presumably the same spot where Gary Twill had come plummeting down out of nowhere to splash his brains out on the cement. Just before 6:00 P.M. would have been a very busy hour at this location, as they both knew.

"It was only by the grace of God that the fool didn't take some innocent passerby with him on his trip to the Hereafter," observed Oscar Piper. "As it was—according to the reports—three people were knocked down, and one woman had to be hospitalized."

"Another argument against suicide," pointed out the retired school-teacher. "Unless Gary Twill had no compassion."

Unfortunately there had been no actual eyewitnesses. If Twill had stood for a few moments in the window, or had hesitated on the narrow ledge outside while he screwed up his courage, nobody had seen him. It had all happened during one of Manhattan's sudden, blustering rainstorms. With no buildings across the street, nothing there except the reaches of a practically deserted Central Park, no one had been in position to catch an accidental glimpse of the beginning of the high dive—if indeed it had been a voluntary dive. Naturally, all the people in the street below were either shielded by umbrellas or by folded newspapers held over their heads; no eyes had been turned up against the slashing, icy rain.

"The first cruise car got here just two minutes after six," Oscar Piper was patiently explaining. "The officers took statements from several persons, including one newsboy—"

"Who very probably might be that little man in the kiosk over there," Miss Withers interrupted impatiently. "I wonder!"

For once she wondered correctly. Mr. Herman Gittel, age 56, professional newsvendor, proved reasonably amenable to conversation after Miss Withers had purchased one copy of each of his evening newspapers, noting with sadness that the *Herald-Tribune* was gone.

"Sure, I seen it," said Mr. Gittel. "And I heard him yelling all the way down. He sounded real weird, like he was nuts or something. Stuff musta blown out of his pockets, because the air was like a snowstorm with bits of paper."

"I really wish I knew exactly what bits of paper," remarked the school-teacher wistfully. "But I suppose the street cleaners have done their work." She surveyed the gutter, poking into a storm drain with her umbrella.

"I kept me one sheet as sort of a souvenir," offered Mr. Gittel. And from his well-worn leather jacket he produced a wrinkled, rain-stained piece of manuscript paper—which proved to be Page 172 of what seemed to be a teleplay script. Miss Withers and the Inspector read:

SCENE 88—EXT COLDWATER CANYON HOUSE—MED CLOSE
SHOT—DAY Cecily and Norman, she in daring and revealing swimsuit,
he in smart yachting costume of the time. They are seated on a stone
bench with profusion of flowers in B.G. He is concealing displeasure.
Cecily is, however, mistress of the situation.
CECILY (moving closer): Don't be difficult, Normie-pie. Isn't it enough
   to be my lover—do you have to be my leading man, too? It really isn't
   your type of role anyway, Mr. Lasky says. And when *The Hunchback
   of Notre Dame* is released, you can write your own ticket at Essanay
   or anywhere.
NORMAN: It isn't just that, beautiful. You're a lovely cheat. We were
   supposed to have a date to go down to Ensenada and gamble a little
   over the weekend—you broke it because you had to stay home and
   read the script of *Passion's Pawn* or something, and then you were
   seen dancing at the Miramar with somebody whose name I intentionally
   don't remember.
CECILY: Don't be difficult, darling. You have your career and I have
   mine. Let's leave it that way.

The rest was undecipherable. Which, Miss Withers thought, might be
all for the best. "Oscar," she said on impulse, "will you buy this for me?"
Somewhat reluctantly, the Inspector invested two dollars for the tattered
souvenir.
"So the guy took his rejected manuscript with him," he said. "You
getting morbid or something, collecting mementoes yet?"
"One never knows," the schoolteacher pronounced mysteriously.
"Anyway," Oscar Piper pointed out impatiently, "whatever personal
stuff blew out of his pockets on the way down, his billfold was there and
he was immediately identified."
"Did the airline ticket show up?"
"Not according to the report. Somebody probably found it and cashed
it in. But he had a California driver's license, membership cards in the
Writers Guild West, Greater Los Angeles Press Club, Ace Hudkins Health
Club and Gym, Civil Liberties Union, and NAACP and CORE, and the
usual jumble of credit cards. There was also over $300 in currency,
and his room key tagged Hotel Harlow Towers 2466. Our men went right
in and upstairs and reported that 2466, a single, was something of a
shambles. Bed unmade, a litter of coffee cups and empty liquor bottles,
and manuscript pages scattered all over the floor. The room was sealed
off, but if you insist on taking a gander at it—"
Miss Withers had been vainly trying to count up to the windows of the

24th floor, but had only managed to get a crick in her neck. "If you count the lobby and presumably the mezzanine, and skip the thirteenth floor which no hotel ever has, then—" She sighed, and gave it up.

"It was the twenty-fourth all right," put in the cooperative Mr. Gittel. "I seen the open windows."

"*Saw,*" corrected the schoolteacher absently. "But are you sure?"

"The hotel is forty stories, and I counted down to where I saw the open windows—"

"Windows? *Plural?*"

"Well, the one on the left was wide-open, curtains flying, and the second over to the right was just a little open. Before the cops got here it was closed."

"Very interesting," said the schoolteacher.

Inspector Oscar Piper found it less so. "Well," he grumbled, "there doesn't seem to be any question about the guy going out the window of his own room. I suppose you're hell-bent to go up to the pad and have a look for clues; but Hildegarde, I warn you, those were trained investigators who handled this case, working on modern scientific lines."

"And using computers, no doubt!" she said scornfully.

"Computers don't guess, like you do! Well, do we go upstairs?"

Miss Withers was deep in thought. "I suppose so. But I am more interested in *people* than in the scene of the crime. I want to see Cecily Barth and make sure that the poor crippled old woman isn't the victim of another 'accidental' suicide or something, and I want to meet the various people who had reasons, large or small, for disliking Gary Twill."

"Okay," said the Inspector resignedly. "Let's go."

They entered the ornate but somewhat musty lobby of the old hotel, almost but not quite a relic of the Gaslight Era, and immediately learned from a supercilious desk clerk that Miss Barth wasn't seeing anybody or taking calls, and furthermore—

"Who's your house dick?" demanded Oscar Piper.

"Why—our security officer is Mr. Durkin, but—"

"Get him here, fast." For once the schoolteacher had to admit the usefulness of a shiny gold badge (denoting over 30 years with the Department) which the Inspector flashed briefly. Because wheels turned, and Mr. Durkin (who had given her a sort of bum's rush earlier in the day) made an instant appearance from the restaurant-bar, where he must have been enjoying a very late lunch or a very early dinner for he was sucking his teeth and chewing chlorophyll mints.

"Was there something, Inspector?"

"There was and is."

The stubby, choleric house detective lost no time getting into the record that he was very shocked that a thing like this should have occured at a quiet, respectable hotel like the Harlow Towers but what can you do? A suicide is a suicide, and the least said about it, the better. And after all, this Twill twerp wasn't the sort of guest who would have been made welcome at the hotel, only he was working for Mr. Abbas, a long-time resident of the penthouse and anything Mr. Abbas asks for—

"Okay. Abbas took a room here for his imported Hollywood writer, and a suite next door for Cecily Barth—is that right?" The Inspector was getting more than a little impatient, perhaps because he had a light lunch and was thinking of dinner. "Anybody else?"

"Just Miss Lawrence, the star. She's in 2634. There's a reservation for the director when they pick one, and for the casting director and costumer. Mr. Abbas likes to have all his staff right on hand. Only his secretary, Jane Roberts, lives home—I think in Brooklyn Heights. And Miss Bixby, the receptionist, who doesn't really count. I'll be glad to take you upstairs—"

"You better be," said the Inspector. "You know, Mr. Durkin, I seem to remember something. You were a sergeant, working out in Queens or Staten Island or somewhere. There was a mishmash, and you were allowed to resign rather than stand charges. So you went out to California and didn't make out and then you came back to Manhattan and got this job."

They were going up in a rocky old elevator. "Can you cool it, Inspector?" Durkin was sweating. "I need this job, and what's past is past. You know how it is, Inspector."

"Maybe," said Oscar Piper. "We'll see how it plays. Where's the room the guy jumped out the window of?"

Durkin led the way down a long hall and then to the right, past a door which he pointed out as Miss Barth's. Then they came to Gary Twill's door. "It's been sealed," said the house detective.

"Then I'll just unseal it," said Oscar Piper.

They went into the room, Miss Withers entering with some trepidation for the place was—from her point of view—in a mess. The bed looked as if some insomniac hippopotamus had been in it, the desk and surrounding territory were littered with pages of crumpled manuscript, the bureau bore an empty whiskey bottle, and clothes were strewn everywhere.

"Yet he seems to have died," the schoolteacher pointed out, "rather nattily dressed in tweed jacket and slacks, including a necktie. Suicides usually don't care how they look. I think I have 'cased the joint,' as you would say. Let us go."

"Okay, okay," said the weary Inspector as he resealed the door. "So now you're satisfied?"

"Not at all! There were no signs of a fight or struggle, no broken furniture or other indications of combat. Yet still—"

"So it was suicide!"

"With the airline ticket?" The schoolteacher shook her head. Then she turned suddenly on the house detective. "Mr. Durkin, just why did you intimate that Gary Twill wasn't the type of guest welcomed at the sacrosanct Harlow Towers?"

Durkin said uneasily, "Well, he was a sort of Bohemian type—loud stereo music at all hours, hipped on the liberal bit and fraternizing with the help and giving 'em ideas. He had Felicio all steamed up about becoming a writer. And he had all sorts of people visiting his room. We can't have that sort of thing."

"Dear me, no! We must live in the last century, mustn't we?" Her glance was scathing.

"Okay, okay!" put in the Inspector. "Let's go see the movie queen."

"Miss Barth isn't going to let us in," predicted Durkin. "Since this happened she's been locked in tight, and she won't hardly even let the maids in to do her rooms."

"No room service? How does she eat?" asked Piper sensibly.

"Didn't you know? Miss Barth is a vegetarian, and lives mostly on wheat germ and crackers and stuff like that, all out of cans and boxes." They were now standing outside the door of the suite, and Durkin knocked. He knocked again and then called out in a wheedling tone, "It's just Durkin, Miss Barth. Can we see you for a minute?"

There was not the slightest sound from within. Inspector Oscar Piper, who was not the most patient man in the world, saw a bell and leaned on it. "Open up, lady—this is the police!"

"Go away!" came a querulous voice from within. "You're not fooling me with that old one!"

Oscar Piper sighed, and nodded at the house dick—who reluctantly produced his master key. It worked, at first. The door swung open and then held, caught by a heavy chain.

Miss Withers felt that this had been mismanaged enough, and spoke up. "Cecily, will you please listen?" she said in her best classroom voice of authority. "Mr. Durkin and Inspector Piper of the New York Police Department are with me, but I started the whole thing. You may not know me but my name is Hildegarde Withers and I happen to live next door to Marcia, out in Santa Monica, and she showed me your letter—"

"Prove it!" The voice was still hostile.

"Well, Marcia is on a new diet and has lost three pounds. John is working the swing shift at Douglas. Loramae had summer flu but got over it and she and her brothers are now trampling my flowerbeds again. Is that enough?"

"All right, I guess," came the disembodied voice. The door closed, a chain rattled free, and then they were permitted inside—all but Mr. Durkin, who found his way blocked by the Inspector's right arm.

"Look, I got my job to do," complained Durkin. "I got to tell her we got rules about not installing chains and keeping pets and—"

"Blow," said Oscar Piper, with the disdain of an honest cop for one who had cheated. Mr. Durkin blew.

And Miss Withers and the Inspector were entering a big, dimly lighted drawing room that smelled of perfume and cat and cigarette smoke. The schoolteacher had eyes only for the woman in the lightweight wheel chair who faced them, sitting on it grandly as if it were some sort of throne. She wore a flowered housecoat as if it were ermine and velvet, and her chin was high and defiant.

What was left of Cecily Barth, presumably in her seventies, was mostly spirit and spunk, though there were traces of ruined beauty under the heavy makeup and in her deep dark eyes. And her hair was still as raven-black and as sleekly arranged as it had been back in the halcyon days when this woman had rivaled Theda Bara and Nita Naldi and Clara Kimball Young.

"It was so good of you to come," Cecily was saying, holding out her hand. "You must forgive my seeming rudeness at the door. But my nerves are in a dither. However, any friend of dear Marcia's—"

Her words were for Miss Withers, but her attention was turned to Oscar Piper; he was a man. For a few seconds she was a faint echo of the Screen Vamp, the Sex Goddess of the Silver Screen, unquote. Quite evidently she expected the Inspector to kiss her hand, but he only held it for a second and then sheepishly dropped it.

Meanwhile Miss Withers was gathering impressions, as was her habit. This elderly, crippled old woman was in fear of her life; the schoolteacher could almost feel the fear, could almost smell it above Cecily's perfume.

"You must excuse the way the place looks," Cecily was saying, waving her hand vaguely. Indeed, the room was a jumble of untidiness. The tables, chairs, and even the mantlepiece suggested Christmas Eve in the family of a dozen or more small children: everything was piled high with toys, plus rolls of fancy wrappings, balls of vari-colored string, and boxes of bright Santa Clause stickers. There was a stack of packages, wrapped and ready for mailing, in one corner.

"Christmas—in September?" said the Inspector, unbelieving.

"I'm afraid I went simply mad in your New York toy stores," admitted

Cecily as she made ineffectual efforts to find them a place to sit. "I had such fun shopping before—before I got too scared to go out any more, even with dear Felicio pushing my wheel chair. But now, I really don't trust anybody!"

The Inspector was seated uneasily on the edge of a sofa and had taken out a fresh cigar, while Miss Withers prowled the room, the packages, the typewriter table. There were many scrapbooks, many old newsclips and photos of an earlier era. But what she was interested in was *now*.

"About this suicide next door—" the Inspector began.

"If indeed it *was* suicide," said Cecily Barth meaningfully.

"You didn't hear any sounds of a struggle, any raised voices?"

"No," admitted Cecily. "But there is an unused bathroom between, where I keep my cat's litterbox. Mr. Twill and I were working very closely together on the script, and we never locked the connecting doors. That would have made a fine scandal once upon a time, wouldn't it? But I'm afraid I wasn't here to notice anything yesterday afternoon; my cat had got out and down the hall and I was looking for him, as I often have to do when I can't get anybody to do it for me."

"Let's get down to cases," the Inspector went on firmly. "When did you last see Gary Twill?"

"Well, he brought in the last sequence of the script early in the morning, around eight o'clock. He'd worked on it all night, poor dear boy. Like most writers, he hated to make carbons and he always made a lot of typographic errors, so I had to type the final version of everything."

Cecily nodded toward the corner of the room, where they saw a bridge table, a portable electric typewriter similar to the one used by Gary Twill, and several piles of white and yellow paper.

"It wasn't actually as intimate and deep a collaboration as I had hoped it would be, but I'm still going to try for co-screenplay credit. The lovely TV residuals, you know! That's the payment to writers for re-runs, and it can go on for years." She beamed at them. "A sensational life story like mine will be released and re-released over and over again."

"You were satisfied with the script, then?" asked Miss Withers.

"More than satisfied! Gary had caught the spirit of the really great days of Hollywood. Such a dear brilliant man! I can't believe he took his own life."

"Who would have done it, then?" demanded Oscar Piper.

"Really, my dear man!" Cecily made a dramatic gesture. "How on earth should I know? I'm a stranger in town."

" 'I a stranger and afraid, in a world I never made,' " said Miss Withers softly. Cecily was obviously winding the Inspector around her little finger, with a practiced charm that dated back two generations. The schoolteacher was less easily impressed. "You're quite sure you heard nothing in the next room yesterday afternoon, and that you were out chasing your kitten at the time Gary Twill died?"

"Quite sure."

"And you received Twill's version of the last sequence of the script about eight yesterday morning, and retyped it with carbons and then took it up to Mr. Abbas say around ten or ten thirty?"

"Exactly. Only I gave it to Jane, his confidential secretary. I can manage these automatic elevators very well, if I take my time. I told Jane that I was delighted with the script and that I would sign formal approval anytime—I have that right in my contract."

"And did you hear anything from Mr. Abbas yesterday?"

"Nothing directly. I phoned Jane Roberts sometime after lunch to learn what the great man's verdict was, and she said he was still studying the script but that storm warnings were out. That didn't worry me; he's the sort of producer who never likes anything on paper in the first reading."

She broke off when there was a sudden interruption from the bedroom. What erupted was at first sight a rather furious battle between two small black kittens. The fracas moved into the drawing room—and then it turned out to be a mimic battle between one black kitten, and one very naturalistic toy kitten, with the former naturally getting the upper hand—or upper paw. Then just as suddenly it was all over; the live kitten turned its back on the stuffed kitten-on-a-string, stalked over to Cecily, and leaped lightly into her lap.

"Asmodeus baby!" said Cecily Barth. She turned to her visitors. "I almost named him Lucifer—only then his nickname would have been 'Loose,' and I couldn't have that, could I?"

"We'll wait and see the film," said Miss Withers ironically, conscious that they weren't getting anywhere. "Miss Barth, I moved heaven and earth to get the Inspector to come up here with me and look into this affair, and all because of Marcia. But I don't think you're being altogether frank with us. We happen to know that you saw Gary Twill die. So you weren't chasing your kitten—you were looking out of your open window. A newsvendor in the street below looked up and saw two open windows—and then yours was swiftly closed. Right?"

If the sally was supposed to put Cecily into one of her dithers, it failed completely. "I wasn't going to admit that," the aged screen star said. "I just wanted to keep out of it. Yes, I had recovered Asmodeus, and I was sitting here and I heard the commotion. I did rush to the window and it was raining so hard I had to raise it to see anything—and I wish I hadn't."

She faced them defiantly, like an angry child caught with a hand in the cookie jar. But Miss Withers was thinking. This ridiculous old woman knew something which she was not prepared to disclose. It might be important, it might be minor. But it was something.

"What I am really interested in," said the schoolteacher, "is the bottle of champagne. The one Gary Twill went out to buy shortly before his death. But he didn't drink it as a sort of stirrup cup into Eternity, because the empty bottle wasn't found among the other empties. Can you help us there, Miss Barth?"

Cecily hesitated for a very long second, and then she smiled. "I thought that some things could be kept private," she said, as she put the black kitten gently down out of her lap. "All right, since you press me, I'll tell you."

She wheeled herself over to the hall closet and almost immediately reappeared with an unopened, gold-topped bottle of champagne in her hand. It was, Miss Withers noticed, of 1938 vintage—whether a good year or a bad year she didn't know. But that did not matter.

"A going-away present," Cecily explained. "Just like Gary."

"But no note with it?" pressed Miss Withers. "I know writers."

Cecily hesitated. "I don't know just when Gary left the bottle. It was in the connecting bathroom, just inside the door on my side. And since you make such a point of it—yes, there *was* a note."

Wheeling herself with a certain calculated dexterity, Cecily went over to the typewriter table and came back with a sheet of manuscript paper, which the Inspector and Miss Withers read as one.

"Cecily dear, the hell with everything. I am taking it on the lam (as we used to say in the old Cagney pictures) and getting outa here. Don't say it hasn't been fun, because it hasn't. Drink this in good health, and think of me as not one who is dead but just gone far away. (Quote from Elizabeth Barrett Browning, I think.) Anyway, I have had it. Your affectionate collaborator, Gary."

It was the Inspector who spoke first. "Well, Hildegarde? You said you would be happier with an eyewitness or a suicide note. You now have the latter. Okay? Let's go somewhere and have dinner."

"Let's not," said Miss Withers, who was in a state of confusion but who had a little red light flashing on and off in the back of her brain. She faced Cecily. "You have, you know, been withholding evidence and in essence you have been resisting police officers in the performance of their duty and otherwise impeding justice. I am quite sure that Inspector Piper can find some grounds for having you held as a material witness in Women's Jail for a few days—"

"It might be a most interesting experience," said Cecily Barth. "But if he did something foolish like that to me—while Jane Roberts, who is the one person who actually might have had real animosity to Gary, goes free—well, Inspectors have become sergeants overnight. Or even sent to a beat over in Canarsie?"

The dear old lady had claws, it appeared. Longer than those of Asmodeus (named after a minor demon) who now was purring contentedly in a chair. A live prop for an ageless actress who was determined always to be on stage . . . Cats, Miss Withers had observed, always had means of taking care of themselves.

"I think—" began Miss Withers. And then the telephone rang.

"I'm not supposed to have any phone calls," Cecily pouted. But she wheeled herself over to the instrument. "Yes?" Her voice changed into a dulcet tone. "Yes, Mr. Abbas?"

The voice at the other end was loud and emphatic; it could be heard across the room. "Cecily, mine darlink, ve got problem. Somebody making stink about that fool Twill. Some old dame who minds other people's business. So ve haf a conference here in de office at eight dis evening, right? All of us! So ve agree on our stories. Hokay?"

"I think I can arrange to be there," said Cecily. She hung up and turned back to her guests. "You perhaps heard," she said. "Mr. Abbas is disturbed at this reopening of the case. So he is calling a conference—"

"We know," said Miss Withers. "Things get more complicated all the time. And my best advice to you is—"

Just then the doorbell rang. Cecily wheeled herself over, put on the chain, then opened. Both Miss Withers and the Inspector caught a glimpse of a frightened girlish face through the crack.

"It's me—Lilith!" came the voice. "Miss Barth, I have to tell you something, but the switchboard girl won't ring you."

"Those were my personal instructions, dear. I—I'm not feeling well and I'm not seeing anybody or talking to—"

"But you don't understand!" the voice from the hall persisted. "We're all in trouble and the picture is in trouble. This whole thing is going to hell in a handbasket. Somebody is trying to reopen the mess and make out like Gary didn't kill himself! There's some old biddy rampaging around—she has some sort of *in* with the fuzz—and she's here only to try to make trouble. And any more bad publicity might frighten away Mr. Abbas' backers. So if anybody asks you, don't tell them about Gary and me—it was only a night or two anyway and all in the course of show business. Really, it doesn't count!"

"Yes, dearie," said Cecily calmly. "My lips are sealed."

"And another thing," said the voice through the crack in the door. "His Nibs wants us all up in the penthouse at eight tonight, for a sort of council of war. It's an ultimatum. We have to get our stories all straight or this picture isn't ever going to get made!"

"Roger—out and over," said Cecily. She closed the door and turned back to her uninvited guests. "You see what I mean?" she demanded a bit plaintively. "I just don't know how to cope with it all."

"You don't have to cope with it all by yourself, not now," said the schoolteacher. "But these are deep waters, and I feel there is more here than meets the eye, unquote." She gave the Inspector a signal, and they made their departure—with Asmodeus the black kitten making a determined but vain effort to go out with them.

"Well, Hildegarde?" said Oscar Piper as they approached the elevator. "Did you see anything I didn't see? I figure that was a genuine twenty-four-carat suicide note, and—"

"And a genuine, twenty-four-carat plane ticket, don't forget. Oscar, I'm afraid I can't take you up on that dinner invitation, I have other things to do. But I suggest that we both crash Mr. Abbas' party at eight."

"Well—if you say so. In for a nickel, in for a dime. Fine old dramatic tradition—to have all the suspects gathered together in one place, while the great Hawkshaw unravels the mystery. Only, in this case, I don't see any possible motive for murder."

"So then it might be an *impossible* motive," Hildegarde retorted. "I am not trying to be cryptic, Oscar. But a little red light is flashing on and off in the back of my head, a warning that perhaps I have missed something. And besides, I have an errand to do—some shopping, as it were."

"Not another hat—when I was just getting used to this one!"

"No, not a hat. Something more in the line of a toy, but a rather unusual toy." She nodded. "And now, if you will be kind enough to hail me a taxi, I'll be off. We'll meet here again in the lobby at eight o'clock, right?"

"Right or wrong, we'll meet," said the Inspector wearily.

The penthouse apartment-cum-office where the self-admittedly great Mr. Abbas lived and had his being was originally a magnificent (if now a somewhat rundown) center of operations. The drawing-room office, in which he was now having a supposedly secret conference with his employees, protégés, and disciples, was large enough for a tennis court or at least a badminton court; it had been furnished in 1932 Moderne—plenty of glass and everything in black and silver, with sharp angles.

The paintings were early imitations of Picasso, the books were sumptuously leather-bound copies of Mr. Abbas' scripts, the lighting was soft and slightly off-green. Miss Bixby loved it; Jane Roberts wished she had kept her date to go bowling; Lilith Lawrence thought belatedly that she should have taken up some other line of work. Hymie Rose sat beside his client and was chewing on an enormous but unlighted cigar. *He should get me out of here and find me some nightclub bookings*, Lilith was thinking.

But a TV picture was a TV picture, with audiences in the millions. One mustn't forget that. And it meant so much to dear old Cecily . . .

Abbas was speaking, as from the mountaintop. He was directing his diatribe at them all, but looking at Cecily in her wheel chair. "Ve got troubles," said Mr. Abbas. "Troubles vith script and troubles vith publicity. Everybody here, including me myself, has goofed. But ve don't got to go on goofing. Don't any of you talk to no more reporters, understand? So vat is it if a fool bellboy suggests that maybe I trun—I trew—Gary Twill over the parapet? The script vas bad, but not dat bad. He musta kill himself, de no-goodnik."

Just then there was a shrill alarm from the doorbell, which Miss Bixby hastily arose to answer. And in came Felicio, smiling apologetically. "Sorry, Mr. Abbas—but he have badge and what am I to do?"

So Inspector Oscar Piper, followed closely by Miss Hildegarde Withers, joined the party, though very much uninvited. "As you were!" commanded the Inspector. "At ease! This isn't a pinch, yet." Again he flashed the persuasive badge.

But the situation was obviously strained, and Miss Withers was, so to speak, up in arms. "We are gathered together," she began, "all of those who knew Gary Twill here in Manhattan, to try to find out how and why he died—"

"Everybody but Mr. Durkin," put in Cecily Barth softly. "A very nasty man."

"Thank you," said the schoolteacher. "Which gives me an idea." She winked to the Inspector, who frowned and then caught on. He stepped catlike to the door and threw it open, disclosing the house detective crouching outside.

"Come in and join the party," said Miss Withers. "I had a hunch you wouldn't want to miss this."

"I was only keeping tabs—" began Durkin defensively. Then he came sheepishly in.

"I shall continue," the schoolteacher said firmly. "But this is not a simple matter."

"Understatement of de year," put in Boris Abbas. "I resent—"

"Go ahead and resent," said Oscar Piper. "But shut up when the lady is talking."

"We have the case," continued Miss Withers as if in a classroom, "of an athletic, two hundred-pound man, in full possession of his faculties, who went to his death out of a hotel window. I discount the theory advanced by Felicio in one press interview that Gary Twill was hurled over the parapet by Mr. Abbas—"

"I do not really mean it—I am a writer of fiction!" cut in the bellboy hastily. "I let the imaginations run wild."

"Because that would have required premeditation and an accomplice down on the twenty-fourth floor to open Twill's window. So I eliminated Mr. Abbas."

The producer bowed.

"But may I see the script which you found so disappointing?" she went on. Abbas nodded to Jane, who got it from the files. As she continued, Miss Withers riffled through the neatly typed pages. "I also had to eliminate Mr. Hymie Rose, who, though he possibly had motive, could hardly have thrown Gary Twill out of the window without creating a battlefield in the room."

"But if poor dear Gary had been sandbagged and was therefore unconscious?" suggested Cecily helpfully.

"He wasn't unconscious—he screamed all the way down. And pages of a manuscript went flying with him. I have one page of that manuscript which was rescued from the gutter and is still legible, and I note that it doesn't match the corresponding page just handed to me. On page 172, in the version Gary Twill took with him to his death, Cecily is playing a love scene in a garden with another Hollywood star of the time, one Norman Kerry—"

"Dat vas in the original outline!" cut in Abbas.

"And in the final version just given to me the scene is played with the Prince of Wales, no less! And later Cecily romances with Jack Dempsey and Charles Lindbergh and heaven knows who else!"

"Vich is vat makes me so infurious!" yelled Abbas. "How to get releases from such big names?"

"Let me explain," Cecily cooed. "I simply took a few liberties as I typed the final version and livened it up a bit. Who remembers dear Norman today? Now Edward, later King of England—"

"His intimates, I understand, always called him by his real name, which was David," said the schoolteacher pedantically.

"I met him once at a party," Cecily said defensively. She looked like a child who had just been told there is no Santa Claus.

"To continue," said Miss Withers. "I once liked Mr. Durkin for the killer. He had left the police force under a cloud, and lived for a while in Los Angeles until the heat was off and he could come back and get this sinecure of a job as hotel security officer. If Twill had known him out west and learned of the old scandal, and if Mr. Durkin had been afraid that Twill would talk and cost him this job—"

"You're dreaming, Hildegarde," said the Inspector.

"I know. I was clutching at straws. But again we face the problem of why the window was open on a stormy, rainy day, and why there were no signs of a struggle. I had to come to the conclusion that this was not a strong-arm job, to use the vernacular. Even though Jane Roberts here has obviously strong arms—"

"*And* the only real motive!" Cecily put in gleefully. "You should have heard them quarreling!"

"You bitch!" said sweet Jane, with feeling.

"I must confess that at one time I even considered Miss Barth herself as a suspect," continued Miss Withers, glancing in her direction.

"I wouldn't want to be ignored!" the old lady said happily. "This is the most exciting thing that's happened to me in years!" She was obviously enjoying every moment of it.

"But it's only in old B-movies that a supposed cripple suddenly arises from a wheel chair and performs deeds of mayhem and murder."

"I really am crippled," Cecily said sadly. "Look at my legs, once the most famous in Hollywood!" She lifted her skirt and displayed pitifully atrophied legs, like pipestems. "So if strong men couldn't have pushed poor dear Gary out of a window, how could poor little me?"

"Exactly. How could you?"

"So that seems to leave only me," spoke up the fair Lilith with some spirit. "But how on earth—"

"You could possibly have called his attention to something down in the street, and then—"

"But *why?* He played fair with me, I got the job. And since we are getting down to cases, I didn't just romance him for the job, I really went for him!" And Lilith gave Hymie Rose a defiant stare.

There was a silence. Then the Inspector coughed and murmured, "Well, Hildegarde? Having eliminated everybody, we come back to suicide."

"Not quite, Oscar. Not with that plane ticket." She turned back to Cecily Barth. "Cecily, you took liberties with Twill's script. Didn't you know he'd scream with rage and insist that Mr. Abbas read the correct version—if he was still around? And that your machinations would all go for nothing?"

Cecily was suddenly quiet.

"It may seem to some of you that this is an insufficient motive for taking a man's life. But the human ego is a strange thing—especially the Hollywood ego. Cecily, you convinced yourself that with Gary Twill out of the way you could talk Mr. Abbas here into using the more sensational version of your life story. True or false?"

The people in the big room were hardly breathing; you could have heard a soap bubble explode.

"Utter nonsense," said Cecily finally, in a small voice. "Granting for a moment what you say about the script, how could I, a ninety-pound cripple, throw a big strong man out of a window?" She finished on a high squeak of triumph.

"To make a long story longer," said Miss Withers almost sadly, "I suggest to you, as they say in British trials, that you worked out a clever and devilish scheme—playing on Gary Twill's good-hearted willingness to help you search for your kitten who was always getting out. You bought a life-like stuffed black kitten, which could easily have been mistaken for the real thing in a rainstorm, and with a cane or some other implement shoved it out on the ledge that runs beneath your room, the bathroom, and Twill's room. Then you rushed to him and asked him to try to reach out of his window and rescue it."

"Pure fantasy!" said Cecily. "I suppose I was right behind him in my wheel chair and gave him a superhuman shove? What jury would believe that?"

"I'm not quite through," Miss Withers said quietly. "I remembered that for years you've been an ardent worker for the Humane Society and the SPCA and kindred organizations, and that once you tried to lead a protest march against the Chicago stockyards. You had seen how they force cattle into the chutes. So you got an inspiration and you bought this."

From her capacious handbag the schoolma'am produced an Xmas-wrapped parcel, and slowly and dramatically unwrapped it. The article inside looked something like a large flashlight, with no bulb.

"What on earth is that?" demanded Oscar Piper.

"It's known as a Shock Rod. At the stockyards it's called a cattle goad. Oscar, I don't suppose you would let me demonstrate, with you as the subject? I guarantee that if this instrument is applied to your anatomy you will automatically and involuntarily jump farther than you have ever jumped before."

"No, thanks," said Oscar.

Miss Withers pressed the button, and the Shock Rod buzzed like an angry rattlesnake. "Cecily, now we know why Gary Twill went out the window. And how can you explain why we found this nasty thing among the Christmas toys wrapped up for your grandnieces and grandnephews?"

"You didn't! You couldn't! I mailed it—" Then the ex-movie star realized what she had said.

Miss Withers and the Inspector had their spaghetti dinner after all, if a bit late. Over the zabaglione he suddenly frowned. "One thing bothers me. Oh, it's not the old woman; she won't stand trial—"

"Psychiatric care?" asked the schoolteacher.

"Some private place, with bars. For the rest of her days. No, I'm wondering how you got into her suite and found the gadget."

"But I didn't! I hunted all over town until I found a place where you can buy them, and I got some Christmas gift paper like Cecily's and wrapped it, figuring it would shock her into a confession. Shock treatment can work both ways, Oscar."

He grinned, and lifted his glass of Chianti. "To you, Hildegarde. Long may you wave!"

THE QUALITY OF MERCY
Eleazar Lipsky

MAMASITA! MAMASITA!" . . . SHE was a good baby and she never cried, but the night was muggy and she had wet herself. She lay in the crib and waited, then called softly again.

"Mamasita!"

No one came.

She lay flat on the mattress with her tiny hands opening and closing. There was comfort in the motion and her eyes were attracted to their wiggling. She studied her fingers. She was not frightened. The room was empty but the street lamp threw a pattern of light on the ceiling. Her solemn eyes turned up, then got tired. As her face fell sidewards, she looked through the slats toward the kitchen door.

A bed with a patchwork design caught her gaze. On occasions the bed meant to her a musky blend of smells and her mother's warmth. The room was heavy with the familiar smell and she put a finger in her mouth.

"Mamasita?"

She got up and clung to the rail and craned her head. A yellow glow came from the kitchen. Voices sometimes came from the kitchen and at such times her mother would answer to the call. Then there would be quick, tapping footsteps, an opening door, and a quiet soothing voice.

There was a rushing in the water pipes, but still no one came.

"Mamasita?"

A mouse darted along the wall and into the kitchen with a whispery scratch of sound. The baby followed the fleeting shadow with saucered eyes and then went back to calling.

339

"Mama!" she cried angrily.

It was taking too long. She needed to be dried and changed and put back to sleep with a firm rubbing hand on her back. She was suddenly unhappy.

"I want *mamasita!*" She screamed and rattled the crib with fury. "I want *mama!*"

In the warm dank night, all windows were open on the airshaft, and the crying baby roused the building. In the room above, an irascible middle-aged woman with a milk-white face, Anna Farley, thrashed about as the baby's yelling kept on. She covered her head with a pillow, but it was no use. She ached with arthritis and the effort brought her up swearing.

Anna threw back the sheet and ran a hand through her hair. "Ah, my God, my God!" She shook her fist in invocation. "It's that baby again!"

Chris Farley, a red-faced subway guard, raised himself. He had a nodding friendship with the new family below, the Faustos, and he wanted no part of the trouble Anna was bent on starting. "Let it alone," he grumbled. "The baby's got to live too."

"You stand for anything!" With an air of scorn, Anna went to the airshaft and pushed aside an oilcloth curtain. "What's wrong with that baby down there? What's the matter with you people? My husband's got to have his sleep! D'you hear?"

"Count me out of it, Annie," Chris called, annoyed. "Do your own dirty work!"

The baby was quiet for a while and then broke out again with long yelling gasps, her little body swelling with rage.

"What the hell down there?" a man called hoarsely.

Other voices joined in, taking both sides of the issue. In the bedlam, some berated the baby, others called for quiet all around. It was not yet midnight, but it was a working-class dwelling in a poor neighborhood. The main outcry came from those who needed sleep. A waitress with an ailing daughter was shrill with complaint.

The clamor did not help, and toward midnight Anna Farley could stand it no longer. "I swear I'll kill them," she groaned. She wrapped herself in a nightrobe and went down to the floor below, wincing as the arthritis throbbed in her shoulder. She paused at the flimsy door to the Fausto apartment.

"What kind are you in there?" she shouted. "Give that baby some milk, or something! What's the matter? Don't you care?"

The baby heard the shouting and suddenly became silent. There was no other response.

"Is anything wrong?" Anna paused irresolute, rubbing her shoulder, then went down into the street with her mind made up. She was too irascible to care about her appearance, or, more likely, it made no difference in the neighborhood. A knot of hoarse-voiced loafers at the door let her pass.

It was a dark street running to decayed brownstone dwellings. The gutters were littered and an open trench showed construction work for a water main. Anna looked around. Except for the loitering youths no one was about. A candy store was still open at the corner.

Anna walked painfully to Columbus Avenue. Neon lights, green and red, showed some life in the taverns. In the dim bars she could see dull-faced men and women drinking. She stood swearing softly to herself and then a green and white car passed.

Anna waved. "Hey, police!"

The patrol car swept around and drew up at the curb. A young police officer put out his head and said pleasantly, "Are you all right, lady?"

"And what's wrong with me?" she demanded.

The blond man in uniform looked at her robe. "Now is that a way to run around the streets?"

Anna sniffed with annoyance. "Never mind me. There's a baby making a racket." She tossed her head in the direction of the building and explained. "You'd better come. Nobody answers the door. They might be dead in there."

"Or covering the gin mills," the officer said drily.

"There's no telling with these new people," she agreed. "Now I've done my share. It's up to you, the rest of it."

Patrolman Kenneth Holden exchanged a tired glance with an older man at the wheel. "What do you say, Herman?"

Patrolman Herman Brewer rubbed a bristly jowl. "I guess we got to check," he sighed.

"Hop in." Holden opened the door and Anna squeezed in tightly, gasping for breath. They drove into the side street.

Anna said finally, "Here's the building."

Holden opened the door. "I won't need you, Herman. You stay with the calls."

"Don't get tangled, Ken. We're almost through." Brewer settled down.

Holden followed Anna past the sullen toughs at the entrance and up to the second landing. His nose was blind to the smells of cookery, nor did he find the poor lighting exceptional. All this was like his own neighborhood. Three women in threadbare wrappers with white naked ankles showing were now at the Faustos' door, chatting indignantly in loud voices. One said ironically, "Ah, the police, the police, they take their time. It's an easy life."

"What's it about?" Holden said easily.

A young woman in braids pointed. "In there, officer."

Holden knocked.

"Sure, he knocks!" a worn older woman said with sarcasm. "We thought of that one too."

Inside, at the sound of knocking, the baby gripped the side of the crib and hushed. She faced toward the sound of strange voices, heavier and slower than those she knew.

Holden tried knocking again, then asked, "Where's the janitor?"

"He won't like to wake up," the older woman said.

"He'll wake up," Holden promised and found his way down to a cellar apartment. A stocky man, James Mahan, was routed from the bosom of his family, a wet-nosed bunch, and was prodded into action. Mahan was sullen as he hiked into trousers while his wife kept up a firecracker line of advice, but he kept respectful enough and followed Holden back upstairs.

"There you are." Mahan opened the door with a squeak. "Good thing you didn't break in. The assemblyman wouldn't like rough stuff. He owns this building."

Holden saw a neat small kitchen. Plaster and paint were needed, but everything else—food, dishes, scrubbing tub, and brooms—were in order. Tiny baby garments, all pink, were drying over the sink where a faucet dripped.

Inside, the baby began to dance in her crib like a monkey on a stick.

"Where's the kid?" Holden's large frame filled the kitchen.

"Give her two seconds and you'll hear." Anna Farley jerked a thumb toward the bedroom. "That's a neglected baby, officer. It's a real crime sure. And you'd better do something."

"Take it easy," Holden said.

The women crowded at the door while Holden entered a combined living and bedroom, sparsely furnished. An oilcloth-covered table held a milk bottle on a centerpiece of daisies. A double bed was neatly made up with khaki army blankets. He noticed religious pictures and family photographs on the walls, especially an expensive portrait of a plump infant girl with curly black hair and shoe-button eyes. There was, of course, a small television set.

"Mama?"

The sound was like a kitten's mew. The baby gripped the crib with fat little fingers. She looked up at strange faces and her eyes went awash with tears. "Mama?"

Holden squatted and tilted back his hat. "Hello, honey," he said softly. "What's the trouble? You can tell me."

The smell of her wetness was strong.

"She don't talk yet at all!" Anna Farley said with scorn, rubbing her shoulder. "The thing's damn young."

The little fat lip trembled. "I want Mama!" When the strange big man tried to lift her, she clung to the crib and squalled. He touched her forehead, turned, and spoke sharply. "This kid's got a temperature."

"Sure! A neglected baby!" Anna Farley folded her arms, her white face pointed with satisfaction. "I could've told you. These people!"

The baby wailed as Holden returned to the women in the kitchen where he asked, annoyed, "When are these people supposed to get home?"

The janitor, James Mahan, said stolidly, "They're a new kind around here, officer. Who knows if they'll come back at all?"

Holden wiped his hat band methodically. "What's the tale here?"

The women's view was that if the Faustos were out drinking, there was no telling when they would return. A street accident was ruled unlikely. There was no useful opinion and Holden found himself sweating in the muggy flat.

"Would anybody mind this kid?" he asked.

"Don't look at me!" Anna winced as her arthritis stabbed her. "That temperature might be the measles, or the diphtheria, or something else filthy. I got my own to consider first. I wouldn't take in that dirty kid for anything."

"Who knows what that kid's got?" the girl with the braids agreed.

"She's not sick." Holden paused at the sound of fresh wailing. "It's just too much crying. That can give temperature."

"Now he's a doctor!" the sarcastic older woman said. "Ah, that badge, that badge, it means a lot."

"It's common sense," Holden argued. "I got two of my own."

The women were unmoved by his parenthood and his plea brought no volunteer.

"Ah, forget it!" Holden went down to the patrol car, where his partner, Herman Brewer, thrice a father, received the news with disgust.

"Still, we got to do something." Brewer rubbed his jowls, vexed. "Temperature can be a tricky thing in babies. You should've rung in one of them biddies."

"It was too sweating hot to argue." Holden paused. "They don't like the idea. These new people ain't their kind."

"That's natural. The trouble is, it's twelve, time to knock off. My old lady is waiting up for me." Brewer paused while a series of call signals filled the car. "We can't stick around till morning waiting for that kid's pa and ma. If the parents don't care, why should we?"

"What about an ambulance?"

"Let's forget about that. It would take too long."

They decided on quicker action. After a call to a detective on duty at the precinct station house, Holden went back to gather a change of clothing and to express his vigorous opinion of the neighbors. They then drove downtown to the New York Home of Mercy in the Sixties, where the receiving room was open.

Wrapped in her blanket, the baby's body heat swelled to lap her in comfort. Her wailing dropped to a whimper under the firm grip of a man's hand. There was the rocking motion of the car and the passing lights, then short lifting jolts which meant stairs. The air changed and brightness told her of a big room. She felt the rumble of a man's chest tones, then another voice, a woman's. Perhaps dimly she understood that they were talking of her, since her name, Carmen, was spoken several times. She felt hot and drowsy and her eyes were swimming.

A woman's kind face, framed in a white coif, bent over and there was a clean smell of soap. Then, suddenly, Carmen Fausto was asleep. . . .

While the baby slept, the street grew deserted and quiet. A small couple, hardly more than a boy and a girl, turned in from a main street which still had traffic. They walked along, swinging hands with a dreamy expression. They laughed with an occasional gentle word to each other, thinking back to their evening's pleasure.

The girl wore a flowered cotton frock. Her face was heart-shaped and delicate, and her hair fell in black curls. The boy, or he might have been a man, was no taller or heavier. His smiling face was thin and irregular and beardless. He wore a sporty jacket.

They entered the building and went up one flight. The hall was dim. No one was about and the man, Vincente Fausto, gave his wife, Juana, a kiss just before they opened the door to their flat, and she giggled.

Thus there was no warning as they entered through the kitchen. At first, Juana noticed nothing as she turned on the light and loosened her hair, nor did she see the note under the milk bottle on the table. She went smiling to the crib with a sense that things were too quiet. She looked down and began to shake. "My baby!" she gasped. "My baby!"

Fausto had remained in the kitchen. He was at the ice box with its cheesey smell. "What about the baby?" he called.

Juana screamed.

"My baby! She's not here!"

"What kind of a joke?" He turned over a chair in his haste. A look was enough. "Oh, my God!"

Juana stood shaking, ashen and sallow, too terrified for speech.

Fausto rummaged behind a hanging drape and under the bed.

It was no joke. He stood in the center of the room and clutched his hands.

"Don't be scared, *querida!*" He spoke bravely, but his heart seemed squeezed by an icy hand. "She's some place. Maybe a neighbor! Just don't get scared!"

She gave him a dreadful look. "You wouldn't come home when I asked!"

He had no answer.

"They stole my baby!" she shrieked. *"Ai! Ai!* I want my baby back!"

"Take it easy, *querida.*" He bit his finger and it bled, but he did not taste the saltiness. "What do I do?" he muttered. "Where do I start?" He looked to his young wife for guidance, but none came. Her eyes were glaring white. "You wait here!"

He rushed out and began banging doors on his floor. The annoyed neighbors either knew nothing or pretended not to know. It took a stretch of agony and three tries before an elderly man, a widower, suggested he ask the Farleys.

Anna Farley came to the door rubbing her shoulder. "What do you want?" she asked stolidly.

"The baby!" he begged. "She's gone! You know anything about the baby?"

She scornfully placed her arms akimbo. "Ah, so you're the fine one leaves a sick baby crying alone! What kind of a man are you?"

"Please!" he entreated.

"Sure I know something! Now why should I tell the likes of you?"

"You know something?" He was small with a boy's face, not as heavy or large as the woman before him. "You know about the baby?" he repeated stupidly.

"What if I do?"

A look flared in his eyes like a spurting match. He took out a knife and pressed a button and the blade flung itself into position. He raised the cutting edge to touch her heart.

"Where's the baby?"

His voice trembled.

Anna Farley saw the wildness in his eyes and she knew she was close to death. It was something she had faced with each birth, always with calm, but in the dim hall with the sharp steel pricking her skin, it was sickish to her taste. She knew she must speak with care.

"It was the police who came, Mister. The baby was crying and somebody called them. They took her."

"You called them?" he demanded.

"It was not me, Mister, I swear it. I didn't even know till after they came."

"It was you that called them!" he muttered thickly.

She saw that he knew the truth, but she had to keep denying it. She remained utterly still, facing the staring little man. "Please don't hurt me, Mister," she begged. "I've got three kids of my own back in there. I had nothing to do with it."

Her robe had fallen open, partly exposing her heavy breasts, but neither was aware of that.

He asked in a low voice. "Where is the baby now?"

"They took her downtown. The Home of Mercy, they said. They left a note. It's a fine place. She'll be all right."

From within, her husband called, "What the hell is it out there, Annie?"

She kept her eyes on the man with the knife. "It's nothing, Chris. Go back to sleep."

Fausto took a deep breath and stepped back.

"Please excuse me, lady." He put away the knife. "I'm sorry about this. You know how it is."

"Get away!" she cried hoarsely. "Go away!" She slammed the door and put her back against it. "Get him away, for the love of God!" she said, over and over. "Oh, God, get him away!"

Fausto turned and ran down into the street. He passed his own flat, forgetting to tell his wife what he had learned. When finally she found the note under the milk bottle, he had already gone.

An hour later, Vincente Fausto was at the entrance to the New York Home of Mercy. His breath was coming in sobs. He stood with his forehead pressed against the door, his thumb rigidly on the button.

Somewhere within the massive pile the bell was ringing.

The old red brick building looked like a hospital, which indeed it once had been. It stood on a square block behind an iron picket fence, sheltered from the street by an old shade tree. It was dark except at the point where Fausto stood.

A patrolman noticed the bowed small figure at the entrance, but passed on, swinging his nightstick.

There was finally a tap at the plate glass.

Fausto looked up. Silhouetted against the inside light, the shadow of a coif loomed above him and he made out a woman's face. He shook with the effort to keep himself in tight control.

"What is it?" the nun asked sharply, her voice muted by the glass. Her voice was cross, something Fausto had not expected. He caught his hand to his side.

"My little girl," he gasped. "I'm here to take her home. I'm the father."

Sister Ursula had had a vexing day. There had been a suspicion of whooping cough among the seven-year-olds and her food accounts refused to balance. Her answer was short.

"You know the rules. We're closed now. Come back tomorrow."

"Not tomorrow, now!" he insisted. "There's some mistake. The cops brought the kid here when they had no right. I want her back now. It was just a mix-up."

"A police case?"

Her voice had changed. There was a sharp ring in her tones. She looked behind her. Except for a workman scrubbing the stairs, the tiled foyer was empty. The man outside the door looked harmless and she threw the bolt. This was against the rule that no one should be admitted after 10 o'clock.

"Come in."

Fausto entered with a quick step and glanced nervously about. There was a smell of disinfectant from the stairs ahead. A sign indicated the nursery up one flight. He nodded with his chin.

"Is the baby up there?"

"Step into the office," the nun said curtly. "I must talk with you."

Fausto heard the voice of authority. Sister Ursula had the practical air of a graduate nurse, used to dealing with the slow and ignorant. She was tall and heavy, he saw, with a look of strong common-sense. Perhaps she was fifty, but this was hard to know since her round stout face showed no lines. Nor could her hair under the coif tell her age. He held back.

"Talk? I don't want talk!" he said in a loud voice. "Just tell me where she is. The mama is waiting. I don't see what this is all about."

The workman on the stairs put down his scrubbing brush and called, "Any trouble, Sister?"

"It's nothing, Anton," she replied, then said firmly, "Come in here, young man."

Something inside Fausto began to quake, but he followed into the office where he took a seat at her desk. He sat twisting his hands. This severe room with its filing cabinets smacked of officialdom and he knew he had to behave.

"Now then."

Sister Ursula affixed her spectacles, large horn-rimmed affairs, and put aside her fiscal accounts with regret. The figures were tormenting but absorbing after the day's work. She turned to the admittance book for the day and studied a dozen entries, in and out. When she finally spoke, it was with a ringing accent that Fausto found strange.

"The child's name?"

"Carmen Fausto."

"Your name and your wife's?"

"I'm Vincente Fausto. My wife is Juana. We live in Rattigan Place."

She ran a finger down a page, then looked up. "We have a child by that name. She came in filthy. She's asleep upstairs."

His breath escaped.

"Then she's here," he said stupidly. "She's all right?"

"We won't know until she's examined."

"Can I take her home now?"

She placed the book aside and closed her tired eyes to consider. This was always disagreeable, this sort of case, and she longed to get back to her accounts; but she had a duty. She had no patience for these fools. She could look back over the years to thousands of children, sick, wounded, burned in flaming tenements, all who came to the Home. She was always moved to anger, but instead of answering, she dialed the telephone and spoke briefly.

"Mr. Cavanaugh, please come over now."

Fausto asked suspiciously, "Who was that?"

She slipped back her cuffs. "What happened tonight? Why did you leave the child?"

Fausto did not know what to say. He felt panic growing within him. The baby, his baby, was in the building and they meant to keep her. He wanted to rush out to get her but he was afraid and guilty before the nun. Her severity loomed large in his eyes. He felt a sense of awe. The bold words he wanted to say came out defiant but trembling.

"If I answer questions, can I get the kid now? I got to know. The wife—if I don't come home with the baby, she'll go out of her mind."

She ignored the question. "What do you do?"

"I'm a shipping clerk. I work. I could get reference." He came back to his point. "Who was that Cavanaugh?"

"Never you mind."

"I got a right to know. I'm the father."

"Ah, indeed!" She studied him almost with irony. "The father! Well, Mr. Cavanaugh is a city detective. He's in charge of this baby's case. You'll have to talk to him in a moment."

The child had to be held till morning to be examined for disease or neglect. The detective might wish to return the baby, or the parents might face a criminal charge.

Fausto asked, unbelieving. "The cops can keep a man's kid from him?"

"They can. It depends on the facts."

"Some cop takes away my own kid? I'm supposed to tell that to the wife?"

"The detective is in charge."

He smashed the desk with his fist and the sound was like a pistol crack.

"Be quiet!" she ordered angrily. "A fine one, you are! The baby came in filthy and hot! It might have burned to death while you were out drinking, man!"

He shouted. "Maybe they try to take the kid for good, hey? Nobody does that! I'm getting that baby!"

"Now, see here—"

Fausto threw back his chair. He paused a moment as she arose with him, an imposing figure in her black habit, and twice his size.

"I'm getting that baby!" he shouted.

She grasped his sleeve as he tried to rush past.

"Behave yourself, young man—"

He screamed hoarsely and he turned and his hand darted out. She saw the steel clearly—frozen, it seemed, in midflight—the flecks of rust, the serrations on the blade.

She could not believe it.

It felt as though a fiery tooth went through her side.

In all her life, not even as a girl before her novitiate, had she ever been struck in anger. No hand had ever been raised against her. Her habit had walled her off even from the sense of such things.

Fausto stared at her in terror.

She felt sick. This boy with wild eyes had walked in from the streets and had struck at her life.

"I didn't—" he cried.

The first shock of pain died like an echo, then surged back. She felt her side and looked down at a smear of blood.

"The baby!" he explained hoarsely. "It was on account of the kid—"

He dropped the knife and rushed off into the foyer.

"Anton!" she called. "Anton!"

There was no fright in her, only a sense of disbelief. She heard sounds of a struggle in the foyer. There was shouting and a banging, like a pail falling downstairs. Her office with its neat filing cabinets was suddenly strange.

She felt weak.

How bad was it? she wondered.

She started to grope for her crucifix when she fell into blackness . . .

Some hours later, Fausto found himself at the police station, weeping and abject, facing a man with hard eyes, blue and cold, who put questions.

The yellow-haired man in authority, he understood, was an assistant district attorney named Wiley. The room was crowded with heavy-faced detectives, all with angry loud voices. He rubbed a bruised shinbone where he had been kicked. Wiley put a question.

"Do you want to tell your story?"

"I don't know what made me do it!" Fausto wept.

"Would you like to smoke?"

"I'm too nervous."

"All right." Wiley sat back, balancing a cigarette, while a man beside him tapped a few notes on a stenotype machine. "Let's start at the beginning."

Fausto wretchedly was taken over the facts, large and small, from the time he had come home with Juana. The questions were skilled and methodical. It surprised him to see how much this man with the hard blue eyes knew or guessed about the events of the night.

"Isn't it a fact that you meant to cut down anyone who got in your way?" Wiley charged. "Wasn't that your intent when you reached the Home of Mercy?"

"I just knew I wanted the baby," Fausto said listlessly.

Wiley pointed a finger.

"You were carrying a switchblade knife, you knew that!"

"I use it at my work. I got to cut a lot of cord making bundles." Fausto dashed the blurring tears away. "I should've killed myself before using it! Why would I want to do a thing like that? I couldn't help myself."

He looked around at the disdainful heavy faces. He felt disliked and unclean and despised. "Can't nobody believe that?" he cried.

"Stabbing a nun!" a sharp-faced man with a brogue burst out. "I ought to cut your hands off, you son of a—"

"I didn't mean it!" Fausto protested weakly.

"They never mean it!" the man with the brogue cried. "Stabbing a nun!"

The lawyer broke in to protect the record. "What made you leave the baby alone last night?"

"Such a good baby!" Fausto could not stop his tears. "She never cried before. She sleeps a lot. I got this job just a short time. I'm working for this concern that makes coat fronts—you know, for men's suits. It's not bad pay, but with one thing and another, I'm paying back some money I owe. There's some loan sharks working that part of town and they take me plenty."

"What's the point?"

Fausto paused. "I'm awful short. I got no money for baby sitters. Then we moved into this strange house. These people—they don't like our kind and they don't talk to us. But I can't keep the wife cooped up. She's a young girl, sir, she's got to get out sometime. Sure, I can sit home when she goes to the movie, but that's no fun for her. So we take a chance. The baby is always so good."

"Go on."

"That's all. Once every other week I take the wife out for *pizza* dinner at this place downtown. It's cheap and good and they serve this wine. Maybe we took too much because for once I was flush. I played policy and I drew the number yesterday and we were celebrating. Our mistake was we took in a movie. The wife wanted to go home, but I said it would be all right, and I talked her into it. This night the baby cried. That's the whole story."

"Is there anything else you want to say?"

Fausto put a begging question. "Was that so wrong, sir? Lots of people do it. It was just a little extra time we took. Can they take away a man's baby for that?"

The assistant district attorney finished a cigarette without reply. He exchanged glances with the angry-faced detectives and swung about in the swivel chair. They had no suggestions and he concluded abruptly.

"No further questions. Examination closed 5 A.M."

It was over.

Fausto waited, but nothing happened, and he asked, "How is the nun, sir? I'm worried about that."

Wiley put on his hat to leave. He stood for a moment, a tall lean man with hard lines about his face, towering above the wretched little prisoner. He spoke slowly.

"You're a lucky man you missed, Fausto. She's going to live."

Perhaps three months later, on a brisk day in October, Sister Ursula entered the great Criminal Courts Building with a troubled look on her face. She asked directions at the circular desk in the lobby and took an elevator to the eleventh floor where a uniformed officer found her a seat in a crowded courtroom.

She whispered to the officer, "Has a man named Fausto been sentenced yet?"

"I'll see." The officer went forward, and returned. "Not yet."

She folded her hands and settled down in the rear while a long sentence calendar was disposed of by a stern judge whose glacial eyes were devoid of compassion. The cases went fast. Prisoners mutely accepted the sentences of the Court without any great show of emotion, and then when the courtroom was somewhat empty, a clerk announced, "Call Vincente Fausto for sentence."

There was a small stir of interest. In the rear, the door opened and the small dejected man walked quietly to his place and humbly bowed his head while four court officers gathered about him. Sister Ursula was conscious that her heart was beginning to distress her with its powerful hastening beat.

The court crier, a man with silvered hair, demanded, "Vincente Fausto, have you anything to say why judgment of this court should not now be imposed on you?"

A sensible-looking woman, a lawyer employed by the Legal Aid Society, arose from the counsel table and stated in a low musical voice, "The defendant is ready for sentence."

The judge removed his chin from his palm and asked disagreeably, "Do you wish to say anything in his behalf, Miss Collier?"

The lawyer bent down and whispered to the prisoner who shook his head. She looked up and said, "He wants to throw himself on the mercy of the court. He says he's sorry."

"I know that," the judge stated in an implacable voice. "For that reason, Miss Collier, I'm going to show him as much mercy as my conscience permits. Is that all?"

"That is all," the lawyer responded.

Sister Ursula half arose, then sank back as the court officer placed a finger to his lips for silence. The judge proceeded to impose sentence. After reciting the facts, he stated in a grating voice:

"It is the judgment of this Court that you be sentenced to a State's Prison for a term of not less than three and not more than five years."

"Three years?" Fausto said stupidly, then bowed his head, "Yes, Your Honor, thank you!" There was a hoarse sound behind him and Juana Fausto stood in the aisle and began to scream, her hands shaking, her voice cracking, as all her strength went into the gasping cries.

"Ai! Ai! Ai!"

Fausto clasped his hands and turned to her miserably, "Oh, please, querida, its not so bad! Please!"

"Remove that woman," the judge ordered.

"Ai!" she screamed.

The girl twisted and squirmed and her hair fell in disorder as she resisted the court officers who tried to drag her from the courtroom. They were gentle and considerate, but it was a hard business and they were panting as the door closed behind them.

It suddenly seemed to the assistant district attorney, standing at the prosecution table, that this case, which he had concluded as a job well done, a credit in its small way to his office and to himself, had been a piece of cruel folly.

When the chamber was again in order, Fausto was taken aside to answer pedigree questions put by the clerk. In this interval, Sister Ursula came forward and introduced herself and asked for permission to address the court.

"Yes, Sister, what is it?" the judge asked courteously.

She placed her hands together and asked strongly, "Why wasn't I called as a witness?"

"A witness?" The puzzled judge turned to the assistant district attorney. "This man pleaded guilty. There was no need for a witness."

Wiley explained, "Sister Ursula feels concerned with the sentence."

"I see," the judge answered.

The nun measured the judge with her level stare. "Three years in prison, Your Honor! That's a great deal of time to separate a man from his family."

The chamber was suddenly quiet. As Fausto turned, he recognized the nun. The other events of that night were confused in his mind, but the strong face of the nun was not something he would ever forget.

Judge Matthew Brady's face was granite. He drummed quietly at the bench, staring at the court officers, measuring the sound of his harsh voice. "I think, Sister Ursula," he said gently, "that I understand these problems better than you possibly can. I suggest you let me fix the sentence."

"I understand this man's heart," the nun replied.

"Perhaps so," the judge answered. "But he might have killed you. Under the circumstances, he is fortunate in the sentence imposed."

"This man pleaded guilty to obtain the mercy of the Court!" The nun's voice was strained. "This man was not acting with reason, but with his heart. He wanted his baby. There was no criminal intent within him. It would be cruel to punish him further."

"I'm sorry—" the judge began.

"At the very moment it happened, I forgave him," she went on strongly. "Why should the Court be less compassionate? A man with so much love in him should not be placed in prison."

Wiley caught the direction of the judge's glance, and looked to the press table where the reporters were wearing delighted grins. He could visualize the newspaper stories the following morning, and, he reflected with grim amusement, the judge was not less discerning.

"Ah, yes!" Judge Brady finally agreed. "As you say."

His face was scarlet, but with judicial aplomb the judge called the prisoner back and suspended the sentence on condition of good behavior. He pointed a strong moral and threw a strong tongue-lashing at the prisoner into the bargain.

"Oh, thank you, Judge!" Fausto cried. "God bless you!"

"And now, get out of my Court!" the judge exclaimed, and swept aside from the bench into his private chambers, where he went for a nerve-soothing cigar.

In the corridor there was a firecracker babble of delight as Juana understood that Vincente was going home with her to the child, and only after a time did the excited couple leave the corridor.

Wiley led Sister Ursula to the elevator. The morning sun was pouring into the marble corridor, and the day looked bright and clear outside.

"What could that judge have been thinking of?" Sister Ursula mumured.

"I have no idea what judges think about," Wiley said drily.

She looked at him sharply. "It was inexcusable to wait so long to call me, Mr. Wiley. I was almost too late. You were quite negligent."

"I'm afraid," Wiley confessed, "that I never expected this judge to agree to your request. He has strong ideas of his own."

There was a constrained silence before she spoke again.

"Thank you for being kind to me. I needed it less than that poor man. The mercy of the Court, indeed!"

She stepped into the elevator and left.

MURDER IN ONE SCENE

Q. Patrick

LIEUTENANT TRANT OF the New York Homicide Bureau was dawdling over breakfast in his pleasant apartment. He buttered a piece of brioche and glanced at the three letters which had come in the mail.

They didn't look interesting. One was from his mother in Newport. He opened it and read Mrs. Trant's usual garrulous account of her social life with its usual undercurrent of pained surprise that her son should choose to be a New York policeman pursuing murderers when he might be escorting the toniest dowagers through the best drawing rooms of the Eastern seaboard.

The second letter came from a Princeton classmate who was starting a cultured magazine and thought Trant might like to sacrifice five hundred dollars on the altar of Art.

The third was even less promising. The long envelope bore his name and address in type and, on its left hand top corner, the printed words: *Big Pal*. Trant knew the organization. It was a worthy one which found sponsors for delinquent boys on parole. Lieutenant Trant, who preferred his criminals delinquent rather than rehabilitated, had no great desire to become a Big Pal. He slit the envelope, anticipating the printed plea beginning: *Dear Friend* . . .

But the envelope did not contain the usual form letter. Inside was a folded sheet of elegant blue stationery. Lieutenant Trant blinked. He unfolded the sheet and looked at what was written on it. He blinked again.

Beneath an embossed Park Avenue address had been written in a round feminine hand:

"Dear George:

"Since you insist, come at five tomorrow. But this is to warn you. I shall have Eddie there. I have also bought a gun. If you try what you tried last time, I will use it.

"Marna."

Lieutenant Trant, whose passion for the unorthodox was unbridled, smiled happily. Offhand he could think of nothing less orthodox than the arrival of so personal and interesting a communication in the envelope of an impersonal and unexciting charitable organization.

He realized that a mistake must have been made with envelopes. Appeals are usually sent out by volunteer ladies who have been given a sucker list and envelopes and who salve their social consciences by typing addresses and providing stamps. This particular volunteer lady—this unknown Marna—must have been very absent-minded or very jittery.

Judging by the nature of the letter she had mailed in the wrong envelope, she had been very jittery.

Trant looked at the date. It had been written the day before. "Five tomorrow" therefore meant five o'clock that afternoon. He let his thoughts toy pleasingly with a picture of the jittery Marna with her gun and Eddie waiting at five for the mysterious George who might "try" again what he had "tried" last time.

It was, of course, his duty as an officer of the law to investigate what might prove to be a very antisocial encounter.

He put the envelope and the letter in his pocket.

He was humming as he left his apartment . . .

A few minutes before five Lieutenant Trant, in an elegantly inconspicuous gray suit, arrived at the house whose address appeared at the head of Marna's letter. Although the house had a Park Avenue number, its door was on a side street. It was an old private residence which had been converted into apartments.

Since he did not know Marna's name, he stepped into the small outside hall and studied the names above the door buzzers. There was no Marna anything. Most of the names were discouraging. But above the buzzer of the penthouse apartment were two printed cards. One said: *Miss Joan Hyde*. The other said: *Mrs. George Hyde*.

Marna could be Mrs. George Hyde. That would make her the wife of the potentially sinister George. Miss Joan Hyde might be her daughter. Lieutenant Trant was disappointed. Romantic about mystery and the possibly mysterious, he had imagined Marna blonde, beautiful—and young.

He was about to press the Hyde buzzer when a girl came in from the street behind him and, fumbling through her pocketbook, brought out a key and opened the door. She glanced at him questioningly and kept the door half open. He smiled and followed her into the house.

The girl had started through the neat mirrored hallway toward a self-service elevator, but she stopped and turned back to him a little suspiciously.

"Are you looking for someone?"

She was young and pretty with shining dark hair, cool eyes and a sort of lazy self-assurance which went with the silver fox coat she was wearing.

How nice, thought Lieutenant Trant, if Marna had looked like that.

He said: "As a matter of fact, I'm looking for Marna Hyde."

"Oh." She smiled. "How interesting."

"Is it?"

"To me it is." She moved to the elevator. "I'll take you up."

Lieutenant Trant got into the elevator, too. The girl's perfume was pleasant. As she made the elevator ascend, she glanced at him sidewise.

"Don't say Marna's got herself a new beau."

"Do I look like a beau?"

"Very. But I wouldn't have thought Marna'd have the energy to take on a new man—what with George to get rid of and the faithful Eddie hovering."

So far so good, thought Lieutenant Trant.

The elevator reached the top floor. They got out to face a single door. The girl started to fumble in her pocketbook again.

"So you live here, too," said Trant.

"I moved in when George moved out. I'm a bodyguard. Hasn't Marna mentioned me? I'm Joan."

"George's sister."

"Yes."

"And you're not on George's side?"

"About the divorce?" Joan Hyde turned. "Are you kidding?"

"I never kid," said Lieutenant Trant. "I am a very sedate young man."

Joan Hyde had found the key. "I don't imagine Marna's home yet but come in and have a drink."

"I'd like to very much."

She opened the door, chattering: "I've just been to that French movie with Barrault and Arletty. It's quite wonderful, but at the beginning I never dreamed he wouldn't get her at the end. Why are foreign movies always so gloomy?"

Trant followed her into a charmingly casual living room. His trained eye saw several very valuable pieces.

Joan Hyde said: "It's nothing much. They wanted a hangout in New York and Marna brought up some of the junk from their Long Island attic. I'll rustle up a drink. Sit down."

As the girl disappeared into the kitchen, Trant moved to a small Chippendale breakfront desk, reflecting that anyone who had "junk" like this in a Long Island attic had no financial problems. On the desk he saw what he hoped he would see. Beside a portable typewriter, there was a pile of unused *Big Pal* envelopes; a pile of form letters; a mimeographed list of addresses; and a second neat pile of letters which had been addressed on the typewriter and stamped ready for mailing.

He glanced at the name on the top and saw that a Mr. and Mrs. LeRoy Jones of Seventy-eighth Street were about to be urged to take an interest in delinquent boys. He had just enough time to glance at the letter below which was for a Mrs. Samuel Katzenbach when he heard Joan returning and dropped into a chair.

"I'm afraid there's only rye." Joan Hyde appeared with a tray. "After having put up with George for so long, Marna and I are a little cautious about alcohol." She put the tray down and glanced at him curiously. "I suppose you do know what I'm talking about? You're not someone who's come to look at the plumbing, are you?"

"I was never good with my hands," said Lieutenant Trant.

Joan made drinks and chattered on. As Trant listened, the situation became increasingly clear. Marna had married George. George was a drunk. Marna had met Eddie. Marna had wanted a divorce. The drunken George had made terrible scenes; at one time he had drunkenly tried to kill Marna. Joan, entirely sympathetic with her sister-in-law, had moved in as protection.

"It's dreary," meditated Joan. "You can't help feeling fond of your own brother, but George is quite frightening. And he still has a key. I'm always telling Marna she should get the lock changed. But she's always putting it off. I . . ."

Trant was losing interest. In spite of the fascinating accident which had made him conscious of it, this was basically a trite situation. A wealthy alcoholic with a temper; probably a frivolous wife.

His thought train snapped because a noise had come from the room, presumably a bedroom, behind Joan. It was a very slight sound but enough to tell him someone was there.

He glanced at his watch. "Five-ten. Marna made a fuss about my being on time. You don't suppose she's in the bedroom? Maybe asleep?"

Joan put her drink down. "I strenuously doubt it. Want me to look?"

"Would you?"

A newspaper lay on the arm of Trant's chair. To feign indifference he picked it up and glanced at it. It had been turned to a review of the opening of the circus. He looked down the columns.

Joan Hyde reached the bedroom door. She opened it. She gasped. "Marna!"

Instantly Trant ran to her side. Oblivious of him, Joan took a step into the room. Trant followed. A blonde girl in a black dress sat huddled on one of the twin beds. Her hair tumbled in disorder around her beautiful but stricken face. Fantastically she was wearing white suede gloves and over the knuckles of the right hand glove stretched a red damp stain.

Joan ran to her. "Marna, what's the matter?"

Trant gazed as if hypnotized at the red stain. Marna turned to look at him from blank eyes.

"Joan, tell that man to go."

"But, Marna, he has a date with you."

"Tell him to go away."

Trant took a step forward, his eyes darting about the room. He passed the foot of the bed. He moved toward the window.

Marna jumped up and screamed: "No, no."

He came to the second bed. He looked down at the area of carpet between the bed and the window. Sprawled on his stomach was the body of a young man. A revolver lay on the floor close to him.

The back of his head had been shot away. He was dead. There was no doubt about that.

Joan came running to Trant's side. "George!" she cried. "Oh, Marna, he tried to attack you again. He . . ."

Trant turned to Marna Hyde. She stood quite still. She was as lovely as he could have wanted her to be.

Rather sadly he said: "Since you bought the gun, Mrs. Hyde, I suppose you felt you should get your money's worth."

Both the girls were staring at him.

He added: "By the way, do you always wear gloves in the house?"

"She has a milk allergy." It was Joan who spoke. "Her hands broke out again this afternoon. She always wears gloves when it's bad. But—who are you? Why are you here?"

Trant shrugged. "I'm sorry to give you such good service. I'm from the Homicide Bureau." He took Marna's elbow. "Shall we move into the next room?"

Marna let him guide her into the living room. She dropped into a chair. Joan Hyde came after them.

"Homicide Bureau. I don't understand."

"You're not meant to." Trant was watching Marna. "You have been sending out appeals for the *Big Pal* people, haven't you?"

The girl shivered. She did not seem to have heard the question. He repeated it. She whispered: "Yes."

"You sent some off yesterday and did some more today?"

"Yes."

Trant took from his pocket the letter he had received and handed it to her. "You wrote this, Mrs. Hyde?"

"Yes, but how . . ."

"It's all fairly obvious, isn't it? Your husband didn't want the divorce. He'd been acting violently. He was coming at five. You were afraid of him so you bought a gun. He got violent again. You shot him."

Marna Hyde did not say anything.

Trant went on: "There's just one thing that seems to be missing. Eddie was supposed to be here. Where is he?"

Marna was looking at the blood stain on her glove. There was dead silence. The buzzer shrilled. Joan started for the door, but Trant outdistanced her to the hall. He opened the door onto a blond young man with broad shoulders and very blue eyes.

Trant said: "Hello, Eddie."

The young man glared. "Who are you?"

"Just a stray policeman. You're a little late for the murder."

"Murder? Nothing's—nothing's happened to Marna?"

Roughly the young man pushed past Trant and ran into the living room. Trant followed. The young man hurried to Marna and dropped at her side, his face gaunt with anxiety.

"Marna, baby. Marna, are you all right?"

"It's George, Eddie," said Joan. "He's dead."

Marna turned so that she was looking straight at the young man. "Eddie, you didn't . . .?" Slowly the expression of horror faded from her eyes. "No." She got up and confronted Trant. She seemed almost calm.

"I haven't any idea how you got here, but presumably you want to ask me questions. It's all quite simple. I did buy the gun. I did write George that letter. But that's all I did. I've been out this afternoon. I got back just before five. I went into the bedroom. I—I found George. I was still bending over him when I heard Joan come in with you. I heard a strange voice. It was all a terrible shock. I didn't want a stranger involved. I decided to wait in the bedroom until you had gone."

Lieutenant Trant lit a cigarette. He was thinking hard and he discovered that he was beginning to relish this situation which, whatever it turned out to be, was no longer trite.

He sat down on the arm of a chair. All three of them were watching him as if he were a time bomb.

He glanced at Marna. "So that's your story. Your husband was dead when you came home?"

"It's true."

Trant smiled. "You would hardly admit that it was a lie, Mrs. Hyde. Of course, with those gloves, there'd be no fingerprints on the gun. You picked a lucky time for your disagreement with milk."

"Marna's milk allergy is on the level," barked Eddie. "Show him your hands, Marna."

Marna peeled off her right glove. There was no doubt about the allergy. Her thumb, the tips of her second and first fingers and the whole middle of her palm were sprinkled with little white blisters. She turned the hand over. Her knuckles were split. She put the glove on again.

Lieutenant Trant looked apologetic. "I'm sorry, Mrs. Hyde. I shouldn't have doubted your word." He eyed her almost with affection. "I might as well explain my presence. There's no magic involved. I'm on the *Big Pal* sucker list. This morning I got what should have been the appeal. It wasn't. I got George's letter instead. I came to see what would happen here at five o'clock."

The drinks were still on the tray. Eddie poured himself a shot of straight rye. Neither of the girls spoke.

"I thought," continued Trant, "that I had received the letter by mistake. That, of course, was what I was supposed to think. Unhappily, I don't think it any more."

Marna said: "What do you think?"

Trant did not reply. "When you're sending out appeals to people on an alphabetical list, the only way to do it without driving yourself crazy is to send them in alphabetical order."

"That's what I did."

"Exactly. Yesterday you got up to the I's. I took a look at your desk. Today you began with the J's and K's. My name's Trant. Certainly you hadn't got to the T's yesterday. You couldn't inadvertently have put George's letter in an envelope for me by yesterday."

Eddie asked: "Which means?"

"That the letter was sent to me by-mistake-on-purpose. Someone saw my name on the sucker list and knew my reputation as a sort of crackpot policeman. They knew if I received the letter I'd be intrigued enough to show up here at five."

The two girls together asked: "But why?"

"Because they wanted me to come. The letter would have given me a preconceived idea of motive. I would have found George's body and realized right away that he had attacked his wife and she had shot him in self-defense. I would have written George off as a victim of justifiable homicide. I might even have made a little speech to Mrs. Hyde about Valiant American Womanhood. Yes, it was a neat trap, a very neat trap."

Eddie asked belligerently: "Are you suggesting that Marna . . ."

"I'm not suggesting that Mrs. Hyde did anything at all." Trant looked at Eddie. "Do you have a key to this apartment?"

"Of course I don't."

"But you were hoping to marry Mrs. Hyde once she got the divorce?" He flushed. "I was and I am."

Trant turned to Marna. "I imagine your husband was quite rich."

"He was very well off."

"Seems to have been a kind of irresponsible character. Didn't make the money himself, did he?"

"No. It's a trust. When his parents died, they left it all to him in trust. He can't touch the capital. Just the income."

Lieutenant Trant was still watching Marna. "Lucky accident my arrival coincided with your sister-in-law's, wasn't it? If I'd come a minute earlier, you wouldn't have let me in. If I'd arrived a minute later, you'd have told Joan about George and you would not have let anyone in either."

Trant continued musingly: "I always rather suspect lucky accidents. They're not always as accidental as they seem."

He shifted his quiet attention to Joan Hyde. "You live here, Miss Hyde. Perhaps you saw Marna writing that letter to George yesterday. Perhaps you even offered to mail it."

Joan Hyde looked back at him blankly.

"I suppose," he went on in his soft, almost gentle voice, "you called George in Marna's name and asked him to come a little before five. After you'd killed him, you went downstairs, saw Marna come home and waited for me. That was an ingenious device, assuming I was a beau of Marna's. It gave you a chance to sell me once and for all on the manslaughter set-up. The violent George, the unchanged lock . . ."

Her dark eyes blazing, Joan snapped: "You're mad."

Lieutenant Trant looked disappointed. "Why do murderers always say: *You're mad?* Do you suppose they pick it up in the movies?"

"You . . ."

"In any case, I'm afraid the movies have been your downfall, Miss Hyde. You got just a little too chatty about your French film. You told me you never dreamed at the beginning that Barrault wouldn't get Arletty in the end. To be in doubt about the end of a movie at the beginning proves quite definitely that you saw the beginning first."

He picked up the newspaper from the arm of the chair. "That French movie happens to be playing at only one Manhattan house. I notice here in the timetable that it begins at 1:20, 3:20 and 5:20. Since you saw the beginning before the end you could not possibly have seen the 3:20 show and arrived here just before five. If you went to the movie at all today, you went to the show which was over just before 3:20. That gave you plenty of time to eliminate George." He paused. "That does horrid things to your alibi, doesn't it?"

Joan Hyde seemed stunned. So did Eddie and Marna.

Eddie asked: "But why would Joan . . .?"

"Failing offspring, a trust fund reverts to the family." Trant's amiable gaze moved to Marna. "Am I right in assuming that Miss Hyde is the family?"

"Why, yes," faltered Marna. "She's the only other child. I suppose the trust goes to her."

"Money." Lieutenant Trant sighed. "Such an orthodox motive. Perhaps you'd give me the name of your husband's lawyer. Just to check."

He produced a pencil and a piece of paper. Marna took the pencil in her right hand and scribbled. Trant put the paper in his pocket. He was still watching Marna.

"When you discovered the corpse, you thought Eddie must have done it, didn't you? Once you'd realized no court would convict you, you'd almost certainly have taken the rap for his sake. Yes, it was quite an expert little scheme for disposing of an alcoholic brother and living happily ever after on his trust fund."

He moved to Joan Hyde. He always felt a slight pang when the time came to arrest an attractive and clever murderess.

She was still quite calm and her eyes were hard with anger. "You'll never prove it. Never."

Trant grinned. "You'll be surprised at what I can prove when I put my mind to it. For example, we've hardly scratched that milk allergy, have we?"

He turned to Marna. "Would you take off your glove again?"

The girl obeyed. Trant drew Joan toward her sister-in-law.

"Your sister-in-law wrote down the lawyer's name for me. See how the pressure of the pencil broke those little blisters? Blisters are very sensitive, Miss Hyde. I challenge even you to have fired a gun and kept your blisters intact." He shrugged. "Mrs. Hyde couldn't have fired the gun. Eddie, who didn't have a key, couldn't have got in. So . . . Like me to do some more proving?"

Eddie was gazing at Marna's hand. He muttered: "For heaven's sake, he's proved it, Marna. It took him just ten minutes."

Trant had a firm hold on Joan Hyde's arm. He still liked her perfume.

"A good detective," he said modestly, "would have solved it before it happened. It's too bad, Miss Hyde. If I'd been a little brighter, we might be going to the theater tonight, instead of to the Tombs . . ."

THE MISSING MAN

Katherine Maclean

"YOU ARE NOT ALONE" announced the sign, flashing neon red in the dark sky. People in the free mixed streets looked up and saw it as they walked back from work. It glowed red behind them in the sky as they entered the gates of their own Kingdoms; their own incorporated small country with its own laws inside its gates. They changed into their own strange costumes, perhaps light armor, and tourneyed, tilting lances against each other, winning ladies. Or in another Kingdom, with a higher wall around its enclosed blocks of city, the strange lotteries and rites of the Aztec sadist cult, or the simple poverty and friendliness of the Brotherhood Love Communes. They were not alone.

Nonconformists who could not choose a suitable conformity lived in the mixed public areas, went to mixing parties, wondering and seeking. Seeking who? To join with to do what? Returning from the parties late and alone, they passed the smaller signs flashing red in the store windows.

YOU ARE NOT ALONE
Find your own Kind, Find your own Hobby.
Find your own Mate, Find your own Kingdom.
Use "Harmony" personality diagnosis and matching service.

Carl Hodges was alone. He stood in a deserted and mined section of the city and saw the red glow of the sign reflecting against the foggy air of the sky of New York, blinking on and off like the light of a flickering red flame. He knew what the glow said. *You are not alone.*

365

He shut his eyes, and tears trickled from under his closed eyelids. Damn the day he had learned to do time track. He could remember and return to Susanne, he could even see the moment of the surfboard and his girl traveling down the front slope of a slanted wave front, even see the nose of the board catch again under the ripple, the wave heaving the board up, up and over, and whipping down edge first like an ax. He knew how to return for pleasure to past events, but now he could not stop returning. It happened again before his eyes, over and over. *Think about something else!*

"'Crying again, Pops?" said a young insolent voice. A hand pushed two tablets against his mouth. "Here, happy pills. Nothing to cry about. It's a good world."

Obediently Carl Hodges took the pills into his mouth and swallowed.

Soon memory and grief would stop hurting and go away. Think about something else. Work? No, he should be at work, on the job instead of vacationing, living with runaway children. Think about fun things.

It was possible that he was a prisoner, but he did not mind. Around him, collecting in the dark, stood the crowd of runaway children and teenagers in strange mixed costumes from many communes across the United States. They had told him that they had run away from the Kingdoms and odd customs of their parents, hating the Brotherhood, and conformity, and sameness of the adults they had been forced to live with by the law that let incorporated villages educate their own children within the walls.

The teeners had told him that all rules were evil, that all customs were neurotic repetition, that fear was a restriction, that practicality was a restriction, and mercy was a restriction.

He told himself they were children, in a passing phase of rebellion.

The pill effect began to swirl in a rosy fog of pleasure into his mind. He remembered fun. "Did I tell you," be muttered to the runaway teener gang that held him as a prisoner-guest, "about the last game of Futures I played with Ronny? It was ten-thirty, late work, so when we finished we disconnected the big computer from its remote controls and started to play City Chess. We had three minor maintenance errors as our only three moves. He wiped out my half of the city, by starting an earthquake from a refrigerator failure in a lunchroom. It wiped out all the power plant crew with food poisoning, and the Croton power plant blew up along a fault line. That was cheating because he couldn't prove the fault line. I wiped out his technocrats in Brooklyn Dome just by reversing the polarity on the air-conditioning machine. It's a good thing our games aren't real. Everyone is wiped out totally by the end of a good game."

A blond kid who seemed to be the leader stepped forward and took

Carl Hodges's arm, leading him back toward his cellar room. "You started to tell me about it, but tell me again. I'm very interested. I'd like to study Maintenance Prediction as a career. What does reversing the leads on the air-conditioning machine do to destroy a place?"

"It changes the smell of the air," said Carl Hodges, the missing man who knew too much. "You wouldn't think that would make a lot of difference, would you?"

Since June 3, every detective the police could spare had been out looking for a missing computerman who had been last seen babbling about ways to destroy New York City.

Judd Oslow, Chief of Rescue Squad, sounded excited on the phone. "Your anti-chance score is out of sight, George. I want you to guess for us where Carl Hodges is and give us another hit like the first three. I'm not supposed to send my men after Carl Hodges, it's not my department, but that's my neck on the block, not yours. Brace yourself to memorize a description."

"Sure." George made ready to visualize a man.

"Carl Hodges, twenty-nine years old, a hundred and forty pounds, five feet nine inches tall, brown hair, hazel eyes."

George visualized someone shorter and thinner than himself. He remembered some short underweight men who were always ready to fight to prove they were bigger.

"His job is assistant coordinator of computer automation city services," read Judd Oslow.

"What's that?" George wanted to get the feel of Carl Hodges's job.

"Glorified maintenance man for the city, the brains for all the maintenance and repair teams. He uses the computer to predict wear and accidents and lightning-strikes and floods that break down phone lines, power and water lines and he sends repair teams to strengthen the things before they are stressed so they don't break. He prevents trouble."

"Oh." George thought: *Carl Hodges will be proud of his job. He won't want to be bigger.* "How does he act with his friends? How does he feel?"

"Wait for the rest." Judd read, "Hobbies are chess, minimax, and surfing. No commune. Few friends. One girl who met with a fatal accident when they were on a love trip last month. He's not happy. He was last seen at a Stranger's introduction party, Thirty-sixth Street and Eighth. He might have been spaced out on drugs, or he might have been psychotic, because he was reported as mumbling continuously on a dangerous subject he was usually careful to keep quiet about."

"What subject?"

"Secret."

"Why?"

"Panic."

"Oh." George restrained his natural anger at being confronted with a secret, and remembered an excuse for the authorities. Panic, or any other group stimulation that could send many people unexpectedly in the same direction, could cause destructive crowding and clogging in the walkways and transportation. People could get jammed in, pushed, trampled, suffocated. In a city of tremendous population and close and immediate access to everything, safety from crowding was based on a good scatter of differences, with some people wanting to be in one place and others in another, keeping them thinly spread. Sometimes the authorities kept secrets, or managed the news to prevent interesting things from pulling dangerous jammed crowds into one place.

The chief of Rescue Squad got the TV connection to the public phone turned on, and let George look at a photograph of the missing man. A wiry undersized scholar with a compressed mouth and expressionless eyes. George tried to tune in by pretending it was his own face in the mirror. Staring into its eyes he felt lonely.

He started by going to the Stranger's introduction party. He followed his impulses, pretending to be Carl Hodges. He wandered the city closely on the trail of Carl Hodges, but he did not feel it with any confidence, because he thought that the trail of feelings that urged him from one place to another were his own lonely feelings and sad thoughts. After he was given a few bad events to be sad about, he was sure it was his own mood.

George woke at dawn and watched pink sunlight touch the bushes along the top of a building so they brightened up like candle flames on the top of a birthday cake. He lay with his eyes open and watched while the light brightened and the pink faded. Crickets sang and creaked in the deep grass and bending tall grass tickled against his face.

He lay still, feeling the kind of aches you get from being kicked. There were a lot of aches. The teener gang that had attacked him had even put chain bruises on his legs. They had not been trying to kill him, only to warn him against trespassing again.

But George still felt strange and without friends. Usually he could join any group. Usually he could be anybody's friend. Was he forgetting how to be buddy with strangers? The teeners had left him on the sidewalk tied in a ridiculous knot with fingers and toes hooked together by Chinese fingertrap tubes. He had worked his fingers free, and walked down to his girlfriend's Brotherhood Love Commune to sleep. He felt strange and inferior, and hoped no one would look at him, when he entered the commune. The brothers in the front rooms said he was giving out bad vibes, and upsetting an important group meditation, and they gave him a cup of tea and put him out with his sleeping bag.

Four A.M., wondering what he was doing wrong, he went to sleep in a shape-hiding shadow in the grass belt opposite the Rescue Squad midtown headquarters. Now awakened again by dawn, he felt his bruises and felt sad and unsuccessful. He had wandered through many places in the city the night before, but he had not found Carl Hodges. The computerman was still an unlucky prisoner somewhere.

By the time the sun was high, George was going across George Washington Bridge the hard way, on the understruts, clinging with bare hands and feet, clambering up and down slopes of girders and cables, sometimes sitting and watching the sun sparkle on the water more than a hundred feet below while huge ships went slowly by, seeming like toys.

The wind blew against his skin, warm sometimes and sometimes cold and foggy. He watched a cloud shadow drift up from the south along the river. It darkened the spires of tall buildings, became a traveling island of dark blue in the light blue of the river, approached and widened, and then there was cool shadow across the bridge for long moments while George looked up and watched a dark cotton cloud pass between him and the sun.

The cloud left and the light blazed. George looked away, dots of darkness in front of his eyes, and watched the cloud shadow climb a giant cliff to the west and disappear over the top. He started picking his way along a downslope of girder, moving carefully because the dazzle of sun dots was still inside his eyes, dancing between his vision and the girders. Overhead the steady rumble of traffic passing along the roadway was a faraway and soothing sound.

A gull in the distance flapped upward through the air towards him. It found an updraft and drifted with it, wings spread and motionless, then paused in front of him, floating, a white beautiful set of wings, a sardonic cynical head with downcurved mouth and expressionless inspecting eyes.

George was tempted to reach out and grab. He shifted to the grip of one hand on the cross strut and hooked one knee over a bar.

The gull tilted the tips of his wings and floated upward and back, a little farther out of reach in the sky, but still temptingly close.

George decided that he was not stupid enough to let a gull trick him into falling off the bridge.

The gull slanted and slid sideways down a long invisible slope of air and squalled, "Creee. Ha ha ha ha. Ha ha ha . . ." in a raucous gull laugh. George hoped he would come back and make friends, but he had never heard of anyone making friends with a gull. He climbed on toward the New Jersey shore, going up and down slopes of girders, found a steel ladder fastened to the side and climbed it straight up to a paint locker and a telephone. He dialed Rescue Squad, and asked for Judd Oslow.

"Chief, I'm tired of taking a vacation."

"This morning Ahmed reported you walked like a cripple. How late did you work last night?"

"Three-thirty."

"Find any clues to Carl Hodges?"

"Not exactly." George looked at the far, high planes and helicopters buzzing through the blue sky. He did not feel like discussing the failure of last night.

"Where are you now?"

"In a painter's crow's nest on George Washington Bridge."

"Climbing George Washington Bridge is your idea of a rest?"

"It's away from people. I like climbing."

"Okay, your choice. You are near Presbyterian Medical Center. Report to the Rescue Squad station there and fill out some reports on what you've been doing all week. Some of the things you've been doing, we would probably like to pay you for. The information girl there will help you fill out the forms. You'll like her, George. She doesn't mind paper work. Let her help you."

Ahmed Kosavakats, George's superior and childhood friend, was ready to admit defeat He had reasoned in trying to find Carl Hodges and reasoned well.

Any commune which had Carl Hodges could ask him how to bias the city services computer in their favor. Ahmed had been checking the routine deliveries of repairs and improvements and rebuilding and projects to each commune, by running a comparison check against the normal deliveries through the statistics computer. Negative. There was no sign of a brilliant manipulator changing the city services.

Ahmed stood up and stretched long arms, thinking. Whoever had Carl Hodges was not using him. If Ahmed could rescue Carl Hodges and become his friend, he would not miss the opportunity to use him. If a man wanted to influence the future of his city . . .

If he could not use his own logic to find Carl Hodges, then the kidnappers were not thinking logically, and could not be predicted by logic. If they were thinking emotionally, then George Sanford could probably tune to them and locate them. But Ahmed would have to tell him what kind of people to tune to, and how they felt.

George Sanford's intuition was a reliable talent. Once, when George was a fattish, obliging kid in Ahmed's gang, Ahmed had added up how often George's simple remarks and guesses had turned out right. George had guessed right every time. But George didn't think. Half envious, Ahmed had told the others that George's head was like a radio; you could tune his brain to any station and get the news and weather and the right time in Paris, San Francisco, and Hong Kong, but a radio isn't going to add anything up, not even two plus two; it works because it's empty.

George Sanford had grown up to a big silent cat of a man. Extremely strong, not caring apparently whether he ate, drank, or slept, a rather blank expression, but he still tuned in on people. His goals were the simple ones of being with friends, helping out, and being welcome, and he had friends everywhere.

Behind the apparent low IQ there were untapped abilities that could only be brought into action by demanding a lot of George when you asked him to help. It was not certain yet how much George could do. George did not know. He probably did not even think about it. He had no demands on himself.

The thing to do, Ahmed thought, was to keep the pressure on George. Keep him working.

Ahmed found George filling out reports by dictating them to a pretty girl. The pretty office worker had her hands poised over the typewriter and was listening to George with an expression of surprise and doubt. George, with his brow knotted, was plodding through a narrative of something he had done the day before. The girl rolled the report sheet through the typewriter opposite a different blank and asked a question timidly; a tape recorder showed its red light, recording the questions and answers. George hesitated, looking at the ceiling desperately for inspiration, his brow more knotted than before.

George always had trouble understanding the reasoning behind red tape. He did not know why certain answers were wanted. They both looked up with relief when Ahmed interrupted by turning off the tape recorder.

"They told me to team up with you this afternoon," Ahmed said to George. "They give this job priority over reports or any other job. Are you feeling okay now?"

"Sure, Ahmed," George said, slightly surprised.

"Let's go outside and see if we can tune to the subject. Okay?"

"Okay." George got up, moving easily. A bruise showed at his hairline on the side of his head, almost hidden by hair. On George's right arm were two blue bruises, and below his slacks on the right ankle was a line of red dents with bruises. A left-handed assailant with a club, or a right-handed assailant with a chain, swinging it left to right, would bruise a man on one side like that.

Walking out of the Rescue Squad office, Ahmed indicated with a gesture the bruise on George's arm.

"May I ask?"

"No," George replied and closed his mouth tightly, staring straight ahead as they went through the double doors.

George didn't want to talk about it, Ahmed thought, because he had lost that fight. That meant he had been outnumbered. But he was not dead or seriously hurt. The assailants then were not killers, or he had escaped them. Probably a trespassing problem. Probably George had trespassed onto some group's territory or Kingdom last night while searching for Carl Hodges by himself. Ahmed put the thought aside. They stopped on a walk among the bushes and trees and looked up at the towering buildings of Presbyterian Medical Center, like giant walls reaching to the sky. Helicopter ambulances buzzed around landing steps like flies.

"Let's not waste time, George, let's get you tuned into Carl Hodges," Ahmed said, pulling out a notebook and pen. "Do you have a picture of Hodges with you?"

"No." The big young man looked uneasy. "You going to do it that same way, Ahmed? If he's sick, will I get sick?"

"I've got a picture here." Ahmed reached for a folder in his pocket and passed a photo to George.

The ground jolted in a sort of thud that struck upward against their feet.

Nine miles or more away, and two minutes earlier, Brooklyn Dome, the undersea suburb, suddenly lost its dome. The heavy ocean descended upon it, and air carrying a torrent of debris that had been houses and people blurted upward through an air shaft. A fountain of wreckage flung upward into the sky, falling in a circular rain of shattered parts to float upon the sea.

All morning a mass wish to escape from the enclosure of walls had driven George happily into the heights and winds and free sky. Now that note in the blend of the mood of the city suddenly changed and worsened to panic, helplessness, defeat, and pain, and then an end. The event telescoped in speed, compressed into a blow of darkness. The broadcast of many thousand minds ended and their background hum in the vibes of the city diminished.

Reaching out with his mind for information, George encountered the memory of that impact. It went by like the thunder wave of breaking the sound barrier, like a wave of black fog. He shut his eyes to tune in, and found nothing, except that the world had lightened. A burden of fear had been suddenly erased.

George opened his eyes and took a deep breath. "Something big," he said. "Something . . ."

Ahmed was watching the sweep-second hand on his watch. "Fifty-five hundred feet, one mile," he muttered.

"What are you doing?"

"It's an explosion somewhere. I'm counting the distance. Sound arrives first through the ground, second through the air. I'm waiting for the sound. I'll get the distance by the time lag."

At thirty seconds the sound of the death of an undersea city reached them, a strange sort of grinding roar, muffled, low and distant.

George shut his eyes again, and felt the world change around him to another place.

"Got something, George?" Ahmed asked alertly. "That was about seven miles."

"Someone knows what happened. I'm picking him up. Brooklyn Dome just collapsed."

"Twelve thousand inhabitants," Ahmed said, dialing his wrist radio grimly, his earphone plugged into his ear. "No one answering at headquarters, just busy signals."

George shut his eyes again, exploring the other place. "Someone's having a nightmare," he said. "He can't wake up."

"Don't flip out, George, keep in touch with facts. A lot of people just died, is all. Keep a grip on that. I'm trying to get our orders."

George stood with his eyes shut, exploring the sensation inside his head. Somewhere a man was trapped in a nightmare, half asleep in a dark prison or closet. It was some kind of delirium.

The real world was a cruel place that bright day, but the black and coiling fragments of that man's world were worse. There was something important about the man's thoughts. He had felt the explosion thud at a distance, as they had, and he had known what it meant. He had expected it.

"Can't locate where he is," George said, opening his eyes and regaining his grip on the bright sunshine world around him.

Ahmed squinted and tilted his head, listening to the obscure and rapid voices on the earplugs of his radio.

"Never mind about that case, George. That's Carl Hodges probably. He'll keep. Headquarters is broadcasting general orders for the emergency.

Repair and services inspection people are ordered to make quick inspections at all danger points in the automatic services, looking for malfunction and sabotage. Repair and inspection teams are ordered into Jersey Dome, to check out every part of it and make sure it is not gimmicked to blow the way Brooklyn Dome went. They are instructed to describe it as a routine safety check."

"What do we do? What about us?"

"Wait, I'm listening. They mentioned us by name. We go to Jersey underseas and try to locate and stop a sabotage agent who might have sabotaged Brooklyn Dome and might be preparing to use the same method on Jersey Dome."

"What method?"

"They don't know. They don't even know if there is a saboteur. They're sending us to make sure."

"If there is a saboteur, he's probably working on it right now." George walked, and then ran for the subway steps down into the underground moving chair belts. Ahmed followed and they caught a brace of abandoned chairs just as they slowed and accelerated them again out into the fast lanes.

"Dirty dogs! Let me out of here. I'll kill you." Furiously Carl Hodges kicked and thrashed and bit at restraining straps, remembering at last, believing his conclusions about the group of teeners that had him prisoner. "You decerebrate lizards. Let me out of here, you fools! You killed Brooklyn Dome. I've got to get back to work and level off the exchanges before something else happens. Let me out of here!"

They backed off, their smiles fading at the barrage of his anger. The tallest one answered with a trace of resentment. "Don't get upset, Pops. They weren't real people, just technocrats and objectivists and fascists and like that."

"They were techs. This city needs techs. People with tech jobs run the city, remember?"

The tall one leaned over him, glowering. "I remember what my tapes tell me. The objectivists passed the law that the compulsory sterility of women can't be reversed without paying five hundred dollars for the operation. That means if I ever want to get married I'll have to save five hundred dollars for my woman to have a kid. They're trying to wipe us all out. Nobody has that kind of money but techs. In the next generation we'll all be gone. We're just getting back at them, wiping them out."

"But faster," chuckled a small kid. "Like *boom!*"

"The objectivists got that law through legally. Why don't your people pull enough votes to get it wiped?" Carl Hodges demanded.

"They ship us out to the boondocks. We can't vote. You're talking like an objectivist. Maybe you believe everyone without money should be wiped?"

"I believe anyone without brains should be wiped!" Carl Hodges snarled suddenly. "Your mothers wouldn't have paid ten cents to have you. Too bad the law wasn't passed sooner."

"Genocide." The tall one reached over and hit him across the mouth. "We were nice to you. To *you!*" He turned and spat in revulsion.

Others surged forward.

"Steady." The leader spread arms and leaned back against the pressure. He addressed Carl. "We don't want to hurt you. You tell us things, you're a good teacher. We'll let you have what you want. Money for rights. Lie there until you have enough money to buy your way out. It will cost you five dollars to get out. That's cheaper than five hundred dollars to be born. That's a bargain."

The kids crowding behind him laughed, and laughed again under-standing the idea slowly. After a time of clumsy humor they untied him and went off, leaving him locked in a narrow windowless bedroom.

Carl Hodges went around the room, inspecting it and thinking coldly of escaping. He had to get out and straighten up the mess the city was in after the collapse of Brooklyn Dome. He had to get out and have the kids arrested before they sabotaged anything else. According to his best logic, there was no way to get out. He was stuck, and deserved it. He pushed his mind, thinking harder, fighting back a return of weakness and tears. He reached for a happy pill, then took the bottle of white pills and poured its contents down a hole in the floor.

The two Rescue Squad men shifted their chairs through acceleration bands to the inner fast slots, and passed the other chairs, each leaning forward on the safety rail of his chairs, as if urging it on. The people they passed were holding portable TV screens like magazines, watching in the same way that people used to read.

The voice of the announcer murmured from a screen, grew louder as they passed, and then again fell to a murmur. "Brooklyn Dome. Fifteen pounds atmosphere pressure to sixty-five pounds per square inch. Exploded upward. Implosion first, then explosion." The voice grew louder again as they approached another sliding chair in the slower lane. Another person listened, propping the screen up on the safety rail to stare into it, with the sound shouting. "Debris is floating for two square miles around the center from which the explosion came. Coast Guard rescue ships, submarines and scuba divers are converged into the area, searching for survivors."

"This is the way the explosion looked from the deck of a freighter, the *Mary-Lou*, five miles south at the moment it occurred." They neared and passed a TV screen which showed a distant picture of an explosion like an umbrella rising and opening on the horizon.

George settled himself in his seat and shut his eyes to concentrate. He had to stop that explosion from happening again to the other undersea dome. Whoever had done it would be laughing as he watched on TV the explosion unfold and settle. Whoever had done it would be eager for destruction, delighting in the death and blood of a small city.

The peculiarly wide range of perceptions that was George Sanford groped out across the city.

"The police department is still investigating the cause of the explosion," said the murmur, growing louder as they passed another TV watcher in the slow lane. Someone handed the announcer another note. "Ah, here we have some new information. Bell Telephone has opened up to the investigators eight recordings taken from public phones in Brooklyn Dome. These phone calls were being made at the moment Brooklyn Dome was destroyed."

A face appeared on a screen behind the announcer, a giant face of a woman telephoning. After an instant of mental adjusting of viewpoint the woman's face became normal in the viewer eye, the announcer shrank to ant size and was forgotten as the woman spoke rapidly into the phone. "I can't stand this place another minute. I would have left already, but I can't leave. The train station is jammed and there are lines in front of the ticket booth. I've never seen such lines. Jerry is getting tickets. I wish he'd hurry." The anxious woman's face glanced sideways either way out of the booth. "I hear the funniest noise, like thunder. Like a waterfall."

The woman screamed and the background tilted as the screaming face and the booth went over sideways. A hand groped past the lens, blackness entered in sheets, and the picture broke into static sparks and splashes. The screen went blank, the antlike announcer sitting in front of it spoke soothingly and the camera rushed forward to him until he was normal size again. He showed a diagram.

George opened his eyes and sat up. Around him on the moving chairs people were watching their TV screens show the pictures he had just seen in his mind's eyes. It showed a diagram of the location of the phone booths at Brooklyn Dome, and then another recording of someone innocently calling from a videophone booth, about to die, and not knowing what was about to happen, an innocent middle-aged face.

Expressionlessly, the people in the traveling subway seats watched, hands bracing the sides of the TV screen, grip tightening as they waited for the ceilings to fall. Audience anticipation; love of power, greatness, crash . . . total force and completeness . . . admiring triumph of completeness in such destruction. Great show. Hope for more horror.

All over the city people looked at the innocent fool mouthing words and they waited, watching, urging the doom on as it approached. *This time be bigger, blacker, more frightening, more crushing.*

George shut his eyes and waited through the hoarse screams and then opened his eyes and looked at the back of the neck of the TV watcher they were passing, then turned around and looked at her face after they passed. She did not notice him; she was watching the TV intently, without outward expression.

Did that woman admit the delight she felt? Did she know she was urging the thundering waterfall on, striking the death blow downward with the descending ocean? She was not different from the others. Typical television viewer, lover of extremes. It was to her credit that when TV showed young lovers she urged them to love more intensely, and rejoiced in their kisses. Lovers of life are also lovers of death.

George slid down further in his seat and closed his eyes, and rode the tidal waves of mass emotion as the millions of watchers, emotions synchronized by watching, enjoyed their mass participation in the death rites of a small city. Over and over, expectancy, anticipation, panic, defeat, death, satisfaction.

The secretly worshiped god of death rode high.

In twenty minutes, after transfers on platforms that held air-lock doors to pass through into denser air, they arrived, carried by underseas tube train, at the small undersea city of Jersey Dome. Population: ten thousand; residents: Civil Service administrators and their families.

The city manager's office building was built of large colored blocks of lightweight translucent foam plastic, like children's large building blocks. There was no wind to blow it away. Inside, the colors of the light tinted the city man's desk. He was a small man sitting behind a large desk with one phone held to his ear and another blinking a red light at him, untouched. "I know traffic is piling up. We have all the trains in service that city services can give up. Everyone wants to leave, that's all. No. There isn't any panic. There's no reason for panic." He hung up, and glared at the other phone's blinking light.

"That phone," he snarled, pointing, "is an outside line full of idiot reporters asking me how domes are built and how Brooklyn Dome could have blown up, or collapsed. It's all idiocy. Well. What do you want?"

Ahmed opened his wallet to his credentials and handed it over, "We're from Metropolitan Rescue Squad. We're specialists in locating people by predicting behavior. We were sent over to locate a possible lunatic who might have sabotaged Brooklyn Dome or blown it up, and might be here planning to blow up Jersey Dome."

"He just might," replied the manager of Jersey Dome with a high-pitched trembling earnestness in his voice. "And you might be the only dangerous lunatics around here. Lunatics who talk about Jersey Dome breaking. It can't break. You understand? The only thing we have to fear is panic. You understand?"

"Of course," Ahmed said soothingly. "But we won't talk about it breaking. It's our job to look for a saboteur. Probably it's just a routine preventative checkup."

The manager pulled a pistol out of a desk drawer and pointed it at them, with a trembling hand. "You're still talking about it. This is an emergency. I am the city manager. I could call my police and have you taken to a mental hospital, gagged."

"Don't worry about that," Ahmed said soothingly, picking his wallet back off the desk and pocketing it. "We're only here to admire the design and the machinery. Can we have a map?"

The manager lowered the pistol and laid it on the desk. "If you cooperate, the girl in the front office will give you all the maps of the design and structure that you'll need. You will find a lot of technicians already in the works, inspecting wires and checking up. They're here to design improvements. You understand?" His voice was still high-pitched and nervous, but steady.

"We understand," Ahmed assured him. "Everything is perfectly safe. We'll go admire their designs and improvements. Come on, George." He turned and went out, stopped at the receptionist's desk to get a map, consulted it, and led the way across the trimmed lawn of the park.

Out on the curved walk under the innocent blue-green glow of the dome, Ahmed glanced back. "But I'm not sure he's perfectly safe himself. Is he cracking up, George?"

"Not yet, but near it." George glanced up apprehensively at the blue-green glow, imagining he saw a rift, but the dark streak was only a catwalk, near the dome surface.

"What will he do when he cracks?" asked Ahmed.

"Run around screaming, 'The sky is falling!' like Chicken Little," muttered George. "What else?" He cocked an apprehensive glance upward at the green glow of the dome. Was it sagging in the middle? No, that was just an effect of perspective. Was there a crack appearing near the air shaft? No, just another catwalk, like a spiderweb on a ceiling.

Making an effort, he pulled his eyes away from the dome and saw Ahmed at a small building ahead labeled "Power Substation 10002." It looked like a child's building block ten feet high, pleasantly screened by bushes, matching the park. Ahmed was looking in the open door. He signaled to George and George hurried to reach him, feeling as if the pressurized, thickened air resisted, like water.

He looked inside and saw a man tinkering with the heavy power cables that provided light and power for the undersea dome. Panels were off, and the connections were exposed.

The actions and mood of the man were those of a workman, serious and careful. He set a meter dial and carefully read it, reset it and made notes, then read it again. George watched him. There was a strange kind of fear in the man, something worse than the boxed-in feeling of being underwater. George felt a similar apprehension. It had been growing in him. He looked at Ahmed, doubtfully.

Ahmed had been lounging against the open door watching George and the man. He took a deep sighing breath and went in with weight evenly balanced on his feet, ready for fast action. "Okay, how are the improvements coming?" he asked the workman.

The man grinned over his shoulder. He was slightly bald in front.

"Not a single improvement, not even a small bomb."

"Let's check your ID. We're looking for the saboteur." Ahmed held out his hand.

Obligingly the man unpinned a plastic ID card from under his lapel, and put a thumbprint over the photographed thumbprint so that it could be seen that the two prints matched. He seemed unafraid of them, and friendly.

"Okay." Ahmed passed his badge back.

The engineer pinned it back on. "Have fun, detectives. I hope you nail a mad bomber so we can stop checking for defects and go home. I can't stand this air down here. Crazy perfume. I don't like it."

"Me, too," George said. A thick perfumed pressure was in the air. He felt the weight of water hanging as a dome far above the city pressing the air down. "Bad air."

"It has helium in it," Ahmed remarked. He checked the map of the small city and looked in the direction of a glittering glass elevator shaft. A metal mesh elevator rose slowly in the shaft, shining in the semidark, like a giant birdcage full of people hanging above a giant living room.

George tried to take another deep breath and felt that whatever he was breathing was not air. "It smells strange, like fake air."

"It doesn't matter how it smells," Ahmed said, leading the way. "It's to keep people from getting the bends from internal pressure when they leave here. Why didn't you okay the man, George? His ID checked out."

"He was scared."

"What of?" Ahmed asked him.

"Not of us. I don't know."

"Then it doesn't matter. He's not up to any bad business."

The two walked across the small green park, through the thick air, toward the glittering glass shaft that went up from the ground into the distant green dome that was the roof of the city. Inside the huge glass tube a brightly lit elevator rose slowly, carrying a crowd of people looking out over the city as a canary would look out above a giant room.

"Next we check the air-pump controls," Ahmed said. "They're near the elevator." People went by, looking formal and overdressed, pale and quiet, stiff and neat. Not his kind of people. Civil servants, government administration people, accountants.

George followed, trying to breathe. The air seemed to be not air, but some inferior substitute. Glittering small buildings rose on either side of the park in rows, like teeth, and he felt inside a tiger mouth. The air smelled like lilies in a funeral parlor. The people he passed gave out vibes of a trapped hopeless defeat that made his depression worse. They passed a crowd of quiet miserable people waiting to get on the elevator, carrying fishing poles and swimming equipment.

High above them the elevator descended slowly.

"That's bad," George said. "You feel it, don't you, Ahmed?"

"Feel what?" Ahmed stopped beside a small rounded building attached to the side of the shaft. The building throbbed with a deep steady *thump, thump, thump,* like a giant heart.

"I want to get out of here," George said. "Don't you feel it?"

"I ignore that kind of feeling," Ahmed said expressionlessly, and pulled on the handle of the door to the pump room. It was unlocked. It opened. The thumping was louder. "Should be locked," Ahmed muttered. They looked inside.

Inside, down a flight of steps, two workmen were checking over some large warm thumping machinery. The two detectives went down the steps.

"Identity check, let's see your ID," George said, and looked at the two badges they handed him, in the same way he had seen Ahmed and other detectives checking them over. He took thumbprints and matched them to the photo thumbprints; he compared the faces on the photos to the faces before him. One big one with a craggy, stone-chiseled face and vertical grim lines on the cheeks; one short weathered one, slightly leaner, slightly more humor in the face. Both identified as engineers of Consolidated Power and Light, inspectors of electrical motor appliance and life support services.

"What are the pumps doing?" Ahmed asked, looking around.

"Pumping air in, pumping water out," replied one of the men. "There's the pump that pushes excess water up to the top where it comes out as a little ornamental fountain in an artificial island. The pressure equalizes by itself, so it doesn't need elaborate equipment, just power."

"Why pump water out?" Ahmed asked. "The air pressure is supposed to be so high that it pushes the water out."

The man laughed. "You make it sound so simple. The air pressure is approximately the same here as up at the top surface of the dome, but the water pressure rises every foot of the way down. Down here at the bottom it is higher than the air pressure. Water squeezes in along the edges of the cement slab, up through the ground cover and the dirt. We have drains to catch the seepage and lead it back to this pump. We expect seepage."

"Why not pump in more air? Higher air pressure would keep all the water out."

"Higher air pressure would burst the top of the dome like a balloon. There isn't enough weight of water to counterpush."

George got an uncertain picture of air pushing to get out the top and water pushing to get in the bottom. "It's working all right?" He handed the ID badges back to them.

"Right," said the explanatory man, pinning on his badge. "It would take a bomb to get those pumps out of balance. Don't know why they sent us to check the pumps. I'd rather be out fishing."

"They're looking for a bomb, dummy," said the other one sourly.

"Oh." The bigger one made a face. "You mean, like Brooklyn Dome blew up?" He looked around slowly. "If anything starts to happen, we're right near the elevator. We can get to the top."

"Not a chance," said the sour one. "The elevator is too slow. And it has a waiting line, people ahead of you. Resign yourself. If this place blows, we blow."

"Why is the elevator so slow?" George asked. *Fix it!* He hoped silently. They listened to the hum of the elevator engine lowering the elevator. It was slow.

"It can go faster; the timer's right here." The sour engineer walked over and inspected the box. "Someone has set it to the slowest speed. I wonder why."

"For sightseeing," George said. "But I saw the crowd waiting. They have fishing poles. They want to get to the top, they don't want to wait in the middle of the air, just viewing."

"Okay." The big talkative one walked over and firmly set the pointer over to "fast." The elevator reached the ground on the other side of the wall, rumbled to a stop, and the doors whirred open.

They listened, hearing voices and the shuffle of feet as people crowded into the elevator, then the doors rumbled shut and the elevator started for the top. The whirr was high and rapid. In less than a third of the time the trip up to the surface had taken before, the whirr stopped.

The two engineers nodded at each other. "I hope they are happy with it."

"They are getting there faster."

George said, "That makes sense," and Ahmed nodded agreement. They went out and watched the elevator return. As rapidly as falling, the great silver birdcage came down the glass shaft and slowed, and stopped, and opened. It was empty. No one who was up there was coming back in to the city.

More people got on.

"What is up there?" George asked, holding himself back from a panic desire to get in the elevator with the others and get out of the enclosed city. "I have a feeling we should go up there," he said, hoping Ahmed would misunderstand and think George was being called by a hunch.

"What do you feel?" Ahmed looked at him keenly. The doors shut and the elevator rose rapidly, leaving them behind on the ground.

"What I feel is, we shouldn't have let that elevator go without us. We've had it, old buddy. It's been nice knowing you. I didn't expect to die young."

"Snap out of it." Ahmed clicked his fingers under George's nose. "You're talking for somebody else. Hold that feeling separate from your thinking. It's not your kind of feeling. George Sanford isn't afraid, ever. You don't think like that."

"Yes, I do," George said sadly. He heard the elevator doors rumble open far overhead. Somewhere above people had escaped to the top of the ocean instead of the bottom. A dock? An island? Somewhere fresh winds were blowing across ocean waves.

"Locate that feeling of doom," Ahmed said. "Maybe our mad bomber is a suicider and plans to go down with the ship. Shut your eyes. Where are you in your head?"

"On top, on an island in the daylight," George said sadly, looking at his imagination of sand and seagulls. "It's too late, Ahmed. We're dead." A few new people arrived and lined up behind him waiting for the elevator. The sound of its descent began far above. People approached through the park from the direction of the railway station, and George remembered that there had been fenced-in crowds waiting for trains, waiting to get out. Maybe some people had grown impatient and wanted to get to fresh air. The crowd behind him grew denser and began to push. The elevator doors opened in front of George.

"Get in, George," said Ahmed, and pushed his elbow. "We're going to the top."

"Thanks." George got on. They were pushed to the back of the cage and the doors shut and the elevator rose with knee-pressing speed. Over the heads of the people before him George saw a widening vision of the undersea city, small buildings circling a central park, dimly and artistically lit by green and blue spotlights on trees and vines, with a rippling effect in the light like seaweed and underwater waves. Paths and roads were lit with bead chains of golden sodium lights. On the other side of the park the railroad station, squares of soft yellow light, fenced in by lacework metal walls. Many people around it. Too many. Dense crowds. The paths across the park were moving with people approaching the elevator shaft.

The elevator reached the top of the dome and went through into a tube of darkness. For a few moments they rose through the darkness and then they felt the elevator slow and stop. The doors rumbled open and the people pressed out, hurried through a glass door and down a staircase, and were gone from the top floor.

George looked around. There was the sky and ocean spaces he had dreamed of, but the sky was cloudy, the ocean was gray, and he was looking at them through thick glass. The island viewing platform was arranged in a series of giant glass steps, and the elevator had opened and let them into the top step, a glass room that looked out in all directions through thick glass, giving a clear view of the horizon, the glass rooms below, and the little motorboats that circled the docks of an artificial island.

"How's your hunch? What do you feel?" Ahmed snapped out, looking around alertly, weight on the balls of his feet, ready to spring at some mad bomber that he expected George to locate.

"The air is faked. I can't breathe it," George said, breathing noisily through his mouth. He felt like crying. This was not the escape he had dreamed of. The feeling of doom persisted and grew worse.

"It's the same air and the same pressure as down undersea in the dome," Ahmed said impatiently. "They keep the pressure high so people can come here from under without going through air locks. They can look, take pictures, and go back down. It smells lousy, so ignore it."

"You mean the air is under pressure here, as bad as all the way down at the bottom of the ocean?"

"Yes, lunk. That's what makes sense to them, so that's the way they have it set up."

"That's why the wall is so thick then, so it won't burst and let the pressure out," George said, feeling as if the thickness of the wall were a deliberate coffin wall, keeping him from escaping. He looked out through the thick glass wall and down through the glass roof of the observation room that was the next step down. He saw chairs and magazines like a waiting room, and the crowd of people that had come on the elevator with him, lined up at a glass door, with the first one in line tugging at the handle of the door. The door was not opening. "What are they doing?"

"They are waiting for the air pressure in the room to go down and equalize with the air pressure in the stairwell and the next room. Right now the pressure in the room presses the door shut. It opens inward as soon as the pressure goes down." Ahmed looked bored.

"We have to go out." George strode over to the inside door that shut off a stair leading down to the next room. He tugged. The glass door did not open. "Air pressure?"

"Yes, wait, the elevator is rising. It seems to be compressing the air, forcing it upward." Thick air made Ahmed's voice high-pitched and distant.

George tugged on the handle, feeling the air growing thicker and press on his eardrums. "'We have enough pressure here already. We don't need any more fake air. Just some real air. I want to be out of here."

The elevator door opened and a group of people, some carrying suitcases, some carrying fishing gear, pressed out and milled and lined up at the door behind George, pushing each other and murmuring complaints about pushing in tones that were much less subdued than the civil service culture usually considered to be polite.

The elevator closed its doors and sank out of sight, and air pressure began to drop as if the air followed the piston of the elevator in pumping up and down. George swallowed and his eardrums clicked and rang. He yanked hard on the handle of the stairwell door. It swung wide with a hiss and he held it open. The crowd hurried down the stairs, giving him polite thanks as they passed. With each thanks received he felt the fear of the person passing. He stared into the faces of a woman, a teener, a young woman, a handsome middle-aged man, looking for something beside fear, and finding only fear and a mouselike instinctive urge to escape a trap, and a fear of fear that kept them quiet, afraid to express the sense of disaster that filled their imaginations.

"Argh," said George as the last one went down the stairs. "Hurry up, Ahmed, maybe they are right." He gestured his friend through the door and ran down after him onto the lower step of a big glass viewing room with tables and magazines to make waiting easy. Behind him he heard the door lock shut and the whirr of the elevator returning to the top with more people.

George leaned his forehead against the thick glass walls and looked out at a scene of little docks and a buzz of small electric boats circling the platform, bouncing in a gray choppy sea, under thick gray clouds.

"What's out there?" Ahmed asked.

"Escape."

"What about the saboteur?" Ahmed asked with an edge of impatience. "What is he thinking, or feeling? Are you picking anything up?

"One of those boats is it," George answered, lying to avoid Ahmed's duty to return to the undersea city. "Or a small submarine, right out there. The top's going to be blasted off the observation platform. Get rescue boats in here. Use your radio, hurry, and get me a helicopter. I want to be in the air to spot which boat."

It wasn't all lies, some of it felt like the truth. He still leaned his forehead against the wall and looked out, knowing he would say anything to get out. Or do anything. He tried to tune to the idea of sabotage, and open to other people's thoughts, but the urge to escape came back in a greater sickness and swamped other thoughts. *"Why?"* he asked the fear. *"What is going to happen?"* An image came of horses kicking down a barn from inside, of cattle stampeding, of a chick pecking to get out of an egg, with the chick an embryo, not ready yet to survive in air. Kicking skeleton feet broke through from inside a bubble and the bubble vanished. The images were confusing. He looked away from his thoughts and watched the outside platform.

The platform was crowded with people, shivering in a cold wind, apparently waiting their turn to enjoy a ride in the little boats. George knew that they were outdoors because they could not stand being indoors.

Ahmed tapped on his arm. He had the wrist-radio earphones plugged into both ears, and his voice sounded odd and deaf. "Headquarters wants to know why, George. Can you give details?"

"Tell them they have five minutes, seven minutes if they're lucky. Get the patrol boats here to stop it and"—George almost shouted into Ahmed's wrist mike—"GET ME THAT HELICOPTER. Get it over here fast! We need it as soon as we get through the air locks!"

The glass air-lock door opened and people tumbled and shoved through.

On the other side was another room surrounded by glass. They lined up against the glass walls like moths against a lighted windowpane, looking out.

"Why do we have to wait so long?" It was a wail, a crying sound like an ambulance siren in the night. The group muttered agreement and nodded at the woman who clutched her hands against the glass as though trying to touch the scene outside.

"I'm not worried about the bends," said a portly older man. "They adjust the waiting time for people with bad sinus and eardrum infections. Does anyone here have a sinus, or eardrum infection?"

"We don't need to wait then," said the same man louder when there was no reply. "Does anyone here know how to make the door open? We can go out right now."

"My son has a screwdriver," suggested a woman, pushing the teenage young man toward the door. Ahmed moved to protest and the woman glared at him and opened her mouth to argue.

An old woman was tugging at the door. It opened suddenly and they forgot quarreling and went out through the door to the open docks and the cold salt wind, and the sound of cold choppy waves splashing against the cement pillars.

An air-beating heavy whirring sound hovered above the docks.

Ahmed looked up. A ladder fell down and dangled before them. Ahmed grabbed the rope rungs and pulled. They sagged lower. He fitted his foot into a rung and climbed.

George stood, breathing deeply of an air that smelled sweet and right and tingled in his lungs like life and energy. The clouds of panic and resignation faded from his mind and he heard the seagulls screaming raucous delight, following the small boats and swooping at sandwiches. The people clustered at the edge of the docks, beginning to talk in normal tones.

The ladder dangled before him, bobbing up and down. The rope rungs brushed against his head and he brushed them aside. What had been happening? What was the doom he had just escaped from? He tried to remember the trapped moments and tried to understand what they had been.

"Come on, George," a voice called from above.

He reached up, gripped, and climbed, looking into a sky of scudding gray and silver clouds and a white and blue police helicopter bouncing above him, its rotating blades shoving damp cool air against him in a kind of pressure that he enjoyed fighting. At the top the ladder stiffened into a metal stair with rails, and opened into the carpeted glass-walled platform of a big observation helicopter.

Ahmed sat cross-legged on the floor, twitching with hurry and impatience, holding his wrist radio to his lips. "Okay, George, tune to it. *What will blow the observation building? Who, what, where? Coast Guard is waiting for information.*"

Still with his memory gripped onto the strange depression he had felt inside the observation building, in the air of Jersey Dome, George looked down and tuned to it and knew how the people still inside felt, and what they wanted.

In the four-step glittering observation building, each glass room was full of people waiting at the doors. He saw the central elevator arrive and open its door and let out another crowd of people to wait and push and pull at the first door at the top. Desperation. A need to get out.

With a feeling of great sorrow, George knew who the saboteurs were. All the kids with screwdrivers, all the helpful people with technical skill who speed elevators, all the helpful people without mechanical understanding who would prop open dime-operated toilet doors for the stranger in need. They were going to be helpful, they were going to go through the air-lock doors and leave the doors jammed open behind them. No resistance behind them to hold back sixty-five pounds per square inch air pressure forcing up from below in the compressed city, pushing upward behind the rising elevator.

He had been pretending to believe it was a mad bomber. How could he tell the police and Coast Guard that it was just the residents of the city, mindless with the need to get out, destroying their own air-lock system?

George held his head, the vision of death strong and blinding. "They are jamming the air-lock system open in the observation building, Ahmed. Tell someone to stop them. They can't do that. It will blow!" The panic need to escape blanked his mind again.

"Lift," George said, making nervous faces at the view below. "Lift this damned copter."

"Is he all right?" the pilot asked Ahmed.

Ahmed was talking intensely into the wrist radio, repeating and relaying George's message. He made a chopping gesture to shut up.

The copter pilot gave them both a glance of doubt for their sanity and set the copter to lift, very slowly.

Slowly beating the air, the copter rose, tilting, and lifted away from the dwindling platform of glinting glass in the middle of the gray ocean.

George gripped the observation rail and watched, ashamed that his hands were shaking.

He saw something indefinable and peculiar begin to happen to the shape of the glass building. "There it goes," he muttered and abruptly sat down on the floor and put his hands over his face. "Hang on to the controls. Here we go. Ahmed, you look. Take pictures or something."

There was a crash, and a boom like a cannon. Something that looked like a crushed elevator full of people shot upward at them, passed them slowly, and then fell, tumbling over and over downward.

A roaring uprush of air grabbed the copter and carried it into the sky, the plane tilted sideways and began to fall sideways. For a moment it was upside down, falling in a rain of small objects that looked like briefcases and fishing rods and small broken pieces that could not be recognized. George hung on to a railing to keep from falling, then suddenly the copter turned right side up, beating its heavy spinning blades in a straining pull upward away from the rising tornado that tried to tilt it over again.

With a tearing roar Jersey Dome spat its contents upward through the air shaft, squeezing buildings and foam blocks and people and furniture into the shaft and upward in a hose of air, upward to the surface and higher in a fountain of debris, mangled by decompression to the surface of the ocean.

For a long moment the fountain of air was a mushroom-shaped cloud of debris, then it subsided.

With one arm and one leg still hooked around the rail, Ahmed listened intently to his radio, hands cupped over his ears to make the speaker plugs in his cars louder. He spoke.

"The city manager is alive down there and broadcasting. He says the canopy of the dome did not break, it just lowered. The air shaft sucked in everything near it and is now plugged shut with foam blocks from buildings but the blocks are slowly compressing into it, and they can hear an air hiss. Survivors are putting on scuba air equipment and finding places to survive another hurricane if the tube blows free again, but he's afraid of water leaks coming in and drowning them out from underneath because the pressure is going down. He wants the air shaft plugged from the top. Suggests bombing it at the top to prevent more air escaping."

Ahmed listened, tilting his head to the sounds in his cars.

"People in the water," George said. "Bombs make concussion. Let's get the people out."

"Affirmative," said the police pilot. "Look for people."

The helicopter swept low and cruised over the water, and they looked down at the close passing waves for a human swimmer needing help.

"There." Ahmed pointed at a pink shiny arm, a dark head. They circled back and hovered, let down the ladder, and the two Rescue Squad men climbed down and maneuvered a web mesh sling around a limp young unconscious naked woman. Her head bobbed under and came up as they slid the sling under her. The waves washed up against their knees as they leaned out from the rope ladder.

"NOW HEAR THIS, NOW HEAR THIS," proclaimed a giant amplified voice. "ALL BOATS IN THE AREA CIRCLE IN THE DISASTER AREA AND TAKE IN SURVIVORS. IN FIVE MINUTES, AT THE NEXT SIGNAL, ALL BOATS MUST WITHDRAW FROM THE AIR SHAFT CENTER TO A DISTANCE OF FIVE HUNDRED YARDS TO PERMIT BOMBING. AWAIT SIGNAL. REPEAT. YOU HAVE FIVE MINUTES TO SEARCH FOR AND TAKE IN SURVIVORS."

Ahmed and George shouted up to the pilot, "Ready." And the hoist drew the mesh sling with the young woman in it upward and into the copter through a cargo door in the bottom. The door hatch closed. They climbed back inside, dripping, and spread the unconscious and pretty body out on the floor for artificial respiration. She was cold, pulseless, and bleeding from ears, nose, and closed eyes. There were no bruises or breaks visible on the smooth skin. George tried gentle hand pressure on the rib cage to start her breathing again, and some blood came from her mouth with a sigh. He pushed again. Blood came from her eyes like tears.

Ahmed said wearily, "Give it up, George, she's dead."

George stood up and retreated from the body, backing away, "What do we do, throw her back?"

"No, we have to take bodies to the hospital. Regulations," muttered the pilot.

They circled the copter around over the choppy gray seas, wipers going on the windshield. The body lay on the floor between them, touching their feet.

They saw an arm bobbing on the waves.

"Should we haul it in?" George asked.

"No, we don't have to take pieces," said the pilot, tone level.

They circled on, passing the little electric boats of the people who had been fishing when the dome blew. The faces were pale as they looked up at the passing helicopter.

The corpse lay on the floor between them, the body smooth and perfect. The plane tilted and the body rolled. The arms and legs moved.

Ahmed seated himself in the copilot's seat, fastened the safety harness, and leaned forward with his head in his hands, not looking at the corpse. George looked out the windshields at the bobbing debris of furniture and unidentifiable bits, and watched Coast Guard boats approaching and searching the water.

The copter radio beeped urgently. The pilot switched it on. "Coast

Guard command to Police Helicopter PB 1005768. Thank you for your assistance. We now have enough Coast Guard ships and planes in the search pattern; please withdraw from the disaster area. Please withdraw from the disaster area."

"Order acknowledged. Withdrawing," the pilot said and switched the radio off. He changed the radio setting and spoke briefly to Rescue Squad headquarters, and turned the plane away from the area of destruction and toward the distant shore.

"What's your job in police?" he asked over his shoulder.

George did not answer.

"Rescue, Detection, and Prevention," Ahmed answered for him. "We were in Jersey Dome ten minutes ago." Behind them the bombs boomed, breaking and closing the air shaft.

"You sure didn't prevent this one," said the copter pilot.

Ahmed did not answer.

"This is a blackmail tape. One copy of this tape has been mailed to each of the major communes and subcities in the New York City district.

"We are responsible for the destruction of Brooklyn Dome. It was a warning, and demonstrated our ability to destroy. We have in our possession a futures expert whose specialty was locating and predicting accidental dangers to the city complex caused by possible simple mechanical and human failures. He is drugged and cooperative. We asked him how Brooklyn Dome could self-destruct from a simple mechanical failure, and he explained how. We are now prepared to offer his services for sale. Our fee will be fifteen thousand dollars a question. If you are afraid that your commune has enemies, your logical question would be, What and who can destroy my commune, and how can I prevent this attack? We will provide the answer service to your enemies, if they pay. They might be asking how to destroy your commune as you listen to this tape. Remember Brooklyn Dome. The name and address enclosed is your personal contact with us. No one else has this name. Keep it secret from the police, and use it when you decide to pay. If you give your contact up to the police, you will cut yourself off from our advice, your enemies will contact us through other names and buy methods to destroy you. Remember Brooklyn Dome. Act soon. Our fee is fifteen thousand dollars a question. The price of survival is cheap."

"Every police department has a copy. Want me to play it again?" Judd Oslow asked. He sat cross-legged on top of his desk like a large fat Buddha and sipped coffee.

"Once was enough," Ahmed said. "Paranoia, and war among the communes. What do those nuts think they are doing with that tape?"

"Making money," Judd Oslow sipped his coffee, carefully staying calm. "They mailed one to each commune in the city area, and only two have turned in the entire tape, or admitted receiving it. Only one has turned in his address. The others must be keeping their addresses, planning to ask attack, or defense, questions."

"Armageddon," said Ahmed.

Judd said, "George, why don't you get off your rump and bring in Carl Hodges? These nuts can't sell his brains if we get him back."

Ahmed said, "You just gave George the job last night. He almost had him this morning, but we were reassigned when Brooklyn Dome blew, and had to get off Carl Hodges's trail to go to Jersey Dome."

"So there's some of the day left. George has spoiled me with success. I'm used to instant results. Come on, George. Carl Hodges, right here in this office, packaged and delivered."

George looked up at him, eyes round and puzzled. "I'm supposed to help people. Every time I start trying to help Carl Hodges something bad happens. It doesn't come out right. Maybe he likes being in trouble. Bodies all over the place. You don't want me helping, with my luck!"

"Snap out of it, George. This is no time for pessimistic philosophy. Get together with Ahmed and hypnotize yourself and tell me where Carl Hodges is."

"What's the use?" George ran his hands over his head in a weary gesture that was not typical of his usual gestures, "Brooklyn Dome people are dead already. Jersey Dome people are mostly dead already. Everybody that ever died is still dead. Billions of people since the beginning of time. How are you going to rescue *them*? Why not let a few more die? What difference does it make?"

"Let's not have an essay on Eternity, George. Nothing makes any difference to Eternity. We don't live in Eternity, we live in now. We want Carl Hodges now."

"What's the use? My advice just makes trouble. I didn't save those people in Jersey Dome. I wasn't smart enough to understand that they'd want to break their own air locks. No, it wasn't the panic, it was the depression. The air changed its charge. Lab animals act irrational when you reverse the ground-to-air static-charge gradient. I should have . . ."

Judd shouted, "George, I'm not interested in your bad conscience. If you want to help people, just answer the question."

George winced at the loudness and squinted up at him with his eyes seeming crossed. "George?"

"*Wow!*" Ahmed stepped forward. "'Wait a minute. George did it already. That was Carl answering you."

Judd hesitated between confident forward and back motions. He started and stopped a gesture. His confusion reached his expression. He shouted, "Get out of here, you kooks. Go do your lunacy somewhere else. When you bring back Carl Hodges, don't tell me how you did it."

"Affirmative," Ahmed said. "Come on, Carl."

In confusion and guilt George followed and found himself on the open sidewalk, standing under a row of maple trees. The wind blew and the trees shed a flutter of green winged seeds about him. He knew he had failed his job somehow, and couldn't figure out how to get back to it. He walked to a bench and sat down.

"Do you understand what was just happening?" Ahmed asked.

"Yes." He felt in his mind and found confusion. "No."

"Shut your eyes. You seem to be on a bench in a park. It is an illusion. This is not where you are. Where are you really?"

George had shut his eyes. The voice went in deeply into a place in his mind where he knew he was in a room, a prisoner, and it was his fault. He did not like that knowledge. Better to pretend. He opened his eyes. "I want to be here in the park. Pretend you are real." He bent and touched some green vetch at his feet and felt the tiny ferns. "History doesn't matter. Sensation matters," he said earnestly. "Even these illusions are real because they are happening now. We live in now. Memory isn't real. The past doesn't exist. Why should we feel anything about the past, or care about it?"

Ahmed computed that it was a good probability that Carl Hodges was speaking through George and looking through his eyes as a form of escape. The rationalization was fluent, the vocabulary not George's. Vocabulary choice is as constant as fingerprints.

The person speaking had to be Carl Hodges.

"Carl Hodges. Do you want to get away from where you are and lie down in this park?"

"You are a questioner. I should not speak."

"Is it wrong to answer questions?"

"Yes, answers kill. People are dead. Like Susanne, they are all dead. Does mourning one person kill others? They drowned too, and floated. Saw girl in water . . . Connection . . . ?"

George had been speaking dreamily, eyes wide and round and sightless. He closed his eyes and every muscle in his face and body tightened in a curling spasm like pain. He slid off the bench and fell to his knees in the soft vetch. "Get me out of this. Make it unhappen. Reverse time. Wipe me out before I did it." The spasmed crouch, was it pain or prayer?

Watching the figure of misery, Ahmed made urgent calculations. The shame-driven need to escape memory was there to work with. Use it.

"Carl, you are in a green field in a small park on East E Avenue and Fifth Street. This is a future scene. Two hours from now, you will be rescued and free, without guilt, relaxed and enjoying being outdoors. We are the police, we are getting into a skytaxi to come and get you. What directions are we giving the driver?"

"Amsterdam Avenue and Fifty-third Street to Columbus Avenue, the wrecked blocks, one of the good cellars near the center of the flattened part of the ruins. Buzz it twice. Thanks. I think I can knock down a kid when I hear you and come out and wave. Land and pick me up fast."

"Okay," said Ahmed, straightening and stepping back from the crouched praying figure.

George took his hands from his face. "Okay what?" His voice was George's usual voice. He got up and brushed small green fronds from his knees.

"Okay, let's make a raid into another kid gang's territory," Ahmed said.

"Where's Biggy?" George looked around as if expecting to see their own gang of kids around them. "Oh, he went to the Canary Islands. And the others, they went to the Sahara. They all went . . ." He shook his head as if waking up. "Ahmed, what do you mean, raid a kid gang territory? That's all over. We're grown up now."

"We're going to rescue that kidnapped computerman. A mixed gang of teener kids are holding him in the ruins near West Fifty-third Street. We know how to handle a kid gang fight."

George was not going to let go of common sense. He settled back on the bench and looked around at the green warm comfort of the park, and rubbed one of the bruises on his arm. "Let's call the police, let them do it."

"We are the police, lunk." Ahmed still stood, smiling, depending on the force of his personality, the habit of command, to get George to obey. George looked up at him, squinting into the light of the sky, one eye half closed. A half of a bruise showed at the side of his face, most of it hidden by the hairline.

"Ahmed, don't be a nut. Logical thinking doesn't fight chains and clubs for you. I mean your brains are great, but we need muscle against a juv army, because they don't know about thinking, and they don't listen."

"What if they are all in their cellars, lunk, and we want to drop them before they get in deeper and carry Carl Hodges away? What kind of thing could get them all out into the open where a helicopter could drop them with gas?"

George absently rubbed the dark mark on the side of his face. "They come out when somebody gets onto their territory, Ahmed. Not an army of cops or a helicopter, I don't mean that. I mean some poor goof is crossing, looking for a shortcut to somewhere else, and they all come out and beat him up."

"That's for you."

"How did you figure . . . Oh, yeah, you don't mean yesterday. You mean strategy, like. They come out to beat me up again and the copter drops them with a gas spray, and maybe there's no one left underground to kill Carl Hodges, or take him away." George got up. "Okay, let's do it."

They came up out of the subway at Fifty-third Street and walked together on the sidewalk opposite the bombed-out shells of old buildings. A distant helicopter sound buzzed in the air.

"Separate, but we keep in touch. Leave your radio open to send, but shut it for receive so there won't be any sound coming out of it. The copter pilot will be listening. I'll circle the block and look in doorways and hallways for trouble. You cut across. We both act like we have some reason to be here, like I'm looking for an address. We're strangers."

"Okay," George said. "I've got a story for them for cutting across. Don't worry about me." He turned and walked nonchalantly around the corner, across the street, past some standing ruins and into the flattened spaces and the area that had once been paved backyard, with steps down to doors that had opened into the cellars of gone buildings. Flattened rubble and standing walls showed where the buildings had been.

He stood in the middle of a backyard, near two flights of cement stairs that led down into the ground to old doors, and he walked onward slowly, going in an irregular wandering course, studying the ground, acting a little confused and clumsy, just the way he had acted the last time he had been there.

The setting sun struck long shadows across the white broken pavement. He turned and looked back at his own long shadow, and started when another person's shadow appeared silently on the pavement alongside of his. He glanced sideways and saw a tall, husky teener in a strange costume standing beside him holding a heavy bat. The teener did not look back at him, he looked off into space, lips pursed as though whistling silently.

George winced again when a short teener with straight blond hair stepped out from behind a fragment of standing wall.

"Back, huh?" asked the blond kid.

George felt the shadows of others gathering behind him.

George said, "I'm looking for a pocket watch I lost the night you guys beat me up. I mean, it's really an antique, and it reminds me of someone.

I've got to find it."

He looked at the ground, turning around in a circle. There was a circle of feet all around him, feet standing in ruined doorways, feet on top of mounds of rubble, the clubs resting on the ground as the owners leaned on them, the chains swinging slightly.

"You must be really stupid," said the leader, his teeth showing in a small smile that had no friendship.

Where was Carl Hodges? The area George stood in was clean, probably well used by feet. The stairs leading down to a cellar door were clean, the door handle had the shine of use. The leader had appeared late, from an unlikely direction. He was standing on dusty, rubble-piled ground which feet had not rubbed and cleared. The leader then had not wanted to come out the usual way and path to confront George. Probably the usual way would have been the door George was facing, the one that looked used.

It was like playing hot and cold for a hidden object. If Carl Hodges was behind that door, the teeners would not let George approach it. George, looking slow and confused, shuffled his feet two steps in that direction. There was a simultaneous shuffle and hiss of clothing as the circle behind him and all around him closed in closer. George stopped and they stopped.

Now there was a circle of armed teeners close around him. Two were standing almost between him and the steps. The helicopter still buzzed in the distance, circling the blocks. George knew if he shouted, or even spoke clearly, and asked for help the copter pilot would bring the plane over in a count of seconds.

The blond kid did not move, still lounging, flashing his teeth in a small smile as he studied George up and down with the expression of a scientist at a zoo studying an odd specimen of gorilla.

"I got something important to tell you," George said to him. But they didn't listen.

"It's a kind of a shame," the blond kid said to the others. "He's so stupid already. I mean, if we just bashed out his brains he wouldn't even notice they were gone."

George faced the leader and sidled another small step in the direction of the steps and the door, and heard the shuffle of feet closing in behind him. He stopped moving and they stopped moving. For sure that door was hiding something. They wanted to keep strangers away from it! "Look, if you found my watch I lost, and if you give it to me, I'll tell you about a thing you ought to know."

If he talked long and confusingly enough, every member of the gang would come out on the surface to hear what he was trying to say. They would all be out in the open. The helicopter was armed for riots; it could spray sleep gas and get every one of them.

He didn't even feel the blow. Suddenly he was on his knees, a purple haze before his eyes. He tried to get up and fell over sideways, still in the curled-up position. He realized he wasn't breathing.

Could a back-of-the-neck karate chop knock out your breathing centers? What had the teacher said? His lungs contracted, wheezing out more air, unable to let air in. It must have been a solar plexus jab with a stick. But then how come he hadn't seen the stick? The purple haze was turning into spinning black spots. He couldn't see.

"What was it he wanted to tell us?"

"Ask him."

"He can't answer, dummy. He can't even grunt. You'll have to wait."

"I don't mind waiting," said the voice of the one carrying a chain. George heard the chain whistle and slap into something, and wondered if it had hit him. Nothing in his body registered anything but a red burning need for air.

"You don't want to trespass on our territory," said a voice. "We're just trying to teach you respect. You stay on the free public sidewalks and don't go inside other people's Kingdoms. Not unless they ask you." The chain whistled and slapped again.

George tried to breathe, but the effort to inhale knotted his chest together, forcing breath out instead of in.

It is a desperate thing having your lungs working against you. The knot tightening the lungs held for another second and then loosened. He drew in a rasping breath of cool air, and another. Air came in like waves of light, dispelling the blindness and bringing back awareness of arms and legs. He straightened out from the curled-up knot and lay on his back breathing deeply and listening to the sounds around him.

The helicopter motor hummed in the distance. *The copter pilot is listening,* he thought, *but he doesn't know I'm in trouble.*

He heard a clink and a hiss of breath like someone making an effort. He rolled suddenly over to one side and covered his face. The chain hit where he had been. He rolled to a crouch with both feet under him, and for the first time looked at the circle of faces of the teeners who had beaten and made fun of him when he was pretending to be drunk and making believe to be Carl Hodges, and had stumbled into this forbidden territory. He had been retracing Carl Hodges's actions, but he had not been sure it was working. He had been near Carl Hodges here, but he had no proof, no reason to protest when they punished him for violating their boundaries. The faces were the same. Young but cold, some faces were uncertain about punishing an adult, but gaining courage from the others. All sizes of teeners in costumes from many communes, but the fellowship and good nature he was used to seeing in groups was missing.

"I used to be in a gang like yours once," he said rapidly to inform the radio listener. "I thought you wouldn't jump me. I didn't come here to get stomped. I just want my antique watch and to tell you something."

He finished the sentence with a quick leap to one side, but the swinging chain swung up and followed, slapped into his skin and curled a line of dents around ribs, chest, and arms. The magnet on the end clanked and clung against a loop of chain. The owner of the chain yanked hard on his handle and the metal lumps turned to teeth and bit in and the chain tightened like rope. George staggered and straightened and stood wrapped up in biting steel chain.

He stood very still. "Hey," he said softly. "That ain't nice."

"Tell us about your news." The circle of teeners and juvs around him were curious about the message he wanted to deliver to them.

George said, "A friend of mine was figuring from my lumps that I got here last time that you've got something important you want me to keep away from. He figures you got the missing computerman. The one who blew up Brooklyn Dome. There's a reward out for him."

A ripple of shock ran through the group surrounding him but the blond kid did not need time to assimilate the threat. Without change of expression he made a gesture of command. "Three of you check the streets. Maybe he brought somebody with him." Three ran silently in different directions.

"I'm just doing you a favor telling you what people say," George said in stupid tones. "Now you gotta do me a favor and help me get my watch back."

"Favor?" screamed the tall, misproportioned one with the chain. "Favor? You stupid fink, you should have kept your stupid mouth shut." He yanked hard on the chain to make its teeth extend more sharply.

An outraged force had been expanding in George's chest. He stood still, looking meek and confused one more second, watching his captors snarl and hate him for having "told his friend." Then he bent forward and butted the chain holder down, rolled over his form to the cement and rolled rapidly down three small cement steps, unrolling the chain behind him. He came up on one knee, reaching for the chain as a weapon. It was a seven-foot chain with a handle at each end. A heavy chain is a terrible weapon in the hands of a strong man. If it had been behind him at the moment of impulse, he would have swept it around and forward and cut them down like grass. He gathered it looped into his hands, eyeing the crowd of oddly dressed teeners that was his target. His speed was too fast to intercept, his motions too smooth to look fast. He threw the chain up into the air behind him, then arched back with every muscle tight and bent forward with a grunt of effort, ignoring two clubs that bounced off his shoulders, bringing the chain forward with a tremendous released surge of force that was rage. The teen gang scattered and fled and the chain swung its cutting deadly circle through the air where they had been.

"Dumb punks." George breathed noisily with the effort. "Whyncha act like brothers? Can't let anybody be your friend. Trying to be smart, not knowing . . ."

He stopped and let the swinging chain drag along the ground, slowing. He rippled it in and let it wrap around his arm, with a short murderous loop of it in his hand. The sun had set and it was growing darker in the corners and harder to see. George fended off a flung stick by deflecting it with the chain, then grabbed a club for his other hand. Something whistled by and clanged against a wall. Probably a knife. The teener leader would see that George knew too much, and instruct the gang to kill him. The boy was logical and ruthless and would decide a stranger's life was less important to him than the million he hoped to gain from selling the computerman's answers.

"Carl Hodges," George bellowed. "Ally ally infree. I need help. Computerman Carl Hodges, come out." The police riot control man in the circling copter would at last hear a request for help, and bring his plane in fast. The teeners would only hear him yelling Carl Hodges's name and still not be sure the police were near.

The cellar door gave two thumps and a crash and fell forward off its rusty hinges across the steps. A man fell out on top of it and scrambled across the door and up the steps without bothering to straighten from all fours.

At the top he straightened and looked at George. The other man was thin and balding, wiry and a little under average in size, totally unlike George in either shape or face, but the impression of lifetime familiarity was overwhelming. His own eyes looked out of the strange face.

George handed him a club from the ground. "Guard my back. They are going to try to take you alive, I think, but not me." He spun slowly, looking and listening, but all was quiet. Teeners lurked in a distance along the routes George would use if he tried to escape.

George looked back at Carl Hodges and saw the thin computerman inspecting George's appearance with a knot of puzzlement between his brows. Looking at him was like looking into a mirror.

"Hello, me over there," George said.

"Hello, me over there," the man said. "Are you a computerman? When I get back on the job do you want to come play City Chess with me? Maybe you could get a job in my department."

"No, buddy, we are us, but I don't play City Chess. I'm not like you."

"Then why . . ." Carl Hodges ducked a flung club and it clattered against the cement. *Then why do I have this impression of two people being the same person?* he meant.

"We have an empathy link in our guts," George said. "I don't think like you. I just feel what you feel."

"God help anyone who feels the way I feel," Hodges said. "I see some kids advancing on my side."

"Hold them off. Back to back. All we need is a little time." George turned away from him again, and searched the comers with his eyes, ready for a rush. "About the way you feel. It's not all that bad. I'll get over it."

"I did it," Carl Hodges said. "How do I get over it? I feel . . . I mean, I have a reason for feeling . . . I got drunk and the egg hit the fan. How do I get over *that*?" His voice was broken by grunts of effort, and things clattered by, deflected, missing them and hitting walls and cement flooring.

They stood back to back and fended off bricks, sticks, and glittering objects that he hoped were not knives. "We can get killed if we don't watch it. That's one way," George said. A stick came through the air and rapped George's ear as he fended it off with his club. The attackers advanced, silhouettes against the dimming view of stone walls. Another attacker shadow picked up the clattering stick from the ground and threw it back as he advanced.

"Ouch," said Carl Hodges. "Duck." They both ducked and a flung net went by. "We fight well together. We must get together and fight another teen gang sometime. Right?" said his brisk voice. "Ouch, damn."

George received a rush by the tallest of the gang, caught at the outstretched staff and yanked the enemy past. He tried to trip the teener as he hurtled by, but missed and turned to see him neatly tripped by a stick between the ankles by Carl. The teener went face forward to the ground and rolled, getting out of range.

"Good pass!" Several new and heavy blows on head and shoulders reminded George to watch his own side. Dizzied, he spun, bracing the staff for a pushing blow with both hands, and felt it strike twice against blurred forms. He reversed it and struck down at an attacker with a contented growl.

With a heavy thrumming and a push of air the police helicopter came over a wall, swooping low, like an owl settling over a nest of mice, and released a white cloud of gas over them all.

George took a deep breath of the clear air before the cloud reached him. Beside him Carl Hodges took a deep startled breath of the white cloud and went down as suddenly as if a club blow had hit.

Still holding his breath, George straddled him and stood alert, peering through the fog at shapes that seemed to be upright and moving. Most of the teeners had run away, or gone down flat on the ground. What were these shapes? Eighteen seconds of holding his breath. Not hard. He could make two minutes usually. He held his breath and tried to see through the white clouds around him. The sound of the helicopter circled, in a wider and wider spiral, laying a cloud of gas to catch all the running mice from the center of the area to its edges.

The shapes suddenly appeared beside him, running, and struck with a double push, flinging him back ten feet so that he skidded on his back on the sandy concrete. He remembered to hold his breath after one snort of surprise and silently rolled to his feet and charged back.

Carl Hodges's unconscious form was missing. George saw movement through the white fog ahead, heard feet scuffing cement and across hollow wood, and he charged in pursuit of the sounds. He half fell, half slid down the cement steps, across the wooden door on the ground and into a corridor, and glimpsed motion ahead, and heard a closet door shutting. Holding his breath, groping, he opened the door, saw broken wall with an opening, smelled the wet smell of cement and underground drafts, and leaped over a pile of ancient trash brooms into the opening.

Safe to breathe here. As he took a deep breath a brilliant flashlight suddenly came on, shining blindingly in his face from only two feet away. "I have a gun pointed at you," said the precise voice of the blond short teener. "Turn left and walk ahead in the directions I tell you. I could kill you here, and no one would find your body, so try to keep my good will."

"Where is Carl Hodges?" George asked, walking with his hands up. The flashlight threw his shadow ahead of him big and wavering across the narrow walls.

"We're all going to be holing down together. Turn left here." The voice was odd.

George looked back and saw that the short teener was wearing a gas mask. As he took a breath to ask why, the white fog rolled down from a night-sky crevice above them. It smelled damp and slightly alcoholic.

"Keep moving," said the teener, gesturing with his gun. George turned left, wondering what happened next when you breathed that fog. A busy day, a busy night. An experience of symbolic insight was often reported by people who had been flattened by police anti-riot gas. What had the day meant? Why were such things happening?

Floating in white mist, George floated free of his body over the city and saw a vast spirit being of complex and bitter logic who brooded over the city and lived also in its future. George spoke to it, in thoughts that were not words. "Ahmed uses the world view of his grandmother, the gypsy. He believes that you are Fate. He believes you have intentions and plans."

It laughed and thought: *The wheels of time grind tight. No room between gear and gear for change. Future exists, logical and unchangeable. No room for change in logic. When it adds up, it must arrive at the same concluding scene. The city is necessity. The future is built. The gears move us toward it. I am Fate.*

George made a strange objecting thought. "The past can change. So everything that adds up from the past can change."

There was a wail from the atmosphere. The vast spirit that brooded over the city vanished, destroyed, dwindling to nowhere, uncreated, never true, like the Wicked Witch of the West when Dorothy poured a bucket of water over her, leaving behind the same dwindling wail. "But all my beautiful disasters, the logic, the logic . . ."

"No arithmetic," George said firmly. "If you can see the future, you can change it. If you can't see the past, it can change by itself and be anything. It won't add up the same twice."

All the crystallized visions of the city of the future shattered and dissolved into white fog, a creative fog that could be shaped to anything by thought. George stood at the center of creation and felt stubborn. They were tempting him again, trying to get him into the bureaucratic game of rules and unfreedom. "No," he said. "I won't fence anyone in with my idea. Let them choose their own past."

He came to consciousness lying on the floor in a small tight room with the blond kid sitting on a bed pointing a gun at him.

"They got Carl Hodges back," the kid said. "You ruined everything. Maybe you are a cop. I don't know. Maybe I should kill you."

"I just had a wild dream," George said, lifting his head, but not moving because he did not want to be shot. "I dreamed I talked to the Fate of New York City. And I told Fate that the future can change anytime, and the past can change anytime. In the beginning was the middle, I said. And Fate started crying and boo-hooing and vanished. I mean, no more Fate. Vanished."

There was a long pause while the short blond kid held the pistol pointed at George's face and stared at him over the top of it. The kid tried several tough faces, and then curiosity got the better of him. He was basically an intellectual, even though a young one, and curiosity meant more to him than love or hate. "What do you mean? The past is variable? You can change it?"

"I mean, we don't know what happened in the past exactly. It's gone anyhow. It's not real anymore. So we can say anything happened we want to have happened. If one past is going to make trouble, we can change it just by being dumb, and everything will straighten out. Like, for example, we just met, right now, right here, we just met. Nothing else happened."

"Oh." The kid put away his gun, thinking about that. "Glad to meet you. My name's Larry."

"My name's George." He arranged himself more comfortably on the floor, not making any sudden moves.

They had a long philosophical discussion, while Larry waited for the police outside to finish searching and go away. Sometimes Larry took the gun out and pointed it again, but usually they discussed things and exchanged stories without accepting any past.

Larry was serious and persuasive in trying to convince George that the world had too many technicians. "They don't know how to be human beings. They like to read about being Tarzan, or see old movies and imagine they are Humphrey Bogart and James Bond, but actually all they have the guts to do is read and study. They make money that way, and they make more gadgets and more computers that do all the thinking and take all the challenge and conquest out of life. And they give a pension to all the people who want to go out into the woods, or surf, instead of staying indoors pushing buttons, and they call the surfers and islanders and forest-farmers Free Loaders, and make sure they are sterilized and don't have children. That's genocide. They are killing off the real people. The race will be descended from those compulsive button pushers, and forget how to live."

It was a good speech. George was uneasy, because it sounded right, and he was sure no man was smart enough to refute the killer, but he tried.

"Couldn't a guy who really wanted children earn enough money to get a breeding permit for himself and an operation for his wife?"

"There aren't that many jobs anymore. The jobs that are left are button-pusher jobs, and you have to study for twenty years to learn to push the right button. They're planning to sterilize everyone but button pushers."

George had nothing to say. It made sense, but his own experience did not fit. "I'm not sterilized, Larry, and I'm a real dope. I didn't get past the sixth grade."

"When did your childhood support run out?"

"Last year."

"No more free food and housing. How about your family—they support you?"

"No family. Orphan. I got lots of good friends, but they all took their pensions and shipped out. Except one. He got a job ."

"You didn't apply for the unemployable youth pension yet?"

"No. I wanted to stay around the city. I didn't want to be shipped out. I figured I could get a job."

"That's a laugh. Lots of luck in getting a job, George. How are you planning to eat?"

"Sometimes I help out around communes and share meals. Everyone usually likes me in the Brotherhood communes." George shifted positions uneasily on the floor and sat up. This was almost lying. He had a job now, but he wasn't going to talk about Rescue Squad, because Larry might call him a cop and try to shoot him. "But I don't bum meals."

"When's the longest you've gone without meals?"

"I don't feel hungry much. I went two days without food once. I'm healthy."

The kid sat cross-legged on the bed and laughed. "Really healthy! You got muscles all over. You've got muscles from ear to ear. So you're trying to beat the system! It was built just to wipe out muscleheads like you. If you apply for welfare, they sterilize you. If you take your unemployable support pension, they sterilize you. If you are caught begging, they sterilize you. Money gets all you muscleheads sooner or later. It's going to get you, too. I'll bet when you are hungry you think of the bottle of wine and the big free meal at the sterility clinic. You think of the chance of winning the million-dollar sweepstakes if the operation gives you the right tattoo number, don't you?"

George didn't answer.

"Maybe you don't know it, but your unemployable pension is piling up, half saved for every week you don't claim it. You've been avoiding it a year almost? When it piles high enough, you'll go in and claim your money and let them sterilize you and ship you out to the boondocks, like everyone else."

"Not me."

"Why not?"

George didn't answer. After a while he said, "Are you going to let them sterilize you?"

Larry laughed again. He had a fox face and big ears. "Not likely. There are lots of ways for a smart guy to beat the system. My descendants are going to be there the year the sun runs down and we hook drives to Earth and cruise away looking for a new sun. My descendants are going to surf light-waves in space. Nobody's going to wipe me out, and nobody's going to make them into button pushers."

"Okay, I see it." George got up and paced, two steps one way, two steps the other way in the narrow room. "Who are you working for, Larry? Who are you crying over? People who let themselves be bribed into cutting off their descendants? They're different from you. Do they have guts enough to bother with? Are they worth getting your brain wiped in a court of law? You're right about history, I guess. I'm the kind of guy the techs are trying to get rid of. You're a tech type of guy yourself. Why don't you be a tech and forget about making trouble?"

At the end of the room, faced away from Larry, George stopped and stared at the wall. His fists clenched. "Kid, do you know what kind of trouble you make?"

"I see it on television," Larry said.

"Those are real people you killed." George still stared at the wall. "This afternoon I was giving artificial respiration to a girl. She was bleeding from the eyes." His voice knotted up. Big muscles bulged on his arms and his fists whitened as he tried to talk. "She was dead, they told me. She looked all right, except for her eyes. I guess because I'm stupid." He turned and his eyes glittered with tears and with a kind of madness. He glanced around the small room looking for a thing to use for a weapon.

Larry took out his gun and pointed it at George, hastily getting off the bed. "Oh, oh, the past is real again. Time for me to leave!" Holding the gun pointed steadily and carefully at George's face, he used his other hand to put on black goggles and slung the gas mask around his neck. "Hold still, George, you don't want a hole through your face. If you fight me, who are you working for? Not your kind of people. Think, man." He backed to the door. George turned, still facing him, his big hands away from his sides and ready, his eyes glittering with a mindless alertness.

Larry backed into the dark hall. "Don't follow. You don't want to follow me. This gun has infrasights, shoots in the dark. If you stick your head out the door, I might shoot it off. Just stand there for ten minutes and don't make any trouble. The gun is silenced. If I have to shoot you, you don't get any medal for being a dead hero. No one would know."

The short teener backed down the dark corridor and was gone.

George still stood crouched, but he shook his head, like a man trying to shake off something that had fallen over his eyes.

He heard Larry bump into something a long way down the corridor.

"I would know," a voice said from the ceiling. Ahmed let himself down from a hole in the ceiling, hung by both long arms and then dropped, landing catlike and silent. He was tall and sooty and filthy and covered with cobwebs. He grinned and his teeth were white in a very dark face. "You just missed a medal for being a dead hero. I thought you were going to try to kill him."

He twiddled the dial of his wrist radio, plugged an earphone into one ear and spoke into the wrist radio. "Flushed one. He's heading west on a cellar corridor from the center, wearing a gas mask and infragoggles, armed and dangerous. He's the kingpin, so try hard, buddies."

George sat down on the edge of the bunk, sweating. "I get too mad sometimes. I almost did try to kill him. What he said was probably right. What he said."

Ahmed unplugged the speaker from his ear. "I was mostly listening to you, good buddy. Very interesting philosophical discussion you were putting out. I kept wanting to sneeze. How come you get into philosophical arguments today and I just get beat up? Everything is backward."

"You're the smart one, Ahmed," said George slowly, accepting the fact that he had been protected. "Thanks for watching." He looked at his own hands, still worrying slowly on an idea. "How come everything the kid said made sense?"

"It didn't," Ahmed said impatiently. "*You* made sense."

"But Larry said that techs are wiping out nontechs."

"Maybe they are, but they aren't killing anybody. The kid kills."

George pushed his hands together, felt them wet with sweat and wiped them on his shirt. "I almost killed the kid. But it felt right, what he was saying. He was talking for the way things are and for the way they're going to be, like Fate."

"Killing is unphilosophical," Ahmed said. "You're tired, George. Take it easy, we've had a long day."

They heard a police siren wail and then distant shots. Ahmed plugged the earphone into his ear. "They just dropped somebody in goggles, gas didn't work on him. They had to drop him with hypo bullets. Probably Larry. Let's try to get out of here."

They put a wad of blankets out into the corridor, head high. No shots, so they went out cautiously and started groping down the long black hall, looking for an exit.

Ahmed said, "So you think Larry was the fickle finger of Fate on the groping hand of the future. No power on Earth can resist the force of an idea whose time has come, said somebody once. But, good buddy, when I was listening to you whilst lying in the ceiling with the spiders crawling on me, I thought I heard you invent a new metaphysics. Didn't you just abolish Fate?"

The corridor widened, and George felt a draft of fresh air without dust, and saw a glimmer of light through a hole. They climbed through and saw a doorway, and a broken door. "I don't know, Ahmed," he said vaguely. "Did I?"

They climbed up the broken door and a flight of stone steps and found themselves in a deserted yard at the center of the ruin. It was quiet there. In the distance around the edges of the block police copters buzzed, landed in the streets.

"Sure you did," Ahmed said. "You abolished Fate. I heard you."

George looked up at the moon. It was bright and it shone across the entire city, like the evil Fate in his dream, but it was only the moon, and the city was quiet. Suddenly George leaped into the air and clicked his heels. "I did. I did." He bellowed. "Hey, everybody! Hey, I did it! I abolished Fate!"

He landed and stopped leaping, and stood panting. The red glow in the sky over New York blinked on and off, on and off from the giant sign they could not see.

"Congratulations," said Ahmed and rested an arm briefly across his shoulders. "May I offer you a tranquilizer?"

"No, you may offer me a meal," George said. "No, cancel that, too. Judd gave me money yesterday. Steaks, hot showers, hotel room. *Wow*. I've got a job." He turned abruptly and walked away. See you tomorrow. *Wow*."

Left alone, tall and tired, smeared with dirt and itchy with cobwebs, Ahmed stared after him, feeling betrayed. Where was all the respect George used to give him? George was a short fat kid once, and treated Ahmed like a boss. Now he was beginning to loom like a Kodiak bear, and he walked away without permission.

Ahmed looked up at the lopsided moon. "Mirror, mirror, on the wall, who's the smartest guy of all? Don't answer that, lady. It's been a long day. I'm tired."

THE GARRULOUS
GARRITY GRAND SCAM
Francis M. Nevins, Jr.

HOW I GOT to be George Boyd belongs in another story. A bunch of us confidence persons teamed up to pull the scam of the century on the Multinat Technologies conglomerate, with me as one of the side men, but after months of sweat the thing went haywire and the perpetrators had to make like moles. All but Milo; blessed with the Turner luck, I weathered the storm in my cover as an editor at Majestic Publications, a Multinat subsidiary. Six uneventful weeks after the crisis I realized that my George Boyd persona was not going to be yanked from me by some cop, and actually began to enjoy the new identity. The job paid nicely, my Central Park South apartment was cozy, I had ample leisure to take in plays and movies and Manhattan's finest eating places with suitably dazzling women. All I had to do in return was to spend business hours behind my desk on the tenth floor of the steel-and-glass hive at 49th and Madison, running a Majestic enterprise known as *Great American Mystery Magazine*. I could almost see myself retiring permanently into this new life.

Until that Monday morning late in April when the sky fell in.

It was 9:22 by my digital when the smooth-gliding elevator let me out at 10. The morning *Times* under my arm, I made a brisk right and trotted down the carpeted corridor past the CPA's office and the psychiatric counselor's and the law firm's and pushed open the full-length glass door whose gold letters read MAJESTIC PUBLICATIONS, INC.—GREAT AMERICAN MYSTERY MAGAZINE—ENTER. I good-morninged politely to Mrs. Blumeyer the receptionist, who was noshing prune danish behind the switchboard counter, and headed back to my corner office at the rear of the suite. Majestic's main office was on the sixteenth floor— every square foot of the sixteenth floor—but *GAMM* was kept on ten where it had been before its vertical neighbor had swallowed it. In terms of office luxury, privacy and freedom from excessive supervision from the head clowns upstairs, that was a break for me. I could cope with a lot of the magazine's day-to-day problems without interference.

That Monday the problems crowded in on me like shoppers at Blooming-dale's on bargain day. Almost before I was in my executive swivel the phone screamed and it was the printer announcing another surcharge on the bill for the next issue of *GAMM*. Then while I was tuning in WNCN on the office radio the phone squalled again and it was the warehouse superinten-dent telling me that the truckers had called a wildcat strike which would delay the shipment of the July issue to the distributors.

But it wasn't until Deb brought in the morning mail that Monday truly became funday.

"Have a nice weekend?" I asked my associate editor casually as she placed a neat stack of letters and manuscripts on my desk blotter.

"So-so," she said.

"Anything from Alan Ovel today?"

"The morning mail hasn't come yet, this is Saturday's stack. But you'd better read the top letter first." The office door clicked gently shut behind her as she left.

Dear sweet Deb. Deborah K. Howard, Associate Editor. Tall, perfectly shaped, with streaked-blonde hair worn loose and curly and twilight blue eyes and a soft mocking voice that could send ripples down a man's spine. But she kept herself inside such a thick wrap-around shield of unapproacha-bility that I would never have dared ask her how she spent her weekends, let alone whether she'd do me the honor of spending one with me. I knew she'd wanted a career as an actress, that she'd played small parts off-off-Broadway and TV soap operas but had thrown in the towel a year ago and landed a full-time job with Majestic. She handled the routine corre-spondence with writers, kept track of foreign sales, gave incoming manu-scripts their first reading—and their last if they were unsalvageable junk— and supervised the other employees. Without her efficiency and common sense I could never have kept up the pretense that I was an experienced editor.

But all thoughts of Deb skittered out of my mind as I read that topmost letter in the stack.

At the head of the sheet of cheap dime-store paper ETHICAL REDISTRI-BUTION ALLIANCE was typed in caps. No address, no phone number, no date. The body of the letter looked like the same type as the heading.

THESES

1. In an unjust and repressive society, crimes are acts not of evil but of heroic defiance.

2. Crime fiction is 50% mental chewing gum and 50% deliberate propaganda for the establishment pigma that crime is a bad thing.

3. *Great American Mystery Magazine* is owned by Majestic Pub-lications, which is owned by Multinat Technologies, which owns two-thirds of America. It does not own us!!!

4. Mr Boyd, you will donate $10,000 to Ethical Redistribution Alliance within one week and an additional $10,000 each and every month hereafter.

The manifesto wasn't signed and made no specific threats if we didn't comply.

I picked up the theatrical prop paperknife from the desk top and tapped it against my fingernails as thoughts stampeded through the old cerebel-lum. Then I stabbed the phone dial and spun an 8.

"Yes?" Deb's cool voice responded.

"Conference," I snapped. "Now."

Three minutes later we were sitting on the black leather divan facing the west window, the letter on the coffee table between us.

"It's some kind of practical joke," she insisted. "Urban guerrilla groups died off years ago. The members that didn't go to jail went to Wall Street in vested suits. And no one in their right mind could honestly resent the fact that the bad guys in mystery stories get caught."

"Why not? If we use a black villain we get called racists, if there's a woman villain we're sexists. If one of our writers sent a story about a midget murderer and we ran it, some group would crawl out of the woodwork and call us sizists! Why can't criminals go after us for saying crime doesn't pay?"

Deb's fingers picked at the material of her midnight-blue pant suit. "You're going to take it seriously then?"

"Let's just say I won't dismiss it as a prank. Look at that letterhead again. No address, no phone number. And no instruction how to deliver the money if we did decide to pay. They've deliberately made it impossible for us to meet their demands. Which might mean simple incompetence, or that they'll send instructions later. After softening us." I let loose a deep and weary sigh. "Where's the envelope this letter came in?"

"In the shredder like all the others. I didn't know it was important till too late."

"Well," I concluded as I stood and stretched, "all we can do for now is ignore it. If they contact us again I'll kick the problem upstairs to Fedunka. Do we have any other crises brewing?"

"It's only 11:30," Deb smiled, grimly determined to be gay. "Give us time!"

Right after I came back from a solitary burger-and-salad lunch, Deb brought in a pile of manuscripts from the morning's mail. "Alan Ovel strikes again," she proclaimed as she handed me the papers. "Another letter *and* another story. And it's a Garrulous Garrity to boot." Across my face passed the look of a man who has just stepped into a meat grinder, and Deb tiptoed discreetly out of the office. I bent cautiously over the letter as if it were an artifact from a distant galaxy.

> Box 1294
> Peter Stuyvesant Station
> NYC, NY
>
> Dear Boydbrain:
>   Well you did it again I see. Rejected "Garrulous Garrity and the Tube of Terror" just like all my others. I might have known it would be too good for you and over your head. Someday you'll beg me to write for that lousy mag of yours and I'll laugh. And just in case you didn't know it, Georgie Porgie, five of the stories in your last issue came straight out of stories I sent you last year and you gave them the brush and passed on all the ideas to your regular stable of burned-out hacks. Is literary ethics dead? *Why won't somebody publish me????* Oh hell, what the use? Here's another story you can use for toilet paper.
>
> Disgustedly,
> Alan Ovel

With feet lifted to the desk top and ankles crossed I proceeded to skim the fifty-fourth submission from the persistent Mr. Ovel during my tenure with *GAMM*. The first of them had come about two weeks after I'd taken over as editor-in-chief, when Deb had brought me a manuscript entitled "Death Is Twelve Cats in a Paint Box" and said: "See what you make of this." The thing was so hopelessly bad it was almost good, and I'd asked Deb to show me any and all of his future submissions. Ovel's plots were totally inconsistent, his characters behaved like distant cousins of any recognizable human beings, his sentences resounded in the mind like the work of a drunk chimpanzee running amok through the abandoned instruments of the New York Philharmonic. I kept hoping that someday he'd include some information about himself with one of his gems, for I regularly suffered dizzy spells trying to figure out what kind of brain could have birthed them. Within a few days of each rejection letter I would find on my desk a letter from Ovel, full of irk and brimming with miff as he might have phrased it, protesting the last rejection and offering me a new epic. His series character was a motor-mouthed clown of a parody private eye with ridiculous fake-Irish speech mannerisms and the improbable name of Garrulous Garrity. A new adventure of Garrulous had become a sort of weekly event for Deb and me.

Before finishing his latest, "Garrulous Garrity and the Mini-Skirt Menace," I paused to reach into the bottom drawer of the desk and pluck out the little schoolkid notebook I kept there, the one labeled OVELISMS. Then I went back to page one of the story and transcribed into the notebook the juiciest of the author's many malapropisms. Beginning with the very first sentence: "Garrulous Garrity stood there, all his faculties rooted to the floor, hard to swallow in a hurry, staring at the cookie-covered corpse." I filled three pages of the notebook before I reached the end of the story. Then I pulled a piece of office stationery from the middle drawer, scrawled a quick note—"Dear Mr. Ovel: Close but no cigar. Keep 'em flying!"— signed it and paperclipped it to the manuscript for return mailing. I felt like St. Francis for having taken a few seconds to encourage the poor klutz.

The week crept by with just the usual office routine and miscellaneous messes. An illiterate who was turned down for a secretarial job filed a sex discrimination complaint against us. The truckers' strike kept July's *GAMM* in the warehouse. A fire in the warehouse turned 20% of the July press run to ash. The air conditioning chose the first day of a heat wave to go kaput.

And then in Thursday morning's mail came the letter. "You won't like it," Deb predicted gravely as she brought it to my desk.

The typed heading was the same as on Monday's manifesto. ETHICAL REDISTRIBUTION ALLIANCE. As before, there was no address and no date. Taped to the sheet of el cheapo paper was the brief clipping from Wednesday's *Times* describing the warehouse fire. Beneath the clipping, typed in caps with what looked like a fresh ribbon, was the simple message: PAY OR SUFFER WORSE.

"I was right." I said, taking no pleasure in the fact. "They're softening us up. Did you save the envelope this time?"

Deb nodded. "It's under my blotter for safekeeping. But with these new postmarks all you can tell is that it was mailed from somewhere in the city. And since with that clipping it must have been mailed yesterday, we know that already."

I swiveled to the phone and spun the dial. "Time to bring in Fedunka." I said. "And the cops."

Detective Sergeant Ponzio had a face that reminded me of Secretariat, the Triple Crown winner. He was pleasant and efficient and not the least help in the world. He interviewed Deb, he interviewed me, he used my phone to call the sixteenth floor and make an appointment to see Mr. Fedunka. He put in a call to the Arson unit that had checked out the warehouse fire two days ago and found there wasn't a shred of evidence of suspicious origin. He called the unit that kept an eye out for political activist groups and found that no one had ever heard of the Ethical Redistribution Alliance.

"Beautiful," I sighed. "So an organization that isn't, committed an act of arson that wasn't." It occurred to me that Garrulous Garrity could have done better than this.

"Now, now, take it easy, Mr. Boyd. Give us a chance to work on it. I'll call you if we learn anything." Sergeant Ponizio smiled pleasantly, as prescribed by the police handbook on Community Relations, and departed for his precinct station to make out a report and throw it in the junk file.

A con man, like a good cop or a good actor, develops professional instincts, and if the instincts are off he is in deep career trouble. At some point during that Thursday morning a little voice in my head whispered advice to me. *Milo,* it said, *you are mixed into some new kind of scam. And not as the creator the way by rights you should be. This time you're the pigeon.*

I was left with such a deep sense of unease that after Ponzio left the office I couldn't settle down to cope with the morning's work. Not even a new Alan Ovel in the mail relieved my discomfort, and I skimmed it rapidly, tore a form rejection slip from a pad, stapled it to the manuscript and was just about to seal the return envelope when the voice whispered to me again.

Read that story one more time, dummy, it said.

The second time around, there was something dimly familiar about "Garrulous Garrity's Hippie Homicide," and after a few minutes of concentration I had it. The story was a retread. We'd turned it down three or four months ago when it was a non-series tale under some other title. "Hippiecide," that was it. Ovel had simply revised the thing slightly, spliced in his ridiculous eyeball from Erin as the main character, and resubmitted.

That was the first familiar thing about the story. No sooner had I caught that than I had the other. *Thanks,* I said to the voice. *I'll do the same for you sometime.*

There it was, on page nine. A pungent denizen of the counterculture was addressing Garrity. "You're a fat Establishment pig," he said, "spouting Establishment pigma. Go swill in the mud, Porkulous Piggity!"

The line wasn't quite on the same level with the Ovelisms I had recorded for posterity in my notebook but it was well worth preserving anyway. Very gingerly I tucked the manuscript in a file folder, walked it out to the secretary's office, and made a photocopy of the entire story. I went back to my own sanctum, slipped the copy into Ovel's return envelope with the rejection form, and gummed it shut.

I had the envelope under my arm when I left for lunch. In the downstairs lobby I found a vacant phone booth, fed coins into the slot and dialed the hangout of an old compadre who was in perpetual need of quick money.

"Yeah, Minky, it's Milo. . . . No, I'm in town, but don't blab it. Want to work? . . . Just a shadowing job at a post office. Peter Stuyvesant Station, Box 1294. Wait till somone opens the box, trail him, get me a name and address. And don't wear that stupid Bogart trenchcoat, he'll spot you a mile off." We agreed on a price, wished each other well, and I hung up.

On my way out to Madison I dropped the Ovel envelope down the mail slot and hoped to heaven the United States Postal Service wouldn't lose it between here and Stuyvesant Station.

When I got back to my office there was a visitor waiting on the divan, but I'd been expecting him. Mr. Fedunka, the general manager of Majestic Publications, the man I'd conned with magnificently phony credentials into hiring me as editor in chief of *GAMM*. He was short, gray, thickly jowled and gutted, with a voice like a pneumatic drill and a personality to match. He has his nose buried in some magazine when I stepped into the office but as soon as I walked in he reared up, stuffed whatever he was reading into the side pocket of his rumpled jacket, stormed over to the desk and shoved a letter at my face. "What the hell is going on in this shop?" he thundered. "A cop named Ponzio came up this morning and told me about this terrorist group you've teed off. And on top of that mess you stick us with a lawsuit!"

I didn't like his body language and I didn't like his words, reading between the syllables of which I sensed a subtle hint that I'd been picked as the corporate scapegoat. "What are you talking about, sir?" I asked with what deference I could muster. "What lawsuit?"

"A law firm on Broadway sent me that letter today. They represent some clown named Alan Ovel who claims you rejected more than fifty of his stories this year alone."

"Ah, yes," I sighed. "The immortal adventures of Garrulous Garrity, fast-talking hard-drinking wild Irish eye. You're damn right I rejected them. They stink. What kind of basis for a lawsuit is that?"

"Read the letter," he croaked. "The lawyer claims you've been pulling ideas out of Ovel's stories, feeding them to the writers that regularly sell to you and buying those stories from the other writers. He says eleven stories you ran this year were direct steals from Ovel manuscripts. Along with the letter he sent copies of the eleven you ran and of his eleven. The lawyer wants $50,000 or he'll file suit."

"So he photocopied eleven stories from GAMM, did he?" I stared straight into Fedunka's cold porcine eyes. "Those stories are copyrighted," I declaimed righteously. "If he sues us, we countersue for infringement. Then the judge can laugh us both out of court! Look, Mr. Fedunka, there's no need to worry. This Ovel is a grade-A nutcake." I proceeded to give my employer a consise summary of my dealings over the months with the elusive Mr. Ovel, leaving out my private arrangement with Minky to hunt the man down. When I finished, Fedunka leaned back and rolled his bull neck against the back of the visitor's chair.

"Could you be telling the gist of Ovel's stories to other writers at cocktail parties or something?" he demanded peevishly. "Could they be sort of borrowing from the guy secondhand without knowing it?"

"Impossible. For one thing, Ovel's stories *have* no gist. They're just slapped down on paper as if he made them up on the spur of the moment. Now, it's true I've jotted down some of his worst lines in a notebook, and a few of the gang at MWA have treated me to drinks on the strength of them." I pulled the treasury of Ovelisms out of the bottom drawer and recited a few of my all-time favorites to prove my point. "'The jumbojet touched Garrity down on Oahu, the most omnipotent of the Hawaiian isles.' That's from 'Garrulous Garrity's Kona Koast Kaper.' Now here's his description of a high-rise office building like this one. 'The Soybean

Exchange Building was a towering slab of mince pie standing proudly on Manhattan's dirty feet.' And, oh yes, this is the opening paragraph of 'Malpractice Is Murder': 'Doctor Cutter's office was partly ajar. The small blonde walked in and over to a picture window that overlooked eleven stories of sidewalk.' And I swear, Mr. Fedunka, that kind of line is all I've ever told anyone about Alan Ovel."

I had expected at least a mild chuckle or two from Fedunka during my recital, but his reaction seemed one of anger rather then delight, and I decided that despite his Broderick Crawford facade he must be linguistic purist, incapable of savoring an outrageous sentence. His scowling face actually reddened as I read.

"Okay," he said when I'd put down the notebook. "I've got an appointment this afternoon with Sheldon Rogers, the copyright lawyer. He'll tell me for sure if anything you've done is actionable." He indulged in what is laughingly called a pregnant pause. "You'd better hope it isn't." And with that final subtle hint that my head was on the chopping block he flung himself out of the visitor's chair and stalked out of the office.

"This is a conspiracy against me," I confided to the neutral gray walls. "A conspiracy!"

For the next twenty-four hours life at *Great American Mystery Magazine* returned to a semblance of normality. Not a peep was to be heard out of Fedunka, or Alan Ovel, or the Ethical Redistribution Alliance. When I called the number where Minky was to leave messages for me, there weren't any, and I visualized him slouching nobly against a wall of Peter Stuyvesant Station, waiting to connect with the tenant of Box 1294. The warehouse superintendent gave me solemn assurances that the truckers' strike would collapse over the weekend. Deb brought me three unsolicited manuscripts that were actually first-rate.

Early Friday afternoon I decided that for the rest of the day the shop could run without me. I'd seen in the morning's *Times* that there would be a panel discussion of writers and experts on mystery fiction at 2:00 P.M. at the John Jay School of Criminal Justice. What a golden chance, I thought, to pick brains on the question that had been bugging me since Monday: Was the Redistribution Alliance's statement about the nature of mystery fiction somewhat plausible, or was it totally off the wall? If the former, there was at least a possibility that a terrorist group was after me. If the latter, I was being targeted for a scam, and professional pride required me to teach the Alliance a stern lesson.

I cabbed west across town and walked the few blocks south to John Jay. A framed poster in the entrance lobby read PANEL DISCUSSION

"CRIME SOLVING: FICTION AND REALITY"—THIRD FLOOR AUDITORIUM.

I caught an elevator, followed arrows, and joined the sparse audience in the chamber just as the panelists were being introduced. Some administrator from John Jay stood on the stage and presented the chairperson of the group, Captain Tuckett of the NYPD, who took the microphone and proceeded to introduce the rest of the gang, glaring ferociously at the audience as he did. There were a woman FBI agent, a John Jay criminology prof, a wild-bearded character in blue jeans who taught a course in detective fiction at the New School, and a white-thatched chairman-of-the-board type in a $500 three-piece suit whom I recognized as John Belt, the mystery writer. Belt wrote police procedurals about a character named Luis Skyhawk, half Mexican and half Cheyenne, who was the homicide specialist of the Los Angeles PD. He'd gotten rich on residuals when the *Skyhawk* TV series ran in prime time for five years. With the modest rates *GAMM* paid, it was no wonder he'd never written for us.

I sat back in the auditorium, surrounded by empty chairs, and listened with half an ear to everyone's spiel and the ensuing crosstalk until the time came for what I was waiting for, the Question and Answer period. I raised my hand and waited to be acknowledged.

"Yes, sir," Captain Tuckett said. "The gentleman on the aisle in the middle row." He glared in my direction. "Yes, you." He held the glare even after I'd risen.

"It's been said," I began, "that mystery fiction is mostly propaganda for Establishment values, like crime doesn't pay, everyone should obey the law, things like that. Do the panelists think that theory has any validity?"

John Belt extended a perfectly cultured hand for the microphone, coughed importantly and commenced an oration. "Detective fiction presupposes a stable society, a regime of law and order, where the police and the authorities are seen as good, decent, honest people. Its enduring popularity among Anglo-American readers can best be attributed to this aspect of the form. . . ."

In mid-sentence Belt was interrupted by the bearded prof, who roared an eight-letter word denoting an object frequently found in cow pastures in a voice so loud he didn't need the mike. "That is *not* what the genre is about! Mr. Belt is describing one tiny subtype, the old-fashioned, racist, sexist, deductive kind of detective story which has been justly called the recreation of narrow, life-hating and ignoble minds. Read Hammett, read Chandler, *there's* the American detective story. The private eye, the loner as hero, the outsider who sees through the crap we call Establishment values. The murderer's a pretty nice guy compared with the plutocrats and politicians. . . ."

At which point the FBI lady took the mike from John Belt and called the prof a pinko and the panel quickly degenerated into a shouting match, with my question long forgotten in the melee. The only speaker who didn't get into the act was Tuckett, who sat still as a waxwork on the stage, glaring out at me. I vacated my seat and walked. Wasted afternoon. How could I get a straight answer if the experts went at each other's throats? I cabbed disgustedly uptown to my pad on Central Park South and poured myself a very large glass of white wine.

Halfway into my third glass I pulled over the phone and put in another call to Minky. "You did? . . . And you stayed on the trail all the way from Peter Stuyvesant to . . . Is *that* so? . . . You bet you've earned your money, pal, thanks a few mil." I hung up and started pacing the shag carpet of the living room. Start of a weekend or no start of a weekend, I had to do some fast and furious cogitation.

Saturday morning I walked east and south to the office to put in the time I'd missed Friday afternoon. Except for me the *GAMM* suite on the tenth floor was empty. I sat behind my desk and tried to work out my next move. Around 10:30 I heard a sort of soft clatter out front: mail being pushed through the slot in the entrance door. I went down the corridor, past the vacant switchboard and scooped up the one item that lay on the linoleum.

It was a copy of *GAMM* for July. Paperclipped to the gaudy cover was a folded sheet of dime-store paper with that old familiar typed heading ETHICAL REDISTRIBUTION ALLIANCE. The message beneath the heading was short and simple.

> All incidents of anti-crime propaganda in this issue are underlined. Have $10,000 in cash ready by 12:00 noon Monday and wait for delivery instructions. You now by now that we mean business.

Feeling as if the hind end of an elephant had just rammed my solar plexus, I skimmed the pages of the issue. I took less than five minutes to complete the count: twenty-two separate sentences or paragraphs underlined with a red felt pen.

And then I reread the last sentence of the covering letter, only with a different emphasis. You know *by now* that we mean business. And with the office locked up this Saturday, the Ethical gang must have expected that the letter wouldn't be found till Monday morning.

So what was going to happen over the weekend that would convince us by then that they meant business?

I raced down the interior corridor to the doorless doorway of Deb's office and grabbed a volume from the shelf of telephone directories. She had a place on Staten Island but I'd never bothered to look up the number before now. I found her listed in the Staten Island directory and went over to her desk and sat and dialed.

"Hel-hello?" It was her voice and it could still send ripples down my spine, because there was terror in it.

"It's me, Deb. George. Are you okay?" My voice was quivering like a taut bowstring. "What happened?"

"I'm still shook up. About two hours ago I went to the corner newsstand for a paper and someone tried to push me out into a street full of cars. Luckily I recovered my balance and got back on the sidewalk, but I was almost run over. There were a lot of people around but no one will admit they saw anything. The police think it was just someone wanting to grab my purse. A precinct detective left here a few minutes ago."

"That wasn't a purse snatcher," I told her. "It was our buddies from the Ethical Redistribution Alliance. Letting us know they mean business." I filled her in on the morning's communique from the terrorists. "Look, stay bottled up in your apartment the rest of the weekend. If you've got a boy friend, have him come over. And for God's sake keep your door locked! Want me to take the ferry over and stay with you awhile?"

"No, I'll, I'll be all right." The way she said it gave me no clue at all whether there was a man in her life or not. "See you Monday morning, George."

I hung up, and sat there a minute, running my eyes absently over the wall-to-wall steel shelving that faced Deb's desk. The shelves were jammed to capacity with the ten office file copies of each issue of *GAMM* from its beginning in the late sixties to the new July issue.

The issue that was still stuck in the warehouse thanks to the truckers' wildcat strike.

I got up, stalked over to the shelves like a cat after a plump juicy mouse, and counted the copies of the July issue.

Nine.

And suddenly the whole lunatic skein of events made sense.

I whirled back to the phone and dialed Deb again and asked her one precise question about an incident in her office early Thursday afternoon. And got precisely the answer I was hoping for.

The final scene of the farce was played out in the living room of a high-ceilinged, ornately furnished old apartment in the Nineties a block from Broadway. There were two actors in the scene, but all the good lines, I say in modesty, were mine. Toadface Fedunka just sort of sat there deflated in a high-back wing chair like a lifesize balloon the night after Macy's Thanksgiving Day parade.

"No wonder you looked so upset Thursday when I read you some of the worst of Alan Ovel. I was kicking your dear little brain children! Judging from all the outdated references to things like miniskirts and hippies I'd say most of them were written several years ago, right?"

"I inherited a little money in the late Sixties," Fedunka mumbled wretchedly. "Quit the job I had, left my wife and started writing. I thought I'd be the new Raymond Chandler. I couldn't sell a word and in a couple of years the money ran out."

"But all those stories stayed in your trunk," I continued, "until you dreamed up a way to use them in a scam. Bombard my magazine with them, then after a few months fake a letter from a lawyer threatening plagiarism suit and, with luck, pick up a nice out-of-court settlement from Majestic. Only the scam had the same weakness your stories have. It was flying by the seat of the pants stuff. If you'd bothered to do some research you'd have learned that the copyright law doesn't protect ideas but only the expression of ideas. To prove infringement you have to establish substantial similarity between your work and the other guy's, and any similarities between the Alan Ovel stories and what we run in *GAMM* were only the level of ideas, like a private eye, or a tough cop, things so general that no one legally owns them and anyone can use them. You learned that when you consulted Sheldon Rogers the other day, didn't you?

"But it didn't ruin your plans completely because you had a second scam in the works at the same time, the Ethical Redistribution caper. Mail us a few threatening letters, keep us on edge, build up a terrorist reputation by claiming responsiblilty for a few accidents like the warehouse fire, and pretty soon you might scare Majestic into paying off. Only you couldn't come up with a safe way to arrange for the payment. With your bullfrog voice you couldn't give us instructions over the phone or you'd be recognized, and if you gave them to us in writing we might call the cops and set a trap. So while you tried to think up a foolproof answer to that problem you decided to soften us up a bit more by going out to Staten Island this morning and attacking Deb. Then on your way back you stopped at the office and shoved a copy of *GAMM* for July into the mail slot with a new threatening note. And that was where you blew it to smithereens, Fedunka. That issue isn't on the stand yet! The truckers are striking the warehouse, and the only copies around are the standard ten file copies the printers mail to the office every month. I went into Deb's office and saw that one was missing, and then I remembered that when I came back from lunch Thursday and found you in my office, you were reading some magazine that you put in your pocket and took out with you when you left. That was the tenth copy. That's how I knew it was you."

"Rotten luck," Fedunka muttered. "Nothing but rotten luck."

"Nothing but carelessness and stupidity," I told him. "The first Redistribution letter, the one that came Monday, was written in the usual straightforward business English, except for one phrase: 'Establishment Pigma.' I just thought it was a neat little coinage, pigma for dogma, and didn't pay any more attention to it—until later in the week when you sent us an old Garrulous Garrity story where the exact same word, pigma, popped up again! Of course it could have been coincidence, two writers happening to use the identical coined word in communicating with *GAMM* during the same week. But it gave me a huge hint that the terrorists were connected somehow with Alan Ovel."

And of course once Minky had identified the tenant of Box 1294 as Fedunka, even a Garrulous Garrity could have figured out that the Ethical Redistribution Alliance must be Fedunka too. But it sounded far more impressive and devastating with that part left out. Milo's Maxim #36: Always make the most of your material.

"All right, Boyd," he croaked. "I needed more money and tried a few fast ones and you caught me. What happens now?"

That was the problem *I* hadn't been able to solve. Turn a fellow con artist, even an inept one like Fedunka, over to the cops? Professional ethics forbade, and even if I did turn him in, my own George Boyd persona would be closely scrutinized during the investigation and probably wouldn't survive. Tell him to forget the whole thing? But then he'd be bound to wonder why I'd been so generous, and again good old George would be threatened. Take a chunk of cash from him and scram from the scene? Unfortunately it was late Saturday afternoon and the banks were closed, so where would he find the money?

"I haven't decided that yet," I told him honestly. "So you can sweat it out till Monday morning, and then we'll both know. And don't think up something cute like trying to zap me between now and then, because I sent a tape cassette with the a report of the entire scam plus all the physical evidence to a lawyer friend of mine, and if I don't call him every eight hours till Monday morning it goes straight to the cops." It was a good lie, I thought. I would have done just that except that the office tape machine was on the fritz.

I found Fedunka slouched over in his chair like a broken toy and found my way out of the apartment.

It was a little after 7:00 P.M. when I stepped into the lobby of my building on Central Park South. As I was heading for the elevator two men eased up off the low-slung foyer couch and started to close in on me. I saw their reflections in the floor-to-ceiling mirror ahead of me at the end of the lobby. Both had plainclothes cop written all over them. The young one was a stranger to me but the middle-aged guy I recognized. Captain Tuckett, the moderator of the John Jay panel, who had spent so much of yesterday afternoon glaring in my direction. Running my face through his memory bank.

I ran to a corner of the lobby and slipped through the service door into a back corridor and raced through the laundry room and the parking garage and out another service door and into the night streets of Manhattan with their shouts and running sounds echoing behind me and as I ran I tried frantically to recall if it was legal for New York cops to shoot at a fleeing confidence person.

How I got out of the city with nothing but the clothes on my back and the stuff in my wallet belongs in another story. A few months later, safely ensconced in a San Francisco hideaway, I ventured out to Union Square one evening and on impulse bought the latest number of *GAMM* at a newsstand. The first item I turned to was the masthead to see who had replaced me.

Deborah K. Howard, Editor in Chief. And the quality of the stories hadn't dropped the least bit.

GOD SAVE THE MARK: A NOVEL
Donald E. Westlake

Forgetting those things which are behind, and reaching forth unto those things which are before, I press toward the mark.

The Epistle of Paul to the Philippians

You must make your mark.

Horatio Alger

1

FRIDAY THE NINETEENTH of May was a full day. In the morning I bought a counterfeit sweepstakes ticket from a one-armed man in a barbershop on West 23rd Street, and in the evening I got a phone call at home from a lawyer saying I'd just inherited three hundred seventeen thousand dollars from my Uncle Matt. I'd never heard of Uncle Matt.

As soon as the lawyer hung up I called my friend Reilly of the Bunco Squad at his house in Queens. "It's me," I said. "Fred Fitch."

Reilly sighed and said, "What have they done to you this time, Fred?"

"Two things," I said. "One this morning and one just now."

"Better watch yourself, then. My grandma always said troubles come in threes."

"Oh, my Lord," I said. "Clifford!"

"What's that?"

"I'll call you back," I said. "I think the third one already came."

I hung up and went downstairs and rang Mr. Grant's bell. He came to the door with a large white napkin tucked under his chin and holding a small fork upright in his hand, a tiny curled shrimp impaled on it. Which was a case of sweets to the sweet, Mr. Grant being a meek curled-shrimp of a man himself, balding, given to spectacles with steel rims, employed as a history teacher at some high school over in Brooklyn. We met at the mailboxes every month or so and exchanged anonymities, but other than that our social contact was nil.

I said, "Excuse me, Mr. Grant, I know it's dinnertime, but do you have a new roommate named Clifford?"

425

He blanched. Fork and shrimp drooped in his hand. He blinked very slowly.

Knowing it was hopeless, I went on anyway, saying, "Pleasant-looking sort, about my age, crewcut, white shirt open at the collar, tie loose, dark slacks." Over the years I've grown rather adept at giving succinct descriptions, unfortunately. I would have gone on and given estimates of Clifford's height and weight but I doubted they were needed.

They weren't. Shrimp at half-mast, Mr. Grant said to me, "I thought he was *your* roommate."

"He said there was a COD package," I said.

Mr. Grant nodded miserably. "Me, too."

"He didn't have enough cash in the apartment."

"He'd already borrowed some from Wilkins on the second floor."

I nodded. "Had a fistful of crumpled bills in his left hand."

Mr. Grant swallowed bile. "I gave him fifteen dollars."

I swallowed bile. "I gave him twenty."

Mr. Grant looked at his shrimp as though wondering who'd put it on his fork. "I suppose," he said slowly, "I suppose we ought to . . ." His voice trailed off.

"Let's go talk to Wilkins," I said.

"All right," he said, and sighed, and came out to the hall, shutting the door carefully after himself. We went on up to the second floor.

This block of West 19th Street consisted almost entirely of three- and four-story buildings with floor-through apartments sporting fireplaces, back gardens, and high ceilings, and how the entire block had so far missed the wrecker's sledge I had no idea. In our building, Mr. Grant had the first floor, a retired Air Force officer named Wilkins had the second, and I lived up top on the third. We all three were bachelors, quiet and sedentary, and not given to disturbingly loud noises. Of us, I was at thirty-one the youngest and Wilkins was much the oldest.

When Mr. Grant and I reached Wilkins' door, I rang the bell and we stood around with that embarrassed uneasiness always felt by messengers of bad tidings.

After a moment the door opened and there stood Wilkins, looking like the Correspondence Editor of the *Senior Citizens' Review*. He wore red sleeve garters with his blue shirt, a green eyeshade was squared off on his forehead, and in his ink-stained right hand he held an ancient fountain pen. He looked at me, looked at Mr. Grant, looked at Mr. Grant's napkin, looked at Mr. Grant's fork, looked at Mr. Grant's shrimp, looked back at me, and said, "Eh?"

I said, "Excuse me, sir, but did someone named Clifford come to see you this afternoon?"

"Your roommate," he said, pointing his pen at me. "Gave him seven dollars."

Mr. Grant moaned. Wilkins and I both looked at his shrimp, as though *it* had moaned. Then I said, "Sir, this man Clifford, or whatever his name is, he isn't my roommate."

"Eh?"

"He's a con man, sir."

"Eh?" He was squinting at me like a man looking across Texas at midday.

"A con man," I repeated. "Con means confidence. A confidence man. A sort of crook."

"Crook?"

"Yes, sir. A con man is someone who tells you a convincing lie, as a result of which you give him money."

Wilkins put his head back and looked at the ceiling, as though to stare through it into my apartment and see if Clifford weren't really there after all, in shirtsleeves, quietly going about the business of being my new roommate. But he failed to see him—or failed to see through the ceiling, I'm not sure which—and looked at me again, saying, "But what about the package? Wasn't it his?"

"Sir, there wasn't any package," I said. "That was the con. That is, the lie he told you was that there was a package, a COD package, and he—"

"Exactly," said Wilkins, pointing his pen at me with a little spray of ink, "exactly the word. COD. Cash on delivery."

"But there wasn't any package," I kept telling him. "It was a lie, to get money from you."

"No package? Not your roommate?"

"That's it, sir."

"Why," said Wilkins, abruptly outraged, "the man's a damn fraud!"

"Yes, sir."

"Where is he now?" Wilkins demanded, going up on tiptoe to look past my shoulder.

"Miles from here, I should think," I said.

"Do I get you right?" he said, glaring at me. "You don't even *know* this man?"

"That's right," I said.

"But he came from your apartment."

"Yes, sir. He'd just talked me into giving him twenty dollars."

Mr. Grant said, "I gave him fifteen." He sounded as mournful as the shrimp.

Wilkins said to me, "Did *you* think he was your roommate? Makes no sense at all."

"No, sir," I said. "He told me he was Mr. Grant's roommate."

Wilkins snapped a stern look at Mr. Grant. "Is he?"

"Of course not!" wailed Mr. Grant. "I gave him fifteen dollars myself!"

Wilkins nodded. "I see," he said. Then, thoughtfully, ruminatively, he said, "It seems to me we should contact the authorities."

"We were just about to," I said. "I thought I'd call my friend on the Bunco Squad."

Wilkins squinted again, under his eyeshade. "I beg your pardon?"

"It's part of the police force. The ones who concern themselves with the confidence men."

"You have a friend in this organization?"

"We met in the course of business," I said, "but over the years we've become personal friends."

"Then by all means," said Wilkins decisively. "I've never seen going through channels accomplish anything yet. Your friend it is."

So the three of us went on up to my place, Wilkins still wearing his eyeshade and carrying his pen, Mr. Grant still wearing his napkin and carrying his fork and shrimp. We entered the apartment and I offered them chairs but they preferred to stand. I called Reilly again, and as soon as I said who I was he said, "COD Clifford."

"What?"

"COD Clifford," he repeated. "I didn't connect the name at first, not till after you hung up. That's who it was, wasn't it?"

"It sounds about right," I said.

"He was some other tenant's new roommate."

"And a COD package had come."

"That's him, all right," Reilly said, and I could visualize him nodding at the telephone. He has a large head, with a thick mass of black hair and a thick bushy black mustache, and when he nods he does so with such judicious authority you can't help but believe he has just thought an imperishable truth. I sometimes think Reilly does so well with the Bunco Squad because he's part con man himself.

I said, "He got twenty dollars from me, fifteen from Mr. Grant on the first floor, and seven from Mr. Wilkins on the second."

Wilkins waved his pen at me, whispering hoarsely, "Make it twelve. For the official record, twelve."

Into the phone I said, "Mr. Wilkins says, for the official record make it twelve."

Reilly laughed while Wilkins frowned. Reilly said, "There's a touch of the con in everybody."

"Except me," I said bitterly.

"Some day, Fred, some psychiatrist is going to do a book on you and make you famous forever."

"Like Count Sacher-Masoch?"

I always make Reilly laugh. He thinks I'm the funniest sad sack he knows, and what's worse he tells me so.

Now he said, "Okay, I'll add your name to Clifford's sucker list, and when we get him you'll be invited to the viewing."

"Do you want a description?"

"No, thanks. We've got a hundred already, several with points of similarity. Don't worry, we'll be getting this one. He works too much, he's pushing his luck."

"If you say so." In my experience, which is extensive, the professional workers of short cons don't usually get caught. Which is nothing against Reilly and the others of the Bunco Squad, but merely reflects the impossibility of the job they've been given. By the time they arrive at the scene of the crime, the artist is invariably gone and the sucker usually isn't even sure exactly what happened. Aside from dusting the victim for fingerprints, there really isn't much the Reillys can do.

This time he had me give him my fellow pigeons' full names, assured me once again that our complaint would go into the bulging Clifford file downtown, and then he asked me, "Now, what else?"

"Well," I said, somewhat embarrassed to be telling about this in front of my neighbors, "this morning a one-armed man in a barbershop on West—"

"Counterfeit sweepstakes ticket," he said.

"Reilly," I said, "how is it you know all these people but you never catch any?"

"We got the Demonstration Kid, didn't we? And Slim Jim Foster? And Able Mabel?"

"All right," I said.

"Your one-armed man, now," Reilly said, "that's Wingy St. Charles. How come you tipped so soon?"

"This afternoon," I said, "I suddenly got a suspicion, you know the way I always do, five hours too late."

"I know," he said. "God, how I know."

"So I went up to the Irish Tourist Board office on East 50th Street," I said, "and showed it to a man there, and he said it was a fake."

"And you bought it this morning. Where?"

"In a barbershop on West 23rd Street."

"Okay. It's soon enough, he might still be working the same neighborhood. We've got a chance. Not a big chance, but a chance. Now, what else do you have?"

"When I came home," I said, "the phone was ringing. It was a man said he was a lawyer, Goodkind, office on East 38th Street. Said I'd just inherited three hundred seventeen thousand dollars from my Uncle Matt."

"Did you check with the family? Is Uncle Matt dead?"

"I don't have any Uncle Matt."

"Okay," said Reilly. "This one we get for sure. When do you go to his office?"

"Tomorrow morning, ten o'clock."

"Right. We'll give it five minutes. Give me the address."

I gave him the address, he said he'd see me in the morning, and we both hung up.

My guests were both staring at me, Mr. Grant in amazement and Wilkins with a sort of fixed ferocity. It was Wilkins who said, "Lot of money, that."

"What money?"

"Three hundred thousand dollars." He nodded at the phone. "What you're getting."

"But I'm not getting three hundred thousand dollars," I said. "It's another con game, like Clifford."

Wilkins squinted. "Eh? How's that follow?"

Mr. Grant said, "But if they give you the money . . ."

"That's just it," I said. "There isn't any money. It's a racket."

Wilkins cocked his head to one side. "Don't see it," he said. "Don't see where they make a profit."

"There's a thousand ways," I said. "For instance, they might talk me into putting all the money into a certain investment, where my so-called Uncle Matt had it, but there's a tax problem or transfer costs and they can't touch the capital without endangering the whole investment, so I have to get two or three thousand dollars in cash from somewhere else to pay the expenses. Or the money's in some South American country and we have to pay the inheritance tax in cash from here before they'll let the money out. There's a new gimmick every day, and ten new suckers to try it on."

"Barnum," suggested Wilkins. "One born a minute, two to take him."

"Two," I said, "is a conservative number."

Mr. Grant said, faintly, "Does this happen to you all the time?"

"I couldn't begin to tell you," I said.

"But why you?" he asked. "This is the first time anything like this ever happened to me. Why should it happen to you so much?"

I couldn't answer him. There just wasn't a single thing I could say in response to a question like that. So I stood there and looked at him, and after a while he and Wilkins went away, and I spent the evening thinking about the question Mr. Grant had asked me, and trying out various answers I might have given him, ranging from, "I guess that's just the breaks of the game," to, "Drop dead," and none of them was really satisfactory.

2

I SUPPOSE IT all began twenty-five years ago, when I returned home from my first day of kindergarten without my trousers. I did have the rather vague notion they'd been traded to some classmate, but I couldn't remember what had been given to me in exchange, nor did I seem to have anything in my possession that hadn't already belonged to me when I'd left for school, a younger and happier child, at nine that morning. Nor was I sure of the identity of the con infant who had done me in, so that neither he nor my trousers were ever found.

From that day forward my life has been an endless series of belated discoveries. Con men take one look at me, streamline their pitches, and soon go gaily off to steak dinners while poor Fred Fitch sits at home and once again dines on gnawed fingernail. I have enough worthless receipts and bad checks to paper my living room, I own miles of tickets to nonexistent raffles and ball games and dances and clambakes and shivarees, my closet is full of little machines that stopped working miracles as soon as the seller went away, and I'm apparently on just about every sucker mailing list in the Western Hemisphere.

I really don't know why this should be true. I am not the typical mark, or victim, not according to Reilly or to all the books I've read on the subject. I am not greedy, nor uneducated, nor particularly stupid, nor an immigrant unfamiliar with the language and customs. I am only—but it is enough—gullible. I find it impossible to believe that anyone could lie to another human being to his face. It has happened to me hundreds of times already, but for some reason I remain unconvinced. When I am alone I am strong and cynical and unendingly suspicious, but as soon as the glib stranger appears in front of me and starts his spiel my mind disappears in a haze of belief. The belief is all-encompassing; I may be the only person in New York City in the twentieth century with a money machine.

This endless gullibility has, of course, colored my entire life. I left my home town in Montana to come to New York City at the very early age of seventeen, much sooner than I would have preferred if it had not been that I was surrounded at home by friends and relatives all of whom had seen me played for a fool more often than I could count. It was embarrassment that drove me from my home to the massive anonymity of New York, when otherwise I might have stayed forever within ten blocks of the place of my birth.

My relationship with women has also been affected, and badly. Since high school I have avoided any but the most casual acquaintance with the opposite sex, and all because of my gullibility. In the first place, any girl who became close friends with me would sooner or later—probably sooner—see me humiliated by a passing bunco artist. In the second place, were I to grow more than fond of a particular girl, how could I ever really know her opinion of me? She might say she loved me, and when she was saying it I would believe her, but an hour later, a day later . . .

No. Solitude has its dreary aspects, but they don't include self-torture.

Similarly my choice of occupation. Not for me the gregarious office job, side by side with my mates, typing or writing or thinking away in our companionable white-shirted tiers. Solitude was the answer here as well, and for the past eight years I have been a free-lance researcher, numbering among my clients many writers and scholars and television producers, for whom I plumb the local libraries in search of specific knowledge.

So here I was at thirty-one, a confirmed bachelor and a semi-recluse, with all the occupational diseases of my sedentary calling: round shoulders and round spectacles and round stomach and round forehead. I seemed inadvertently to have found the way to skip the decades, to go from the middle twenties to the middle fifties and there to stay while the gray years drifted silently by and nothing broke the orderly flow of time but the occasional ten-dollar forays of passing confidence men.

Until, on that Friday the nineteenth of May, I received the phone call from the lawyer named Goodkind that changed—and very nearly ended—my life.

3

IN AN EFFORT to eliminate, or at least contain, my pot belly, I've taken to walking as much as possible whenever I go out, and so on Saturday morning I walked from my apartment on West 19th Street to the office of the alleged lawyer, Goodkind, on East 38th Street. I made one stop along the way, in a drugstore on the corner of West 23rd and Sixth Avenue, where I purchased a packet of tobacco.

I'd gone half a block farther up Sixth Avenue when I heard someone behind me call, "Say, you!" I turned, and a tall and rather heavy-set man was striding toward me, motioning at me to stay where I was. He wore a dark suit, the jacket flapping open, a white shirt bunched at the waist, and a wrinkled brown tie. He looked like an ex-Marine who has only recently started to get flabby.

When he reached me he said, "You just bought some tobacco in the store on the corner, right?"

"Yes, I did," I said. "Why?"

He pulled his wallet from his hip pocket and flipped it open to show me his badge. "Police," he said. "All we want you to do is cooperate."

"I'll be happy to," I said, with that sudden flutter of guilt we all feel when abruptly confronted by the law.

He said, "What sort of bill did you use back there?"

"What sort? You mean—? Well, it was a five."

He pulled a crumpled bill from his jacket pocket and handed it to me, saying, "This one?"

I looked at the bill, but of course there's no way to tell one piece of money from another, so eventually I had to say, "I guess it is. I can't be sure."

"Take a close look at it, brother," he said, and he suddenly sounded much tougher than before.

I took a close look, but how did I know if this was the bill I'd used or not? "I'm sorry," I said, feeling very nervous about it, "but I just can't be positive one way or the other."

"The counterman says you're the one passed it on him," he said.

I looked at him, saw him glowering at me. I said, "Passed it on him? You mean it's counterfeit?"

"That's exactly right," he said.

"It's happened again," I said, sadly studying the bill in my hand. "People pass counterfeit money on me all the time."

"Where'd you get this one?"

"I'm sorry, I just don't know."

I could tell by his face that he was somewhat suspicious of me, and he confirmed it by saying, "You don't seem too anxious to cooperate, brother."

"Oh, I am," I said. "It's just I don't remember where I got this particular bill."

"Come over to the car," he said, and led me to a battered green unmarked Plymouth parked near a fireplug. He had me get in on the passenger side in front, and then he came around and slid in behind the wheel. A police radio under the dashboard was crackling and giving occasional spurts of words.

The detective said, "Let's see some identification."

I showed him my library and Social Security cards, and he carefully wrote down my name and address in a black notebook. He'd taken the five-dollar bill back by now, and he wrote its serial number on the same page, then said to me, "You got any more bills on you?"

"Yes, I do."

"Let's see."

I had thirty-eight dollars in bills, two tens, three fives and three ones. I gave them to him and he studied each of them at length, holding them up to the light, rubbing them between thumb and finger, listening to them crinkle, and then putting them atop the dashboard in two piles.

When he was done, it turned out three more of them had been counter-feit, a ten and two fives. "We'll have to impound these," he said, and gave me the other bills back. "I'll give you a receipt, but of course you know you can't collect good money for these. If there's ever a conviction based on these bills it's possible you'll be able to make a partial recovery from the people who made them, but otherwise I'm afraid you've been had."

"That's all right," I said, and grinned weakly. In the first place, I was used to being had, and in the second place, I was delighted that he no longer thought I was potentially a member of the gang passing them.

He had a receipt book in the glove compartment. He got it out and wrote out an involved receipt, including the serial numbers of the bills, and when he handed it to me he said, "You want to be more careful from now on. Look at your change when it's given to you and you won't make these costly mistakes."

"I'll do that," I promised. I got out of the car, looked at my watch, and saw I'd have to move fast if I intended to reach Goodkind's office by ten o'clock. I began walking briskly uptown.

I reached 32nd Street before it occurred to me I'd been taken. Then I stood stock-still on the sidewalk, and as I felt the blood drain from my head, I took out the receipt and looked at it.

Twenty dollars. I had just bought this scribbled piece of paper for twenty dollars.

I turned around and ran, but of course by the time I got to 24th Street he was long gone. I started looking around for a phone booth, intending to call Reilly at Headquarters, but then I remembered I'd be seeing him at the supposed lawyer's office a little after ten.

A little after ten? I looked at my watch and it was just one minute before the hour. I was supposed to be there now!

I flagged a cab, which meant another dollar the bogus policeman had cost me. I got into the back seat, the driver started the meter, and we raced uptown directly into the middle of the garment center's perpetual traffic jam.

I got to Goodkind's office at twenty after ten. The hallway and reception room and Goodkind's private office were all crawling with Bunco Squad men, who had sprung the trap before the cheese had arrived. I threaded my way through them, muttering hello to the ones I knew and identifying myself to the rest and found Reilly in Goodkind's office with two other Bunco Squad men and, seated at his desk, a hungry lupine sharpie with onyx eyes who had to be Goodkind himself.

Reilly said to me, "Where the hell have you been?"

"A phony policeman worked the counterfeit ploy on me for twenty dollars," I said.

"Oh, Christ," said Reilly, and suddenly looked too weary to stand.

Goodkind, grinning hungrily at me, said, in a voice like the one Eve must have heard from the serpent, "Hello there, Fred. It's really too bad you're my client."

I looked at him. "What?"

Reilly said, "He's legit, you goofball. He's on the up-and-up."

"You mean—?"

"What a suit I'd have against you," Goodkind said gleefully. "And you with all that money."

"It's square," Reilly told me. "You really did inherit three hundred and seventeen thousand dollars, and God help us all."

"Still," said Goodkind, rubbing his hands together, "maybe we can work something out."

I stretched out on the floor and became unconscious.

4

JACK REILLY IS a great bear of a man, sprinkled with pipe tobacco. Two hectic hours after my subsidence on the floor of Attorney Goodkind's office, Reilly and I entered a bar on East 34th Street, and he said, "Fred, if you're going to drive me to drink, the least you can do is pay for it."

"I guess I can," I said. "Now." And my knees got weak again.

Reilly steered me to a booth in the back, hollered till a waitress came, ordered Jack Daniels on the rocks for both of us, and said to me, "If you'll take my advice, Fred, the first thing you'll do is get yourself another lawyer."

I said, doubtfully, "That doesn't seem fair, does it? After all, he's the one handling the estate."

"He handles it the way I handle my girl," he said, and made a fondling motion in the air. "Goodkind's a little too much in love with your money, Fred. Unload him."

"All right," I promised, though secretly I doubted if I had the nerve to just walk into Goodkind's office and fire him. But maybe I could hire another attorney and *he* could fire Goodkind.

Reilly said, "And the second thing you better do, Fred, is figure out a safe place to put that money."

"I'd rather not think about it," I said.

"Well, you've got to think about it," he told me. "I don't want you calling me every hundred dollars till it's gone."

"Let's talk about it later," I said. "After I've had a drink and a chance to calm down."

"It's an awful lot of money, Fred," he said.

I already knew that. It was three hundred and seventeen thousand dollars, give or take a nickel. Not only that, it was three hundred and seventeen thousand dollars *net*, after inheritance taxes and legal fees and all the rest of it, the actual amount of the inheritance being nearly five hundred thousand. Half a million.

Five million dimes.

It seems I really did have an Uncle Matt, or that is, a grand-uncle by that name. My great-grandmother on my mother's mother's side married twice and had one son by the second marriage, who in his turn had three wives but no children. (A quick phone call to my mother in Montana from Goodkind's office had garnered this information.) Uncle Matt, or Matthew Grierson, which was his real name, had spent most of his life as a ne'er-do-well and—presumably—alcoholic. Every single relative he had reviled him and snubbed him and refused him entry to their homes. Except me, of course. I never did an unkind thing to Uncle Matt in my life, primarily because I'd never heard of him, my parents being too genteel to mention such a bad character in the presence of children.

But it was this kindness by default which had produced my windfall. Uncle Matt hadn't wanted to leave his money to a dog and cat hospital or a scholarship fund for underprivileged spastics, but he detested all his relations just as severely as they had all detested him. Except me. So it seems that Uncle Matt took an interest in me, studying me from afar, and decided that I was a loner like himself, cut off from the rotten family and living my own life the way I wanted. I don't know why he never introduced himself to me, unless he was afraid that close up I'd turn out to be as bad as the rest of his relations. At any rate he studied me, and thought he sensed some sort of affinity between us, and in the end he left his money to me.

The source of the money itself was a little confusing. Eight years ago Uncle Matt had gone off to Brazil with an unspecified amount of capital which he'd apparently saved over a long period of time, and three years later he'd come back from Brazil with over half a million dollars in cash and gems and securities. How he'd done it no one seemed to know. In fact, so far as my mother had been able to tell me over the phone, no one in the family had even known Uncle Matt was rich. As Mother said, "A lot of people would have treated Matt a heap different if they *had* known, believe you me."

I believed her.

In any case, Uncle Matt had spent the last three years living right here in New York City, in an apartment hotel on Central Park South. Twelve days ago he had died, had been buried without fanfare, and his will had been opened by his attorney, Marcus Goodkind. Among this document's instructions, it had commanded the attorney to complete all the possible legal rigmarole before informing me either of my uncle's death or of the bequest. "My nephew Fredric is of a sensitive and delicate nature," the will read on this point. "Funerals would give him the flutters and red tape would give him hives."

It had taken twelve days, and so far as I felt right now I wished it had taken twelve years. Twelve hundred years. I sat in this booth with Reilly, a hundredthousandaire waiting for a Jack Daniels on the rocks, and all I felt was sick and terrified.

And there was worse to come. After the belated arrival of our drinks, and after I'd downed half of mine in the first swallow, Reilly said, "Fred, let's get this business of the money straightened away. I've got some other things to talk to you about."

"Like what?"

"The money first."

I leaned forward. "Like where the money came from?"

He seemed surprised. "Haven't you figured that out yet?"

"Figured it out? I don't get you."

"Fred, have you ever heard of Matt 'Short Sheet' Gray?"

The name rang a faint distant bell. I said, "Did Maurer write about him?"

"I don't know, he might. Midwest con man, over forty years. Spread a swath of receipts across the middle of the country as thick as fallen leaves in October."

I said, "My uncle's name was Matthew Grierson."

"So was Short Sheet's. Matt Gray was what you might call his professional name."

I reached unsteadily for my drink. Though it was half gone I still managed to slop some on my thumb. I drank what was left, licked my thumb, blinked at Reilly, and said, "I've inherited three hundred thousand dollars from a con man."

"And the question is," he said, "where's a good safe place for it."

"From a con man," I said. "Reilly, don't you get it?"

"Yeah yeah," he said impatiently. "Fred, this is serious."

I chuckled. "Talk about casting your bread on the waters," I said. I laughed. "A con man," I said. I guffawed. "I'm inheriting my own money back," I said. I whooped.

Reilly leaned across the table and slapped me across the face. "You're getting hysterical, Fred," he pointed out.

I was. I took two pieces of ice from my glass, put one in my mouth, and held the other against my stinging cheek where Reilly had given me his Irish hand. "I suppose I needed that," I said.

"You did."

"Then thanks."

The waitress came over, looking suspicious, and said, "Anything wrong here?"

"Yes," Reilly told her. "These drinks are empty."

She picked up the glasses, looked at us suspiciously some more, and went away.

Reilly said, "The point is, what are you going to do with the money?"

"Buy a gold brick with it, I suspect."

"Or the Brooklyn Bridge," Reilly agreed gloomily.

"Verrazano Narrows Bridge," I said. "Only the newest and most modern for my money."

"Where's the money now?" he asked me.

"The securities are in a couple of safe-deposit boxes, the gems are in the Winston Company vault, and Uncle Matt had seven savings accounts in different banks around town. Plus a checking account. Plus he owned some property."

The waitress brought our fresh drinks, looked at us suspiciously, and went away again.

Reilly said, "The securities and gems are all right where they are. Just leave them there and have your lawyer switch the paperwork over to you. The cash we'll have to work out. There's got to be a way to keep you from getting your hands on it."

I said, "There was something else you wanted to talk to me about."

"You haven't had enough to drink yet," be said.

"Tell me now," I said.

"At least drink some of it," he said. "You'll spill it all over yourself."

"Tell me now," I insisted.

He shrugged. "Okay, buddy. A couple of people from Homicide are coming to see you at your home at four o'clock this afternoon."

"Who? Why?"

"Your Uncle Matt was murdered, Fred. Struck down with the well-known blunt instrument."

I poured cold Jack Daniels in my lap.

5

HALF AN HOUR later, as I walked homeward through Madison Square Park, a girl with marzipan breasts flung herself into my arms, kissed me soundly, and whispered in my ear, "Pretend you know me!"

"Oh, come *on*," I said irritably, "how much of a fool do you think I am?" I pushed her roughly away.

"Darling!" she cried bravely, holding her arms out to me. "It's so good to see you again!" Panic gleamed in her eyes, and lines of tension marred her beautiful face.

Could it be real? After all, strange things *do* happen. And this was New York City, with the United Nations just a few blocks away. For all I knew, some sort of spy ring could—

No! For once in my life I had to remain the skeptic. And if this wasn't the opening shot of a variation on the badger game, I wasn't the good old Fred Fitch known and loved by grifters from coast to coast. ("After all," as Reilly had once said, "if they don't have songs about you, Fred, it's only because they don't sing.")

I said, "Young lady, you have made a mistake. I've never seen you before in my life."

"If you don't help me," she said rapidly under her breath, "I'll tear my clothes and swear you attacked me."

"In Madison Square Park? At ten minutes to one in the afternoon?" I gestured at the hordes of lunch-munching office workers, pigeon-feeding widows, and auto-hypnotic retirees filling the benches and paths around us.

She looked around and shrugged. "Oh, well," she said. "It was a good try. Come on, Fred, let's go have a drink and talk it over."

"You know who I am?"

"Of course I know who you are. Didn't your Uncle Matt talk about you all the time? How he used to dandle you on his knee when you were no higher—"

"I never met Uncle Matt in my life," I said. "That one wasn't even a good try."

She got very irritated, put her hands on her hips, and said, "All right, smart guy. Do you want to know what's going on or don't you?"

"I don't." Although, of course, I did. The other half of gullibility is curiosity.

She stepped closer to me again, so close the marzipan nearly touched my shirtfront. "I'm on your side, Fred," she said softly. She began fingering my tie. Watching her fingers, looking both little-girlish and sexy, she murmured, "Your life's in danger, you know. Powerful interests in Brazil. The same ones who murdered your Uncle Matt."

"What's your part in all this?"

She looked quickly around and said, "Not here. Come to my place tonight—160 West 78th. Smith. Be there at nine."

"But what's it all about?"

"We can't be seen together," she said. "Too dangerous. Tonight at nine." With which she spun away from me and walked briskly off toward Madison Avenue, her skirt twitching about her legs as she walked. Even the retirees on the benches roused themselves from their stupor enough to watch her walk by.

I murmured to myself, "160 West 78th," committing the address to memory. But then I shook my head, angry with myself; I was on the verge of falling into another trap. Forcing determination, I walked on southward, met with no further incidents, and found waiting on my doorstep as brassy a blonde as I ever want to see. If the other one had been made of marzipan, this one was made of pillows encased in steel. She looked like the model for all those cartoons about tough-looking broads being led into paddy wagons.

She'd been leaning against my door, arms folded—probably running through a few choruses of *Lili Marlene*—but when I arrived she straightened up, put her hands on her hips—that's two women who'd faced me that way in fifteen minutes—and said, "So you're the nephew, huh? You don't look like much."

"Don't start," I told her. "Whatever you're up to, I'm on the alert."

"I bet you look a lot like the milkman," she said. "I told Matt you were nothing but a fruit, but he wouldn't listen to me."

"A what?"

"A fruit," she said. "A fig. A fuzzy peach. An apperycot."

"Now, look—"

"You look," she said, and opened a patent-leather black purse and handed me a letter. "Read that," she said.

My name was written on the envelope in a scrawling and shaky masculine hand. I took the letter and turned it around without opening it and said, "I suppose inside here there's a note purporting to be from my Uncle Matt."

"Purporting? What kind of word is that? You been seeing that fag lawyer?"

"You mean Goodkind?"

"That's the one. And never mind purporting, that letter's the jake."

"I'll do you a favor," I said. "I won't even open this letter. You just take it back and go on about your business. I won't turn you over to the police, and we'll just call it even."

"You're a sweetheart," she told me. "You're a goddam prince. Read the letter there while I find my violin."

"I'm not going to read it," I said, "and if I did read it I wouldn't believe it."

She looked at me with a very cold eye, and continued to stand in front of my door with arms akimbo. "Is that right?" she said.

"That's right," I said, expecting her any instant to go into a crouch and start throwing left jabs.

Instead, she pointed a scarlet-tipped finger at me and said, "Let me tell you something, honey. It'll take a better man than you to pull a fast one on little Gertie. You just better wise up."

"Little Gertie? Is that supposed to be you?"

"Oh, you are a one," she said. "Read the damn letter and quit fooling around."

"You really want to go through with this, do you?"

"Read the letter."

"All right. Excuse me one minute. Just step aside, there, I want to unlock the door."

She stepped aside, I unlocked the door, and we went into the apartment. "Oh, isn't this sweet," she said, looking around the living room. "Of course, it could use the masculine touch."

"Well, you'd be the one to give it," I said, and went over to the telephone.

She watched me for five seconds of surprise, and then she barked with sudden laughter, saying, "Well, well, he's got a little sting in his little tail, hasn't he?" She tossed her patent-leather purse on the sofa—the sofa cringed away from it—and said, "You got anything to drink in here? I mean, besides peach brandy."

"You won't be staying that long," I said, and began to dial Reilly's office number.

"Don't make a complete horse's ass of yourself, honey," she said, strolling around the room and grimacing at my paintings. "Call Goodkind first and ask him about me. Gertie Divine, the Body Secular." She raised her arms above her head, half-turned toward me, and did a bump that caused a sonic boom.

She seemed so sure of herself. And yet, didn't they all seem sure of themselves? Hadn't the one-armed man, and Clifford, and this morning's phony cop?

Still, I'd already made one bad mistake, sicking Reilly on Goodkind. Was it possible that this was another? I stopped dialing Reilly's number, hung up, found the phone book, found Goodkind's number, and phoned him instead.

He was all oil. "Well, well, if it isn't my favorite client. Not to mention the man I'm about to sue for defamation of character. Heh, heh."

I said, "Have you ever heard of Gertie Divine?"

"What?" He sounded as startled as if I'd hit him with a cattle prod. "Where have you heard about her?"

"She's right here."

"Get her out of there! Don't listen to her, don't listen to a word she says! As your attorney, Fred, I urge you, I urge vou vehemently, get that woman out of there this instant."

I said, "I really wish you wouldn't call me Fred."

"Get her out of there," he said, a bit more quietly. "That's the long and the short of it, get her out of there."

"She says she's got a letter from Uncle Matt," I said.

That set him off again. "Don't read it! Don't even touch it! Close your eyes, close your ears, get her out!"

"Should I call Reilly?"

"For God's sake, no! Just get her out of there!"

"Will you tell me one thing?" I asked. "Will you tell me who she is?"

There was a brief pause while he got hold of himself, and then very quietly he said, "Why do you want to concern yourself with this woman, Fred? She isn't a good type of woman, believe me."

"I'd prefer it," I said, "if you didn't call me Fred."

"She's cheap," he said. "She's uneducated. She's lower class. She's not your sort at all."

"What did she have to do with Uncle Matt?"

"Uhhhhhh. Well, she lived there."

"On Central Park South?"

"The doormen hated her."

"Wait a second. You mean, she lived with Uncle Matt?"

"Your uncle was a different sort of man," he said. "Rough and ready, a sort of pioneer type. Not like you at all. Naturally, his taste in women differs from yours, and so the sort of woman he would—"

"Thank you," I said, and hung up.

She was seated on the sofa, legs crossed, one arm stretched out across the top of the sofa back. She was wearing black spike-heel shoes with straps halfway up the shin, nylons, a black skirt, and a white blouse with a frill at the throat. The blouse was coming out of the skirt at the side, revealing pale skin. She had also been wearing a black jacket, but that was now hanging on the doorknob.

She said, "So he gave you the word, did he?"

"He said I should get you out of here. I shouldn't listen to you. You're lower class."

"Is that right?" She bridled a bit, and said, "*He's* the one you shouldn't listen to, the shyster crook. He'd peddle his sister for candy bars and cheat her on the split."

That about summed up my own impression of Attorney Goodkind, but the fact that this woman—could she possibly be named Gertie Divine?— and I shared an enmity did not necessarily mean I could trust her. I said, "I suppose I might as well look at this letter."

"I suppose you might as well," she said. She picked it up from her lap and handed it to me. "While you're reading," she said, "how about a little hospitality?"

I didn't want to offer her a drink because I didn't want her to have an excuse to stay any longer than necessary, so I pretended not to have heard, turned my back, and opened the letter.

It was short, pungent, and difficult to read, being also in the same scrawled shaky masculine handwriting. It said:

Nepheu Fred,

This will interduce Gertie Divine, who used to headline at the Artillery Club in San Antonio. She has been my faithful companion and nurse, and she is the best thing I got to pass on to you. You keep her happy and I give you a garantee she'll keep you happy.

Your long lost uncle,

Matt

I looked up from the letter and found myself alone in the living room. Then I heard a clink of ice cubes, and went out to the kitchen to find Gertie Divine making a screwdriver with tomorrow morning's orange juice. "You want something, gracious host," she said to me, "You can make it yourself."

I held the letter up. I said, "What does this thing mean?"

"It means I'm yours now, honey," she said. She picked her drink up and went off the other way. "Is this the bedroom back here?"

6

A FEW MINUTES after Gertie Divine went out to the supermarket there was a tentative tapping at my door, and when I opened it Wilkins from the second floor was there, lugging an ancient scuffed black suitcase all done up with broad leather straps. He set the suitcase down, puffed, shook his head, and said, "Not as young as I used to be."

There didn't seem to be anything to say to that. Besides, my head was still full of the problem of Gertie Divine, and what was I to do with her when she came back. If she came back. Anyway, I simply stood there and looked at Wilkins and his suitcase and continued to think about Miss Divine.

Wilkins was all in blue, as usual; one of his old Air Force blue shirts and a blue ink-stained right hand. After puffing a while longer and shaking his head some more, he finally said, "Like to see you, my boy. Like to take a minute of your time."

"Certainly, sir," I said, though I wasn't certain at all. "Come on in. Here, let me take that—"

But before I could get to the suitcase he'd swooped onto it himself, grasping its ancient handle and lifting it out of my reach. "S'all right," he said hastily, like the hero of embezzlement movies when a redcap has offered to carry the bag of swag, "I'll take it myself."

In order to carry the suitcase at all, he had to lean far over in the opposite direction, so that he stood like a number 7, in which position he could just barely walk, clumping one foot forward at a time and swiveling his whole body with each step. Thus he came staggering into my apartment, looking as comic and deformed as a Beckett hero.

In the center of the living room he finally set the suitcase down again, and proceeded to puff some more. He also wiped his hand across his forehead, using the ink-stained hand, leaving above his brows the cartoonist's triple streak representing speed, so that he now reminded me of an ancient and wizened Mercury.

Hospitality seemed required of me, I had no idea why, so I said, "Uh, would you care for a drink?"

"Alcohol? No, no, thanks, I never touch alcohol. My late wife broke me of the habit thirty-seven years ago. Thirty-eight, come September. Wonderful woman."

"How about some coffee?"

He cocked a quizzical brow at me. "Tea?" he asked.

"Of course," I said. "No trouble. I'll just be a minute, take a seat there."

I went to the kitchen to make the tea, and there I could get back to my interior monologue about Gertie Divine. She had apparently moved in, though not exactly with bag and baggage, and so far as I could tell she intended to stay here. What she intended the arrangements to be I could only guess, but I thought the guess a good one, and the prospect a bad one.

But what was I to do? She just *assumed* everything; she marched cheerfully along without the faintest thought that someone else might not agree with her plans. Like searching my kitchen, announcing I had no food at all worthy of the name, and then snapping her fingers at me and saying, "Give me ten bucks, I'll go to the store."

Had I argued? Had I refused? Had I asked her who she thought she was? No. What I'd done was take out my wallet, give her the ten-dollar bill the bogus cop hadn't taken, and open the door for her when she left, patent-leather purse swinging from her forearm.

I had brave thoughts about refusing to let her in when she returned, I had bittersweet thoughts about her running off with my ten dollars and not returning at all, but in my heart I knew what was going to happen. She was going to come back with a double sack of groceries, she was going to order me to put them away while she ripped down the curtains in my living room, and I was going to put those awful groceries away.

Ah, well. In the meantime there was Wilkins. I made us both cups of tea, and when I brought them into the living room he was still standing beside his suitcase, exactly as I'd left him.

I said, "Why don't you sit down, sir?"

"Ah, tea!" he exclaimed, and took a cup from me, and stood there holding it, smiling brightly and falsely at me. "Heard about your good fortune," he said. "Want to offer my congratulations."

"You heard? How?"

"Phoned the authorities. What did you call it? Bunco Squad. Wondered how things had gone this morning."

"And they told you."

"Said I was neighbor, friend. Polite young man, most helpful."

"I see." I glanced at the suitcase. "And, uh, that?"

He looked down and smiled more broadly than ever, saying, "Life's work, my boy. Planned to show it you, never got around till now."

"Life's work? You mean, something to do with the Air Force?"

He smirked, and winked, and screwed his face up into remarkable expressions, and said archly, "You could say so, my boy, you could say so."

I had no idea what it was all about and with my distraction over Gertie Divine, I really didn't care. I carried my cup of tea over to my reading chair and sat down. Wilkins could either take the hint and sit down himself or he could go on standing guard over the suitcase indefinitely, the choice was up to him.

Wilkins watched me avidly, waiting for me to express burning curiosity about his damn suitcase, but when it finally became obvious to him that no burning was about to begin he abruptly went over to the rocker, sat down, put his tea on the marble-top table to his left, and said, "Really a nice place you've got here. Fixed up first-rate."

"Thank you very much."

"So difficult to get just the right furnishings these days."

"Yes, it is," I said.

"Specially on retired pay. Can't do much on short rations, can we?" He did a sort of barking laugh, picked up his teacup, and slurped down a huge swallow.

"It does take careful shopping," I said, wondering what on earth we were talking about and why we were talking about it. Meanwhile, in the middle of the room the suitcase had begun to grow. Not literally, of course, but in my mind. While Wilkins had been making such a fuss about it I couldn't have cared less about the thing, but now that we appeared to be talking about furniture or shopping or short rations or whatever it was, now that we weren't concerning ourselves with the suitcase at all, its enigmatic presence in the middle of the floor, all wrapped in leather straps with blackened buckles, was beginning to prey on my mind. What could be inside the thing, what could it contain? A model airplane? A set of spaceship plans? An H bomb?

"What a man really needs, these days," Wilkins was meanwhile saying, oblivious of my growing curiosity, "is a lot of money. Cash on the line. Of course, the best way to do it is your way, inherit the lot, don't lift a finger, let it fall your way. But those of us not so lucky, we've got to scrounge around, find a way to make ends meet and hope to build up for a windfall, something to put us on Easy Street."

Although this entire speech had been said in an open and friendly and chipper fashion, I suddenly found myself feeling guilty at having come so abruptly into unearned wealth. I said, "Well, I suppose it is different on a fixed income . . ."

"Not fixed for long," he announced, even more chipper than before. He nodded his head toward the huge suitcase. "That's what that's all about, of course. Make a killing."

"You said you wanted to show it to me," I said, as casually as possible, trying my best to cover my curiosity.

"Naturally," he said, beaming in a friendly fashion at me but not getting up from the rocker. "Any time at all. Any time you're free."

"Then there's no time like the present," I said. But an instant later I thought that had sounded too eager, and added, "If you don't have to hurry off anywhere, that is."

"Not at all, not at all. Happy to show you." Now at last he did get into motion, clinking the teacup back into its saucer, bounding to his feet, and dropping immediately to his knees in front of the suitcase. Wrestling the suitcase over onto its side and going to work undoing the leather straps, he said, "Young man like—you—be very interested I'm—sure. Thirty-one years—work here, thirty-one. Got it all worked—*there* it is!—all worked out."

With which he opened the top of the suitcase and looked up at me like the genie delivering treasure to Aladdin.

Treasure? The suitcase was full of paper, typewriter paper, six stacks of it filling the interior. The top page of each stack—and, I suspected, all the pages underneath—was completely covered with writing in ink in a tiny but neat hand. The ink was the same shade of dark blue as Wilkins' right hand.

I said, "What is it?"

"My book," he said reverently. He patted the nearest stack of papers. "This is it."

"Your book?" A sort of dread overtook me, and I said, "You mean, your autobiography?"

"Oh, no! Not at all, no. I didn't have that sort of career, not me, no. Quiet tour, quiet tour." He gazed down fondly at his stacks of paper. "No, this isn't fact at all. But based on fact, naturally, based on fact."

"A novel, then," I said.

"In a way, in a certain way. But the history is accurate." He squinted at me as though to demonstrate how accurate he'd been, and said, "To the finest detail. Facts almost impossible to find, all in here, all accurate. Studied the era, got it all down."

Still groping in the dark, I said, "It's a historical novel."

"In a manner of speaking," he said. Kneeling there beside his suitcase full of paper, he leaned toward me, braced one hand on his manuscript, and whispered, "It's a retelling of the campaigns of Julius Caesar, with the addition of aircraft."

I said, "I beg your pardon?"

"I call it," he said, "*Veni, Vidi, Vici Through Air Power*. Pretty good, eh?"

"Pretty good," I said faintly.

He peered at me shrewdly, squinting only one eye. "You don't see it yet," he said. "You think the notion's a little loony."

"Well, it's just new," I said. "I'm not used to it yet."

"Of course it's new! That's half the point. What makes it to the big time, ever ask yourself?"

"I'm not sure," I said.

"Originals! It isn't the imitations that get on the best-seller list, it's the new ideas, the original thoughts. Like this!"

He thumped his manuscript for emphasis and we both looked with surprise at the sound of the thud. I said, "Well, it does sound original."

"Naturally it's original!" Now he was warmed to his task; crouched forward, hands gesturing, he explained it all to me. "I've kept the historical facts, kept them all. The names of the barbarian tribes, strength of armies, the actual battles, kept everything. All I've added is air power. Through a fluke of fate the Romans have aircraft, at about World War I level. So we see the sort of difference air power makes by putting it in a historical setting where it wasn't there."

I said, "You mean, how it changes history and all?"

"Well, it doesn't change history that much," he said. "After all, Caesar won almost all the battles he was in anyway. So not much is different afterwards. But the *battles* are different. And the psychology of the commanders is different. I've got it all down here, all down here. Julius, now, Julius Caesar himself, he's really something. Quite a character, quite a character. Wait till you read it."

"You want me to read it?" But that didn't sound right, so I immediately said, "I'll be glad to read it. I'd like very much to read it."

"It's an exciting idea, that's why," he told me. "You look at it right off the bat, you say to yourself, that's loony. Loony idea. But then it gets to you, you see how it has to be. Rickety little airplanes coming over the hills into Gaul, dropping spears and rocks—"

"They don't have guns?"

"Of course not. Gunpowder wasn't invented till a long time after that, long time. What I'm keeping here, I'm keeping accuracy. Aircraft is all they've got."

"But," I said, "if they have airplanes, that means they have the internal combustion engine. And gasoline. And refined oils. And if they've got all that, they'd just about have to have everything else, all the things we've got right now. Automobiles. Elevators. And bombs, too, maybe even atomic bombs."

"Don't worry about that," he said, smiling, sure of himself, and he patted his manuscript again. "It's all in here, all worked out in here."

I said, "Have you got a publisher?"

"Publisher!" Sudden rage flushed his face dark red, and his hands closed into fists. "Blind!" he shouted. "Every last one of them! Either they want to steal a man's work, or they don't see the potential. Potential, that's the word, and they don't see it. Stick with the tried and true, that's all they know. A man comes along with something really new, really different, really exciting, they don't know what to do with it."

"They've been rejecting it?"

"Went to one fellow," he said more quietly. "Said he'd publish it. Some sort of cooperation thing, I pay the expenses, printing costs and all that, he publishes it and sends the copies around to the bookstores. I don't know, I didn't think that was how they worked it, but he says so. Showed me a lot of books he published that way. Looked good, some of them, nice job, bright colors on the front, good paper, nice printing. Never heard of the books, though. That worries me. Of course, I'm not a reader, not that much, not outside my specialty. You, now, you probably heard of all of them. Some, anyway."

"I don't do much reading myself," I said. "Contemporary reading. Most of my reading is research."

"Like myself," he said happily. "Two of a kind, we are." He smiled at me, then smiled at his manuscript. "Done now," he said.

"That's good," I said.

"Fellow said all the big names started out that way," he said, gazing off into the middle distance. "Publishing their own books, going in with fellows like him. D. H. Lawrence, he says. James Joyce. All sorts of big names."

"It could be," I said. "I really don't know that much about literary history."

"Naturally it costs a few thousand dollars," he said. "And then more after that, for the publicity. You don't get anywhere in this world today without publicity, believe you me. Got my own ideas for publicizing this book. Ad copy to knock your eye out, put it right in the *New York Times*.

Papers all over the country. Get the message across to the reading public."

"That sounds expensive," I said, feeling tremors of a premonition.

"Takes money to make money," he said. "But think of the profits. Book sales, that's only the beginning. Foreign publishers. Movies, there's bound to be a movie in this. Got a suggested cast list here, Jack Lemmon for the young Julius Caesar, Barbara Nichols—got it right . . ." He began rooting around among the stacks of manuscript, without success, until he said, "Oh, here's this. Cover. Rough idea."

He held toward me a sheet of paper containing a drawing of sorts, also done in the inevitable dark-blue ink. Two lines of lettering across the top, done shakily in a style reminiscent of the Superman logo, read:

VENI, VIDI, VICI

THROUGH AIR POWER

"That's just a rough sketch," Wilkins told me unnecessarily. "I'm no artist. Have to hire someone to do it right."

He seemed to know his limitations; anyway, he was right about not being an artist. I couldn't for the life of me figure out what the drawing was supposed to be. It contained any number of lines, some straight and some curved, some long and some short, most crossing several others, but what they were supposed to represent I couldn't begin to guess. Could this possibly be a rickety biplane coming over the hills into Gaul? There was no way to tell. I very nearly turned the sheet upside down, to see if it made any more sense that way, but stopped myself in time, knowing it would surely insult Wilkins, who would think I'd done it deliberately to make fun of his drawing ability.

I said, "I don't seem to be able to—this doesn't—"

"It's Caesar and his staff," Wilkins explained, "standing beside one of the airplanes." He was still kneeling there, beside his suitcase, and now he clumped over to me on his knees and began pointing at various scawls on the sheet, saying, "There's the plane," and, "There's Julius," and, "There's one of the loyal Goth commanders."

There was nothing to do but nod and say, "Yes, of course. Very nice." Which is what I did.

When we were done looking at the drawing, Wilkins took it back, clumped over to his suitcase again, and returned it to its spot somewhere in the middle of the manuscript. Doing so, not looking at me, he said, "What I need now, naturally, is financing. Split the profits fifty-fifty with the right man. Kindred spirit, money to invest. Fellow at the publishing house does the printing, distributing, simply for cash, no percentage of profits. I do the book, ad copy, all publicity, appearances, *Tonight Show*, et cetera, take fifty per cent. Third fellow finances, gets it started, sits back, gets fifty per cent."

I was beginning to feel very nervous. Wilkins was by no means a con man, he wasn't trying here to cheat me out of any money, but it was by now patently obvious he wanted me to invest in the publication of his novel, and I had no idea how I could possibly refuse him. What could I say? Any refusal at all would be an aspersion on the novel, and that would be insulting.

Actually I liked Wilkins, liked his ink-stained appearance, his offbeat way of speaking, his neat and mouselike air of self-containment. I didn't want to hurt his feelings, didn't want us avoiding each other's eyes during chance meetings by the mailbox.

Besides, what did I know about publishing, or novels? Though it did seem unlikely that Wilkins had actually written a best seller, think how many best sellers there have been that must have looked at least as unlikely beforehand. But the right people got behind them and pushed, the time was right, *something* was right, and there you are. And with publicity, a strong, well-financed ad campaign, Wilkins just might have something after all.

But I had to be sensible about it. After all, I had money now, a great deal of money, and if I was ever going to learn to be alert about money, this was the time. It was true that Wilkins wasn't a con man. But that didn't necessarily mean his novel wasn't a gold brick.

The thing for me to do, before even considering an investment, was talk to this publisher he had in mind, see what the man said, what he thought the prospects were. Always go to a specialist in the field, that's the rule.

I said, "Have you signed any contract with this publisher yet?"

"Well, it can't be done," he said, "without the guarantee of cash. Chap has his own expenses, after all, he can't just go around signing contracts with every crackpot walks into the office. A man has to show he's serious about it, has to put the money on the line."

"You're supposed to see him again, is that it?"

"We left it open," Wilkins said eagerly. "I'm to call if I get a fellow to go in with me."

"I suppose the thing to do—" I started, and there came a sudden loud knocking at the door. "One minute," I said to Wilkins, and went over and opened the door.

I'd completely forgotten about Gertie Divine, but in she came now with two sacks of groceries, just as I'd anticipated. "You owe me three bucks," she said, and came on into the living room, and looked with some surprise at Wilkins, kneeling there on the floor beside the open suitcase. "What's this?" she asked. "A prayer meeting?"

"My neighbor, Mr. Wilkins," I said. "Mr. Wilkins, this is, uh, Miss Divine. She was a friend of my uncle."

Still holding the sacks of groceries, she gazed down at Wilkins and said, "What's that you got there, Pop, the minutes of the last meeting?"

Wilkins abruptly shut the lid of the suitcase and said to me, "Can she be trusted?"

Gertie met his suspicion with an equal dose of her own. Turning around, peering at me from between the grocery bags, she said, "What's this geezer got in mind, Fred?"

Wilkins answered her, saying frostily, "Mr. Fitch and I are in partnership. It's a confidential matter at the moment."

"Oh, is it?"

I said, "Mr. Wilkins has written a novel—"

"And he wants it published," she finished. "And you're supposed to spring the geetus to some vanity house."

I blinked. "Vanity house?"

"When you write a stinking book and nobody wants it," she said, "you go to a vanity house and they soak you for whatever you got. I had a girl friend once, she did this exposé, The Real True Life of a Stripper, called *The Shame of the Ecdysiast.* Cost her sixty-five hundred bucks to get the thing published, sold eight hundred copies, got one stinking review. And they hated it."

Frozen-voiced and frozen-faced, Wilkins said, "The gentleman I have been in contact with happens to be president of a respectable old-line firm, they publish a full line of—"

"Crap." She looked at me, made a motion of her head toward Wilkins, and said, "Throw the old bum out."

"Now, see here," said Wilkins, getting creakily up from his knees.

"Never mind," Gertie told me. "Just hold these." She dumped the two sacks in my arms, turned around, grasped Wilkins by the arm, and walked him briskly to the door. As he went by me I saw him looking absolutely blank with astonishment, an astonishment that kept him speechless until he was already out in the hallway, where he managed to wail, "My manuscript!"

"Coming up," Gertie told him. Back she came, gathered up the suitcase as though it were a six-pack of beer, carried it to the hallway, and heaved it out the door. I seemed to hear a repeated and receding series of thumps, as though something heavy were falling down stairs. I seemed also to hear a fluttering sound, as though from the beating of many tiny wings. I know I heard, before Gertie slammed the door, Wilkins give vent to a cry of despair.

I stood there knowing I should do something about this, stop Gertie, help Wilkins, assert myself, but all I did was stand there. And it wasn't simply cowardice, though that was a part of it. It was also relief, the knowledge that the decision about Wilkins' novel had been taken out of my hands. It wouldn't have been possible for me to say no to Wilkins, though in the back of my mind I had known all along I should say no to him, and it was with great relief and guilty pleasure that I permitted Gertie to wrest the decision out of my hands.

Gertie came back into the living room, brushing her hands and looking pleased with herself. She looked at me, stopped, put her hands on her hips, and said, "What are you doing, standing there? Put the goods away."

I said, plaintively, "You won't tear down my living-room curtains, will you?"

"Why the hell should I do something like that?"

"God alone knows," I said, and went off to the kitchen to put the groceries away.

7

WHAT WITH ONE thing and another I'd completely forgotten Reilly's having told me about the visit I would be getting from Homicide, so when someone knocked at my door at four o'clock my first impulse — since I believed it was probably Wilkins with a shotgun — was to ignore it.

Unfortunately — or maybe fortunately — my impulses no longer mattered around this place. As I sat there in the living room, trying to assemble the jigsaw puzzle of my mind, Gertie came striding through from the kitchen, carrying a sharp knife speckled with celery in her right hand, and opened the door before I could think of how to stop her.

God knows what the detectives thought, having the door opened to them by a woman with a knife in her hand. But they recognized her, so I suppose that cut short their shock. In any case, I heard a masculine voice say, "We'll, if it isn't Gertie. You part of the inheritance, honey?"

"That's just what I am, Steve," she said. "You boys here on business?"

"Official is as official does," said the voice known as Steve.

"Then come on in," said Gertie, and stepped back to allow into my home two men who looked almost exactly like the phony cop who'd worked the counterfeit con on me this morning.

Gertie said to me, "Here's Steve and Ralph, a couple of dicks." Motioning at me, she told them, "That's Fred Fitch, Matt's nephew. I suppose he's the one you want to see."

"You're the one I want to see, Gertie," said Steve, as roguish as a bulldozer, "but Fred here is the one I want to talk to."

"I got dinner on," she said. "You boys will excuse me."

"For almost anything, Gertie," said Steve, laying his gallantry on with a trowel.

She gave him an arch grin and walked out, and Steve turned to me, his manner suddenly becoming Prussian. He said, "You are Fredric Fitch?"

"That's right," I said. I got to my feet and said, "Would you like to sit down?"

They promptly sat down, the both of them, and then I sat down again and began to feel very foolish. I said, "Uh, Jack Reilly told me you'd be coming to see me."

"We got a report," Steve told me. "As we understand it, you didn't know about this bequest you got until today, is that it?"

"That's right," I said. "Well, no, not exactly. I heard about it yesterday, but I didn't believe it until today."

"That's kind of a shame," Steve said, straight-faced. "Knocks you out of being our number one suspect."

Ralph, speaking for the first time, explained, "You see, you've got the best motive we know about."

"*Only* motive we know about," said Steve.

"So naturally," said Ralph, "we're disappointed about you not knowing about the inheritance in advance."

"And naturally," said Steve, "we'd like to bust that story if we could, because then we could have our number one suspect back."

Feeling the faint flutter of butterfly wings in my belly, I said, "You don't really suspect me, do you?"

"Well, that's just it," said Steve. "We can't, can we?"

"It's not having the choice," Ralph explained, "that's what bothers us so."

"And of course," said Steve, "there are what you might call weird elements to the case."

"Which we don't like either," said Ralph.

"Weird elements make us nervous," said Steve.

I said, "I don't know what you mean, weird elements."

Steve said, "According to our information, you never met your Uncle Matt, is that right?"

"That's right."

"Never even heard of him, in fact."

"That's right."

"Yet he left you almost half a million bucks."

"Three hundred thousand," I corrected.

"Before taxes," he said. "Half a million before taxes."

"Yes."

"To a nephew he'd never met, a nephew that didn't even know he existed."

"That's right," I said.

"That strikes us," Ralph explained, "as a weird element."

"Then there's this business about not telling you about the inheritance until a couple weeks after the old guy's dead. Right in the will it says this." Steve spread his hands. "That's also what we like to call between ourselves a weird element."

"Not to mention Gertie," said Ralph.

"Exactly," said Steve. "Here you have this old guy dying of cancer, he's got about as much get up and go as a wet noodle, and yet he—"

I said, "Dying?"

"Isn't that something?" said Ralph. "One foot in the grave already and the proverbial other one on a banana peel, and somebody has to hurry him along."

"I didn't know about that," I said.

"So that's another element of the sort we call a weird element," said Steve. "Bumping a guy going in a day or two anyway. Not to mention Gertie, like Ralph said."

I said, "Was he really that close to death? A day or two?"

"He's been that close the last five years," Ralph told me. "That's what his doctor says. He was down in Brazil, Matt Grierson was, and he found out he had cancer, and he came home to die."

"Not to mention Gertie," said Steve. "Except I think maybe it's time we did mention Gertie."

I said, "What about her?"

"That's what your uncle picks for a nurse," said Steve. "Gertie Divine, the Body Secular."

"Was she really a stripper?" I asked.

Steve was surprised at me. "Certainly," he said. "I seen her myself, over in Passaic, not so many years ago. And you ask me, she's still got the old pizzazz."

Ralph said, "Steve's had the hots for Gertie ever since we come on this case."

"Longer," Steve's said. "Since Passaic. But anyway, that isn't the point. The point is a terminal cancer patient, what the doctors call a terminal cancer patient, and an old bozo to boot, that's what he picks for his nurse. Then he gets bumped and his nephew gets all his loot, and when we come around for a nice talk with the nephew, who's here? Gertie. There's another weird element, what we think of around the station house as a weird element."

Ralph said, "How long have you known Gertie, Fred?"

I wanted to call him Ralph, I really wanted to call him Ralph. I wanted to start my answer with Ralph and end my answer with Ralph and put Ralphs in here and there in the middle of the answer, and answer only in words which were anagrams of Ralph. But I'm a coward. I didn't even call him Ralph once. I said, "I just met her today. She was here when I came back from the lawyer's."

They blinked at me, in unison. Steve said, "You mean, she just walked in? Cold?"

"Not cold, Steve," said Ralph.

"All right," conceded Steve, "not cold. But just walked in. You never saw her before."

"Let me show you something," I said, and got to my feet.

"I'd be delighted to see it," said Steve. "We both would."

"Delighted," said Ralph.

I went over to the desk and took Uncle Matt's letter of introduction out of the pigeonhole I'd filed it in, and brought it to Steve, and handed it to him. He read it, and grinned, and said, "Now, isn't that something new." He handed the letter to Ralph. "Here's something entirely different, Ralph," he said.

Ralph read the letter. When he was done he said, "There's a thing I notice about this letter."

Steve said, "What's that, Ralph?"

"It doesn't seem to have a date on it," said Ralph.

"She just brought it here today," I said, somewhat defensively.

"I accept that," said Ralph. "What I wonder about, I wonder when he wrote it. You follow me?"

"Why don't we ask her?" I said.

Steve said, "I don't think that'll be necessary, Fred. Do you, Ralph?"

"Not at the moment," said Ralph.

With me standing up and then sitting down I felt better than before, and more sure of myself. I said, "If my uncle was dying anyway, and if he was hit with a blunt instrument, isn't it likely he was killed in a quarrel with somebody? Some sort of rage, no real motive at all."

"It is a possibility," said Steve. "I certainly do go along with you on that, Fred, what you bring up there is a possibility. And I believe we're doing some work along those lines already. Aren't we, Ralph?"

"Routine work along those lines," said Ralph. "That's what we're doing, yes."

"Of course, at the same time," said Steve, "I admit to you in all frankness and honesty I wouldn't mind turning up with somebody saw you and your Uncle Matt together six months ago. Or you and Gertie. Right, Ralph?"

"Help us considerably," said Ralph.

"I'm sorry," I said, "but I'm telling the truth."

"Oh, I don't doubt it," Steve said fatalistically. "But a fella can dream, can't he?"

Ralph said, "You wouldn't have anything you might want to tell us that we don't already know, would you?"

"About the murder?"

"That's the case we're working on, yes."

"I never heard about it myself till this afternoon, I don't know a thing about it. Only what Ralph told me and what you told me."

"And what Gertie told you."

"Gertie doesn't tell me a thing. At least, she hasn't yet."

Steve laughed. "A good old girl, Gertie," he said. He heaved to his feet, looking very strong and tough. "Don't let me hear about you giving her a bad time, Fred," he half-joked.

"I don't think that's the way it'll go," I said.

Ralph also stood up. "I guess we'll be going along," he said. "Any time you want to get in touch with us, call Homicide South. Or try through your friend Reilly."

"I will," I said. "If I have any reason to call."

"That's right," said Ralph.

As they headed for the door, Steve said, "Tell Gertie so long for us, Fred. Tell her she's still my girl."

"It do that," I said, and stood fidgeting from one foot to the other until they finally left.

The slamming of the door brought Gertie out of the kitchen, looking around, saying, "They're gone?"

"Steve said to tell you so long."

"Cops are bums," she said philosophically. Then she frowned at me, saying, "Sweetie, this place is a mausoleum. Haven't you got a record player?"

"I doubt you'll care much for my records," I said.

"Honey, I figured that out already, but like the fella says, music is better than no music at all. Put on some of your string quartets, will you?"

I put on Beethoven's Ninth, full volume. If it was rock and roll she wanted, it was rock and roll she was going to get.

8

THE NEXT FEW hours were for me a time of muted panic. How totally Gertie had made herself at home! All I could think about was bed, and what she thought the sleeping arrangements were going to be. Though I did not consider myself a prude, and though technically I was not a virgin (I mean my abstinence had now lasted so long I could be thought of having returned, at least honorarily, to virginal status), the notion of casually hopping into the sack with a stripper from the Artillery Club within a few hours of meeting her—or even within a few months of first meeting her, to be honest—was paralyzing. On the other hand, to refuse any woman, much less a woman with the blunt strength of Gertie, is an extremely delicate operation at which I have not had a whole heck of a lot of practice.

Not that Gertie's presence was all bad, not by a long shot. She'd saved me from Wilkins, for instance, and the more I thought about that episode the more it seemed to me I had been in the process of being conned after all, via remote control, by the fellow who had offered to publish Wilkins' book for him at a price.

Besides that, Gertie turned out to have a really unexpected genius at cookery, producing a dinner the like of which I hadn't eaten for years, if ever. The basic ingredients were steak and potatoes and broccoli and salad, but the extras turned these basics into so many variations on manna. I ate myself round-faced.

During dinner, to make conversation and thus to distract myself from my panic, I asked Gertie what she thought about Uncle Matt having been murdered, and if she had any idea who might have done it.

"Not a one," she said. "Nobody saw nobody, nobody heard a thing. I wasn't home when it happened and nobody else was around."

I said, "It's been almost two weeks. I guess the police must be stuck."

"Cops," she said, in offhand contempt, and shrugged her shoulders, as though to say what-do-you-expect?

I felt as though I should take some sort of interest in Uncle Matt's death, since he *had* given me over three hundred thousand dollars, but it was hard to concentrate with Gertie over there carving away on her steak with such gusto. Nevertheless, I managed to keep on the track, saying, "Do you suppose it might have been someone he swindled? You know, getting revenge."

"Matt was retired for years," she said, and filled her mouth with salad.

"Well, out of the past," I said. "Someone who finally caught up with him."

She held up a hand for me to wait, sat there chewing salad, swallowed, put the hand down again, and said, "You mean a mark? From like twenty years back?"

"Maybe," I said.

"Forget it, honey," she said. "If a sucker catches on while he's still in the store he might take a poke at you but not later on. That's the thing about suckers, they're *suckers*. They just go home and feel sorry for themselves, they don't go around tracking people down and bumping them off."

I felt my face getting red. She had described me so accurately that the next time I brought a forkful of potatoes up to my mouth I stuck the tines into my upper lip.

Meanwhile, Gertie was going on in a reminiscing sort of way, saying, "That's what Professor Kilroy used to say all the time, 'A sucker is a sucker.' It was like a philosophy with him."

"Professor who?"

"Professor Kilroy. Him and Matt was partners for years."

"Where's he these days?"

She shrugged. "Beats me. Probably still in Brazil. What's the matter, you don't like your food?"

I had put my fork down. "I'm full," I said. "It was delicious, but I'm full."

"What an appetite," she said in disgust. "Why'd I waste my time?"

We finished the meal with nectar reminiscent of coffee, and then I staggered to my reading chair in the living room, where I lolled for the next hour, digesting and trying not to think about the events yet to come tonight and holding this morning's *Times* in front of my face upside down.

Until, at about seven-fifteen, Gertie appeared before me with her black jacket on and her patent-leather purse dangling from her left forearm. "Put yourself out a little," she said. "Walk me to the subway."

I looked up uncertainly and said, "Where are you going?"

"Home," she announced. "You think I got nothing better to do than hang around here all the time?"

A feeling of such relief washed over me then that I very nearly tossed my *Times* into the air and shouted whoopee, refraining only for fear it might hurt her feelings. But to know that Gertie was leaving, that she considered somewhere other than this place home, that she did not intend to remain here permanently like Bartleby, there was good news indeed.

Smiling, I said, "I'll be glad to walk you, Gertie." I folded the newspaper, got out of the chair, put my jacket on, and we left the apartment.

I felt strangely comfortable walking along the sidewalk with Gertie, felt none of the embarrassment I'd anticipated on the way downstairs. We walked to Eighth Avenue in companionable silence, and up to 23rd Street, where the subway entrance was and where it belatedly occurred to me—as I may have mentioned before, the word *belatedly* is my capsule autobiography—to offer Gertie money for a cab instead.

She instantly overreacted. Putting her hand to her heart—a not easy thing for Gertie to do—she pretended to be on the verge of a faint, and cried, "Oh, the spendthrift! He throws it around like it was pianos."

I knew how to handle Gertie now, so I said, "Of course, if you'd feel more at home in the subway—"

Her answer was to put two fingers in her mouth and give a whistle that shattered windows as far away as the UN Building. A cab yanked itself out of traffic and stopped, panting, at our feet.

I handed Gertie a dollar, at which she looked as though she'd never seen anything so small before. Then she said, in weary disgust, "A Hundred-twelfth Street, big spender."

In some confusion, I handed her another dollar, saying, "Is that enough?"

"No more," she said "You'll spoil me."

I held the cab door for her, and after she got in I said through the window, "When will I see you again?" More in trepidation than anything else.

"Never," she said. "Unless you get my phone number."

"Oh," I said, and patted myself all over for paper and pencil, finding neither. (I rarely carry pen or pencil, as it makes it too easy for me to sign things.)

Finally the cab driver, who was probably Gertie's brother, or at least her cousin, leaned toward me with a filthy pencil stub and a gum wrapper in his outstretched hand, saying, "Here you go, Casanova."

I smoothed the gum wrapper out on the cab roof and copied down Gertie's number as she reeled it off to me with all the care of instructions being given to a retarded child: "University five—that's U N, you know—University five nine nine seven oh. You got it?"

She wouldn't take my word for it, but made me read it back to her. Then I put it in my wallet, stepped back up onto the sidewalk, and the cab driver called to me, "Hey, Willie Sutton!"

I bent and squinted at him. "Eh?"

"The pencil," he said.

So I took his pencil out of my pocket and gave it to him and at last they raced away uptown. I could—although I didn't want to—imagine the conversation between them as they traveled, and my ears burned in sympathy.

And what was this other feeling? Jealousy? Jealous of Gertie Divine (the Body Secular, let's not forget that) and a cab driver? I felt like taking out my wallet again and checking to see who I was.

That's why I was so distracted as I walked back home, and why I paid no attention to the things around me. I was thinking about Gertie, whose phone number was unexpectedly in my wallet, and I was wondering what I was going to do about that phone number in future.

I had been far from tranquil about the apparent arrangements up till Gertie's abrupt departure, but one thing could be said in their favor: I wasn't in charge. Whatever was happening or going to happen was completely out of my hands, which can be a really liberating feeling, particularly for a tongue-tied recluse.

But now all that had been changed. All at once everything was up to me. I had no doubt Gertie would never re-enter my life without a specific invitation from me, and that fact left me hip-deep in a quandary. Did I *want* to call her? And if I did, what on earth for?

These questions took about ninety-five per cent of my attention, leaving very little for the world around me. I did hear the backfire as I crossed 21st Street, but paid it no mind. And I heard the second backfire as I turned into 19th Street almost simultaneous with the sound of someone breaking glass nearby, but ignored that one as well.

The third backfire should have made more impression than it did, particularly since it was immediately followed by a *brrringgg* sound from a trash can in front of the building I was passing, but I paid it no more attention than the others, and so I was totally unprepared when a street urchin of about twelve came up to me, tugged at my sleeve, and said, "Say, mister. That car just took a shot at you."

I looked at him, my mind still full of Gertie. "What's that?"

"That car," he said, pointing down the street. "They just took a shot at you."

Assuming I was being kidded, I said, "Of course. Very funny."

"You think I'm lying? Take a look at the garbage can there."

Was he serious? I said, "Why?"

" 'Cause that's what they plugged," he said. "Take a look at the hole."

Suddenly I remembered the backfires, the sound of glass breaking, the ringing of the trash can. The boy was right, somebody was shooting at me!

While I was gaping at him, trying to encompass this incredible idea, he pointed down the street behind me and said, "Here they come again."

"What? Who?"

"Comere," he said urgently, grabbed my sleeve, and the two of us ducked into a cellar entranceway. "Keep cool," the boy advised me. "They didn't see us come in here."

I tried to see what was happening out in the street but it was difficult while at the same time trying to keep from being seen. Also, the street was lined with parked cars. Nevertheless, I did see the black car go slowly by, as ominous as the silence in the middle of a storm. I couldn't see who was driving or how many people were in the car, but it seemed to me the aura of menace around it was inescapable.

After they'd gone the boy said, "You want me to go get a cop?"

"No, that's all right," I said. "I live just a few doors from here." I got out my wallet, fished a bill from it without exactly knowing its denomination—I only knew it had to be either a single or a five—and in some embarrassment pressed it into the boy's hand, saying, "A small token of my esteem."

He took it casually and said, "Sure. They tryna keep you from testifying?"

"I don't think so," I said. "I'm not sure what they're doing."

"They're shooting at you," he said reasonably.

"Yes. Well, goodbye."

"See you around," he said.

I took the remaining half-block to my building at a dead run, went up the stairs to the third floor at the same breakneck speed, and stopped short at my door with the sudden thought: *What if they're in there?*

I stood indecisively in the hallway a minute or two, trying to think of some way to test for the presence of assassins in my apartment, but ultimately decided there was no way to test other than actually entering the apartment and seeing what happened. What finally emboldened me to do so was the thought that if they—whoever they were—had access to my apartment it was unlikely they would be driving around the city taking potshots at me from moving cars.

My supposition was correct; the apartment was as empty as I'd left it. After a quick search of all the rooms and all the closets I got on the phone and called Reilly at home, but he wasn't there. So I tried him at Headquarters and he wasn't there either.

Now what? I wanted to report this to the police, of course, but on the other hand I felt a little foolish just calling up some strange policeman and saying, "Someone is shooting at me from a car." It would require so much explanation, and in fact, most of the explanation I wouldn't even be able to offer.

I thought of phoning Steve and Ralph, the Homicide detectives— it seemed to me very likely that the people shooting at me were the same ones who had killed my Uncle Matt—but there was just something so oppressive about that vaudeville team that I doubt I would have phoned them if there'd been an assassin in every closet in the place.

No, what I wanted was my friend Reilly. Let *him* tell the other police. I called him again at home, hoping against hope, but there was still no answer, so I returned disconsolately to my reading chair, sat down in it, and failed to read the *Times*.

Every five minutes between then and eight-thirty I tried Reilly again, and never did find him home. Then at eight-thirty, I remembered the girl who had approached me in Madison Square Park, the one who had warned me I was in danger and claimed to be on my side. I hadn't believed her on either count at the time, but now it seemed that at least the first half of her statement was true. If people were shooting at me, it seemed fair to say that I was in danger.

Could the second half also be true? Was it possible she *was* on my side? Was it possible she could tell me who was shooting at me and why?

Nine o'clock, she'd said, that was when I was supposed to meet her at her place tonight—160 West 78th, I'd remembered the address without wanting to.

Should I go? It would mean leaving here now, because to get there later than nine o'clock might be useless. But I hated to go up there alone, without Reilly, without at least talking it over with Reilly, telling him what had happened and asking him what he thought we should do about it.

I'll give him one last chance, I thought. I'll call him at home, and if he's there I'll tell him the whole story. But if he isn't there I'll go up to 78th Street myself and find out what's going on. Anything is better than just sitting here, twiddling my thumbs.

Naturally enough, he wasn't home.

Fine. Having made my decision, I was left with one other small problem; namely, how to leave this building and this neighborhood without being shot at any more. After all, they couldn't reasonably be expected to go on missing forever.

Disguise myself? No. There were a total of three tenants in this building, and any watcher would readily guess who I had to be no matter what disguise I chose for myself.

Just bolt out the door and down the street, pell-mell? No again. A car can outrun a man every time. And if I were to betray the fact that I was now aware of them, they would throw aside subterfuge and attack much more openly.

The back way? There was a small garden behind the building, Mr. Grant's domain, enclosed by high fencing on three sides. I wasn't entirely sure, but it seemed to me that if one could get over that fence at the rear, it should be possible to get through the building behind this one and thus out onto the street one block away.

At any rate, it was worth a try. I changed to my black suit, put a dark sweater on under the jacket, and went downstairs to knock on Mr. Grant's door.

Didn't he ever do anything but eat? This time he had a chicken leg in his hand, as well as the inevitable napkin tucked into his collar. I said, "I'm sorry to interrupt you again, but I wonder if I could go out your back door."

He was so bewildered I felt sorry for him. He said, "My back door?" He turned around, as though looking for it.

"It would take too long to explain," I said. "It really would. But if you'd just let me go through your apartment and out the back door. . . "

"You mean, into my garden?"

"Well, through your garden. I want to go over the fence and into the building across the way."

"Across the way?"

"I promise to explain the first chance I get," I said.

I think he only stepped to one side, allowing me to enter, because it was easier than trying to understand me. He shut the door, then preceded me through his neat apartment to the rear door, unlocked and opened it, and stood aside again to let me out. As I stepped through he said, "You won't be coming back?"

"Not this way," I said. Which shows how little we know our own futures.

THERE WAS MORE than enough light, spilling from windows on all sides. I traversed the winding slate walk to the board fence at the far end of the garden, climbed up on a steel lawn chair there, hoisted myself the rest of the way up, and slid down the other side into a million rusting metal coils. Springs of some sort they were, attaching themselves to my feet or bounding off with mighty *sprongs* or merely clustering under me as I tried to regain my balance. There was nothing for it but that I should fall over, and so I did, with a crash and a clatter and a bi-di-*ding*.

I lay there unmoving, waiting for silence, which eventually arrived, to be immediately followed by the sound of a window being hurled open. A hoarse male voice shouted, "Shoo! Damn it, you cats shoo the hell out of there!"

I didn't move.

We both waited and listened for half a minute or so, and then he gave vent to a couple more half-hearted shoos and shut his window again.

It was impossible to move without sound effects. *Boing* under my left knee, *greeek* under my chest, *chinkle* in the vicinity of my right arm. With many a *plink* and *tunkle* I crawled away from the fence and the ubiquitous springs, until I was at last clear of all of them except those which had attached themselves to my belt and cuffs. These I removed, with muffled *brangs,* and got rather shakily to my feet.

I was in a much darker yard than Mr. Grant's, and one not nearly so well kept. Directly in front of me was the building I was headed for, with a barred window and a shut door at ground-level. Though lights were on in the upper windows, the ground floor was in total darkness.

It hadn't occurred to me before that I would probably have to go through an apartment in this building, that the physical setup would more than likely be similar to my own building, with the rear entrance only to a ground-floor apartment. But I was apparently in luck; from the absence of light, and the time only a little past eight-thirty, it seemed this apartment must be empty.

I had never burgled a door before, and wasn't entirely sure how to go about it. I began with this one by rattling the knob and proving to my own satisfaction that it was, like every other door in New York City, locked.

But then I noticed that one of the panes of glass in the door was broken, replaced—temporarily, I suppose—by a piece of cardboard. How securely could a piece of cardboard be fastened? I pushed on it experimentally, and it gave, being attached on the inside only by masking tape. I pushed it farther open, reached in, opened the door from the inside, and stepped cautiously into pitch blackness.

My only guide was the faint gray rectangle of the window. If I kept that always behind me, and if I moved with extreme care, it seemed to me I must sooner or later navigate the entire apartment and emerge at the front of the building. Slowly, therefore, I began to shuffle forward.

I had shuffled about six shuffles when I heard a creak. I stopped. I listened.

A light went on. Bedside lamp, directly ahead of me ten feet or so. Hand still touching the lamp switch, long bare arm leading my eye to the right, where a naked woman was sitting up in a double bed, staring at me with the blank stunned gaze of someone awakened by the incomprehensible. Beside her, farther from the lamp, the mound of a second person, still asleep.

But not for long. Neither taking her hand from the lamp nor her eyes from me, the woman began to pummel the mound with her other fist, crying, "George! George, wake up! A prowler, George!"

I was frozen. I was incapable of movement or speech, and so could neither escape nor explain. I just stood there, like Lot's wife.

The mound abruptly sat up, proving to be a man with a remarkably heavy jaw and a remarkably hairy chest. He didn't look at me at all. Instead, he looked at the woman and said, slowly and dangerously, "Who's this George?"

She looked at him. She blinked. She put her hands to her face. She said, "Oh, my God, it's Frank!"

I didn't wait for any more, since I'd suddenly found my feet capable once again of motion. To the right of the bed was a doorway. I ran to it and full tilt into a closet full of female clothing.

I backed out again, sputtering and beating off dresses, and found Frank gradually becoming aware of my presence, if not my identity. He looked at me, staggering past with a white blouse wrapped around my neck, and said, "George? This is George?"

My only chance was out the door I'd come in. Flinging the blouse at Frank, I spun out the door, across the yard in the direction of the fence and home, and back again into the Sargasso Sea of rusty springs. I flailed through these, and back there somewhere that window was flung up again and the hoarse male voice bellowed, "All right, cats, you asked for it!"

I attained the fence, but could do no more. I sagged against it, waiting for whatever was going to happen next. Behind me, in the doorway of the apartment I'd just left, Frank was standing buck-naked and shouting, "Come back here, George! Come back and fight like a man!" Meanwhile, the woman was tugging at him from behind and crying, "Frank, it's all a mistake, let me explain, Frank, please!"

Now another female voice suddenly cried, "Harry, you'll get the cops on us!"

The hoarse male voice roared, "Outa the way, Mabel, this time they're gonna get it!"

"Harry, don't!"

"Frank, please!"

"George, you bastard!"

From somewhere back there, something made a small sound. It sounded like pah. Near me a piece of metal went *ting*.

It happened again. First pah behind me, and then *ting* close by. And a third time. And a fourth time.

Pah-*ting*.

Pah-*ting*.

I didn't get it until there was a pah, and instead of a *ting* there was a sudden burning sensation in my right leg, just above the knee, as though I'd been stung by a wasp. Then I realized what was happening.

Harry was shooting at me with a BB gun.

Pah-*ting*.

I suddenly found new reserves of strength. Up and over the fence I went, clawing my way, and collapsed in a heap across the lawn chair on the other side.

After a minute or two I had my wind back sufficiently to get to my feet, remove the springs that had attached themselves to my clothing, toss them back over the fence—which set off a new paroxysm of fury back there—and limp on down the path to Mr. Grant's back door.

I knocked, and soon he opened the door an inch; looked at me with some astonishment, and said, "Are you coming back?"

"Change of plans," I panted.

He looked past me, in the direction of all the noise. Over there beyond his fence it sounded as though a war were going on: shouts and shrieks and clamoring. Mr. Grant said, mildly, "What on earth is all that?"

"Some sort of wild party," I said. "Nothing to do with us." I slipped past him into the apartment. "Thank you very much," I said. "I'll be going now."

When I left him, he was a very baffled man.

10

THERE WAS A black car double-parked across the street, its motor throbbing. I stood in the vestibule, in darkness, and watched it for a while without seeing it do anything but sit there and throb. A liveried chauffeur sat in semi-darkness behind the wheel, and black side curtains were drawn to hide the rear seat.

It was them, there was no question of it. They didn't know I'd finally become aware of them shooting at me before—or, that is, I'd finally been warned by a passing child—so they were waiting as bold as brass right in front of my door, expecting me sooner or later to come blithely out and down the steps and directly into a hail of gunfire.

Not a bit of it. I had to get out of here, and I was resigned to going out the front way, but something had to be done about that hail of gunfire.

I had one advantage. They didn't know that I knew that they were trying to kill me. With a little luck, plus the element of surprise, I might be able to get past them after all. Zip out the door, leap down the steps, race away along the sidewalk, be gone before they knew what was happening.

It sounded good, all right, but somehow I just wasn't doing it. Seconds ticked away forever, and I continued to lurk in the vestibule.

Until, looking far down the street to the right, I saw a police car coming, meandering along slowly the way they do, and I knew I was saved. They wouldn't dare shoot at me with a police car right next to them.

I tensed, I crouched, I closed my hand on the doorknob, I waited while the police car inched its way down the street and every nerve in my body slowly tied itself into a half-hitch. Until, until . . .

The police car approached the double-parked black automobile, started past it, came even with it . . .

And out the door I went, zip, according to plan. Down the steps, leap, and away along the sidewalk, race, and not a single shot was fired.

Also, it was a one-way street. They couldn't merely U-turn and come swooping after me, they would have to completely circle the block. With any luck, I could be in a cab and racing uptown long before they made it.

Of course, there's no such thing as a taxicab in New York City when you want one. That is, there are cabs, thousands and thousands of cabs, but they're all off-duty. They streamed by me in schools, in coveys, in congeries, every bloody one of them off-duty, while I waved my arms around like the signal-giver on an aircraft carrier.

At last there showed up a cab whose driver had apparently decided to work a second hour today. Into it I leaped, shouting, "Uptown! Hurry!" So up he dawdled to the next corner, where the light was red, and stopped there.

"These lights are set at twenty-two miles an hour, my friend," he said. "So that's the speed I'll hurry at, if it's okay with you."

"Whatever you say," I said, while simultaneously trying to hide myself from the world and look all around for the black car. I failed to see it, and I hoped it was failing to see me, and several weeks later the light changed and we began to crawl uptown at twenty-two miles an hour.

I was encouraged to see, when we turned onto 78th Street, that the only car that made the turn after us was a little gray Peugeot, driven by a woman in a huge floppy hat. As the Peugeot went on by us I paid the driver, left his cab, and hurried across the sidewalk and into the building.

Locked glass doors were in front of me, with a panel on the wall to their right containing nameplates and doorbells. But what was the name the girl had given me? I couldn't for the life of me remember.

Maybe if I looked at all the names, the right one would ring a bell. I ran my finger down the rows, looking at all the names . . .

Smith?

Could it possibly have been Smith? Surely no one would use the name Smith in a situation like this. And yet that was the only one that caught my attention at all. And it did seem as though I remembered her having used that name, giving me this address and then the name Smith.

Well. Obviously there was nothing to do but try. It was already ten minutes past nine, and getting later every second.

I pressed the button beside "Smith 3-B," and after a minute a metallic and vaguely female voice said through the grill above the nameplates, "Who is it?"

"Fitch," I told the grill. "Fred Fitch."

The door buzzed. I pushed it open and went into a long thirtyish lobby with the elevator at the far end.

The elevator was also on the ninth floor. I pushed the button and watched the numbers over the doors light slowly one after the other in reverse order. A while after the number 1 went on, the doors slid open and there was the elevator.

Apartment 3-B was to my right when I got off the elevator on the third floor. I rang its bell and the door immediately opened and standing there was the girl from Madison Square Park, wearing red canvas slacks and a sleeveless blouse in a kaleidoscope design. She was barefoot, and a highball glass in her right hand tinkled its ice at me.

"You're ten minutes late," she said.

"I had a little trouble," I said.

"Well, you're here," she said, "and that's the important thing. Come on in."

I entered a white hall, at the end of which I could see a portion of the living room. Miss Smith closed the door and said, "You're worth fifty bucks to me, do you know that?"

"What?"

"Come on along," she said, and preceded me along the carpeted hall to the living room.

There was nothing to do but follow. As she entered the living room she said to someone out of sight, "Okay, smart boy, pay up. You lose."

Something was wrong. I stepped hesitantly into the living room, ready to flee.

But it wouldn't do any good to flee. Reilly heaved his big frame up out of the sofa, put his drink down on the coffee table, and said to me in great disgust, "Okay, you silly bastard, explain yourself."

11

EXPLAIN MYSELF, HE said. Well, he also had some explaining to do, and so for a while the apartment was knee-deep in explanations, as I described to them my having been shot at and they told me what they'd had in mind in inveigling me up here.

It seems Miss Smith, whose first name was Karen, was a friend of Reilly's, and he'd put her up to this. They had been talking about me—my ears burned at the idea—and it had been Reilly's contention that the windfall I had just received would make me, at long last, cautious in my dealings with strangers. Karen Smith had insisted she could work her wiles on me, inheritance or no inheritance. Reilly had said that if she could do it—that is, if I was still the same incorrigible sucker I'd always been—he wanted to know about it. If Karen could talk me into coming to this apartment tonight, without telling me any truth other than her last name and address, Reilly would owe her fifty dollars. If she failed, she owed Reilly fifty dollars.

I believed them about this harebrained bet, because that's the sort of plot that just naturally springs up around me, but Reilly for a long time wouldn't believe me about the shooting. When finally he did come grudgingly around to accept it, he wanted to know why I hadn't reported it to the police. "I'm not the only cop in the world, you know," he said.

"You're the only cop in the world I know," I reminded him. "And I kept calling you, but you weren't home."

"So you thought you'd come up here."

"Well, Miss Smith had said—"

"Karen," she said, and smiled at me.

I smiled back at her. "Karen," I agreed. To Reilly I said, "She'd talked in the park there as though my life was in danger and she knew what it was all about, so I thought I'd come up and find out."

He sighed heavily and shook his head. "Let me give you a for instance, Fred. For instance, Karen is a gun moll in cahoots with the people that shot at you. So you come up here, and *they're* here."

"Well," I said. I looked helplessly at Karen. "I didn't think it could be like that," I said. "You just weren't that kind of girl."

She laughed and said, "Thank you, Mr. Fitch, thank you very much."

"Fred," I said.

"Fred," she agreed.

Reilly said, "Fred, that's just the kind of thing always gets you in trouble. When will you get it through your head that people aren't what they look like?"

"Sometimes they are," I said.

"Which times?"

I didn't have an answer, and Reilly was a little mad at me—the fifty dollars he owed Karen had something to do with that, I believe—so the conversation stalled there for a minute, with everybody looking at nobody, until Karen said brightly, "Let me get drinks for everybody. Fred?"

"Oh, Scotch, I suppose."

"Ice?"

"Please."

While she was away in the kitchen rattling ice-cube trays, Reilly said to me, "I don't suppose you got the kid's name."

I had no idea what he meant, and so said, "Who?"

"The kid," he said, not very patiently. "The one told you you'd been shot at."

"Oh. No, he didn't tell me. He was just a boy, one of the boys from the neighborhood."

He sighed again. "Fred," he said softly, "may I tell you how you should have handled this?"

"I wish you would."

"Then I will. You should have collared the kid and taken him straight to a phone and called your local precinct. The kid might have been able to describe the car. He might even have seen the people inside it."

"I don't think so," I said.

"You don't think so. In any case he was your witness. So you call the precinct, and when the officers arrive you tell them, 'This kid says some-body was shooting at me.' It's simple."

"It sounds simple," I admitted, "the way you say it. But I don't know, it just didn't seem to work out that way."

"It never does, with you," he said. He sighed, and shook his head, and heaved to his feet. "I'll make the call now," he said. "I don't suppose there's any detail you forgot to tell me, is there? Like the license plate of the car, for instance."

"Don't get sore at me," I said. "After all, you're a professional at this, I'm not."

"God knows," he said. He went away to another room to use the phone, and for a while I could hear him muttering and murmuring in there. Karen came back from the kitchen during this, carrying drinks, and the two of us sat in the living room and made small talk about the weather and television and so on while waiting for Reilly to come back.

I found that I liked Karen Smith very much. She was a stunningly beautiful girl, and normally I think stunningly beautiful girls have a way of cramping conversation on first meeting—not that it's *their* fault—but Karen was different. She had such an open manner, such easy humor, that it was easy to relax with her, as though we'd been casual buddies for years.

Reilly spoiled the mood, on his return, by being gruff and impatient, exactly as he'd been when he'd left. "They'll want to talk to you again," he said, coming in, and sat down next to Karen on the sofa.

I said, "Who? Those detectives?"

"Right. Call them in the morning and make arrangements. Early in the morning."

"I will," I promised.

He said, "The other thing is, you better find some place else to stay for a while."

"You mean, not go home?"

"They've got your place staked out," he said. "That's obvious. With any luck you've shaken them now, let's try and keep it that way."

"You think I ought to go to a hotel?"

"Some friend's place would be better," he said. "Somebody they wouldn't think of."

"If it's a friend," I said, "they'd think of it."

Karen said, "You could stay here, if you want. The sofa's comfortable."

"Oh, no," I said. "I wouldn't want to put you out."

"No problem," she assured me. "I have more space here than I need, we wouldn't get in each other's way at all."

"I'll stay in a hotel," I said. "That's all right. Thank you anyway."

Reilly said, "Wait a second, wait a second." He turned to Karen. "You sure it's okay?"

She spread her hands. "Why not? I work all day, half the time I've got dates in the evening, the place is empty practically all the time."

I said, "Really, I appreciate it, but—"

"Shut up," Reilly told me. He leaned closer to Karen, lowered his voice slightly, and said, "You know one thing it means."

She blushed, and smiled, and then we all knew the one thing it meant. She turned toward him and murmured, "There's still your place."

I was beginning to be embarrassed. "Uh," I said. "I'll stay at a hotel. I'd really rather stay at a hotel."

Reilly turned to me and said, "You would. Listen, Fred. Number one, nobody knows you even know Karen, so nobody will look for you here. Number two, you're already here, so you won't have to do any traveling out on the streets. Number three, if you're here Karen and I can both keep an eye on you."

I said, "You want me to stay?"

"I wouldn't say that, exactly," he said. "But I know it's best. So do it."

I looked at Karen. "Are you sure?"

"The place is yours," she said.

"Well. Thank you."

She got to her feet. "Shall I get you another drink?"

"I think you'd better," I said.

12

THE TWO DAYS I spent in Karen's apartment were among the oddest of my entire life. She did have a large place, as she'd said, but even a large apartment is a relatively small area when two people are living in it, and the first part of my stay was full of abrupt embarrassments, flashes of leg, confusions in the hallway, and excessive politeness on all sides.

The embarrassments began promptly on Saturday night, about half an hour after it had been decided I would stay there. Reilly and Karen began to look cow-eyed at each other, I began to get very much a fifth-wheel feeling, and when finally Reilly suggested to Karen that they "go out" for a while I was as relieved at the idea as they were.

After they left, of course, I felt a little eerie being alone in a strange apartment, and with some sheepishness I went around to every room and turned all the lights on. I spent a fruitless hour or so trying to figure out why anyone would want to kill Uncle Matt and me, and wondering why after two weeks the police couldn't seem to manage to solve the case. As boredom began to get a really good grip on me, I scrounged around the apartment until I found paper and pencil, then sat down in the living room and began to make up a crossword puzzle, something I hadn't done since high school. Back when I was fifteen and sixteen years old I actually sold a number of crossword puzzles to magazines specializing in that sort of thing. I still remember the definition of which at the time I was the proudest: "The poet's on the pumpkin." Five letters.

After a while I gave up the crossword puzzle, watched television instead, and ultimately went to sofa about midnight, falling asleep with less trouble than I'd anticipated.

And Karen, heels in hand and a trifle drunk, inadvertently woke me a little after two when she came in and switched on the living-room light before she remembered she had a house guest. Then, as long as I was awake anyway, and since she had a hankering to talk, we sat awhile and chatted, me in underwear and blanket and she in tight knit dress and stockinged feet.

She wanted to talk about Reilly, mostly, wondering how long I'd known him and what did I think of him and so on. "I can't help it," she told me. "I'm out of my mind for that man, absolutely off my head."

"Are you two going to, uh, get married?"

"Ah, well," she said, and looked tragic, and I knew I'd just made a bad mistake.

I tried to save the situation, saying, "Yes, I remember the first time I ever met Reilly, in the Bunco—" But it was too late; I'd pushed the button and I was going to get the recorded announcement whether I wanted it or not.

"Don't you know about Jack?" she asked me. Because she was tipsy, her speech had great precision in the middle but got fuzzy out around the edges. "Don't you know about his wife?" she asked.

"You mean he's married? Now? Already?"

"Separated. For years and years and years." She gestured, waving away hosts of years. "Separated, but no divorce." She leaned toward me, making her balance in the chair precarious, and whispered confidentially, "Religious problems."

"Oh," I said. "I didn't know that. Reilly never mentioned—but I guess he wouldn't—I mean, he doesn't—uhhh—it wouldn't come up, I suppose. Between him and me."

"Religious problems," she whispered again, and winked at me, and sat back in the chair. "So here I sit," she said. "Completely out of my skull over that man, and nothing to be done. Nothing to be done."

"That's too bad," I said. What else can you say to something like that at two in the morning when you've been awakened in a strange living room by a beautiful woman who's had too much to drink? And who isn't yours?

Well, we talked awhile longer, and then she staggered off to bed, and I disarranged myself on the sofa once again and slept poorly but dreamlessly until seven in the morning, when someone began to dent garbage cans in the areaway.

That was Sunday, the morning our ménage scaled undreamed-of heights of awkwardness. It seemed as though I couldn't turn a corner without running into Karen dressing or undressing or adjusting or bathing or scratching or burping, and it also seemed as though every time she lurched through a doorway I was on the other side just about to put the second leg of my pants on.

In the long run, though, this rotten morning was beneficial. After a couple of hours of it, we were so inured to one another's presence that by mutual unspoken agreement we just stopped getting flustered about it all. No more gulps, no more pardon mes, no more abruptly slammed doors. We relaxed with one another, and promptly the embarrassing situations themselves came to a stop.

After breakfast we made up a shopping list. I was going to be needing things—all sorts of things from socks to a toothbrush—and Karen thought it best if I kept out of sight, so we made up a list and she went shopping for me. The doorbell rang while she was gone, but I didn't answer it. It kept ringing and I kept not answering it. Finally it stopped, and when Karen came back in a minute later Reilly was with her. Reilly said to me, "What's the matter with you now? You deaf?"

"I was playing it safe," I said.

He grumbled.

I asked him if the police were getting anywhere, and how much longer he thought I'd have to stay here, and he told me grumpily he didn't think anyone in the world was getting anywhere with anything, and he supposed I'd be living in Karen's apartment the rest of my life. He then took Karen away with him—for a ride in the country, they said—and I was left to my own devices.

I had the apartment to myself again, and wandered around it with all the boredom I could muster. I read a *Cosmopolitan*, I read a Cheerios box, I read the medicine cabinet. I turned on the television set and switched back and forth for a while without finding anything. I stood at the living-room window and looked out at the gray brick walls and black windows facing me all around, looked down at the concrete areaway at the bottom with its array of dented garbage cans, looked up at the angular triangle of gray sky visible above the roofs, and wound up looking at my own pale reflection in the glass. Even that got dull after a while, so I went to the bedroom and opened the closet doors and poked through all the dresser drawers; not to be nosy, but just for something to do. Karen had what I would consider a lot of clothes. There was also a faint and musky perfume hovering over all her things, and it soon drove me back to the neuter corner of the living room again, where I set to work once more on the crossword puzzle, in which I found myself tending to use words I shouldn't use.

Karen came back at about one-thirty in the morning, arriving just as I was taking the second leg of my pants off. Since Reilly wasn't with her, since I was going to bed no matter what, and since we weren't worrying about that sort of thing any more, I continued to take my pants off, hung them over a chair, and said, "How are you?"

"Dreadful," she said, and began to weep buckets.

Well, what could I do? I went over and put my arms around her and consoled her, and there I stood in my shorts while Karen wept onto my shoulder and told me how she couldn't stand it any more, being *with* Reilly but not *of* Reilly, having to lead this double-life or half-life or whatever it was, and I said, "That's too bad," which seemed to be the only thing I ever said to her after sundown, and in a while she raised her tear-stained face and I kissed her.

It wasn't actually a long kiss, but it would do. When it was over we stood looking at each other, wide-eyed, and I said, "I'm sorry, I shouldn't have done that."

She smiled wanly and said, "You're very sweet, Fred," and turned away and went snuffling off to bed, and I went to sofa, and silence reigned.

Monday morning, nothing was said about last night's kiss. In fact, about all Karen said to me was, "I forgot to tell you, Jack says the two men from Homicide are coming to see you today." She also said she was going to be late for work, but I think she was talking to herself rather than me; in any case, five minutes later she'd torn out of the apartment and I was alone again. Back I went to the sofa, to rest and wait for my vaudeville team from Homicide.

The doorbell rang about quarter to ten, but when I went to the voicebox and asked who was there, I got no answer. I kept saying, "Hello? Hello?"

until the doorbell rang a second time, and I realized it was the hall door they were at, not the door downstairs.

Except it wasn't them. I opened the door and an elderly Jewish man was there, dressed in black, with a flat black hat and a long gray beard. He squinted at me and muttered something in what I took to be Yiddish, and I said, "I think you've got the wrong apartment." He consulted a grubby scrap of paper in his palm, turned away from me, and went shuffling toward an apartment across the hall. I shrugged, shut the door, and went back to sofa. But I was awake now, so I turned on the television set and watched a quiz show with celebrities.

The bell rang again ten minutes later. The upstairs bell. I switched off the set, went to the door, and once again it wasn't the police.

Instead, it was a chipper young man with a clipboard. "Hello there, sir," he said brightly, and consulted his clipboard. "I believe a Miss Karen Smith lives here?"

"She isn't in right now," I said.

"Ah. Well, she may have told you I'd be calling."

"She didn't say anything," I said.

He raised an eyebrow. "Mitchell?" he suggested. "Neighborhood Beautification Committee?"

"No, I'm sorry," I said. "She didn't say anything at all."

"That does create a problem," he said, tapping his pencil against his clipboard. "We have her down here for a fifteen-dollar donation. She didn't leave the money with you?"

I felt obscurely as though he half-believed I'd been given the money and was planning to keep it. I said, "No, she didn't leave anything, didn't even mention it."

"Mmm. That's ungood. All this stuff has to be in by noon today."

I remembered having seen some bills tucked away in a change purse in a bureau drawer in Karen's bedroom. I said, "Just a minute. I may be able to get the money for you."

There was more than enough there, over thirty dollars, I took three fives and gave them to the man at the door. "Thank you, sir," he said. "Here, I'll give you the receipt, you'll need that for tax purposes. Do I make it out to you or Miss Smith?"

"Miss Smith," I said.

He wrote out the receipt and gave it to me and I went back to lie down on the sofa again.

Twenty minutes later I sat up and looked at the receipt on the coffee table beside me. Fifteen dollars! I'd just bought another receipt!

And this time I hadn't even used my own money.

I dashed from the apartment and ran up and down the stairwell, checking all the halls, but of course he was gone. I'd have to replace that money, but how? I didn't have enough cash on me, and to give her a check I'd have to admit having poked through her personal things. But I couldn't just permanently steal fifteen dollars from her.

I went back to the apartment and paced the living room and thought about it, and I promised myself—as I had done once or twice in the past—that from now on I was going to be *suspicious*.

Sure.

At eleven-thirty the doorbell rang again, the street bell this time, and this time it was actually Steve and Ralph. When they came up they let me know they were unhappy about my not calling them right away when I'd been shot at, but I apologized and said I knew they were right and it wouldn't happen again, so they dropped the subject and went on to other things.

Such as why anybody would want to kill little me. Ralph said, "What we like to do, Fred, you understand, we like to start with a theory, just to have a place to start."

Steve said, "Kind of a direction to move in, Ralph means."

"That's what I mean," agreed Ralph. "Naturally, if in the subsequent investigation we happen to run across facts that don't fit in with this theory, we change the theory."

"Or maybe sometimes the facts," Steve said, and he and Ralph both laughed.

When he was done laughing, Ralph said, "Now, in this particular case we do have a theory. About the guy that shot at you last night."

"Our theory," said Steve, "is he's the same guy that did for your uncle."

"That's just our theory," Ralph explained. "Admittedly, it's got features we aren't too crazy about."

"Like modus operandi, for instance," said Steve.

Ralph looked at Steve and frowned. "Steve," he said, "I don't think Fred is really interested in this sort of technical details. I think what he's more interested in is what you might call the overall design."

"In other words," said Steve, "the theory."

"Exactly," said Ralph. He looked at me, raised his eyebrows, and said, "Well?"

I looked back at him, having no idea what he wanted, and said, "Well what?"

"Well, what do you think of the theory?"

Steve added, "We'd like your opinion of it, Fred, since you're involved, you might say."

I shrugged and said, "I guess it sounds all right. It makes sense, the same person both times."

Ralph said, "Why, Fred?"

"What?"

"You say it makes sense, the same guy killed your Uncle Matt and shot at you. Why does it make sense?"

"Well," I said, at a loss, and instead of finishing the sentence I waved my hands around a little. "It just makes sense, that's all," I said.

"Less sloppy," Ralph suggested. "One murderer for the whole thing. Like a blanket policy."

"I suppose so," I said.

Ralph said, "Then he'd have the same reason, I guess, both times. Kill your uncle, kill you, both the same motive."

"It might be," I said. I had the uncomfortable feeling these two wanted to trap me somehow, but I didn't know where or why.

Steve said, "What do you figure, Fred? Is he after the money?"

"I don't know," I said. "I don't know who he is or what he's after."

"But that looks like a good bet, doesn't it? Maybe he's some second cousin, he figures he'll just keep bumping people off till he inherits."

"That doesn't make any sense," I said. "It'd be too obvious."

Ralph said, "Then let's try another theory. He doesn't want to kill you for your money, Fred, he wants to kill you to shut you up."

Steve smiled happily and said, "How's about that one, Fred? Better?"

"Shut me up? Shut me up from saying what?"

Ralph said, "You tell us, Fred."

Well, I couldn't tell them, which made them unhappy again. We went around in circles awhile longer and finally they left, telling me to keep in touch and to let them know if I moved anywhere else. I promised I would, and sat down on the sofa, and started a new crossword puzzle.

At ten minutes to three that afternoon the phone rang. I picked it up and a muffled male voice said, "Fred Fitch?"

"Yes?"

"So there you are," he said, and chuckled, and the phone clicked as he hung up.

13

GERTIE OPENED THE door and said, "Well, if it isn't the Eagle Scout. How's your knots coming?"

"Loose," I said, and stepped into her apartment. "I don't think I was followed," I said.

She raised a caustic eyebrow. "Not followed! How do you stand such obscurity?"

I said, "Would you like to hear what's been happening, or would you rather go on with this endless chain of exit lines?"

"Well, you're nasty for a ninety-seven-pound weakling," she said, "I'll say that much for you. Come on to the kitchen, I'm making supper."

This apartment, on West 112th Street down the block from St. John's Cathedral, was much smaller and cheaper than Karen's place, and not at all like my own neat den on 19th Street, but I felt immediately at home in it and shortly found myself sitting with my elbows on the kitchen table, a white mug of coffee in front of me, as I filled Gertie in on what had been happening to me since I'd put her into a cab Saturday night. When I got to the part about the telephone call from the muffled male voice she turned away from the cheese sauce she was making and said, "How'd they get on to you?"

"I don't know. But when I got the call, I panicked. All I could think of was I had to find some place else to go, and fast. I couldn't go back home, they might still be watching there. I didn't want to take the time to call the police or anything, because I didn't know how close these people already were. They could have been calling from the drugstore on the corner."

"So you called your old pal Gertie," she said.

"I remembered I still had your phone number in my wallet. I called and you said come up and here I am."

"Here you are." She nodded. "Little man," she said, "you've had a busy week. So what now?"

"Now I call Reilly," I said.

"Are you sure?"

I looked at her. "Why not?"

"I still ask you how they got on to you. You never knew this Smith broad till Saturday, so how'd they know you were there?"

I winced at her calling Karen a broad, but I also considered the import of her question. I said, "Reilly? Not Reilly."

"Why not? He hates money?"

"Reilly's my friend," I said.

"Honey," she said, "there's something your Uncle Matt used to say, and he was right. 'A man with half a million bucks can't afford friends.' Money changes things, that's my words of wisdom for today."

"Reilly wouldn't do a thing like that," I said.

"I'm glad to hear it. How'd they get on to you?"

"I don't know. Maybe your friends Steve and Ralph."

She nodded judiciously. "Could be. I never figured those two were exactly priests."

I felt a chill breeze blow across the back of my neck. I said, "What you're saying is, I can't trust anybody in the world."

"You got a pretty way with a phrase, honey," she said.

"So you don't think I should call Reilly or anybody else and tell them I'm here."

"Not unless you want another phone call. Or maybe this time a visit in person. Which believe me, sweetheart, I don't want. Not here. The landlord's down on show-biz people as it is."

"Then what should I do?"

"Stick here till it blows over," she said. "I can get you an army cot from someplace, we'll work it out."

"How will it blow over? When's it going to be safe?"

"When they get the guy knocked off your Uncle Matt. He's the one behind all this, that's the safest bet of the month."

"But what if they never get him?"

"They'll get him. He keeps doing things, agitating, moving around. A guy that can't quit, him they'll get."

"I hope you're right," I said.

"Sure I'm right."

But I wasn't convinced, one way or the other. On the one side I felt I should call Reilly right away—or, instead of Reilly, Steve and Ralph—and tell him what had happened and where I was now, because if the police didn't know what was going on, how could they possibly help me? On the other side there was the problem of how the killer had found out where I was, and the real possibility that Gertie was right, that I could trust absolutely no one now that I was a hundredthousand-aire.

I couldn't think about it yet, I was still too confused. So I changed the subject, asking Gertie to tell me about my Uncle Matt, which she was more than willing to do. As he came across in her exuberant description, he was a happy-go-lucky sharpie with a heart full of larceny but without any vestige of a mean streak, a chipper quick-witted con man with a deck of cards in one hand and a stack of uranium stock in the other, a heavy drinker but not a sloppy one, a big spender and a good-time Charlie, a man whose sense of responsibility and need for security were about as well developed as that of the lilies of the field.

"He made it big down there in Brazil," she said. "Him and Professor Kilroy. He never talked about it much, how he did it, but I knew him before he went south and he never had that kind of cabbage before in his life. I figure he must of hit a couple of those absconding big businessmen, those Wall Street tycoons that duck out to Brazil with a million or two when things get hot. And when he come back he was already sick, he knew he could go any day, and he was what you might call retired. He did some like consultant work for kak, but that was just for kicks."

"For what? He did what?"

"Consultant work," she said.

"No," I said, "the other word. Kak?"

"Oh, yeah. Citizens Against Crime, you heard of them,"

"I did?"

"They're one of these reform outfits," she said negligently. "You see about them in the paper all the time."

"I didn't recognize the name," I explained. "What was it you called it? Kak?"

"C," she spelled, "A, C. Kak. Citizens Against Crime."

"Okay," I said. "I've got it now."

"You are fast," she said, not entirely as though she meant it.

I said, "What did Uncle Matt do for, uh, kak?"

"Told em about cons, how the stores work these days and like that."

"Oh. So he wasn't actually working anywhere."

"Naw. Strictly retired, Matt was. Used to play gin sometimes, with me or the elevator man, just to keep his hand in, but he had the shakes so bad the last couple of years he couldn't even deal seconds any more."

"Deal seconds?"

"Dealing the second card from the top," she explained. "When Matt was on, sauced just enough and in his health, he could deal fifths all night long and you'd never hear a rustle."

"Fifth card from the top?"

"You know it," she said, and the doorbell rang. We looked at each other. She said, "Just keep cool and don't make a sound."

"I won't," I promised.

She left the kitchen. I sat at the table and didn't make a sound.

High on one wall was the kind of white plastic kitchen electric clock you get for trading stamps. It had a red sweep second hand, which I watched go round fifteen times, then didn't watch for a while, then watched five times more.

When I figured half an hour had gone by, and when in all that time I hadn't heard a sound from the front of the apartment, I went investigating, moving cautiously through the rooms, listening, pausing, looking around corners.

The apartment was empty. The hall door was ajar. I went to it and peeked outside and the hall was also empty, except that lying on the floor out there, on its side, was a shoe made entirely of white plastic straps and a red plastic wedgie heel.

The other one must still have been on Gertie's foot.

14

NOW WHAT?

I stood in the middle of Gertie's crowded messy tiny living room, I held Gertie's wedgie in my right hand, and I asked myself that question aloud: "Now what?"

There was no answer.

When a person has been kidnapped—and with this shoe for mute testimony what else was there to believe but that Gertie had been kidnapped by party or parties (probably parties) unknown?—one's first reaction is, "Call the police!" so that on coming back into the apartment I'd headed straight for the phone. But in the nick of time I'd brought myself up short, remembering something Gertie herself had pointed out to me just a few minutes before she'd disappeared:

Only four people had known I was at Karen Smith's apartment, and three of them were cops.

Dare I call the police? Dare I let the likes of Steve and Ralph know where I was? I'd instinctively mistrusted those two from the very first time I'd met them, and now it seemed probable my instinct had been—for once—correct.

Then what about Reilly? He was my friend, he'd been my friend for years, surely *he* wouldn't betray me.

But hadn't Reilly been acting oddly the last few days, grumpy and sullen and strangely distant? And didn't he turn out to be living some sort of double life, with Karen on one side and an invisible wife on the other? And hadn't I always suspected him of containing at least as much con man as the criminals he was charged with apprehending? Was this a man I could completely trust?

Or what of Karen herself? Hadn't she, on our very first meeting in Madison Square Park, lied to me and gulled me? What did I know about her, after all, other than that she was a convincing liar and was having an affair with a married man?

No, no, I could trust none of these people, not if I valued my skin.

To whom, then, could I turn? I went farther afield, to my so-called lawyer, the brave attorney Goodkind; *there* was a man I wouldn't trust with a subway token in the Sahara. And when my neighbor Wilkins had come to me with his trunk full of novel had he in actuality been casing the joint for the mob? Was that less unlikely than his claim to have written a book about airborne Roman legions dropping rocks on the primitives of Gaul? And what about Mr. Grant, wasn't he in a way too good to be true, melting into the background, seeming so meek and inoffensive, the surest sign of the arch-conspirator? Couldn't he or Wilkins—or both, why not?—have been planted in my building years ago, just waiting for the right moment?

Was all this far-fetched? Of course it was, but three hundred thousand dollars was far-fetched in the first place. Being shot at and hounded was far-fetched. Gertie's being kidnapped from under my nose was far-fetched. My Uncle Matt's murder was far-fetched.

As far as that went, my Uncle Matt's very *existence* was far-fetched.

And who knew to what lengths some people might not go to get their hands on three hundred thousand dollars?

Very well, Uncle Matt had been right; a man with three hundred thousand dollars can't afford friends. From now on, whatever happened, I would be able to rely on no one but myself.

The thought was not encouraging. I was aware of my capabilities and of my limitations, and I knew which was the longer list.

But what was I to do? And if I didn't even dare *report* Gertie's kidnapping, how would anyone ever find her?

Somehow or other that was now up to me too, and I knew it, and I quailed before the responsibility. How would I go about finding Gertie, and rescuing her, and bringing her kidnappers to justice? How would I even begin? All I knew anything about was library research, and I strongly doubted I'd be finding Gertie in any library.

In true researcher style, I tried marshaling my facts, and found them in short supply. Fogs and suspicions and confusions littered the landscape all around me, but of facts there were very few. Only three, in fact: (1) Gertie had been kidnapped. (2) I had been shot at. (3) Uncle Matt had been murdered.

Was that a starting point, number three? The murder of Uncle Matt actually had been the beginning of all this, so was that where I should begin? At the very least it was, in this sea of shifting ambiguities, a fact that stood firm, something that could be studied, something I could be sure of: my Uncle Matt *had* been murdered.

Had he?

Oh, come *on*. After all, *something* had to be true. If you couldn't believe anything at all, how could you move, how could you think, how could you act? It was necessary to start somewhere.

I had meandered this far in my thinking when the doorbell suddenly shrilled and I leaped at once to attention. Could this be them? Could they have found out—perhaps by torturing Gertie—that I was here, and had they returned to get me?

My initial impulse was to hide in the nearest closet or under the nearest bed, shut my eyes, and wait for them to go away. In fact I even took a quick tiptoeing step toward the rear of the apartment before I remembered that I *wanted* to see them, that I'd just been straining my brain to think of a way to *find* them. If now they had come to me, so much the better.

At least that's what I told myself, while glancing in quick panic around the room for some sort of weapon; after all, I was out to capture them, not to let them capture me.

Atop the television set in one corner of the living room was a lamp of such monumental ugliness as to be magnificently impressive, like Chicago. Its porcelain base represented an endless chain of Cupids, in white and pink and gold, doing things together. It may all have been very obscene, there was no real way to be sure. At any rate, I hurried over and removed this monstrosity's fringed shade, pulled its cord from the wall plug, and hefted the lamp in my right hand, finding it pleasingly weighty. Holding this weapon of love behind my back I went over and opened the door, ready to start smashing Cupids into every face I saw.

The gray-haired, full-jowled, black-suited minister on the threshold smiled sweetly upon me and said, in a soft and gentle voice, "Good afternoon to you, my dear sir. Would Miss Gertrude Divine be at home?"

Was the lamp really out of sight? Flustered, jamming the lamp into the small of my back, I said, "Well, no, she isn't. She had to, uh, go out for a while. I don't know exactly when she'll be back."

"Ah, well," he said, and sighed, and transferred the brown paper package from his right arm to his left. "I'll try again another time," he said. "My apologies for having intruded."

Anything might have relevance, anything at all, so I said, "Could you tell me what it was about?"

"Mr. Grierson's Bible," he said. "Perhaps I could come back tomorrow afternoon."

"I'm not sure she'll be here," I said. "What do you mean, Mr. Grierson's Bible?"

"The Bible he ordered, the inscribed Bible."

So Uncle Matt, the famous boulevardier and con man, had gotten religion toward the end. It was small of me, I know, but I found myself taking a nasty little pleasure in the thought of the supremely confident confidence man losing some of that confidence as he saw the end approaching.

I think I managed to hide this unworthy pleasure as I said, "I'm Mr. Grierson's nephew, maybe I could help."

"Ah, are you?" His smile of pleasure was tinged with sadness as he said, "I am most happy to meet you, sir, though one could wish it were under happier circumstances. I am the Reverend Willis Marquand."

"How do you do? I'm Fredric Fitch. Won't you, uh, won't you come in?"

"If you're sure I'm not disturbing you?"

"Not at all, sir."

Reverend Marquand noticed the lamp as I was closing the door. I held it up and laughed foolishly and said, "Just putting this up when you rang." I went over and put it back in its place on the television set, then offered Reverend Marquand a seat.

When we were both seated, he said, "A real loss, your uncle. A fine man."

"You knew him well?"

"Only telephonically, I'm afraid. We chatted awhile when he phoned the Institute to order the Bible." He patted the brown paper package, now resting on the sofa beside him.

"Is that it?"

"Would you care to see it? It's our finest model, and really beautiful. We're all quite proud of it."

He removed the wrappings and showed it to me, and it was impressive in much the same way as the lamp, and with the same color scheme. It was bound in white leatherette with an ornate gilt cross on the front and ornate gilt lettering on the spine. The page edges were all gilt, and gold and red ribbons were available to mark one's place. Inside, intricately illuminated letters were the rule, ornate brightly colored illustrations on heavy glossy paper were scattered throughout, and much of the dialogue was in red. The first page was inscribed in flowing gilt script:

> To Dearest Gertrude,
> with all my love forever
> *Whither Thou Goest, I Will Go*
>   *Ruth 1:16*
> Matthew Grierson

Now, this was odd. I could visualize Uncle Matt turning to religion himself in his old age, particularly knowing he was suffering from terminal cancer, but that he or anybody else would consider a gold and white leatherette Bible the right gift for Gertie Divine—despite her name—was hard to believe. There was more here than met the eye.

Then I understood. This was a message of some kind, a clue that Gertie would understand.

A clue to what?

Well, maybe three hundred thousand dollars wasn't all there was to it. After all, Brazil was where Uncle Matt made his money, and Brazil is a great new raw nation, its wealth hardly tapped. Maybe there was more, much more, and the three hundred thousand was only the visible part of the iceberg, and the clue to the rest of it was somehow here in this Bible.

Of course! Why else give the three hundred thousand to a perfect stranger, even if he is technically a relative? Because it's chicken feed, because the really *big* money is tied up somewhere else.

That's why Uncle Matt sent Gertie to me. He was leaving it up to her whether she would tell me about the rest of it or not. The three hundred thousand was a kind of test to see if I was worthy of all of it. And Gertie had been kidnapped by people intent on forcing the information out of her.

I said, "You're delivering this, is that it?"

"Well—" He smiled in some embarrassment. "There is the question of payment. Your uncle was to have sent us a check, but unfortunately he passed on before—"

"Well, how much is it?"

"Thirty-seven dollars and fifty cents."

"I'll write you a check," I said. I'd brought along my checkbook when I'd first left home, not knowing how long I'd be gone, but this was the first time I'd had to use it so far.

Reverend Marquand loaned me a pen and said, "Just make it out to Dear Hearts Institute."

I wrote out the check and gave it to him, and he seemed ready to settle down, minister-like, and discuss my own religious affiliations with me at some length. I begged off, saying I did have some work to get done, and he was very good about it, leaving at once and letting me get to the job of studying the Bible.

I spent nearly an hour at it, and got nowhere. How was this Bible different from all other Bibles? I couldn't figure it out. But of course Gertie was the one the message was for, and I had no doubt it would be meaningful to her in one glance.

Finally I had to give it up. I hid the Bible in the oven, put it completely out of my mind, and went back to the train of thought I'd been on when the Reverend Marquand had arrived, which had been the decision that the only fact of which I could be at all sure was the murder of Uncle Matt. Starting from there, and with the luck of a Daily Double winner, maybe I could eventually find some other facts about which to be sure.

Very well. I left a note for Gertie, telling her I'd phone in from time to time just in case she should escape from her captors, and went out to look up the murder reports in the newspapers at the library.

The Lone Researcher was on the trail.

15

THE *DAILY NEWS* found my Uncle Matt dull, but didn't like to say so. He was, after all, a semi-mysterious old demi-millionaire with an oddball will and a weird history and a photogenic ex-stripper nurse, and as if that weren't enough, he'd also been murdered in his luxury penthouse apartment on Central Park South and the murderer was still at large. It was clear the *News* felt it *should* have a field day with Uncle Matt, and yet somehow it just couldn't seem to get a good grip on him. Every item that started out to be a story about Uncle Matt's murder ultimately wound up being a story about something else instead, usually the Collier brothers, with whom my uncle, so far as I could tell, had shared no characteristics at all, other than being dead, having money and belonging to the white race.

Still, the *Daily News* was the only game in town. The *Times* had given the story one bare useless item the day after the murder, and the other papers had been almost as bad. Only the *News* had persisted in follow-up stories, I suppose out of a sense of noblesse oblige.

Ah, well. Intermixed with the references to Jack London and Peaches Browning (don't ask *me* how they did it) I did find the facts of the case, such as they were, and copied them laboriously into the notebook I'd just bought for the purpose.

Uncle Matt had been murdered the night of Monday, May 8, seventeen days ago. Gertie had gone out to a movie that evening with a friend identified as one Gus Ricovic and hadn't returned to the apartment until one-thirty in the morning, at which time she discovered the body and phoned the police. The actual murder was assumed to have taken place somewhere between ten and eleven. Death had resulted from a single blow to the back of the head made by some blunt instrument, not found on the premises nor turned up in the subsequent investigation. There was no sign of forcible entry into the apartment nor was there any indication of a fight or any other struggle. So far as Gertie knew (or at least so far as she had told the police and reporters), Uncle Matt hadn't expected any visitors that evening.

The *Daily News* was so taken with the notion of someone murdering a man who's expected to die momentarily from cancer anyway that they even interviewed Uncle Matt's doctor, one Lucius Osbertson, who from his manner in the interview I took to be both rotund and orotund; in the spaces between the lines Dr. Osbertson could faintly be heard lamenting the loss of a steady source of fees.

The follow-up stories added little. The police appeared to be wandering dispiritedly in an ever-diminishing spiral, like a band of defeatist Indians who've lost their warpath. Gertie came in for a lot of attention, with photos and interviews and her show-biz biography. Gus Ricovic was never mentioned at all after the initial story. Here and there references were made to the strange will Uncle Matt was supposed to have left behind, but of course its details had not as yet been made public, so there were no references to me, and by the time I would have been available for the spotlight the story was as dead as Uncle Matt. By the sixth day after the murder, in fact, even the *Daily News* had nothing left to say about it any more.

When I left the newspaper library, my new notebook bristling with the facts in the case, it was five o'clock, the height of that daily self-torture known as the rush hour. I was on 43rd Street west of Tenth Avenue and decided it would be saner to walk than to try to find a cab or squeeze myself aboard a Ninth Avenue bus, so walk is what I did. It was probably also quicker; I made it, walking at a leisurely pace, in twenty-five minutes, and so far as I could tell I wasn't shot at once.

I had thought at first, while in the library, of going back to Gertie's place, of maybe using that as my base of operations, but then it seemed to me that Gertie might be forced into admitting that I'd been there, and in that case her kidnappers would naturally stake the place out on the assumption that I'd be back. After that I'd considered staying at a hotel, but the idea of signing a false name to a hotel register while a desk clerk stood directly in front of me and looked at me was far too nerve-racking to consider. As to staying with some friend, my friends were too few and precious for me to want to involve any of them in kidnappings and murder attempts, not to mention the fact that God alone knew if I could trust any of them.

When all was said and done, there was only one place I could go and that place was home. My own apartment. Surely no one would expect to find me in my own apartment, so it was unlikely that anyone would be looking for me there, and that meant I could expect to be at least as safe there as anywhere else in the world. And a good deal more comfortable; I could change my suit, I could sleep in my own bed, I could begin to lead again at least some small remnant of my former life.

Thus went my thinking, and I could find no flaws in it. Still and all, as I approached my own block my feet did begin to drag a little, my shoulders to hunch, and the small of my back just slightly to itch. I found myself peering into every parked car, and flinching away from every moving one. I alternately stared into the faces of pedestrians coming the other way or ducked my own face behind my hand, neither tactic being particularly brilliant since I left in my wake a long line of immobile pedestrians standing flat-footed on the sidewalk and staring after me. As a result, my return was not entirely as unobtrusive as I had hoped it might be.

Nevertheless, I came to my own building without incident, and entered, and found my mailbox filled to overflowing. Actually overflowing; letters were sticking out of the slot above the door like darts out of a dartboard. When I unlocked the little door it sprang open with a sound like *phong!*, only faster, and a whole wad of mail burst out and scattered all over the floor.

I filled my jacket pockets with letters, held another stack in my left hand, and went on upstairs. As I reached the second-floor landing, the door there opened, Wilkins appeared, and the two of us faced each other for the first time since Gertie had thrown him—and his suitcase—out of my apartment. Wilkins raised his ink-stained hand, pointed a rigid ink-stained finger at me, and said, icily, "Just you wait." Then he snapped the door shut again.

I hesitated there on the landing, wanting to knock on that slammed door and see if I could make it up to Wilkins somehow, because after all I did truly owe him an apology. The very worst that could be said of the man was that he was deluded, and if I had come perilously close to entering his delusion that was my fault, not his. And I did have more money now than I could possibly use, so why not put some of it into the publication of his novel, regardless of whether or not it was any good?

But there was no time for all that now, so making a mental note to talk to Wilkins when the rest of this was all over, I went on past his door and up the stairs to the third floor and walked into my apartment.

Where a woman with impossibly red hair, sequined tortoise shell glasses and a mostly yellow plaid suit leaped up from my reading chair, flung her arms out, and came rushing toward me on spike-heel shoes, beaming and crying, "Darling! I'm here and the answer is yes!"

16

I DIDN'T EVEN know what the question was. Quickly I side-stepped the embrace, ran around the sofa, and with a little distance between us said, "What now? What's all this?"

She had turned, like the bull still after the cape, and paused on tippy-heel, arms still oufflung as she cried, "Darling, don't you *recognize* me? Have I changed so much?"

Was there really something familiar about her, or was it merely the old suggestibility at work again? Taking no chances, I said, "Madam, I have never seen you before in my life. Explain yourself. What are you doing here?"

"Darling, I'm *Sharlene!*"

"Sharlene?" I squinted, trying to get the picture. There had been a Sharlene back in high school, a shy little girl I'd managed to go steady with for a while, a wistful ephemeral little thing who'd had it in her head she wanted to be a poetess. Most of the kids in school had called her Emily Dickinson, which she had taken as a compliment.

"Sharlene *Kester!*" yelled this garden-club monstrosity, giving in truth the full name of that frail girl-child.

"You?" In my bafflement I actually pointed at her. "*You're* Emily Dickinson?"

"You *remembered!*" The thought so enraptured her that she charged me again, arms outstretched as though she were doing her impression of a Flying Fortress, and it was only the nimblest of footwork that enabled me to keep the sofa between us.

I shouted, "Wait a minute, *wait* a minute!" I held up my hand like a traffic cop.

Amazingly enough, she stopped. Tilted somewhat forward, seemingly ready to leap into action again at any instant, she inquired, "Darling, what is it? I'm here, I'm yours, the answer is yes! Why don't you take me?"

"Answer?" I asked. "Answer to what?"

"Your letter!" she cried. "That beautiful beautiful letter!"

"What letter? I didn't write you any letter."

"The letter from *camp*. I know how long it's been, believe me I know, but you told me to take my time, to answer only when I was sure, and now I'm sure. The answer is *yes!*"

My mind was empty. I said, in bafflement, "Camp?"

"Boy Scout camp!" Then, abruptly, the manic look on her face switched to something much sterner, and in a quick cold voice she said, "You aren't going to say you didn't *write* that letter."

Then I remembered. The summer I was fifteen I had spent two weeks in a Boy Scout camp, two of the most disastrous weeks of my life; of all the gear I'd taken to camp with me, I'd returned with nothing but my left sneaker, and it without its laces. That was also the year I'd been going steady with Sharlene Kester, and in a fit of depression while at camp I had written her a letter; yes, I had. But what the letter had said I could no longer remember at all.

Nor could I understand why, sixteen years later, Sharlene—could this gaily daubed hippo really be Sharlene?—why she should out of a clear blue sky decide to answer that letter.

Unless she'd heard about the inheritance. Eh? Eh?

While I was wasting time thinking, Sharlene was still talking. She was saying, "Just let me tell you something, Fred Fitch. You remember my Uncle Mortimer, who used to be assistant district attorney back home? Well, he's a judge now, and I showed him your letter, and he says it's a clear proposal of marriage, and it'll stand up in any court in the United States. And he told me, if you've gone big-city and think you're going to trifle with me, he told me he'll handle the whole thing *himself*, and *you'll* be slapped with a breach of promise suit just faster than you can think, so you'd better be careful what you say to me. Now. Do you remember that letter or don't you?"

No, not this. I didn't have time for this, that's all. I didn't know whether or not Sharlene—my God!—had a case against me, and at the moment I really didn't care. All I knew was that I already had too much to think about and it was time to set the excess wolves at each other's throats for a change. So, "Excuse me," I said, and went over to the telephone.

"You go ahead and call anyone you want to," she said loudly. "I know my rights. You can't trifle with my affections."

It was five-thirty by now, and no longer normal office hours, but Goodkind had struck me as the sort of man who'd be liable to stay late in the office, gloating over the law volumes dealing with mortgage foreclosures. If he weren't there, I'd just have to take a chance on calling Reilly.

Fortunately, Goodkind was true to his character and present in his office. When he answered I identified myself, and he said, "Fred! I've been looking all over for you! Where are you?"

"Never mind," I said. "I want to—"

"Are you home?"

"No. I want to—"

"Fred, I've got to talk to you."

"In a minute. I want to—"

"This is important! Vital!"

"I want to—"

"Can you come to the office?"

"No. I want to—"

"We've got to meet, and talk. There are things—"

"God damn it," I shouted, "shut up for a minute!"

There was stunned silence all over the world. Out of the corner of my eye I saw Sharlene staring at me in blank astonishment.

Into the silence, I said, "If you're my attorney, you'll listen to me for one minute. If you don't want to listen, you're not my attorney."

"Fred," said a voice composed entirely of cholesterol, "of course I'll listen to you. Anything, Fred."

"Good. When I was fifteen years old I spent two weeks at a Boy Scout camp."

"Wonderful places," he said, a trifle vaguely, but obviously wanting to please.

"While there," I said, "I wrote a letter to a girl I knew in high school. She's here now, in New York. Her uncle's a judge in Montana. She claims the letter's a proposal of marriage, and if I don't marry her she'll sue me for breach of promise."

I held the phone away from my ear so Sharlene could join me in listening to Goodkind laugh. His laughter reminded me of the witch in Walt Disney's *Snow White*.

Behind her sequined harlequin tortoise-shell spectacles, Sharlene had begun to blink a lot. Her expression had now become nervous, but determined.

When Goodkind was down to little giggles and chuckles, I put the phone back to my head and said, "What should I do? Should I tell her no?" Then I held the phone out again, so we could both hear his answer.

I must admit the answer surprised me, because what he said was, "Oh, no, not a bit. Fred? Act worried, boy. Bluster if you can. Act as though you don't want to marry her, and you're trying to bluff, and you're afraid you don't have a leg to stand on. If we can con these people to actually taking us to court—" Instead of ending the sentence, he began to giggle again.

I brought the mouthpiece close, and said to my mouthpiece, "What good does that do me?"

"Does her family have any money?" he asked me. "Do they own their house, have a business of any kind?"

"Excuse me a second," I said. "She just left the door open, and there's a draft coming in."

I walked over to the door, and clearly I could hear the tickety-tick of her heels as she raced down the stairs. Then, up the stairwell came the faintly receding cry, "You'll pay for thiiiiisss!!!"

With a feeling rare to me in life—the feeling called triumph—I quietly closed the door.

17

WHEN I GOT back to the phone, Goodkind was saying, "Hello? Hello? Hello?"

"Hello," I said.

"There you are. Where are you?"

"I'm not at liberty to say right now," I said.

"Fred, it is imperative that we get together—"

He was wrong. What was imperative was that I assume control somehow. Steeling myself, I said, "For the last time, don't call me Fred."

"You can call me Marcus," he said.

"I don't want to call you Marcus," I told him, which may have been the harshest thing I'd ever said to anybody in my life. "I want to call you Mr. Goodkind. I want you to call me Mr. Fitch."

"But . . . but that isn't the way it's done. Everybody calls everybody by his first name.

"Everybody but you and me," I said.

"Well," he said doubtfully, "you're in charge." Which made me glow all over.

Keeping the smile out of my voice, I said, "The other reason I called, I want some money."

"Well, naturally, Fr—uh. Naturally. It's yours."

"Is there any of it you can get hold of without any documents from me?"

"Well, uh—"

"I'm not accusing you of anything," I said. "I just want to know if there's any way you can transfer some funds without my having to sign anything or show up anywhere."

"It would be best if you came here, you know. Or if you want I could meet you some—"

"Is—there—any—way?"

Silence, then: "Yes."

"Good. I want you to take four thousand dollars and put it into my account at Chase Hanover, the branch at Twenty-fifth and Seventh. Just a second, I'll get you my account number."

I went away and looked for my checkbook, found it at last in my jacket pocket, where it had been for the last five days—I didn't seem to be able to think about more than one thing at a time—went back to the telephone, and heard Goodkind saying, with some urgency, "Hello? Hello? Hello?"

"Stop saying hello," I said.

"I thought you'd hung up. Ff—uh. Are you feeling all right?"

"I'm fine. My account number is seven six oh, dash, five nine two, space, six two two nine three, space, eight. Have you got that?"

He read it back to me.

"Good," I said. "Transfer the money first thing tomorrow morning. And do it in cash so I can start drawing on it right away."

"I will," he promised. "Is there anything else?"

"Yes. My uncle's apartment. Has it been rented to anybody else or can I still get into it?"

"It's yours," he said. "Part of the estate. It's a co-op, your uncle owned it."

"Get a set of keys to the doorman," I said. "Tonight," I added, though I had no intention of going there before tomorrow sometime. I was beginning to learn a little about subterfuge.

"Will do," he said.

"And when I get there," I told him, "don't you be snooping around."

"I'm your attorney, Ffuff."

"Who?"

"I'm your attorney. There are important things—"

"The keys to the doorman," I said. "That's the important thing."

"I'll do it," he promised. "And now we've got to talk."

"Later," I said, and hung up. I well knew the dangers in allowing me to be talked to.

Evening was coming on by now, and it seemed a good idea to show no light at my windows, just in case, so for the next twenty minutes I went about the task of erecting makeshift blackout curtains, composed of blankets and towels and my bedspread and shower curtain. When I was done, the apartment had a strangely underground appearance, possibly a fallout shelter for the Budapest String Quartet, but I was reasonably certain no light would show to any watcher outside, and that was the important part.

While I'd been at work the phone had rung several times, once continuing for eighteen rings before the caller had given up. This was my first experience at not answering a telephone and I found it surprisingly difficult, much like giving up smoking. My mind kept trying to betray me, kept insisting that it was unnatural not to answer the telephone (or not to smoke), and I found it physically difficult to stay in the other room. As the evening wore on, the phone sounded a few more times, and it never did get any easier to ignore.

At any rate, once I'd completed the blackout arrangements I took a look at my incredible stack of mail, now piled up on the drop-leaf table near the door. I began by sorting the one stack into three stacks, separated into bills, personal letters and others, and for the first time in my life the smallest stack was of bills. These I immediately tucked away in the bill pigeonhole in my desk, and then I sat down to see what my personal mail was all about.

It was all about money, though hardly any of my correspondents actually used the word. There were seven letters from relatives—four cousins, two aunts and a niece-in-law—none of whom had ever written me a letter before in their lives. The letters were chatty and newsy, in a gimme sort of way: Cousin James Fisher had a golden oportunity to buy a Shell station out to the new highway, and Aunt Arabella needed an operation on her back in the worst way, and Cousin Wilhelmina Spofford surely wished she could afford to go to the University of Chicago. And so on.

I read all the letters, and I began to backslide. I *wanted* to believe, against all the evidence of the world, that these people were writing to me because they liked me and wanted to be in communication with me, and because I wanted to believe it I came perilously close to letting myself believe it.

In order to fortify myself against my structural weaknesses, when I finished the last of my relations' advertisements for themselves I looked up and spoke aloud. "Bah," I said. "Humbug." I then used the seven letters to start a warming little blaze in my fireplace, and sat in front of it to read the third stack of mail, the miscellaneous pile.

The word *miscellaneous* has perhaps never been so aptly employed. This stack included an advertisement for a company that was bound and determined to save me money on slacks if I would only send them my measurements and choice of color, and a notice from a bunch of monks in California alerting me to the news that they intended to say Mass for me en masse every day for the next hundred years and if I wished to express my appreciation for this religious frenzy I could use the enclosed envelope no stamp needed, and a newsletter informing me that the Kelp-Chartle Non-Sectarian Orphanage of Augusta, Georgia, is on the brink of bankruptcy won't I help, and a badly typed note from a man in Baltimore who if I write song lyrics he writes music why don't we get together, and a notice from an organization called Citizens Against Crime (Senator Earl Dunbar, Honorary Chairman)—and wasn't that the outfit Uncle Matt was "consultant" for?—telling me that if I wanted to help stamp out racketeers and gangsters all I had to do was send a check to further CAC's good work, and a form letter from an insurance man who if I would tell him how old I was he would tell me how much money he could save me on life insurance use the enclosed envelope no stamp needed, and half a dozen mixed charity appeals, and a notice that I'd won a free dance lesson, and a notice that I'd won a free crate of Florida oranges, and a letter from a lawyer informing me that his client Miss Linda Lou McBeggle intends to mount a paternity suit against me unless I do right by her having already done wrong by her, and a scented envelope containing a notice about Miss Crystal St. Cyr's at-home massage service, and a warning that I was in big trouble if I didn't give all my money to the Saints Triumphant World Universal Church because it's harder for a rich man to get into Heaven than for a camel to pass through a needle's eye, and a notice that I had a library book overdue.

You know, if I had been approached by any one of these things separately I would more than likely have fallen for it—if I didn't have so much else on my mind—but having them all piled up together like this was eye-opening, because for the first time I could see just how ridiculous they were. Just as one nude woman is beautiful but a nudist colony is only silly.

How the fire roared.

18

I SET MY alarm for nine o'clock, but the telephone woke me at twenty past eight. I was almost groggy enough to answer it but woke up slowly as I staggered into the living room, and came to consciousness just as my fingers touched the receiver. I jerked my hand back as though the plastic were hot, and stood weaving there until one of the silences between rings stretched and stretched and stretched and changed key and became the silence of an apartment in which no telephone is ringing.

At that point I had my first coherent thought of Tuesday, the twenty-fifth of May: "Now that I have three hundred thousand dollars, I can get an extension phone."

This thought pleased me and I smiled, and then, not to waste the expression, I went into the bathroom and brushed my teeth.

It was hard to believe it was really eight-thirty in the morning, headed for nine o'clock. My blackout curtains were still covering all the windows at both front and rear of the apartment, so that inside it was not very long after midnight. All the while I was preparing breakfast I had to fight the feeling I was actually having a midnight snack, and when at five minutes to ten I went downstairs and out to a bright and sunshiny world, all this glaring light seemed wrong somehow, the way it does when you've gone to the movies in the middle of the afternoon and you come outside and it's still day. It shouldn't be still day, but it is.

Combined with this feeling of temporal displacement was another, much worse: an itching between the shoulder blades. Though I didn't see that long black limousine awaiting me out front, and though both sidewalks seemed conspicuously empty of conspicuously lounging men, I felt very strange and uneasy about going out into all that bright sunlight, exposing myself as the biggest target in the world. Going down the stoop my mind was full of notions of high-powered rifles on roofs across the way, sub-machine guns jutting out the windows of parked cars, passing pedestrians suddenly whirling about with blazing automatics in their hands. When I got all the way down to the sidewalk with none of this happening, I actually felt a sense of anticlimax. A welcome anticlimax, but an anti-climax just the same.

I hurried directly to the bank, where I learned that Goodkind had made the exchange of funds for me as I'd asked, and where I cashed a check for a hundred dollars. I also did some heavy peering around, on the possibility that Goodkind might stake out the bank in hopes I'd show up, but he was nowhere in sight. Any number of suspicious characters avoided my eye while I was doing this scanning, but that's normal for New York and didn't mean that any of them were following me or had any connection with me.

498

I went from the bank to a street-corner phone booth. I had calls to make and I didn't know but what someone might be tapping my line at home to see if I was there. I was pleased at having thought of this precaution and felt almost cheery as I dialed the operator and asked her to connect me with Police Headquarters.

I was far less cheery three and a half minutes later when I finally got someone who would listen to me. An emergency would have to happen very slowly in New York City for a telephone call to the police to have any effect on it. The operator had given me a good long stretch of dead air punctuated by tiny faraway clicks before at last a crashingly loud close-up click shattered my eardrum and heralded the start of ringing. Four rings went by, well spaced, as I sweated in the phone booth, and at last I was in contact with a man with a gravel voice and a Brooklyn accent, who would listen to nothing from me other than my location. I pleaded, I shouted, I started a dozen different sentences, and when at last I gave up and told him the intersection I was calling from he promptly went away, I was treated to another spate of dead air, and I leaned against the phone-booth glass and watched the cabs go by until a sudden voice said, "Fraggis-Steep Frecinct."

"Oh," I said. "I want to report—"

"Fummation or complaint?" he asked me.

"I beg your pardon?"

He sighed. "You want fummation?" be asked me. "Or you wanna regista complaint?"

"Oh," I said, at last understanding. "*In*formation, you mean!"

"Fummation? Right." Click.

"No!" I cried. "Not fummation! Complaint! Complaint!" But it was too late.

Dead air again, followed by another male voice, this one saying, "Sergeant Srees, Fummation."

"I don't want fummation," I said. "I want to register a complaint."

"You got the wrong office," he told me. "Hold on." And he began clicking very loudly in my ear.

I held the phone away from my head, listened to the tiny clicking, and finally the tiny voices as a male operator came on and was told by my friend of Fummation to switch me over to Complaint. I brought the phone cautiously back to my ear, and after a little more silence, got yet another voice, this one saying, "Sergeant Srees, Desk."

"I want to register a complaint," I said.

"Felony or misdemeanor?"

"What?"

"You wanna regista felony? Or you wanna regista misdemeanor?"

"Kidnapping," I said. "That's a felony, I think."

"You want Tectivision," he told me. "Hang on." And clicked to let me know there was no use talking to him any more.

I did anyway. "You people are crazy," I said into the dead air. "Somebody could steal the whole city, sell it to Chicago, you wouldn't even hear about it till a week later."

"Srees, Tectivision."

"What's that?"

"Tectivision."

I concentrated. "Once more," I said.

"Smatter with you?" he asked me. "You want a Spanish-speakin tective?"

"Detective Division," I said, as the light dawned.

"Hold on," he said, and clicked.

"Wait!" I shouted. A young couple walking past my phone booth flinched. I saw them hurry away, trying not to act as though they were walking very fast. They didn't look back.

"Mendez, Tectivision."

"Look," I said, but before I could say any more he said two million words in Spanish, all in the space of ten seconds. When he was done I was a little groggy, but I kept trying. "I don't speak Spanish," I said. "Do you have anybody there that speaks English?"

"I speak English," he said, enunciating with beautiful clarity.

"God bless you," I said. "I want to report a kidnapping."

"When did this occur?"

"Yesterday. Her name is Gertrude Divine, she was kidnapped from her apartment yesterday afternoon."

"Your name, sir?"

"This is one of those anonymous calls," I said.

"We must have your name, sir."

"No, no. That's the whole point of an anonymous call, I don't give you my name. Now, Miss Divine's address is 727 West 112th Street, apart—"

"Not this precinct?"

"I beg your pardon?"

"Why are you calling this precinct, sir? This event occurred way uptown. Just a moment, I'll connect you with the correct precinct."

"No, you won't," I said. "I've reported the kidnapping, and now I'm hanging up."

"Sir—"

I hung up.

After this experience I needed to rest my nerves awhile before making my other call, so I left the phone booth and walked a block to another outdoor booth, where I called Dr. Lucius Osbertson, he being Uncle Matt's doctor, the one who'd been interviewed by the *Daily News*. I didn't want to give Dr. Osbertson advance warning that I was coming to see him, just to be on the safe side, so when his receptionist or nurse or whoever she was answered the phone I asked if the doctor had office hours at all today.

"Twelve till two," she said. "Name, please?"

I panicked, not having a name quick to hand. Staring out the phone-booth glass in desperation, seeing the stores and diners all around me, I opened my mouth and said, "Fred Nedick."

Fred Nedick? What kind of a name was that? I stood there in the phone booth and waited for her to say something like oh-come-off-it, or ha-ha-very-funny, or oh-another-drunk-eh?

Instead, she said, "Has the doctor seen you before, Mr. Nedick?"

This part I *had* prepared in advance. "No," I said. "I was recommended by Dr. Wheelwright." I actually did know a Dr. Wheelwright, who gave me a penicillin shot every February when I got the current year's virus. My feeling was that no doctor would just blindly turn away a patient who claimed a recommendation from another doctor, even if Doctor A didn't recognize the name of Doctor B. (Is any of this making sense?)

The nurse, at any rate, said, "Excuse me one minute, please, Mr. Nedick," and left me standing there under the foolish weight of the name I'd given myself. I scratched myself and felt inadequate and uncomfortable until she returned and said, "The doctor can see you at the end of office hours today. If you could be here at one forty-five?"

"One forty-five. Yes, thank you."

"That's quarter till two."

"Yes," I said, "I know it is."

"Some people get confused," she said. And hung up.

19

MINETTA LANE IS an L-shaped street, one block long, in the heart of Green-wich Village. It is a beautiful street, in a Little Old New York sort of way, and is almost the only area that still looks like Greenwich Village, the rest of it looking mostly like Coney Island. Except West 8th Street which looks like Far Rockaway.

In any case, I was going to Minetta Lane because that was where Gus Ricovic lived.

Remember Gus Ricovic? According to the *Daily News* he had taken Gertie
out for a date the night my Uncle Matt was murdered. Who he was beyond
that the *Daily News* had not said, nor was it clear whether or not he had
accompanied Gertie into the apartment and become a co-discoverer of the
body, nor had there been any mention of him in any of the follow-up stories.
But I wanted to know more about him, so when I'd gotten up this morning
I'd looked him up in the phone book—everybody is in the phone book—and
there he was, living on Minetta Lane.

The address was an old dark-brick apartment building, and the name G.
Ricovic was next to the bell-button for apartment 5-C. I rang, and waited,
and had about decided nobody was home when all at once the door buzzer
sounded. I leaped to the door and got it open just in time.

When I got to the fifth floor the door of apartment 5-C was standing
open, showing a large square living room full of bad furniture from the
Salvation Army. There was no one in sight. I stood tentatively in the doorway
a second or two, and then tapped on the door.

A voice called, "Come on in!"

I entered, and the voice called, "Shut it, will ya?"

I shut it, and the voice called, "Take a seat."

I took a seat, and the voice was quiet.

To the right of where I was sitting an arched doorway led to a long hall,
this in semi-darkness. From somewhere down there came the sound of
running water, and the brisk scrub-scrub of someone brushing his teeth. This
was followed by an interminable period of repulsive gargling sounds, and
then a great deal of splashing—as though dolphins were at play nearby and
then what sounded like a towel repeatedly being snapped.

At last there was silence. I listened, and nothing seemed to be happening
at all.

My mouth had become very dry. What was I doing here? What did I
know about questioning people, about investigating murder cases, about
unraveling complex schemes? Nothing. Less than nothing, in fact, because
what little I did remember from my reading, I didn't know how to use.

I had come here to ask a man named Gus Ricovic some questions. What
questions? And what did I hope to gain from his answers? If I asked him
straight out if he was part of the gang that had killed Uncle Matt and
kidnapped Gertie and shot at me, he would naturally say no, he wasn't. And
what would that prove?

While trying to decide what it would prove, I looked up and saw someone
coming down the dark hall toward me. At first l thought it was a young boy,
and wondered why he was smoking a cigar, but then I realized he was an
adult and merely unusually short.

He was wearing a white terrycloth robe, and he was barefoot, and yet the only word that possibly describes him is "dapper." A dapper little man with neat narrow feet, a neat narrow head, neat slicked-down black hair, neat tiny mustache, and a neat economy of movement. His right hand was in a pocket of his robe, in the manner of English nobility at the races, and with his left hand he removed the long and slender cigar from his mouth in order to say, "Don't believe I've had the pleasure, man."

"Fred Fitch," I said, getting to my feet. "Are you Gus Ricovic?"

"That's why I live here," he said, moving the cigar around like George Burns. "This is Gus Ricovic's pad, so this is where Gus Ricovic lives. What's a Fred Fitch?"

"I'm a friend of Gertie's," I said. "Also Matt Grierson's nephew."

"Ah, the money boy," he said, and smiled in Levantine pleasure. "Any friend of money is a friend of Gus Ricovic," he said. "Have you breakfasted?"

"Yes."

"Come watch," he said, and turned away.

I followed him into the dark hall and off to the right into an even darker kitchen. He hit a light-switch, nothing happened, and he said conversationally, "Have a seat, man. We talk while I ingest."

I couldn't see a thing. Did *he* think the light had gone on? I stood in the doorway, trying to decide what to say and/or do, and all at once a furious flickering began all around me, with a white-on-white kitchen appearing and disappearing like a midnight thunderstorm with lightning outside the windows.

But it was only a fluorescent ceiling fixture, somewhat more sluggish than most. It was pinging and buzzing up there, in time with its flickers, and with a final *zizzop!* it came completely on and stayed that way.

Gus Ricovic—for I supposed this was indeed he—was already at a cabinet across the way, reaching for a box of something called Instant Breakfast. "Fantastic invention," he commented, and took a paper packet out of the box.

Wondering if he meant fluorescent lighting, I pulled out one of the chrome-tube chairs by the formica table and sat down. "Yes, it is," I said, since comment seemed to be expected of me.

"The only breakfast that makes sense, man," he said, plunking the packet onto the counter beside the sink, so he hadn't meant the light after all. He went over to the refrigerator and got out a quart of milk. *En passant,* he said, "What's your will with me, pal?"

I said, "You were with Gertie the night my uncle was murdered."

"Ungood, man," he said, getting a glass from a cupboard. "Blood. Fuzz. Iron everywhere." He shuddered, and put the glass with the milk and the packet on the counter.

"You were in the apartment?"

"Wall-to-wall bluecoats," he said. "Looked like a civil rights meeting." He went over to another cupboard, opened it, and got down a bottle of Hennessy brandy.

"Did you meet Gertie through Uncle Matt?" I asked, because it suddenly seemed important to know whose circle this odd little man had originally belonged to. I had no idea why it was important, but it seemed important, and so I asked.

Carrying brandy to the counter, he said, "Nah, man. The other way around."

"You knew Gertie first."

He ripped open the packet. "Knew her for years," he said. "Buddy system." He shrugged.

"Would you mind telling me where you met her?"

He poured yellow powder from the packet into the glass. "Club in Brooklyn. We both worked there one time."

"You worked there?"

"Bongos, my friend," he said, and put down the packet and drummed the counter a hot lick to demonstrate. "Strippers need bongos," he said, "like folk singers need guitars."

"Then you don't have any connection with my uncle."

He shrugged, and poured milk into the glass. "Got to know him some. Played him gin while the lady put her face on." He made dealing motions. "Dishonest old geezer, your uncle," he said.

"He cheated?"

"Not so's you couldn't notice it. Old and slow, man." He held his hands up close to his face and studied them as though they were recent acquisitions. "Some day these hands," he said, "will not know bongos. Hard to imagine."

"What did he say when you caught him?"

Ricovic shrugged, put his hands down, and used them to pour brandy in on top of the milk and the yellow powder. "A few dollars to make an old man happy," he said. "Besides, Gertie made good on it."

"You mean you let him get away with it."

He took a spoon from a drawer and began stirring the contents of the glass. "It's what Gertie wanted." He put the spoon down and faced me: "The question is, what do you want."

"Information," I said.

"Information." He smiled slightly, picked up his glass, and said, "Follow."

We went back to the living room, where he motioned me back to the chair I'd been sitting in before, and then seated himself on the sofa. "Information," he repeated, seeming to enjoy the feel of the word in his mouth.

"Like, vengeance is yours, is that how it goes?"

"I want to know who killed my uncle," I said. "For reasons of my own."

"Reasons of your own. You're a rich boy now."

"What's that got to do with anything?"

"When rich boys want information," he said, smiling at me, "all they have to do is wave money." He raised his glass in salute. "Your health," he said, and downed the whole glassful chugalug.

Carefully I said, "You mean *you* might know something?"

"I know the value of a dollar," he said. He put the empty glass on the coffee table, and wiped his mouth with the sleeve of his robe.

Was this for real, or was he trying to pull something, trying to peddle some cock-and-bull story made up out of his head? I said, "Naturally I'd pay a reward for information leading—"

"Yeah, yeah," he said. "Leading to the arrest and conviction of the guy that killed your uncle. I've read those cards, too."

"Well?"

"I tell you, man," he said, "my personal feeling is, there's many a slip twixt the arrest and the conviction. COD is not my style."

"You'd want your money beforehand."

"I'd feel safer that way."

I said, "Do you really have something to sell?"

He smiled. "Gus Ricovic," he said, "doesn't dicker for practice."

"The name of the killer?"

"That's the special of the week, my friend," he said.

"And proof," I said.

He shrugged. "Indications," he said. "I have the finger to point with, you have the eyes to see."

"I wouldn't want to give you money," I said, "for information I couldn't use."

"Fiscally sound, man. Maybe you shouldn't buy at all."

Damn him, he was in a seller's market and he knew it. He didn't care if I bought or not, or at least he could afford to act that way. I was the one approaching him, so the decision was up to me.

I said, "How much?"

"A thousand now," he said.

"Now?"

"Installment plan. Another thousand when the law puts the collar on the boy I name. And another thousand when he goes to trial win or lose."

"Why so complicated?"

"Gus Ricovic has scruples," he told me. "If my information does nothing, it costs you one grand. If it helps, but not enough, it costs two grand. If it does the whole job, it costs three grand." He spread his hands. "Absolutely honest," he said.

I sat back to think about it, but I already knew I was going to do it. I said, "All right, I'll write you a check."

"Not hardly, my friend. You'll write me cash."

I could understand that, but I said, "I don't have a thousand dollars in cash."

"Who does? You take it out of your bank, you come back at six o'clock."

"Why six o'clock?"

"I'll need time to talk to the other party."

"What other party?"

"The party that did for your uncle. Naturally."

I didn't see anything naturally about it. I said, "You're going to *talk* to him?"

"You want some sort of unfair advantage? Naturally I have to give him the opportunity to meet your price."

"Meet my—! But you—You can't—*You're* the one—"

"Excuse me pointing this out, man," he said, "but you're sputtering."

"You're damn *right* I'm sputtering! What kind of—I'll come back here at six o'clock, you'll say oh, no, the price went up, the other party offered such and such, you'll have to pay at least so and so."

"Possibly," he said, judiciously granting me the point. "I tell you what we'll do, we'll limit it to two rounds of bidding. You play pinochle?"

"Pinochle?" I said.

"Two rounds of bidding? It's a phrase from pinochle."

I felt like a man with a wasp's nest in the attic of his skull. "What do I care?" I demanded. "Pinochle? What do you mean, pinochle? First you say you know something you'll sell, then you've got to talk to the other *party*, for God's sake, then it's two rounds of bidding, now it's pinochle. Maybe you don't know anything, what do you think of that? Maybe you're some kind of four-flusher, how does that grab you? That's a term from blackjack, it means you don't really have anything, you're bluffing." I got to my feet, driven upward in an excess of frustration. "I don't believe a word you've said," I told him, "and I wouldn't give you a thousand *cents.*"

"Poker," he said.

"What?"

"Four-flush is a term from poker. It means you give the appearance of having five cards all in the same suit, but you only have four." He got to his feet. "I have five," he said. "And I'll see you at six o'clock."

"I knew that," I said. I pointed a finger at Gus Ricovic. "I *knew* it was poker. That's how upset you got me."

"My apologies, man," he said. "When you come back at six, I'll try not to increase the agitation."

20

BLACKJACK IS A game where you're dealt two cards face down, and if you want more cards they're dealt face up, and the object of the game is to get as close as possible to twenty-one points—picture cards count ten—without getting more than twenty-one points. If at the end of the hand your cards come closer to twenty-one points than do the dealer's cards, you win.

Poker is a game where you're dealt five cards, and if you get one pair that's good but if you get two pair that's better, and three of a kind is better than that, and there are also straights and flushes and straight flushes and full houses and four of a kind.

I just want to point out that I did know all that. I don't know why I said four-flush was a term from blackjack. The only term from blackjack is *blackjack*.

Anyway, when I staggered out of Gus Ricovic's apartment I immediately took a cab back uptown to the bank, on my way to make the second withdrawal of the day.

Sitting in the back of the cab as slowly we progressed through New York's perpetual traffic snarl, I wondered if I was in the process of being played for a sucker yet a millionth time. Did Gus Ricovic really know who had killed Uncle Matt? If he did know, would he really tell me? If he did know and he really told me, would it ultimately do me any good?

In private-eye books, of which I've read my share, people are always buying information, and the information is always one hundred per cent accurate. Nobody ever sells a private eye a lie, Lord knows why. But I wasn't a private eye, and Gus Ricovic might at this very moment be constructing for my special use a green and blue, six-sided, open-topped, reversible, large economy-size thousand-dollar whopper.

But I'd buy it, I knew that as well as he did. I had no idea how else to learn anything and I might as well throw my money away at least *attempting* something.

But before you can throw money away you have to get your hands on it. Not always an easy thing to do, that, not if you've entrusted your money to a bank.

"Lot of money," said the teller dubiously, looking at the check I'd written and shoved across the counter to him.

"I'll take it in hundreds," I said.

"One moment," he said, and picked up his phone and checked my account. He seemed troubled by what he heard, put the phone down again, and studied my check with fretful eyes.

I said, "I have enough to cover it."

"Yes, of course," he said, not taking his eyes from the check. "Lot of money," he repeated.

"Hundreds," I repeated. "In a little envelope, if you have one."

"One moment," he repeated, and for a second I thought I was caught in a loop of time, endlessly backing on itself, circling around and around and around and never getting anywhere. But then, instead of picking up the phone and checking my account again, the teller walked away, carrying the check with him.

I leaned against the counter and waited. The woman behind me, Xmas Club booklet in hand, gave me a dirty look and went off to join another line.

The teller came back with another man, who was trying to look as dapper as Gus Ricovic but was failing. Of course, he had a gray suit on instead of a white terrycloth bathrobe, which may have made the difference. He smiled at me like a mechanical store-window Santa Claus and said, "Can I be of service?"

"You could cash my check," I said. "I'd like hundreds, if you have any."

The teller had already given this new one my check. The new one looked at it, seemed vaguely disturbed, and said, "Lot of money."

"Not really," I said. "Considering the national debt—"

He put my check on the counter and pointed over my shoulder. "I'm afraid you'll have to have this okayed," he said. "Mr. Kekkleman over there can help you, I'm sure."

"It's my money," I pointed out. "I'm just letting you people hold it for me."

"Yes, sir, naturally. Mr. Kekkleman will take care of everything for you."

So I went over to see Mr. Kekkleman, who sat at a desk behind an altar rail. He looked up at me with the bright expression of a man prepared instantly to make loans for solid collateral, and I said, "I need you to okay this check."

He took the check, looked at it, and his expression turned constipated. Before he could say it, I said, "Lot of money."

"Yes, it is," he said. "Would you have a seat?"

I sat down in the chair beside the desk. When he picked up the phone I said, "The man over there already checked my account."

He gave me a blank distracted smile and checked my account. It took longer this time. I said, conversationally, "I'm thinking of taking all my money out of this stupid bank," and he gave me the same plastic smile.

Finally he put the phone down and said, "Yes, sir, Mr. Fitch. Would you give me a specimen signature?"

I burst out laughing.

His smile grew pained and puzzled. "Sir?"

"You just made me think," I told him, "about the specimens you have to give when you go see the doctor. You know, you take the little bottle into the men's room and all. And then I remembered a story I read once about some drunks who wrote their names in the snow that way. Specimen signatures, you see?"

He didn't think it was funny, and smiled so as to let me know it. Then he extended me a pen and a memo pad and I signed my name the old-fashioned way. He compared this signature with the one on the check, and this satisfied him. I have no idea why this satisfied him, since I'd written that check over on the other side of this same room not five minutes ago. Do crooks' signatures change every five minutes?

Well, I didn't make a fuss. He did some runes on the back of my check, I went over and stood in line behind the woman with the Xmas Club booklet, and in more time than it takes to tell about it I had ten hundred-dollar bills in a tiny manila envelope tucked away inside my wallet.

Free at last.

21

DR. OSBERTSON'S PARK Avenue office was everything the Park Avenue office of a Park Avenue doctor should be, and his nurse blended in icy beauty with the décor.

I sat for a while in the waiting room with three dowagers. Then I sat for a while with two dowagers. Then I sat with one dowager. In the last stage I sat for a period of time alone. But at last the nurse held a door open and looked at me and said, "Mr. Nedick?"

I was afraid the name would make me blush, if I heard it too often. "Coming," I mumbled, and put down the copy of *Forbes* magazine I'd been leafing through—in some amazement, I might add—and followed her down a shiny corridor into a gleaming examination room, all white enamel and stainless steel.

"The doctor will be with you in just a moment," she said, and put a folder on a table, and went away, shutting the door behind her. The folder was empty, and on the tab was lettered very carefully in ink: *Nedick, F.*

Her idea of a moment was pretty unusual. It was two-thirty when she left me in that room, and ten minutes to three—that's two-fifty, some people get confused—when Dr. Osbertson came briskly in, rubbing pudgy clean hands together and saying, "Well, now, what seems to be the trouble today?"

Seldom do people in real life resemble the fictional clichés erected to represent them, but Dr. Osbertson was the exception to the rule. He was fiftyish, distinguished, well padded, complacent and obviously well-off. He had the smile of an evil baby, and I swear I could feel his eyes undressing my wallet, though they seemed to miss the envelope full of hundreds.

I said, "Doctor, my name is Fitch. I'm—"

"What's this? The nurse has given me the wrong folder." He picked it up and started for the door with it.

"No, she didn't," I said. "I told her my name was Nedick. I didn't want you to know who I really was until I got here." He stopped with one hand on the doorknob, the other clutching the empty folder, and looked at me with the attentive frown of a baby trying to understand why the watch ticks. Then he said, "I believe you've come to the wrong sort of physician. Mental disorders are not my—"

"Matthew Grierson was my uncle," I said.

He blinked at me, very slowly, and then said, "Ah, I see." He removed his hand from the doorknob, replaced the folder on the table, and smiled falsely at me, saying, "Well, this is a pleasure. Frankly, I don't understand—" He gestured at the folder.

"Some odd things have been happening," I said. "But they aren't important. The important thing is I want to talk to you about my uncle."

"Well, of course, his death wasn't from natural causes, was it? No, indeed. Actually, I should think the police would be the ones for you to talk to." He made a smallish movement toward the phone on the wall near the door. "Shall I call them for you?"

"I've already talked to them," I said. "Twice. Now I want to talk to you."

"Yes, of course." His smile had grown nervous, and he turned with some reluctance away from the phone. Whether this meant he had something to hide or merely thought he was dealing with a potential nut, I couldn't tell.

I said, "I understand my uncle had cancer."

"Yes, he did, that's right, that's what he had. Cancer." Osbertson was babbling, because of his nervousness, and he was looking around like a man who's lost something important and can't quite remember what it is.

I refused to be sidetracked. Hoping that calm and reasonable questioning would have a beneficial effect on him, so that sooner or later he'd settle down and begin to talk to me, I said, "I understand he'd had the cancer for several years."

"Yes, that's right. Six years, I believe, six years going on seven." He had drifted over to a side table and was fussily and distractedly moving things around on it: a little bottle, a tongue depressor, a package of disposable rubber gloves.

I said, "I understand he hadn't originally been expected to live this long."

"Oh, yes, that's true," he said forcefully, actually turning around to face me. "Very true," he said earnestly. "The original prognosis was death within a year. Within a year. Of course, that was a diagnostician in Brazil, but I myself was flown down not long afterwards and examined the subject and I must say I agreed with that diagnosis exactly. And other physicians since then have confirmed the diagnosis. Of course, there can't be any real precision in cases like this, the literature is full of cases of individuals who lived a greater or lesser time than was assumed in the diagnosis, and this man Grierson merely happened to be one of them. He could have gone at any moment. He would *not* have lived another six months, that I will state without equivocation. As to the general diagnosis in cases of this sort, no physician presumes to be offering an exact timetable, and the physician can't be blamed if the individual patient behaves in a manner differing from the norm."

Smiling, I said, "Well, I don't suppose Uncle Matt exactly *blamed* you for keeping him alive."

"Eh?" He'd been caught up in his explanation, and now all at once he seemed to remember whom he was talking to and what the subject was. "Oh, of course," he said. "Your uncle. Astonishing case, astonishing." With the return of memory had come the return of distraction; once again he was half-turned from me, pottering among the implements on his table.

I said, "You were his doctor for a long time, eh? I mean, even before he went to Brazil."

"What?" He touched a hypodermic syringe, a thermometer, a stethoscope. "Oh, no, not a bit. Never treated him till I went down to see him in Brazil. No, no, no previous history at all, not with me."

"I don't understand," I admitted. "How did he happen to pick you to come all the way to Brazil, if you'd never treated him before?"

He seemed startled. He put on a disposable rubber glove, took it off, disposed of it. "Mutual acquaintance, I suppose," he muttered, half-swallowing the words. "Some other patient."

"Who?"

"Couldn't say, couldn't possibly remember. Have to look it up in the records." He picked up the syringe, depressed the plunger, put it down. "Might not even be there."

"Well," I said, "I do want to talk to people who knew Uncle Matt. If it wouldn't be too much trouble, could you take a look and see if you do have it in the records?"

"Well, of course," he mumbled, "medical records, it's all confidential, not supposed to do that sort of thing." He picked up a bottle marked *Alcohol,* put it down. "Laymen," he said.

"I don't want to *see* anybody's records," I said. "If I could just know the name of the patient who recommended you to my uncle . . ."

He picked up a box of cotton pads, took out a pad, put the box down, put the pad down on the box. "Of course," he said indistinctly, talking into his chest, "those would be the old records, might be difficult to find . . ."

"If you'd look. Would you please look?"

"I'm not sure I'd—" He broke off, and turned even farther away from me. He picked up a small bottle, picked up the syringe, stuck the needle of the syringe through the stopper of the small bottle. He mumbled something I didn't catch, though the general rambling nature of it came through clearly enough.

What was he planning to do, inject me with something? Knock me out? Maybe even kill me. I backed farther away from him, looking around, and on a bench to my left I saw one of those little rubber hammers used by doctors to tap people on the knee. I edged closer to it.

Meanwhile, the doctor had raised his voice again, was saying, "All of this is most unorthodox, of course. Naturally, you understand a physician must be careful whom he deals with, who gets information and who does not. A physician has an obligation to his patients." And all the while he was drawing the fluid from the little bottle into the syringe, removing the needle from the bottle, putting the now-full syringe down on the table, discarding the bottle. He was obviously trying to keep me from noticing any of this, keeping his back to me, muttering away, trying to appear random and distracted.

I was close now to the rubber hammer. If he came toward me with that syringe I could get to the hammer in one leap. With luck I'd knock the syringe from his hand and overpower him before he could do whatever he had in mind. I was his last patient of the day; if necessary I'd hold him prisoner here all night to get the information I wanted, and an explanation for his weird behavior.

In the interim, I was acting as though unaware of his preparations. I said, "You can understand my interest, I hope. After all, I did profit from my uncle's death, profited a great deal, and I feel a certain obligation to get to know him, even if it is only posthumously."

"Oh, naturally," he blathered. "Completely understandable, completely." As he spoke he was rolling up his left shirt sleeve. Was he trying to lull my suspicions, trying to make me think he was diabetic or some such thing and preparing his normal injection?

He really went quite far with it, opening the alcohol bottle, wetting the cotton pad, cleaning a patch of skin on his inner left elbow. "Most natural instinct in the world," he nattered, while doing this. "One feels a certain—kinship—to relatives who leave us money. Particularly a great deal of money. Oh, particularly."

He picked up the syringe.

I edged closer to the rubber hammer.

He stuck the needle in his arm and injected himself.

My mouth hung open like a sprung drawbridge. I watched him put the syringe down, place the cotton pad against the injection, bend his elbow, and turn at last away from the table. "I can understand your coming to see me," he said, still rambling, as he walked over to the paper-covered gray-leather examination table, sat down on it, and then stretched out. "I'm sorry I can be of no real help to you," he said drowsily.

More loudly than I'd expected, I shouted, "What have you done?"

"One hundred," he said. "Ninety-nine. Ninety-eight. Ninety-seven."

I raced over to him. His eyes were closed, his features relaxed, his hands crossed on his chest. He looked very peaceful. "Wake up!" I shouted. "You've got to answer my questions! Wake up!"

"Ninety-six," he said. "Ninety-fi. Nine-four. Ni-th. Ni. Nnnnnnn."

I shook him. I slapped his cheeks. I screamed in his ear. I half-climbed atop him, straddling him with one leg the better to grasp his shoulders and shake him, and I was in that position when the door opened and the nurse came in.

She screamed. She shrieked, "Murder!" She went tearing away down the corridor, screaming, "He's murdered the doctor!"

Dr. Osbertson slept on, faintly smiling. As for me, I fled.

22

MY RETURN HOME bore a marked similarity to Napoleon's departure from Russia. I had gone out with a head full of grand plans and predetermined goals, and I was coming back without my army. As for my six o'clock appointment with Gus Ricovic, I did not right now have very high hopes.

I approached my block circumspectly, but once again there was no sign of my would-be assassins. With one last quick look around, I ducked into my doorway.

The mailbox was full again. I emptied it into my pockets and went on upstairs.

For once there was no one to greet me at my door, not even Wilkins. I went inside, emptied the mail from my pockets to the table near the door, and went out to the kitchen to prepare myself one of the first pre-sundown drinks of my life.

If I had ever thought there was any chance of my being a detective, I now knew better. I'd gone out to question two men, and one of them had put himself to sleep rather than answer me. Unconscious, he had routed me.

Of course, it might be construed as progress of a kind. After all, Dr. Osbertson wouldn't have knocked himself out if he hadn't had something to hide, would he?

I considered briefly the notion that Dr. Osbertson had murdered Uncle Matt himself, in a fit of pique at Uncle Matt's having proved his diagnosis to be so completely off the beam. To a professional man, it might seem a sort of insult to say a man will die in a year and then have the man live *five* years beyond the diagnosis. If Uncle Matt hadn't been hit on the head with a blunt instrument he might have outlived his physician.

But that was a fairly silly reason for murder. No, it wouldn't do. The murder had something to do with money, the money I'd inherited. There was no reason for any of the rest of this, otherwise.

So what was Dr. Osbertson hiding? The identity of the patient who had recommended him to Uncle Matt? But why would that be something worth hiding?

The extent of my ignorance in this sea of occurrences sometimes startled me and sometimes disheartened me. At the moment it was doing both.

How could I find out what Dr. Osbertson knew and didn't want me to know? If I went back to see him again, God alone knew what he might do. Shoot himself in the foot. Operate on his vocal cords. Inject himself with German measles and put himself in quarantine.

My first drink didn't solve any problems, so I had a second. As I sipped at it, I dialed Gertie's number on the off-chance, but there wasn't any answer. I then went through today's inpouring of mail and found it—with one exception—to be another dose of yesterday's avalanche. I threw the rest away and took a closer look at my exception.

It was a plain envelope, with no name or address or any other writing on it. Nor a stamp; it hadn't been mailed but had been dropped into my mailbox by someone while I was out.

Inside was a small sheet of stationery, folded once. I opened it up and found a typed message inside, short and sweet. It read:

Call me.
Professor Kilroy
CH2-2598

Professor Kilroy. Where had I heard that name before? Somewhere . . .

Gertie. She'd said Professor Kilroy was my Uncle Matt's partner down in Brazil!

Maybe at last I'd start finding out what was going on!

I had the number almost all dialed when caution suddenly reasserted itself. This was a Chelsea number, which meant somewhere in this neighborhood. The note claimed to be from Professor Kilroy, but what if it wasn't? What if it was a trick, to get me to announce when I was home? The gang could be a block from here, three buildings from here, just waiting for the phone to ring.

No, the thing to do was get out of the neighborhood, get uptown, and call from there. And for once in my life I was going to *do* the thing that was the thing to do. Back on went my coat, into my pocket went Professor Kilroy's note, and out the door went I.

23

I KNEW JUST the place to go: the newspaper library. At least when I began to read a newspaper it didn't put itself to sleep on me or start auctioning its information. And it had occurred to me that some of the characters in this cast of thousands might from time to time have been newsworthy. Professor Kilroy, for instance. Or Uncle Matt. Or Gus Ricovic. Anything I found out about their past activities might be of help to me.

Or, on the other hand, it might not.

In any case, it seemed best to leave the apartment, and the newspaper library was as good a place to go as any, and better than some. So I left my snug lair once again, and as I hurried away toward Eighth Avenue, I found myself amazed at the neighborhood's continued lack of assassins. It seemed I'd just managed to double-think them somehow; I was a sort of living purloined letter, hidden in the most obvious place and therefore unseeable.

It was twenty past three when I arrived at the library. By five o'clock, when I left, I'd learned a little but I'd also run across some surprising blanks. Professor Kilroy, for example, hadn't appeared at all, nor—except for his murder—had my Uncle Matt. Reilly had showed up a few times, in connection with Bunco Squad arrests, but Karen Smith had never appeared at all. Wilkins had appeared once, having something obscure to do with the 1949 Berlin airlift. Mr. Grant had never made the *Times*. I'd expected Goodkind to be in constantly, but he appeared only once, when a former client for whom he had successfully prosecuted a damage suit against a large elevator corporation turned around and sued him for having kept over half the proceeds. Neither Gertie nor Gus Ricovic appeared, but Dr. Lucius Osbertson did, just once. Seven years ago he'd been the physician for a man named Walter J. Cosgrove, a financier whose testimony was wanted in a fraudulent stock deal. Dr. Osbertson had sworn his client was too ill to testify at that time. I looked up Cosgrove, and discovered that three days after Dr. Osbertson's testimony Cosgrove escaped to Brazil, taking with him, in the newspaper's estimation, "upwards of two million dollars in cash and negotiable securities." I've never been sure whether *upwards of* means *more than* or *almost,* but I got the general idea.

Cosgrove's departure for Brazil took place a year after Uncle Matt's, and two years before Uncle Matt's return. I wondered if Cosgrove and Uncle Matt had gotten to know one another down there in Brazil, if it was Cosgrove who had called Osbertson down to see to Uncle Matt when Uncle Matt had fallen ill.

I wondered if any of the money Uncle Matt had brought back had at one time belonged to Walter J. Cosgrove.

It seemed to me likely that the name Cosgrove was what Dr. Osbertson had been hiding this afternoon; he was probably still trying to live down the blot to his reputation. But if that was all it was, his action seemed a little extreme. No, there was still more to this than I understood.

When I left the newspaper library, I walked over to the gas station at Tenth Avenue and 42nd Street and used the phone booth there. I dialed the number on Professor Kilroy's note, and it was answered after three rings by a gravelly voice saying, "Yes? What is it?"

"Professor Kilroy, please," I said. The name sounded as foolish in its way as did Fred Nedick, but I didn't feel as silly pronouncing it; *I* wasn't Professor Kilroy.

The gravelly voice said, "Who is this?"

"Fred Fitch," I said. "Is this Professor Kilroy?"

"Where are you? You to home?"

"Never mind where I am. Is this Professor Kilroy?"

"Sure. Who do you think it is? You think I give you somebody else's number? Where you want to meet, your place or mine?"

"Neither," I said. I'd thought about this part of it, and had finally decided on the safest place to meet this man, whoever he was. "I'll meet you," I said, "at Grand Central, the main waiting room."

"How come?"

"I have no way to be sure who you are."

"Listen, kid, all I'm doing is helping out the nephew of an old pal, that's my only interest in this."

"My only interest," I told him, "is protecting myself. I'll meet you at Grand Central or nowhere."

"Sure, what the hell, Grand Central. Any special time?"

"I'll leave that up to you."

"Eight o'clock, okay? After the rush hour."

"All right by me," I said. "How will I recognize you?"

"Don't worry," he said. "I'll recognize you."

Click.

24

NOW FOR UNCLE Matt's apartment.

I had waited this long to go there because I was fairly certain that Goodkind would be spending at least part of today hanging around its vicinity in hopes of getting my ear for a fast lesson in hypnosis. I had no idea what his role in all this might be, whether he was connected with the murderer/kidnappers or if he had some separate plot of his own afoot, but I did know enough about my own guillibility and I had seen enough of his smiling face to know that my only safety lay in avoiding him.

But he couldn't stake out Uncle Matt's apartment forever. Sooner or later he would have to give it up, called away by the pressure of his business. Surely by now he had to be somewhere suborning a jury, or foreclosing on a widow, or pursuing an ambulance. Hoping this assumption was correct, I sidled under cover of the rush hour up to that part of West 59th Street known as Central Park South, found the right building, and lurked around until I was fairly certain Attorney Goodkind was nowhere in the vicinity. Then I approached the doorman, who looked mainly like an admiral in the Bolivian Navy.

At first he pretended I wasn't there, as I'm sure he fervently wished. I suppose I just didn't look the Central Park South type, and I assume he thought me a tourist, wanting him to point out to me the passing celebrities: Killer Joe Piro, Barbra Streisand, General Hershey.

When I finally took the tactic of standing directly in front of him and obstructing his attempt to flag cabs, he reluctantly acknowledged my existence by giving me an impatient, "Yes? What is it?"

"The keys to the Grierson apartment," I said.

If I'd expected any sudden change in manner, any abrupt shift to bowing and scraping, I was to be disappointed. With the same gruff impatience, he reached into the trouser pocket of his admiral's uniform, produced two keys attached by a bit of dirty string to a round red tag, and handed it to me without a word or a look. Then he stepped around me and blew his whistle violently at the world.

Inside, I was stopped by another naval officer, this one a mere commander in the Swiss Maritime, who with barely concealed hostility wanted to know who it was I hoped to see.

"Nobody," I said. "I own an apartment in this building. The Matthew Grierson apartment."

This time there was a change, to a rather offensive sort of chumminess. The commander said, "Oh, yeah? You inherited, huh? Rags to riches, huh?"

How was it that people like this instinctively knew they could get away with such treatment of me? Money isn't everything, a fact of which rotters like this one were endlessly eager to remind me.

I said, "Not exactly," knowing it to be a weak response, and went on by him and across the long low-ceilinged lobby to the elevator. I told the operator, "The Grierson apartment," he slid his doors shut, and up we went.

On the way, the operator—green uniform, possibly a passed-over captain in the Merry Men Brigade—said, "You the nephew?"

Not another one. With a sinking heart I said, "Yes, I am."

But he wasn't exactly another one. He was simply the garrulous type. "Mr. Grierson used to talk about you a lot," he said. He was a gnarled and weather-beaten man of about fifty, thin and somewhat stoop-shouldered. "We used to play cards together sometimes," he went on, "when my tour was done. Sometimes he'd be reading a report on you."

"Is that right?"

"Yes, sir," he said. "My favorite tenant, your uncle. Never uppity, like a lot of these people. Paid his debts, too, on the button. If he'd lose, he'd write you a check right then and there."

"Did he lose a lot?" I asked, wondering if this little man had been picking my uncle in a small-time way.

But he said, "No, sir, he mostly won. He was real lucky, your uncle."

It seemed as though that last had been said with some kind of an edge in the voice, but I couldn't be sure, and before I could say anything more the elevator came to a stop, the doors opened, and he was pointing away to the left, saying, "That's it there, sir, 14-C. It's really the thirteenth floor, but most people are superstitious, you know? So they call it fourteen."

"That's interesting," I said, as I stepped out of the elevator.

"But it's still the thirteenth floor," he said. "Ain't that so? You go outside and count the windows, this here's the thirteenth floor, ain't it?"

"I suppose it is," I said.

"Sure it is," he said. Then he shook his head, said, "Rich people," shut his doors, and went away.

It took two keys on two locks to get into Uncle Matt's apartment, which had the musty smell of disuse and which, when I began switching on lights, sprang into existence like a series of no-longer-needed movie sets.

The style represented here was surely not Uncle Matt's, not from all I'd heard about the old man. Undoubtedly the building itself had an interior decorator on tap who had designed and furnished this apartment. It was the sort of thing Uncle Matt would more than likely leave to someone else to take care of; I doubted he cared very much what his surroundings looked like, so long as they sufficiently had the appropriate smell of money.

The rooms went on and on. A long broad living room on two levels, with a lot of long low sofas and on the walls long abstract paintings, and great drape-flanked windows at the end giving a beautiful long view of Central Park. Following a curve of wrought-iron railing away from all this grandeur, one came to a small formal dining room with dark red fabric wall covering and heavy wood antique furnishings. A shiny white compact but very complete kitchen was off this, through a swinging door with a porthole in it.

Away from the dining room in the other direction one came to a game room, with a pool table *and* a poker table, the latter with chip trays and glass holders. Past this were two large elaborate bedrooms, both with canopied king-size beds and outsize views of Central Park. Each bedroom had its own Pompeiian bathroom, in one of which was a sauna. Beyond the second bedroom was a sort of den or office, with a desk and with built-in bookshelves containing books I'm sure no one had ever read. And off in yet another direction was a smallish plain bedroom with its own attached prim bath; servant's quarters, no doubt.

Uncle Matt had done well for himself. He'd spent his declining years in comfort.

I wandered around the rooms, not sure what I was looking for and not sure what I was finding. If it was Uncle Matt's personality, some aura of him, I had hoped to find here, I doubted I was getting it. The dominant personality here was the interior decorator's. Other than that, I suppose I mostly just wanted to take a look at the scene of the crime.

Which was the game room. Uncle Matt had been found, according to the text and photo in the *Daily News,* face-down in the game room, between the pool table and the poker table. A pool game had been in progress, with only one cue out, so it was assumed Uncle Matt had been shooting a solitary game of pool when he'd been struck down.

I stood looking at the very spot on the carpet for a while, learned nothing, theorized nothing, and finally went away to wander through the other rooms, getting nowhere until I settled down at the desk in the office.

Then I'm not sure where I got. I found a few odd pieces of stationery here and there, letters from this person and that, nothing very enlightening. There was a bill from Goodkind, with an ingratiating, palsy-walsy, yet obsequious letter accompanying it that made me think most of Uriah Heep. There was a letter from another attorney, a Prescott Wilks, taking exception to Uncle Matt's having done with the service of his firm, and one paragraph of this letter struck me as a little odd:

> You know the circumstances as well as I, Mr. Grierson, and I needn't tell you our mutual friend is as upset as I am at this abrupt and unjustifiable termination of your relationship with this firm. I have been asked to communicate to you the information that any alteration in the arrangements or any plans you might have for "striking out on your own," as it were, will not be treated lightly. Kindly bear this in mind in your future dealings with Latham, Courtney, Wilks & Wilks.

Apparently there had been no future dealings with Latham, Courtney, Wilks & Wilks; the letter was dated four months ago, there was no more recent correspondence that I could see, and Goodkind seemed securely in control of the situation by the time I had entered the affair.

What interested me was the veiled threat I seemed to distinguish in that one paragraph of Wilks' letter. Who was the mutual friend? What sort of relationship had Uncle Matt had with Prescott Wilks' firm? What exactly did the phrase "will not be treated lightly" mean? Did it mean murder?

I was bothered a bit by the knowledge that surely Steve and Ralph had seen this letter and had investigated its meaning, but against this fact I put the uncertainty I felt about Steve and Ralph, who might have sold out to the gang, who might have been the ones to tell the gang where I was hiding, and who might be covering for the murderers instead of seeking them out. After all, as Gertie had said, nobody was likely to accuse Steve and Ralph of being priests.

Thinking of Gertie, I decided to try her apartment again, but when I picked up the phone the line was dead. Goodkind must have seen to cutting off the service, which was very alert and thrifty of him, but with three hundred thousand dollars I could surely afford to keep the phone going in my other apartment.

Would I live here? Somehow I thought not; the place was too much like the lobby of Radio City Music Hall. I'd keep expecting tourist groups to be led through by guides. Besides, I couldn't spend my entire life being cowed by doormen. No, I'd have Goodkind put the place up for sale. All in all, I thought I'd stay in my own place on West 19th Street. I'd never found it less than satisfactory before, so why should I change it now?

Ah, but that was in the future, when all this mess was over and I could lead my normal life again. As to now, I was allegedly investigating Uncle Matt's apartment, for reason or reasons unknown. Therefore I copied the address of Latham, Courtney, Wilks & Wilks from the letter onto a piece of scrap paper, tucked the paper into my pocket, and went on with my search.

I made my next discovery in the closet off the maid's bedroom. That's where I found the crumpled-up body of Gus Ricovic.

25

AT FIRST I didn't realize he was dead. He was sitting on the floor, knees up, back against the wall, chin on knees, all tucked in the corner. His eyes were open, wide open, and on his face he had a sort of bland and faintly quizzical smile. He appeared to be looking at my ankles, and all in all the naturalness of his expression and posture had me absolutely fooled for perhaps ten seconds, during which time I was (a) amazed and (b) cynical.

I was (a) amazed because who wouldn't be, opening a closet door and finding Gus Ricovic tucked away on the floor inside? And I was (b) cynical because the immediate explanation for his presence which came to me was, "Oh ho! He's come looking for something to sell." That is, in the instant of seeing him I leaped to the assumption that when he had offered to sell me information he had actually been possessed of no information to sell and had therefore come rushing over here to see if by some rare stroke of luck he might find some information I'd later be willing to buy. This thought took much less time to think than it does to describe.

In any case, it very quickly became superseded by (c) horror. That was when I noticed that Gus Ricovic wasn't moving, his eyes weren't blinking, and there seemed to be something stickily wrong with the top of his bead. "Oh," I said, and slammed the door.

Then the noise of the slam scared me. Was the killer still somewhere close by? Had I spent the last half-hour playing hide and seek, all unknowing, with a multiple murderer? And now that I had found the latest body, would this murderer think it necessary to add me to his collection?

No, that couldn't be right. Whoever had killed Uncle Matt was already out to kill me and had made his intentions perfectly plain. And could there be any doubt that the same Mister X had done for Gus Ricovic? Whether Ricovic had come here hoping to find information to sell, or whether he had been killed as a result of trying to blackmail the killer, there was still no doubt that the same murdering hand had clubbed down both Uncle Matt and the thing in the closet.

So I had to be alone in the apartment, just me and Gus Ricovic. I didn't open the closet door any more, I already knew what he looked like. I turned by back, started walking, and three rooms later my brain at last caught up with me.

The first thing my brain wanted to know was what now? Call the police? No, for the same reasons that I hadn't called them when Gertie was kidnapped. In fact, I could handle this the same way, getting to the safe ground of a neutral phone booth somewhere. Aside from its other advantages, this plan had the admirable feature of getting me out of this apartment, in which the air suddenly seemed to have gotten both damp and chilly. Clammy. Like a mausoleum.

Gus Ricovic's body seemed to vibrate way back in its dark closet at the far end of the apartment. As though invisible strings were attached to it, leading to every other room, the air seemed to ring and echo with his presence. It was like being in a cave inside an iceberg, with something rotting off in a corner.

Anyway, it was time for my meeting with Professor Kilroy.

I left the apartment at a fast walk, fumbled with the keys as I locked the door, and even with that door between us, still felt the clammy tendrils of Gus Ricovic trailing along the back of my neck. I shivered, and pushed the button for the elevator.

My friendly elevator operator arrived, not soon enough, and as soon as I boarded he turned a worried face to me and said, "I been thinking about things, Mr. Grierson."

"Fitch," I said, distracted. I was thinking that I had never seen a dead body before and would prefer never to see a dead body again. Ever. Particularly not in closets in empty apartments.

"Yeah, that's right," the operator was saying. "I remember. Mr. Grierson explained me that one time, how you had different names."

"Did he?" I said.

"Mr. Fitch," he said urgently, "I hope you won't say nothing to the management here about me playing cards with your uncle or anything like that. We're not supposed to mingle with the tenants, you know. I mean, I wouldn't of done it if your uncle hadn't wanted me to."

"I won't say anything," I said.

"It could cost me my job," he said. "I wouldn't know what to do without this job."

I said nothing to that, having problems of my own to think about, and when at last the elevator doors opened on the ground floor I went away without reassuring him any more about his tenure. Besides, hadn't he heard of self-service elevators? Sooner or later automation must spread even to Central Park South, whether I finked on his chumming with Uncle Matt or not.

I wondered how the Bolivian admiral out front had liked having Uncle Matt for a tenant.

I wondered how I could manage so many irrelevant thoughts with Gus Ricovic sitting up there in that dark closet.

Three blocks from the apartment building I found an outdoor phone booth. Being wise in the ways of the Police Department by now, I succeeded in anonymously reporting the body in the closet in under five minutes, having run through the inevitable battery of Sergeant Sreeses and Tective Sreeses and Friggum-Steen Precincts like Roger Bannister through the four-minute mile.

As I was coming out of the phone booth, it occurred to me to wonder by how narrow a margin had I missed the murderer or murderers of Gus Ricovic. Had they left half an hour before I'd come? Or five minutes? Or thirty seconds?

Had they perhaps been going down in one elevator while I was going up in the other?

It was almost time to go meet Professor Kilroy, but the growing realization of how close perhaps I had come to taking the long walk hand in hand with Gus Ricovic made a preliminary stop necessary.

There was the place, just down the block, its door under the red neon
sign that said BAR.

26

I HAD ABOUT decided he wouldn't show up. It was ten minutes past eight,
the cavernous interior of Grand Central was sparsely populated. I sat on
a bench where I could watch most of the great room, waiting to see any
familiar face, any one at all. I would flee as though pursued by demons,
which I might as well be. I could still remember, only too clearly, having
been shot at not so very long ago. Not to mention the quizzical smile
and unblinking eyes of Gus Ricovic.

But the man who emerged out of nowhere and plopped down onto the
bench beside me was no one I had ever seen before in my life. He had
a great scraggly bushy black beard with great streaks of gray in it, his
hair was long and unkempt and also black with streaks of gray, his face
seemed to be just slightly dirty, and he wore great thick spectacles with
horn rims, the right wing of which was broken and haphazardly fixed
with Scotch tape. He was of medium height, but dressed in an old tweed
suit a good two or three sizes too large for him. His shirt was also too
large for him, and his orange-and-red tie was put together with the largest
knot I'd seen in years, the sort of knot we used to call a Windsor when
it was sported by all the sharpest blades in high school.

"Hello, kid," he said, in the most gravelly voice I ever heard in my
life, "I'm Professor Kilroy."

I said, "I guess you already know who I am."

"Sure," he said. "Short Sheet pointed you out to me one time."

"Short—? Oh, you mean Uncle Matt."

"Matt, yeah." He wiped the back of his hand across his mouth and
looked vaguely out around the terminal. "Let's go some place and get a
drink," he said.

"I'd rather stay right here," I told him.

"Yeah," he said. He squinted at me through his glasses. "You gone
paranoid, huh?"

"If you mean I've finally learned you can't trust anybody, you're
right."

"Smart kid," he said. "I figured no nephew of Matt's could be one
hundred per cent shlemiel."

I wondered what per cent shlemiel he figured I was, but I said, "You wanted to talk to me about something."

"Yeah, that's right." He wiped his mouth again, glanced out around the terminal some more, and said, "I could do with a drink, you know? I'm kinda nervous, to be seen with you."

That made *me* nervous. I looked quickly around, saw no one with a machine gun, and said, "Why should you be nervous?"

"I don't want em mad at me any more."

"Who?"

"The Coppo boys."

"The who?"

He looked at me. "You don't know nothing about nothing, do you?"

"I never heard of the Coppo boys," I said.

"Where do you think all that dough came from?"

"I don't know. From Brazil somewhere."

"That's right. From Pedro Coppo."

"He's one of the Coppo boys?"

He shook his head. "Naw. He was their father."

"Was?"

"Lemme start at the beginning, will ya?" he asked me.

"Sure," I said.

"You heard of Brasilia, right?"

"I think so. It's a new city."

"Right. Started about ten years ago, in the back country, way the hell away from anywhere. There was a lot of money made there, kid, a lot of money. Me, I operated a little store there myself for a while, down in the workers' part. Shack City, you know?"

"A store?"

He made dealing motions. "Cards," he said. "Like that. They love to gamble, those South Americans. It's the hot Latin blood."

"Did Uncle Matt have a store there, too?"

"For a while. We known each other for years, sometimes we put in with each other, sometimes we work single-o. You know what I mean?"

"I think so," I said.

"So there was this bird Coppo," Professor Kilroy said. "Pedro Coppo. He was one of the boys cleaning up there in Brasilia. Construction, you know? Trucking. Trucking companies made a fortune. Coppo was in all over the place, finger in this pie, finger in that pie." He demonstrated with downward jabbing motions.

"I've got it," I said.

"So Short Sheet had him a con figured, a really sweet con. Complicated, you know? Land tracts and like that. He needed somebody to be a surveyor from General Motors, so I stood in. He took that Coppo for almost a million bucks." He waved his hands around in remembered excitement. "I got a hundred grand for myself," he said, "and Short Sheet got the rest. He went to Rio and had himself a time."

Trying a long shot, I said, "Is that where he met Walter Cosgrove?" Because Walter Cosgrove was the only other patient of Dr. Lucius Osbertson that I knew of, and he and Uncle Matt had been in Brazil at the same time.

Professor Kilroy looked startled, then began briskly to wipe his mouth and scratch inside his coat. "Cosgrove?" he asked me. "Who's Cosgrove?"

"It doesn't matter," I said. I was convinced Professor Kilroy knew who Walter Cosgrove was, but I didn't see any point in pressing the issue. I didn't want to scare him away before he'd finished telling me the part he was willing to talk about. So I said, "What happened next? After Uncle Matt went to Rio?"

"What happened next," he said, "is Pedro Coppo killed himself. Who would of thought it? He was a smart type, he could of made himself another million easy. But out a window he went, right there in Brasilia. To show you how new everything was then, he landed in wet cement."

"Oh," I said. "In other words, I've inherited blood money."

"There's a lot of blood on that dough, by now," he said. "Pedro Coppo. Short Sheet. Almost me, and maybe you."

And Gus Ricovic, but there was no point my mentioning that.

"The Coppo boys," I said, beginning to understand. "The sons. They're out to revenge their father."

"You got it," he said. He looked around nervously. "And they're rough boys. Two of them, twin brothers."

"They're here in the States?"

"They been here for years," he said. "They come up here long before their old man went out the window." He leaned closer to me and whispered harshly, "They're in the rackets. They got the whole mob behind them."

"Then they're the ones that killed my uncle."

"Or ordered it done," he said. "They're big boys now, they don't have to do the rough stuff themselves. All they do is point, and you're dead."

I was thinking of the shots from the moving car. That was gangland style, certainly. What sort of inheritance was this, that came with professional killers attached?

Professor Kilroy was wiping his mouth continually now, and looking more and more agitated. It was no surprise at all when he said, "Kid, I'm sorry, but I need a drink. Will you come with me?"

"I'd rather not," I said. "I feel safer here, in the open."

"You aren't safe anywhere, kid," he said. "That's the point I'm trying to get across." He wiped his mouth so vigorously he almost knocked his glasses off. "I really need that drink," he said. "I tell you what, you wait here and I'll be right back."

"I don't like that either," I said.

"You think I'm going to sell you out, call somebody and say here he is? I didn't have to show up at all if that's what I had in mind."

That was true enough. I said, "All right. I'll wait ten minutes, no more."

"It's a deal." He sprang to his feet, then hesitated, hanging over me, and said, "You wouldn't have a dollar on you."

"A dollar?"

"I told you a lot already," he said, "and I got a lot more to tell you. It's worth a dollar. It's worth a lot more than a dollar."

I took out my wallet, found a dollar bill, and handed it to him. It disappeared at once somewhere within his outsize clothing, and away he shambled, with a funny rushing sort of limp, scrabbling across the terminal floor like some weird bird, reminding me most of Emmett Kelly all made up in his sad-clown costume.

While he was gone I sat and thought over what he'd so far told me. It was all beginning to make sense now; Uncle Matt's mysterious acquisition of riches in Brazil, his murder, the try at killing me, the kidnapping of Gertie. That too was gangland style. I suppose they thought Gertie might know where I was, or maybe they were holding her for ransom and sooner or later I'd be hearing from them.

That presented a problem. If they did find me, what crime would they have in mind, extortion or murder? If murder, my job was to cut and run. If extortion, if they wanted me to pay for Gertie's release, of course I would.

I determined to ask Professor Kilroy about Gertie when he came back.

But would he come back? I looked at my watch and eight minutes had gone by. I was beginning to get a little nervous. Or, that is, I had already been a little nervous and I was now getting a little *more* nervous.

It's astonishing how many people look like members of the mob, if you look at them closely. Carrying suitcases full of bombs, carrying overcoats slung over their arms to hide sawed-off shotguns. There were even three tough-looking guys carrying violin cases.

Professor Kilroy *had* sold me out, I was suddenly sure of it. His ten minutes had wound themselves out and he wasn't here. The terminal was filling up with professional killers, slowly closing in on me.

I got to my feet, dithering, not knowing which way to turn, and finally just walked briskly off to the nearest bank of lockers. I stood half out of sight behind these and watched the bench I had just left.

Nothing happened.

Nothing happened for one hundred and eighty seconds. I thought I might make a dash for the door. On the other hand, that might be exactly what they were waiting for.

But could they guard all the doors? What if I went out onto the platform and around and out to the taxi stand? Or was there someone out on the platform waiting to throw me onto the third rail?

Professor Kilroy appeared, hurrying, and scrambled over to the bench where we'd been sitting. He stood there in obvious perplexity, looking around and seeming very agitated. There was no one with him.

Still hesitant, I came out from behind the lockers and walked slowly over to rejoin the Professor. He saw me coming and rushed over to me, saying, "What happened? You see one of them?"

"I'm not sure," I said. "I guess not." I sat down again where I'd been.

He stayed on his feet, very agitated, looking all around. "Maybe we oughta get outa here," he said.

"No. I feel safe here . . .

"It's bad to stay in one place too long."

"Sit down," I said. "Tell me the rest. There can't be much more."

"There ain't." He sat down, but he was still very nervous, moving his hands and feet a lot. "After the old man kicked off," he said, "his sons swore to get us. Matt and me. They caught up with me three years ago."

"They didn't kill you," I pointed out.

"They knew I was small potatoes," he said. "They knew Short Sheet was the artist on that one. I give em back all the money I had left, they roughed me up a little, and that was it. They wouldn't even of roughed me up, but they thought I knew where Short Sheet was."

"You didn't?"

He winked, and leaned closer, and whispered, "I did, but I conned them. I wouldn't sell out an old pal." I could smell whiskey on his breath.

I said, "But they did kill Uncle Matt."

"Because he was the brains. And because he wouldn't give em back the dough. At least, that's what I figure. I figure it took em all this time to find him 'cause they couldn't believe he'd be right here under their noses in New York City, and of course they didn't know his real name. But they found him finally. They kept on looking till they did."

"And now they're after me," I said.

"They're after the money," he said. "They don't care about you, any more than they cared about me. Less, you didn't have nothing to do with the con. But they don't like the idea anybody getting the advantage of that money. That's why they made me give it back." He wiped his mouth and said, "I shouldn't of done it. You know what I should of done?"

"What?"

"I should of give it to some charity," he said. "Some orphanage or something."

"But wouldn't they have killed you if they didn't get the money back?"

"What do they care about the money? They got all the dough they need. It's just they didn't want me getting the benefit." Bitterly, he added, "And I shouldn't of let *them* get the benefit."

I said, "I think they kidnapped a friend of mine. Maybe you know her, Gertie Divine. She lived with my uncle."

He squinted at me. "The stripper? They kidnapped her?"

"What do you suppose? Do they want to kill me, or do they want me to pay ransom for her?"

"Did she inherit anything?"

"Not that I know of," I said. "I think I was the only one inherited anything."

"Don't count on it," he said. "That wouldn't be like Short Sheet, leave his pal Gertie out in the cold. He seen to it she got something, don't you worry."

"You think that's why they kidnapped her?"

"Sure. Squeeze the dough out of her, what else? Why ask you to pay ransom for her? She ain't your kid."

"I thought that might be what they had in mind," I said.

"You worry about yourself, kid," he said, and patted my knee. "You got plenty to worry about right there, believe you me."

"I believe you," I said.

He said, "Listen, what was that name you brought up before? Cosgrove?"

"Walter Cosgrove."

"Yeah. That name's got like a familiar ring to it. Who is he?"

"Nobody important," I said. I had the feeling Professor Kilroy had it in his mind to pump me about Walter Cosgrove, to find out how much I knew about the man and where I'd gotten my information, and something I suppose what the Professor had termed paranoia—told me that any knowledge I could keep to myself was nothing but points for my side.

He persisted though, saying, "I feel like I know the name from somewhere is all. Walter Cosgrove. What is he, another grifter?"

"It doesn't matter," I said. "What do you think I ought to do about the Coppo brothers? Go to the police?"

"Listen," he said, "those boys already got half the cops in the city on their payroll, just in the normal line of business. You go to a cop, how do you know he isn't somebody'll turn you right over to the Coppos?"

"I was thinking that myself," I said gloomily. "In fact, I'd suspected there might be some crooked police involved in this somewhere."

"You think there's any other reason they never solved your uncle's murder?"

"I guess not."

"Some of these amateur outfits," he said, "like kak and the Crime Commission, they do pretty good work sometimes, but there ain't enough of them. The cops still have it all their own way."

"So what should I do?"

"If you think you can disappear," he said, "go ahead and do it. If not, my advice is unload that inheritance. Turn it all over to some charity, every bit of it. And do it loud and clear, with your picture in the papers and everything. Just so they know."

"But," I said, "all that money."

"It'll never bring you nothing but grief, kid," he said. "You called it yourself. Blood money, you said, and that's what it is. Two men are dead already for that money. Maybe Short Sheet's stripper is dead too, by now. And maybe you'll be dead in a couple days. I don't know how you kept away from them so long already. Beginner's luck maybe."

"Maybe that's it." I gazed dismally between my knees at the dirty floor. "I suppose I ought to get out of town," I said.

"Don't do it, kid. They know that kind of dodge, they expect it. Once you're out on the run it's all over. They've got you in their kind of situation."

I could see what he meant, and he was right. I said, "What can I do, then? I need time to think, time to decide. Where can I go?"

"You been staying around your home, haven't you? That's where you got my note."

"I've been staying there mostly, yes."

"That's why you lasted so long," he said. "That's so dumb they can't believe it. You're on the run, and you know you're on the run, and they know you're on the run, and you stay home. They'll never think of it in a million years. You just stay to home, like you been doing. Don't go out on the street very much, if you can help it. And my advice is, unload that dough. It'll never bring you nothing but a bullet in the back."

"I don't know," I said. "I just don't know."

"You work it out for yourself," he said. "All know is what I'd do. Just don't give the dough to the Coppos, that's all I ask. I hate the thought of them getting all that cash."

"They won't get it," I promised.

"Good." He got to his feet. "I can't hang around any longer," he said, and, wiped his mouth again. "Say, what I told you, that's worth something, ain't it?"

"It is." I admitted. I took out my wallet again, found a ten, hesitated, put another ten with it, and gave them to him.

He took the money with a sardonic grin. "Three years ago," he said, "I was buying cigarettes at the Playboy Club with these, and telling the Bunny keep the change. You never know, kid, you never know how things'll turn out."

"I guess not," I said.

He scampered away across the terminal. I watched him, and when he was a good distance away I got up and followed him. There was a lot he'd already told me, but I had the suspicion there was also a lot more Professor Kilroy *hadn't* told me. I wanted to know more about him.

At first I thought he suspected he was being followed, the way he kept looking around, and the fact that he was wandering around inside the terminal, doubling back on himself and hurrying along in great circles, but I kept well back and I'm sure he never did see me.

After a lot of this aimless rushing back and forth, upstairs and down, he finally headed for a bank of lockers, pulled out a key, unlocked one of the doors, and took out a neat new black attache case of the kind being carried by half the men in the terminal. On all the others it looked normal, but on Professor Kilroy it looked incongruous. Carrying this unexpected bit of luggage, he headed for the nearest men's room and went on inside.

I waited outside. I waited for twenty minutes. Men went in and men came out, but no Professor Kilroy. Was there another exit? Dare I go in and look for him?

At last I did. There was no other exit and there was no Professor Kilroy. I looked all over the place, even peeking over the tops of stall doors — which got me called a few names — and he just wasn't there.

He wasn't there.

27

I CAME OUT of the men's room feeling baffled and uneasy and irritable. How had he done it? Where was he now?

As I stood there, with no doubt an expression of absolute stupidity on my face, a hearty man of middle age, robust appearance, good suit, nice pencil mustache, came up to me and said, "Say there, my friend, would this happen to be your suitcase?"

Distracted, I looked at the expensive-seeming blue suitcase he was holding up for my inspection and said, "No, it isn't."

"I just found it here," he said.

"Is that right?" I continued to look around the terminal, hoping to see the scuttling form of Professor Kilroy somewhere out there on the great floor.

"Do you suppose there's anything valuable in it?"

I looked at him, finally hearing what he was saying. "What was that?"

"I said, I wonder if there's anything valuable in here."

A great rage was swelling within my breast. I said, "Are you actually trying to work the lost-bag swindle on me?"

He blinked, and looked very innocent and very confused. "Well, of course not," he said. "I just found this—"

"If that isn't the last straw," I said. Enraged, I kicked him soundly in the shin, and went away from there.

28

I WAS BEING followed.

I had chosen to walk home, for a number of reasons. There was my normal reason of pot belly, of course, but in addition I wanted a chance to think about what Professor Kilroy had told me—particularly his idea that I should give the money away to save my life—and sometimes I could think best if I went for a walk. And I must admit there was also a third reason; in how many movies on the Late Late Show had I seen it happen, where the hero gets into a taxi he thinks is being operated by an ordinary hack, only to discover that the man behind the wheel is in actuality a hireling of the mob? More than I could count, that's bow many. I'm sure Professor Kilroy would have called it paranoiac, but every taxi I saw seemed to glitter with a yellow evil, to be pregnant with malevolent potential. And never had I seen so many thuggish-looking cab drivers.

Therefore I walked.

And therefore I was being followed.

I had chosen to take Fifth Avenue, that being a broad and well-lighted thoroughfare as well as more scenic than some of the avenues to the west, and I had gone two or three blocks before I became aware of them. They were in a long black Cadillac, the same car that had been parked across the street from my apartment the other day. It was traveling now with only its amber parking lights on, and there were black side curtains drawn over the windows, hiding the back seat. In the darkness within the car I could make out little about the driver other than that he wore a chauffeur's cap.

Their method of keeping track of me was an odd one. They would drive slowly past me and stop at the curb just short of the next intersection. Then they would wait as I walked by and went about halfway down the next block before once again they passed me and came to a stop near the intersection.

It was more frightening in its own way than an out-and-out attack; that sleek and silent car rolling slowly by me, its tires crunching on the blacktop, then coming to rest like a great panther just a little way ahead. The driver always faced forward. The side curtains never moved.

Every time I went by I expected roaring gunfire from that curtained window, or a sudden leap of burly thugs out the doors, grabbing me up, hustling me into the back seat, taking me for the final ride. But nothing happened, and our slow silent terrifying game of follow the leader continued for block after block.

What could I do? Obviously they were hoping for a time when the sidewalk in my general vicinity would be free of other pedestrians, so they could at their leisure and without witnesses shoot me down or kidnap me or whatever they had in mind for me. Failing that, I suppose they hoped to follow me to the place where I was hiding out.

Ah, but the crosstown streets were all one-way, and maybe that was my salvation. Coming up was 36th Street, one-way eastbound, if I were to turn right, to turn west on that street, how could the Cadillac follow me?

It couldn't.

Just this side of the intersection the Cadillac throbbed like a panther feigning languor. It had sidled past me again and slid to the curb and stopped. I walked on by it, feeling the old tightening of muscles in the middle of my back, and once again nothing happened. I came to the corner, made an abrupt right turn, and strode briskly away down 36th Street.

And behind me a car door slammed.

I looked back in time to see the Cadillac shoot across the intersection, headed south, no doubt meaning to cut across 35th Street and come around in front of me, cutting me off at the Sixth Avenue end of this block. Meantime, a bulky man in a cloth cap had come around the corner and was walking at a steady pace after me, his hands in the pockets of his leather jacket.

I walked faster, pulling ahead of the bulky man, but without hope of getting down to the other corner before the Cadillac could come around and seal it off.

Ahead of me, about the middle of the block, there was light spilling from a small luncheonette, the only store still open along this stretch. And except for the bulky man behind me, I was the only pedestrian in sight. My shoulder blades itched and itched, and I hurried toward the luncheonette. There I would find people, safety, an island of light. If worst came to worst, I could phone the police; there was at least a chance the call would be answered by someone not in the employ of the Coppo brothers.

At the far corner, the black Cadillac nosed around the corner, its amber parking lights like the eyes of a sea monster. It stopped down there, near the corner, waiting for me.

I was nearing the luncheonette, nearing it, nearing it.

I was half a dozen steps away when its lights went out.

I almost stopped in my tracks. I did falter a bit, but then I remembered the bulky man behind me and I hurried on again. Only the occasional streetlight now gave homage to the memory of Thomas Alva Edison, a great man who should have statues erected to him on every side street in town. Well-illuminated statues. Next door to all-night diners with large clientele.

As I came even with the luncheonette, out its door came a man wearing white pants and a black coat, a jangling set of keys in his hand. I promptly veered right, walked past him, and went on through the open door and inside. "Power failure?" I asked pleasantly, and strode on into the darkness.

"Hey!" said an outraged voice behind me. "Whatcha think you're doin?"

"Coffee and a cheese Danish," I said cheerily, and fell over a table.

"Come outa there!"

"Make it a prune Danish, then," I said, got to my feet, and fell over a chair.

"We're closed, ya numskull!"

"How about the flank steak, hash fried, and green peas?" I asked him. I was crawling around the floor trying to find some way to stand up without hitting my head on the underside of a table.

"What are ya doin? Ya wreckin the joint? Come *outa* there!"

"Oh, I get it," I said. "Everything I want's on the dinner."

"Out! Out! Out!"

"When's the Swede get here?"

He wasn't a literary type. He said, "Do you come outa there or do I call the cops?"

I was on my feet again, albeit shakily. "Nyaa nyaa," I said provocatively, "you can't catch me."

"Okay, buster," he said, came striding in after me, and fell over a chair.

In an attempt to circle around him, I walked into a wall, backed away from that into a booth, caromed off a hat rack, and wound up with my arms wrapped around a cash register. I felt like the ball in a pinball machine.

But at least I was up front again, with him no longer between me and the exit. I could hear him blundering around somewhere in the interior, falling over things and muttering, "Where are ya? Lemme get my hands on ya. Where are ya?" Apparently he was in too much of a rage to think about turning the lights on, which was fine by me.

I tippy-toed toward the door, fell over a planter—what was *that* doing here, full of artificial flowers with sharp points?—and went the rest of the way on hands and knees. Still on hands and knees, I peeked out around the corner of the door, and saw the bulky man leaning against a store-front window about twenty feet to my left. And the amber-eyed Cadillac parked down at the corner to my right.

But coming toward me from the direction of Sixth Avenue was a group of teen-agers, all talking at the same time, most waving their arms, moving in a compact mass as though enclosed in an invisible box. They may all have been boys and they may all have been girls and they may have been a mixture of the two, it was impossible to tell. They all wore slacks and jackets and were slender without any particular shape. Their hair was too long if they were boys and too short if they were girls. Their voices were changing if they were boys and showed they'd been smoking too much if they were girls. They all walked as though they'd just gotten off motorcycles.

I got to my feet, brushed myself off, and as the group drew abreast of me I stepped quickly from the doorway, inserted myself in the middle of them, and said loudly, "Say there, gang, you hear the one about the centipede with athlete's foot?"

They paid absolutely no attention to me. They just kept walking along the same as ever, all talking at the same time, most waving their arms, the compact mass unaltered in the slightest by my presence in its middle. One of them on my left was relating the plot of a motion picture, another one a little farther forward was describing a coat he/she had seen at some airport, one to my right rear was discussing American foreign policy, one out front was talking about the advantages of the university at Mexico City, and one on the left fringe was giving an impassioned defense of the birth control pill.

The bulky man had retired into a dark doorway. All I could see of him as we trundled by was a pair of malevolently gleaming eyes.

The Cadillac slithered by and came to a stop down near the corner.

At Fifth Avenue my platoon turned right. I was still trying to confound the Cadillac with one-way streets, and Fifth Avenue was one-way southbound, so I parted from the group there, turning to go in the opposite direction, saying, "See you later, alligator," as a way of dating myself for them.

"See you, man," one of them called after me, which I thought was very nice.

The bulky man was after me again, but the Cadillac was hampered from circling the block once more by a red light facing it at Fifth Avenue. Still, no light stays red forever, unfortunately, and before I had reached 37th Street I heard the swoosh of it back there, setting off on my roundabout trail once again.

May I point out that throughout this entire time I was absolutely terrified? It was the spasm of panic that had kept me going so far, and I was now finding out about myself that panic had a tendency to make me manic. The shyness I had always assumed to be an integral part of my character appeared now to be excess baggage, to be hurled overboard when the going got rough.

But how much longer could I keep it up? They were chasing me both by car and afoot. As nine o'clock neared, the business and shopping district in which we were buffeting was busy closing down; soon the streets would be more or less empty, the last of the stores and luncheonettes would be closed, the traffic along Fifth Avenue would slow to a trickle. In all that darkness and silence and emptiness they could finish me off like a man slapping a mosquito between his palms.

I crossed 37th Street, looked down to my right, and didn't see the Cadillac yet in sight; more red lights, I assumed. I kept going north. Behind me, the bulky man had receded to almost a full block back.

As I crossed 38th Street, I glanced over my shoulder and saw the Cadillac streak across the intersection a block south, jouncing like an ocean liner in a rough sea.

Well, at least I was giving them trouble. As I strode briskly northward on Fifth, the Cadillac was forced to zigzag like a skier on a slalom; east to Madison, up a block, west to Sixth, up a block, east to Madison, up a block, and so on.

Fine. They might get me, but I'd take some of their gas with me.

But 37th Street was the last I saw of the yellow-eyed monster until I approached 40th Street, where I saw they'd decided not to play that game. The Cadillac was parked north of 40th Street, in front of the library, waiting for me to come to it.

Well, I wouldn't. I turned left on 40th Street, which was again the wrong way for the Cadillac, hurried along beside the library, and beyond it on my right there was the inviting darkness of Bryant Park. Too inviting; the bulky man and I might go in there, but only the bulky man would be coming out. In the morning I'd be found among the ivy, if someone didn't steal me before then.

I hurried past the park, turned right on Sixth Avenue, and made for the bright lights and movement of 42nd Street. Reaching that corner, I came across another group, and promptly joined in. This time I knew what sex they were but they didn't. They twittered at my arrival and made quite a fuss over me. "Well, look what we have here," one of them said, batting his store-bought eyelashes at me. "Rough trade."

All things considered, I suppose I'll have to accept that as having been a compliment.

"Where did you come from, honey?" another asked me. "You off a ship?"

It seemed all at once as though I were only a few seconds from a fate worse than death, so I took the other choice, extricated myself—with some difficulty—from the aviary, and entered a handy bookstore.

From one extreme to the other. This place reeked of heterosexuality; men with furrowed brows and furtive eyes dipped through the racks of girlie magazines and sexy paperbacks. There was a kind of shabbiness overlying everything here, as though no one connected with any part of this could quite afford even second best.

The store was narrow and shallow and full of silent browsing men who weren't meeting each other's eyes. I threaded my way through them, saw a smallish green door at the very rear of the store, made for it, opened it, and stepped on through as the man at the cash register up front shouted, "Hey! Where you—?"

I heard no more, because I'd shut the door again.

I was in a small bare empty room with a single fifteen-watt bulb glowing sullenly in a ceiling fixture. Across the way was a curtained doorway. I went through there and into another small room, in which three men were standing around a table looking at a lot of pictures of naked women. They looked up, startled, saw me in the doorway, and dropped the pictures as though they'd suddenly caught fire. "A raid!" one of them shouted, and all three went tearing through a doorway on the opposite side of the room.

I paused to glance at some of the photos, saw that they were of men and women combined in activities which seemed anatomically improbable, and went on through the further doorway after the departed trio.

They were long gone; not even the sound of a footfall or a hoarse cry of despair sounded ahead of me. I was now in a long dim hallway with a door at the far end boasting a frosted-glass window. I made for it, found it locked, and turned uncertainly back just in time to see two men entering the hallway at the other end. One was the man who'd been sitting at the cash register in the bookstore, and the other was a tall and heavily built man in a maroon sweater. Both carried short lengths of pipe in their hands, and both seemed very stern.

Midway between us there was a closed door in the left-hand wall. Crossing my fingers, I dashed for this—apparently my two pursuers thought I was dashing for them, because they stood where they were and braced themselves—and wonder of wonders I found it unlocked. I ducked through, saw a flight of stairs leading up, and went up them three at a time.

Four flights later, I was winded and on the roof. This struck me as being poor planning; if any of the people now chasing me caught up with me, all they had to do was throw me over the side. I went near the edge, glanced over, and saw the street several miles below. Ooogg.

Yes, but. Over to my right, three or four buildings away, was one of the 42nd Street movie houses. The building roof was the same height as this one, there seemed to be a fire escape or ladder of some kind leading down to the marquee, and alongside the marquee was a very tall ladder atop which a very thin young man was engaged in changing the lettering announcing the movies playing within.

While I considered the unlikelihood of what I was considering, I heard the roof door behind me grate open and I wasted no more time in idle consideration. Without looking back to see who had caught up with me, I took off across the roofs as far as the movie theater, and down the fire escape to the marquee.

I wouldn't say that I have an abnormal fear of heights, but that's probably because I don't consider a fear of heights abnormal. I mean, you can get killed if you're up high and all of a sudden you're down low. People who aren't afraid of heights are people who haven't stopped to think about what happens when you reach the sidewalk in too much of a hurry. I have stopped to think about it, and I therefore felt very small, weak, nervous, terrified and top-heavy as I went down those iron rungs on the front of the movie theater, expecting at any second to lose my grip, fall through the marquee like a dropped safe, and make an omelet of myself on the sidewalk.

Amazingly enough, I made it. The top of the marquee was some sort of thin sheet metal, painted black, which bucked and dipped and went *sprong* as I walked across it. Looking back and up, I saw the two men from the the bookstore still up there on the roof, looking down; they made no move to follow me, but contented themselves with threateningly shaking their pipes.

The head of the young man atop the ladder was just short of the top of the marquee. When I leaned down and said, "Hello," he started with surprise and very nearly took himself and his ladder completely away from me for good and all. But he managed to grab hold of the marquee and steady himself, which was lucky for both of us.

"Excuse me," I said, swinging my legs over the side and cautiously lowering myself toward the ladder. "I just want to—"

He was holding onto the marquee with both hands and gaping at me open-mouthed, his eyes popping. Fortunately his feet were on the second rung down from the top, so it was possible for me to get a good footing on the very top of the ladder and then to shift my hold from the top of the marquee to the metal letter guides across its face.

"I'll just be a minute," I said, trying to reassure him, not wanting to get into any sort of argument or fight or anything up here on top of a ladder. "If I could just, uhh, just swing around—"

I went down a step, edged slowly around him, skipping the rung he was on and feeling with my right foot for the rung just below him. Our faces were inches apart, he still hadn't said a word, and he was staring at me as though his face had been frozen in that expression.

"Just two seconds more," I said. I was babbling and I knew it, and I knew he wasn't really listening, but I went on babbling anyway. Panic takes different people in different ways, that's all. Him it made freeze, me it made babble.

I was finally past him. "Thanks," I said. "I appreciate it, thank you very much, I'll go on now, you do what you were doing, I'll—" And thus, babbling away, I continued on down the ladder.

I was almost down to street-level when, above me, my inadvertent benefactor finally found his voice and shouted down at me, "Why don't you watch where you're going?"

29

FOR SOME REASON I had a little trouble getting to sleep that night, and so didn't awaken Wednesday morning until nearly quarter of eleven. I dressed myself haphazardly, still somewhat under the influence of my dreams, which had consisted primarily of my falling from great heights into the open jaws of huge amber-eyed cats with faces like Cadillacs, and as a result had to try three times before I finally got on a pair of matching socks. But I felt a little better after washing my face and drinking a cup of coffee, and decided to begin my day by seeing what the mailman had to offer.

He had junk to offer, as usual. I carried it all upstairs, sat down in the chair near the fireplace, and started to read.

My Cousin Maybelle wanted to study at Actor's Studio. Citizens Against Crime (Senator Earl Dunbar, Honorary Chairman) was back with another request for me to help stamp out crime by giving them money. The *Saturday Evening Post* wanted me to put the Golden Disk in the YES pocket and get eighteen years of their magazine for twenty-seven cents. A self-sufficient blind person had knit my initials onto some cheap handkerchiefs, which were being sent along for my inspection. Some crazy company sent me a little square of clear plastic and the information that if I acted fast I could have my automobile seats completely encased in the awful stuff. The National Minuscule Mitosis Association needed my help to rid the world of this dread crippler.

I read each letter—and each initial—with a great deal of care, and then threw everything into the fireplace. Except the square of plastic, which I suspected might melt instead of burn, and in any case would surely smell bad.

The letter from Citizens Against Crime I almost kept, it seemed so specifically to be directed at me; in fact, I found myself wondering if Uncle Matt himself might have written it. "Dear Citizen," it began, "Have you ever been bilked by one of the estimated eighteen thousand confidence men currently plying their nefarious racket in these United States? Are you one of the more than three million annual burglary victims?" And so on. The rest was more general, but that opening sentence hit me where I lived. Have I been bilked by *one* of the eighteen thousand con men? Listen, Senator Earl Dunbar, Honorary Chairman and signer of this letter, I, Fred Fitch, Honorary Chump, have been bilked by *all* of them.

In went that letter, too.

A little later, as I was putting breakfast on, I found myself thinking about the money again, trying to decide what to do about it. Was Professor Kilroy right, did my only safety lie in getting rid of it, giving it all to some charity so the Coppo brothers would leave me alone? I had gnawed at that question during my sleepless hours last night without coming up with any useful answer, and now I was at it again.

The trouble was, the question had a thousand sides and each side had a thousand arguments for and against and maybe-maybe. I should give up the money because it was blood money, bought with murder and lies. But I shouldn't allow the Coppos to intimidate me. But they did intimidate me. But with all that money I should be able to buy some sort of protection for myself. But how could I trust anyone at all so long as I still had the money? But the money was mine, I should be allowed to do with it what *I* wanted to do with it. But I didn't really need the money, I already had whatever I wanted. And so on, and so on, and so on.

Well, there was one thing I could do with the money, if I decided to give it up. Donate some of it to every nut that sent me a letter. In no time at all it'd be gone.

But would the Coppos take my word for it?

More important, did I really want the Coppos to dictate my life for me?

Even more important than that, did I want the Coppos to *end* my life for me?

What did I want with all that money, when you came right down to it? I didn't want to live in Uncle Matt's apartment, or any other apartment like it. I had an occupation that suited me and that I would prefer to keep up with anyway; what would I do with myself all day if I didn't work? All the money could do was make me its nervous watchman, keep me permanently what Professor Kilroy had so accurately termed paranoid. With my record as a sucker, I could see a nervous breakdown within six months. So maybe, after all, I should simply find an appropriate charity, turn the whole wad over to them with a lot of public fanfare, and return quietly to the life I was used to and content with.

But doggone it, that would be admitting defeat! Pushed around by a bunch of thugs. Harassed, browbeaten and conquered.

And so on and so on, around and around and around. So the heck with it. I would make no decision at all just yet, I still had another string to my bow. It was my intention today to call upon Prescott Wilks, the attorney whose piqued and somewhat cryptic letter I'd found in Uncle Matt's apartment. I wanted to know what sort of legal services his firm had done for Uncle Matt, why Uncle Matt had terminated those services, and just what that veiled threat in his letter had been all about.

After breakfast I looked up Wilks' address in the phone book, and there he was: Latham, Courtney, Wilks & Wilks, 630 Fifth Avenue. That would be Rockefeller Center. Right.

I left the apartment just after noon, went outside, and ran directly into the arms of Reilly, who grabbed me tight, said, "*There* you are, you damn fool," and hustled me across the sidewalk to an unmarked car.

30

I WASN'T TAKEN for a one-way ride to the Jersey swamps after all. Reilly drove me to a police station and marched me inside.

"I get a phone call," I said.

"Later," he said.

He went with me to the cells at the back, and watched me locked away. "I'm doing this for your own good," he said.

"I want my phone call," I said.

He shook his head and went away.

I made a great deal of noise for a while, shouting, rattling the barred door of my cell and so on, but no one paid any attention to me at all, so after a while I subsided.

It's a good thing I'd eaten a large breakfast; the lunch they brought me didn't even *look* edible. A phlegmatic guard came a while later and took the tray away again, and when I told him I wanted to make a phone call he didn't appear to hear me. In any case, he just picked up the tray and shuffled off.

A little after two o'clock another guard came and unlocked my cell. I told him, "I want to make a phone call."

"You got a visitor," he said.

"A what?" I peeked mistrustfully out at the corridor. Who would be coming to see me here?

"A visitor," he repeated patiently. "A nice young lady. Don't keep her waiting."

"Gertie?" I hadn't meant to say the name aloud, but I did.

"She didn't tell me her name," he said. "Come along."

I went along. I was taken to a scruffy-looking room with a long table in it, the table surrounded by chairs, at one of which was sitting Karen Smith. I looked at her and said, "Oh."

"Jack told me you were here," she said. "He doesn't know I'm coming to see you."

"Is that right?" I looked at the guard, standing in the doorway, not seeming to be listening at all to the conversation. I looked again at Karen, who didn't seem particularly dangerous sitting there with her coat open showing pink sweater and white skirt, and I decided to see what everybody was up to now, so I went over and sat down across the table from her and said, "Now what?"

"You're mad at me," she said. "I know you are. Is it that receipt?"

"Receipt?"

"The one you left on the coffee table. Neighborhood Beautification or something."

"Oh!" I'd completely forgotten that damn thing in all that had happened since. Now, remembering it, I also remembered where I'd gotten the money to pay for it, and I felt my face getting red.

Meanwhile, Karen was saying, "I feel as though I'm responsible for that. You didn't have any way to know it wasn't something I'd agreed to give money to, and it just as well might have been. So I feel as though I ought to give you your money back, and when Jack catches the man he—"

She was opening her purse. I began to wave my hands in front of myself, saying, "No, no, please. No, that's all right. Really."

"No, I *want* to," she said. "After all, you were my guest."

"No," I said. "Please. Listen, you don't owe me anything at all."

"But I feel do."

"Uh. Well, you don't. As a matter of fact—" I cleared my throat, and looked around at the guard—he seemed to be asleep on his feet—and finally I said, "As a matter of fact, I'm the one that owes you money. You see, I didn't have enough myself to pay him, so—uhhh . . ."

"But I didn't have any money there," she said.

"Well, yes, you did. Uhh . . ."

"Oh! The money in the dresser!"

I didn't meet her eye.

She said, "But how did you know about that?"

I studied my fingernails. They were clean, but I went on studying them. "I'm not normally like that," I mumbled, "I want you to know that. But there just wasn't anything to do there, I didn't know what to do with myself . . ."

"So you went through all my things."

I nodded miserably.

"Well, you poor man! I didn't even think! There we left you all alone all that time, it's a wonder you didn't have a fit or something."

Well, it wasn't *that* bad."

"No, that was *terrible* of us. Is that why you left?"

I finally chanced a look at her, and her expression was serious but sympathetic. Apparently she hadn't chosen after all to look on me as a sex maniac who'd gone slobbering through her bedroom, for which I was grateful. I said, "No, that wasn't it. What happened, I got a phone call Monday afternoon."

"A phone call?"

"A man's voice. He said my name, and when I said yes he sort of chuckled and said, 'So there you are,' and hung up."

Her eyes widened. "The killer?"

"Who else?"

"Oh, Fred, no wonder you ran away!"

"They could have been calling from right down at the corner."

"Of course! But why didn't you let us know? Why didn't you call me in the evening, when I was home from work? Or why not call Jack?"

"The question I couldn't answer," I said, "is how they found out where I was. I still can't answer it."

With her eyes even wider than before, she said, "You mean *us?* Jack and *me?* Why would we—how could we—how *could* you!"

"How did they find out, Karen?"

"Well, *I* didn't tell them! I didn't tell *anybody!*"

Looking at her now, torn between outraged shock and sympathetic understanding, I was prepared to believe her. Karen Smith, I was now convinced, was no more than an innocent pawn in all this, as I was. I said so: "I believe you, Karen. But when I left there, how could I be sure? And how can I be sure now of Reilly?"

"Jack? But he's your *friend!*"

"I'm told a favorite line of my uncle's was, 'A man with half a million dollars can't afford friends.' "

"Oh, Fred, that's so cynical. Don't get cynical, please, don't let money change you."

"I'm changed already," I said.

"Jack is your friend," she insisted. "You know that as well as I do."

"Jack Reilly," I said, "is half con man himself, I've known that about him for years. That's how he knows so much how to handle other con men. Look how he's conned you."

Her face paled and she said, "What do you mean? What has he done to me?"

"All that jazz about the religious reasons," I said. "Reilly's got himself set up with—"

"I don't want to hear anything like that!" She stood up so quickly she almost knocked the chair over. "If you were a true friend of Jack's, you wouldn't say such despicable things! If you were a friend of *mine*—" She stopped and bit her trembling lower lip. Clasping her purse in both hands, she fled from the room.

Now what had I done? What kind of idiotic wrong thing had I said this time?

Knowing exactly what I'd done, and wanting only to turn the world backward and erase the last three minutes and run through it all again without that stupid business about Reilly, I headed around the table after Karen, calling her name, going out the door after her and down the corridor.

The guard caught me halfway to the front door, and grabbed me in a very painful hammerlock. "Not so fast, my bucko," he panted. "You're a guest here, you remember?"

He trotted me back to my suite.

31

ABOUT THREE-THIRTY the corridor in front of my cell suddenly grew dark with cops. All of my favorites were there; Steve and Ralph and Reilly. Steve and Ralph had on their faces the slight smiles of an old vaudeville team waiting in the wings to go out and do their favorite number for the ten thousandth time, but Reilly looked sore.

When the guard opened the door and let them in, Reilly was the first one to speak, saying, "All right, Fred, you've done it this time. I don't know what smart ideas you've got about Karen, but you can—"

"What do you mean, smart ideas?"

"Turning her against me," he said. "I just had a bad session with that girl, and you owe me for that."

"Oh, stop it," I said. "I'm not the one with smart ideas about Karen. You come around here waving your finger at me, why don't you marry the girl or give her up?"

"That's none of your business, Fred. You just keep your nose out of my personal affairs."

Ralph cleared his throat at this point saying, "Gents, if we could get to the business at hand here—"

"Which is the phone call I'm supposed to get," I told him.

Steve said, "Well, no, not exactly. We wouldn't be the ones to see about that. Would we, Ralph?"

"No," agreed Ralph, "that wouldn't be our department."

"We're more interested in homicide," Steve explained.

"I'm not talking," I said.

Reilly said, "Fred, will you start cooperating, for God's sake? What's the matter with you?"

"What's the matter with me? I'll tell you what's the matter with me. Somebody sold me out to the Coppo brothers, that's what's the matter with me. Somebody told them I was at Karen's place, and only four people knew that besides me, and three of them are in this cell."

Steve said, "How's that again, my friend?"

"You people are too funny to talk to," I told him.

Reilly said, "And me, Fred? Am I too funny to talk to?"

"I don't know what you are, Reilly. Until I find out, I don't talk to you either."

"Say it in plain language, Fred."

I met his eye firmly. "I don't trust you, Reilly," I said.

Before he could say anything in reply, the cell door opened and an elderly guard stood there blinking at us. "Which one's the prisoner?" he asked.

I was tempted to point at Steve, but I said, "Me."

"Come on along," he said.

Reilly said, "Hold on, there."

Ralph said, "What's up, my friend?"

"Gotta let this bird go," said the old man. "They's a lawyer out here with all the paperwork."

The last I saw of Reilly, he was standing in the middle of the cell with his face purple.

32

IT WAS GOODKIND. As lupine as ever, he stood out by the front desk with a smile of self-satisfaction on his face, waiting for me.

"I only heard about this an hour ago," he greeted me. "I got right to work on it."

"Thank you."

"You should have called me, I'd have had you out before this."

"They wouldn't let me use a phone."

"Ho ho?" His nose twitched, smelling a suit. "In front of witnesses? Non-police witnesses."

"No. They kept it in the family."

"Well. We'll have to talk about that later." He took my elbow, led me toward the door. "We have other things to talk about first," he said. "Important things."

I said, "Like the Coppo brothers?"

"Who?" He looked at me with such an absurd attempt at an innocent expression that I almost laughed in his face.

Instead, I said, "Or maybe Walter Cosgrove."

That got a reaction. Clutching at my elbow he said, "Where did you hear that name? Who's been at you?"

We were just inside the station house main door, and several uniformed policemen now trooped in, separating us. I went on outside, and Goodkind caught up with me on the sidewalk, grasping my elbow again, saying hurriedly in my car, "Don't let them get at you, Fred. Keep away from Cosgrove's people. Don't listen to them."

"Everybody calls me Fred," I said.

"For God's sake, it's your *name!* Will you stop that, we have *important* things to discuss."

"We have not," I said, and then I shouted, "Help! Police!"

Well, of course, there we were in front of a police station, so we were immediately surrounded by nobody. There's never a cop around when you want one, including in front of the precinct house.

"Help!" I demanded. "Police!" I insisted.

Goodkind had released my elbow as though he'd just got word about my leprosy, and was looking at me as though he'd just got word about my psychopathic personality. "What are you doing?" he asked me.

"Calling for help." I demonstrated again: "Help! For Pete's sake, police!"

Abruptly we were surrounded by a trio of uniformed patrolmen, all of whom wanted to know what was going on. I pointed at Goodkind and said, "This bird just tried to pick my pocket."

Goodkind gaped in astonishment. "Me? Fred, are you out of your mind?"

"Okay, buddy," said one of the cops, and grabbed Goodkind the way Goodkind had been grabbing me—by the elbow.

Another of the cops said to me, "You'll have to come in and sign a complaint, pal."

"I can't," I said. "I'm supposed to meet my wife, if I'm late again she'll kill me. Let me come back later."

"Listen, pal," cop number two said. "If you want this guy held, you got to sign a complaint against him."

"I'll come back," I promised. "My name's Minetta, Ff—Frank Minetta, 27 West 10th Street. I'll be back in an hour." I started backing out of our little group. "In an hour," I said.

"We won't hold him any more than that," one of the cops warned me.

"I'll be back," I lied, and turned around, and trotted away down the sidewalk.

I got half a block when I heard a bellow behind me: "Fred!" I looked back and there was Reilly on the station house steps, waving his arms at me. Goodkind was yakking at him, clutching at his lapels, and the three cops were trying to wrestle Goodkind around Reilly and into the building.

It wouldn't take them long to straighten things out back there, and then everybody would be after me.

I started to run.

33

WHEN KAREN OPENED the door I said, "First of all, I want to apologize again."

"Don't be silly," she said. "We took care of all that on the phone. Come on in."

I went on in.

When I'd run away from Goodkind and Reilly and the police force, at first I hadn't been able to think of a place to go. The Coppo brothers and their mob might not believe a man would be dumb enough to hide out in his own apartment, but Reilly knew me and he could believe it with no trouble at all. That's how he'd gotten me the last time.

So where else was there? I wasn't sure I could get back into Gertie's apartment, nor was I sure it would be a good idea for me to be there; the mob knew about that place and might have it staked out just to be on the safe side. Since Gus Ricovic's occupancy, Uncle Matt's apartment was also too dangerous now.

Then I thought of Karen. She'd been angry at me when last we'd parted company, and I did want to get that straightened out, make my apologies, and whatnot. But besides that, she was apparently mad at Reilly now, at least according to what he'd said in that cell, and she just might be inclined to help me against him.

At any rate, I thought it worth a phone call, which I made from a stuffy phone booth in a dark and crowded drugstore on Eighth Avenue. When Karen answered, I identified myself and launched at once into my apology, but she cut me off midway through the first sentence, saying, "No, Fred, you were right. I'm *glad* you opened my eyes, *glad*."

I kept on trying to apologize anyway, but she would have none of it, so I switched to the other reason for my call, and she said she'd be glad to hide me out again, and now here I was.

"I'm pretty sure I wasn't followed," I said, as I walked down the hall into the living room. "That's what took me so long getting here. Back-tracking and whatnot."

"You're getting skillful at all this," she said, smiling at me. "Tell me what you've been doing since you went away from here."

"Oh, wow. You wouldn't believe half of it."

But she did believe it, all of it. She laughed at the idea of Dr. Osbertson knocking himself out rather than answer questions, she was wide-eyed at all I'd been told by Professor Kilroy, she shivered delicately at the discovery of Gus Ricovic, and she grew as incensed as I was at the treatment I'd been given in jail.

As I was finishing, the street bell rang, and when Karen went to the callbox to ask who was there we both heard the gruff angry voice say, "It's Jack. Let me in."

"No," she said, and walked away from the callbox.

The bell rang again.

I said, "Karen, listen, I really don't want to come between—"

"Don't worry about it, John Alden," she said. She came over and sat down beside me on the sofa. As the bell sounded yet again she said, "Well, now. What shall we do this evening?"

34

WHAT WE DID mostly was talk. Or, that is, I talked, Karen being one of those rarities, a good listener. I think I talked so much primarily because I was terrified that if I ever did stop talking about my troubles she'd start talking about hers, and I really didn't want to hear the sad saga of Karen and Reilly and the hypotenuse.

What I talked about mostly was the money. "It's brought me nothing but grief," I said several times. "Nothing but trouble and worry. I don't see that it ever will bring me anything but trouble and worry."

"It just doesn't seem right to give it up," she said. "Not that you need it or anything, you're right about that. It's just—I don't know, it's as though if you give it up you've let the world beat you somehow."

"That's all right," I said. "I'm no fanatic, if I'm beaten I'll cry uncle."

"Well, what would you do with the money?" she asked me. "If you didn't keep it, I mean."

"I don't know. Give it to some charity. CARE, maybe, if they promise to send packages around to all the city jails. Or the Red Cross. I wish that's what Uncle Matt had done. Let the Coppos take out their mad on the Salvation Army."

"It just doesn't seem right," she said.

That was the conversation, with variations, that we kept having all evening. In a way I agreed with her, it would be admitting defeat to give the money up. But that was pride, nothing but pride. I didn't need the money, I didn't really even want the money. To keep it simply out of pride, when to have it in my possession meant I was marked for death, was only foolish.

Oh, well. Another thing we did during the evening was not answer the phone. Karen did once, and it was Reilly, and she hung up on him. "My eyes have been opened about that man," she said to me.

Quickly I said, "I wonder if maybe the USO would be a good place to give the money?"

Then also I spent a part of the evening planning what I would do tomorrow. I would go see Wilks—it had been too late this afternoon by the time I finally got away from the jail—and I would also go to the newspaper library and see what I could learn about the Coppo brothers.

Would it be smart to get in touch with them direct? The Coppos, I mean. Maybe if I was to call them, explain to them I'd never even met my Uncle Matt, I hadn't asked for this money, I was intending at once to turn it over to my favorite charity, maybe they'd leave me alone.

And maybe they'd come wiggling through the telephone line and bite me on the throat.

Ugh. I gave up that line of thought at once.

I also spent a lot of time not saying anything in response to Karen's line about John Alden. I knew this girl only slightly, she was having an affair with a friend of mine—or at least a former friend of mine, time would tell—we'd never dated, and yet that comment about John Alden had certainly seemed like a suggestion that I make some sort of move in her direction. It was true I'd kissed her once, but the circumstances had been a little unusual and I didn't think the kiss should count as having been a step in any sort of courtship.

Besides, my attitude toward Karen was as confused and ambivalent as my attitude toward the money. In a way I wanted very much to follow up the John Alden line, but at the same time I was very much intimidated by her beauty and her—what shall I call it?—her sexual emancipation, if you'll excuse the expression. In any case, I did nothing, and Karen dropped no more hints on the subject, and our conversation seemed to travel along well enough without it.

A little before midnight it occurred to me to try phoning Gertie again. I explained to Karen, "I don't have much hope, but I try once or twice a day anyway."

"I'll make us fresh drinks," Karen said, and took our glasses out to the kitchen.

I dialed the number, it rang twice, there was a click, and a voice that was surely Gertie's very own said, "Hello?"

35

"GERTIE?"

"Fred?"

"Gertie, is that you?"

"Is that *you*, Fred?"

"You got away!" I shouted, and Karen came in from the kitchen to see what was going on.

"I been calling your place, Fred," Gertie was saying. "You at home, or where are you?"

"When did you get away? How did you do it?"

"I climbed out a window. You should of seen me: Daredevil Gertie, the Human Fly. I only got in here a little while ago."

"Gertie, you better get out of there. They're liable to come looking for you again."

"I figured to go to kak in the morning," she said.

Karen was waving frantically at me, and pointing at the floor with her other hand. I nodded at her, and said into the phone, "Gertie, come on over here. You'll be safe and we can talk."

"Here? Where's here?"

"I'm at Karen Smith's place."

"Oh, yeah? You and her are a thing, huh?"

"I'll give you the address," I said. "You got pencil and paper?"

"Hold on."

She was gone so long I was beginning to think she'd been kidnapped again, but at last she did come back and I gave her the address and she promised to be right over.

"Be circuitous," I said.

"What's that?"

"Make sure you're not followed."

"Oh. You betcha."

We hung up and I said to Karen, "She'll be here in a little while."

Karen said, "Well?" She had a very odd expression on her face, sort of waiting and humorous and fatalistic.

I had no idea what she meant, and therefore said, "Well what?"

"Fred," she said, and shook her head, and gave a long-suffering sigh. "I can see you're going to be a lot of trouble," she said. "I only hope you're worth it."

"Karen, I don't—"

"Don't you realize," she said, "that if you're going to kiss me before Gertie gets here you should start now?"

36

TIME PASSED WHICH is no one's business but my own.

Gertie arrived about forty-five minutes later, looking none the worse for her experience. She marched in, grinned at Karen, and said, "So this is the competition. I better lose a few pounds."

"I was just thinking I should fill in a little," Karen told her. "Come in, sit down."

"Tell me what happened," I said. "I thought they'd killed you."

Gertie dropped into an armchair, adjusted her skirt, plunked her patent-leather purse down on the floor beside the chair, and said, "If you ask me, they didn't know what they were up to. First off I figured like you, I figured it was all over for little Gertie. But no, they took me out to Queens some place, some cruddy section, little houses, all grimy, locked me away in a room upstairs. Then I figured, oh ho, it's the fate worse than death. Well, I've had worse than that. But no, it wasn't that either. All they did was keep me there, and talk a lot on the phone. They didn't know *what* they were doing, those boys, they were a couple of lunkheads. I told them so myself."

"Two of them?"

"Yeah. The same two that grabbed me. They used chloroform on me in the hallway, or it would have taken more than two."

"Then that's why I didn't hear you scream or anything."

"You kidding? I didn't get a *chance* to scream. Listen, Fred, you ever hear of anybody named Coppo? Some name like that."

"You're darn right I did," I said. "Where'd you hear it?"

"That's who they were calling all the time," she said. "With my ear down by the keyhole I could hear part of what they said. Mostly bitching about having to keep guard on me, wanting to know what was up, what should they do with me, stuff like that. And the guy they talked to mostly was this Coppo. 'Lemme talk to Coppo,' I heard them say that a dozen times."

"There's two of them," I told her. "Two Coppos. They're brothers. I heard about them from Professor Kilroy."

That startled her. "Kilroy? That old buzzard's in town? I figured he was still down in South America some place."

"No," I said. "He's in town, and he got in touch with me." Then I told her about meeting Professor Kilroy, and what he'd told me about Pedro Coppo and the Coppo brothers.

When I was done, she said, "So it's the dough they're after, huh?"

"Professor Kilroy thought I should give it all to some charity."

"Give it all to putting those bums in the chair, you mean," she said. "What about the police? Did you go to them yet?"

"Are you kidding? There's cops in on this somewhere, I heard that part, too. Those two lunkheads telling each other the only good thing about the whole caper was the cops were cooled off."

"I thought so!" I jumped to my feet, excited and angry at having my suspicions verified. "They're all around us," I said. "You don't know who to trust, you just don't know who."

"I know where *I'm* going," said Gertie. "First thing in the morning I'm headed for kak."

"That's what you said on the phone," I said. "But why go to them? What can they do?"

"They can maybe give me some protection," she said. "Besides, they're one outfit you *can* trust."

"How can you be sure?"

"From what Matt told me," she said. "Matt was no sucker, he knew when an outfit was legit or not."

Karen said, "What are you two talking about?"

"Kak," I explained.

When Karen continued to look confused, Gertie took over the explanation, telling her what CAC was and about Uncle Matt having been a consultant to them. Karen listened, and then said, "But can they really do anything? What kind of power do they have?"

"Some senator runs it," Gertie said.

"Senator Earl Dunbar," I said, remembering the letters I'd gotten from them.

"Right," said Gertie, "that's the guy. Senator Dunbar. The way I figure, with a senator running things they got to have something going. Besides, wheres else do we turn? We go to the cops, we're right back in the laps of the Coppo boys again."

Karen said, "But what can they do if the police are corrupt? There must be some honest policemen, why not go to them?"

"Honey," said Gertie, "the tricky part is separate the sheep from the wolves, you know what I mean? The cop on the take don't have a sign on his back."

Karen turned to me, saying, "Fred, do you really think Jack could be involved in something like that?"

"I don't know any more," I told her. "I don't like to think of him that way, but I just can't be sure of him any more."

"Kak's our best bet," said Gertie. "Fred, how come you didn't go there yourself?"

"It never occurred to me," I admitted. "They sent me a couple of fund-raising letters, so I guess I just naturally lumped them in with everybody else, out to take me for a dollar."

She shook her head. "You're a nutty guy, Fred," she said.

"Maybe so."

"Come to kak with me in the morning," she said. "You tell them the part you know, I'll tell them the part I know."

I hesitated, saying, "I just don't know . . ."

"What else are you going to do, Fred?"

"You're right," I said. I turned to Karen, saying, "What do you think?"

"I suppose it's best," she said doubtfully.

"Good," said Gertie decisively. "Then that's settled. Now the only question is, how slow a worker are you, Fred?"

"What say?"

"I want to know who sleeps where," she explained.

It took me a few seconds for the question to sink in, during which Gertie kept watching my face. Then I got it.

She nodded. "That's what I figured," she said, and got to her feet. "Come on, Karen," she said. "Let's leave Don Juan to his beauty sleep."

I think Karen could at least have had the charity not to laugh.

37

AFTER BREAKFAST, KAREN announced that she was coming with us.

"No," I said firmly.

"I'll just call the office and say I'm sick today," she said.

Gertie said, "Fred's right, honey. Neither of us is liable to be very healthy to be near right now."

"That's all right," said Karen. "I'll help watch for them."

I said, "If this outfit's as good as Gertie thinks it is, maybe the mob has their headquarters watched or something. Anything could happen, and I don't want you mixed up in it."

"Fred," Karen said, "I think you're dramatizing this a little bit."

"Dramatizing? I've been shot at and followed and hounded, Gertie was kidnapped, for Pete's sake, my uncle was murdered, Gus Ricovic was murdered! If I'm dramatizing, what the heck are the Coppos doing?"

Gertie said, "Gus? What happened to Gus?"

"I'll just phone the office," Karen said, and went into the living room.

Gertie said, "What's this about Gus?"

So I told her about Gus, which seemed to shake her up quite a bit. "I can't understand it," she said. "What would Gus know? Why bump off Gus?"

"Somebody found a reason," I said.

Karen came back, saying, "Ready to go."

Gertie frowned at her and said to me, "Can't you talk her out of it, Fred?"

I just looked at her.

"Oh, yeah," she said fatalistically. "I forgot."

So we were an army of three as we marched out to the sunlight to strike our blow for decent society.

38

WE'D WALKED LESS than a block when Gertie said, "I guess I must of been followed last night."

I stopped where I was, and without turning my head to left or right, said, "Why do you say a thing like that, Gertie?" The sun was shining, the morning air was crisp and clear and clean, and I couldn't have felt more like an exposed target if I'd stood on a sand dune in the Sahara.

"Because of the car half a block behind us," she said. "It looks like the same one they took me away in. Don't look around at it."

"I wasn't going to," I assured her.

Karen was standing on my other side, and now she leaned in front of me to say under her breath to Gertie, "Are you sure it's the same car?"

"Looks like it."

I said, faintly, "What sort of car is it?"

"Black Caddy."

"Uh huh," I said. "We're doomed."

"They won't do nothing out in the open like this," Gertie said.

Karen said, "We can get a cab down at the corner."

"No!" I said. "That's what they want. We get into a cab, and the driver's one of them."

Karen looked at me as though she might make a comment about dramatization again, but then she changed her mind and said, "Then what can we do?"

"Split up," Gertie suggested.

Karen said, "But wouldn't we be better off sticking together?"

"We're just a bigger target this way," Gertie told her. "If we split up, at least one of us'll get through to kak."

"Maybe," said Karen doubtfully.

"Gertie's right," I said, as though I knew what I was talking about. But at least if we split up there was less likelihood of anything happening to Karen. I had no illusions about which of the three of us the black Cadillac would follow.

Gertie said, "Start walking again. Casual, like we don't know nothing's going on."

We started walking again, stiffly, as though we knew exactly what was going on.

Out of the corner of her mouth, Gertie said, "When we get to the corner, we go three different ways. Remember, kak's office is at Rockefeller Center."

"I remember," I said.

As we approached the corner, I said, "Should we synchronize watches?"

I felt Karen give me a long and very slow look. "Guess not," I said.

39

THE CADILLAC WAS following me.

We had split up at the corner of 79th Street and Broadway, executing a maneuver like toy soldiers on parade, Karen turning left, Gertie going straight ahead, and me turning right.

The Cadillac also turned right.

At 79th Street I turned right again, and so did the Cadillac. It was keeping well behind me, but it was the same car, no doubt of it. I was sure the side curtains were drawn, too, the same as always.

Never had the sun seemed so bright. Never had the store-fronts along

79th Street seemed set back so far from the curb, leaving such a wide expanse of sidewalk. Never had any block in New York looked quite so deserted at ten o'clock on a May morning.

We crossed Amsterdam Avenue, like an unobservant matador being followed by the bull.

At Columbus Avenue, 79th Street is blocked by the planetarium and the Museum of Natural History. There were bicycles parked out in front of both buildings. Driven by a wild surmise, I hurried across the street, but all the bikes had locks on them. Naturally. Everything in New York has a lock on it, much good it does anybody.

Across the street, the Cadillac was stopped by a red light. If I only had a vehicle of some sort, now was the time to get clean away from them.

A flock of boys on bikes suddenly swarmed around me, dismounting with the bicycles still in motion, kicking down the kick-stands, reaching with practiced knowledge for their locks. I looked around me and knew my chance had come.

The boy nearest me was very short, and stout, and wore glasses. I said to him, "Excuse me," and took his bicycle.

He looked at me without comprehension.

I got on his bicycle and rode away.

Behind me, there was a sudden flurry of shouts. Looking back, I saw the rest of the boys leaping onto their own cycles and setting off after me. And the Cadillac, finally having a green light to deal with, was nosing around the corner.

I faced front, bent grimly over the handlebars, and pedaled furiously around the museum and down 78th Street.

It had been years since I'd ridden a bike. While it may be true that a skill once learned is never forgotten, it is also true that if you haven't ridden a bicycle for years you're going to be dreadful at it. Particularly when you're driving down a sidewalk alive with garbage cans, young trees, fire hydrants and old ladies walking Pekinese.

How I threaded through all that I'll never know, but one way and another I did survive it, with a pack of howling bike-riding children in my wake, and with the black Cadillac snorting in muffled impatience at a red light back on Columbus Avenue.

At the far end of the block was Central Park, and I made for it like a bicycling bear headed for his cave. Ahh, but between me and the potential sanctuary of the park lay Central Park West, a broad avenue blazing with traffic. Buses, cabs, MG's, Rolls Royces, doctors in Lincolns, college boys in Ferraris, kept women in Mustangs, tourists in Edsels, interior decorators in Dafs, all tearing back and forth, all knowing they have sixty seconds of green light before the red light will return, all knowing that the unofficial world record is seventeen blocks on one green light and all trying to beat that record, and absolutely none of them prepared to deal with a nut on a bicycle abruptly crossing their bows.

But what was I to do? I was going far too fast—and was far too shaky—to attempt a left or right turn. With all those screaming children behind me—not to mention the Cadillac, which must surely have a green light of its own again by now—I dared not stop. There was only one thing to do, and I did it.

I closed my eyes.

Oh, the shrieking of brakes. Oh, the tinkling of smashed headlights against smashed taillights. Oh, the screams of disbelief and rage. Oh, the panic.

I opened my eyes and saw curb dead ahead. Some reflex left over from childhood made me yank up on the handlebars, so that the bicycle climbed the curb rather than stopping abruptly at it and leaving me to go airborne over the low stone wall and into the park. A similar reflex enabled me to turn right without capsizing. Down the sidewalk I raced, amid the strollers in the sun, leaving chaos, outrage, and crushed straw hats in my wake. So many fists were raised and shaking back there it looked like a mob of Romans come to hear Mussolini.

There was a break in the stone wall, and a path, blacktop, going into the park and sloping away downhill to the right. I turned in there, gasping for breath, still pumping furiously, and let the incline take me.

Beautiful. I could sit at last, and stop pumping, and feel the wind rush past my sweating brow. Down the slope I sailed, and even the yelping of the children still dogging my trail sounded suddenly remote and unimportant. I almost smiled, and then looked down at the bottom of the slope and stopped almost smiling.

A pond lay dead ahead. Possibly the most polluted body of water in the United States, it sported a necklace of beer cans, milk cartons, bits of wax paper, latex products, abandoned toy dump trucks, dill pickles, broken switchblade knives, half-pint muscatel bottles, cardboard coffee containers, copies of *Playboy,* brown shoes, and crib springs.

No. Please no.

I applied the brakes. That is, I applied what were the brakes on a bike when I was a kid, which is to say that I began to pedal backward. When I was a kid, if you were on a bike and you wanted to slow down you pushed the pedals backward against pressure and the bike slowed down.

Plus ça change, plus c'est change. Bicycles aren't bicycles any more. I began to pedal backward, encountered no pressure at all, and kept on trying. Meanwhile, the bike was picking up speed. I was pedaling back-ward, the bike was going faster and faster forward, and that murky pond lay sprawled down there in front of me like an extra circle of Hell.

I couldn't think what was wrong. Was the rotten cycle broken? Why on earth wasn't I stopping? Furiously I pedaled backward, and more furiously I streaked forward.

The pond was scant feet away when at last I saw the little levers attached to the handlebars quite near my knuckles. Slender cables of some sort meandered away from these levers and disappeared into the bike's plumb-ing.

Could these be the brakes? I had no time to think, to ponder, to do anything but close my fingers about both those levers at once and squeeze. Hard.

The bike stopped on a dime, and gave four cents' change.

It's too bad there weren't any levers on me. The bike stopped but I did not. I sailed through the air with the greatest of ease, out over the olive-drab water, and seemed to hang there in midair while a peculiar yellow stench lovingly embraced me. Then I shut my mouth and my eyes, folded my body up in the fetal position, plummeted downward, smashed into the water, and sank like a safe.

40

WHEN I EMERGED, soaking and sputtering and spitting out candy bar wrappers, on the far side of the pond, I looked about me and saw the pack of boys splitting into two groups and circling the pond on both sides, still intent on my capture even though I no longer had anybody's bicycle. Is it good for little children to bear grudges like that?

At the top of the slope I'd lately left I saw a cop, just making up his mind to trot down and ask me one or two questions. I didn't have time for all that now, nor to be set upon by a thousand enraged children, so I faced the other way and saw ahead of me a jagged escarpment of bare rock. Perfect. Up this it was possible for me to scramble, but no one would be able to pursue me on bike.

I had never in my life before been quite this wet, nor had I ever run across water quite this slippery and greasy. My hands and shoes and elbows kept sliding on the rocks as I climbed, leaving green smears behind. But I did at last attain the top, looked to my left, and saw across a bit of greensward the south-bound lanes of the road that makes a long oval inside the park. A traffic light was there—red, because all traffic lights are red—and among the vehicles hunched at the white line there was a taxicab with its vacancy light aglow.

Saved! I squished in a sodden dogtrot across the greensward, pulled open the cab door, collapsed on the seat, and gasped, "Rockefeller Center."

The cabby turned around in some surprise, looked at me, and did a double-take. He then leaned way over to look out his right side window toward the direction from which I'd come, saying, "It's raining?"

"The light's green," I said.

He immediately straightened, tromped the accelerator, and we joined the race to the next red light. On the way, he said, in a reasonable tone, "It ain't raining here."

"This isn't rain," I said, very near the end of my rope. "I had some trouble."

"Oh," he said.

He was quiet for two more red lights, but while we were stopped at the third he turned around with a peculiar expression on his face and said, "I hope you don't mind me pointing this out, mister, but you smell something awful."

"I know," I said.

"I would go so far as to say you stink," he told me.

"The light's green," I said.

He faced front, gunned, and off we went again. I sat in the rear of the cab and spoiled.

"You get some nuts," the driver decided. Since he didn't appear to have been talking to me, I made no reply.

41

THE ELEVATOR OPERATOR at Rockefeller Center didn't like my aroma much either. The CAC headquarters were on a very high floor, so that we spent a lot of time together, comparatively speaking; when I left, he was looking around his elevator for a window to open.

The door I wanted had no name on it, only a number. I entered and found myself in a small and scruffy reception room, with a receptionist at a desk and with Gertie and Karen reading respectively *Holiday* and *Time* on a bench to my right.

They both leaped to their feet at my entrance. Karen came running toward me, arms outstretched, saying, "Darling! I was so—" And recoiled.

"I'm sorry," I said.

Gertie looked at me, wide-eyed. "Wha'd you do?" she asked me. "Hide out in the sewer?"

"I had a little trouble," I said.

The receptionist said, "Sir, is that—is that you? The smell. Is it you?"

"I couldn't go back to the apartment," I said. "I'd just managed to get away."

The receptionist went over and opened the window all the way.

I said, "Excuse me." I walked over to the window—the receptionist circled around me like a dog avoiding a horse—took off my jacket and tie, and flung them out into the world. Then, facing the room, I told the three women, "I'll stay here by the window."

The receptionist said to Gertie, "Is this the man you were waiting for?" She sounded as though she couldn't believe the answer would be yes.

But it was. "That's him," Gertie admitted. "But he ain't always quite that bad."

"Maybe I can get you something else to wear," the receptionist told me, and hurried from the room.

Karen, keeping her distance, said, "I was so worried about you, Fred. You didn't get here, and you didn't get here."

"I had some trouble," I said, for the millionth time, thereby managing the difficult feat of overstating an understatement.

"I wanted to phone the police," Karen told me. "But Gertie was sure you'd make it."

"I'm not sure I was right," said Gertie.

The receptionist came back at that point, carrying a white laboratory smock, saying, "This is all I could find, sir."

"Thank you," I said. "Anything." I headed toward her.

Quickly she put the smock down on a chair and retreated to the other side of the room.

It's discouraging to be a pariah. Feeling very hangdog, I went over and picked up the smock and asked the receptionist to direct me to the men's room. She did, and I left them, taking my green miasma with me.

In a stall in the men's room I stripped down to the skin and put on the smock, which was—happily—too large for me. My hands disappeared inside the sleeves, and the bottom of the smock reached to my shins. I rolled the sleeves up till I could see my hands, and then went over to a sink and washed as best I could, patting myself dry with paper towels.

At one point a portly man smoking a cigar came in, looked at me, made a U-turn, and went out again.

My clothing was ruined, all of it, even my shoes. I threw everything into the trash can and then, wearing nothing but my smock, I padded barefoot back down the corridor to the offices of CAC.

The door was propped open, held by a Manhattan phone book. Both windows were open wide. A faint trace of my previous perfume still hung at nose-level in the air.

This time everybody was pleased to see me. Or maybe amused to see me. In any case, they all smiled broadly when I came into the room. Karen said, "Oh, that's much better, Fred. Come sit down beside me."

The receptionist spoke briefly into the phone and then told us, "Our Mr. Bray will see you in just a few minutes."

"Thank you," we said.

Karen said, "Tell me what happened to you, Fred."

Gertie said, "You looked like they tried to drown you in garbage. Nobody's *that* mean."

I told them about my getaway. Karen tried to keep a straight face and failed. Gertie didn't even try.

"I'll laugh tomorrow," I said shortly, picked up a *Kiplinger* magazine, and read about life among the rest of the paranoids.

A few minutes later a very distinguished-looking man came in—gray hair, fawn topcoat, well-fed look—and said to the receptionist, "Ah, there, Mary, is Callahan in?"

"Good morning, Senator," she said. "No, he had to see the Commissioner this morning. Did he expect you?"

"No, I just thought I'd drop by, see how things are doing." He looked at his watch. "When did be expect to be back, did he say?"

"No later than eleven-thirty, he said. I think he meant it this time."

The Senator laughed, saying, "We'll take him at his word, I think. I'll wait." He turned toward the bench where we were sitting, and apparently took a good look at us for the first time: two comely women of wildly disparate types, and sitting between them like a hospital patient waiting for the operation on his gall bladder a sort of sheepish madman in white coat and bare feet.

Political training has probably never come in handier. The Senator's smile turned glassy for barely a second, and other than that he gave no visible reaction at all. Recovering, he gave the three of us the sort of blank cheerful smile an outgoing man always offers when taking a seat with others in a waiting room. I gave him back a weak version of the same smile, while Karen studied the floor and Gertie studied the ceiling.

Then for a while the four of us sat there with magazines open in front of us, like a surrealist's painting.

Finally the door to our right opened and a harried-looking young man in shirt sleeves came out. He had a pencil behind one ear, his collar was open, and his tie was loose. He gave me a brief odd look, and then said, "Senator! Nice to see you again."

The Senator stood up, and they shook hands. The Senator said, "Good to see you, Bob. I believe these people have been waiting."

"Yes, of course." Bob now turned his full attention on us. "I'm terribly sorry to keep you waiting, folks," he said. "We're a little understaffed around here. You said something about reporting a crime?"

"A whole box full of crimes," Gertie told him. "Murder, kidnapping, attempted murder, bribing cops, you name it."

Bob seemed a little taken aback. Chuckling a bit, he said, "That's quite a list, madam. Have any idea who's been doing all this?"

"Two brothers named Coppo."

The Senator suddenly burst out, "The Coppos again! They're becoming a two-man crime wave, Bob."

"You can say that again," said Gertie.

The Senator said, "Bob, with your permission I'd like to sit in on this interview." He turned to me. "That is, if you wouldn't mind."

Gertie said, "You're Senator Dunbar, aren't you?"

He smiled acknowledgment. "Former Senator, I'm afraid. Otherwise, guilty as charged."

"You run this outfit."

"Honorary Chairman only," said the senator, smiling graciously. "A mere figurehead."

"You can sit in as far as we're concerned," Gertie said, and turned to me. "Right, Fred?"

"Of course," I said. I was pleased to have him; if we could get somebody important interested right away, it couldn't hurt and it might even help.

"Then come along," said the Senator. "You lead the way, Bob."

We all trooped on into Bob's tiny office, settled ourselves in chairs, and for the next twenty minutes Gertie and Karen and I told our combined story.

42

"THAT," SAID THE Senator, "is one of the most incredible stories I've ever heard."

"Well, it's all true," said Gertie. "Every word of it."

"Oh, I believe you," the Senator assured her. "I merely mean that it is incredible to me that in this day and age this sort of thing can still be permitted to go on. Vendettas, mob killings, kidnappings of innocent individuals from their very doorsteps—no, it's unforgivable."

"The question is," I said, "is it stoppable."

The Senator turned to me. "I wish I could tell you, Mr. Fitch," he said, without my having to ask him not to call me Fred, "that it is stoppable, that an easy solution awaits you here in this office. But I'm afraid I can't. We already have an extensive file on the Coppo brothers, I believe they're in our top ten—Bob?"

"Numbers seven and eight, I believe," said Bob seriously.

"Not that it matters," the Senator said, "unless we can show results. But we want those two, we want to see them behind bars. We have our top ten here, the same as the FBI. All it means is, those are the criminals we concentrate on. Buy information when we can, try to find witnesses who are willing to testify—"

"Well, we're willing to testify," Gertie said. "Aren't we, Fred?"

"Of course," I said.

"Ah, well," said the Senator, "but it isn't really that easy. The Coppo brothers can afford the best attorneys, you know. And what do you have, really, to bring into court against them? What proof?" He turned to me, "You have the word of a dubious character, someone calling himself Professor Kilroy, whom you can't even produce to verify what he told you. Hearsay, nothing more."

"But the shots at me," I said. "The car that followed me. The phone calls."

"Proof," the Senator said. "You have no proof, no witnesses, no corroboration." He smiled sadly, and leaned toward me, saying, "I'm sorry, Mr. Fitch, I truly am, but these are facts I'm telling you. Our legal system does seem to offer more protection to the criminal than to his victim, but a democracy could hardly operate otherwise."

"Why not?" Gertie demanded. "Why not just toss bums like those Coppos in jail and get em out of the way?"

"Would you really want to do that, Miss Divine? Let's change the words from criminal and victim to accused and accuser. A small exercise in semantics, but notice how everything changes. Our legal system offers more protection to the accused than to the accuser. Would you truly want it any other way?"

"I know what you mean, Senator," I said, "and I suppose you're right. But that's abstraction, and I'm here in the concrete." I laughed self-consciously and said, "Maybe with my feet in the concrete."

"I sympathize, Mr. Fitch," he said, "and I wish I could offer you a brighter prospect, but it would be unfair. You see how understaffed we are here, and even with a full staff, and adequate financing, we could hardly do more than scratch the surface. Oh, we might dispatch our top ten, but there's always ten more behind them, and ten more behind them. Believe me, Mr. Fitch, the criminal statistics are frightening."

"It isn't just the statistics," I said.

Gertie said, "What about *me* on the witness stand? I was kidnapped, that isn't any hearsay."

The Senator smiled sadly at her. "Again, have you any proof? Witnesses? Did the Coppo brothers themselves kidnap you, and could you identify them?"

"The guys that guarded me called the Coppos on the phone."

"Can you prove that? The use of a name doesn't prove a thing, Miss Divine." The Senator sat back and spread his hands. "Forgive my taking the role of the devil's advocate, but I do want you to see what we're up against. The enemy is an elusive one, and well represented by counsel."

"What does it take to win?" Karen asked.

"To be honest," he said, "it takes money. Most of our success has come as a result of information bought and paid for. For instance, if we could know for certain which police officers have been corrupted by the Coppo gang, we could by-pass them, go to the honest officers, arrange traps to catch the bribe-taking police red-handed. If we could buy from informants, for instance, the names of the two men who kidnapped Miss Divine, if we could offer one of them an inducement to turn state's evidence—" He spread his hands. "We can do it," he said, "but only a little at a time. We chop off the tentacles, slowly, but the head seems always to remain."

"And meanwhile," Gertie said, "the Coppos are still after Fred and me."

"All I can suggest," the Senator said, "is that you leave the city, perhaps even leave the country, until such time as these criminals have been put safely behind bars."

Karen said, "But what if they never *get* behind bars?"

"I really don't know what to tell you," the Senator said.

I had been mulling things over the last couple of minutes, and now I said, "Senator, could you use a donation?"

He smiled wistfully. "We could always use donations," he said.

"I've got one for you," I said.

Both women were looking at me oddly. Karen said, "Fred, what are you going to do?"

"I'm giving it away," I told her. "Here's my good cause, putting people like the Coppo brothers behind bars."

The Senator said, "Mr. Fitch, what are you driving at?"

Karen said, "Fred, don't!"

But I was determined. "Your organization gets the whole thing, "I told the Senator. "Three hundred thousand dollars. I don't want the damn stuff, and it can do you people a lot of good."

43

OF COURSE, THEY all tried to talk me out of it. Karen just kept doggedly telling me not to do it, while Gertie was vehement, telling me I was crazy, nobody in his right mind would give away three hundred grand, and so on. The young man, Bob, kept saying, "You don't want to do this on the spur of the moment, Mr. Fitch." And the Senator said such things as, "You really should think this over, you know," and, "Why don't you talk to your clergyman first, see what he has to say," and, "You don't want to do something today you'll regret tomorrow."

But I knew what it was I wanted. I'd suspected for a couple of days that I wasn't going to be keeping the money, that the only thing left was to decide where was the best place to donate it. And when we'd come in here, when I'd seen this place and heard the Senator talk, I'd known then where my money could do the most good.

My money. But it wasn't my money, not really. I'd inherited under false pretenses, surely; if Uncle Matt had known the kind of goofball and born mark I am he would hardly have left me in charge of his ill-gotten loot. And it wasn't Uncle Matt's money, any more than mine, because he too had gotten it under false pretenses, stolen it from a man who'd ended his life as a result. If it belonged to anybody, really, it was the heirs of Pedro Coppo, his two sons. But the idea of giving those crooks any of the money just stuck in my craw; they were worse than Uncle Matt, worse than any con man. A con man may pick you for a hundred dollars, but when he goes away he's hurt nothing but your pocketbook. He doesn't beat people up, or kidnap them, or kill them.

No, here was the best place for blood money. Let it go to the Citizens Against Crime, let it do good for a change. Let it put the Coppo brothers in jail, let it keep them there the rest of their lives. The rest of my life, anyway, that was good enough for me.

When at last they saw I was adamant about giving the money to CAC, and about doing it right now, the Senator said, "Well, sir, I hardly know what to say. Your donation will do a great deal of good, I can tell you that much. And it's the sort of windfall we don't even dream about around here, do we, Bob?"

"Not hardly, sir," said Bob, smiling weakly. "Frankly, I'm stunned by all this."

"I suppose what you'll want now is a lawyer," said the Senator. "Would you like to phone your attorney from here?"

Goodkind? Oh, no. "Let's use your lawyer," I said. "He probably knows more about this sort of thing than mine does. All we have to do now is draw up some sort of paper for me to sign, guaranteeing delivery of the full inheritance. That way, if anything happens to me in the meantime, you can still collect."

"Oh, I'm sure nothing will happen to you," the Senator said. "In fact, I think what we'll do is send a team direct to the Coppo brothers to tell them about this. What say, Bob?"

"I'd like to do it myself, sir."

"Good boy. You and Callahan." The Senator turned back to me, saying, "All right, we'll get the organization's attorney right up here. Bob, would you see to it?"

"Certainly, sir." Bob got up from his desk, excused himself to the rest of us, and left.

Senator Dunbar turned to me and said, "I wonder if you'd be interested in a job with us here, Mr. Fitch?" He smiled and said, "We'll be able to add to our staff now, of course."

"I don't know anything about this kind of work," I said, but I was pleased and flustered at having been asked.

"What sort of work do you do?" he asked me, and for the next few minutes we discussed my profession as researcher and the possibilities of adapting that profession to something useful to CAC. I finally said I'd think it over, and then the Senator told us something about CAC's history and record, and some specific anecdotes about the activities of the organization. All in all, we chatted about ten minutes before Bob came back in and said, "All set, sir. I cleared the conference room for us, we'll have more space there."

"Very good, Bob," said the Senator, getting to his feet. He and I spent a few seconds bowing each other out the door, and then I gave in and went first. Karen and Gertie, both still disapproving, though silently now, trailed after us.

We crossed the reception room and went through a door on the other side, into a long and rather narrow room dominated by a gleaming conference table flanked by comfortable-looking chairs with wooden arms and red-leather upholstered seats. A man was standing at the far end of the table, with a black attaché case open on the table in front of him; he was taking papers and pens from it and lining them up.

There was something immediately familiar about this man, but I couldn't think what. He was perhaps fifty, medium height, slightly stocky but not overweight in any real sense, well dressed; the sort of man you see at half the tables every lunch hour in midtown restaurants. Was that it, merely that he reminded me of a type? But why did I have this odd feeling that I had seen *him* somewhere before?

Senator Dunbar came around me, saying, "Ah, Prescott, good to see you again." He and the new man shook hands, and then the Senator turned to me, saying, "Mr. Fitch, may I introduce the man who has donated his legal services to our organization free of charge ever since its founding. Mr. Prescott Wilks, here's perhaps our greatest benefactor, Mr. Fredric Fitch."

Prescott Wilks. The lawyer who'd written the letter to Uncle Matt.

All at once I felt a chill in the back of my neck. Something was wrong somewhere. I was surrounded by smiling, amiable, *convincing* people; we were all sliding effortlessly down the chute together.

It was happening again!

Then Prescott Wilks came toward me, his hand outstretched, a pleasant smile on his face, and all at once I knew where I'd seen him before, and that meant I knew who he was, and that meant . . .

"Professor Kilroy!" I shouted. "You're Professor Kilroy!"

44

I WAS SURROUNDED by blank stares of incomprehension, but I didn't care. I felt as though a great fog were suddenly lifting and all at once the landscape was clear all around me.

"He is!" I told everybody, told myself. "He put on a fake beard and a fright wig and those glasses, he dirtied his face, he put on old clothes that were too big for him to make him look smaller and scrawnier, he walked funny, he talked with that gravel voice—"

Senator Dunbar approached me with a concerned look, saying,

"Mr. Fitch, do you feel unwell? Has the strain—?"

"No strain at all," I said. "You know how I know? That attaché case there. You had it in a locker, with your regular clothes in it. You went and got it and went into the men's room and changed your clothes in a stall, and that's why Professor Kilroy never came out again. Because *you* came out! The minute I walked in here I knew I'd seen you somewhere, but I couldn't remember where. It was at Grand Central. You were one of the men that came *out* of that men's room."

Prescott Wilks offered me a beautiful imitation of a baffled smile. "I confess I don't follow you, young man," he said. He turned the smile to Senator Dunbar, saying, "Should I, Earl?"

Karen, looking troubled, touched my arm and said, "Fred? Are you all right?"

"This young man's been under a severe strain," the Senator said. "You've heard of the Coppo brothers."

Wilks nodded. "Of course."

"It's all a con," I told Karen. "The whole thing was a huge con."

The Senator went blithely along, explaining things to Wilks. "They've been making life difficult for Mr. Fitch," he said. "I don't think we could really blame him if he starts imagining things."

Gertie came over on my other side and said, "Fred, what's happened to you? You snap a cable or something?"

"I trusted you, Gertie," I said. "And you're in it with them."

The Senator said, "Bob, perhaps it would be best if you called a doctor."

"Doctor Osbertson," I said. "Let's get the whole gang here."

Bob didn't go anywhere. The room got quieter and quieter. Everyone was looking at me, and behind their worried, amiable, puzzled countenances I could see the beginnings of wariness.

Karen sensed it, too. Her hand tightened on my arm as she faced them, and the lines had been drawn: we two against the rest of them.

I said, "Prescott Wilks wrote a letter to my uncle. I've got it. I suppose the word for that is coincidence."

Gertie said, "Fred, you flipped. All of a sudden you don't trust nobody."

"And you weren't kidnapped," I told her. "That was just part of the buildup."

"Fred, believe me, I know whether I was kidnapped or not."

"You do, do you?" I look around at the concerned false faces. "I'm going to find out what's behind all this," I said. "Walter Cosgrove has something to do with it, and I'm going to find out what."

"Bob," said the Senator, somewhat grimly, "I believe that doctor should be called at once."

"Yes, sir," he said, and backed hurriedly out the door.

"He won't call any doctors," I said. "He knows when the boat's going down. You take a look out there, you'll see him running for the elevators."

The Senator's smile was a little crooked. "I think not," he said. "Bob is a trusted assistant."

"Trusted?" I backed away, holding Karen's arm. "We're leaving here," I said. "Don't try to stop us."

The Senator said, "Are you sure the Coppos aren't after you? Before you go out on that street, before you expose yourself to the world, you had better be sure. You *were* shot at, you know. You were harassed, hounded."

For just a second I felt my grip on reality weakening, but I steeled myself and said, "That was you people. You were the ones shot at me. Professional mobsters don't miss three times, I should have thought of that long ago. You weren't trying to hit me, you just wanted to scare me. And it took three shots to attract my attention."

"I have no idea what you're talking about," said the Senator. "As for me, I've been on the West Coast the last three weeks, and can produce any number of responsible citizens to bear me out."

"Then it was Wilks," I said. "He ran the whole thing. He took the shots at me, played Professor Kilroy, followed me in the car, called me at Karen's place—"

"That's the most fantastic thing I ever heard of," said Wilks. "I'm an attorney, not an—an—acrobat."

"I'll bet you seventeen dollars," I told him, "you were in your senior class play in college. In the drama society. I'll bet you've always had a yen for the stage. I bet you invest in shows. I bet you've been in amateur theater."

I could see my bets hitting home. Wilks turned to the Senator for help, and the Senator said to me, "Fortunately, young man, we're all friends in here, or these incredible charges of yours might have some serious results."

"Serious results? How's this for a serious result—it was Wilks that killed Uncle Matt!"

"Now, that's too much!" cried Wilks. "I have never raised a hand against a human being in my life!"

The Senator turned to Gertie, saying, "Miss Divine, this young man is your friend, isn't there anything you can do with him?"

But Gertie laughed and shook her head and said, "Forget it, Senator, the kid tumbled. You're not gonna get him back on the track now."

I said to her, "You admit it?"

"Sure," she said. "Why not?"

"You'll go to jail," I said. "That's why not."

"Not on your life," she said. "You got to have a lot of proof first, and you don't have a thing "

"You weren't kidnapped," I said.

"No kidding," she said. "And it wasn't always Wilks in the Caddy, sometimes it was me. You like me in my driver's hat?"

The thought of that Cadillac, so menacing, being driven by Gertie in a chauffeur's cap, with the curtained back seat as empty as the inside of my head, filled me with humiliation and rage. "What about murder?" I demanded. "You think there's no proof there? Wilks'll pay for that, and so will the rest of you. Accessories!"

"Come off it, Fred," Gertie said. "Wilks didn't kill anybody. Look at him, he ain't the type. If this crowd was gonna kill Matt, they'd of done it years ago. He held them up five years, you know."

The Senator suddenly burst out, "I've heard enough! You people come in here with a story of harassment, we offer you our assistance, and suddenly you start making these wild accusations—If you don't leave at once, I'll call the police!"

"I'll do it for you," I said. "Come on, Karen."

We backed cautiously out to the reception room. Beside me, Karen seemed as tense as an overwound watch. Her face was very white, except for two small circles of high color on her cheeks. She gazed at each speaker in turn, and when no one was speaking she looked at the Senator, much the way I suspect the bird looks at the snake.

The reception room was empty, the receptionist having abandoned her post. Bob didn't seem to be around anywhere, either. I moved toward the desk and the phone.

The Senator had followed me. "I would prefer it," he said coldly, "if you would not make your personal calls on my telephone."

"There's other phones," I said. "Gertie? Are you coming with us?"

She grinned at me and shook her head. "Naw, I better stick here with these birds and get our story straight. See you later, Fred."

When Karen and I backed out, Gertie was still grinning at me, standing there flanked by Wilks and the Senator, both of whom were looking very grim.

I had the funny feeling Gertie was proud of me.

45

"GERTIE'S NOTE FROM Uncle Matt," I told Karen as we waited for the elevator, "was a fake. They had to get her close to me so she could set me up for the con. She's the one told me about Professor Kilroy and about kak."

"I'm lost, Fred," Karen said. She looked dazed. "All of a sudden, everything is something else."

"I've gone through my life that way," I said. I began counting, saying, "How many parts did Wilks play? He took the shots at me. Then he was the rabbi. Then he—"

"The rabbi? Fred, *do* you feel all right?"

I said, "The day I got the call at your place, a rabbi came around to the door. Old man with a heavy beard, mumbling. They knew I was in the building, but they didn't know which apartment. So Wilks got out the makeup kit and kept knocking on doors till he found me."

"How did they know you were in the building?"

"Followed me from my place."

She said, "And you thought it was Jack, you thought he betrayed you. You owe him an apology, Fred."

"I know it. Back to Wilks. After the rabbi, he was Professor Kilroy. They couldn't take a chance on Gertie giving me the whole con, it might not ring true, so they filled in with Professor Kilroy. Then Gertie drove the car and Wilks was the man in the cap. And this morning it was Wilks in the Cadillac again."

The elevator door slid open. The operator and a half-dozen passengers looked at me in absolute astonishment. For just a second I couldn't think why anybody would look at me like that, but when I glanced down to see if my fly was shut and saw that I was still barefoot and wearing the laboratory smock, I understood. I felt my face light up like an exit sign. Looking as dignified and unconcerned as I could manage, I took Karen's arm and we boarded the elevator.

On the way down Karen said, "What do we do now?"

"Call the police," I said. "First thing."

But I didn't have to call the police. The second my bare foot hit the sidewalk of Fifth Avenue, I was arrested.

46

THAT EVENING REILLY brought me some clothing and the news I was no longer to be kept in jail. I'd had a long session already with Steve and

Ralph, about which the less said is believe me the better, and now they were done with me.

The meeting with Reilly was very awkward at first, with me apologizing and being defensive all at once, and he simultaneously understanding and swallowing rage.

"Fred," he said, "all I ask is you find the happy medium. First, you trust everybody. Then, you trust nobody. Can't you get in the middle someplace?"

"I'll try," I said. "I really will."

"All right, enough of that," he said. "That's behind us, that isn't what I came here for. I thought you'd like to know what else I found out."

"I'd love to know it," I said.

"I got most of it from Goodkind," he said. "He swears he would've told you if you'd given him a chance, but I don't believe it. I think he had another song and dance for you, something to cover the facts without giving the facts."

"Like Senator Dunbar and company," I said.

"Same style. Anyway, what Goodkind says, that money never did belong to your uncle. He didn't steal it or make it or win it or anything. You were right about Walter Cosgrove being involved in this; it was his money."

"He had to be involved," I said. "Dr. Osbertson knew him. Wilks obviously knew him, from the way he acted when I said the name to him while he was being Professor Kilroy."

"The way Goodkind got the story," Reilly said, "Matt was down and out in Brazil when Cosgrove found him. Matt was dying of cancer and he knew it. Cosgrove had to get half a million dollars into the States and into the hands of Earl Dunbar. Dunbar has influence, he could wangle some sort of pardon or amnesty for Cosgrove, so Cosgrove could come back to this country. Half a million was Dunbar's price, in advance."

"This is too complicated," I said.

"Not really," he said. "Not when you get down to the core of it. Anyway, Dunbar had this Citizens Against Crime gimmick, he's had it for years, a safe front for any money he wanted to collect without soiling his hands. The sort of cash a lesser politician would call campaign contributions. But Dunbar was smarter than that; money never went directly to him. CAC got it, and then he siphoned it off, leaving just enough to maintain the organization. That office you saw is the extent of it."

"But what about Cosgrove and the money?"

"Cosgrove gave it to Matt," Reilly said, "because Matt was supposed to die in less than a year, and he was supposed to leave a will in which he repented his evil life and left all his money to CAC to continue its good work."

"He double-crossed them," I said.

"He double-crossed them six ways from Sunday. First, by staying alive five years instead of six months. And second, by leaving his money to you."

"That's why Wilks killed him then," I said. "Because Matt fired him, and he suspected a double-cross."

Reilly shook his head. "No. In the first place, Wilks desperately didn't want Matt to die until he found out what the cross was. In the second place, Wilks has a rock-solid alibi for the time of the murder."

"It wasn't Wilks?"

"Definitely not."

"Well, it wasn't the Coppo brothers," I said. "If there are any Coppo brothers."

"Oh, there are," Reilly said. "But they don't come from Brazil, they come from Canarsie. And they never had anything to do with you or your uncle or anybody else in this mess."

"But they're real," I said. "Just in case I should happen to look them up in the newspaper files, I suppose."

"Something like that."

"But all that complicated machinery they had working around me," I said. "Why go through all that?"

"They couldn't just go to you and say your uncle made a mistake, the money's supposed to be theirs. Dunbar was putting pressure on Wilks from one side, and I suppose Cosgrove was putting pressure on him from the other side. You had a reputation for gullibility, so they started setting this thing up, making it up as they went along, hustling you around as best they could. Also, I think Wilks enjoyed it. You were right about him, he's a frustrated ham."

"If I hadn't seen that letter from him in Uncle Matt's desk," I said, "I might never have tipped. I'd have signed the papers, and it would have been all over."

"It was close," Reilly agreed. "You're a born sucker, Fred, and a born sucker's worst enemy is himself."

"I'm getting better," I said. "I think I've learned something these last few days."

"Maybe so," he said, but he didn't sound convinced.

I said, "The only question is, which one of them killed Uncle Matt? And Gus Ricovic? If Wilks didn't, which one did?"

"None of them," Reilly said. "They're all clean. Besides, it wouldn't make sense for them to wait five years and then kill Matt. And besides that, they suspected he was up to something, and they hoped he *wouldn't* die until they found out what it was."

"Then who killed Uncle Matt?"

"I have no idea," he said.

I said, "I've been figuring it was all tied together, the con and the murder. But that was what they wanted me to think, wasn't it? Tying everything together."

"As best as we can tell," said Reilly, "there's no tie-in at all. Wilks and Gertie Divine simply used the fact of the murder to hang their con on."

"Oh, for Pete's sake," I said, feeling sudden relief. "In that case, I know who did it."

Reilly looked at me dubiously. "You do?"

"The elevator operator."

"The what?"

"At this apartment house," I said. "The night elevator operator."

"Fred, do you feel all right?"

"I feel fine. Listen to me. Matt used to play cards with the elevator operator, and you know Matt had to be cheating him, just naturally, not even thinking about it. But he was getting sloppy. Gertie and Gus Ricovic both used to catch him all the time, but they let him get away with it."

"You're sure of this?" Reilly asked me. He was looking less dubious and more interested.

"Positive," I said. "And that elevator operator is nowhere near as sharp as Gertie, so he never knew Matt was cheating him until the last night they played. Then when he caught him Matt must have gotten sore, maybe threatened to tell the management, and the management would fire anybody who socialized with the tenants, the elevator man told me so himself. He got frantic when Matt headed for the phone, and killed him. Hit him with a bottle, maybe, and took the bottle away with him."

"You're sure he and Matt played cards?"

"Positive. Gertie told me, for one. And the elevator man himself told me so."

"I don't think our people knew about that," Reilly said thoughtfully.

"Everybody was covering for him, because they didn't want him to get in trouble for socializing."

"But what about Ricovic?" Reilly asked me.

"That's the clincher," I said. "The only reason Gus Ricovic would have been in that building at that time was to talk to the killer, tell him it would take a bid of over three thousand dollars to keep him from selling the truth to me. I think Gus had an odd attitude toward life, it would never occur to him anybody might try to kill him, no matter what."

"The MO was the same," Reilly said. "Both hit over the head with blunt instruments."

"Elevator operator," I said. "I'd have seen it long ago if I hadn't convinced myself all this other stuff was tied in with the killing."

"I'll be right back," said Reilly. "I've got to make a call."

I spent the time while he was gone getting dressed, setting aside the laboratory smock with something less than reluctance.

When Reilly returned he said, "The boys are checking it."

I said, "What about Wilks and Dunbar and the rest? What happens to them now?"

"Nothing, unfortunately," he said. "There's no real proof of anything they did, no way to successfully bring them into court. Earl Dunbar won't be doing much to help Walter Cosgrove get back into the country, but that's about the best you can say for the whole affair."

"And Gertie? What about her fake kidnapping?"

"You're the only one reported her kidnapped, Fred. She says no, she was out of town is all. She never claimed to be kidnapped."

"So everybody's scot-free," I said.

"Including you, Fred," Reilly pointed out. "Try looking at it that way, why don't you?"

I tried looking at it that way.

47

Two days later, on Saturday, I was in Gertie's apartment. She was making us a quick lunch before we went for a ride in my new car—she would be driving until I got my license—and when the phone rang she said, "You git it, honey, will you?"

It was Reilly. When he heard my voice he said, "Karen said you'd be there, but I didn't believe it."

"Why not? I told Karen when I talked to her—"

"Yeah, yeah, I know." Grumpily he said, "I suppose I owe you thanks for that."

"For what?"

"For talking to Karen."

"Oh," I said. "Heck, I figured I owed you something, mistrusting you that way. And it was pretty much my fault that Karen broke up with you, so I thought I'd see if I could fix it up again."

"I had it all wrong about you," he said. "The way I saw it, you were out to get Karen for yourself."

"Not me," I said. "In the first place, she's your girl. And in the second place, she really isn't my type, and I'm not really her type. You're her type."

He said, "What do you mean, she isn't your type?"

"She's too—uhh—normal for me, Reilly. I'm more of a—"

Gertie came in from the kitchen, brandishing a table-knife covered with mayonnaise, saying, "What was that?"

"Just a second." I turned to Gertie, saying, "I hate mayonnaise."

"Not *my* mayonnaise. I make it myself, in a blender."

I made a doubtful face, and turned back to the phone. "You and Karen were meant for each other, Reilly," I said. Gertie went back to the kitchen.

Reilly said, "Well, I don't know what you said to her, but it did the job, I've got to admit it. There's no more trouble around here."

"I just told her," I said, "that you and she made a perfect couple and that men are like loaves of bread. Half is better than none. And when she said women also didn't live on bread alone I told her about the phallic significance of the staff of life and suggested that we invent our lives for ourselves anyway, so why didn't she live the romantic fantasy you were offering her, and she—"

"You did *what?*"

"It worked, Reilly," I pointed out.

"I don't know," he said pensively, "it shouldn't work." He sighed and said, "All right, never mind that. The other thing I called about, your elevator operator confessed an hour ago. You were right on all counts. He caught Matt cheating, got mad, swore some, and Matt threatened to phone the doorman and have him thrown out. They'd been drinking, the two of them. The elevator man grabbed up an empty bottle, clubbed Matt with it, and left. He dropped the bottle down the elevator shaft. The lab boys are over there now, putting the pieces together."

"What did he use on Gus Ricovic?"

"Eight ball from the pool table. Ricovic knew about the setup, and guessed it was the elevator man who'd killed Matt. He asked for an offer better than three thousand, but the elevator man didn't have any money, so he took Ricovic into the apartment to talk it over, hit him with the eight ball, hid the body, washed the eight ball in the bathroom sink, and went back to work."

"Where'd he get the apartment key?"

"From Matt. So he could come in any time, to play cards, or bring booze, or whatever."

"So it's all cleared up."

"Right."

"Good. I'm glad to hear it."

"But what about you? I heard you were going to give the money away after all."

"I was considering it," I said.

"Why?"

"Well, mostly because it was ill-gotten gains. Blood money. And I'd gotten along all right without it for thirty years."

"So who gets it all?"

"I do."

"You what?"

"Gertie explained it to me," I explained to him. "She pointed out that I could still live my old life as much as I wanted, but much more comfortably now. Instead of paying rent on my apartment 1 could buy the house. That way nobody'll ever buy it to build a parking lot there. And so on."

"So you're keeping it," he said faintly.

"Gertie won't let me do anything but."

(Actually, what Gertie had said, more frequently than anything else, was, "Are you crazy? That's *money!*")

He said, "You aren't buying any more gold bricks, are you?"

"Not too many," I said. "I'm being a little careful."

"But not paranoid any more."

"No, I don't think so. I'm trying for a balance."

"Glad to hear it. Is Goodkind still your lawyer?"

"No, I let him go. Uncle Matt hired him because he was a crook and they could get along. I fired him for the same reason."

"Who's your new lawyer? Anybody I know?"

"Oh, sure. You know him pretty well. Prescott Wilks."

"What?"

"Dunbar fired him, in a fit of pique. So I figured, there's a man that really hustles for his clients. So I hired him. I think he's going to work out all right." I sniffed. There was a very odd and unpleasant odor coming from the kitchen. Gertie's mayonnaise?

Reilly was saying, "You with Gertie for the same reason?"

I got a little offended at that. "Gertie and I," I said stiffly, "are good friends. She's teaching me some things."

"I don't doubt it."

"Listen, Reilly, just because a girl dances at the Artillery Club in San Antonio doesn't mean she has loose morals. Gertie is—"

"Whatever you say, Fred."

"Well, she is." The smell was getting worse.

"I'm sure of it."

"I've got to hang up now, Reilly," I said. "There's something wrong here. I'll talk to you later."

I hung up, and started toward the kitchen, and met Gertie and a cloud of smoke coming out. I said, "What's going on?"

"You tell me, buster," she said, giving me the gimlet eye.

"Me? Why me?"

"Ten minutes ago I started to preheat the oven. I just looked in there now, and you know what's in there?"

"It smells like naugahyde," I said.

"I don't know about any of those places," she said. "All I know is, in my oven there's a burning Bible."

"A bur—" I said, and the last of the cons perpetrated on me suddenly opened like a flower before my eyes.

Of course, it was too late to stop payment on the check. But at least it gave us a neat ending, and that's one thing all good cons must have.

A neat ending.